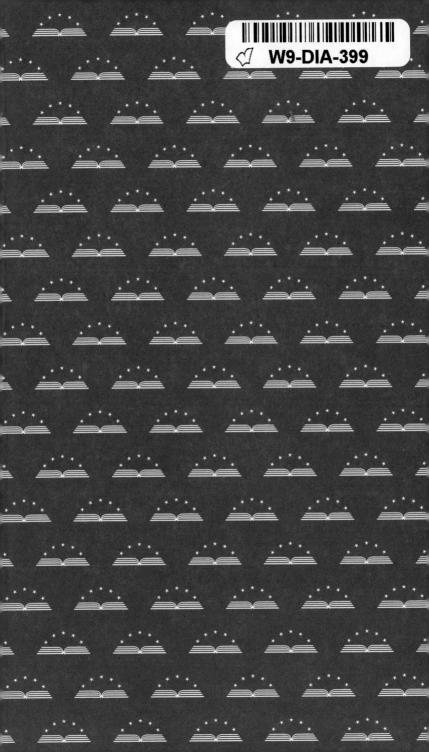

# LOUISA MAY ALCOTT

# LOUISA MAY ALCOTT

WORK
EIGHT COUSINS
ROSE IN BLOOM
STORIES & OTHER WRITINGS

Susan Cheever, *editor*

THE LIBRARY OF AMERICA

Distributed to the trade in the United States
by Penguin Group (USA) Inc.
and in Canada by Penguin Books Canada Ltd.

Library of Congress Control Number: 2013949838
ISBN 978–1–59853–306–4

First Printing
The Library of America—256

Manufactured in the United States of America

# Contents

# WORK

## *A STORY OF EXPERIENCE*

"An endless significance lies in work; in idleness
alone is there perpetual despair."
—CARLYLE

TO

## MY MOTHER,

WHOSE LIFE HAS BEEN A LONG LABOR OF LOVE,
THIS BOOK IS GRATEFULLY INSCRIBED

BY

## HER DAUGHTER.

# CONTENTS

## LIST OF ILLUSTRATIONS,

*FROM DRAWINGS BY SOL EYTINGE.*

# Chapter I

CHRISTIE.

"Aunt Betsey, there's going to be a new Declaration of Independence."

"Bless and save us, what do you mean, child?" And the startled old lady precipitated a pie into the oven with destructive haste.

"I mean that, being of age, I'm going to take care of myself, and not be a burden any longer. Uncle wishes me out of the way; thinks I ought to go, and, sooner or later, will tell me so. I don't intend to wait for that, but, like the people in fairy tales, travel away into the world and seek my fortune. I know I can find it."

Christie emphasized her speech by energetic demonstrations in the bread-trough, kneading the dough as if it was her destiny, and she was shaping it to suit herself; while Aunt Betsey stood listening, with uplifted pie-fork, and as much astonishment as her placid face was capable of expressing. As the girl paused, with a decided thump, the old lady exclaimed:

"What crazy idee you got into your head now?"

"A very sane and sensible one that's got to be working out, so please listen to it, ma'am. I've had it a good while, I've thought it over thoroughly, and I'm sure it's the right thing for me to do. I'm old enough to take care of myself; and if I'd been a boy, I should have been told to do it long ago. I hate to be dependent; and now there's no need of it, I can't bear it any longer. If you were poor, I wouldn't leave you; for I never forget how kind *you* have been to me. But Uncle doesn't love or understand me; I *am* a burden to him, and I must go where I can take care of myself. I can't be happy till I do, for there's nothing here for me. I'm sick of this dull town, where the one idea is eat, drink, and get rich; I don't find any friends to help me as I want to be helped, or any work that I can do well; so let me go, Aunty, and find my place, wherever it is."

"But I do need you, deary; and you mustn't think Uncle don't like you. He does, only he don't show it; and when your odd ways fret him, he ain't pleasant, I know. I don't see why you can't be contented; I've lived here all my days, and never found the place lonesome, or the folks unneighborly." And Aunt Betsey looked perplexed by the new idea.

"You and I are very different, ma'am. There was more yeast put into my composition, I guess; and, after standing quiet in a warm corner so long, I begin to ferment, and ought to be kneaded up in time, so that I may turn out a wholesome loaf. You can't do this; so let me go where it can be done, else I shall turn sour and good for nothing. Does that make the matter any clearer?" And Christie's serious face relaxed into a smile as her aunt's eye went from her to the nicely moulded loaf offered as an illustration.

"I see what you mean, Kitty; but I never thought on't before. You be better riz than me; though, let me tell you, too much emptins makes bread poor stuff, like baker's trash; and too much workin' up makes it hard and dry. Now fly 'round, for the big oven is most het, and this cake takes a sight of time in the mixin'."

"You haven't said I might go, Aunty," began the girl, after a long pause devoted by the old lady to the preparation of some compound which seemed to require great nicety of measurement in its ingredients; for when she replied, Aunt Betsey curiously interlarded her speech with audible directions to herself from the receipt-book before her.

"I ain't no right to keep you, dear, ef you choose to take (a pinch of salt). I'm sorry you ain't happy, and think you might

AUNT BETSEY'S INTERLARDED SPEECH.

be ef you'd only (beat eggs' six yolks and whites together). But ef you can't, and feel that you need (two cups of sugar), only speak to Uncle, and ef he says (a squeeze of fresh lemon); go, my dear, and take my blessin' with you (not forgettin' to cover with a piece of paper)."

Christie's laugh echoed through the kitchen; and the old lady smiled, benignly, quite unconscious of the cause of the girl's merriment.

"I shall ask Uncle to-night, and I know he won't object. Then I shall write to see if Mrs. Flint has a room for me, where I can stay till I get something to do. There is plenty of work in the world, and I'm not afraid of it; so you'll soon hear good news of me. Don't look sad, for you know I never could forget *you*, even if I should become the greatest lady in the land." And Christie left the prints of two floury but affectionate hands on the old lady's shoulders, as she kissed the wrinkled face that had never worn a frown to her.

Full of hopeful fancies, Christie salted the pans and buttered the dough in pleasant forgetfulness of all mundane affairs, and the ludicrous dismay of Aunt Betsey, who followed her about rectifying her mistakes, and watching over her as if this sudden absence of mind had roused suspicions of her sanity.

"Uncle, I want to go away, and get my own living, if you please," was Christie's abrupt beginning, as they sat round the evening fire.

"Hey! what's that?" said Uncle Enos, rousing from the doze he was enjoying, with a candle in perilous proximity to his newspaper and his nose.

Christie repeated her request, and was much relieved, when, after a meditative stare, the old man briefly answered:

"Wal, go ahead."

"I was afraid you might think it rash or silly, sir."

"I think it's the best thing you could do; and I like your good sense in pupposin' on't."

"Then I may really go?"

"Soon's ever you like. Don't pester me about it till you're ready; then I'll give you a little suthing to start off with." And Uncle Enos returned to "The Farmer's Friend," as if cattle were more interesting than kindred.

Christie was accustomed to his curt speech and careless manner; had expected nothing more cordial; and, turning to her aunt, said, rather bitterly:

"Didn't I tell you he'd be glad to have me go? No matter! When I've done something to be proud of, he will be as glad to see me back again." Then her voice changed, her eyes kindled, and the firm lips softened with a smile. "Yes, I'll try my experiment; then I'll get rich; found a home for girls like myself; or, better still, be a Mrs. Fry, a Florence Nightingale, or" —

"How are you on't for stockin's, dear?"

Christie's castles in the air vanished at the prosaic question; but, after a blank look, she answered pleasantly:

"Thank you for bringing me down to my feet again, when I was soaring away too far and too fast. I'm poorly off, ma'am; but if you are knitting these for me, I shall certainly start on a firm foundation." And, leaning on Aunt Betsey's knee, she patiently discussed the wardrobe question from hose to head-gear.

"Don't you think you could be contented any way, Christie,

ef I make the work lighter, and leave you more time for your books and things?" asked the old lady, loth to lose the one youthful element in her quiet life.

"No, ma'am, for I can't find what I want here," was the decided answer.

"What *do* you want, child?"

"Look in the fire, and I'll try to show you."

The old lady obediently turned her spectacles that way; and Christie said in a tone half serious, half playful:

"Do you see those two logs? Well that one smouldering dismally away in the corner is what my life is now; the other blazing and singing is what I want my life to be."

"Bless me, what an idee! They are both a-burnin' where they are put, and both will be ashes to-morrow; so what difference *doos* it make?"

Christie smiled at the literal old lady; but, following the fancy that pleased her, she added earnestly:

"I know the end is the same; but it *does* make a difference *how* they turn to ashes, and *how* I spend my life. That log, with its one dull spot of fire, gives neither light nor warmth, but lies sizzling despondently among the cinders. But the other glows from end to end with cheerful little flames that go singing up the chimney with a pleasant sound. Its light fills the room and shines out into the dark; its warmth draws us nearer, making the hearth the cosiest place in the house, and we shall all miss the friendly blaze when it dies. Yes," she added, as if to herself, "I hope my life may be like that, so that, whether it be long or short, it will be useful and cheerful while it lasts, will be missed when it ends, and leave something behind besides ashes."

Though she only half understood them, the girl's words touched the kind old lady, and made her look anxiously at the eager young face gazing so wistfully into the fire.

"A good smart blowin' up with the belluses would make the green stick burn most as well as the dry one after a spell. I guess contentedness is the best bellus for young folks, ef they would only think so."

"I dare say you are right, Aunty; but I want to try for myself; and if I fail, I'll come back and follow your advice. Young folks always have discontented fits, you know. Didn't you when you were a girl?"

"Shouldn't wonder ef I did; but Enos came along, and I forgot 'em."

"My Enos has not come along yet, and never may; so I'm not going to sit and wait for any man to give me independence, if I can earn it for myself." And a quick glance at the gruff, gray old man in the corner plainly betrayed that, in Christie's opinion, Aunt Betsey made a bad bargain when she exchanged her girlish aspirations for a man whose soul was in his pocket.

"Jest like her mother, full of hifalutin notions, discontented, and sot in her own idees. Poor capital to start a fortin' on."

Christie's eye met that of her uncle peering over the top of his paper with an expression that always tried her patience. Now it was like a dash of cold water on her enthusiasm, and her face fell as she asked quickly:

"How do you mean, sir?"

"I mean that you are startin' all wrong; your redic'lus notions about independence and self-cultur won't come to nothin' in the long run, and you'll make as bad a failure of your life as your mother did of her'n."

"Please, don't say that to me; I can't bear it, for *I* shall never think her life a failure, because she tried to help herself, and married a good man in spite of poverty, when she loved him! You call that folly; but I'll do the same if I can; and I'd rather have what my father and mother left me, than all the money you are piling up, just for the pleasure of being richer than your neighbors."

"Never mind, dear, he don't mean no harm!" whispered Aunt Betsey, fearing a storm.

But though Christie's eyes had kindled and her color deepened, her voice was low and steady, and her indignation was of the inward sort.

"Uncle likes to try me by saying such things, and this is one reason why I want to go away before I get sharp and bitter and distrustful as he is. I don't suppose I can make you understand my feeling, but I'd like to try, and then I'll never speak of it again;" and, carefully controlling voice and face, Christie slowly added, with a look that would have been pathetically eloquent to one who could have understood the instincts of a strong nature for light and freedom: "You say I am discontented, proud and ambitious; that's true, and I'm glad of it. I am discontented, because I can't help feeling that there is a better sort of life than this dull one made up of everlasting work, with no object but money. I can't starve my soul for the sake of my body, and I mean to get out of the treadmill if I can. I'm proud, as you call it, because I hate dependence where there isn't any love to make it bearable. You don't say so in words, but I know you begrudge me a home, though you will call me ungrateful when I'm gone. I'm willing to work, but I want work that I can put my heart into, and feel that it does me good, no matter how hard it is. I only ask for a chance to be a useful, happy woman, and I don't think that is a bad ambition. Even if I only do what my dear mother did, earn my living honestly and happily, and leave a beautiful example behind me, to help one other woman as hers helps me, I shall be satisfied."

Christie's voice faltered over the last words, for the thoughts and feelings which had been working within her during the last few days had stirred her deeply, and the resolution to cut loose from the old life had not been lightly made. Mr. Devon had listened behind his paper to this unusual outpouring with a sense of discomfort which was new to him. But though the words reproached and annoyed, they did not soften him, and when Christie paused with tearful eyes, her uncle rose, saying, slowly, as he lighted his candle:

"Ef I'd refused to let you go before, I'd agree to it now; for you need breakin' in, my girl, and you are goin' where you'll get it, so the sooner you're off the better for all on us. Come, Betsey, we may as wal leave, for we can't understand the wants of her higher nater, as Christie calls it, and we've had lecterin' enough for one night." And with a grim laugh the old man quitted the field, worsted but in good order.

"There, there, dear, hev a good cry, and forget all about it!" purred Aunt Betsey, as the heavy footsteps creaked away, for the good soul had a most old-fashioned and dutiful awe of her lord and master.

"I shan't cry but act; for it is high time I *was* off. I've stayed for your sake; now I'm more trouble than comfort, and away I go. Good-night, my dear old Aunty, and don't look troubled, for I'll be a lamb while I stay."

Having kissed the old lady, Christie swept her work away,

and sat down to write the letter which was the first step toward freedom. When it was done, she drew nearer to her friendly *confidante* the fire, and till late into the night sat thinking tenderly of the past, bravely of the present, hopefully of the future. Twenty-one to-morrow, and her inheritance a head, a heart, a pair of hands; also the dower of most New England girls, intelligence, courage, and common sense, many practical gifts, and, hidden under the reserve that soon melts in a genial atmosphere, much romance and enthusiasm, and the spirit which can rise to heroism when the great moment comes.

Christie was one of that large class of women who, moderately endowed with talents, earnest and true-hearted, are driven by necessity, temperament, or principle out into the world to find support, happiness, and homes for themselves. Many turn back discouraged; more accept shadow for substance, and discover their mistake too late; the weakest lose their purpose and themselves; but the strongest struggle on, and, after danger and defeat, earn at last the best success this world can give us, the possession of a brave and cheerful spirit, rich in self-knowledge, self-control, self-help. This was the real desire of Christie's heart; this was to be her lesson and reward, and to this happy end she was slowly yet surely brought by the long discipline of life and labor.

Sitting alone there in the night, she tried to strengthen herself with all the good and helpful memories she could recall, before she went away to find her place in the great unknown world. She thought of her mother, so like herself, who had borne the commonplace life of home till she could bear it no longer. Then had gone away to teach, as most country girls are forced to do. Had met, loved, and married a poor gentleman, and, after a few years of genuine happiness, untroubled even by much care and poverty, had followed him out of the world, leaving her little child to the protection of her brother.

Christie looked back over the long, lonely years she had spent in the old farm-house, plodding to school and church, and doing her tasks with kind Aunt Betsey while a child; and slowly growing into girlhood, with a world of romance locked up in a heart hungry for love and a larger, nobler life.

She had tried to appease this hunger in many ways, but found little help. Her father's old books were all she could command,

and these she wore out with much reading. Inheriting his refined tastes, she found nothing to attract her in the society of the commonplace and often coarse people about her. She tried to like the buxom girls whose one ambition was to "get married," and whose only subjects of conversation were "smart bonnets" and "nice dresses." She tried to believe that the admiration and regard of the bluff young farmers was worth striving for; but when one well-to-do neighbor laid his acres at her feet, she found it impossible to accept for her life's companion a man whose soul was wrapped up in prize cattle and big turnips.

Uncle Enos never could forgive her for this piece of folly, and Christie plainly saw that one of three things would surely happen, if she lived on there with no vent for her full heart and busy mind. She would either marry Joe Butterfield in sheer desperation, and become a farmer's household drudge; settle down into a sour spinster, content to make butter, gossip, and lay up money all her days; or do what poor Matty Stone had done, try to crush and curb her needs and aspirations till the struggle grew too hard, and then in a fit of despair end her life, and leave a tragic story to haunt their quiet river.

To escape these fates but one way appeared; to break loose from their narrow life, go out into the world and see what she could do for herself. This idea was full of enchantment to the eager girl, and, after much earnest thought, she had resolved to try it.

"If I fail, I can come back," she said to herself, even while she scorned the thought of failure, for with all her shy pride she was both brave and ardent, and her dreams were of the rosiest sort.

"I won't marry Joe; I won't wear myself out in a district-school for the mean sum they give a woman; I won't delve away here where I'm not wanted; and I won't end my life like a coward, because it is dull and hard. I'll try my fate as mother did, and perhaps I may succeed as well." And Christie's thoughts went wandering away into the dim, sweet past when she, a happy child, lived with loving parents in a different world from that.

Lost in these tender memories, she sat till the old moon-faced clock behind the door struck twelve, then the visions vanished, leaving their benison behind them.

As she glanced backward at the smouldering fire, a slender spire of flame shot up from the log that had blazed so cheerily, and shone upon her as she went. A good omen, gratefully accepted then, and remembered often in the years to come.

# Chapter II

## SERVANT

A FORTNIGHT later, and Christie was off. Mrs. Flint had briefly answered that she had a room, and that work was always to be found in the city. So the girl packed her one trunk, folding away splendid hopes among her plain gowns, and filling every corner with happy fancies, utterly impossible plans, and tender little dreams, so lovely at the time, so pathetic to remember, when contact with the hard realities of life has collapsed our bright bubbles, and the frost of disappointment nipped all our morning glories in their prime.

The old red stage stopped at Enos Devon's door, and his niece crossed the threshold after a cool handshake with the master of the house, and a close embrace with the mistress, who stood pouring out last words with spectacles too dim for seeing. Fat Ben swung up the trunk, slammed the door, mounted his perch, and the ancient vehicle swayed with premonitory symptoms of departure.

Then something smote Christie's heart. "Stop!" she cried, and springing out ran back into the dismal room where the old man sat. Straight up to him she went with outstretched hand, saying steadily, though her face was full of feeling:

"Uncle, I'm not satisfied with that good-bye. I don't mean to be sentimental, but I do want to say, 'Forgive me!' I see now that I might have made you sorry to part with me, if I had tried to make you love me more. It's too late now, but I'm not too proud to confess when I'm wrong. I want to part kindly; I ask your pardon; I thank you for all you've done for me, and I say good-bye affectionately now."

Mr. Devon had a heart somewhere, though it seldom troubled him; but it did make itself felt when the girl looked at him with his dead sister's eyes, and spoke in a tone whose unaccustomed tenderness was a reproach.

Conscience had pricked him more than once that week, and he was glad to own it now; his rough sense of honor was

15

touched by her frank expression, and, as he answered, his hand was offered readily.

"I like that, Kitty, and think the better of you for't. Let bygones be bygones. I gen'lly got as good as I give, and I guess I deserved some on't. I wish you wal, my girl, I heartily wish you wal, and hope you won't forgit that the old house ain't never shet aginst you."

Christie astonished him with a cordial kiss; then bestowing another warm hug on Aunt Niobe, as she called the old lady in a tearful joke, she ran into the carriage, taking with her all the sunshine of the place.

Christie found Mrs. Flint a dreary woman, with "boarders" written all over her sour face and faded figure. Butcher's bills and house rent seemed to fill her eyes with sleepless anxiety; thriftless cooks and saucy housemaids to sharpen the tones of her shrill voice; and an incapable husband to burden her shoulders like a modern "Old man of the sea."

A little room far up in the tall house was at the girl's disposal for a reasonable sum, and she took possession, feeling very rich with the hundred dollars Uncle Enos gave her, and delightfully independent, with no milk-pans to scald; no heavy lover to elude; no humdrum district school to imprison her day after day.

For a week she enjoyed her liberty heartily, then set about finding something to do. Her wish was to be a governess, that being the usual refuge for respectable girls who have a living to get. But Christie soon found her want of accomplishments a barrier to success in that line, for the mammas thought less of the solid than of the ornamental branches, and wished their little darlings to learn French before English, music before grammar, and drawing before writing.

So, after several disappointments, Christie decided that her education was too old-fashioned for the city, and gave up the idea of teaching. Sewing she resolved not to try till every thing else failed; and, after a few more attempts to get writing to do, she said to herself, in a fit of humility and good sense: "I'll begin at the beginning, and work my way up. I'll put my pride in my pocket, and go out to service. Housework I like, and can do well, thanks to Aunt Betsey. I never thought it degradation to do it for her, so why should I mind doing it for others if they pay for it? It isn't what I want, but it's better than idleness, so I'll try it!"

Full of this wise resolution, she took to haunting that purgatory of the poor, an intelligence office. Mrs. Flint gave her a recommendation, and she hopefully took her place among the ranks of buxom German, incapable Irish, and "smart" American women; for in those days foreign help had not driven farmers' daughters out of the field, and made domestic comfort a lost art.

At first Christie enjoyed the novelty of the thing, and watched with interest the anxious housewives who flocked in demanding that *rara avis*, an angel at nine shillings a week; and not finding it, bewailed the degeneracy of the times. Being too honest to profess herself absolutely perfect in every known branch of house-work, it was some time before she suited herself. Meanwhile, she was questioned and lectured, half engaged and kept waiting, dismissed for a whim, and so worried that she began to regard herself as the incarnation of all human vanities and shortcomings.

"A desirable place in a small, genteel family," was at last offered her, and she posted away to secure it, having reached a state of desperation and resolved to go as a first-class cook rather than sit with her hands before her any longer.

A well-appointed house, good wages, and light duties seemed things to be grateful for, and Christie decided that going out to service was not the hardest fate in life, as she stood at the door of a handsome house in a sunny square waiting to be inspected.

Mrs. Stuart, having just returned from Italy, affected the artistic, and the new applicant found her with a Roman scarf about her head, a rosary like a string of small cannon balls at her side, and azure draperies which became her as well as they did the sea-green furniture of her marine boudoir, where unwary walkers tripped over coral and shells, grew sea-sick looking at pictures of tempestuous billows engulfing every sort of craft, from a man-of-war to a hencoop with a ghostly young lady clinging to it with one hand, and had their appetites effectually taken away by a choice collection of water-bugs and snakes in a glass globe, that looked like a jar of mixed pickles in a state of agitation.

MRS. STUART.

Madame was intent on a water-color copy of Turner's "Rain, Wind, and Hail," that pleasing work which was sold upside-down and no one found it out. Motioning Christie to a seat she finished some delicate sloppy process before speaking. In that little pause Christie examined her, and the impression then received was afterward confirmed.

Mrs. Stuart possessed some beauty and chose to think herself a queen of society. She assumed majestic manners in public and could not entirely divest herself of them in private, which often produced comic effects. Zenobia troubled about fish-sauce, or Aspasia indignant at the price of eggs will give some idea of this lady when she condescended to the cares of house-keeping.

Presently she looked up and inspected the girl as if a new servant were no more than a new bonnet, a necessary article to be ordered home for examination. Christie presented her rec-ommendation, made her modest little speech, and awaited her doom.

Mrs. Stuart read, listened, and then demanded with queenly brevity:

"Your name?"

"Christie Devon."

"Too long; I should prefer to call you Jane as I am accus-tomed to the name."

"As you please, ma'am."

"Your age?"

"Twenty-one."

"You are an American?"

"Yes, ma'am."

Mrs. Stuart gazed into space a moment, then delivered the following address with impressive solemnity.

"I wish a capable, intelligent, honest, neat, well-conducted person who knows her place and keeps it. The work is light, as there are but two in the family. I am very particular and so is Mr. Stuart. I pay two dollars and a half, allow one afternoon out, one service on Sunday, and no followers. My table-girl must understand her duties thoroughly, be extremely neat, and always wear white aprons."

"I think I can suit you, ma'am, when I have learned the ways of the house," meekly replied Christie.

Mrs. Stuart looked graciously satisfied and returned the paper with a gesture that Victoria might have used in restoring a granted petition, though her next words rather marred the effect of the regal act, "My cook is black."

"I have no objection to color, ma'am."

An expression of relief dawned upon Mrs. Stuart's counte-nance, for the black cook had been an insurmountable obstacle to all the Irish ladies who had applied. Thoughtfully tapping her Roman nose with the handle of her brush Madame took another survey of the new applicant, and seeing that she looked neat, intelligent, and respectful, gave a sigh of thank-fulness and engaged her on the spot.

Much elated Christie rushed home, selected a bag of neces-sary articles, bundled the rest of her possessions into an empty closet (lent her rent-free owing to a profusion of cockroaches), paid up her board, and at two o'clock introduced herself to Hepsey Johnson, her fellow servant.

Hepsey was a tall, gaunt woman, bearing the tragedy of her race written in her face, with its melancholy eyes, subdued expression, and the pathetic patience of a wronged dumb animal. She received Christie with an air of resignation, and speedily bewildered her with an account of the duties she would be expected to perform.

A long and careful drill enabled Christie to set the table with but few mistakes, and to retain a tolerably clear recollection of the order of performances. She had just assumed her badge of servitude, as she called the white apron, when the bell rang violently and Hepsey, who was hurrying away to "dish up," said:

"It's de marster. You has to answer de bell, honey, and he likes it done bery spry."

Christie ran and admitted an impetuous, stout gentleman, who appeared to be incensed against the elements, for he burst in as if blown, shook himself like a Newfoundland dog, and said all in one breath:

"You're the new girl, are you? Well, take my umbrella and pull off my rubbers."

"Sir?"

Mr. Stuart was struggling with his gloves, and, quite unconscious of the astonishment of his new maid, impatiently repeated his request.

"Take this wet thing away, and pull off my overshoes. Don't you see it's raining like the very deuce!"

Christie folded her lips together in a peculiar manner as she knelt down and removed a pair of muddy overshoes, took the dripping umbrella, and was walking away with her agreeable burden when Mr. Stuart gave her another shock by calling over the banister:

"I'm going out again; so clean those rubbers, and see that the boots I sent down this morning are in order."

"Yes, sir," answered Christie meekly, and immediately afterward startled Hepsey by casting overshoes and umbrella upon the kitchen floor, and indignantly demanding:

"Am I expected to be a boot-jack to that man?"

"I 'spects you is, honey."

"Am I also expected to clean his boots?"

"Yes, chile. Katy did, and de work ain't hard when you gits used to it."

"It isn't the work; it's the degradation; and I won't submit to it."

Christie looked fiercely determined; but Hepsey shook her head, saying quietly as she went on garnishing a dish:

"Dere's more 'gradin' works dan dat, chile, and dem dat's bin 'bliged to do um finds dis sort bery easy. You's paid for it, honey; and if you does it willin, it won't hurt you more dan washin' de marster's dishes, or sweepin' his rooms."

"There ought to be a boy to do this sort of thing. *Do* you think it's right to ask it of me?" cried Christie, feeling that being servant was not as pleasant a task as she had thought it.

"Dunno, chile. I'se shore I'd never ask it of any woman if I was a man, 'less I was sick or ole. But folks don't seem to 'member dat we've got feelin's, and de best way is not to mind dese ere little trubbles. You jes leave de boots to me; blackin' can't do dese ole hands no hurt, and dis ain't no deggydation to me now; I's a free woman."

"Why, Hepsey, were you ever a slave?" asked the girl, forgetting her own small injury at this suggestion of the greatest of all wrongs.

"All my life, till I run away five year ago. My ole folks, and eight brudders and sisters, is down dere in de pit now, waitin' for the Lord to set 'em free. And He's gwine to do it soon, *soon!*" As she uttered the last words, a sudden light chased the tragic shadow from Hepsey's face, and the solemn fervor of her voice thrilled Christie's heart. All her anger died out in a great pity, and she put her hand on the woman's shoulder, saying earnestly:

"I hope so; and I wish I could help to bring that happy day at once!"

For the first time Hepsey smiled, as she said gratefully, "De Lord bress you for dat wish, chile." Then, dropping suddenly into her old, quiet way, she added, turning to her work:

"Now you tote up de dinner, and I'll be handy by to 'fresh your mind 'bout how de dishes goes, for missis is bery 'ticular, and don't like no 'stakes in tendin'."

Thanks to her own neat-handed ways and Hepsey's prompting

through the slide, Christie got on very well; managed her salver dexterously, only upset one glass, clashed one dish-cover, and forgot to sugar the pie before putting it on the table; an omission which was majestically pointed out, and graciously pardoned as a first offence.

By seven o'clock the ceremonial was fairly over, and Christie dropped into a chair quite tired out with frequent pacings to and fro. In the kitchen she found the table spread for one, and Hepsey busy with the boots.

"Aren't you coming to your dinner, Mrs. Johnson?" she asked, not pleased at the arrangement.

"When you's done, honey; dere's no hurry 'bout me. Katy liked dat way best, and I'se used ter waitin'."

"But *I* don't like that way, and I won't have it. I suppose Katy thought her white skin gave her a right to be disrespectful to a woman old enough to be her mother just because she was black. I don't; and while I'm here, there must be no difference made. If we can work together, we can eat together; and because you have been a slave is all the more reason I should be good to you now."

If Hepsey had been surprised by the new girl's protest against being made a boot-jack of, she was still more surprised at this sudden kindness, for she had set Christie down in her own mind as "one ob dem toppin' smart ones dat don't stay long nowheres." She changed her opinion now, and sat watching the girl with a new expression on her face, as Christie took boot and brush from her, and fell to work energetically, saying as she scrubbed:

"I'm ashamed of complaining about such a little thing as this, and don't mean to feel degraded by it, though I should by letting you do it for me. I never lived out before: that's the reason I made a fuss. There's a polish, for you, and I'm in a good humor again; so Mr. Stuart may call for his boots whenever he likes, and we'll go to dinner like fashionable people, as we are."

There was something so irresistible in the girl's hearty manner, that Hepsey submitted at once with a visible satisfaction, which gave a relish to Christie's dinner, though it was eaten at a kitchen table, with a bare-armed cook sitting opposite, and three rows of burnished dish-covers reflecting the dreadful spectacle.

After this, Christie got on excellently, for she did her best, and found both pleasure and profit in her new employment. It gave her real satisfaction to keep the handsome rooms in order, to polish plate, and spread bountiful meals. There was an atmosphere of ease and comfort about her which contrasted agreeably with the shabbiness of Mrs. Flint's boarding-house, and the bare simplicity of the old home. Like most young people, Christie loved luxury, and was sensible enough to see and value the comforts of her situation, and to wonder why more girls placed as she was did not choose a life like this rather than the confinements of a sewing-room, or the fatigue and publicity of a shop.

She did not learn to love her mistress, because Mrs. Stuart evidently considered herself as one belonging to a superior race of beings, and had no desire to establish any of the friendly relations that may become so helpful and pleasant to both mistress and maid. She made a royal progress through her dominions every morning, issued orders, found fault liberally, bestowed praise sparingly, and took no more personal interest in her servants than if they were clocks, to be wound up once a day, and sent away the moment they got out of repair.

Mr. Stuart was absent from morning till night, and all Christie ever knew about him was that he was a kind-hearted, hot-tempered, and very conceited man; fond of his wife, proud of the society they managed to draw about them, and bent on making his way in the world at any cost.

If masters and mistresses knew how skilfully they are studied, criticised, and imitated by their servants, they would take more heed to their ways, and set better examples, perhaps. Mrs. Stuart never dreamed that her quiet, respectful Jane kept a sharp eye on all her movements, smiled covertly at her affectations, envied her accomplishments, and practised certain little elegancies that struck her fancy.

Mr. Stuart would have become apoplectic with indignation if he had known that this too intelligent table-girl often contrasted her master with his guests, and dared to think him wanting in good breeding when he boasted of his money, flattered a great man, or laid plans to lure some lion into his house. When he lost his temper, she always wanted to laugh, he bounced and bumbled about so like an angry blue-bottle fly; and when he got himself up elaborately for a party, this disrespectful hussy confided to Hepsey her opinion that "master was a fat dandy, with nothing to be vain of but his clothes,"—a sacrilegious remark which would have caused her to be summarily ejected from the house if it had reached the august ears of master or mistress.

"My father was a gentleman; and I shall never forget it, though I do go out to service. I've got no rich friends to help me up, but, sooner or later, I mean to find a place among cultivated people; and while I'm working and waiting, I can be fitting myself to fill that place like a gentlewoman, as I am."

With this ambition in her mind, Christie took notes of all that went on in the polite world, of which she got frequent glimpses while "living out." Mrs. Stuart received one evening of each week, and on these occasions Christie, with an extra frill on her white apron, served the company, and enjoyed herself more than they did, if the truth had been known.

While helping the ladies with their wraps, she observed what they wore, how they carried themselves, and what a vast amount of prinking they did, not to mention the flood of gossip they talked while shaking out their flounces and settling their topknots.

Later in the evening, when she passed cups and glasses, this demure-looking damsel heard much fine discourse, saw many famous beings, and improved her mind with surreptitious studies of the rich and great when on parade. But her best time was after supper, when, through the crack of the door of the little room where she was supposed to be clearing away the relics of the feast, she looked and listened at her ease; laughed at the wits, stared at the lions, heard the music, was impressed by the wisdom, and much edified by the gentility of the whole affair.

After a time, however, Christie got rather tired of it, for there was an elegant sameness about these evenings that became intensely wearisome to the uninitiated, but she fancied that as each had his part to play he managed to do it with spirit. Night after night the wag told his stories, the poet read his poems, the singers warbled, the pretty women simpered and dressed, the heavy scientific was duly discussed by the elect precious, and Mrs. Stuart, in amazing costumes, sailed to and fro in her most swan-like manner; while my lord stirred up the lions he had captured, till they roared their best, great and small.

"Good heavens! why don't they do or say something new and interesting, and not keep twaddling on about art, and music, and poetry, and cosmos? The papers are full of appeals for help for the poor, reforms of all sorts, and splendid work that others are doing; but these people seem to think it isn't genteel enough to be spoken of here. I suppose it is all very elegant to go on like a set of trained canaries, but it's very dull fun to watch them, and Hepsey's stories are a deal more interesting to me."

Having come to this conclusion, after studying dilettanteism through the crack of the door for some months, Christie left the "trained canaries" to twitter and hop about their gilded cage, and devoted herself to Hepsey, who gave her glimpses into another sort of life so bitterly real that she never could forget it.

HEPSEY.

Friendship had prospered in the lower regions, for Hepsey had a motherly heart, and Christie soon won her confidence by bestowing her own. Her story was like many another; yet, being the first Christie had ever heard, and told with the unconscious eloquence of one who had suffered and escaped, it made a deep impression on her, bringing home to her a sense of obligation so forcibly that she began at once to pay a little part of the great debt which the white race owes the black.

Christie loved books; and the attic next her own was full of them. To this store she found her way by a sort of instinct as sure as that which leads a fly to a honeypot, and, finding many novels, she read her fill. This amusement lightened many heavy hours, peopled the silent house with troops of friends, and, for a time, was the joy of her life.

Hepsey used to watch her as she sat buried in her book when the day's work was done, and once a heavy sigh roused Christie from the most exciting crisis of "The Abbot."

"What's the matter? Are you very tired, Aunty?" she asked, using the name that came most readily to her lips.

"No, honey; I was only wishin' I could read fast like you does. I's berry slow 'bout readin' and I want to learn a heap," answered Hepsey, with such a wistful look in her soft eyes that Christie shut her book, saying briskly:

"Then I'll teach you. Bring out your primer and let's begin at once."

"Dear chile, it's orful hard work to put learnin' in my ole head, and I wouldn't 'cept such a ting from you only I needs dis sort of help so bad, and I can trust you to gib it to me as I wants it."

Then in a whisper that went straight to Christie's heart, Hepsey told her plan and showed what help she craved.

For five years she had worked hard, and saved her earnings for the purpose of her life. When a considerable sum had been hoarded up, she confided it to one whom she believed to be a friend, and sent him to buy her old mother. But he proved false, and she never saw either mother or money. It was a hard blow, but she took heart and went to work again, resolving this time to trust no one with the dangerous part of the affair, but when she had scraped together enough to pay her way she meant to go South and steal her mother at the risk of her life.

"I don't want much money, but I must know little 'bout readin' and countin' up, else I'll get lost and cheated. You'll help me do dis, honey, and I'll bless you all my days, and so will my old mammy, if I ever gets her safe away."

With tears of sympathy shining on her cheeks, and both hands stretched out to the poor soul who implored this small boon of her, Christie promised all the help that in her lay, and kept her word religiously.

From that time, Hepsey's cause was hers; she laid by a part of her wages for "ole mammy," she comforted Hepsey with happy prophecies of success, and taught with an energy and skill she had never known before. Novels lost their charms now, for Hepsey could give her a comedy and tragedy surpassing any thing she found in them, because truth stamped her tales with a power and pathos the most gifted fancy could but poorly imitate.

The select receptions upstairs seemed duller than ever to her now, and her happiest evenings were spent in the tidy kitchen, watching Hepsey laboriously shaping A's and B's, or counting up on her worn fingers the wages they had earned by months of weary work, that she might purchase one treasure,—a feeble, old woman, worn out with seventy years of slavery far away there in Virginia.

For a year Christie was a faithful servant to her mistress, who appreciated her virtues, but did not encourage them; a true friend to poor Hepsey, who loved her dearly, and found in her sympathy and affection a solace for many griefs and wrongs. But Providence had other lessons for Christie, and when this one was well learned she was sent away to learn another phase of woman's life and labor.

While their domestics amused themselves with privy conspiracy and rebellion at home, Mr. and Mrs. Stuart spent their evenings in chasing that bright bubble called social success, and usually came home rather cross because they could not catch it.

On one of these occasions they received a warm welcome, for, as they approached the house, smoke was seen issuing from an attic window, and flames flickering behind the half-drawn curtain. Bursting out of the carriage with his usual impetuosity, Mr. Stuart let himself in and tore upstairs shouting "Fire!" like an engine company.

In the attic Christie was discovered lying dressed upon her bed, asleep or suffocated by the smoke that filled the room. A book had slipped from her hand, and in falling had upset the candle on a chair beside her; the long wick leaned against a cotton gown hanging on the wall, and a greater part of Christie's wardrobe was burning brilliantly.

"I forbade her to keep the gas lighted so late, and see what the deceitful creature has done with her private candle!" cried Mrs. Stuart with a shrillness that roused the girl from her heavy sleep more effectually than the anathemas Mr. Stuart was fulminating against the fire.

Sitting up she looked dizzily about her. The smoke was clearing fast, a window having been opened; and the tableau was a striking one. Mr. Stuart with an excited countenance was dancing frantically on a heap of half-consumed clothes pulled from the wall. He had not only drenched them with water from bowl and pitcher, but had also cast those articles upon the pile like extinguishers, and was skipping among the fragments with an agility which contrasted with his stout figure in full evening costume, and his besmirched face, made the sight irresistibly ludicrous.

Mrs. Stuart, though in her most regal array, seemed to have left her dignity downstairs with her opera cloak, for with skirts gathered closely about her, tiara all askew, and face full of fear and anger, she stood upon a chair and scolded like any shrew.

The comic overpowered the tragic, and being a little hysterical with the sudden alarm, Christie broke into a peal of laughter that sealed her fate.

"Look at her! look at her!" cried Mrs. Stuart gesticulating on her perch as if about to fly. "She has been at the wine, or lost her wits. She must go, Horatio, she must go! I cannot have my nerves shattered by such dreadful scenes. She is too fond of books, and it has turned her brain. Hepsey can watch her to-night, and at dawn she shall leave the house for ever."

"Not till after breakfast, my dear. Let us have that in comfort I beg, for upon my soul we shall need it," panted Mr. Stuart, sinking into a chair exhausted with the vigorous measures which had quenched the conflagration.

Christie checked her untimely mirth, explained the probable cause of the mischief, and penitently promised to be more careful for the future.

Mr. Stuart would have pardoned her on the spot, but Madame was inexorable, for she had so completely forgotten her dignity that she felt it would be impossible ever to recover it in the eyes of this disrespectful menial. Therefore she dismissed her with a lecture that made both mistress and maid glad to part.

She did not appear at breakfast, and after that meal Mr. Stuart paid Christie her wages with a solemnity which proved that he had taken a curtain lecture to heart. There was a twinkle in his eye, however, as he kindly added a recommendation, and after the door closed behind him Christie was sure that he exploded into a laugh at the recollection of his last night's performance.

This lightened her sense of disgrace very much, so, leaving a part of her money to repair damages, she packed up her dilapidated wardrobe, and, making Hepsey promise to report progress from time to time, Christie went back to Mrs. Flint's to compose her mind and be ready *à la* Micawber "for something to turn up."

# *Chapter III*

ACTRESS

FEELING that she had all the world before her where to choose, and that her next step ought to take her up at least one round higher on the ladder she was climbing, Christie decided not to try going out to service again. She knew very well that she would never live with Irish mates, and could not expect to find another Hepsey. So she tried to get a place as companion to an invalid, but failed to secure the only situation of the sort that was offered her, because she mildly objected to waiting on a nervous cripple all day, and reading aloud half the night. The old lady called her an "impertinent baggage," and Christie retired in great disgust, resolving not to be a slave to anybody.

Things seldom turn out as we plan them, and after much waiting and hoping for other work Christie at last accepted about the only employment which had not entered her mind.

Among the boarders at Mrs. Flint's were an old lady and her pretty daughter, both actresses at a respectable theatre. Not stars by any means, but good second-rate players, doing their work creditably and earning an honest living. The mother had been kind to Christie in offering advice, and sympathizing with her disappointments. The daughter, a gay little lass, had taken Christie to the theatre several times, there to behold her in all the gauzy glories that surround the nymphs of spectacular romance.

To Christie this was a great delight, for, though she had pored over her father's Shakespeare till she knew many scenes by heart, she had never seen a play till Lucy led her into what seemed an enchanted world. Her interest and admiration pleased the little actress, and sundry lifts when she was hurried with her dresses made her grateful to Christie.

The girl's despondent face, as she came in day after day from her unsuccessful quest, told its own story, though she uttered no complaint, and these friendly souls laid their heads together, eager to help her in their own dramatic fashion.

"I've got it! I've got it! All hail to the queen!" was the cry that one day startled Christie as she sat thinking anxiously, while sewing mock-pearls on a crown for Mrs. Black.

Looking up she saw Lucy just home from rehearsal, going through a series of pantomimic evolutions suggestive of a warrior doing battle with incredible valor, and a very limited knowledge of the noble art of self-defence.

"What have you got? Who is the queen?" she asked, laughing, as the breathless hero lowered her umbrella, and laid her bonnet at Christie's feet.

"*You* are to be the Queen of the Amazons in our new spectacle, at half a dollar a night for six or eight weeks, if the piece goes well."

"No!" cried Christie, with a gasp.

"Yes!" cried Lucy, clapping her hands; and then she proceeded to tell her news with theatrical volubility. "Mr. Sharp, the manager, wants a lot of tallish girls, and I told him I knew of a perfect dear. He said: 'Bring her on, then,' and I flew home to tell you. Now, don't look wild, and say no. You've only got to sing in one chorus, march in the grand procession, and lead your band in the terrific battle-scene. The dress is splendid! Red tunic, tiger-skin over shoulder, helmet, shield, lance, fleshings, sandals, hair down, and as much cork to your eyebrows as you like."

Christie certainly did look wild, for Lucy had burst into the room like a small hurricane, and her rapid words rattled about the listeners' ears as if a hail-storm had followed the gust. While Christie still sat with her mouth open, too bewildered to reply, Mrs. Black said in her cosey voice:

"Try it, me dear, it's just what you'll enjoy, and a capital beginning I assure ye; for if you do well old Sharp will want you again, and then, when some one slips out of the company, you can slip in, and there you are quite comfortable. Try it, me dear, and if you don't like it drop it when the piece is over, and there's no harm done."

"It's much easier and jollier than any of the things you are after. We'll stand by you like bricks, and in a week you'll say it's the best lark you ever had in your life. Don't be prim, now, but say yes, like a trump, as you are," added Lucy, waving a pink satin train temptingly before her friend.

"I will try it," said Christie, with sudden decision, feeling that something entirely new and absorbing was what she needed to expend the vigor, romance, and enthusiasm of her youth upon.

With a shriek of delight Lucy swept her off her chair, and twirled her about the room as excitable young ladies are fond of doing when their joyful emotions need a vent. When both were giddy they subsided into a corner and a breathless discussion of the important step.

Though she had consented, Christie had endless doubts and fears, but Lucy removed many of the former, and her own desire for pleasant employment conquered many of the latter. In her most despairing moods she had never thought of trying this. Uncle Enos considered "play-actin'" as the sum of all iniquity. What would he say if she went calmly to destruction by that road? Sad to relate, this recollection rather strengthened her purpose, for a delicious sense of freedom pervaded her soul, and the old defiant spirit seemed to rise up within her at the memory of her Uncle's grim prophecies and narrow views.

"Lucy is happy, virtuous, and independent, why can't I be so too if I have any talent? It isn't exactly what I should choose, but any thing honest is better than idleness. I'll try it any way, and get a little fun, even if I don't make much money or glory out of it."

So Christie held to her resolution in spite of many secret misgivings, and followed Mrs. Black's advice on all points with a docility which caused that sanguine lady to predict that she would be a star before she knew where she was.

"Is this the stage? How dusty and dull it is by daylight!" said Christie next day, as she stood by Lucy on the very spot where she had seen Hamlet die in great anguish two nights before.

"Bless you, child, it's in curl-papers now, as I am of a morning. Mr. Sharp, here's an Amazon for you."

As she spoke, Lucy hurried across the stage, followed by Christie, wearing any thing but an Amazonian expression just then.

"Ever on before?" abruptly asked a keen-faced, little man, glancing with an experienced eye at the young person who stood before him bathed in blushes.

"No, sir."

"Do you sing?"

"A little, sir."

"Dance, of course?"

"Yes, sir."

"Just take a turn across the stage, will you? Must walk well to lead a march."

As she went, Christie heard Mr. Sharp taking notes audibly:

"Good tread; capital figure; fine eye. She'll make up well, and behave herself, I fancy."

A strong desire to make off seized the girl; but, remembering that she had presented herself for inspection, she controlled the impulse, and returned to him with no demonstration of displeasure, but a little more fire in "the fine eye," and a more erect carriage of the "capital figure."

"All right, my dear. Give your name to Mr. Tripp, and your mind to the business, and consider yourself engaged,"—with which satisfactory remark the little man vanished like a ghost.

"Lucy, did you hear that impertinent 'my dear'?" asked Christie, whose sense of propriety had received its first shock.

"Lord, child, all managers do it. They don't mean any thing; so be resigned, and thank your stars he didn't say 'love' and 'darling,' and kiss you, as old Vining used to," was all the sympathy she got.

Having obeyed orders, Lucy initiated her into the mysteries of the place, and then put her in a corner to look over the scenes in which she was to appear. Christie soon caught the idea of her part,—not a difficult matter, as there were but few ideas in the whole piece, after which she sat watching the arrival of the troop she was to lead. A most forlorn band of warriors they seemed, huddled together, and looking as if afraid to speak, lest they should infringe some rule; or to move, lest they be swallowed up by some unsuspected trapdoor.

Presently the ballet-master appeared, the orchestra struck up, and Christie found herself marching and counter-marching at word of command. At first, a most uncomfortable sense of the absurdity of her position oppressed and confused her; then the ludicrous contrast between the solemn anxiety of the troop and the fantastic evolutions they were performing amused her till the novelty wore off; the martial music excited her; the desire to please sharpened her wits; and natural grace made it easy for her to catch and copy the steps and poses given her to imitate. Soon she forgot herself, entered into the spirit of the

thing, and exerted every sense to please, so successfully that
Mr. Tripp praised her quickness at comprehension, Lucy applauded heartily from a fairy car, and Mr. Sharp popped his
head out of a palace window to watch the Amazon's descent
from the Mountains of the Moon.

When the regular company arrived, the troop was dismissed
till the progress of the play demanded their reappearance. Much
interested in the piece, Christie stood aside under a palm-tree,
the foliage of which was strongly suggestive of a dilapidated
green umbrella, enjoying the novel sights and sounds about her.

Yellow-faced gentlemen and sleepy-eyed ladies roamed languidly about with much incoherent jabbering of parts, and
frequent explosions of laughter. Princes, with varnished boots
and suppressed cigars, fought, bled, and died, without a change
of countenance. Damsels of unparalleled beauty, according to
the text, gaped in the faces of adoring lovers, and crocheted
serenely on the brink of annihilation. Fairies, in rubber-boots
and woollen head-gear, disported themselves on flowery barks of
canvas, or were suspended aloft with hooks in their backs like
young Hindoo devotees. Demons, guiltless of hoof or horn,
clutched their victims with the inevitable "Ha! ha!" and vanished
darkly, eating pea-nuts. The ubiquitous Mr. Sharp seemed to
pervade the whole theatre; for his voice came shrilly from
above or spectrally from below, and his active little figure
darted to and fro like a critical will-o-the-wisp.

The grand march and chorus in the closing scene were easily
accomplished; for, as Lucy bade her, Christie "sung with all
her might," and kept step as she led her band with the dignity
of a Boadicea. No one spoke to her; few observed her; all were
intent on their own affairs; and when the final shriek and bang
died away without lifting the roof by its din, she could hardly
believe that the dreaded first rehearsal was safely over.

A visit to the wardrobe-room to see her dress came next;
and here Christie had a slight skirmish with the mistress of that
department relative to the length of her classical garments. As
studies from the nude had not yet become one of the amusements of the *élite* of Little Babel, Christie was not required to
appear in the severe simplicity of a costume consisting of a
necklace, sandals, and a bit of gold fringe about the waist, but
was allowed an extra inch or two on her tunic, and departed,

much comforted by the assurance that her dress would not be "a shock to modesty," as Lucy expressed it.

"Now, look at yourself, and, for my sake, prove an honor to your country and a terror to the foe," said Lucy, as she led her *protégée* before the green-room mirror on the first night of "The Demon's Daughter, or The Castle of the Sun!! The most Magnificent Spectacle ever produced upon the American Stage!!!"

Christie looked, and saw a warlike figure with glittering helmet, shield and lance, streaming hair and savage cloak. She liked the picture, for there was much of the heroic spirit in the girl, and even this poor counterfeit pleased her eye and filled her fancy with martial memories of Joan of Arc, Zenobia, and Britomarte.

"Go to!" cried Lucy, who affected theatrical modes of speech. "Don't admire yourself any longer, but tie up your sandals and come on. Be sure you rush down the instant I cry, 'Demon, I defy thee!' Don't break your neck, or pick your way like a cat in wet weather, but come *with effect*, for I want that scene to make a hit."

CHRISTIE AS QUEEN OF THE AMAZONS.

Princess Caremfil swept away, and the Amazonian queen climbed to her perch among the painted mountains, where her troop already sat like a flock of pigeons shining in the sun. The gilded breast-plate rose and fell with the quick beating of her heart, the spear shook with the trembling of her hand, her lips were dry, her head dizzy, and more than once, as she waited for her cue, she was sorely tempted to run away and take the consequences.

But the thought of Lucy's good-will and confidence kept her, and when the cry came she answered with a ringing shout, rushed down the ten-foot precipice, and charged upon the foe with an energy that inspired her followers, and quite satisfied the princess struggling in the demon's grasp.

With clashing of arms and shrill war-cries the rescuers of innocence assailed the sooty fiends who fell before their unscientific blows with a rapidity which inspired in the minds of beholders a suspicion that the goblins' own voluminous tails tripped them up and gallantry kept them prostrate. As the last groan expired, the last agonized squirm subsided, the conquerors performed the intricate dance with which it appears the Amazons were wont to celebrate their victories. Then the scene closed with a glare of red light and a "grand tableau" of the martial queen standing in a bower of lances, the rescued princess gracefully fainting in her arms, and the vanquished demon scowling fiercely under her foot, while four-and-twenty dishevelled damsels sang a song of exultation, to the barbaric music of a tattoo on their shields.

All went well that night, and when at last the girls doffed crown and helmet, they confided to one another the firm opinion that the success of the piece was in a great measure owing to their talent, their exertions, and went gaily home predicting for themselves careers as brilliant as those of Siddons and Rachel.

It would be a pleasant task to paint the vicissitudes and victories of a successful actress; but Christie was no dramatic genius born to shine before the world and leave a name behind her. She had no talent except that which may be developed in any girl possessing the lively fancy, sympathetic nature, and ambitious spirit which make such girls naturally dramatic. This was to be only one of many experiences which were to show her her own weakness and strength, and through effort, pain, and disappointment fit her to play a nobler part on a wider stage.

For a few weeks Christie's illusions lasted; then she discovered that the new life was nearly as humdrum as the old, that her companions were ordinary men and women, and her bright hopes were growing as dim as her tarnished shield. She grew unutterably weary of "The Castle of the Sun," and found the "Demon's Daughter" an unmitigated bore. She was not tired of the profession, only dissatisfied with the place she held in it, and eager to attempt a part that gave some scope for power and passion.

Mrs. Black wisely reminded her that she must learn to use her wings before she tried to fly, and comforted her with stories of celebrities who had begun as she was beginning, yet who had suddenly burst from their grub-like obscurity to adorn the world as splendid butterflies.

"We'll stand by you, Kit; so keep up your courage, and do your best. Be clever to every one in general, old Sharp in particular, and when a chance comes, have your wits about you and grab it. That's the way to get on," said Lucy, as sagely as if she had been a star for years.

"If I had beauty I should stand a better chance," sighed Christie, surveying herself with great disfavor, quite unconscious that to a cultivated eye the soul of beauty was often visible in that face of hers, with its intelligent eyes, sensitive mouth, and fine lines about the forehead, making it a far more significant and attractive countenance than that of her friend, possessing only piquant prettiness.

"Never mind, child; you've got a lovely figure, and an actress's best feature,—fine eyes and eyebrows. I heard old Kent say so, and he's a judge. So make the best of what you've got, as I do," answered Lucy, glancing at her own comely little person with an air of perfect resignation.

Christie laughed at the adviser, but wisely took the advice, and, though she fretted in private, was cheerful and alert in public. Always modest, attentive, and obliging, she soon became a favorite with her mates, and, thanks to Lucy's good offices with Mr. Sharp, whose favorite she was, Christie got promoted sooner than she otherwise would have been.

A great Christmas spectacle was brought out the next season, and Christie had a good part in it. When that was over she thought there was no hope for her, as the regular company was full and a different sort of performance was to begin. But just then her chance came, and she "grabbed it." The first soubrette died suddenly, and in the emergency Mr. Sharp offered the place to Christie till he could fill it to his mind. Lucy was second soubrette, and had hoped for this promotion; but Lucy did not sing well. Christie had a good voice, had taken lessons and much improved of late, so she had the preference and resolved to stand the test so well that this temporary elevation should become permanent.

She did her best, and though many of the parts were distasteful to her she got through them successfully, while now and then she had one which she thoroughly enjoyed. Her Tilly Slowboy was a hit, and a proud girl was Christie when Kent, the comedian, congratulated her on it, and told her he had seldom seen it better done.

To find favor in Kent's eyes was an honor indeed, for he belonged to the old school, and rarely condescended to praise modern actors. His own style was so admirable that he was justly considered the first comedian in the country, and was the pride and mainstay of the old theatre where he had played for years. Of course he possessed much influence in that little world, and being a kindly man used it generously to help up any young aspirant who seemed to him deserving.

He had observed Christie, attracted by her intelligent face and modest manners, for in spite of her youth there was a native refinement about her that made it impossible for her to romp and flirt as some of her mates did. But till she played Tilly he had not thought she possessed any talent. That pleased him, and seeing how much she valued his praise, and was flattered by his notice, he gave her the wise but unpalatable advice always offered young actors. Finding that she accepted it, was willing to study hard, work faithfully, and wait patiently, he predicted that in time she would make a clever actress, never a great one.

Of course Christie thought he was mistaken, and secretly resolved to prove him a false prophet by the triumphs of her career. But she meekly bowed to his opinion; this docility pleased him, and he took a paternal sort of interest in her, which, coming from the powerful favorite, did her good service with the higher powers, and helped her on more rapidly than years of meritorious effort.

Toward the end of that second season several of Dickens's dramatized novels were played, and Christie earned fresh laurels. She loved those books, and seemed by instinct to understand and personate the humor and pathos of many of those grotesque creations. Believing she had little beauty to sacrifice, she dressed such parts to the life, and played them with a spirit and ease that surprised those who had considered her a dignified and rather dull young person.

"I'll tell you what it is, Sharp, that girl is going to make a capital character actress. When her parts suit, she forgets herself entirely and does admirably well. Her Miggs was nearly the death of me to-night. She's got that one gift, and it's a good one. You'd better give her a chance, for I think she'll be a credit to the old concern."

Kent said that,—Christie heard it, and flew to Lucy, waving Miggs's cap for joy as she told the news.

"What did Mr. Sharp say?" asked Lucy, turning round with her face half "made up."

"He merely said 'Hum,' and smiled. Wasn't that a good sign?" said Christie, anxiously.

"Can't say," and Lucy touched up her eyebrows as if she took no interest in the affair.

Christie's face fell, and her heart sunk at the thought of failure; but she kept up her spirits by working harder than ever, and soon had her reward. Mr. Sharp's "Hum" did mean yes, and the next season she was regularly engaged, with a salary of thirty dollars a week.

It was a grand step, and knowing that she owed it to Kent, Christie did her utmost to show that she deserved his good opinion. New trials and temptations beset her now, but hard work and an innocent nature kept her safe and busy. Obstacles only spurred her on to redoubled exertion, and whether she did well or ill, was praised or blamed, she found a never-failing excitement in her attempts to reach the standard of perfection she had set up for herself. Kent did not regret his patronage. Mr. Sharp was satisfied with the success of the experiment, and Christie soon became a favorite in a small way, because behind the actress the public always saw a woman who never "forgot the modesty of nature."

But as she grew prosperous in outward things, Christie found herself burdened with a private cross that tried her very much. Lucy was no longer her friend; something had come between them, and a steadily increasing coldness took the place of the confidence and affection which had once existed. Lucy was jealous for Christie had passed her in the race. She knew she could not fill the place Christie had gained by favor, and now held by her own exertions, still she was bitterly envious, though ashamed to own it.

Christie tried to be just and gentle, to prove her gratitude to her first friend, and to show that her heart was unchanged. But she failed to win Lucy back and felt herself injured by such unjust resentment. Mrs. Black took her daughter's part, and though they preserved the peace outwardly the old friendliness was quite gone.

Hoping to forget this trouble in excitement Christie gave herself entirely to her profession, finding in it a satisfaction which for a time consoled her.

But gradually she underwent the sorrowful change which comes to strong natures when they wrong themselves through ignorance or wilfulness.

Pride and native integrity kept her from the worst temptations of such a life, but to the lesser ones she yielded, growing selfish, frivolous, and vain,—intent on her own advancement, and careless by what means she reached it. She had no thought now beyond her art, no desire beyond the commendation of those whose opinion was serviceable, no care for any one but herself.

Her love of admiration grew by what it fed on, till the sound of applause became the sweetest music to her ear. She rose with this hope, lay down with this satisfaction, and month after month passed in this feverish life, with no wish to change it, but a growing appetite for its unsatisfactory delights, an ever-increasing forgetfulness of any higher aspiration than dramatic fame.

"Give me joy, Lucy, I'm to have a benefit next week! Everybody else has had one, and I've played for them all, so no one seemed to begrudge me my turn when dear old Kent proposed it," said Christie, coming in one night still flushed and excited with the good news.

"What shall you have?" asked Lucy, trying to look pleased, and failing decidedly.

"'Masks and Faces.' I've always wanted to play Peg, and it has good parts for you and Kent, and St. George. I chose it for that reason, for I shall need all the help I can get to pull me through, I dare say."

The smile vanished entirely at this speech, and Christie was suddenly seized with a suspicion that Lucy was not only jealous of her as an actress, but as a woman. St. George was a comely young actor who usually played lovers' parts with Christie, and played them very well, too, being possessed of much talent, and a gentleman. They had never thought of falling in love with each other, though St. George wooed and won Christie night after night in vaudeville and farce. But it was very easy to imagine that so much mock passion had a basis of truth, and Lucy evidently tormented herself with this belief.

"Why didn't you choose Juliet: St. George would do Romeo so well?" said Lucy, with a sneer.

"No, that is beyond me. Kent says Shakespeare will never be my line, and I believe him. I should think you'd be satisfied with 'Masks and Faces,' for you know Mabel gets her husband safely back in the end," answered Christie, watching the effect of her words.

"As if I wanted the man! No, thank you, other people's leavings won't suit me," cried Lucy, tossing her head, though her face belied her words.

"Not even though he has 'heavenly eyes,' 'distracting legs,' and 'a melting voice?'" asked Christie maliciously, quoting Lucy's own rapturous speeches when the new actor came.

"Come, come, girls, don't quarrel. I won't 'ave it in me room. Lucy's tired to death, and it's not nice of you, Kitty, to come and crow over her this way," said Mamma Black, coming to the rescue, for Lucy was in tears, and Christie looking dangerous.

"It's impossible to please you, so I'll say good-night," and Christie went to her room with resentment burning hotly in her heart.

As she crossed the chamber her eye fell on her own figure

reflected in the long glass, and with a sudden impulse she turned up the gas, wiped the rouge from her cheeks, pushed back her hair, and studied her own face intently for several moments. It was pale and jaded now, and all its freshness seemed gone; hard lines had come about the mouth, a feverish disquiet filled the eyes, and on the forehead seemed to lie the shadow of a discontent that saddened the whole face. If one could believe the testimony of that countenance things were not going well with Christie, and she owned it with a regretful sigh, as she asked herself, "Am I what I hoped I should be? No, and it is my fault. If three years of this life have made me this, what shall I be in ten? A fine actress perhaps, but how good a woman?"

With gloomy eyes fixed on her altered face she stood a moment struggling with herself. Then the hard look returned, and she spoke out defiantly, as if in answer to some warning voice within herself. "No one cares what I am, so why care myself? Why not go on and get as much fame as I can? Success gives me power if it cannot give me happiness, and I must have some reward for my hard work. Yes! a gay life and a short one, then out with the lights and down with the curtain!"

But in spite of her reckless words Christie sobbed herself to sleep that night like a child who knows it is astray, yet cannot see the right path or hear its mother's voice calling it home.

On the night of the benefit, Lucy was in a most exasperating mood, Christie in a very indignant one, and as they entered their dressing-room they looked as if they might have played the Rival Queens with great effect. Lucy offered no help and Christie asked none, but putting her vexation resolutely out of sight fixed her mind on the task before her.

As the pleasant stir began all about her, actress-like, she felt her spirits rise, her courage increase with every curl she fastened up, every gay garment she put on, and soon smiled approvingly at herself, for excitement lent her cheeks a better color than rouge, her eyes shone with satisfaction, and her heart beat high with the resolve to make a hit or die.

Christie needed encouragement that night, and found it in the hearty welcome that greeted her, and the full house, which proved how kind a regard was entertained for her by many who knew her only by a fictitious name. She felt this deeply, and it helped her much, for she was vexed with many trials those before the footlights knew nothing of.

The other players were full of kindly interest in her success, but Lucy took a naughty satisfaction in harassing her by all the small slights and unanswerable provocations which one actress has it in her power to inflict upon another.

Christie was fretted almost beyond endurance, and retaliated by an ominous frown when her position allowed, threatening asides when a moment's by-play favored their delivery, and angry protests whenever she met Lucy off the stage.

But in spite of all annoyances she had never played better in her life. She liked the part, and acted the warm-hearted, quick-witted, sharp-tongued Peg with a spirit and grace that surprised even those who knew her best. Especially good was she in the scenes with Triplet, for Kent played the part admirably, and cheered her on with many an encouraging look and word. Anxious to do honor to her patron and friend she threw her whole heart into the work; in the scene where she comes like a good angel to the home of the poor play-wright, she brought tears to the eyes of her audience; and when at her command Triplet strikes up a jig to amuse the children she "covered the buckle" in gallant style, dancing with all the frolicsome *abandon* of the Irish orange-girl who for a moment forgot her grandeur and her grief.

That scene was her best, for it is full of those touches of nature that need very little art to make them effective; and when a great bouquet fell with a thump at Christie's feet, as she paused to bow her thanks for an encore, she felt that she had reached the height of earthly bliss.

In the studio scene Lucy seemed suddenly gifted with unsuspected skill; for when Mabel kneels to the picture, praying her rival to give her back her husband's heart, Christie was amazed to see real tears roll down Lucy's cheeks, and to hear real love and longing thrill her trembling words with sudden power and passion.

"That is not acting. She does love St. George, and thinks I mean to keep him from her. Poor dear! I'll tell her all about it to-night, and set her heart at rest," thought Christie; and when Peg left the frame, her face expressed the genuine pity that she felt, and her voice was beautifully tender as she promised to restore the stolen treasure.

Lucy felt comforted without knowing why, and the piece went smoothly on to its last scene. Peg was just relinquishing the repentant husband to his forgiving wife with those brave words of hers, when a rending sound above their heads made all look up and start back; all but Lucy, who stood bewildered. Christie's quick eye saw the impending danger, and with a sudden spring she caught her friend from it. It was only a second's work, but it cost her much; for in the act, down crashed one of the mechanical contrivances used in a late spectacle, and in its fall stretched Christie stunned and senseless on the stage.

A swift uprising filled the house with tumult; a crowd of actors hurried forward, and the panic-stricken audience caught glimpses of poor Peg lying mute and pallid in Mabel's arms, while Vane wrung his hands, and Triplet audibly demanded, "Why the devil somebody didn't go for a doctor?"

Then a brilliant view of Mount Parnassus, with Apollo and the Nine Muses in full blast, shut the scene from sight, and soon Mr. Sharp appeared to ask their patience till the after-piece was ready, for Miss Douglas was too much injured to appear again. And with an unwonted expression of feeling, the little man alluded to "the generous act which perhaps had changed the comedy to a tragedy and robbed the beneficiary of her well-earned reward at their hands."

All had seen the impulsive spring toward, not from, the danger, and this unpremeditated action won heartier applause than Christie ever had received for her best rendering of more heroic deeds.

But she did not hear the cordial round they gave her. She had said she would "make a hit or die;" and just then it seemed as if she had done both, for she was deaf and blind to the admiration and the sympathy bestowed upon her as the curtain fell on the first, last benefit she ever was to have.

## Chapter IV

GOVERNESS

MR. PHILIP FLETCHER.

---

DURING the next few weeks Christie learned the worth of many things which she had valued very lightly until then. Health became a boon too precious to be trifled with; life assumed a deeper significance when death's shadow fell upon its light, and she discovered that dependence might be made endurable by the sympathy of unsuspected friends.

Lucy waited upon her with a remorseful devotion which touched her very much and won entire forgiveness for the past, long before it was repentantly implored. All her comrades came with offers of help and affectionate regrets. Several whom she had most disliked now earned her gratitude by the kindly thoughtfulness which filled her sick-room with fruit and flowers, supplied carriages for the convalescent, and paid her doctor's bill without her knowledge.

Thus Christie learned, like many another needy member of the gay profession, that though often extravagant and jovial in their way of life, these men and women give as freely as they spend, wear warm, true hearts under their motley, and make misfortune only another link in the bond of good-fellowship which binds them loyally together.

Slowly Christie gathered her energies after weeks of suffering, and took up her life again, grateful for the gift, and anxious to be more worthy of it. Looking back upon the past she felt that she had made a mistake and lost more than she had gained in those three years. Others might lead that life of alternate excitement and hard work unharmed, but she could not. The very ardor and insight which gave power to the actress made that mimic life unsatisfactory to the woman, for hers was an earnest nature that took fast hold of whatever task she gave herself to do, and lived in it heartily while duty made it right, or novelty lent it charms. But when she saw the error of a step, the emptiness of a belief, with a like earnestness she tried to retrieve the one and to replace the other with a better substitute.

In the silence of wakeful nights and the solitude of quiet days, she took counsel with her better self, condemned the reckless spirit which had possessed her, and came at last to the decision which conscience prompted and much thought confirmed.

"The stage is not the place for me," she said. "I have no genius to glorify the drudgery, keep me from temptation, and repay me for any sacrifice I make. Other women can lead this life safely and happily: I cannot, and I must not go back to it, because, with all my past experience, and in spite of all my present good resolutions, I should do no better, and I might do worse. I'm not wise enough to keep steady there; I must return to the old ways, dull but safe, and plod along till I find my real place and work."

Great was the surprise of Lucy and her mother when Christie told her resolution, adding, in a whisper, to the girl, "I leave the field clear for you, dear, and will dance at your wedding with all my heart when St. George asks you to play the 'Honeymoon' with him, as I'm sure he will before long."

Many entreaties from friends, as well as secret longings, tried and tempted Christie sorely, but she withstood them all, carried her point, and renounced the profession she could not follow without self-injury and self-reproach. The season was nearly over when she was well enough to take her place again, but she refused to return, relinquished her salary, sold her wardrobe, and never crossed the threshold of the theatre after she had said good-bye.

Then she asked, "What next?" and was speedily answered. An advertisement for a governess met her eye, which seemed to combine the two things she most needed just then,—employment and change of air.

"Mind you don't mention that you've been an actress or it will be all up with you, me dear," said Mrs. Black, as Christie prepared to investigate the matter, for since her last effort in that line she had increased her knowledge of music, and learned French enough to venture teaching it to very young pupils.

"I'd rather tell in the beginning, for if you keep any thing back it's sure to pop out when you least expect or want it. I don't believe these people will care as long as I'm respectable and teach well," returned Christie, wishing she looked stronger and rosier.

"You'll be sorry if you do tell," warned Mrs. Black, who knew the ways of the world.

"I shall be sorry if I don't," laughed Christie, and so she was, in the end.

"L. N. Saltonstall" was the name on the door, and L. N. Saltonstall's servant was so leisurely about answering Christie's meek solo on the bell, that she had time to pull out her bonnet-strings half-a-dozen times before a very black man in a very white jacket condescended to conduct her to his mistress.

A frail, tea-colored lady appeared, displaying such a small proportion of woman to such a large proportion of purple and fine linen, that she looked as if she was literally as well as figuratively "dressed to death."

Christie went to the point in a business-like manner that seemed to suit Mrs. Saltonstall, because it saved so much trouble, and she replied, with a languid affability:

"I wish some one to teach the children a little, for they are getting too old to be left entirely to nurse. I am anxious to get to the sea-shore as soon as possible, for they have been poorly all winter, and my own health has suffered. Do you feel inclined to try the place? And what compensation do you require?"

Christie had but a vague idea of what wages were usually paid to nursery governesses, and hesitatingly named a sum which seemed reasonable to her, but was so much less than any other applicant had asked, that Mrs. Saltonstall began to think she could not do better than secure this cheap young person, who looked firm enough to manage her rebellious son and heir, and well-bred enough to begin the education of a little fine lady. Her winter had been an extravagant one, and she could economize in the governess better perhaps than elsewhere; so she decided to try Christie, and get out of town at once.

"Your terms are quite satisfactory, Miss Devon, and if my brother approves, I think we will consider the matter settled. Perhaps you would like to see the children? They are little darlings, and you will soon be fond of them, I am sure."

A bell was rung, an order given, and presently appeared an eight-year-old boy, so excessively Scotch in his costume that he looked like an animated checkerboard; and a little girl, who presented the appearance of a miniature opera-dancer staggering under the weight of an immense sash.

"Go and speak prettily to Miss Devon, my pets, for she is coming to play with you, and you must mind what she says," commanded mamma.

The pale, fretful-looking little pair went solemnly to Christie's knee, and stood there staring at her with a dull composure that quite daunted her, it was so sadly unchildlike.

"What is your name, dear?" she asked, laying her hand on the young lady's head.

"Villamena Temmatina Taltentall. You mustn't touch my hair; it's just turled," was the somewhat embarrassing reply.

"Mine's Louy 'Poleon Thaltensthall, like papa's," volunteered the other young person, and Christie privately wondered if the possession of names nearly as long as themselves was not a burden to the poor dears.

Feeling that she must say something, she asked, in her most persuasive tone:

"Would you like to have me come and teach you some nice lessons out of your little books?"

If she had proposed corporal punishment on the spot it could not have caused greater dismay. Wilhelmina cast herself upon the floor passionately, declaring that she "touldn't tuddy," and Saltonstall, Jr., retreated precipitately to the door, and from that refuge defied the whole race of governesses and "nasty lessons" jointly.

"There, run away to Justine. They are sadly out of sorts, and quite pining for sea-air," said mamma, with both hands at her ears, for the war-cries of her darlings were piercing as they departed, proclaiming their wrongs while swarming up stairs, with a skirmish on each landing.

With a few more words Christie took leave, and scandalized the sable retainer by smiling all through the hall, and laughing audibly as the door closed. The contrast of the plaid boy and beruffled girl's irritability with their mother's languid affectation, and her own unfortunate efforts, was too much for her. In the middle of her merriment she paused suddenly, saying to herself:

"I never told about my acting. I must go back and have it settled." She retraced a few steps, then turned and went on again, thinking, "No; for once I'll be guided by other people's advice, and let well alone."

A note arrived soon after, bidding Miss Devon consider herself engaged, and desiring her to join the family at the boat on Monday next.

At the appointed time Christie was on board, and looked about for her party. Mrs. Saltonstall appeared in the distance with her family about her, and Christie took a survey before reporting herself. Madame looked more like a fashion-plate than ever, in a mass of green flounces, and an impressive bonnet flushed with poppies and bristling with wheat-ears. Beside her sat a gentleman, rapt in a newspaper, of course, for to an American man life is a burden till the daily news have been absorbed. Mrs. Saltonstall's brother was the possessor of a handsome eye without softness, thin lips without benevolence, but plenty of will; a face and figure which some thirty-five years of ease and pleasure had done their best to polish and spoil, and a costume without flaw, from his aristocratic boots to the summer hat on his head.

The little boy more checkered and the little girl more operatic than before, sat on stools eating *bonbons*, while a French maid and the African footman hovered in the background.

MRS. SALTONSTALL AND FAMILY.

Feeling very much like a meek gray moth among a flock of butterflies, Christie modestly presented herself.

"Good morning," said Madame with a nod, which, slight as it was, caused a great commotion among the poppies and the wheat; "I began to be anxious about you. Miss Devon, my brother, Mr. Fletcher."

The gentleman bowed, and as Christie sat down he got up, saying, as he sauntered away with a bored expression:

"Will you have the paper, Charlotte? There's nothing in it."

As Mrs. Saltonstall seemed going to sleep and she felt delicate about addressing the irritable infants in public, Christie amused herself by watching Mr. Fletcher as he roamed listlessly about, and deciding, in her usual rash way, that she did not like him because he looked both lazy and cross, and *ennui* was evidently his bosom friend. Soon, however, she forgot every thing but the shimmer of the sunshine on the sea, the fresh wind that brought color to her pale cheeks, and the happy thoughts that left a smile upon her lips. Then Mr. Fletcher put up his glass and stared at her, shook his head, and said, as he lit a cigar:

"Poor little wretch, what a time she will have of it between Charlotte and the brats!"

But Christie needed no pity, and thought herself a fortunate young woman when fairly established in her corner of the luxurious apartments occupied by the family. Her duties seemed light compared to those she had left, her dreams were almost as bright as of old, and the new life looked pleasant to her, for she was one of those who could find little bits of happiness for herself and enjoy them heartily in spite of loneliness or neglect.

One of her amusements was studying her companions, and for a time this occupied her, for Christie possessed penetration and a feminine fancy for finding out people.

Mrs. Saltonstall's mission appeared to be the illustration of each new fashion as it came, and she performed it with a devotion worthy of a better cause. If a color reigned supreme she flushed herself with scarlet or faded into primrose, made herself pretty in the bluest of blue gowns, or turned livid under a gooseberry colored bonnet. Her hat-brims went up or down, were preposterously wide or dwindled to an inch, as the mode demanded. Her skirts were rampant with sixteen frills, or picturesque with landscapes down each side, and a Greek border or a plain hem. Her waists were as pointed as those of Queen Bess or as short as Diana's; and it was the opinion of those who knew her that if the autocrat who ruled her life decreed the wearing of black cats as well as of vegetables, bugs, and birds, the blackest, glossiest Puss procurable for money would have adorned her head in some way.

Her time was spent in dressing, driving, dining and dancing; in skimming novels, and embroidering muslin; going to church with a velvet prayer-book and a new bonnet; and writing to her husband when she wanted money, for she had a husband somewhere abroad, who so happily combined business with pleasure that he never found time to come home. Her children were inconvenient blessings, but she loved them with the love of a shallow heart, and took such good care of their little bodies that there was none left for their little souls. A few days' trial satisfied her as to Christie's capabilities, and, relieved of that anxiety, she gave herself up to her social duties, leaving the ocean and the governess to make the summer wholesome and agreeable to "the darlings."

Mr. Fletcher, having tried all sorts of pleasure and found that, like his newspaper, there was "nothing in it," was now paying the penalty for that unsatisfactory knowledge. Ill health soured his temper and made his life a burden to him. Having few resources within himself to fall back upon, he was very dependent upon other people, and other people were so busy amusing themselves, they seemed to find little time or inclination to amuse a man who had never troubled himself about them. He was rich, but while his money could hire a servant to supply each want, gratify each caprice, it could not buy a tender, faithful friend to serve for love, and ask no wages but his comfort.

He knew this, and felt the vain regret that inevitably comes to those who waste life and learn the value of good gifts by their loss. But he was not wise or brave enough to bear his punishment manfully, and lay the lesson honestly to heart. Fretful and imperious when in pain, listless and selfish when at ease, his one aim in life now was to kill time, and any thing that aided him in this was most gratefully welcomed.

For a long while he took no more notice of Christie than if she had been a shadow, seldom speaking beyond the necessary salutations, and merely carrying his finger to his hat-brim when he passed her on the beach with the children. Her first dislike was softened by pity when she found he was an invalid, but she troubled herself very little about him, and made no romances with him, for all her dreams were of younger, nobler lovers.

Busied with her own affairs, the days though monotonous were not unhappy. She prospered in her work and the children soon believed in her as devoutly as young Turks in their Prophet. She devised amusements for herself as well as for them; walked, bathed, drove, and romped with the little people till her own eyes shone like theirs, her cheek grew rosy, and her thin figure rounded with the promise of vigorous health again.

Christie was at her best that summer, physically speaking,

for sickness had refined her face, giving it that indescribable expression which pain often leaves upon a countenance as if in compensation for the bloom it takes away. The frank eyes had a softer shadow in their depths, the firm lips smiled less often, but when it came the smile was the sweeter for the gravity that went before, and in her voice there was a new undertone of that subtle music, called sympathy, which steals into the heart and nestles there.

She was unconscious of this gracious change, but others saw and felt it, and to some a face bright with health, intelligence, and modesty was more attractive than mere beauty. Thanks to this and her quiet, cordial manners, she found friends here and there to add charms to that summer by the sea.

The dashing young men took no more notice of her than if she had been a little gray peep on the sands; not so much, for they shot peeps now and then, but a governess was not worth bringing down. The fashionable belles and beauties were not even aware of her existence, being too entirely absorbed in their yearly husband-hunt to think of any one but themselves and their prey. The dowagers had more interesting topics to discuss, and found nothing in Christie's humble fortunes worthy of a thought, for they liked their gossip strong and highly flavored, like their tea.

But a kind-hearted girl or two found her out, several lively old maids, as full of the romance of the past as ancient novels, a bashful boy, three or four invalids, and *all* the children, for Christie had a motherly heart and could find charms in the plainest, crossest baby that ever squalled.

Of her old friends she saw nothing, as her theatrical ones were off on their vacations, Hepsey had left her place for one in another city, and Aunt Betsey seldom wrote.

But one day a letter came, telling her that the dear old lady would never write again, and Christie felt as if her nearest and dearest friend was lost. She had gone away to a quiet spot among the rocks to get over her first grief alone, but found it very hard to check her tears, as memory brought back the past, tenderly recalling every kind act, every loving word, and familiar scene. She seldom wept, but when any thing did unseal the fountains that lay so deep, she cried with all her heart, and felt the better for it.

With the letter crumpled in her hand, her head on her knees, and her hat at her feet, she was sobbing like a child, when steps startled her, and, looking up, she saw Mr. Fletcher regarding her with an astonished countenance from under his big sun umbrella.

Something in the flushed, wet face, with its tremulous lips and great tears rolling down, seemed to touch even lazy Mr. Fletcher, for he furled his umbrella with unusual rapidity, and came up, saying, anxiously:

"My dear Miss Devon, what's the matter? Are you hurt? Has Mrs. S. been scolding? Or have the children been too much for you?"

"No; oh, no! it's bad news from home," and Christie's head went down again, for a kind word was more than she could bear just then.

"Some one ill, I fancy? I'm sorry to hear it, but you must hope for the best, you know," replied Mr. Fletcher, really quite exerting himself to remember and present this well-worn consolation.

"There is no hope; Aunt Betsey's dead!"

"Dear me! that's very sad."

Mr. Fletcher tried not to smile as Christie sobbed out the old-fashioned name, but a minute afterward there were actually tears in his eyes, for, as if won by his sympathy, she poured out the homely little story of Aunt Betsey's life and love, unconsciously pronouncing the kind old lady's best epitaph in the unaffected grief that made her broken words so eloquent.

For a minute Mr. Fletcher forgot himself, and felt as he remembered feeling long ago, when, a warm-hearted boy, he had comforted his little sister for a lost kitten or a broken doll. It was a new sensation, therefore interesting and agreeable while it lasted, and when it vanished, which it speedily did, he sighed, then shrugged his shoulders and wished "the girl would stop crying like a water-spout."

"It's hard, but we all have to bear it, you know; and sometimes I fancy if half the pity we give the dead, who don't need it, was given to the living, who do, they'd bear their troubles more comfortably. I know *I* should," added Mr. Fletcher, returning to his own afflictions, and vaguely wondering if any one would cry like that when he departed this life.

Christie minded little what he said, for his voice was pitiful and it comforted her. She dried her tears, put back her hair, and thanked him with a grateful smile, which gave him another pleasant sensation; for, though young ladies showered smiles upon him with midsummer radiance, they seemed cool and pale beside the sweet sincerity of this one given by a girl whose eyes were red with tender tears.

"That's right, cheer up, take a little run on the beach, and forget all about it," he said, with a heartiness that surprised himself as much as it did Christie.

"I will, thank you. Please don't speak of this; I'm used to bearing my troubles alone, and time will help me to do it cheerfully."

"That's brave! If I can do any thing, let me know; I shall be most happy." And Mr. Fletcher evidently meant what he said.

Christie gave him another grateful "Thank you," then picked up her hat and went away along the sands to try his prescription; while Mr. Fletcher walked the other way, so rapt in thought that he forgot to put up his umbrella till the end of his aristocratic nose was burnt a deep red.

That was the beginning of it; for when Mr. Fletcher found a new amusement, he usually pursued it regardless of consequences. Christie took his pity for what it was worth, and thought no more of that little interview, for her heart was very heavy. But he remembered it, and, when they met on the beach next day, wondered how the governess would behave. She was reading as she walked, and, with a mute acknowledgment of his nod, tranquilly turned a page and read on without a pause, a smile, or change of color.

Mr. Fletcher laughed as he strolled away; but Christie was all the more amusing for her want of coquetry, and soon after he tried her again. The great hotel was all astir one evening with bustle, light, and music; for the young people had a hop, as an appropriate entertainment for a melting July night. With no taste for such folly, even if health had not forbidden it, Mr. Fletcher lounged about the piazzas, tantalizing the fair fowlers who spread their nets for him, and goading sundry desperate spinsters to despair by his erratic movements. Coming to a quiet nook, where a long window gave a fine view of the brilliant scene, he found Christie leaning in, with a bright, wistful

face, while her hand kept time to the enchanting music of a
waltz.

"Wisely watching the lunatics, instead of joining in their
antics," he said, sitting down with a sigh.

Christie looked around and answered, with the wistful look
still in her eyes:

"I'm very fond of that sort of insanity; but there is no place
for me in Bedlam at present."

"I daresay I can find you one, if you care to try it. I don't
indulge myself." And Mr. Fletcher's eye went from the rose in
Christie's brown hair to the silvery folds of her best gown, put
on merely for the pleasure of wearing it because every one else
was in festival array.

She shook her head. "No, thank you. Governesses are very
kindly treated in America; but ball-rooms like that are not for
them. I enjoy looking on, fortunately; so I have my share of
fun after all."

"I shan't get any complaints out of her. Plucky little soul! I
rather like that," said Mr. Fletcher to himself; and, finding his
seat comfortable, the corner cool, and his companion pleasant
to look at, with the moonlight doing its best for her, he went
on talking for his own satisfaction.

Christie would rather have been left in peace; but fancying
that he did it out of kindness to her, and that she had done
him injustice before, she was grateful now, and exerted herself
to seem so; in which endeavor she succeeded so well that Mr.
Fletcher proved he could be a very agreeable companion when
he chose. He talked well; and Christie was a good listener.
Soon interest conquered her reserve, and she ventured to ask a
question, make a criticism, or express an opinion in her own
simple way. Unconsciously she piqued the curiosity of the
man; for, though he knew many lovely, wise, and witty women,
he had never chanced to meet with one like this before; and
novelty was the desire of his life. Of course he did not find
moonlight, music, and agreeable chat as delightful as she did;
but there *was* something animating in the fresh face opposite,
something flattering in the eager interest she showed, and
something most attractive in the glimpses unconsciously given
him of a nature genuine in its womanly sincerity and strength.
Something about this girl seemed to appeal to the old self, so

long neglected that he thought it dead. He could not analyze the feeling, but was conscious of a desire to seem better than he was as he looked into those honest eyes; to talk well, that he might bring that frank smile to the lips that grew either sad or scornful when he tried worldly gossip or bitter satire; and to prove himself a man under all the elegance and polish of the gentleman.

He was discovering then, what Christie learned when her turn came, that fine natures seldom fail to draw out the finer traits of those who approach them, as the little witch-hazel wand, even in the hand of a child, detects and points to hidden springs in unsuspected spots. Women often possess this gift, and when used worthily find it as powerful as beauty; for, if less alluring, it is more lasting and more helpful, since it appeals, not to the senses, but the souls of men.

Christie was one of these; and in proportion as her own nature was sound and sweet so was its power as a touchstone for the genuineness of others. It was this unconscious gift that made her wonder at the unexpected kindness she found in Mr. Fletcher, and this which made him, for an hour or two at least, heartily wish he could live his life over again and do it better.

After that evening Mr. Fletcher spoke to Christie when he met her, turned and joined her sometimes as she walked with the children, and fell into the way of lounging near when she sat reading aloud to an invalid friend on piazza or sea-shore. Christie much preferred to have no auditor but kind Miss Tudor; but finding the old lady enjoyed his chat she resigned herself, and when he brought them new books as well as himself, she became quite cordial.

Everybody sauntered and lounged, so no one minded the little group that met day after day among the rocks. Christie read aloud, while the children revelled in sand, shells, and puddles; Miss Tudor spun endless webs of gay silk and wool; and Mr. Fletcher, with his hat over his eyes, lay sunning himself like a luxurious lizard, as he watched the face that grew daily fairer in his sight, and listened to the pleasant voice that went reading on till all his ills and *ennui* seemed lulled to sleep as by a spell.

A week or two of this new caprice set Christie to thinking. She knew that Uncle Philip was not fond of "the darlings;" it

was evident that good Miss Tudor, with her mild twaddle and
eternal knitting, was not the attraction, so she was forced to
believe that he came for her sake alone. She laughed at herself
for this fancy at first; but not possessing the sweet unconsciousness of those heroines who can live through three volumes with a burning passion before their eyes, and never see it
till the proper moment comes, and Eugene goes down upon
his knees, she soon felt sure that Mr. Fletcher found her society
agreeable, and wished her to know it.

Being a mortal woman, her vanity was flattered, and she
found herself showing that she liked it by those small signs and
symbols which lovers' eyes are so quick to see and understand,—
an artful bow on her hat, a flower in her belt, fresh muslin
gowns, and the most becoming arrangement of her hair.

"Poor man, he has so few pleasures I'm sure I needn't
grudge him such a small one as looking at and listening to me
if he likes it," she said to herself one day, as she was preparing
for her daily stroll with unusual care. "But how will it end? If
he only wants a mild flirtation he is welcome to it; but if he
really cares for me, I must make up my mind about it, and not
deceive him. I don't believe he loves me: how can he? such an
insignificant creature as I am."

Here she looked in the glass, and as she looked the color
deepened in her cheek, her eyes shone, and a smile would sit
upon her lips, for the reflection showed her a very winning
face under the coquettish hat put on to captivate.

"Don't be foolish, Christie! Mind what you do, and be sure
vanity doesn't delude you, for you are only a woman, and in
things of this sort we are so blind and silly. I'll think of this
possibility soberly, but I won't flirt, and then which ever way I
decide I shall have nothing to reproach myself with."

Armed with this virtuous resolution, Christie sternly replaced the pretty hat with her old brown one, fastened up a
becoming curl, which of late she had worn behind her ear, and
put on a pair of stout, rusty boots, much fitter for rocks and
sand than the smart slippers she was preparing to sacrifice.
Then she trudged away to Miss Tudor, bent on being very
quiet and reserved, as became a meek and lowly governess.

But, dear heart, how feeble are the resolutions of womankind! When she found herself sitting in her favorite nook, with

the wide, blue sea glittering below, the fresh wind making her blood dance in her veins, and all the earth and sky so full of summer life and loveliness, her heart *would* sing for joy, her face *would* shine with the mere bliss of living, and underneath all this natural content the new thought, half confessed, yet very sweet, *would* whisper, "Somebody cares for me."

If she had doubted it, the expression of Mr. Fletcher's face that morning would have dispelled the doubt, for, as she read, he was saying to himself: "Yes, this healthful, cheery, helpful creature is what I want to make life pleasant. Every thing else is used up; why not try this, and make the most of my last chance? She does me good, and I don't seem to get tired of her. I can't have a long life, they tell me, nor an easy one, with the devil to pay with my vitals generally; so it would be a wise thing to provide myself with a good-tempered, faithful soul to take care of me. My fortune would pay for loss of time, and my death leave her a bonny widow. I won't be rash, but I think I'll try it."

With this mixture of tender, selfish, and regretful thoughts in his mind, it is no wonder Mr. Fletcher's eyes betrayed him, as he lay looking at Christie. Never had she read so badly, for she could not keep her mind on her book. It *would* wander to that new and troublesome fancy of hers; she could not help thinking that Mr. Fletcher must have been a handsome man before he was so ill; wondering if his temper was *very* bad, and fancying that he might prove both generous and kind and true to one who loved and served him well. At this point she was suddenly checked by a slip of the tongue that covered her with confusion.

She was reading "John Halifax," and instead of saying "Phineas Fletcher" she said Philip, and then colored to her forehead, and lost her place. Miss Tudor did not mind it, but Mr. Fletcher laughed, and Christie thanked Heaven that her face was half hidden by the old brown hat.

Nothing was said, but she was much relieved to find that Mr. Fletcher had joined a yachting party next day and he would be away for a week. During that week Christie thought over the matter, and fancied she had made up her mind. She recalled certain speeches she had heard, and which had more weight with her than she suspected. One dowager had said to another: "P. F. intends to marry, I assure you, for his sister told me so, with tears in her eyes. Men who have been gay in their youth make very good husbands when their wild oats are sowed. Clara could not do better, and I should be quite content to give her to him."

"Well, dear, I should be sorry to see my Augusta his wife, for whoever he marries will be a perfect slave to him. His fortune would be a nice thing if he did not live long; but even for that my Augusta shall not be sacrificed," returned the other matron whose Augusta had vainly tried to captivate "P. F.," and revenged herself by calling him "a wreck, my dear, a perfect wreck."

At another time Christie heard some girls discussing the eligibility of several gentlemen, and Mr. Fletcher was considered the best match among them.

"You can do any thing you like with a husband a good deal older than yourself. He's happy with his business, his club, and his dinner, and leaves you to do what you please; just keep him comfortable and he'll pay your bills without much fuss," said one young thing who had seen life at twenty.

"I'd take him if I had the chance, just because everybody wants him. Don't admire him a particle, but it will make a jolly stir whenever he does marry, and I wouldn't mind having a hand in it," said the second budding belle.

"I'd take him for the diamonds alone. Mamma says they are splendid, and have been in the family for ages. He won't let Mrs. S. wear them, for they always go to the eldest son's wife. Hope he'll choose a handsome woman who will show them off well," said a third sweet girl, glancing at her own fine neck.

"He won't; he'll take some poky old maid who will cuddle him when he is sick, and keep out of his way when he is well. See if he don't."

"I saw him dawdling round with old Tudor, perhaps he means to take her: she's a capital nurse, got ill herself taking care of her father, you know."

"Perhaps he's after the governess; she's rather nice looking, though she hasn't a bit of style."

"Gracious, no! she's a dowdy thing, always trailing round with a book and those horrid children. No danger of his marrying *her*." And a derisive laugh seemed to settle that question beyond a doubt.

"Oh, indeed!" said Christie, as the girls went trooping out of the bath-house where this pleasing chatter had been carried on regardless of listeners. She called them "mercenary, worldly, unwomanly flirts," and felt herself much their superior. Yet the memory of their gossip haunted her, and had its influence upon her decision, though she thought she came to it through her own good judgment and discretion.

"If he really cares for me I will listen, and not refuse till I know him well enough to decide. I'm tired of being alone, and should enjoy ease and pleasure so much. He's going abroad for the winter, and that would be charming. I'll try not to be worldly-minded and marry without love, but it does look tempting to a poor soul like me."

So Christie made up her mind to accept, if this promotion was offered her; and while she waited, went through so many alternations of feeling, and was so harassed by doubts and fears that she sometimes found herself wishing it had never occurred to her.

Mr. Fletcher, meantime, with the help of many meditative cigars, was making up *his* mind. Absence only proved to him how much he needed a better time-killer than billiards, horses, or newspapers, for the long, listless days seemed endless without the cheerful governess to tone him up, like a new and agreeable sort of bitters. A gradually increasing desire to secure this satisfaction had taken possession of him, and the thought of always having a pleasant companion, with no nerves, nonsense, or affectation about her, was an inviting idea to a man tired of fashionable follies and tormented with the *ennui* of his own society.

The gossip, wonder, and chagrin such a step would cause rather pleased his fancy; the excitement of trying almost the only thing as yet untried allured him; and deeper than all the desire to forget the past in a better future led him to Christie by the nobler instincts that never wholly die in any soul. He wanted her as he had wanted many other things in his life, and had little doubt that he could have her for the asking. Even if love was not abounding, surely his fortune, which hitherto had procured him all he wished (except health and happiness) could buy him a wife, when his friends made better bargains every day. So, having settled the question, he came home again, and every one said the trip had done him a world of good.

Christie sat in her favorite nook one bright September morning, with the inevitable children hunting hapless crabs in a pool near by. A book lay on her knee, but she was not reading; her eyes were looking far across the blue waste before her with an eager gaze, and her face was bright with some happy thought. The sound of approaching steps disturbed her reverie, and, recognizing them, she plunged into the heart of the story, reading as if utterly absorbed, till a shadow fell athwart the page, and the voice she had expected to hear asked blandly:

"What book now, Miss Devon?"

"'Jane Eyre,' sir."

Mr. Fletcher sat down just where her hat-brim was no screen, pulled off his gloves, and leisurely composed himself for a comfortable lounge.

"What is your opinion of Rochester?" he asked, presently.

"Not a very high one."

"Then you think Jane was a fool to love and try to make a saint of him, I suppose?"

"I like Jane, but never can forgive her marrying that man, as I haven't much faith in the saints such sinners make."

"But don't you think a man who had only follies to regret might expect a good woman to lend him a hand and make him happy?"

"If he has wasted his life he must take the consequences, and be content with pity and indifference, instead of respect and love. Many good women do 'lend a hand,' as you say, and it is quite Christian and amiable, I've no doubt; but I cannot think it a fair bargain."

Mr. Fletcher liked to make Christie talk, for in the interest of the subject she forgot herself, and her chief charm for him was her earnestness. But just then the earnestness did not seem to suit him, and he said, rather sharply:

"What hard-hearted creatures you women are sometimes! Now, I fancied you were one of those who wouldn't leave a poor fellow to his fate, if his salvation lay in your hands."

"I can't say what I should do in such a case; but it always seemed to me that a man should have energy enough to save himself, and not expect the 'weaker vessel,' as he calls her, to do it for him," answered Christie, with a conscious look, for Mr. Fletcher's face made her feel as if something was going to happen.

Evidently anxious to know what she *would* do in aforesaid case, Mr. Fletcher decided to put one before her as speedily as possible, so he said, in a pensive tone, and with a wistful glance:

"You looked very happy just now when I came up. I wish I could believe that my return had any thing to do with it."

Christie wished she could control her tell-tale color, but finding she could not, looked hard at the sea, and, ignoring his tender insinuation, said, with suspicious enthusiasm:

"I was thinking of what Mrs. Saltonstall said this morning. She asked me if I would like to go to Paris with her for the winter. It has always been one of my dreams to go abroad, and I do hope I shall not be disappointed."

Christie's blush seemed to be a truer answer than her words, and, leaning a little nearer, Mr. Fletcher said, in his most persuasive tone:

"Will you go to Paris as *my* governess, instead of Charlotte's?"

Christie thought her reply was all ready; but when the moment came, she found it was not, and sat silent, feeling as if that "Yes" would promise far more than she could give. Mr. Fletcher had no doubt what the answer would be, and was in no haste to get it, for that was one of the moments that are so pleasant and so short-lived they should be enjoyed to the uttermost. He liked to watch her color come and go, to see the asters on her bosom tremble with the quickened beating of her heart, and tasted, in anticipation, the satisfaction of the moment when that pleasant voice of hers would falter out its grateful assent. Drawing yet nearer, he went on, still in the persuasive tone that would have been more lover-like if it had been less assured.

"I think I am not mistaken in believing that you care for me a little. You must know how fond I am of you, how much I need you, and how glad I should be to give all I have if I might keep you always to make my hard life happy. May I, Christie?"

"You would soon tire of me. I have no beauty, no accomplishments, no fortune,—nothing but my heart and my hand to give the man I marry. Is that enough?" asked Christie, looking at him with eyes that betrayed the hunger of an empty heart longing to be fed with genuine food.

But Mr. Fletcher did not understand its meaning; he saw the humility in her face, thought she was overcome by the weight of the honor he did her, and tried to reassure her with the gracious air of one who wishes to lighten the favor he confers.

"It might not be for some men, but it is for me, because I want you very much. Let people say what they will, if you say yes I am satisfied. You shall not regret it, Christie; I'll do my best to make you happy; you shall travel wherever I can go with you, have what you like, if possible, and when we come back by and by, you shall take your place in the world as my wife. You will fill it well, I fancy, and I shall be a happy man. I've had my own way all my life, and I mean to have it now, so smile, and say, 'Yes, Philip,' like a sweet soul, as you are."

But Christie did not smile, and felt no inclination to say "Yes, Philip," for that last speech of his jarred on her ear. The tone of unconscious condescension in it wounded the woman's sensitive pride; self was too apparent, and the most generous words seemed to her like bribes. This was not the lover she had dreamed of, the brave, true man who gave her all, and felt it could not half repay the treasure of her innocent, first love. This was not the happiness she had hoped for, the perfect faith, the glad surrender, the sweet content that made all things possible, and changed this work-a-day world into a heaven while the joy lasted.

She had decided to say "yes," but her heart said "no" decidedly, and with instinctive loyalty she obeyed it, even while she seemed to yield to the temptation which appeals to three of the strongest foibles in most women's nature,—vanity, ambition, and the love of pleasure.

"You are very kind, but you may repent it, you know so little of me," she began, trying to soften her refusal, but sadly hindered by a feeling of contempt.

"I know more about you than you think; but it makes no difference," interrupted Mr. Fletcher, with a smile that irritated Christie, even before she understood its significance. "I thought it would at first, but I found I couldn't get on without you, so I made up my mind to forgive and forget that my wife had ever been an actress."

Christie had forgotten it, and it would have been well for him if he had held his tongue. Now she understood the tone that had chilled her, the smile that angered her, and Mr. Fletcher's fate was settled in the drawing of a breath.

"Who told you that?" she asked, quickly, while every nerve tingled with the mortification of being found out then and there in the one secret of her life.

"I saw you dancing on the beach with the children one day, and it reminded me of an actress I had once seen. I should not have remembered it but for the accident which impressed it on my mind. Powder, paint, and costume made 'Miss Douglas' a very different woman from Miss Devon, but a few cautious inquiries settled the matter, and I then understood where you got that slight *soupçon* of dash and daring which makes our demure governess so charming when with me."

As he spoke, Mr. Fletcher smiled again, and kissed his hand to her with a dramatic little gesture that exasperated Christie beyond measure. She would not make light of it, as he did, and submit to be forgiven for a past she was not ashamed of. Heartily wishing she had been frank at first, she resolved to have it out now, and accept nothing Mr. Fletcher offered her, not even silence.

"Yes," she said, as steadily as she could, "I *was* an actress for three years, and though it was a hard life it was an honest one, and I'm not ashamed of it. I ought to have told Mrs. Salton-stall, but I was warned that if I did it would be difficult to find a place, people are so prejudiced. I sincerely regret it now, and shall tell her at once, so you may save yourself the trouble."

"My dear girl, I never dreamed of telling any one!" cried Mr. Fletcher in an injured tone. "I beg you won't speak, but trust me, and let it be a little secret between us two. I assure you it makes no difference to me, for I should marry an opera dancer if I chose, so forget it, as I do, and set my mind at rest upon the other point. I'm still waiting for my answer, you know."

"It is ready."

"A kind one, I'm sure. What is it, Christie?"

"No, I thank you."

"But you are not in earnest?"

"Perfectly so."

Mr. Fletcher got up suddenly and set his back against the rock, saying in a tone of such unaffected surprise and disappointment that her heart reproached her:

"Am I to understand that as your final answer, Miss Devon?"

"Distinctly and decidedly my final answer, Mr. Fletcher."

"No, I thank you."

Christie tried to speak kindly, but she was angry with herself
and him, and unconsciously showed it both in face and voice,
for she was no actress off the stage, and wanted to be very true
just then as a late atonement for that earlier want of candor.

A quick change passed over Mr. Fletcher's face; his cold eyes
kindled with an angry spark, his lips were pale with anger, and
his voice was very bitter, as he slowly said:

"I've made many blunders in my life, and this is one of the
greatest; for I believed in a woman, was fool enough to care
for her with the sincerest love I ever knew, and fancied that she
would be grateful for the sacrifice I made."

He got no further, for Christie rose straight up and answered
him with all the indignation she felt burning in her face and
stirring the voice she tried in vain to keep as steady as his own.

"The sacrifice would not have been *all* yours, for it is what we
*are*, not what we *have*, that makes one human being superior to
another. I am as well-born as you in spite of my poverty; my life,
I think, has been a better one than yours; my heart, I know, is
fresher, and my memory has fewer faults and follies to reproach

me with. What can you give me but money and position in return for the youth and freedom I should sacrifice in marrying
you? Not love, for you count the cost of your bargain, as no true
lover could, and you reproach me for deceit when in your heart
you know you only cared for me because I can amuse and serve
you. I too deceived myself, I too see my mistake, and I decline
the honor you would do me, since it is so great in your eyes that
you must remind me of it as you offer it."

In the excitement of the moment Christie unconsciously
spoke with something of her old dramatic fervor in voice and
gesture; Mr. Fletcher saw it, and, while he never had admired
her so much, could not resist avenging himself for the words
that angered him, the more deeply for their truth. Wounded
vanity and baffled will can make an ungenerous man as spiteful
as a woman; and Mr. Fletcher proved it then, for he saw where
Christie's pride was sorest, and touched the wound with the
skill of a resentful nature.

As she paused, he softly clapped his hands, saying, with a
smile that made her eyes flash:

"Very well done! infinitely superior to your 'Woffington,'
Miss Devon. I am disappointed in the woman, but I make my
compliment to the actress, and leave the stage free for another
and a more successful Romeo."

Still smiling, he bowed and went away apparently quite calm
and much amused, but a more wrathful, disappointed man
never crossed those sands than the one who kicked his dog and
swore at himself for a fool that day when no one saw him.

For a minute Christie stood and watched him, then, feeling
that she must either laugh or cry, wisely chose the former vent
for her emotions, and sat down feeling inclined to look at the
whole scene from a ludicrous point of view.

"My second love affair is a worse failure than my first, for I
did pity poor Joe, but this man is detestable, and I never will
forgive him that last insult. I dare say I *was* absurdly tragical,
I'm apt to be when very angry, but what a temper he has got!
The white, cold kind, that smoulders and stabs, instead of
blazing up and being over in a minute. Thank Heaven, I'm not
his wife! Well, I've made an enemy and lost my place, for of
course Mrs. Saltonstall won't keep me after this awful discovery. I'll tell her at once, for I will have no 'little secrets' with

him. No Paris either, and that's the worst of it all! Never mind, I haven't sold my liberty for the Fletcher diamonds, and that's a comfort. Now a short scene with my lady and then exit governess."

But though she laughed, Christie felt troubled at the part she had played in this affair; repented of her worldly aspirations; confessed her vanity; accepted her mortification and disappointment as a just punishment for her sins; and yet at the bottom of her heart she did enjoy it mightily.

She tried to spare Mr. Fletcher in her interview with his sister, and only betrayed her own iniquities. But, to her surprise, Mrs. Saltonstall, though much disturbed at the discovery, valued Christie as a governess, and respected her as a woman, so she was willing to bury the past, she said, and still hoped Miss Devon would remain.

Then Christie was forced to tell her why it was impossible for her to do so; and, in her secret soul, she took a naughty satisfaction in demurely mentioning that she had refused my lord.

Mrs. Saltonstall's consternation was comical, for she had been so absorbed in her own affairs she had suspected nothing; and horror fell upon her when she learned how near dear Philip had been to the fate from which she jealously guarded him, that his property might one day benefit the darlings.

In a moment every thing was changed; and it was evident to Christie that the sooner she left the better it would suit madame. The proprieties were preserved to the end, and Mrs. Saltonstall treated her with unusual respect, for she had come to honor, and also conducted herself in a most praiseworthy manner. How she could refuse a Fletcher visibly amazed the lady; but she forgave the slight, and gently insinuated that "my brother" was, perhaps, only amusing himself.

Christie was but too glad to be off; and when Mrs. Saltonstall asked when she would prefer to leave, promptly replied, "To-morrow," received her salary, which was forthcoming with unusual punctuality, and packed her trunks with delightful rapidity.

As the family was to leave in a week, her sudden departure caused no surprise to the few who knew her, and with kind farewells to such of her summer friends as still remained, she went to bed that night all ready for an early start. She saw nothing more of Mr. Fletcher that day, but the sound of excited voices in the drawing-room assured her that madame was having it out with her brother; and with truly feminine inconsistency Christie hoped that she would not be too hard upon the poor man, for, after all, it was kind of him to overlook the actress, and ask the governess to share his good things with him.

She did not repent, but she got herself to sleep, imagining a bridal trip to Paris, and dreamed so delightfully of lost splendors that the awakening was rather blank, the future rather cold and hard.

She was early astir, meaning to take the first boat and so escape all disagreeable *rencontres*, and having kissed the children in their little beds, with tender promises not to forget them, she took a hasty breakfast and stepped into the carriage waiting at the door. The sleepy waiters stared, a friendly housemaid nodded, and Miss Walker, the hearty English lady who did her ten miles a day, cried out, as she tramped by, blooming and bedraggled:

"Bless me, are you off?"

"Yes, thank Heaven!" answered Christie; but as she spoke Mr. Fletcher came down the steps looking as wan and heavy-eyed as if a sleepless night had been added to his day's defeat. Leaning in at the window, he asked abruptly, but with a look she never could forget:

"Will nothing change your answer, Christie?"

"Nothing."

His eyes said, "Forgive me," but his lips only said, "Good-by," and the carriage rolled away.

Then, being a woman, two great tears fell on the hand still red with the lingering grasp he had given it, and Christie said, as pitifully as if she loved him:

"He *has* got a heart, after all, and perhaps I might have been glad to fill it if he had only shown it to me sooner. Now it is too late."

# Chapter V

## COMPANION

BEFORE she had time to find a new situation, Christie received a note from Miss Tudor, saying that hearing she had left Mrs. Saltonstall she wanted to offer her the place of companion to an invalid girl, where the duties were light and the compensation large.

"How kind of her to think of me," said Christie, gratefully. "I'll go at once and do my best to secure it, for it must be a good thing or she wouldn't recommend it."

Away went Christie to the address sent by Miss Tudor, and as she waited at the door she thought:

"What a happy family the Carrols must be!" for the house was one of an imposing block in a West End square, which had its own little park where a fountain sparkled in the autumn sunshine, and pretty children played among the fallen leaves.

Mrs. Carrol was a stately woman, still beautiful in spite of her fifty years. But though there were few lines on her forehead, few silver threads in the dark hair that lay smoothly over it, and a gracious smile showed the fine teeth, an indescribable expression of unsubmissive sorrow touched the whole face, betraying that life had brought some heavy cross, from which her wealth could purchase no release, for which her pride could find no effectual screen.

She looked at Christie with a searching eye, listened attentively when she spoke, and seemed testing her with covert care as if the place she was to fill demanded some unusual gift or skill.

"Miss Tudor tells me that you read aloud well, sing sweetly, possess a cheerful temper, and the quiet, patient ways which are peculiarly grateful to an invalid," began Mrs. Carrol, with that keen yet wistful gaze, and an anxious accent in her voice that went to Christie's heart.

"Miss Tudor is very kind to think so well of me and my few accomplishments. I have never been with an invalid, but I think I can promise to be patient, willing, and cheerful. My

70

own experience of illness has taught me how to sympathize with others and love to lighten pain. I shall be very glad to try if you think I have any fitness for the place."

"I do," and Mrs. Carrol's face softened as she spoke, for something in Christie's words or manner seemed to please her. Then slowly, as if the task was a hard one, she added:

"My daughter has been very ill and is still weak and nervous. I must hint to you that the loss of one very dear to her was the cause of the illness and the melancholy which now oppresses her. Therefore we must avoid any thing that can suggest or recall this trouble. She cares for nothing as yet, will see no one, and prefers to live alone. She is still so feeble this is but natural; yet solitude is bad for her, and her physician thinks that a new face might rouse her, and the society of one in no way connected with the painful past might interest and do her good. You see it is a little difficult to find just what we want, for a young companion is best, yet must be discreet and firm, as few young people are."

Fancying from Mrs. Carrol's manner that Miss Tudor had said more in her favor than had been repeated to her, Christie in a few plain words told her little story, resolving to have no concealments here, and feeling that perhaps her experiences might have given her more firmness and discretion than many women of her age possessed. Mrs. Carrol seemed to find it so; the anxious look lifted a little as she listened, and when Christie ended she said, with a sigh of relief:

"Yes, I think Miss Tudor is right, and you *are* the one we want. Come and try it for a week and then we can decide. Can you begin to-day?" she added, as Christie rose. "Every hour is precious, for my poor girl's sad solitude weighs on my heart, and this is my one hope."

"I will stay with pleasure," answered Christie, thinking Mrs. Carrol's anxiety excessive, yet pitying the mother's pain, for something in her face suggested the idea that she reproached herself in some way for her daughter's state.

With secret gratitude that she had dressed with care, Christie took off her things and followed Mrs. Carrol upstairs. Entering a room in what seemed to be a wing of the great house, they found an old woman sewing.

"How is Helen to-day, Nurse?" asked Mrs. Carrol, pausing.

"Poorly, ma'am. I've been in every hour, but she only says: 'Let me be quiet,' and lies looking up at the picture till it's fit to break your heart to see her," answered the woman, with a shake of the head.

"I have brought Miss Devon to sit with her a little while. Doctor advises it, and I fancy the experiment may succeed if we can only amuse the dear child, and make her forget herself and her troubles."

"As you please, ma'am," said the old woman, looking with little favor at the new-comer, for the good soul was jealous of any interference between herself and the child she had tended for years.

"I won't disturb her, but you shall take Miss Devon in and tell Helen mamma sends her love, and hopes she will make an effort for all our sakes."

"Yes, ma'am."

"Go, my dear, and do your best." With these words Mrs. Carrol hastily left the room, and Christie followed Nurse.

A quick glance showed her that she was in the daintily furnished boudoir of a rich man's daughter, but before she could take a second look her eyes were arrested by the occupant of this pretty place, and she forgot all else. On a low luxurious couch lay a girl, so beautiful and pale and still, that for an instant Christie thought her dead or sleeping. She was neither, for at the sound of a voice the great eyes opened wide, darkening and dilating with a strange expression as they fell on the unfamiliar face.

"Nurse, who is that? I told you I would see no one. I'm too ill to be so worried," she said, in an imperious tone.

"Yes, dear, I know, but your mamma wished you to make an effort. Miss Devon is to sit with you and try to cheer you up a bit," said the old woman in a dissatisfied tone, that contrasted strangely with the tender way in which she stroked the beautiful disordered hair that hung about the girl's shoulders.

Helen knit her brows and looked most ungracious, but evidently tried to be civil, for with a courteous wave of her hand toward an easy chair in the sunny window she said, quietly:

"Please sit down, Miss Devon, and excuse me for a little while. I've had a bad night, and am too tired to talk just yet. There are books of all sorts, or the conservatory if you like it better."

HELEN CARROL.

"Thank you. I'll read quietly till you want me. Then I shall be very glad to do any thing I can for you."

With that Christie retired to the big chair, and fell to reading the first book she took up, a good deal embarrassed by her reception, and very curious to know what would come next.

The old woman went away after folding the down coverlet carefully over her darling's feet, and Helen seemed to go to sleep.

For a time the room was very still; the fire burned softly on the marble hearth, the sun shone warmly on velvet carpet and rich hangings, the delicate breath of flowers blew in through the half-open door that led to a gay little conservatory, and nothing but the roll of a distant carriage broke the silence now and then.

Christie's eyes soon wandered from her book to the lovely face and motionless figure on the couch. Just opposite, in a recess, hung the portrait of a young and handsome man, and below it stood a vase of flowers, a graceful Roman lamp, and

several little relics, as if it were the shrine where some dead
love was mourned and worshipped still.

As she looked from the living face, so pale and so pathetic in
its quietude, to the painted one so full of color, strength, and
happiness, her heart ached for poor Helen, and her eyes were
wet with tears of pity. A sudden movement on the couch gave
her no time to hide them, and as she hastily looked down upon
her book a treacherous drop fell glittering on the page.

"What have you there so interesting?" asked Helen, in that
softly imperious tone of hers.

"Don Quixote," answered Christie, too much abashed to
have her wits about her.

Helen smiled a melancholy smile as she rose, saying wearily:

"They gave me that to make me laugh, but I did not find it
funny; neither was it sad enough to make me cry as you do."

"I was not reading, I was"—there Christie broke down, and
could have cried with vexation at the bad beginning she had
made. But that involuntary tear was better balm to Helen than
the most perfect tact, the most brilliant conversation. It
touched and won her without words, for sympathy works
miracles. Her whole face changed, and her mournful eyes grew
soft as with the gentle freedom of a child she lifted Christie's
downcast face and said, with a falter in her voice:

"I know you were pitying me. Well, I need pity, and from
you I'll take it, because you don't force it on me. Have *you*
been ill and wretched too? I think so, else you would never
care to come and shut yourself up here with me!"

"I have been ill, and I know how hard it is to get one's spirits
back again. I've had my troubles, too, but not heavier than I
could bear, thank God."

"What made you ill? Would you mind telling me about it? I
seem to fancy hearing other people's woes, though it can't
make mine seem lighter."

"A piece of the Castle of the Sun fell on my head and nearly
killed me," and Christie laughed in spite of herself at the astonishment in Helen's face. "I was an actress once; your mother
knows and didn't mind," she added, quickly.

"I'm glad of that. I used to wish I could be one, I was so
fond of the theatre. They should have consented, it would

have given me something to do, and, however hard it is, it couldn't be worse than this." Helen spoke vehemently and an excited flush rose to her white cheeks; then she checked herself and dropped into a chair, saying, hurriedly:

"Tell about it: don't let me think; it's bad for me."

Glad to be set to work, and bent on retrieving her first mistake, Christie plunged into her theatrical experiences and talked away in her most lively style. People usually get eloquent when telling their own stories, and true tales are always the most interesting. Helen listened at first with a half-absent air, but presently grew more attentive, and when the catastrophe came sat erect, quite absorbed in the interest of this glimpse behind the curtain.

Charmed with her success, Christie branched off right and left, stimulated by questions, led on by suggestive incidents, and generously supplied by memory. Before she knew it, she was telling her whole history in the most expansive manner, for women soon get sociable together, and Helen's interest flattered her immensely. Once she made her laugh at some droll trifle, and as if the unaccustomed sound had startled her, old nurse popped in her head; but seeing nothing amiss retired, wondering what on earth that girl could be doing to cheer up Miss Helen so.

"Tell about your lovers: you must have had some; actresses always do. Happy women, they can love as they like!" said Helen, with the inquisitive frankness of an invalid for whom etiquette has ceased to exist.

Remembering in time that this was a forbidden subject, Christie smiled and shook her head.

"I had a few, but one does not tell those secrets, you know."

Evidently disappointed, and a little displeased at being reminded of her want of good-breeding, Helen got up and began to wander restlessly about the room. Presently, as if wishing to atone for her impatience, she bade Christie come and see her flowers. Following her, the new companion found herself in a little world where perpetual summer reigned. Vines curtained the roof, slender shrubs and trees made leafy walls on either side, flowers bloomed above and below, birds carolled in half-hidden prisons, aquariums and ferneries stood all about, and the soft plash of a little fountain made pleasant music as it rose and fell.

Helen threw herself wearily down on a pile of cushions that lay beside the basin, and beckoning Christie to sit near, said, as she pressed her hands to her hot forehead and looked up with a distressful brightness in the haggard eyes that seemed to have no rest in them:

"Please sing to me; any humdrum air will do. I am so tired, and yet I cannot sleep. If my head would only stop this dreadful thinking and let me forget one hour it would do me so much good."

"I know the feeling, and I'll try what Lucy used to do to quiet me. Put your poor head in my lap, dear, and lie quite still while I cool and comfort it."

Obeying like a worn-out child, Helen lay motionless while Christie, dipping her fingers in the basin, passed the wet tips softly to and fro across the hot forehead, and the thin temples where the pulses throbbed so fast. And while she soothed she sang the "Land o' the Leal," and sang it well; for the tender words, the plaintive air were dear to her, because her mother loved and sang it to her years ago. Slowly the heavy eyelids drooped, slowly the lines of pain were smoothed away from the broad brow, slowly the restless hands grew still, and Helen lay asleep.

So intent upon her task was Christie, that she forgot herself till the discomfort of her position reminded her that she had a body. Fearing to wake the poor girl in her arms, she tried to lean against the basin, but could not reach a cushion to lay upon the cold stone ledge. An unseen hand supplied the want, and, looking round, she saw two young men standing behind her.

Helen's brothers, without doubt; for, though utterly unlike in expression, some of the family traits were strongly marked in both. The elder wore the dress of a priest, had a pale, ascetic face, with melancholy eyes, stern mouth, and the absent air of one who leads an inward life. The younger had a more attractive face, for, though bearing marks of dissipation, it betrayed a generous, ardent nature, proud and wilful, yet lovable in spite of all defects. He was very boyish still, and plainly showed how much he felt, as, with a hasty nod to Christie, he knelt down beside his sister, saying, in a whisper:

"Look at her, Augustine! so beautiful, so quiet! What a comfort it is to see her like herself again."

"Ah, yes; and but for the sin of it, I could find it in my heart to wish she might never wake!" returned the other, gloomily.

"Don't say that! How could we live without her?" Then, turning to Christie, the younger said, in a friendly tone:

"You must be very tired; let us lay her on the sofa. It is very damp here, and if she sleeps long you will faint from weariness."

Carefully lifting her, the brothers carried the sleeping girl into her room, and laid her down. She sighed as her head touched the pillow, and her arm clung to Harry's neck, as if she felt his nearness even in sleep. He put his cheek to hers, and lingered over her with an affectionate solicitude beautiful to see. Augustine stood silent, grave and cold as if he had done with human ties, yet found it hard to sever this one, for he stretched his hand above his sister as if he blessed her, then, with another grave bow to Christie, went away as noiselessly as he had come. But Harry kissed the sleeper tenderly, whispered, "Be kind to her," with an imploring voice, and hurried from the room as if to hide the feeling that he must not show.

A few minutes later the nurse brought in a note from Mrs. Carrol.

"My son tells me that Helen is asleep, and you look very tired. Leave her to Hester, now; you have done enough to-day, so let me thank you heartily, and send you home for a quiet night before you continue your good work to-morrow."

Christie went, found a carriage waiting for her, and drove home very happy at the success of her first attempt at companionship.

The next day she entered upon the new duties with interest and good-will, for this was work in which heart took part, as well as head and hand. Many things surprised, and some things perplexed her, as she came to know the family better. But she discreetly held her tongue, used her eyes, and did her best to please.

Mrs. Carrol seemed satisfied, often thanked her for her faithfulness to Helen, but seldom visited her daughter, never seemed surprised or grieved that the girl expressed no wish to see her; and, though her handsome face always wore its gracious smile, Christie soon felt very sure that it was a mask put on to hide some heavy sorrow from a curious world.

Augustine never came except when Helen was asleep: then, like a shadow, he passed in and out, always silent, cold, and grave, but in his eyes the gloom of some remorseful pain that prayers and penances seemed powerless to heal.

Harry came every day, and no matter how melancholy, listless, or irritable his sister might be, for him she always had a smile, an affectionate greeting, a word of praise, or a tender warning against the reckless spirit that seemed to possess him. The love between them was very strong, and Christie found a never-failing pleasure in watching them together, for then Helen showed what she once had been, and Harry was his best self. A boy still, in spite of his one-and-twenty years, he seemed to feel that Helen's room was a safe refuge from the temptations that beset one of his thoughtless and impetuous nature. Here he came to confess his faults and follies with the frankness which is half sad, half comical, and wholly charming in a good-hearted young scatter-brain. Here he brought gay gossip, lively descriptions, and masculine criticisms of the world he moved in. All his hopes and plans, joys and sorrows, successes and defeats, he told to Helen. And she, poor soul, in this one happy love of her sad life, forgot a little the burden of despair that darkened all the world to her. For his sake she smiled, to him she talked when others got no word from her, and Harry's salvation was the only duty that she owned or tried to fulfil.

A younger sister was away at school, but the others seldom spoke of her, and Christie tired herself with wondering why Bella never wrote to Helen, and why Harry seemed to have nothing but a gloomy sort of pity to bestow upon the blooming girl whose picture hung in the great drawing-room below.

It was a very quiet winter, yet a very pleasant one to Christie, for she felt herself loved and trusted, saw that she suited, and believed that she was doing good, as women best love to do it, by bestowing sympathy and care with generous devotion.

Helen and Harry loved her like an elder sister; Augustine showed that he was grateful, and Mrs. Carrol sometimes forgot to put on her mask before one who seemed fast becoming *confidante* as well as companion.

In the spring the family went to the fine old country-house

just out of town, and here Christie and her charge led a freer, happier life. Walking and driving, boating and gardening, with pleasant days on the wide terrace, where Helen swung idly in her hammock, while Christie read or talked to her; and summer twilights beguiled with music, or the silent reveries more eloquent than speech, which real friends may enjoy together, and find the sweeter for the mute companionship.

Harry was with them, and devoted to his sister, who seemed slowly to be coming out of her sad gloom, won by patient tenderness and the cheerful influences all about her.

Christie's heart was full of pride and satisfaction, as she saw the altered face, heard the tone of interest in that once hopeless voice, and felt each day more sure that Helen had outlived the loss that seemed to have broken her heart.

Alas, for Christie's pride, for Harry's hope, and for poor Helen's bitter fate! When all was brightest, the black shadow came; when all looked safest, danger was at hand; and when the past seemed buried, the ghost which haunted it returned, for the punishment of a broken law is as inevitable as death.

When settled in town again Bella came home, a gay, young girl, who should have brought sunshine and happiness into her home. But from the hour she returned a strange anxiety seemed to possess the others. Mrs. Carrol watched over her with sleepless care, was evidently full of maternal pride in the lovely creature, and began to dream dreams about her future. She seemed to wish to keep the sisters apart, and said to Christie, as if to explain this wish:

"Bella was away when Helen's trouble and illness came, she knows very little of it, and I do not want her to be saddened by the knowledge. Helen cares only for Hal, and Bella is too young to be of any use to my poor girl; therefore the less they see of each other the better for both. I am sure you agree with me?" she added, with that covert scrutiny which Christie had often felt before.

She could but acquiesce in the mother's decision, and devote herself more faithfully than ever to Helen, who soon needed all her care and patience, for a terrible unrest grew upon her, bringing sleepless nights again, moody days, and all the old afflictions with redoubled force.

Bella "came out" and began her career as a beauty and a

belle most brilliantly. Harry was proud of her, but seemed jealous of other men's admiration for his charming sister, and would excite both Helen and himself over the flirtations into which "that child" as they called her, plunged with all the zest of a light-hearted girl whose head was a little turned with sudden and excessive adoration.

In vain Christie begged Harry not to report these things, in vain she hinted that Bella had better not come to show herself to Helen night after night in all the dainty splendor of her youth and beauty; in vain she asked Mrs. Carrol to let her go away to some quieter place with Helen, since she never could be persuaded to join in any gayety at home or abroad. All seemed wilful, blind, or governed by the fear of the gossiping world. So the days rolled on till an event occurred which enlightened Christie, with startling abruptness, and showed her the skeleton that haunted this unhappy family.

Going in one morning to Helen she found her walking to and fro as she often walked of late, with hurried steps and excited face as if driven by some power beyond her control.

"Good morning, dear. I'm so sorry you had a restless night, and wish you had sent for me. Will you come out now for an early drive? It's a lovely day, and your mother thinks it would do you good," began Christie, troubled by the state in which she found the girl.

But as she spoke Helen turned on her, crying passionately:

"My mother! don't speak of her to me, I hate her!"

"Oh, Helen, don't say that. Forgive and forget if she has displeased you, and don't exhaust yourself by brooding over it. Come, dear, and let us soothe ourselves with a little music. I want to hear that new song again, though I can never hope to sing it as you do."

"Sing!" echoed Helen, with a shrill laugh, "you don't know what you ask. Could *you* sing when your heart was heavy with the knowledge of a sin about to be committed by those nearest to you? Don't try to quiet me, I *must* talk whether you listen or not; I shall go frantic if I don't tell some one; all the world will know it soon. Sit down, I'll not hurt you, but don't thwart me or you'll be sorry for it."

Speaking with a vehemence that left her breathless, Helen thrust Christie down upon a seat, and went on with an expression in her face that bereft the listener of power to move or speak.

"Harry has just told me of it; he was very angry, and I saw it, and made him tell me. Poor boy, he can keep nothing from *me*. I've been dreading it, and now it's coming. You don't know it, then? Young Butler is in love with Bella, and no one has prevented it. Think how wicked when such a curse is on us all."

The question, "What curse?" rose involuntarily to Christie's lips, but did not pass them, for, as if she read the thought, Helen answered it in a whisper that made the blood tingle in the other's veins, so full of ominous suggestion was it.

"The curse of insanity I mean. We are all mad, or shall be; we come of a mad race, and for years we have gone recklessly on bequeathing this awful inheritance to our descendants. It should end with us, we are the last; none of us should marry; none dare think of it but Bella, and she knows nothing. She must be told, she must be kept from the sin of deceiving her lover, the agony of seeing her children become what I am, and what we all may be."

Here Helen wrung her hands and paced the room in such a paroxysm of impotent despair that Christie sat bewildered and aghast, wondering if this were true, or but the fancy of a troubled brain. Mrs. Carrol's face and manner returned to her with sudden vividness, so did Augustine's gloomy expression, and the strange wish uttered over his sleeping sister long ago. Harry's reckless, aimless life might be explained in this way; and all that had perplexed her through that year. Every thing confirmed the belief that this tragical assertion was true, and Christie covered up her face, murmuring, with an involuntary shiver:

"My God, how terrible!"

Helen came and stood before her with such grief and penitence in her countenance that for a moment it conquered the despair that had broken bounds.

"We should have told you this at first; I longed to do it, but I was afraid you'd go and leave me. I was so lonely, so miserable, Christie. I could not give you up when I had learned to love you; and I did learn very soon, for no wretched creature ever needed help and comfort more than I. For your sake I tried to be quiet, to control my shattered nerves, and hide my desperate thoughts. You helped me very much, and your unconsciousness made me doubly watchful. Forgive me; don't desert me now, for the old horror may be coming back, and I want you more than ever."

Too much moved to speak, Christie held out her hands, with a face full of pity, love, and grief. Poor Helen clung to them as if her only help lay there, and for a moment was quite still. But not long; the old anguish was too sharp to be borne in silence; the relief of confidence once tasted was too great to be denied; and, breaking loose, she went to and fro again, pouring out the bitter secret which had been weighing upon heart and conscience for a year.

"You wonder that I hate my mother; let me tell you why. When she was beautiful and young she married, knowing the sad history of my father's family. He was rich, she poor and proud; ambition made her wicked, and she did it after being warned that, though he might escape, his children were sure to inherit the curse, for when one generation goes free it falls more heavily upon the rest. She knew it all, and yet she married him. I have her to thank for all I suffer, and I cannot love her though she is my mother. It may be wrong to say these things, but they are true; they burn in my heart, and I must speak out; for I tell you there comes a time when children judge their parents as men and women, in spite of filial duty, and woe to those whose actions change affection and respect to hatred or contempt."

The bitter grief, the solemn fervor of her words, both touched and awed Christie too much for speech. Helen had passed beyond the bounds of ceremony, fear, or shame: her hard lot, her dark experience, set her apart, and gave her the right to utter the bare truth. To her heart's core Christie felt that warning; and for the first time saw what many never see or wilfully deny,—the awful responsibility that lies on every man and woman's soul forbidding them to entail upon the innocent the burden of their own infirmities, the curse that surely follows their own sins.

Sad and stern, as an accusing angel, that most unhappy daughter spoke:

"If ever a woman had cause to repent, it is my mother; but

she will not, and till she does, God has forsaken us. Nothing can subdue her pride, not even an affliction like mine. She hides the truth; she hides me, and lets the world believe I am dying of consumption; not a word about insanity, and no one knows the secret beyond ourselves, but doctor, nurse, and you. This is why I was not sent away, but for a year was shut up in that room yonder where the door is always locked. If you look in, you'll see barred windows, guarded fire, muffled walls, and other sights to chill your blood, when you remember all those dreadful things were meant for me."

"Don't speak, don't think of them! Don't talk any more; let me do something to comfort you, for my heart is broken with all this," cried Christie, panic-stricken at the picture Helen's words had conjured up.

"I *must* go on! There is no rest for me till I have tried to lighten this burden by sharing it with you. Let me talk, let me wear myself out, then you shall help and comfort me, if there is any help and comfort for such as I. Now I can tell you all about my Edward, and you'll listen, though mamma forbade it. Three years ago my father died, and we came here. I was well then, and oh, how happy!"

Clasping her hands above her head, she stood like a beautiful, pale image of despair; tearless and mute, but with such a world of anguish in the eyes lifted to the smiling picture opposite that it needed no words to tell the story of a broken heart.

"How I loved him!" she said, softly, while her whole face glowed for an instant with the light and warmth of a deathless passion. "How I loved him, and how he loved me! Too well to let me darken both our lives with a remorse which would come too late for a just atonement. I thought him cruel then,—I bless him for it now. I had far rather be the innocent sufferer I am, than a wretched woman like my mother. I shall never see him any more, but I know he thinks of me far away in India, and when I die one faithful heart will remember me."

There her voice faltered and failed, and for a moment the fire of her eyes was quenched in tears. Christie thought the reaction had come, and rose to go and comfort her. But instantly Helen's hand was on her shoulder, and pressing her back into her seat, she said, almost fiercely:

"I'm not done yet; you must hear the whole, and help me to

save Bella. We knew nothing of the blight that hung over us till father told Augustine upon his death-bed. August, urged by mother, kept it to himself, and went away to bear it as he could. He should have spoken out and saved me in time. But not till he came home and found me engaged did he have courage to warn me of the fate in store for us. So Edward tore himself away, although it broke his heart, and I—do you see that?"

With a quick gesture she rent open her dress, and on her bosom Christie saw a scar that made her turn yet paler than before.

"Yes, I tried to kill myself; but they would not let me die, so the old tragedy of our house begins again. August became a priest, hoping to hide his calamity and expiate his father's sin by endless penances and prayers. Harry turned reckless; for what had he to look forward to? A short life, and a gay one, he says, and when his turn comes he will spare himself long suffering, as I tried to do it. Bella was never told; she was so young they kept her ignorant of all they could, even the knowledge of my state. She was long away at school, but now she has come home, now she has learned to love, and is going blindly as I went, because no one tells her what she *must* know soon or late. Mamma will not. August hesitates, remembering me. Harry swears he will speak out, but I implore him not to do it, for he will be too violent; and I am powerless. I never knew about this man till Hal told me to-day. Bella only comes in for a moment, and I have no chance to tell her she must *not* love him."

Pressing her hands to her temples, Helen resumed her restless march again, but suddenly broke out more violently than before:

"Now do you wonder why I am half frantic? Now will you ask me to sing and smile, and sit calmly by while this wrong goes on? You have done much for me, and God will bless you for it, but you cannot keep me sane. Death is the only cure for a mad Carrol, and I'm so young, so strong, it will be long in coming unless I hurry it."

She clenched her hands, set her teeth, and looked about her as if ready for any desperate act that should set her free from the dark and dreadful future that lay before her.

For a moment Christie feared and trembled; then pity conquered fear. She forgot herself, and only remembered this poor girl, so hopeless, helpless, and afflicted. Led by a sudden impulse, she put both arms about her, and held her close with a strong but silent tenderness better than any bonds. At first, Helen seemed unconscious of it, as she stood rigid and motionless, with her wild eyes dumbly imploring help of earth and heaven. Suddenly both strength and excitement seemed to leave her, and she would have fallen but for the living, loving prop that sustained her.

Still silent, Christie laid her down, kissed her white lips, and busied herself about her till she looked up quite herself again, but so wan and weak, it was pitiful to see her.

"It's over now," she whispered, with a desolate sigh. "Sing to me, and keep the evil spirit quiet for a little while. To-morrow, if I'm strong enough, we'll talk about poor little Bella."

And Christie sang, with tears dropping fast upon the keys, that made a soft accompaniment to the sweet old hymns which soothed this troubled soul as David's music brought repose to Saul.

When Helen slept at last from sheer exhaustion, Christie executed the resolution she had made as soon as the excitement of that stormy scene was over. She went straight to Mrs. Carrol's room, and, undeterred by the presence of her sons, told all that had passed. They were evidently not unprepared for it, thanks to old Hester, who had overheard enough of Helen's wild words to know that something was amiss, and had reported accordingly; but none of them had ventured to interrupt the interview, lest Helen should be driven to desperation as before.

"Mother, Helen is right; we should speak out, and not hide this bitter fact any longer. The world will pity us, and we must bear the pity, but it would condemn us for deceit, and we should deserve the condemnation if we let this misery go on. Living a lie will ruin us all. Bella will be destroyed as Helen was; I am only the shadow of a man now, and Hal is killing himself as fast as he can, to avoid the fate we all dread."

Augustine spoke first, for Mrs. Carrol sat speechless with her trouble as Christie paused.

"Keep to your prayers, and let me go my own way, it's the

shortest," muttered Harry, with his face hidden, and his head down on his folded arms.

"Boys, boys, you'll kill me if you say such things! I have more now than I can bear. Don't drive me wild with your reproaches to each other!" cried their mother, her heart rent with the remorse that came too late.

"No fear of that; *you* are not a Carrol," answered Harry, with the pitiless bluntness of a resentful and rebellious boy.

Augustine turned on him with a wrathful flash of the eye, and a warning ring in his stern voice, as he pointed to the door.

"You shall not insult your mother! Ask her pardon, or go!"

"She should ask mine! I'll go. When you want me, you'll know where to find me." And, with a reckless laugh, Harry stormed out of the room.

Augustine's indignant face grew full of a new trouble as the door banged below, and he pressed his thin hands tightly together, saying, as if to himself:

"Heaven help me! Yes, I do know; for, night after night, I find and bring the poor lad home from gambling-tables and the hells where souls like his are lost."

Here Christie thought to slip away, feeling that it was no place for her now that her errand was done. But Mrs. Carrol called her back.

"Miss Devon—Christie—forgive me that I did not trust you sooner. It was so hard to tell; I hoped so much from time; I never could believe that my poor children would be made the victims of my mistake. Do not forsake us: Helen loves you so. Stay with her, I implore you, and let a most unhappy mother plead for a most unhappy child." Then Christie went to the poor woman, and earnestly assured her of her love and loyalty; for now she felt doubly bound to them because they trusted her.

"What shall we do?" they said to her, with pathetic submission, turning like sick people to a healthful soul for help and comfort.

"Tell Bella all the truth, and help her to refuse her lover. Do this just thing, and God will strengthen you to bear the consequences," was her answer, though she trembled at the responsibility they put upon her.

"Not yet," cried Mrs. Carrol. "Let the poor child enjoy the

holidays with a light heart,—then we will tell her; and then Heaven help us all!"

So it was decided; for only a week or two of the old year remained, and no one had the heart to rob poor Bella of the little span of blissful ignorance that now remained to her.

A terrible time was that to Christie; for, while one sister, blessed with beauty, youth, love, and pleasure, tasted life at its sweetest, the other sat in the black shadow of a growing dread, and wearied Heaven with piteous prayers for her relief.

"The old horror is coming back; I feel it creeping over me. Don't let it come, Christie! Stay by me! Help me! Keep me sane! And if you cannot, ask God to take me quickly!"

With words like these, poor Helen clung to Christie; and, soul and body, Christie devoted herself to the afflicted girl. She would not see her mother; and the unhappy woman haunted that closed door, hungering for the look, the word, that never came to her. Augustine was her consolation, and, during those troublous days, the priest was forgotten in the son. But Harry was all in all to Helen then; and it was touching to see how these unfortunate young creatures clung to one another, she tenderly trying to keep him from the wild life that was surely hastening the fate he might otherwise escape for years, and he patiently bearing all her moods, eager to cheer and soothe the sad captivity from which he could not save her.

These tender ministrations seemed to be blessed at last; and Christie began to hope the haunting terror would pass by, as quiet gloom succeeded to wild excitement. The cheerful spirit of the season seemed to reach even that sad room; and, in preparing gifts for others, Helen seemed to find a little of that best of all gifts,—peace for herself.

On New Year's morning, Christie found her garlanding her lover's picture with white roses and the myrtle sprays brides wear.

"These were his favorite flowers, and I meant to make my wedding wreath of this sweet-scented myrtle, because he gave it to me," she said, with a look that made Christie's eyes grow dim. "Don't grieve for me, dear; we shall surely meet hereafter, though so far asunder here. Nothing can part us there, I devoutly believe; for we leave our burdens all behind us when we go." Then, in a lighter tone, she said, with her arm on Christie's neck:

"This day is to be a happy one, no matter what comes after it. I'm going to be my old self for a little while, and forget there's such a word as sorrow. Help me to dress, so that when the boys come up they may find the sister Nell they have not seen for two long years."

"Will you wear this, my darling? Your mother sends it, and she tried to have it dainty and beautiful enough to please you. See, your own colors, though the bows are only laid on that they may be changed for others if you like."

As she spoke Christie lifted the cover of the box old Hester had just brought in, and displayed a cashmere wrapper, creamy-white, silk-lined, down-trimmed, and delicately relieved by rosy knots, like holly berries lying upon snow. Helen looked at it without a word for several minutes, then gathering up the ribbons, with a strange smile, she said:

"I like it better so; but I'll not wear it yet."

"Bless and save us, deary; it *must* have a bit of color some-where, else it looks just like a shroud," cried Hester, and then wrung her hands in dismay as Helen answered, quietly:

"Ah, well, keep it for me, then. I shall be happier when I wear it so than in the gayest gown I own, for when you put it on, this poor head and heart of mine will be quiet at last."

Motioning Hester to remove the box, Christie tried to ban-ish the cloud her unlucky words had brought to Helen's face, by chatting cheerfully as she helped her make herself "pretty for the boys."

All that day she was unusually calm and sweet, and seemed to yield herself wholly to the happy influences of the hour, gave and received her gifts so cheerfully that her brothers watched her with delight; and unconscious Bella said, as she hung about her sister, with loving admiration in her eyes:

"I always thought you would get well, and now I'm sure of it, for you look as you used before I went away to school, and seem just like our own dear Nell."

"I'm glad of that; I wanted you to feel so, my Bella. I'll accept your happy prophecy, and hope I may get well soon, very soon."

So cheerfully she spoke, so tranquilly she smiled, that all re-joiced over her believing, with love's blindness, that she might yet conquer her malady in spite of their forebodings.

It was a very happy day to Christie, not only that she was

generously remembered and made one of them by all the family, but because this change for the better in Helen made her heart sing for joy. She had given time, health, and much love to the task, and ventured now to hope they had not been given in vain. One thing only marred her happiness, the sad estrangement of the daughter from her mother, and that evening she resolved to take advantage of Helen's tender mood, and plead for the poor soul who dared not plead for herself.

As the brothers and sisters said good-night, Helen clung to them as if loth to part, saying, with each embrace:

"Keep hoping for me, Bella; kiss me, Harry; bless me, Augustine, and all wish for me a happier New Year than the last."

When they were gone she wandered slowly round the room, stood long before the picture with its fading garland, sung a little softly to herself, and came at last to Christie, saying, like a tired child:

"I have been good all day; now let me rest."

"One thing has been forgotten, dear," began Christie, fearing to disturb the quietude that seemed to have been so dearly bought.

Helen understood her, and looked up with a sane sweet face, out of which all resentful bitterness had passed.

"No, Christie, not forgotten, only kept until the last. To-day is a good day to forgive, as we would be forgiven, and I mean to do it before I sleep." Then holding Christie close, she added, with a quiver of emotion in her voice: "I have no words warm enough to thank you, my good angel, for all you have been to me, but I know it will give you a great pleasure to do one thing more. Give dear mamma my love, and tell her that when I am quiet for the night I want her to come and get me to sleep with the old lullaby she used to sing when I was a little child."

No gift bestowed that day was so precious to Christie as the joy of carrying this loving message from daughter to mother. How Mrs. Carrol received it need not be told. She would have gone at once, but Christie begged her to wait till rest and quiet, after the efforts of the day, had prepared Helen for an interview which might undo all that had been done if too hastily attempted.

Hester always waited upon her child at night; so, feeling that she might be wanted later, Christie went to her own room to rest. Quite sure that Mrs. Carrol would come to tell her what had passed, she waited for an hour or two, then went to ask of Hester how the visit had sped.

"Her mamma came up long ago, but the dear thing was fast asleep, so I wouldn't let her be disturbed, and Mrs. Carrol went away again," said the old woman, rousing from a nap.

Grieved at the mother's disappointment, Christie stole in, hoping that Helen might rouse. She did not, and Christie was about to leave her, when, as she bent to smooth the tumbled coverlet, something dropped at her feet. Only a little pearl-handled penknife of Harry's; but her heart stood still with fear, for it was open, and, as she took it up, a red stain came off upon her hand.

Helen's face was turned away, and, bending nearer, Christie saw how deathly pale it looked in the shadow of the darkened room. She listened at her lips; only a faint flutter of breath parted them; she lifted up the averted head, and on the white throat saw a little wound, from which the blood still flowed. Then, like a flash of light, the meaning of the sudden change which came over her grew clear,—her brave efforts to make the last day happy, her tender good-night partings, her wish to be at peace with every one, the tragic death she had chosen rather than live out the tragic life that lay before her.

Christie's nerves had been tried to the uttermost; the shock of this discovery was too much for her, and, in the act of calling for help, she fainted, for the first time in her life.

When she was herself again, the room was full of people; terror-stricken faces passed before her; broken voices whispered, "It is too late," and, as she saw the group about the bed, she wished for unconsciousness again.

Helen lay in her mother's arms at last, quietly breathing her life away, for though every thing that love and skill could devise had been tried to save her, the little knife in that desperate hand had done its work, and this world held no more suffering for her. Harry was down upon his knees beside her, trying to stifle his passionate grief. Augustine prayed audibly above her, and the fervor of his broken words comforted all hearts but one. Bella was clinging, panic-stricken, to the kind old doctor, who was sobbing like a boy, for he had loved and served poor Helen as faithfully as if she had been his own.

"Can nothing save her?" Christie whispered, as the prayer ended, and a sound of bitter weeping filled the room.

"Nothing; she is sane and safe at last, thank God!"

Christie could not but echo his thanksgiving, for the blessed tranquillity of the girl's countenance was such as none but death, the great healer, can bring; and, as they looked, her eyes opened, beautifully clear and calm before they closed for ever. From face to face they passed, as if they looked for some one, and her lips moved in vain efforts to speak.

Christie went to her, but still the wide, wistful eyes searched the room as if unsatisfied; and, with a longing that conquered the mortal weakness of the body, the heart sent forth one tender cry:

"My mother—I want my mother!"

There was no need to repeat the piteous call, for, as it left her lips, she saw her mother's face bending over her, and felt her mother's arms gathering her in an embrace which held her close even after death had set its seal upon the voiceless prayers for pardon which passed between those reunited hearts.

When she was asleep at last, Christie and her mother made her ready for her grave; weeping tender tears as they folded her in the soft, white garment she had put by for that sad hour; and on her breast they laid the flowers she had hung about her lover as a farewell gift. So beautiful she looked when all was done, that in the early dawn they called her brothers, that they might not lose the memory of the blessed peace that shone upon her face, a mute assurance that for her the new year had happily begun.

"Now my work here is done, and I must go," thought Christie, when the waves of life closed over the spot where another tired swimmer had gone down. But she found that one more task remained for her before she left the family which, on her coming, she had thought so happy.

Mrs. Carrol, worn out with the long effort to conceal her secret cross, broke down entirely under this last blow, and besought Christie to tell Bella all that she must know. It was a hard task, but Christie accepted it, and, when the time came, found that there was very little to be told, for at the death-bed of the elder sister, the younger had learned much of the sad truth. Thus prepared, she listened to all that was most carefully and tenderly confided to her, and, when the heavy tale was done, she surprised Christie by the unsuspected strength she showed. No tears, no lamentations, for she was her mother's daughter, and inherited the pride that can bear heavy burdens, if they are borne unseen.

"Tell me what I must do, and I will do it," she said, with the quiet despair of one who submits to the inevitable, but will not complain.

When Christie with difficulty told her that she should give up her lover, Bella bowed her head, and for a moment could not speak, then lifted it as if defying her own weakness, and spoke out bravely:

"It shall be done, for it is right. It is very hard for *me*, because I love him; he will not suffer much, for he can love again. I should be glad of that, and I'll try to wish it for his sake. He is young, and if, as Harry says, he cares more for my fortune than myself, so much the better. What next, Christie?"

Amazed and touched at the courage of the creature she had fancied a sort of lovely butterfly to be crushed by a single blow, Christie took heart, and, instead of soothing sympathy, gave her the solace best fitted for strong natures, something to do for others. What inspired her, Christie never knew; perhaps it was the year of self-denying service she had rendered for pity's sake; such devotion is its own reward, and now, in herself, she discovered unsuspected powers.

"Live for your mother and your brothers, Bella; they need you sorely, and in time I know you will find true consolation in it, although you must relinquish much. Sustain your mother, cheer Augustine, watch over Harry, and be to them what Helen longed to be."

"And fail to do it, as she failed!" cried Bella, with a shudder.

"Listen, and let me give you this hope, for I sincerely do believe it. Since I came here, I have read many books, thought much, and talked often with Dr. Shirley about this sad affliction. He thinks you and Harry may escape it, if you will. You are like your mother in temperament and temper; you have self-control, strong wills, good nerves, and cheerful spirits. Poor Harry is willfully spoiling all his chances now; but you may save him, and, in the endeavor, save yourself."

"Oh, Christie, may I hope it? Give me one chance of escape,

and I will suffer any hardship to keep it. Let me see any thing before me but a life and death like Helen's, and I'll bless you for ever!" cried Bella, welcoming this ray of light as a prisoner welcomes sunshine in his cell.

Christie trembled at the power of her words, yet, honestly believing them, she let them uplift this disconsolate soul, trusting that they might be in time fulfilled through God's mercy and the saving grace of sincere endeavor.

Holding fast to this frail spar, Bella bravely took up arms against her sea of troubles, and rode out the storm. When her lover came to know his fate, she hid her heart, and answered "no," finding a bitter satisfaction in the end, for Harry was right, and, when the fortune was denied him, young Butler did not mourn the woman long. Pride helped Bella to bear it; but it needed all her courage to look down the coming years so bare of all that makes life sweet to youthful souls, so desolate and dark, with duty alone to cheer the thorny way, and the haunting shadow of her race lurking in the background.

Submission and self-sacrifice are stern, sad angels, but in time one learns to know and love them, for when they have chastened, they uplift and bless. Dimly discerning this, poor Bella put her hands in theirs, saying, "Lead me, teach me; I will follow and obey you."

All soon felt that they could not stay in a house so full of heavy memories, and decided to return to their old home. They begged Christie to go with them, using every argument and entreaty their affection could suggest. But Christie needed rest, longed for freedom, and felt that in spite of their regard it would be very hard for her to live among them any longer. Her healthy nature needed brighter influences, stronger comrades, and the memory of Helen weighed so heavily upon her heart that she was eager to forget it for a time in other scenes and other work.

So they parted, very sadly, very tenderly, and laden with good gifts Christie went on her way weary, but well satisfied, for she had earned her rest.

# Chapter VI

## SEAMSTRESS

---

FOR some weeks Christie rested and refreshed herself by making her room gay and comfortable with the gifts lavished on her by the Carrols, and by sharing with others the money which Harry had smuggled into her possession after she had steadily refused to take one penny more than the sum agreed upon when she first went to them.

She took infinite satisfaction in sending one hundred dollars to Uncle Enos, for she had accepted what he gave her as a loan, and set her heart on repaying every fraction of it. Another hundred she gave to Hepsey, who found her out and came to report her trials and tribulations. The good soul had ventured South and tried to buy her mother. But "ole missis" would not let her go at any price, and the faithful chattel would not run away. Sorely disappointed, Hepsey had been obliged to submit; but her trip was not a failure, for she liberated several brothers and sent them triumphantly to Canada.

"You *must* take it, Hepsey, for I could not rest happy if I put it away to lie idle while you can save men and women from torment with it. I'd give it if it was my last penny, for I can help in no other way; and if I need money, I can always earn it, thank God!" said Christie, as Hepsey hesitated to take so much from a fellow-worker.

The thought of that investment lay warm at Christie's heart, and never woke a regret, for well she knew that every dollar of it would be blessed, since shares in the Underground Railroad pay splendid dividends that never fail.

Another portion of her fortune, as she called Harry's gift, was bestowed in wedding presents upon Lucy, who at length succeeded in winning the heart of the owner of the "heavenly eyes" and "distracting legs;" and, having gained her point, married him with dramatic celerity, and went West to follow the fortunes of her lord.

The old theatre was to be demolished and the company scattered, so a farewell festival was held, and Christie went to it, feeling more solitary than ever as she bade her old friends a long good-bye.

The rest of the money burned in her pocket, but she prudently put it by for a rainy day, and fell to work again when her brief vacation was over.

Hearing of a chance for a good needle-woman in a large and well-conducted mantua-making establishment, she secured it as a temporary thing, for she wanted to divert her mind from that last sad experience by entirely different employment and surroundings. She liked to return at night to her own little home, solitary and simple as it was, and felt a great repugnance to accept any place where she would be mixed up with family affairs again.

So day after day she went to her seat in the workroom where a dozen other young women sat sewing busily on gay garments, with as much lively gossip to beguile the time as Miss Cotton, the forewoman, would allow.

For a while it diverted Christie, as she had a feminine love for pretty things, and enjoyed seeing delicate silks, costly lace, and all the indescribable fantasies of fashion. But as spring came on, the old desire for something fresh and free began to haunt her, and she had both waking and sleeping dreams of a home in the country somewhere, with cows and flowers, clothes bleaching on green grass, bob-o'-links making rapturous music by the river, and the smell of new-mown hay, all lending their charms to the picture she painted for herself.

Most assuredly she would have gone to find these things, led by the instincts of a healthful nature, had not one slender tie held her till it grew into a bond so strong she could not break it.

Among her companions was one, and one only, who attracted her. The others were well-meaning girls, but full of the frivolous purposes and pleasures which their tastes prompted and their dull life fostered. Dress, gossip, and wages were the three topics which absorbed them. Christie soon tired of the innumerable changes rung upon these themes, and took refuge in her own thoughts, soon learning to enjoy them undisturbed by the clack of many tongues about her. Her evenings at home were devoted to books, for she had the true New England woman's desire for education, and read or studied for the love of it. Thus she had much to think of as her needle flew, and was rapidly becoming a sort of sewing-machine when life was brightened for her by the finding of a friend.

Among the girls was one quiet, skilful creature, whose black dress, peculiar face, and silent ways attracted Christie. Her evident desire to be let alone amused the new comer at first, and she made no effort to know her. But presently she became aware that Rachel watched her with covert interest, stealing quick, shy glances at her as she sat musing over her work. Christie smiled at her when she caught these glances, as if to reassure the looker of her good-will. But Rachel only colored, kept her eyes fixed on her work, and was more reserved than ever.

This interested Christie, and she fell to studying this young woman with some curiosity, for she was different from the others. Though evidently younger than she looked, Rachel's face was that of one who had known some great sorrow, some deep experience; for there were lines on the forehead that contrasted strongly with the bright, abundant hair above it; in repose, the youthfully red, soft lips had a mournful droop, and the eyes were old with that indescribable expression which comes to those who count their lives by emotions, not by years.

Strangely haunting eyes to Christie, for they seemed to appeal to her with a mute eloquence she could not resist. In vain did Rachel answer her with quiet coldness, nod silently when she wished her a cheery "good morning," and keep resolutely in her own somewhat isolated corner, though invited to share the sunny window where the other sat. Her eyes belied her words, and those fugitive glances betrayed the longing of a lonely heart that dared not yield itself to the genial companionship so freely offered it.

Christie was sure of this, and would not be repulsed; for her own heart was very solitary. She missed Helen, and longed to fill the empty place. She wooed this shy, cold girl as patiently and as gently as a lover might, determined to win her confidence, because all the others had failed to do it. Sometimes she left a flower in Rachel's basket, always smiled and nodded as she entered, and often stopped to admire the work of her tasteful fingers. It was impossible to resist such friendly overtures, and slowly Rachel's coldness melted; into the beseeching eyes came a look of gratitude, the more touching for its word-lessness, and an irrepressible smile broke over her face in an-swer to the cordial ones that made the sunshine of her day.

Emboldened by these demonstrations, Christie changed her seat, and quietly established between them a daily interchange of something beside needles, pins, and spools. Then, as Rachel did not draw back offended, she went a step farther, and, one day when they chanced to be left alone to finish off a delicate bit of work, she spoke out frankly:

"Why can't we be friends? I want one sadly, and so do you, unless your looks deceive me. We both seem to be alone in the world, to have had trouble, and to like one another. I won't annoy you by any impertinent curiosity, nor burden you with uninteresting confidences; I only want to feel that you like me a little and don't mind my liking you a great deal. Will you be my friend, and let me be yours?"

A great tear rolled down upon the shining silk in Rachel's hands as she looked into Christie's earnest face, and answered with an almost passionate gratitude in her own:

"You can never need a friend as much as I do, or know what a blessed thing it is to find such an one as you are."

"Then I may love you, and not be afraid of offending?" cried Christie, much touched.

"Yes. But remember *I* didn't ask it first," said Rachel, half dropping the hand she had held in both her own.

"You proud creature! I'll remember; and when we quarrel, I'll take all the blame upon myself."

Then Christie kissed her warmly, whisked away the tear, and began to paint the delights in store for them in her most en-thusiastic way, being much elated with her victory; while Ra-chel listened with a newly kindled light in her lovely eyes, and a smile that showed how winsome her face had been before many tears washed its bloom away, and much trouble made it old too soon.

Christie kept her word,—asked no questions, volunteered no confidences, but heartily enjoyed the new friendship, and found that it gave to life the zest which it had lacked before. Now some one cared for her, and, better still, she could make some one happy, and in the act of lavishing the affection of her generous nature on a creature sadder and more solitary than herself, she found a satisfaction that never lost its charm. There was nothing in her possession that she did not offer Rachel, from the whole of her heart to the larger half of her little room.

"I'm tired of thinking only of myself. It makes me selfish and low-spirited; for I'm not a bit interesting. I must love somebody, and 'love them hard,' as children say; so why can't you come and stay with me? There's room enough, and we could be so cosy evenings with our books and work. I know you need some one to look after you, and I love dearly to take care of people. Do come," she would say, with most persuasive hospitality.

But Rachel always answered steadily: "Not yet, Christie, not yet. I've got something to do before I can think of doing any thing so beautiful as that. Only love me, dear, and some day I'll show you all my heart, and thank you as I ought."

So Christie was content to wait, and, meantime, enjoyed much; for, with Rachel as a friend, she ceased to care for country pleasures, found happiness in the work that gave her better food than mere daily bread, and never thought of change; for love can make a home for itself anywhere.

A very bright and happy time was this in Christie's life; but, like most happy times, it was very brief. Only one summer allowed for the blossoming of the friendship that budded so slowly in the spring; then the frost came and killed the flowers; but the root lived long underneath the snows of suffering, doubt, and absence.

Coming to her work late one morning, she found the usually orderly room in confusion. Some of the girls were crying; some whispering together,—all looking excited and dismayed. Mrs. King sat majestically at her table, with an ominous frown upon her face. Miss Cotton stood beside her, looking unusually sour and stern, for the ancient virgin's temper was not of the best. Alone, before them all, with her face hidden in her hands, and despair in every line of her drooping figure, stood Rachel,—a meek culprit at the stern bar of justice, where women try a sister woman.

"What's the matter?" cried Christie, pausing on the threshold.

Rachel shivered, as if the sound of that familiar voice was a

MRS. KING AND MISS COTTON.

fresh wound, but she did not lift her head; and Mrs. King answered, with a nervous emphasis that made the bugles of her
head-dress rattle dismally:

"A very sad thing, Miss Devon,—*very* sad, indeed; a thing
which *never* occurred in my establishment before, and *never*
shall again. It appears that Rachel, whom we all considered a
most respectable and worthy girl, has been quite the reverse. I
shudder to think what the consequences of my taking her
without a character (a thing I never do, and was only tempted
by her superior taste as a trimmer) might have been if Miss
Cotton, having suspicions, had not made strict inquiry and
confirmed them."

"That was a kind and generous act, and Miss Cotton must
feel proud of it," said Christie, with an indignant recollection
of Mr. Fletcher's "cautious inquiries" about herself.

"It was perfectly right and proper, Miss Devon; and I thank

her for her care of my interests." And Mrs. King bowed her acknowledgment of the service with a perfect castanet accompaniment, whereat Miss Cotton bridled with malicious complacency.

"Mrs. King, are you sure of this?" said Christie. "Miss Cotton does not like Rachel because her work is so much praised. May not her jealousy make her unjust, or her zeal for you mislead her?"

"I thank you for your polite insinuations, miss," returned the irate forewoman. "*I* never make mistakes; but you will find that *you* have made a very great one in choosing Rachel for your bosom friend instead of some one who would be a credit to you. Ask the creature herself if all I've said of her isn't true. She can't deny it."

With the same indefinable misgiving which had held her aloof, Christie turned to Rachel, lifted up the hidden face with gentle force, and looked into it imploringly, as she whispered: "Is it true?"

The woful countenance she saw made any other answer needless. Involuntarily her hands fell away, and she hid her own face, uttering the one reproach, which, tender and tearful though it was, seemed harder to be borne than the stern condemnation gone before.

"Oh, Rachel, I so loved and trusted you!"

The grief, affection, and regret that trembled in her voice roused Rachel from her state of passive endurance and gave her courage to plead for herself. But it was Christie whom she addressed, Christie whose pardon she implored, Christie's sorrowful reproach that she most keenly felt.

"Yes, it *is* true," she said, looking only at the woman who had been the first to befriend and now was the last to desert her. "It is true that I once went astray, but God knows I have repented; that for years I've tried to be an honest girl again, and that but for this help I should be a far sadder creature than I am this day. Christie, you can never know how bitter hard it is to outlive a sin like mine, and struggle up again from such a fall. It clings to me; it won't be shaken off or buried out of sight. No sooner do I find a safe place like this, and try to forget the past, than some one reads my secret in my face and hunts me down. It seems very cruel, very hard, yet it is my punishment, so I try to bear it, and begin again. What hurts me now more than all the rest, what breaks my heart, is that I deceived *you*. I never meant to do it. I did not seek you, did I? I tried to be cold and stiff; never asked for love, though starving for it, till you came to me, so kind, so generous, so dear,— how could I help it? Oh, how could I help it then?"

Christie had watched Rachel while she spoke, and spoke to her alone; her heart yearned toward this one friend, for she still loved her, and, loving, she believed in her.

"I don't reproach you, dear: I don't despise or desert you, and though I'm grieved and disappointed, I'll stand by you still, because you need me more than ever now, and I want to prove that I am a true friend. Mrs. King, please forgive and let poor Rachel stay here, safe among us."

"Miss Devon, I'm surprised at you! By no means; it would be the ruin of my establishment; not a girl would remain, and the character of my rooms would be lost for ever," replied Mrs. King, goaded on by the relentless Cotton.

"But where will she go if you send her away? Who will employ her if you inform against her? What stranger will believe in her if we, who have known her so long, fail to befriend her now? Mrs. King, think of your own daughters, and be a mother to this poor girl for their sake."

That last stroke touched the woman's heart; her cold eye softened, her hard mouth relaxed, and pity was about to win the day, when prudence, in the shape of Miss Cotton, turned the scale, for that spiteful spinster suddenly cried out, in a burst of righteous wrath:

"If that hussy stays, *I* leave this establishment for ever!" and followed up the blow by putting on her bonnet with a flourish.

At this spectacle, self-interest got the better of sympathy in Mrs. King's worldly mind. To lose Cotton was to lose her right hand, and charity at that price was too expensive a luxury to be indulged in; so she hardened her heart, composed her features, and said, impressively:

"Take off your bonnet, Cotton; I have no intention of offending you, or any one else, by such a step. I forgive you, Rachel, and I pity you; but I can't think of allowing you to stay. There are proper institutions for such as you, and I advise you to go to one and repent. You were paid Saturday night, so nothing prevents your leaving at once. Time is money here, and we are wasting it. Young ladies, take your seats."

All but Christie obeyed, yet no one touched a needle, and Mrs. King sat, hurriedly stabbing pins into the fat cushion on her breast, as if testing the hardness of her heart.

Rachel's eye went round the room; saw pity, aversion, or contempt, on every face, but met no answering glance, for even Christie's eyes were bent thoughtfully on the ground, and Christie's heart seemed closed against her. As she looked her whole manner changed; her tears ceased to fall, her face grew hard, and a reckless mood seemed to take possession of her, as if finding herself deserted by womankind, she would desert her own womanhood.

"I might have known it would be so," she said abruptly, with a bitter smile, sadder to see than her most hopeless tears. "It's no use for such as me to try; better go back to the old life, for there are kinder hearts among the sinners than among the saints, and no one can live without a bit of love. Your Magdalen Asylums are penitentiaries, not homes; I won't go to any of them. Your piety isn't worth much, for though you read in your Bible how the Lord treated a poor soul like me, yet when I stretch out my hand to you for help, not one of all you virtuous, Christian women dare take it and keep me from a life that's worse than hell."

As she spoke Rachel flung out her hand with a half-defiant gesture, and Christie took it. That touch, full of womanly compassion, seemed to exorcise the desperate spirit that possessed the poor girl in her despair, for, with a stifled exclamation, she sunk down at Christie's feet, and lay there weeping in all the passionate abandonment of love and gratitude, remorse and shame. Never had human voice sounded so heavenly sweet to her as that which broke the silence of the room, as this one friend said, with the earnestness of a true and tender heart:

"Mrs. King, if you send her away, I must take her in; for if she does go back to the old life, the sin of it will lie at our door, and God will remember it against us in the end. Some one must trust her, help her, love her, and so save her, as nothing else will. Perhaps I can do this better than you,—at least, I'll try; for even if I risk the loss of my good name, I could bear that better than the thought that Rachel had lost the work of these hard years for want of upholding now. She shall come home with me; no one there need know of this discovery, and I will take any work to her that you will give me, to keep her from want and its temptations. Will you do this, and let me sew for less, if I can pay you for the kindness in no other way?"

Poor Mrs. King was "much tumbled up and down in her own mind;" she longed to consent, but Cotton's eye was upon her, and Cotton's departure would be an irreparable loss, so she decided to end the matter in the most summary manner. Plunging a particularly large pin into her cushioned breast, as if it was a relief to inflict that mock torture upon herself, she said sharply:

"It is impossible. You can do as you please, Miss Devon, but I prefer to wash my hands of the affair at once and entirely."

Christie's eye went from the figure at her feet to the hard-featured woman who had been a kind and just mistress until now, and she asked, anxiously:

"Do you mean that you wash your hands of me also, if I stand by Rachel?"

"I do. I'm very sorry, but my young ladies *must* keep respectable company, or leave my service," was the brief reply, for Mrs. King grew grimmer externally as the mental rebellion increased internally.

"Then I *will* leave it!" cried Christie, with an indignant voice and eye. "Come, dear, we'll go together." And without a look or word for any in the room, she raised the prostrate girl, and led her out into the little hall.

There she essayed to comfort her, but before many words had passed her lips Rachel looked up, and she was silent with surprise, for the face she saw was neither despairing nor defiant, but beautifully sweet and clear, as the unfallen spirit of the woman shone through the grateful eyes, and blessed her for her loyalty.

"Christie, you have done enough for me," she said. "Go back, and keep the good place you need, for such are hard to find. I can get on alone; I'm used to this, and the pain will soon be over."

"I'll not go back!" cried Christie, hotly. I'll do slop-work and starve, before I'll stay with such a narrow-minded, cold-hearted woman. Come home with me at once, and let us lay our plans together."

"No, dear; if I wouldn't go when you first asked me, much less will I go now, for I've done you harm enough already. I never can thank you for your great goodness to me, never tell you what it has been to me. We must part now; but some day I'll come back and show you that I've not forgotten how you loved and helped and trusted me, when all the others cast me off."

Vain were Christie's arguments and appeals. Rachel was immovable, and all her friend could win from her was a promise to send word, now and then, how things prospered with her.

"And, Rachel, I charge you to come to me in any strait, no matter what it is, no matter where I am; for if any thing could break my heart, it would be to know that you had gone back to the old life, because there was no one to help and hold you up."

"I *never* can go back; you have saved me, Christie, for you love me, you have faith in me, and that will keep me strong and safe when you are gone. Oh, my dear, my dear, God bless you for ever and for ever!"

Then Christie, remembering only that they were two loving women, alone in a world of sin and sorrow, took Rachel in her arms, kissed and cried over her with sisterly affection, and watched her prayerfully, as she went away to begin her hard task anew, with nothing but the touch of innocent lips upon her cheek, the baptism of tender tears upon her forehead to keep her from despair.

Still cherishing the hope that Rachel would come back to her, Christie neither returned to Mrs. King nor sought another place of any sort, but took home work from a larger establishment, and sat sewing diligently in her little room, waiting, hoping, longing for her friend. But month after month went by, and no word, no sign came to comfort her. She would not doubt, yet she could not help fearing, and in her nightly prayer no petition was more fervently made than that which asked the Father of both saint and sinner to keep poor Rachel safe, and bring her back in his good time.

Never had she been so lonely as now, for Christie had a social heart, and, having known the joy of a cordial friendship even for a little while, life seemed very barren to her when she lost it. No new friend took Rachel's place, for none came to her, and a feeling of loyalty kept her from seeking one. But she suffered for the want of genial society, for all the tenderness of her nature seemed to have been roused by that brief but most sincere affection. Her hungry heart clamored for the happiness that was its right, and grew very heavy as she watched friends or lovers walking in the summer twilight when she took her evening stroll. Often her eyes followed some humble pair, longing to bless and to be blessed by the divine passion whose magic beautifies the little milliner and her lad with the same tender grace as the poet and the mistress whom he makes immortal in a song. But neither friend nor lover came to Christie, and she said to herself, with a sad sort of courage:

"I shall be solitary all my life, perhaps; so the sooner I make up my mind to it, the easier it will be to bear."

At Christmas-tide she made a little festival for herself, by giving to each of the household drudges the most generous gift she could afford, for no one else thought of them, and having known some of the hardships of servitude herself, she had much sympathy with those in like case.

Then, with the pleasant recollection of two plain faces, brightened by gratitude, surprise, and joy, she went out into the busy streets to forget the solitude she left behind her.

Very gay they were with snow and sleigh-bells, holly-boughs, and garlands, below, and Christmas sunshine in the winter sky above. All faces shone, all voices had a cheery ring, and everybody stepped briskly on errands of good-will. Up and down went Christie, making herself happy in the happiness of others. Looking in at the shop-windows, she watched, with interest, the purchases of busy parents, calculating how best to fill the little socks hung up at home, with a childish faith that never must be disappointed, no matter how hard the times might be. She was glad to see so many turkeys on their way to garnish hospitable tables, and hoped that all the dear home circles might be found unbroken, though she had place in none. No Christmas-tree went by leaving a whiff of piny sweetness behind, that she did not wish it all success, and picture to herself the merry little people dancing in its light. And whenever she saw a ragged child eying a window full of goodies, smiling even while it shivered, she could not resist playing Santa Claus till her purse was empty, sending the poor little souls enraptured home with oranges and apples in either hand, and splendid sweeties in their pockets, for the babies.

No envy mingled with the melancholy that would not be dispelled even by these gentle acts, for her heart was very tender that night, and if any one had asked what gifts she desired most, she would have answered with a look more pathetic than any shivering child had given her:

"I want the sound of a loving voice; the touch of a friendly hand."

Going home, at last, to the lonely little room where no Christmas fire burned, no tree shone, no household group awaited her, she climbed the long, dark stairs, with drops on her cheeks, warmer than any melted snow-flake could have left, and opening her door paused on the threshold, smiling with wonder and delight, for in her absence some gentle spirit *had* remembered her. A fire burned cheerily upon the hearth, her lamp was lighted, a lovely rose-tree, in full bloom, filled the air with its delicate breath, and in its shadow lay a note from Rachel.

"A merry Christmas and a happy New Year, Christie! Long ago you gave me your little rose; I have watched and tended it for your sake, dear, and now when I want to show my love and thankfulness, I give it back again as my one treasure. I crept in while you were gone, because I feared I might harm you in some way if you saw me. I longed to stay and tell you that I am safe and well, and busy, with your good face looking into mine, but I don't deserve that yet. Only love me, trust me, pray for me, and some day you shall know what you have done for me. Till then, God bless and keep you, dearest friend, your
RACHEL."

Never had sweeter tears fallen than those that dropped upon the little tree as Christie took it in her arms, and all the rosy clusters leaned toward her as if eager to deliver tender messages. Surely her wish was granted now, for friendly hands had been at work for her. Warm against her heart lay words as precious as if uttered by a loving voice, and nowhere, on that happy night, stood a fairer Christmas tree than that which bloomed so beautifully from the heart of a Magdalen who loved much and was forgiven.

# Chapter VII

## THROUGH THE MIST

THE year that followed was the saddest Christie had ever known, for she suffered a sort of poverty which is more difficult to bear than actual want, since money cannot lighten it, and the rarest charity alone can minister to it. Her heart was empty and she could not fill it; her soul was hungry and she could not feed it; life was cold and dark and she could not warm and brighten it, for she knew not where to go.

She tried to help herself by all the means in her power, and when effort after effort failed she said: "I am not good enough yet to deserve happiness. I think too much of human love, too little of divine. When I have made God my friend perhaps He will let me find and keep one heart to make life happy with. How shall I know God? Who will tell me where to find Him, and help me to love and lean upon Him as I ought?"

In all sincerity she asked these questions, in all sincerity she began her search, and with pathetic patience waited for an answer. She read many books, some wise, some vague, some full of superstition, all unsatisfactory to one who wanted a living God. She went to many churches, studied many creeds, and watched their fruits as well as she could; but still remained unsatisfied. Some were cold and narrow, some seemed theatrical and superficial, some stern and terrible, none simple, sweet, and strong enough for humanity's many needs. There was too much machinery, too many walls, laws, and penalties between the Father and his children. Too much fear, too little love; too many saints and intercessors; too little faith in the instincts of the soul which turns to God as flowers to the sun. Too much idle strife about names and creeds; too little knowledge of the natural religion which has no name but godliness, whose creed is boundless and benignant as the sunshine, whose faith is as the tender trust of little children in their mother's love.

Nowhere did Christie find this all-sustaining power, this paternal friend, and comforter, and after months of patient searching she gave up her quest, saying, despondently:

"I'm afraid I never shall get religion, for all that's offered me seems so poor, so narrow, or so hard that I cannot take it for my stay. A God of wrath I cannot love; a God that must be propitiated, adorned, and adored like an idol I cannot respect; and a God who can be blinded to men's iniquities through the week by a little beating of the breast and bowing down on the seventh day, I cannot serve. I want a Father to whom I can go with all my sins and sorrows, all my hopes and joys, as freely and fearlessly as I used to go to my human father, sure of help and sympathy and love. Shall I ever find Him?"

Alas, poor Christie! she was going through the sorrowful perplexity that comes to so many before they learn that religion cannot be given or bought, but must grow as trees grow, needing frost and snow, rain and wind to strengthen it before it is deep-rooted in the soul; that God is in the hearts of all, and they that seek shall surely find Him when they need Him most.

So Christie waited for religion to reveal itself to her, and while she waited worked with an almost desperate industry, trying to buy a little happiness for herself by giving a part of her earnings to those whose needs money could supply. She clung to her little room, for there she could live her own life undisturbed, and preferred to stint herself in other ways rather than give up this liberty. Day after day she sat there sewing health of mind and body into the long seams or dainty stitching that passed through her busy hands, and while she sewed she thought sad, bitter, oftentimes rebellious thoughts.

It was the worst life she could have led just then, for, deprived of the active, cheerful influences she most needed, her mind preyed on itself, slowly and surely, preparing her for the dark experience to come. She knew that there was fitter work for her somewhere, but how to find it was a problem which wiser women have often failed to solve. She was no pauper, yet was one of those whom poverty sets at odds with the world, for favors burden and dependence makes the bread bitter unless love brightens the one and sweetens the other.

There are many Christies, willing to work, yet unable to bear the contact with coarser natures which makes labor seem degrading, or to endure the hard struggle for the bare necessities of life when life has lost all that makes it beautiful. People wonder when such as she say they can find little to do; but to those who know nothing of the pangs of pride, the sacrifices of feeling, the martyrdoms of youth, love, hope, and ambition that go on under the faded cloaks of these poor gentlewomen, who tell them to go into factories, or scrub in kitchens, for there is work enough for all, the most convincing answer would be, "Try it."

Christie kept up bravely till a wearisome low fever broke both strength and spirit, and brought the weight of debt upon her when least fitted to bear or cast it off. For the first time she began to feel that she had nerves which would rebel, and a heart that could not long endure isolation from its kind without losing the cheerful courage which hitherto had been her staunchest friend. Perfect rest, kind care, and genial society were the medicines she needed, but there was no one to minister to her, and she went blindly on along the road so many women tread.

She left her bed too soon, fearing to ask too much of the busy people who had done their best to be neighborly. She returned to her work when it felt heavy in her feeble hands, for debt made idleness seem wicked to her conscientious mind. And, worst of all, she fell back into the bitter, brooding mood which had become habitual to her since she lived alone. While the tired hands slowly worked, the weary brain ached and burned with heavy thoughts, vain longings, and feverish fancies, till things about her sometimes seemed as strange and spectral as the phantoms that had haunted her half-delirious sleep. Inexpressibly wretched were the dreary days, the restless nights, with only pain and labor for companions. The world looked very dark to her, life seemed an utter failure, God a delusion, and the long, lonely years before her too hard to be endured.

It is not always want, insanity, or sin that drives women to desperate deaths; often it is a dreadful loneliness of heart, a hunger for home and friends, worse than starvation, a bitter sense of wrong in being denied the tender ties, the pleasant duties, the sweet rewards that can make the humblest life happy; a rebellious protest against God, who, when they cry for bread, seems to offer them a stone. Some of these impatient souls throw life away, and learn too late how rich it might have been with a stronger faith, a more submissive spirit. Others are kept, and slowly taught to stand and wait, till blest with a happiness the sweeter for the doubt that went before.

There came a time to Christie when the mist about her was so thick she would have stumbled and fallen had not the little candle, kept alight by her own hand, showed her how far "a good deed shines in a naughty world;" and when God seemed utterly forgetful of her He sent a friend to save and comfort her.

March winds were whistling among the house-tops, and the sky was darkening with a rainy twilight as Christie folded up her finished work, stretched her weary limbs, and made ready for her daily walk. Even this was turned to profit, for then she took home her work, went in search of more, and did her own small marketing. As late hours and unhealthy labor destroyed appetite, and unpaid debts made each mouthful difficult to swallow with Mrs. Flint's hard eye upon her, she had undertaken to supply her own food, and so lessen the obligation that burdened her. An unwise retrenchment, for, busied with the tasks that must be done, she too often neglected or deferred the meals to which no society lent interest, no appetite gave flavor; and when the fuel was withheld the fire began to die out spark by spark.

As she stood before the little mirror, smoothing the hair upon her forehead, she watched the face reflected there, wondering if it could be the same she used to see so full of youth and hope and energy.

"Yes, I'm growing old; my youth is nearly over, and at thirty I shall be a faded, dreary woman, like so many I see and pity. It's hard to come to this after trying so long to find my place, and do my duty. I'm a failure after all, and might as well have stayed with Aunt Betsey or married Joe."

"Miss Devon, to-day is Saturday, and I'm makin' up my bills, so I'll trouble you for your month's board, and as much on the old account as you can let me have."

Mrs. Flint spoke, and her sharp voice rasped the silence like a file, for she had entered without knocking, and her demand was the first intimation of her presence.

Christie turned slowly round, for there was no elasticity in her motions now; through the melancholy anxiety her face always wore of late, there came the worried look of one driven almost beyond endurance, and her hands began to tremble nervously as she tied on her bonnet. Mrs. Flint was a hard woman, and dunned her debtors relentlessly; Christie dreaded the sight of her, and would have left the house had she been free of debt.

"I am just going to take these things home and get more work. I am sure of being paid, and you shall have all I get. But, for Heaven's sake, give me time."

Two days and a night of almost uninterrupted labor had given a severe strain to her nerves, and left her in a dangerous state. Something in her face arrested Mrs. Flint's attention; she observed that Christie was putting on her best cloak and hat, and to her suspicious eye the bundle of work looked unduly large.

It had been a hard day for the poor woman, for the cook had gone off in a huff; the chamber girl been detected in petty larceny; two desirable boarders had disappointed her; and the incapable husband had fallen ill, so it was little wonder that her soul was tried, her sharp voice sharper, and her sour temper sourer than ever.

"I *have* heard of folks putting on their best things and going out, but never coming back again, when they owed money. It's a mean trick, but it's sometimes done by them you wouldn't think it of," she said, with an aggravating sniff of intelligence.

To be suspected of dishonesty was the last drop in Christie's full cup. She looked at the woman with a strong desire to do something violent, for every nerve was tingling with irritation and anger. But she controlled herself, though her face was colorless and her hands were more tremulous than before. Unfastening her comfortable cloak she replaced it with a shabby shawl; took off her neat bonnet and put on a hood, unfolded six linen shirts, and shook them out before her landlady's eyes; then retied the parcel, and, pausing on the threshold of the door, looked back with an expression that haunted the woman long afterward, as she said, with the quiver of strong excitement in her voice:

"Mrs. Flint, I have always dealt honorably by you; I always mean to do it, and don't deserve to be suspected of dishonesty like that. I leave every thing I own behind me, and if I don't come back, you can sell them all and pay yourself, for I feel now as if I *never* wanted to see you or this room again."

Then she went rapidly away, supported by her indignation, for she had done her best to pay her debts; had sold the few trinkets she possessed, and several treasures given by the Carrols, to settle her doctor's bill, and had been half killing herself to satisfy Mrs. Flint's demands. The consciousness that she had been too lavish in her generosity when fortune smiled upon her, made the present want all the harder to bear. But she would neither beg nor borrow, though she knew Harry would delight to give, and Uncle Enos lend her money, with a lecture on extravagance, gratis.

"I'll paddle my own canoe as long as I can," she said, sternly; "and when I must ask help I'll turn to strangers for it, or scuttle my boat, and go down without troubling any one."

When she came to her employer's door, the servant said: "Missis was out;" then seeing Christie's disappointed face, she added, confidentially:

"If it's any comfort to know it, I can tell you that missis wouldn't have paid you if she had a been to home. There's been three other women here with work, and she's put 'em all off. She always does, and beats 'em down into the bargain, which ain't genteel to my thinkin'."

"She promised me I should be well paid for these, because I undertook to get them done without fail. I've worked day and night rather than disappoint her, and felt sure of my money," said Christie, despondently.

"I'm sorry, but you won't get it. She told me to tell you your prices was too high, and she could find folks to work cheaper."

"She did not object to the price when I took the work, and I have half-ruined my eyes over the fine stitching. See if it isn't nicely done." And Christie displayed her exquisite needlework with pride.

The girl admired it, and, having a grievance of her own, took satisfaction in berating her mistress.

"It's a shame! These things are part of a present the ladies are going to give the minister; but I don't believe he'll feel easy in 'em if poor folks is wronged to get 'em. Missis won't pay what they are worth, I know; for, don't you see, the cheaper the work is done, the more money she has to make a spread with her share of the present? It's my opinion you'd better hold on to these shirts till she pays for 'em handsome."

"No; I'll keep *my* promise, and I hope she will keep hers. Tell her I need the money very much, and have worked very hard to please her. I'll come again on Monday, if I'm able."

Christie's lips trembled as she spoke, for she was feeble still, and the thought of that hard-earned money had been her sustaining hope through the weary hours spent over that ill-paid work. The girl said "Goodbye," with a look of mingled pity and respect, for in her eyes the seamstress was more of a lady than the mistress in this transaction.

Christie hurried to another place, and asked eagerly if the young ladies had any work for her. "Not a stitch," was the reply, and the door closed. She stood a moment looking down upon the passers-by wondering what answer she would get if she accosted any one; and had any especially benevolent face looked back at her she would have been tempted to do it, so heart-sick and forlorn did she feel just then.

She knocked at several other doors, to receive the same reply. She even tried a slop-shop, but it was full, and her pale face was against her. Her long illness had lost her many patrons, and if one steps out from the ranks of needle-women it is very hard to press in again, so crowded are they, and so desperate the need of money.

One hope remained, and, though the way was long, and a foggy drizzle had set in, she minded neither distance nor the chilly rain, but hurried away with anxious thoughts still dogging her steps. Across a long bridge, through muddy roads and up a stately avenue she went, pausing, at last, spent and breathless at another door.

A servant with a wedding-favor in his button-hole opened to her, and, while he went to deliver her urgent message, she peered in wistfully from the dreary world without, catching glimpses of home-love and happiness that made her heart ache for very pity of its own loneliness.

A wedding was evidently afoot, for hall and staircase blazed with light and bloomed with flowers. Smiling men and maids ran to and fro; opening doors showed tables beautiful with bridal white and silver; savory odors filled the air; gay voices echoed above and below; and once she caught a brief glance at the bonny bride, standing with her father's arm about her, while her mother gave some last, loving touch to her array; and a group of young sisters with April faces clustered round her.

The pretty picture vanished all too soon; the man returned with a hurried "No" for answer, and Christie went out into the deepening twilight with a strange sense of desperation at her heart. It was not the refusal, not the fear of want, nor the reaction of over-taxed nerves alone; it was the sharpness of the contrast between that other woman's fate and her own that made her wring her hands together, and cry out, bitterly:

"Oh, it isn't fair, it isn't right, that she should have so much and I so little! What have I ever done to be so desolate and miserable, and never to find any happiness, however hard I try to do what seems my duty?"

There was no answer, and she went slowly down the long avenue, feeling that there was no cause for hurry now, and even night and rain and wind were better than her lonely room or Mrs. Flint's complaints. Afar off the city lights shone faintly through the fog, like pale lamps seen in dreams; the damp air cooled her feverish cheeks; the road was dark and still, and she longed to lie down and rest among the sodden leaves.

When she reached the bridge she saw the draw was up, and a spectral ship was slowly passing through. With no desire to mingle in the crowd that waited on either side, she paused, and, leaning on the railing, let her thoughts wander where they would. As she stood there the heavy air seemed to clog her breath and wrap her in its chilly arms. She felt as if the springs of life were running down, and presently would stop; for, even when the old question, "What shall I do?" came haunting her, she no longer cared even to try to answer it, and had no feeling but one of utter weariness. She tried to shake off the strange mood that was stealing over her, but spent body and spent brain were not strong enough to obey her will, and, in spite of her efforts to control it, the impulse that had seized her grew more intense each moment.

"Why should I work and suffer any longer for myself alone?" she thought; "why wear out my life struggling for the bread I have no heart to eat? I am not wise enough to find my place, nor patient enough to wait until it comes to me. Better give up trying, and leave room for those who have something to live for."

Many a stronger soul has known a dark hour when the importunate wish has risen that it were possible and right to lay down the burdens that oppress, the perplexities that harass, and hasten the coming of the long sleep that needs no lullaby. Such an hour was this to Christie, for, as she stood there, that sorrowful bewilderment which we call despair came over her, and ruled her with a power she could not resist.

A flight of steps close by led to a lumber wharf, and, scarcely knowing why, she went down there, with a vague desire to sit still somewhere, and think her way out of the mist that seemed to obscure her mind. A single tall lamp shone at the farther end of the platform, and presently she found herself leaning her hot forehead against the iron pillar, while she watched with curious interest the black water rolling sluggishly below.

She knew it was no place for her, yet no one waited for her, no one would care if she staid for ever, and, yielding to the perilous fascination that drew her there, she lingered with a heavy throbbing in her temples, and a troop of wild fancies whirling through her brain. Something white swept by below,— only a broken oar—but she began to wonder how a human body would look floating through the night. It was an awesome fancy, but it took possession of her, and, as it grew, her eyes dilated, her breath came fast, and her lips fell apart, for she seemed to see the phantom she had conjured up, and it wore the likeness of herself.

With an ominous chill creeping through her blood, and a growing tumult in her mind, she thought, "I *must* go," but still stood motionless, leaning over the wide gulf, eager to see where that dead thing would pass away. So plainly did she see it, so peaceful was the white face, so full of rest the folded hands, so strangely like, and yet unlike, herself, that she seemed to lose her identity, and wondered which was the real and which the imaginary Christie. Lower and lower she bent; looser and looser grew her hold upon the pillar; faster and faster beat the pulses in her temples, and the rush of some blind impulse was swiftly coming on, when a hand seized and caught her back.

For an instant every thing grew black before her eyes, and

the earth seemed to slip away from underneath her feet. Then she was herself again, and found that she was sitting on a pile of lumber, with her head uncovered, and a woman's arm about her.

THE RESCUE.

"Was I going to drown myself?" she asked, slowly, with a fancy that she had been dreaming frightfully, and some one had wakened her.

"You were most gone; but I came in time, thank God! O Christie! don't you know me?"

Ah! no fear of that; for with one bewildered look, one glad cry of recognition, Christie found her friend again, and was gathered close to Rachel's heart.

"My dear, my dear, what drove you to it? Tell me all, and let me help you in your trouble, as you helped me in mine," she said, as she tenderly laid the poor, white face upon her breast, and wrapped her shawl about the trembling figure clinging to her with such passionate delight.

"I have been ill; I worked too hard; I'm not myself to-night. I owe money. People disappoint and worry me; and I was so worn out, and weak, and wicked, I think I meant to take my life."

"No, dear; it was not you that meant to do it, but the weakness and the trouble that bewildered you. Forget it all, and rest a little, safe with me; then we'll talk again."

Rachel spoke soothingly, for Christie shivered and sighed as if her own thoughts frightened her. For a moment they sat silent, while the mist trailed its white shroud above them, as if death had paused to beckon a tired child away, but, finding her so gently cradled on a warm, human heart, had relented and passed on, leaving no waif but the broken oar for the river to carry toward the sea.

"Tell me about yourself, Rachel. Where have you been so long? I've looked and waited for you ever since the second little note you sent me on last Christmas; but you never came."

"I've been away, dear heart, hard at work in another city, larger and wickeder than this. I tried to get work here, that I might be near you; but that cruel Cotton always found me out; and I was so afraid I should get desperate that I went away where I was not known. There it came into my mind to do for others more wretched than I what you had done for me. God put the thought into my heart, and he helped me in my work, for it has prospered wonderfully. All this year I have been busy with it, and almost happy; for I felt that your love made me strong to do it, and that, in time, I might grow good enough to be your friend."

"See what I am, Rachel, and never say that any more!"

"Hush, my poor dear, and let me talk! You are not able to do any thing, but rest, and listen: I knew how many poor souls went wrong when the devil tempted them; and I gave all my strength to saving those who were going the way I went. I had no fear, no shame to overcome, for I was one of them. They would listen to me, for I knew what I spoke; they could believe in salvation, for I was saved; they did not feel so outcast and forlorn when I told them you had taken me into your innocent arms, and loved me like a sister. With every one I helped my power increased, and I felt as if I had washed away a little of my own great sin. O Christie! never think it's time to die till you are called; for the Lord leaves us till we have done our work, and never sends more sin and sorrow than we can bear and be the better for, if we hold fast by Him."

So beautiful and brave she looked, so full of strength and yet of meek submission was her voice, that Christie's heart was thrilled; for it was plain that Rachel had learned how to distil balm from the bitterness of life, and, groping in the mire to save lost souls, had found her own salvation there.

"Show me how to grow pious, strong, and useful, as you are," she said. "I am all wrong, and feel as if I never could get right again, for I haven't energy enough to care what becomes of me."

"I know the state, Christie: I've been through it all! but when *I* stood where you stand now, there was no hand to pull me back, and I fell into a blacker river than this underneath our feet. Thank God, I came in time to save you from either death!"

"How did you find me?" asked Christie, when she had echoed in her heart the thanksgiving that came with such fervor from the other's lips.

"I passed you on the bridge. I did not see your face, but you stood leaning there so wearily, and looking down into the water, as I used to look, that I wanted to speak, but did not; and I went on to comfort a poor girl who is dying yonder. Something turned me back, however; and when I saw you down here I knew why I was sent. You were almost gone, but I kept you; and when I had you in my arms I knew you, though it nearly broke my heart to find you here. Now, dear, come home."

"Home! ah, Rachel, I've got no home, and for want of one I shall be lost!"

The lament that broke from her was more pathetic than the tears that streamed down, hot and heavy, melting from her heart the frost of her despair. Her friend let her weep, knowing well the worth of tears, and while Christie sobbed herself quiet, Rachel took thought for her as tenderly as any mother.

When she had heard the story of Christie's troubles, she

stood up as if inspired with a happy thought, and stretching both hands to her friend, said, with an air of cheerful assurance most comforting to see:

"I'll take care of you; come with me, my poor Christie, and I'll give you a home, very humble, but honest and happy."

"With you, Rachel?"

"No, dear, I must go back to my work, and you are not fit for that. Neither must you go again to your own room, because for you it is haunted, and the worst place you could be in. You want change, and I'll give you one. It will seem queer at first, but it is a wholesome place, and just what you need."

"I'll do any thing you tell me. I'm past thinking for myself to-night, and only want to be taken care of till I find strength and courage enough to stand alone," said Christie, rising slowly and looking about her with an aspect as helpless and hopeless as if the cloud of mist was a wall of iron.

Rachel put on her bonnet for her and wrapped her shawl about her, saying, in a tender voice, that warmed the other's heart:

"Close by lives a dear, good woman who often befriends such as you and I. She will take you in without a question, and love to do it, for she is the most hospitable soul I know. Just tell her you want work, that I sent you, and there will be no trouble. Then, when you know her a little, confide in her, and you will never come to such a pass as this again. Keep up your heart, dear; I'll not leave you till you are safe."

So cheerily she spoke, so confident she looked, that the lost expression passed from Christie's face, and hand in hand they went away together,—two types of the sad sisterhood standing on either shore of the dark river that is spanned by a Bridge of Sighs.

Rachel led her friend toward the city, and, coming to the mechanics' quarter, stopped before the door of a small, old house.

"Just knock, say 'Rachel sent me,' and you'll find yourself at home."

"Stay with me, or let me go with you. I can't lose you again, for I need you very much," pleaded Christie, clinging to her friend.

"Not so much as that poor girl dying all alone. She's waiting for me, and I must go. But I'll write soon; and remember, Christie, I shall feel as if I had only paid a very little of my debt if you go back to the sad old life, and lose your faith and hope again. God bless and keep you, and when we meet next time let me find a happier face than this."

Rachel kissed it with her heart on her lips, smiled her brave sweet smile, and vanished in the mist.

Pausing a moment to collect herself, Christie recollected that she had not asked the name of the new friend whose help she was about to ask. A little sign on the door caught her eye, and, bending down, she managed to read by the dim light of the street lamp these words:

> "C. WILKINS, Clear-Starcher.
> Laces done up in the best style."

Too tired to care whether a laundress or a lady took her in, she knocked timidly, and, while she waited for an answer to her summons, stood listening to the noises within.

A swashing sound as of water was audible, likewise a scuffling as of flying feet; some one clapped hands, and a voice said, warningly, "Into your beds this instant minute or I'll come to you! Andrew Jackson, give Gusty a boost; Ann Lizy, don't you tech Wash's feet to tickle 'em. Set pretty in the tub, Victory, dear, while ma sees who's rappin'."

MRS. WILKINS.

Then heavy footsteps approached, the door opened wide, and a large woman appeared, with fuzzy red hair, no front teeth, and a plump, clean face, brightly illuminated by the lamp she carried.

"If you please, Rachel sent me. She thought you might be able"—

Christie got no further, for C. Wilkins put out a strong bare arm, still damp, and gently drew her in, saying, with the same motherly tone as when addressing her children, "Come right in, dear, and don't mind the clutter things is in. I'm givin' the children their Sat'day scrubbin', and they will slop and kite 'round, no matter ef I do spank 'em."

Talking all the way in such an easy, comfortable voice that Christie felt as if she must have heard it before, Mrs. Wilkins led her unexpected guest into a small kitchen, smelling suggestively of soap-suds and warm flat-irons. In the middle of this apartment was a large tub; in the tub a chubby child sat, sucking a sponge and staring calmly at the new-comer with a pair of big blue eyes, while little drops shone in the yellow curls and on the rosy shoulders.

"How pretty!" cried Christie, seeing nothing else and stopping short to admire this innocent little Venus rising from the sea.

"So she is! Ma's darlin' lamb! and ketchin' her death a cold this blessed minnit. Set right down, my dear, and tuck your wet feet into the oven. I'll have a dish o' tea for you in less'n no time; and while it's drawin' I'll clap Victory Adelaide into her bed."

Christie sank into a shabby but most hospitable old chair, dropped her bonnet on the floor, put her feet in the oven, and, leaning back, watched Mrs. Wilkins wipe the baby as if she had come for that especial purpose. As Rachel predicted, she found herself at home at once, and presently was startled to hear a laugh from her own lips when several children in red and yellow flannel night-gowns darted like meteors across the open doorway of an adjoining room, with whoops and howls, bursts of laughter, and antics of all sorts.

How pleasant it was; that plain room, with no ornaments but the happy faces, no elegance, but cleanliness, no wealth, but hospitality and lots of love. This latter blessing gave the place its charm, for, though Mrs. Wilkins threatened to take her infants' noses off if they got out of bed again, or "put 'em in the kettle and bile 'em" they evidently knew no fear, but gambolled all the nearer to her for the threat; and she beamed upon them with such maternal tenderness and pride that her homely face grew beautiful in Christie's eyes.

When the baby was bundled up in a blanket and about to be set down before the stove to simmer a trifle before being put to bed, Christie held out her arms, saying with an irresistible longing in her eyes and voice:

"Let me hold her! I love babies dearly, and it seems as if it would do me more good than quarts of tea to cuddle her, if she'll let me."

"There now, that's real sensible; and mother's bird'll set along with you as good as a kitten. Toast her tootsies wal, for she's croupy, and I have to be extra choice of her."

"How good it feels!" sighed Christie, half devouring the warm and rosy little bunch in her lap, while baby lay back luxuriously, spreading her pink toes to the pleasant warmth and smiling sleepily up in the hungry face that hung over her.

Mrs. Wilkins's quick eyes saw it all, and she said to herself, in the closet, as she cut bread and rattled down a cup and saucer:

"That's what she wants, poor creeter; I'll let her have a right nice time, and warm and feed and chirk her up, and then I'll see what's to be done for her. She ain't one of the common sort, and goodness only knows what Rachel sent her here for. She's poor and sick, but she ain't bad. I can tell that by her face, and she's the sort I like to help. It's a mercy I ain't eat my supper, so she can have that bit of meat and the pie."

Putting a tray on the little table, the good soul set forth all she had to give, and offered it with such hospitable warmth that Christie ate and drank with unaccustomed appetite, finishing off deliciously with a kiss from baby before she was borne away by her mother to the back bedroom, where peace soon reigned.

"Now let me tell you who I am, and how I came to you in such an unceremonious way," began Christie, when her hostess returned and found her warmed, refreshed, and composed by a woman's three best comforters,—kind words, a baby, and a cup of tea.

"'Pears to me, dear, I wouldn't rile myself up by telling any werryments to-night, but git right warm inter bed, and have a good long sleep," said Mrs. Wilkins, without a ray of curiosity in her wholesome red face.

"But you don't know any thing about me, and I may be the worst woman in the world," cried Christie, anxious to prove herself worthy of such confidence.

"I know that you want takin' care of, child, or Rachel wouldn't a sent you. Ef I can help any one, I don't want no introduction; and ef you be the wust woman in the world (which you ain't), I wouldn't shet my door on you, for then you'd need a lift more'n you do now."

Christie could only put out her hand, and mutely thank her new friend with full eyes.

"You're fairly tuckered out, you poor soul, so you jest come right up chamber and let me tuck you up, else you'll be down sick. It ain't a mite of inconvenience; the room is kep for company, and it's all ready, even to a clean night-cap. I'm goin' to clap this warm flat to your feet when you're fixed; it's amazin' comfortin' and keeps your head cool."

Up they went to a tidy little chamber, and Christie found herself laid down to rest none too soon, for she was quite worn out. Sleep began to steal over her the moment her head touched the pillow, in spite of the much beruffled cap which Mrs. Wilkins put on with visible pride in its stiffly crimped borders. She was dimly conscious of a kind hand tucking her up, a comfortable voice purring over her, and, best of all, a motherly good-night kiss, then the weary world faded quite away and she was at rest.

# Chapter VIII

## A CURE FOR DESPAIR

LISHA WILKINS.

WHEN Christie opened the eyes that had closed so wearily, afternoon sunshine streamed across the room, and seemed the herald of happier days. Refreshed by sleep, and comforted by grateful recollections of her kindly welcome, she lay tranquilly enjoying the friendly atmosphere about her, with so strong a feeling that a skilful hand had taken the rudder, that she felt very little anxiety or curiosity about the haven which was to receive her boat after this narrow escape from shipwreck.

Her eye wandered to and fro, and brightened as it went; for though a poor, plain room it was as neat as hands could make it, and so glorified with sunshine that she thought it a lovely place, in spite of the yellow paper with green cabbage roses on it, the gorgeous plaster statuary on the mantel-piece, and the fragrance of dough-nuts which pervaded the air. Every thing suggested home life, humble but happy, and Christie's solitary heart warmed at the sights and sounds about her.

A half open closet-door gave her glimpses of little frocks and jackets, stubby little shoes, and go-to-meeting hats all in a row. From below came up the sound of childish voices chattering, childish feet trotting to and fro, and childish laughter sounding sweetly through the Sabbath stillness of the place. From a room near by, came the soothing creak of a rocking-chair, the rustle of a newspaper, and now and then a scrap of conversation common-place enough, but pleasant to hear, because so full of domestic love and confidence; and, as she listened, Christie pictured Mrs. Wilkins and her husband taking their rest together after the week's hard work was done.

"I wish I could stay here; it's so comfortable and home-like. I wonder if they wouldn't let me have this room, and help me to find some better work than sewing? I'll get up and ask them," thought Christie, feeling an irresistible desire to stay, and strong repugnance to returning to the room she had left, for, as Rachel truly said, it *was* haunted for her.

When she opened the door to go down, Mrs. Wilkins bounced out of her rocking-chair and hurried to meet her with a smiling face, saying all in one breath:

"Good mornin', dear! Rested well, I hope? I'm proper glad to hear it. Now come right down and have your dinner. I kep it hot, for I couldn't bear to wake you up, you was sleepin' so beautiful."

"I was so worn out I slept like a baby, and feel like a new creature. It was so kind of you to take me in, and I'm so grateful I don't know how to show it," said Christie, warmly, as her hostess ponderously descended the complaining stairs and ushered her into the tidy kitchen from which tubs and flat-irons were banished one day in the week.

"Lawful sakes, the' ain't nothing to be grateful for, child, and you're heartily welcome to the little I done. We are country folks in our ways, though we be livin' in the city, and we have a reg'lar country dinner Sundays. Hope you'll relish it; my vittles is clean ef they ain't rich."

As she spoke, Mrs. Wilkins dished up baked beans, Indian-pudding, and brown bread enough for half a dozen. Christie was hungry now, and ate with an appetite that delighted the good lady who vibrated between her guest and her children, shut up in the "settin'-room."

"Now please let me tell you all about myself, for I am afraid you think me something better than I am. If I ask help from you, it is right that you should know whom you are helping," said Christie, when the table was cleared and her hostess came and sat down beside her.

"Yes, my dear, free your mind, and then we'll fix things up right smart. Nothin' I like better, and Lisha says I have considerable of a knack that way," replied Mrs. Wilkins, with a smile, a nod, and an air of interest most reassuring.

So Christie told her story, won to entire confidence by the sympathetic face opposite, and the motherly pats so gently given by the big, rough hand that often met her own. When all was told, Christie said very earnestly:

"I am ready to go to work to-morrow, and will do any thing I can find, but I *should* love to stay here a little while, if I could; I do so dread to be alone. Is it possible? I mean to pay my board of course, and help you besides if you'll let me."

Mrs. Wilkins glowed with pleasure at this compliment, and leaning toward Christie, looked into her face a moment in silence, as if to test the sincerity of the wish. In that moment Christie saw what steady, sagacious eyes the woman had; so clear, so honest that she looked through them into the great, warm heart below, and looking forgot the fuzzy, red hair, the paucity of teeth, the faded gown, and felt only the attraction of a nature genuine and genial as the sunshine dancing on the kitchen floor.

Beautiful souls often get put into plain bodies, but they cannot be hidden, and have a power all their own, the greater for the unconsciousness or the humility which gives it grace. Christie saw and felt this then, and when the homely woman spoke, listened to her with implicit confidence.

"My dear, I'd no more send you away now than I would my Adelaide, for you need looking after for a spell, most as much as she does. You've been thinkin' and broodin' too much, and sewin' yourself to death. We'll stop all that, and keep you so busy there won't be no time for the hypo. You're one of them that can't live alone without starvin' somehow, so I'm jest goin' to turn you in among them children to paster, so to speak. That's wholesome and fillin' for *you*, and goodness knows it will be a puffect charity to *me*, for I'm goin' to be dreadful drove with gettin' up curtins and all manner of things, as spring comes on. So it ain't no favor on my part, and you can take out your board in tendin' baby and putterin' over them little tykes."

"I should like it *so* much! But I forgot my debt to Mrs. Flint;

perhaps she won't let me go," said Christie, with an anxious cloud coming over her brightening face.

"Merciful, suz! don't you be werried about her. I'll see to her, and ef she acts ugly Lisha'll fetch her round; men can always settle such things better'n we can, and he's a dreadful smart man Lisha is. We'll go to-morrer and get your belongins, and then settle right down for a spell; and by-an'-by when you git a trifle more chipper we'll find a nice place in the country some'rs. That's what you want; nothin' like green grass and woodsy smells to right folks up. When I was a gal, ef I got low in my mind, or riled in my temper, I jest went out and grubbed in the gardin, or made hay, or walked a good piece, and it fetched me round beautiful. Never failed; so I come to see that good fresh dirt is fust rate physic for folk's spirits as it is for wounds, as they tell on."

"That sounds sensible and pleasant, and I like it. Oh, it is *so* beautiful to feel that somebody cares for you a little bit, and you ain't one too many in the world," sighed Christie.

"Don't you never feel that agin, my dear. What's the Lord for ef he ain't to hold on to in times of trouble. Faith ain't wuth much ef it's only lively in fair weather; you've got to believe hearty and stan' by the Lord through thick and thin, and he'll stan' by you as no one else begins to. I remember of havin' this bore in upon me by somethin' that happened to a man I knew. He got blowed up in a powder-mill, and when folks asked him what he thought when the bust come, he said, real sober and impressive: 'Wal, it come through me, like a flash, that I'd served the Lord as faithful as I knew how for a number a years, and I guessed he'd fetch me through somehow, and he did.' Sure enough the man warn't killed; I'm bound to confess he was shook dreadful, but his faith warn't."

Christie could not help smiling at the story, but she liked it, and sincerely wished she could imitate the hero of it in his piety, not his powder. She was about to say so when the sound of approaching steps announced the advent of her host. She had been rather impressed with the "smartness" of Lisha by his wife's praises, but when a small, sallow, sickly looking man came in she changed her mind; for not even an immensely stiff collar, nor a pair of boots that seemed composed entirely of what the boys call "creak leather," could inspire her with confidence.

Without a particle of expression in his yellow face, Mr. Wilkins nodded to the stranger over the picket fence of his collar, lighted his pipe, and clumped away to enjoy his afternoon promenade without compromising himself by a single word.

His wife looked after him with an admiring gaze as she said:

"Them boots is as good as an advertisement, for he made every stitch on 'em himself;" then she added, laughing like a girl: "It's redick'lus my bein' so proud of Lisha, but ef a woman ain't a right to think wal of her own husband, I should like to know who has!"

Christie was afraid that Mrs. Wilkins had seen her disappointment in her face, and tried, with wifely zeal, to defend her lord from even a disparaging thought. Wishing to atone for this transgression she was about to sing the praises of the wooden-faced Elisha, but was spared any polite fibs by the appearance of a small girl who delivered an urgent message to the effect, that "Mis Plumly was down sick and wanted Mis Wilkins to run over and set a spell."

As the good lady hesitated with an involuntary glance at her guest, Christie said quickly:

"Don't mind me; I'll take care of the house for you if you want to go. You may be sure I won't run off with the children or steal the spoons."

"I ain't a mite afraid of anybody wantin' to steal them little toads; and as for spoons, I ain't got a silver one to bless myself with," laughed Mrs. Wilkins. "I guess I will go, then, ef you don't mind, as it's only acrost the street. Like's not settin' quiet will be better for you 'n talkin', for I'm a dreadful hand to gab when I git started. Tell Mis Plumly I'm a comin'."

Then, as the child ran off, the stout lady began to rummage in her closet, saying, as she rattled and slammed:

"I'll jest take her a drawin' of tea and a couple of nut-cakes: mebby she'll relish 'em, for I shouldn't wonder ef she hadn't had a mouthful this blessed day. She's dreadful slack at the best of times, but no one can much wonder, seein' she's got nine children, and is jest up from a rheumatic fever. I'm sure I never grudge a meal of vittles or a hand's turn to such as she is, though she does beat all for dependin' on her neighbors. I'm a thousand times obleeged. You needn't werry about the children, only don't let 'em git lost, or burnt, or pitch out a winder;

and when it's done give 'em the patty-cake that's bakin' for 'em."

With which maternal orders Mrs. Wilkins assumed a sky-blue bonnet, and went beaming away with several dishes genteelly hidden under her purple shawl.

Being irresistibly attracted toward the children Christie opened the door and took a survey of her responsibilities.

Six lively infants were congregated in the "settin'-room," and chaos seemed to have come again, for every sort of destructive amusement was in full operation. George Washington, the eldest blossom, was shearing a resigned kitten; Gusty and Ann Eliza were concocting mud pies in the ashes; Adelaide Victoria was studying the structure of lamp-wicks, while Daniel Webster and Andrew Jackson were dragging one another in a clothes-basket, to the great detriment of the old carpet and still older chariot.

Thinking that some employment more suited to the day might be introduced, Christie soon made friends with these young persons, and, having rescued the kitten, banished the basket, lured the elder girls from their mud-piety, and quenched the curiosity of the Pickwickian Adelaide, she proposed teaching them some little hymns.

The idea was graciously received, and the class decorously seated in a row. But before a single verse was given out, Gusty, being of a house-wifely turn of mind, suggested that the patty-cake might burn. Instant alarm pervaded the party, and a precipitate rush was made for the cooking-stove, where Christie proved by ocular demonstration that the cake showed no signs of baking, much less of burning. The family pronounced themselves satisfied, after each member had poked a grimy little finger into the doughy delicacy, whereon one large raisin reposed in proud pre-eminence over the vulgar herd of caraways.

Order being with difficulty restored, Christie taught her flock an appropriate hymn, and was flattering herself that their youthful minds were receiving a devotional bent, when they volunteered a song, and incited thereunto by the irreverent Wash, burst forth with a gem from Mother Goose, closing with a smart skirmish of arms and legs that set all law and order at defiance.

Hoping to quell the insurrection Christie invited the breath-less rioters to calm themselves by looking at the pictures in the big Bible. But, unfortunately, her explanations were so vivid that her audience were fired with a desire to enact some of the scenes portrayed, and no persuasions could keep them from playing Ark on the spot. The clothes-basket was elevated upon two chairs, and into it marched the birds of the air and the beasts of the field, to judge by the noise, and all set sail, with Washington at the helm, Jackson and Webster plying the clothes and pudding-sticks for oars, while the young ladies rescued their dolls from the flood, and waved their hands to imaginary friends who were not unmindful of the courtesies of life even in the act of drowning.

MRS. WILKINS' SIX LIVELY INFANTS.

Finding her authority defied Christie left the rebels to their own devices, and sitting in a corner, began to think about her own affairs. But before she had time to get anxious or perplexed the children diverted her mind, as if the little flibberty-gibbets knew that their pranks and perils were far wholesomer for her just then than brooding.

The much-enduring kitten being sent forth as a dove upon the waters failed to return with the olive-branch; of which peaceful emblem there was soon great need, for mutiny broke out, and spread with disastrous rapidity.

Ann Eliza slapped Gusty because she had the biggest bandbox; Andrew threatened to "chuck" Daniel overboard if he continued to trample on the fraternal toes, and in the midst of the fray, by some unguarded motion, Washington capsized the ship and precipitated the patriarchal family into the bosom of the deep.

Christie flew to the rescue, and, hydropathically treated, the anguish of bumps and bruises was soon assuaged. Then appeared the appropriate moment for a story, and gathering the dilapidated party about her she soon enraptured them by a recital of the immortal history of "Frank and the little dog Trusty." Charmed with her success she was about to tell another moral tale, but no sooner had she announced the name, "The Three Cakes," when, like an electric flash a sudden recollection seized the young Wilkinses, and with one voice they demanded their lawful prize, sure that now it must be done.

Christie had forgotten all about it, and was harassed with secret misgivings as she headed the investigating committee. With skipping of feet and clapping of hands the eager tribe surrounded the stove, and with fear and trembling Christie drew forth a melancholy cinder, where, like Casabianca, the lofty raisin still remained, blackened, but undaunted, at its post.

Then were six little vials of wrath poured out upon her devoted head, and sounds of lamentation filled the air, for the irate Wilkinses refused to be comforted till the rash vow to present each member of the outraged family with a private cake produced a lull, during which the younger ones were decoyed into the back yard, and the three elders solaced themselves with mischief.

Mounted on mettlesome broomsticks Andrew and Daniel were riding merrily away to the Banbury Cross, of blessed memory, and little Vic was erecting a pagoda of oyster-shells, under Christie's superintendence, when a shrill scream from within sent horsemen and architects flying to the rescue.

Gusty's pinafore was in a blaze; Ann Eliza was dancing frantically about her sister as if bent on making a *suttee* of herself, while George Washington hung out of a window, roaring, "Fire!" "water!" "engine!" "pa!" with a presence of mind worthy of his sex.

A speedy application of the hearth-rug quenched the conflagration, and when a minute burn had been enveloped in cotton-wool, like a gem, a coroner sat upon the pinafore and investigated the case.

It appeared that the ladies were "only playing paper dolls," when Wash, sighing for the enlightenment of his race, proposed to make a bonfire, and did so with an old book; but Gusty, with a firm belief in future punishment, tried to save it, and fell a victim to her principles, as the virtuous are very apt to do.

The book was brought into court, and proved to be an ancient volume of ballads, cut, torn, and half consumed. Several peculiarly developed paper dolls, branded here and there with large letters, like galley-slaves, were then produced by the accused, and the judge could with difficulty preserve her gravity when she found "John Gilpin" converted into a painted petticoat, "The Bay of Biscay, O," situated in the crown of a hat, and "Chevy Chase" issuing from the mouth of a triangular gentleman, who, like Dickens's cherub, probably sung it by ear, having no lungs to speak of.

It was further apparent from the agricultural appearance of the room that beans had been sowed broadcast by means of the apple-corer, which Wash had converted into a pop-gun with a mechanical ingenuity worthy of more general appreciation. He felt this deeply, and when Christie reproved him for leading his sisters astray, he resented the liberty she took, and retired in high dudgeon to the cellar, where he appeared to set up a menagerie,—for bears, lions, and unknown animals, endowed with great vocal powers, were heard to solicit patronage from below.

Somewhat exhausted by her labors, Christie rested, after clearing up the room, while the children found a solace for all afflictions in the consumption of relays of bread and molasses, which infantile restorative occurred like an inspiration to the mind of their guardian.

Peace reigned for fifteen minutes; then came a loud crash

from the cellar, followed by a violent splashing, and wild cries of, "Oh, oh, oh, I've fell into the pork barrel! I'm drownin', I'm drownin'!"

Down rushed Christie, and the sticky innocents ran screaming after, to behold their pickled brother fished up from the briny deep. A spectacle well calculated to impress upon their infant minds the awful consequences of straying from the paths of virtue.

At this crisis Mrs. Wilkins providentially appeared, breathless, but brisk and beaming, and in no wise dismayed by the plight of her luckless son, for a ten years' acquaintance with Wash's dauntless nature had inured his mother to "didoes" that would have appalled most women.

"Go right up chamber, and change every rag on you, and don't come down agin till I rap on the ceilin'; you dreadful boy, disgracin' your family by sech actions. I'm sorry I was kep' so long, but Mis Plumly got tellin' her werryments, and 'peared to take so much comfort in it I couldn't bear to stop her. Then I jest run round to your place and told that woman that you was safe and well, along'r friends, and would call in to-morrer to get your things. She'd ben so scart by your not comin' home that she was as mild as milk, so you won't have no trouble with her, I expect."

"Thank you very much! How kind you are, and how tired you must be! Sit down and let me take your things," cried Christie, more relieved than she could express.

"Lor', no, I'm fond of walkin', but bein' ruther hefty it takes my breath away some to hurry. I'm afraid these children have tuckered you out though. They are proper good gen'lly, but when they do take to trainen they're a sight of care," said Mrs. Wilkins, as she surveyed her imposing bonnet with calm satisfaction.

"I've enjoyed it very much, and it's done me good, for I haven't laughed so much for six months as I have this afternoon," answered Christie, and it was quite true, for she had been too busy to think of herself or her woes.

"Wal, I thought likely it would chirk you up some, or I shouldn't have went," and Mrs. Wilkins put away a contented smile with her cherished bonnet, for Christie's face had grown so much brighter since she saw it last, that the good woman felt sure her treatment was the right one.

At supper Lisha reappeared, and while his wife and children talked incessantly, he ate four slices of bread and butter, three pieces of pie, five dough-nuts, and drank a small ocean of tea out of his saucer. Then, evidently feeling that he had done his duty like a man, he gave Christie another nod, and disappeared again without a word.

When she had done up her dishes Mrs. Wilkins brought out a few books and papers, and said to Christie, who sat apart by the window, with the old shadow creeping over her face:

"Now don't feel lonesome, my dear, but jest lop right down on the soffy and have a sociable kind of a time. Lisha's gone down street for the evenin'. I'll keep the children as quiet as one woman can, and you may read or rest, or talk, jest as you're a mind."

"Thank you; I'll sit here and rock little Vic to sleep for you. I don't care to read, but I'd like to have you talk to me, for it seems as if I'd known you a long time and it does me good," said Christie, as she settled herself and baby on the old settee which had served as a cradle for six young Wilkinses, and now received the honorable name of sofa in its old age.

Mrs. Wilkins looked gratified, as she settled her brood round the table with a pile of pictorial papers to amuse them. Then having laid herself out to be agreeable, she sat thoughtfully rubbing the bridge of her nose, at a loss how to begin. Presently Christie helped her by an involuntary sigh.

"What's the matter, dear? Is there any thing I can do to make you comfortable?" asked the kind soul, alert at once, and ready to offer sympathy.

"I'm very cosy, thank you, and I don't know why I sighed. It's a way I've got into when I think of my worries," explained Christie, in haste.

"Wal, dear, I wouldn't ef I was you. Don't keep turnin' your troubles over. Git atop of 'em somehow, and stay there ef you can," said Mrs. Wilkins, very earnestly.

"But that's just what I can't do. I've lost all my spirits and courage, and got into a dismal state of mind. You seem to be very cheerful, and yet you must have a good deal to try you sometimes. I wish you'd tell me how you do it;" and Christie looked wistfully into that other face, so plain, yet so placid, wondering to see how little poverty, hard work, and many cares had soured or saddened it.

"Really I don't know, unless it's jest doin' whatever comes along, and doin' of it hearty, sure that things is all right, though very often I don't see it at fust."

"Do you see it at last?"

"Gen'lly I do; and if I don't I take it on trust, same as children do what older folks tell 'em; and byme-by when I'm grown up in spiritual things I'll understan' as the dears do, when they git to be men and women."

That suited Christie, and she thought hopefully within herself:

"This woman has got the sort of religion I want, if it makes her what she is. Some day I'll get her to tell me where she found it." Then aloud she said:

"But it's *so* hard to be patient and contented when nothing happens as you want it to, and you don't get your share of happiness, no matter how much you try to deserve it."

"It ain't easy to bear, I know, but having tried my own way and made a dreadful mess on 't, I concluded that the Lord knows what's best for us, and things go better when he manages than when we go scratchin' round and can't wait."

"Tried your own way? How do you mean?" asked Christie, curiously; for she liked to hear her hostess talk, and found something besides amusement in the conversation, which seemed to possess a fresh country flavor as well as country phrases.

Mrs. Wilkins smiled all over her plump face, as if she liked to tell her experience, and having hunched sleepy little Andy more comfortably into her lap, and given a preparatory hem or two, she began with great good-will.

"It happened a number a years ago and ain't much of a story any way. But you're welcome to it, as some of it is rather humorsome, the laugh may do you good ef the story don't. We was livin' down to the east'ard at the time. It was a real pretty place; the house stood under a couple of maples and a gret brook come foamin' down the rayvine and away through the medders to the river. Dear sakes, seems as ef I see it now, jest as I used to settin' on the doorsteps with the laylocks all in blow, the squirrels jabberin' on the wall, and the saw-mill screekin' way off by the dam."

Pausing a moment, Mrs. Wilkins looked musingly at the

steam of the tea-kettle, as if through its silvery haze she saw her early home again. Wash promptly roused her from this reverie by tumbling off the boiler with a crash. His mother picked him up and placidly went on, falling more and more into the country dialect which city life had not yet polished.

"I oughter hev been the contentedest woman alive, but I warn't, for you see I'd worked at millineryin' before I was married, and had an easy time on't. Afterwards the children come along pretty fast, there was sights of work to do, and no time for pleasurin', so I got wore out, and used to hanker after old times in a dreadful wicked way.

"Finally I got acquainted with a Mis Bascum, and she done me a sight of harm. You see, havin' few pies of her own to bake, she was fond of puttin' her fingers into her neighborses, but she done it so neat that no one mistrusted she was takin' all the sauce and leavin' all the crust to them, as you may say. Wal, I told her my werryments and she sympathized real hearty, and said I didn't ought to stan' it, but have things to suit me, and enjoy myself, as other folks did. So when she put it into my head I thought it amazin' good advice, and jest went and done as she told me.

"Lisha was the kindest man you ever see, so when I up and said I warn't goin' to drudge round no more, but must hev a girl, he got one, and goodness knows what a trial *she* was. After she came I got dreadful slack, and left the house and the children to Hen'retta, and went pleasurin' frequent all in my best. I always *was* a dressy woman in them days, and Lisha give me his earnin's real lavish, bless his heart! and I went and spent 'em on my sinful gowns and bunnets."

Here Mrs. Wilkins stopped to give a remorseful groan and stroke her faded dress, as if she found great comfort in its dinginess.

"It ain't no use tellin' all I done, but I had full swing, and at fust I thought luck was in my dish sure. But it warn't, seein' I didn't deserve it, and I had to take my mess of trouble, which was needful and nourishin', ef I'd had the grace to see it so.

"Lisha got into debt, and no wonder, with me a wastin' of his substance; Hen'retta went off suddin', with whatever she could lay her hands on, and everything was at sixes and sevens. Lisha's patience give out at last, for I was dreadful fractious,

knowin' it was all my fault. The children seemed to git out of
sorts, too, and acted like time in the primer, with croup and
pins, and whoopin'-cough and temper. I declare I used to
think the pots and kettles biled over to spite each other and me
too in them days.

"All this was nuts to Mis Bascum, and she kep' advisin' and
encouragin' of me, and I didn't see through her a mite, or
guess that settin' folks by the ears was as relishin' to her as bitters is to some. Merciful, suz! what a piece a work we did make
betwixt us! I scolded and moped 'cause I couldn't have my
way; Lisha swore and threatened to take to drinkin' ef I didn't
make home more comfortable; the children run wild, and the
house was gittin' too hot to hold us, when we was brought up
with a round turn, and I see the redicklousness of my doin's in
time.

"One day Lisha come home tired and cross, for bills was
pressin', work slack, and folks talkin' about us as ef they'd
nothin' else to do. I was dishin' up dinner, feelin' as nervous as
a witch, for a whole batch of bread had burnt to a cinder while
I was trimmin' a new bunnet, Wash had scart me most to death
swallerin' a cent, and the steak had been on the floor more'n
once, owin' to my havin' babies, dogs, cats, or hens under my
feet the whole blessed time.

"Lisha looked as black as thunder, throwed his hat into a
corner, and came along to the sink where I was skinnin' pertaters. As he washed his hands, I asked what the matter was; but
he only muttered and slopped, and I couldn't git nothin' out of
him, for he ain't talkative at the best of times as you see, and
when he's werried corkscrews wouldn't draw a word from him.

"Bein' riled myself didn't mend matters, and so we fell to
hectorin' one another right smart. He said somethin' that
dreened my last drop of patience; I give a sharp answer, and
fust thing I knew he up with his hand and slapped me. It warn't
a hard blow by no means, only a kind of a wet spat side of the
head; but I thought I should have flew, and was as mad as ef
I'd been knocked down. You never see a man look so 'shamed
as Lisha did, and ef I'd been wise I should have made up the
quarrel then. But I was a fool. I jest flung fork, dish, pertaters
and all into the pot, and says, as ferce as you please:

"'Lisha Wilkins, when you can treat me decent you may

come and fetch me back; you won't see me till then, and so I tell you.'

"Then I made a bee-line for Mis Bascum's; told her the whole story, had a good cry, and was all ready to go home in half an hour, but Lisha didn't come.

"Wal, that night passed, and what a long one it was to be sure! and me without a wink of sleep, thinkin' of Wash and the cent, my emptins and the baby. Next day come, but no Lisha, no message, no nuthin', and I began to think I'd got my match though I had a sight of grit in them days. I sewed, and Mis Bascum she clacked; but I didn't say much, and jest worked like sixty to pay for my keep, for I warn't goin' to be beholden to her for nothin'.

"The day dragged on terrible slow, and at last I begged her to go and git me a clean dress, for I'd come off jest as I was, and folks kep' droppin' in, for the story was all round, thanks to Mis Bascum's long tongue.

"Wal, she went, and ef you'll believe me Lisha wouldn't let her in! He handed my best things out a winder and told her to tell me they were gittin' along fust rate with Florindy Walch to do the work. He hoped I'd have a good time, and not expect him for a consider'ble spell, for he liked a quiet house, and now he'd got it.

"When I heard that, I knew he must be provoked the wust kind, for he ain't a hash man by nater. I could have crep' in at the winder ef he wouldn't open the door, I was so took down by that message. But Mis Bascum wouldn't hear of it, and kep' stirrin' of me up till I was ashamed to eat 'umble pie fust; so I waited to see how soon he'd come round. But he had the best on't you see, for he'd got the babies and lost a cross wife, while I'd lost every thing but Mis Bascum, who grew hatefuler to me every hour, for I begun to mistrust she was a mischief-maker,— widders most always is,—seein' how she pampered up my pride and 'peared to like the quarrel.

"I thought I should have died more'n once, for sure as you live it went on three mortal days, and of all miser'ble creeters I was the miser'blest. Then I see how wicked and ungrateful I'd been; how I'd shirked my bounden duty and scorned my best blessins. There warn't a hard job that ever I'd hated but what grew easy when I remembered who it was done for; there warn't a trouble or a care that I wouldn't have welcomed hearty, nor one hour of them dear fractious babies that didn't seem precious when I'd gone and left 'em. I'd got time to rest enough now, and might go pleasuring all day long; but I couldn't do it, and would have given a dozin bunnets trimmed to kill ef I could only have been back moilin' in my old kitchen with the children hangin' round me and Lisha a comin' in cheerful from his work as he used to 'fore I spoilt his home for him. How sing'lar it is folks never *do* know when they are wal off!"

"I know it now," said Christie, rocking lazily to and fro, with a face almost as tranquil as little Vic's, lying half asleep in her lap.

"Glad to hear it, my dear. As I was goin' on to say, when Saturday come, a tremenjus storm set in, and it rained guns all day. I never shall forgit it, for I was hankerin' after baby, and dreadful werried about the others, all bein' croupy, and Florindy with no more idee of nussin' than a baa lamb. The rain come down like a reg'lar deluge, but I didn't seem to have no ark to run to. As night come on things got wuss and wuss, for the wind blowed the roof off Mis Bascum's barn and stove in the butt'ry window; the brook riz and went ragin' every which way, and you never did see such a piece of work.

"My heart was most broke by that time, and I knew I should give in 'fore Monday. But I set and sewed and listened to the tinkle tankle of the drops in the pans set round to ketch 'em, for the house leaked like a sieve. Mis Bascum was down suller putterin' about, for every kag and sarce jar was afloat. Moses, her brother, was lookin' after his stock and tryin' to stop the damage. All of a sudden he bust in lookin' kinder wild, and settin' down the lantern, he sez, sez he: 'You're ruthern an unfortinate woman to-night, Mis Wilkins.' 'How so?' sez I, as ef nuthin' was the matter already.

"'Why,' sez he, 'the spilins have give way up in the rayvine, and the brook's come down like a river, upsot your lean-to, washed the mellion patch slap into the road, and while your husband was tryin' to git the pig out of the pen, the water took a turn and swep him away.'

"'Drownded?' sez I, with only breath enough for that one word. 'Shouldn't wonder,' sez Moses, 'nothin' ever did come up alive after goin' over them falls.'

"It come over me like a streak of lightenin'; every thin' kinder slewed round, and I dropped in the first faint I ever had in my life. Next I knew Lisha was holdin' of me and cryin' fit to kill himself. I thought I was dreamin', and only had wits enough to give a sort of permiscuous grab at him and call out:

"'Oh, Lisha! ain't you drownded?' He give a gret start at that, swallered down his sobbin', and sez as lovin' as ever a man did in this world:

"'Bless your dear heart, Cynthy, it warn't me it was the pig;' and then fell to kissin' of me, till betwixt laughin' and cryin' I was most choked. Deary me, it all comes back so livin' real it kinder takes my breath away."

And well it might, for the good soul entered so heartily into her story that she unconsciously embellished it with dramatic illustrations. At the slapping episode she flung an invisible "fork, dish, and pertaters" into an imaginary kettle, and glared; when the catastrophe arrived, she fell back upon her chair to express fainting; gave Christie's arm the "permiscuous grab" at the proper moment, and uttered the repentant Lisha's explanation with an incoherent pathos that forbid a laugh at the sudden introduction of the porcine martyr.

"What did you do then?" asked Christie in a most flattering state of interest.

"Oh, law! I went right home and hugged them children for a couple of hours stiddy," answered Mrs. Wilkins, as if but one conclusion was possible.

"Did all your troubles go down with the pig?" asked Christie, presently.

"Massy, no, we're all poor, feeble worms, and the best meanin' of us fails too often," sighed Mrs. Wilkins, as she tenderly adjusted the sleepy head of the young worm in her lap. "After that scrape I done my best; Lisha was as meek as a whole flock of sheep, and we give Mis Bascum a wide berth. Things went lovely for ever so long, and though, after a spell, we had our ups and downs, as is but natural to human creeters, we never come to such a pass agin. Both on us tried real hard; whenever I felt my temper risin' or discontent comin' on I remembered them days and kep' a taut rein; and as for Lisha he never said a raspin' word, or got sulky, but what he'd bust out laughin' after it and say: 'Bless you, Cynthy, it warn't me, it was the pig.'"

Mrs. Wilkins' hearty laugh fired a long train of lesser ones, for the children recognized a household word. Christie enjoyed the joke, and even the tea-kettle boiled over as if carried away by the fun.

"Tell some more, please," said Christie, when the merriment subsided, for she felt her spirits rising.

"There's nothin' more to tell, except one thing that prevented my ever forgittin' the lesson I got then. My little Almiry took cold that week and pined away rapid. She'd always been so ailin' I never expected to raise her, and more'n once in them sinful tempers of mine I'd thought it would be a mercy ef she was took out of her pain. But when I laid away that patient, sufferin' little creeter I found she was the dearest of 'em all. I most broke my heart to hev her back, and never, never forgive myself for leavin' her that time."

With trembling lips and full eyes Mrs. Wilkins stopped to wipe her features generally on Andrew Jackson's pinafore, and heave a remorseful sigh.

"And this is how you came to be the cheerful, contented woman you are?" said Christie, hoping to divert the mother's mind from that too tender memory.

"Yes," she answered, thoughtfully, "I told you Lisha was a smart man; he give me a good lesson, and it set me to thinkin' serious. 'Pears to me trouble is a kind of mellerin' process, and ef you take it kindly it doos you good, and you learn to be glad of it. I'm sure Lisha and me is twice as fond of one another, twice as willin' to work, and twice as patient with our trials sense dear little Almiry died, and times was hard. I ain't what I ought to be, not by a long chalk, but I try to live up to my light, do my duty cheerful, love my neighbors, and fetch up my family in the fear of God. Ef I do this the best way I know how, I'm sure I'll get my rest some day, and the good Lord won't forgit Cynthy Wilkins. He ain't so fur, for I keep my health wonderfle, Lisha is kind and stiddy, the children flourishin', and I'm a happy woman though I be a humly one."

There she was mistaken, for as her eye roved round the narrow room from the old hat on the wall to the curly heads bobbing here and there, contentment, piety, and mother-love made her plain face beautiful.

"That story has done me ever so much good, and I shall not forget it. Now, good-night, for I must be up early to-morrow, and I don't want to drive Mr. Wilkins away entirely," said Christie, after she had helped put the little folk to bed, during which process she had heard her host creaking about the kitchen as if afraid to enter the sitting-room.

She laughed as she spoke, and ran up stairs, wondering if she could be the same forlorn creature who had crept so wearily up only the night before.

It was a very humble little sermon that Mrs. Wilkins had preached to her, but she took it to heart and profited by it; for she was a pupil in the great charity school where the best teachers are often unknown, unhonored here, but who surely will receive commendation and reward from the head master when their long vacation comes.

# Chapter IX

## MRS. WILKINS'S MINISTER

MR. POWER.

NEXT day Christie braved the lion in his den, otherwise the flinty Flint, in her second-class boarding-house, and found that alarm and remorse had produced a softening effect upon her. She was unfeignedly glad to see her lost lodger safe, and finding that the new friends were likely to put her in the way of paying her debts, this much harassed matron permitted her to pack up her possessions, leaving one trunk as a sort of hostage. Then, with promises to redeem it as soon as possible, Christie said good-bye to the little room where she had hoped and suffered, lived and labored so long, and went joyfully back to the humble home she had found with the good laundress.

All the following week Christie "chored round," as Mrs. Wilkins called the miscellaneous light work she let her do. Much washing, combing, and clean pinaforing of children fell to her share, and she enjoyed it amazingly; then, when the elder ones were packed off to school she lent a hand to any of the numberless tasks housewives find to do from morning till night. In the afternoon, when other work was done, and little Vic asleep or happy with her playthings, Christie clapped laces, sprinkled muslins, and picked out edgings at the great table where Mrs. Wilkins stood ironing, fluting, and crimping till the kitchen bristled all over with immaculate frills and flounces.

It was pretty delicate work, and Christie liked it, for Mrs. Wilkins was an adept at her trade and took as much pride and pleasure in it as any French *blanchisseuse* tripping through the streets of Paris with a tree full of coquettish caps, capes, and petticoats borne before her by a half invisible boy.

Being women, of course, they talked as industriously as they worked; fingers flew and tongues clacked with equal profit and pleasure, and, by Saturday, Christie had made up her mind that Mrs. Wilkins was the most sensible woman she ever knew. Her grammar was an outrage upon the memory of Lindley Murray, but the goodness of her heart would have done honor to any saint in the calendar. She was very plain, and her manners were by no means elegant, but good temper made that homely face most lovable, and natural refinement of soul made mere external polish of small account. Her shrewd ideas and odd sayings amused Christie very much, while her good sense and bright way of looking at things did the younger woman a world of good.

Mr. Wilkins devoted himself to the making of shoes and the consumption of food, with the silent regularity of a placid animal. His one dissipation was tobacco, and in a fragrant cloud of smoke he lived and moved and had his being so entirely that he might have been described as a pipe with a man somewhere behind it. Christie once laughingly spoke of this habit and declared she would try it herself if she thought it would make her as quiet and undemonstrative as Mr. Wilkins, who, to tell the truth, made no more impression on her than a fly.

"I don't approve on't, but he might do wuss. We all have to have our comfort somehow, so I let Lisha smoke as much as he likes, and he lets me gab, so it's about fair, I reckon," answered Mrs. Wilkins, from the suds.

She laughed as she spoke, but something in her face made Christie suspect that at some period of his life Lisha had done "wuss;" and subsequent observations confirmed this suspicion and another one also,—that his good wife had saved him, and was gently easing him back to self-control and self-respect. But, as old Fuller quaintly says, "She so gently folded up his faults in silence that few guessed them," and loyally paid him that respect which she desired others to bestow. It was always "Lisha and me," "I'll ask my husband" or "Lisha'll know; he don't say much, but he's a dreadful smart man," and she kept up the fiction so dear to her wifely soul by endowing him with her own virtues, and giving him the credit of her own intelligence.

Christie loved her all the better for this devotion, and for her sake treated Mr. Wilkins as if he possessed the strength of Samson and the wisdom of Solomon. He received her respect as if it was his due, and now and then graciously accorded her a few words beyond the usual scanty allowance of morning and evening greetings. At his shop all day, she only saw him at meals and sometimes of an evening, for Mrs. Wilkins tried to keep him at home safe from temptation, and Christie helped her by reading, talking, and frolicking with the children, so that he might find home attractive. He loved his babies and would even relinquish his precious pipe for a time to ride the little chaps on his foot, or amuse Vic with shadow rabbits on the wall.

At such times the entire content in Mrs. Wilkins's face made tobacco fumes endurable, and the burden of a dull man's presence less oppressive to Christie, who loved to pay her debts in something besides money.

As they sat together finishing off some delicate laces that Saturday afternoon, Mrs. Wilkins said, "Ef it's fair to-morrow I want you to go to my meetin' and hear my minister. It'll do you good."

"Who is he?"

"Mr. Power."

Christie looked rather startled, for she had heard of Thomas Power as a rampant radical and infidel of the deepest dye, and been warned never to visit that den of iniquity called his free church.

"Why, Mrs. Wilkins, you don't mean it!" she said, leaving her lace to dry at the most critical stage.

"Yes, I do!" answered Mrs. Wilkins, setting down her flat-iron with emphasis, and evidently preparing to fight valiantly for her minister, as most women will.

"I beg your pardon; I was a little surprised, for I'd heard all sorts of things about him," Christie hastened to say.

"Did you ever hear *him*, or read any of his writins?" demanded Mrs. Wilkins, with a calmer air.

"Never."

"Then don't judge. You go hear and see that blessed man, and ef you don't say he's the shadow of a great rock in a desert land, I'll give up," cried the good woman, waxing poetical in her warmth.

"I will to please you, if nothing else. I did go once just because I was told not to; but he did not preach that day and every thing was so peculiar, I didn't know whether to like it or be shocked."

"It is kind of sing'lar at fust, I'm free to confess, and not as churchy as some folks like. But there ain't no place but that big enough to hold the crowds that want to go, for the more he's abused the more folks flock to see him. They git their money's wuth I do believe, for though there ain't no pulpits and pews, there's a sight of brotherly love round in them seats, and pious practice, as well as powerful preaching, in that shabby desk. *He* don't need no commandments painted up behind him to read on Sunday, for he keeps 'em in his heart and life all the week as honest as man can."

There Mrs. Wilkins paused, flushed and breathless with her defence, and Christie said, candidly: "I did like the freedom and good-will there, for people sat where they liked, and no one frowned over shut pew-doors, at me a stranger. An old black woman sat next me, and said 'Amen' when she liked what she heard, and a very shabby young man was on the other, listening as if his soul was as hungry as his body. People read books, laughed and cried, clapped when pleased, and hissed when angry; that I did *not* like."

"No more does Mr. Power; he don't mind the cryin' and the smilin' as it's nat'ral, but noise and disrespect of no kind ain't pleasin' to him. His own folks behave becomin', but strangers go and act as they like, thinkin' that there ain't no bounds to the word free. Then we are picked at for their doin's, and Mr. Power has to carry other folkses' sins on his shoulders. But, dear suz, it ain't much matter after all, ef the souls is well-meanin'. Children always make a noise a strivin' after what they want most, and I shouldn't wonder ef the Lord forgive all our short-comin's of that sort, sense we are hankerin' and reachin' for the truth."

"I wish I *had* heard Mr. Power that day, for I was striving after peace with all my heart, and he might have given it to me," said Christie, interested and impressed with what she heard.

"Wal, no, dear, I guess not. Peace ain't give to no one all of a suddin, it gen'lly comes through much tribulation, and the sort that comes hardest is best wuth havin'. Mr. Power would a' ploughed and harrered you, so to speak, and sowed good seed liberal; then ef you warn't barren ground things would have throve, and the Lord give you a harvest accordin' to your labor. Who did you hear?" asked Mrs. Wilkins, pausing to starch and clap vigorously.

"A very young man who seemed to be airing his ideas and beliefs in the frankest manner. He belabored everybody and every thing, upset church and state, called names, arranged heaven and earth to suit himself, and evidently meant every word he said. Much of it would have been ridiculous if the boy had not been so thoroughly in earnest; sincerity always commands respect, and though people smiled, they liked his courage, and seemed to think he would make a man when his spiritual wild oats were sown."

"I ain't a doubt on't. We often have such, and they ain't all empty talk, nuther; some of 'em are surprisingly bright, and all mean so well I don't never reluct to hear 'em. They must blow off their steam somewheres, else they'd bust with the big idees a swellin' in 'em; Mr. Power knows it and gives 'em the chance they can't find nowheres else. 'Pears to me," added Mrs. Wilkins, ironing rapidly as she spoke, "that folks is very like clothes, and a sight has to be done to keep 'em clean and whole. All on us has to lend a hand in this dreadful mixed-up wash, and each do our part, same as you and me is now. There's scrubbin' and bilin', wrenchin' and bluein', dryin' and foldin', ironin' and polishin', before any of us is fit for wear a Sunday mornin'."

"What part does Mr. Power do?" asked Christie, much amused at this peculiarly appropriate simile.

"The scrubbin' and the bilin'; that's always the hardest and the hottest part. He starts the dirt and gits the stains out, and leaves 'em ready for other folks to finish off. It ain't such pleasant work as hangin' out, or such pretty work as doin' up, but some one's got to do it, and them that's strongest does it best, though they don't git half so much credit as them as polishes and crimps. That's showy work, but it wouldn't be no use ef the things warn't well washed fust," and Mrs. Wilkins thoughtfully surveyed the snowy muslin cap, with its border fluted like the petals of a prim white daisy, that hung on her hand.

"I'd like to be a washerwoman of that sort; but as I'm not one of the strong, I'll be a laundress, and try to make purity as attractive as you do," said Christie, soberly.

"Ah, my dear, it's warm and wearin' work I do assure you, and hard to give satisfaction, try as you may. Crowns of glory ain't wore in this world, but it's my 'pinion that them that does the hard jobs here will stand a good chance of havin' extra bright ones when they git through."

"I know *you* will," said Christie, warmly.

"Land alive, child! I warn't thinking of Cynthy Wilkins, but Mr. Power. I'll be satisfied ef I can set low down somewheres and see him git the meddle. He won't in this world, but I know there's rewards savin' up for him byme-by."

"I'll go to-morrow if it pours!" said Christie, with decision.

"Do, and I'll lend you my bunnit," cried Mrs. Wilkins, passing, with comical rapidity, from crowns of glory to her own cherished head-gear.

"Thank you, but I can't wear blue, I look as yellow as a dandelion in it. Mrs. Flint let me have my best things though I offered to leave them, so I shall be respectable and by-and-by blossom out."

On the morrow Christie went early, got a good seat, and for half an hour watched the gathering of the motley congregation that filled the great hall. Some came in timidly, as if doubtful of their welcome; some noisily, as if, as Mrs. Wilkins said, they had not learned the wide difference between liberty and license; many as if eager and curious; and a large number with the look of children gathering round a family table ready to be fed, and sure that wholesome food would be bountifully provided for them.

Christie was struck by the large proportion of young people in the place, of all classes, both sexes, and strongly contrasting faces. Delicate girls looking with the sweet wistfulness of maidenly hearts for something strong to lean upon and love; sad-eyed women turning to heaven for the consolations or the satisfactions earth could not give them; anxious mothers perplexed with many cares, trying to find light and strength; young men with ardent faces, restless, aspiring, and impetuous, longing to do and dare; tired-looking students, with perplexed wrinkles on their foreheads, evidently come to see if this man had discovered the great secrets they were delving after; and soul-sick people trying this new, and perhaps dangerous medicine, when others failed to cure. Many earnest, thoughtful men and women were there, some on the anxious seat, and some already at peace, having found the clew that leads safely through the labyrinth of life. Here and there a white head, a placid old face, or one of those fine countenances that tell, unconsciously, the beautiful story of a victorious soul.

Some read, some talked, some had flowers in their hands, and all sat at ease, rich and poor, black and white, young and old, waiting for the coming of the man who had power to attract and hold so many of his kind. Christie was so intent on watching those about her that she did not see him enter, and only knew it by the silence which began just in front of her, and seemed to flow backward like a wave, leaving a sea of expectant faces turning to one point. That point was a gray head, just visible above the little desk which stood in the middle of a great platform. A vase of lovely flowers was on the little shelf at one side, a great Bible reposed on the other, and a manuscript lay whitely on the red slope between.

In a moment Christie forgot every thing else, and waited with a curious anxiety to see what manner of man this was. Presently he got up with an open book in his hand, saying, in a strong, cheerful voice: "Let us sing," and having read a hymn as if he had composed it, he sat down again.

Then everybody did sing; not harmoniously, but heartily, led by an organ, which the voices followed at their own sweet will. At first, Christie wanted to smile, for some shouted and some hummed, some sat silent, and others sung sweetly; but before the hymn ended she liked it, and thought that the natural praise of each individual soul was perhaps more grateful to the ear of God than masses by great masters, or psalms warbled tunefully by hired opera singers.

Then Mr. Power rose again, and laying his hands together, with a peculiarly soft and reverent gesture, lifted up his face and prayed. Christie had never heard a prayer like that before; so devout, so comprehensive, and so brief. A quiet talk with God, asking nothing but more love and duty toward him and our fellow-men; thanking him for many mercies, and confiding all things trustfully to the "dear father and mother of souls."

The sermon which followed was as peculiar as the prayer,

and as effective. "One of Power's judgment-day sermons," as she heard one man say to another, when it was over. Christie certainly felt at first as if kingdoms and thrones were going down, and each man being sent to his own place. A powerful and popular wrong was arrested, tried, and sentenced then and there, with a courage and fidelity that made plain words eloquent, and stern justice beautiful. He did not take David of old for his text, but the strong, sinful, splendid Davids of our day, who had not fulfilled the promise of their youth, and whose seeming success was a delusion and a snare to themselves and others, sure to be followed by sorrowful abandonment, defeat, and shame. The ashes of the ancient hypocrites and Pharisees was left in peace, but those now living were heartily denounced; modern money-changers scourged out of the temple, and the everlasting truth set up therein.

As he spoke, not loudly nor vehemently, but with the indescribable effect of inward force and true inspiration, a curious stir went through the crowd at times, as a great wind sweeps over a corn field, lifting the broad leaves to the light and testing the strength of root and stem. People looked at one another with a roused expression; eyes kindled, heads nodded involuntary approval, and an emphatic, "that's so!" dropped from the lips of men who saw their own vague instincts and silent opinions strongly confirmed and nobly uttered. Consciences seemed to have been pricked to duty, eyes cleared to see that their golden idols had feet of clay, and wavering wills strengthened by the salutary courage and integrity of one indomitable man.

Another hymn, and a benediction that seemed like a fit grace after meat, and then the crowd poured out; not yawning, thinking of best clothes, or longing for dinner, but waked up, full of talk, and eager to do something to redeem the country and the world.

Christie went rapidly home because she could not help it, and burst in upon Mrs. Wilkins with a face full of enthusiasm, exclaiming, while she cast off her bonnet as if her head had outgrown it since she left:

"It was splendid! I never heard such a sermon before, and I'll never go to church anywhere else."

"I knew it! ain't it fillin'? don't it give you a kind of spiral h'ist,

and make things wuth more somehow?" cried Mrs. Wilkins, gesticulating with the pepper-pot in a way which did not improve the
steak she was cooking, and caused great anguish to the noses of
her offspring, who were watching the operation.

Quite deaf to the chorus of sneezes which accompanied her
words, Christie answered, brushing back her hair, as if to get a
better out-look at creation generally:

"Oh, yes, indeed! At first it was rather terrible, and yet so
true I wouldn't change a word of it. But I don't wonder he is
misunderstood, belied, and abused. He tells the truth so
plainly, and lets in the light so clearly, that hypocrites and sinners must fear and hate him. I think he *was* a little hard and
unsparing, sometimes, though I don't know enough to judge
the men and measures he condemned. I admire him very
much, but I should be afraid of him if I ever saw him nearer."

"No, you wouldn't; not a grain. You hear him preach agin
and you'll find him as gentle as a lamb. Strong folks is apt to be
ruther ha'sh at times; they can't help it no more than this stove
can help scorchin' the vittles when it gits red hot. Dinner's
ready, so set right up and tell me all about it," said Mrs. Wilkins,
slapping the steak on to the platter, and beginning to deal out
fried potatoes all round with absent-minded lavishness.

Christie talked, and the good soul enjoyed that far more
than her dinner, for she meant to ask Mr. Power to help her
find the right sort of home for the stranger whose unfitness for
her present place was every day made more apparent to the
mind of her hostess.

"What took you there first?" asked Christie, still wondering
at Mrs. Wilkins's choice of a minister.

"The Lord, my dear," answered the good woman, in a tone
of calm conviction. "I'd heard of him, and I always have a
leanin' towards them that's reviled; so one Sabbath I felt to go,
and did. 'That's the gospel for me,' says I, 'my old church ain't
big enough now, and I ain't goin' to set and nod there any
longer,' and I didn't."

"Hadn't you any doubts about it, any fears of going wrong
or being sorry afterwards?" asked Christie, who believed, as
many do, that religion could not be attained without much
tribulation of some kind.

"In some things folks is led; I be frequent, and when them

leadin's come I don't ask no questions but jest foller, and it always turns out right."

"I wish I could be led."

"You be, my dear, every day of your life only you don't see it. When you are doubtful, set still till the call comes, then git up and walk whichever way it says, and you won't fall. You've had bread and water long enough, now you want meat and wine a spell; take it, and when it's time for milk and honey some one will fetch 'em ef you keep your table ready. The Lord feeds us right; it's we that quarrel with our vittles."

"I will," said Christie, and began at once to prepare her little board for the solid food of which she had had a taste that day.

That afternoon Mrs. Wilkins took her turn at church-going, saw Mr. Power, told Christie's story in her best style, and ended by saying:

"She's true grit, I do assure you, sir. Willin' to work, but she's seen the hard side of things and got kind of discouraged. Soul and body both wants tinkerin' up, and I don't know anybody who can do the job better'n you can."

"Very well, I'll come and see her," answered Mr. Power, and Mrs. Wilkins went home well satisfied.

He kept his word, and about the middle of the week came walking in upon them as they were at work.

"Don't let the irons cool," he said, and sitting down in the kitchen began to talk as comfortably as if in the best parlor; more so, perhaps, for best parlors are apt to have a depressing effect upon the spirits, while the mere sight of labor is exhilarating to energetic minds.

He greeted Christie kindly, and then addressed himself to Mrs. Wilkins on various charitable matters, for he was a minister at large, and she one of his almoners. Christie could really see him now, for when he preached she forgot the man in the sermon, and thought of him only as a visible conscience.

A sturdy man of fifty, with a keen, brave face, penetrating eyes, and mouth a little grim; but a voice so resonant and sweet it reminded one of silver trumpets, and stirred and won the hearer with irresistible power. Rough gray hair, and all the features rather rugged, as if the Great Sculptor had blocked out a grand statue, and left the man's own soul to finish it.

Had Christie known that he came to see *her* she would have

been ill at ease; but Mrs. Wilkins had kept her own counsel, so when Mr. Power turned to Christie, saying:

"My friend here tells me you want something to do. Would you like to help a Quaker lady with her housework, just out of town?"

She answered readily: "Yes, sir, any thing that is honest."

"Not as a servant, exactly, but companion and helper. Mrs. Sterling is a dear old lady, and the place a pleasant little nest. It is good to be there, and I think you'll say so if you go."

"It sounds pleasant. When shall I go?"

Mr. Power smiled at her alacrity, but the longing look in her eyes explained it, for he saw at a glance that her place was not here.

"I will write at once and let you know how matters are settled. Then you shall try it, and if it is not what you want, we will find you something else. There's plenty to do, and nothing pleasanter than to put the right pair of hands to the right task. Good-by; come and see me if the spirit moves, and don't let go of Mrs. Wilkins till you lay hold of a better friend, if you can find one."

Then he shook hands cordially, and went walking out again into the wild March weather as if he liked it.

"Were you afraid of him?" asked Mrs. Wilkins.

"I forgot all about it: he looked so kind and friendly. But I shouldn't like to have those piercing eyes of his fixed on me long if I had any secret on my conscience," answered Christie.

"You ain't nothin' to fear. He liked your way of speakin' fust rate, I see that, and you'll be all right now he's took hold."

"Do you know Mrs. Sterling?"

"Only by sight, but she's a sweet appearin' woman, and I wouldn't ask nothin' better'n to see more of her," said Mrs. Wilkins, warmly, fearing Christie's heart might misgive her.

But it did not, and when a note came saying Mrs. Sterling would be ready for her the next week, she seemed quite content with every thing, for though the wages were not high she felt that country air and quiet were worth more to her just then than money, and that Wilkinses were better taken homœopathically.

The spirit did move her to go and see Mr. Power, but she could not make up her mind to pass that invisible barrier which stands between so many who could give one another genuine help if they only dared to ask it. But when Sunday came she went to church, eager for more, and thankful that she knew where to go for it.

This was a very different sermon from the other, and Christie felt as if he preached it for her alone. "Keep innocency and take heed to the thing that is right, for this will bring a man peace at the last," might have been the text, and Mr. Power treated it as if he had known all the trials and temptations that made it hard to live up to.

Justice and righteous wrath possessed him before, now mercy and tenderest sympathy for those who faltered in well-doing, and the stern judge seemed changed to a pitiful father. But better than the pity was the wise counsel, the cheering words, and the devout surrender of the soul to its best instincts; its close communion with its Maker, unchilled by fear, untrammelled by the narrowness of sect or superstition, but full and free and natural as the breath of life.

As she listened Christie felt as if she was climbing up from a solitary valley, through mist and shadow toward a mountain top, where, though the way might be rough and strong winds blow, she would get a wider outlook over the broad earth, and be nearer the serene blue sky. For the first time in her life religion seemed a visible and vital thing; a power that she could grasp and feel, take into her life and make her daily bread. Not a vague, vast idea floating before her, now beautiful, now terrible, always undefined and far away.

She was strangely and powerfully moved that day, for the ploughing had begun; and when the rest stood up for the last hymn, Christie could only bow her head and let the uncontrollable tears flow down like summer rain, while her heart sang with new aspiration:

> "Nearer, my God, to thee,
> E'en though a cross it be
> That raiseth me,
> Still all my song shall be,
> Nearer, my God, to thee.
> Nearer to thee!"

Sitting with her hand before her eyes, she never stirred till the sound of many feet told her that service was done. Then she wiped her eyes, dropped her veil, and was about to rise when she saw a little bunch of flowers between the leaves of the hymn book lying open in her lap. Only a knot of violets set in their own broad leaves, but blue as friendly eyes looking into hers, and sweet as kind words whispered in her ear. She looked about her hoping to detect and thank the giver; but all faces were turned the other way, and all feet departing rapidly.

Christie followed with a very grateful thought in her heart for this little kindness from some unknown friend; and, anxious to recover herself entirely before she faced Mrs. Wilkins, she took a turn in the park.

The snow was gone, high winds had dried the walk, and a clear sky overhead made one forget sodden turf and chilly air. March was going out like a lamb, and Christie enjoyed an occasional vernal whiff from far-off fields and wakening woods, as she walked down the broad mall watching the buds on the boughs, and listening to the twitter of the sparrows, evidently discussing the passers-by as they sat at the doors of their little mansions.

Presently she turned to walk back again and saw Mr. Power coming toward her. She was glad, for all her fear had vanished now, and she wanted to thank him for the sermon that had moved her so deeply. He shook hands in his cordial way, and, turning, walked with her, beginning at once to talk of her affairs as if interested in them.

"Are you ready for the new experiment?" he asked.

"Quite ready, sir; very glad to go, and very much obliged to you for your kindness in providing for me."

"That is what we were put into the world for, to help one another. You can pass on the kindness by serving my good friends who, in return, will do their best for you."

"That's so pleasant! I always knew there were plenty of good, friendly people in the world, only I did not seem to find them often, or be able to keep them long when I did. Is Mr. Sterling an agreeable old man?"

"Very agreeable, but not old. David is about thirty-one or two, I think. He is the son of my friend, the husband died some years ago. I thought I mentioned it."

"You said in your note that Mr. Sterling was a florist, and might like me to help in the green-house, if I was willing. It must be lovely work, and I *should* like it very much."

"Yes, David devotes himself to his flowers, and leads a very quiet life. You may think him rather grave and blunt at first, but you'll soon find him out and get on comfortably, for he is a truly excellent fellow, and my right-hand man in good works."

A curious little change had passed over Christie's face during these last questions and answers, unconscious, but quite observable to keen eyes like Mr. Power's. Surprise and interest appeared first, then a shadow of reserve as if the young woman dropped a thin veil between herself and the young man, and at the last words a half smile and a slight raising of the brows seemed to express the queer mixture of pity and indifference with which we are all apt to regard "excellent fellows" and "amiable girls." Mr. Power understood the look, and went on more confidentially than he had at first intended, for he did not want Christie to go off with a prejudice in her mind which might do both David and herself injustice.

"People sometimes misjudge him, for he is rather old-fashioned in manner and plain in speech, and may seem unsocial, because he does not seek society. But those who know the cause of this forgive any little short-comings for the sake of the genuine goodness of the man. David had a great trouble some years ago and suffered much. He is learning to bear it bravely, and is the better for it, though the memory of it is still bitter, and the cross hard to bear even with pride to help him hide it, and principle to keep him from despair."

Mr. Power glanced at Christie as he paused, and was satisfied with the effect of his words, for interest, pity, and respect shone in her face, and proved that he had touched the right string. She seemed to feel that this little confidence was given for a purpose, and showed that she accepted it as a sort of gage for her own fidelity to her new employers.

"Thank you, sir, I shall remember," she said, with her frank eyes lifted gravely to his own. "I like to work for people whom I can respect," she added, "and will bear with any peculiarities of Mr. Sterling's without a thought of complaint. When a man has suffered through one woman, all women should be kind and patient with him, and try to atone for the wrong which lessens his respect and faith in them."

"There you are right; and in this case all women *should* be kind, for David pities and protects womankind as the only retaliation for the life-long grief one woman brought upon him. That's not a common revenge, is it?"

"It's beautiful!" cried Christie, and instantly David was a hero.

"At one time it was an even chance whether that trouble sent David to 'the devil,' as he expressed it, or made a man of him. That little saint of a mother kept him safe till the first desperation was over, and now he lives for her, as he ought. Not so romantic an ending as a pistol or Byronic scorn for the world in general and women in particular, but dutiful and brave, since it often takes more courage to live than to die."

"Yes, sir," said Christie, heartily, though her eyes fell, remembering how she had failed with far less cause for despair than David.

They were at the gate now, and Mr. Power left her, saying, with a vigorous hand-shake:

"Best wishes for a happy summer. I shall come sometimes to see how you prosper; and remember, if you tire of it and want to change, let me know, for I take great satisfaction in putting the right people in the right places. Good-by, and God be with you."

# Chapter X

MRS. STERLING.

IT was an April day when Christie went to her new home. Warm rains had melted the last trace of snow, and every bank was full of pricking grass-blades, brave little pioneers and heralds of the Spring. The budding elm boughs swung in the wind; blue-jays screamed among the apple-trees; and robins chirped shrilly, as if rejoicing over winter hardships safely passed. Vernal freshness was in the air despite its chill, and lovely hints of summer time were everywhere.

These welcome sights and sounds met Christie, as she walked down the lane, and, coming to a gate, paused there to look about her. An old-fashioned cottage stood in the midst of a garden just awakening from its winter sleep. One elm hung protectingly over the low roof, sunshine lay warmly on it, and at every window flowers' bright faces smiled at the passer-by invitingly.

On one side glittered a long green-house, and on the other stood a barn, with a sleek cow ruminating in the yard, and an inquiring horse poking his head out of his stall to view the world. Many comfortable gray hens were clucking and scratching about the hay-strewn floor, and a flock of doves sat cooing on the roof.

A quiet, friendly place it looked; for nothing marred its

peace, and the hopeful, healthful spirit of the season seemed to haunt the spot. Snow-drops and crocuses were up in one secluded nook; a plump maltese cat sat purring in the porch; and a dignified old dog came marching down the walk to escort the stranger in. With a brightening face Christie went up the path, and tapped at the quaint knocker, hoping that the face she was about to see would be in keeping with the pleasant place.

She was not disappointed, for the dearest of little Quaker ladies opened to her, with such an air of peace and good-will that the veriest ruffian, coming to molest or make afraid, would have found it impossible to mar the tranquillity of that benign old face, or disturb one fold of the soft muslin crossed upon her breast.

"I come from Mr. Power, and I have a note for Mrs. Sterling," began Christie in her gentlest tone, as her last fear vanished at sight of that mild maternal figure.

"I am she; come in, friend; I am glad to see thee," said the old lady, smiling placidly, as she led the way into a room whose principal furniture seemed to be books, flowers, and sunshine.

The look, the tone, the gentle "thee," went straight to Christie's heart; and, while Mrs. Sterling put on her spectacles and slowly read the note, she stroked the cat and said to herself: "Surely, I have fallen among a set of angels. I thought Mrs. Wilkins a sort of saint, Mr. Power was an improvement even upon that good soul, and if I am not mistaken this sweet little lady is the best and dearest of all. I do hope she will like me."

"It is quite right, my dear, and I am most glad to see thee; for we need help at this season of the year, and have had none for several weeks. Step up to the room at the head of the stairs, and lay off thy things. Then, if thee is not tired, I will give thee a little job with me in the kitchen," said the old lady with a kindly directness which left no room for awkwardness on the new-comer's part.

Up went Christie, and after a hasty look round a room as plain and white and still as a nun's cell, she whisked on a working-apron and ran down again, feeling, as she fancied the children did in the fairy tale, when they first arrived at the house of the little old woman who lived in the wood.

Mrs. Wilkins's kitchen was as neat as a room could be, wherein six children came and went, but this kitchen was tidy with the immaculate order of which Shakers and Quakers alone seem to possess the secret,—a fragrant, shining cleanliness, that made even black kettles ornamental and dish-pans objects of interest. Nothing burned or boiled over, though the stove was full of dinner-pots and skillets. There was no litter or hurry, though the baking of cake and pies was going on, and when Mrs. Sterling put a pan of apples, and a knife into her new assistant's hands, saying in a tone that made the request a favor, "Will thee kindly pare these for me?" Christie wondered what would happen if she dropped a seed upon the floor, or did not cut the apples into four exact quarters.

"I never shall suit this dear prim soul," she thought, as her eye went from Puss, sedately perched on one small mat, to the dog dozing upon another, and neither offering to stir from their own dominions.

This dainty nicety amused her at first, but she liked it, and very soon her thoughts went back to the old times when she worked with Aunt Betsey, and learned the good old-fashioned arts which now were to prove her fitness for this pleasant place.

Mrs. Sterling saw the shadow that crept into Christie's face, and led the chat to cheerful things, not saying much herself, but beguiling the other to talk, and listening with an interest that made it easy to go on.

Mr. Power and the Wilkinses made them friends very soon; and in an hour or two Christie was moving about the kitchen as if she had already taken possession of her new kingdom.

"Thee likes housework I think," said Mrs. Sterling, as she watched her hang up a towel to dry, and rinse her dish-cloth when the cleaning up was done.

"Oh, yes! if I need not do it with a shiftless Irish girl to drive me distracted by pretending to help. I have lived out, and did not find it hard while I had my good Hepsey. I was second girl, and can set a table in style. Shall I try now?" she asked, as the old lady went into a little dining-room with fresh napkins in her hand.

"Yes, but we have no style here. I will show thee once, and hereafter it will be thy work, as thy feet are younger than mine."

A nice old-fashioned table was soon spread, and Christie

kept smiling at the contrast between this and Mrs. Stuart's. Chubby little pitchers appeared, delicate old glass, queer china, and tiny tea-spoons; linen as smooth as satin, and a quaint tankard that might have come over in the "May-flower."

"Now, will thee take that pitcher of water to David's room? It is at the top of the house, and may need a little dusting. I have not been able to attend to it as I would like since I have been alone," said Mrs. Sterling.

Rooms usually betray something of the character and tastes of their occupants, and Christie paused a moment as she entered David's, to look about her with feminine interest.

It was the attic, and extended the whole length of the house. One end was curtained off as a bedroom, and she smiled at its austere simplicity.

A gable in the middle made a sunny recess, where were stored bags and boxes of seed, bunches of herbs, and shelves full of those tiny pots in which baby plants are born and nursed till they can grow alone.

The west end was evidently the study, and here Christie took a good look as she dusted tidily. The furniture was nothing, only an old sofa, with the horsehair sticking out in tufts here and there; an antique secretary; and a table covered with books. As she whisked the duster down the front of the ancient piece of furniture, one of the doors in the upper half swung open, and Christie saw three objects that irresistibly riveted her eyes for a moment. A broken fan, a bundle of letters tied up with a black ribbon, and a little workbasket in which lay a fanciful needle-book with "Letty" embroidered on it in faded silk.

"Poor David, that is his little shrine, and I have no right to see it," thought Christie, shutting the door with self-reproachful haste.

At the table she paused again, for books always attracted her, and here she saw a goodly array whose names were like the faces of old friends, because she remembered them in her father's library.

Faust was full of ferns, Shakspeare, of rough sketches of the men and women whom he has made immortal. Saintly Herbert lay side by side with Saint Augustine's confessions. Milton and Montaigne stood socially together, and Andersen's lovely "Märchen" fluttered its pictured leaves in the middle of an open Plato; while several books in unknown tongues were half-hidden by volumes of Browning, Keats, and Coleridge.

In the middle of this fine society, slender and transparent as the spirit of a shape, stood a little vase holding one half-opened rose, fresh and fragrant as if just gathered.

Christie smiled as she saw it, and wondered if the dear, dead, or false woman had been fond of roses.

Then her eye went to the mantel-piece, just above the table, and she laughed; for, on it stood three busts, idols evidently, but very shabby ones; for Göthe's nose was broken, Schiller's head cracked visibly, and the dust of ages seemed to have settled upon Linnæus in the middle. On the wall above them hung a curious old picture of a monk kneeling in a devout ecstasy, while the face of an angel is dimly seen through the radiance that floods the cell with divine light. Portraits of Mr. Power and Martin Luther stared thoughtfully at one another from either side, as if making up their minds to shake hands in spite of time and space.

"Melancholy, learned, and sentimental," said Christie to herself, as she settled David's character after these discoveries.

The sound of a bell made her hasten down, more curious than ever to see if this belief was true.

"Perhaps thee had better step out and call my son. Sometimes he does not hear the bell when he is busy. Thee will find my garden-hood and shawl behind the door," said Mrs. Sterling, presently; for punctuality was a great virtue in the old lady's eyes.

Christie demurely tied on the little pumpkin-hood, wrapped the gray shawl about her, and set out to find her "master," as she had a fancy to call this unknown David.

From the hints dropped by Mr. Power, and her late discoveries, she had made a hero for herself; a sort of melancholy Jaques; sad and pale and stern; retired from the world to nurse his wounds in solitude. She rather liked this picture; for romance dies hard in a woman, and, spite of her experiences, Christie still indulged in dreams and fancies. "It will be so interesting to see how he bears his secret sorrow. I am fond of woe; but I do hope he won't be too lackadaisical, for I never could abide that sort of blighted being."

Thinking thus, she peeped here and there, but saw no one in yard or barn, except a workman scraping the mould off his boots near the conservatory.

"This David is among the flowers, I fancy; I will just ask, and not bolt in, as he does not know me. "Where is Mr. Sterling?" added Christie aloud, as she approached.

The man looked up, and a smile came into his eyes, as he glanced from the old hood to the young face inside. Then he took off his hat, and held out his hand, saying with just his mother's simple directness:

"I am David; and this is Christie Devon, I know. How do you do?"

"Yes; dinner's ready," was all she could reply, for the discovery that this was the "master," nearly took her breath away. Not the faintest trace of the melancholy Jaques about him; nothing interesting, romantic, pensive, or even stern. Only a broad-shouldered, brown-bearded man, with an old hat and coat, trousers tucked into his boots, fresh mould on the hand he had given her to shake, and the cheeriest voice she had ever heard.

What a blow it was to be sure! Christie actually felt vexed with him for disappointing her so, and could not recover herself, but stood red and awkward, till, with a last scrape of his boots, David said with placid brevity:

"Well, shall we go in?"

Christie walked rapidly into the house, and by the time she got there the absurdity of her fancy struck her, and she stifled a laugh in the depths of the little pumpkin-hood, as she hung it up. Then, assuming her gravest air, she went to give the finishing touches to dinner.

Ten minutes later she received another surprise; for David appeared washed, brushed, and in a suit of gray,—a personable gentleman, quite unlike the workman in the yard.

Christie gave one look, met a pair of keen yet kind eyes with a suppressed laugh in them, and dropped her own, to be no more lifted up till dinner was done.

It was a very quiet meal, for no one said much; and it was evidently the custom of the house to eat silently, only now and then saying a few friendly words, to show that the hearts were social if the tongues were not.

On the present occasion this suited Christie; and she ate her dinner without making any more discoveries, except that the earth-stained hands were very clean now, and skilfully supplied her wants before she could make them known.

As they rose from table, Mrs. Sterling said: "Davy, does thee want any help this afternoon?"

"I shall be very glad of some in about an hour if thee can spare it, mother."

"I can, dear."

"Do you care for flowers?" asked David, turning to Christie, "because if you do not, this will be a very trying place for you."

"I used to love them dearly; but I have not had any for so long I hardly remember how they look," answered Christie with a sigh, as she recalled Rachel's roses, dead long ago. "Shy, sick, and sad; poor soul, we must lend a hand and cheer her up a bit," thought David, as he watched her eyes turn toward the green things in the windows with a bright, soft look he liked to see.

"Come to the conservatory in an hour, and I'll show you the best part of a 'German,'" he said, with a nod and a smile, as he went away, beginning to whistle like a boy when the door was shut behind him.

"What did he mean?" thought Christie, as she helped clear the table, and put every thing in Pimlico order.

She was curious to know, and when Mrs. Sterling said: "Now, my dear, I am going to take my nap, and thee can help David if thee likes," she was quite ready to try the new work.

She would have been more than woman if she had not first slipped upstairs to smooth her hair, put on a fresh collar, and a black silk apron with certain effective frills and pockets, while a scarlet rigolette replaced the hood, and lent a little color to her pale cheeks.

"I am a poor ghost of what I was," she thought; "but that's no matter: few can be pretty, any one can be neat, and that is more than ever necessary here."

Then she went away to the conservatory, feeling rather oppressed with the pity and sympathy, for which there was no call, and fervently wishing that David would not be so comfortable, for he ate a hearty dinner, laughed four times, and whistled as no heart-broken man would dream of doing.

No one was visible as she went in, and walking slowly down the green aisle, she gave herself up to the enjoyment of the lovely place. The damp, sweet air made summer there, and a group of slender, oriental trees whispered in the breath of wind that blew in from an open sash. Strange vines and flowers hung overhead;

banks of azaleas, ruddy, white, and purple, bloomed in one place; roses of every hue turned their lovely faces to the sun; ranks of delicate ferns, and heaths with their waxen bells, were close by; glowing geraniums and stately lilies side by side; savage-looking scarlet flowers with purple hearts, or orange spikes rising from leaves mottled with strange colors; dusty passion-flowers, and gay nasturtiums climbing to the roof. All manner of beautiful and curious plants were there; and Christie walked among them, as happy as a child who finds its playmates again.

Coming to a bed of pansies she sat down on a rustic chair, and, leaning forward, feasted her eyes on these her favorites. Her face grew young as she looked, her hands touched them with a lingering tenderness as if to her they were half human, and her own eyes were so busy enjoying the gold and purple spread before her, that she did not see another pair peering at her over an unneighborly old cactus, all prickles, and queer knobs. Presently a voice said at her elbow:

"You look as if you saw something beside pansies there."

David spoke so quietly that it did not startle her, and she answered before she had time to feel ashamed of her fancy.

"I do; for, ever since I was a child, I always see a little face when I look at this flower. Sometimes it is a sad one, sometimes it's merry, often roguish, but always a dear little face; and when I see so many together, it's like a flock of children, all nodding and smiling at me at once."

"So it is!" and David nodded, and smiled himself, as he handed her two or three of the finest, as if it was as natural a thing as to put a sprig of mignonette in his own button-hole.

Christie thanked him, and then jumped up, remembering that she came there to work, not to dream. He seemed to understand, and went into a little room near by, saying, as he pointed to a heap of gay flowers on the table:

"These are to be made into little bouquets for a 'German' to-night. It is pretty work, and better fitted for a woman's fingers than a man's. This is all you have to do, and you can use your taste as to colors."

While he spoke David laid a red and white carnation on a bit of smilax, tied them together, twisted a morsel of silver foil about the stems, and laid it before Christie as a sample.

"Yes, I can do that, and shall like it very much," she said, burying her nose in the mass of sweetness before her, and feeling as if her new situation grew pleasanter every minute.

"Here is the apron my mother uses, that bit of silk will soon be spoilt, for the flowers are wet," and David gravely offered her a large checked pinafore.

Christie could not help laughing as she put it on: all this was so different from the imaginary picture she had made. She was disappointed, and yet she began to feel as if the simple truth was better than the sentimental fiction; and glanced up at David involuntarily to see if there were any traces of interesting woe about him.

But he was looking at her with the steady, straightforward

DAVID AND CHRISTIE IN THE GREENHOUSE.

look which she liked so much, yet could not meet just yet; and all she saw was that he was smiling also with an indulgent expression as if she was a little girl whom he was trying to amuse.

"Make a few, and I'll be back directly when I have attended to another order," and he went away thinking Christie's face was very like the pansies they had been talking about,—one of the sombre ones with a bright touch of gold deep down in the heart, for thin and pale as the face was, it lighted up at a kind word, and all the sadness vanished out of the anxious eyes when the frank laugh came.

Christie fell to work with a woman's interest in such a pleasant task, and soon tied and twisted skilfully, exercising all her taste in contrasts, and the pretty little conceits flower-lovers can produce. She was so interested that presently she began to hum half unconsciously, as she was apt to do when happily employed:

> "Welcome, maids of honor,
>     You do bring
>     In the spring,
> And wait upon her.
> She has virgins many,
>     Fresh and fair,
>     Yet you are
> More sweet than any."

There she stopped, for David's step drew near, and she remembered where she was.

"The last verse is the best in that little poem. Have you forgotten it?" he said, pleased and surprised to find the newcomer singing Herrick's lines "To Violets."

"Almost; my father used to say that when we went looking for early violets, and these lovely ones reminded me of it," explained Christie, rather abashed.

As if to put her at ease David added, as he laid another handful of double-violets on the table:

> "'Y' are the maiden posies,
>     And so graced,
>     To be placed
> 'Fore damask roses.

> Yet, though thus respected,
>     By and by
>     Ye do lie,
> Poor girls, neglected."

"I always think of them as pretty, modest maids after that, and can't bear to throw them away, even when faded."

Christie hoped he did not think her sentimental, and changed the conversation by pointing to her work, and saying, in a business-like way:

"Will these do? I have varied the posies as much as possible, so that they may suit all sorts of tastes and whims. I never went to a 'German' myself; but I have looked on, and remember hearing the young people say the little bouquets didn't mean any thing, so I tried to make these expressive."

"Well, I should think you had succeeded excellently, and it is a very pretty fancy. Tell me what some of them mean: will you?"

"You should know better than I, being a florist," said Christie, glad to see he approved of her work.

"I can grow the flowers, but not read them," and David looked rather depressed by his own ignorance of those delicate matters.

Still with the business-like air, Christie held up one after another of the little knots, saying soberly, though her eyes smiled:

"This white one might be given to a newly engaged girl, as suggestive of the coming bridal. That half-blown bud would say a great deal from a lover to his idol; and this heliotrope be most encouraging to a timid swain. Here is a rosy daisy for some merry little damsel; there is a scarlet posy for a soldier; this delicate azalea and fern for some lovely creature just out; and there is a bunch of sober pansies for a spinster, if spinsters go to 'Germans.' Heath, scentless but pretty, would do for many; these Parma violets for one with a sorrow; and this curious purple flower with arrow-shaped stamens would just suit a handsome, sharp-tongued woman, if any partner dared give it to her."

David laughed, as his eye went from the flowers to Christie's face, and when she laid down the last breast-knot, looking as if she would like the chance of presenting it to some one she knew, he seemed much amused.

"If the beaux and belles at this party have the wit to read your posies, my fortune will be made, and you will have your hands full supplying compliments, declarations, rebukes, and criticisms for the fashionable butterflies. I wish I could put consolation, hope, and submission into *my* work as easily, but I am afraid I can't," he added a moment afterward with a changed face, as he began to lay the loveliest white flowers into a box.

"Those are not for a wedding, then?"

"For a dead baby; and I can't seem to find any white and sweet enough."

"You know the people?" asked Christie, with the sympathetic tone in her voice.

"Never saw or heard of them till to-day. Isn't it enough to know that 'baby's dead,' as the poor man said, to make one feel for them?"

"Of course it is; only you seemed so interested in arranging the flowers, I naturally thought it was for some friend," Christie answered hastily, for David looked half indignant at her question.

"I want them to look lovely and comforting when the mother opens the box, and I don't seem to have the right flowers. Will you give it a touch? women have a tender way of doing such things that we can never learn."

"I don't think I can improve it, unless I add another sort of flower that seems appropriate: may I?"

"Any thing you can find."

Christie waited for no more, but ran out of the greenhouse to David's great surprise, and presently came hurrying back with a handful of snow-drops.

"Those are just what I wanted, but I didn't know the little dears were up yet! You shall put them in, and I know they will suggest what you hope to these poor people," he said approvingly, as he placed the box before her, and stood by watching her adjust the little sheaf of pale flowers tied up with a blade of grass. She added a frail fern or two, and did give just the graceful touch here and there which would speak to the mother's sore heart of the tender thought some one had taken for her dead darling.

The box was sent away, and Christie went on with her work,

but that little task performed together seemed to have made them friends; and, while David tied up several grand bouquets at the same table, they talked as if the strangeness was fast melting away from their short acquaintance.

Christie's own manners were so simple that simplicity in others always put her at her ease: kindness soon banished her reserve, and the desire to show that she was grateful for it helped her to please. David's bluntness was of such a gentle sort that she soon got used to it, and found it a pleasant contrast to the polite insincerity so common. He was as frank and friendly as a boy, yet had a certain paternal way with him which rather annoyed her at first, and made her feel as if he thought her a mere girl, while she was very sure he could not be but a year or two older than herself.

"I'd rather he'd be masterful, and order me about," she thought, still rather regretting the "blighted being" she had not found.

In spite of this she spent a pleasant afternoon, sitting in that sunny place, handling flowers, asking questions about them, and getting the sort of answers she liked; not dry botanical name and facts, but all the delicate traits, curious habits, and poetical romances of the sweet things, as if the speaker knew and loved them as friends, not merely valued them as merchandise.

They had just finished when the great dog came bouncing in with a basket in his mouth.

"Mother wants eggs: will you come to the barn and get them? Hay is wholesome, and you can feed the doves if you like," said David, leading the way with Bran rioting about him.

"Why don't he offer to put up a swing for me, or get me a doll? It's the pinafore that deceives him. Never mind: I rather like it after all," thought Christie; but she left the apron behind her, and followed with the most dignified air.

It did not last long, however, for the sights and sounds that greeted her, carried her back to the days of egg-hunting in Uncle Enos's big barn; and, before she knew it, she was rustling through the hay mows, talking to the cow and receiving the attentions of Bran with a satisfaction it was impossible to conceal.

The hens gathered about her feet cocking their expectant eyes at her; the doves came circling round her head; the cow stared placidly, and the inquisitive horse responded affably when she offered him a handful of hay.

"How tame they all are! I like animals, they are so contented and intelligent," she said, as a plump dove lit on her shoulder with an impatient coo.

"That was Kitty's pet, she always fed the fowls. Would you like to do it?" and David offered a little measure of oats.

"Very much;" and Christie began to scatter the grain, wondering who "Kitty" was.

As if he saw the wish in her face, David added, while he shelled corn for the hens:

"She was the little girl who was with us last. Her father kept her in a factory, and took all her wages, barely giving her clothes and food enough to keep her alive. The poor child ran away, and was trying to hide when Mr. Power found and sent her here to be cared for."

"As he did me?" said Christie quickly.

"Yes, that's a way he has."

"A very kind and Christian way. Why didn't she stay?"

"Well, it was rather quiet for the lively little thing, and rather too near the city, so we got a good place up in the country where she could go to school and learn housework. The mill had left her no time for these things, and at fifteen she was as ignorant as a child."

"You must miss her."

"I do very much."

"Was she pretty?"

"She looked like a little rose sometimes," and David smiled to himself as he fed the gray hens.

Christie immediately made a picture of the "lively little thing" with a face "like a rose," and was uncomfortably conscious that she did not look half as well feeding doves as Kitty must have done.

Just then David handed her the basket, saying in the paternal way that half amused, half piqued her: "It is getting too chilly for you here: take these in please, and I'll bring the milk directly."

In spite of herself she smiled, as a sudden vision of the elegant Mr. Fletcher, devotedly carrying her book or beach-basket, passed through her mind; then hastened to explain the smile, for David lifted his brows inquiringly, and glanced about him to see what amused her.

"I beg your pardon: I've lived alone so much that it seems a little odd to be told to do things, even if they are as easy and pleasant as this."

"I am so used to taking care of people, and directing, that I do so without thinking. I won't if you don't like it," and he put out his hand to take back the basket with a grave, apologetic air.

"But I do like it; only it amused me to be treated like a little girl again, when I am nearly thirty, and feel seventy at least, life has been so hard to me lately."

Her face sobered at the last words, and David's instantly grew so pitiful she could not keep her eyes on it lest they should fill, so suddenly did the memory of past troubles overcome her.

"I know," he said in a tone that warmed her heart, "I know, but we are going to try, and make life easier for you now, and you must feel that this is home and we are friends."

"I do!" and Christie flushed with grateful feeling and a little shame, as she went in, thinking to herself: "How silly I was to say that! I may have spoilt the simple friendliness that was so pleasant, and have made him think me a foolish stuck-up old creature."

Whatever he might have thought, David's manner was unchanged when he came in and found her busy with the table.

"It's pleasant to see thee resting, mother, and every thing going on so well," he said, glancing about the room, where the old lady sat, and nodding toward the kitchen, where Christie was toasting bread in her neatest manner.

"Yes, Davy, it was about time I had a helper for thy sake, at least; and this is a great improvement upon heedless Kitty, I am inclined to think."

Mrs. Sterling dropped her voice over that last sentence; but Christie heard it, and was pleased. A moment or two later, David came toward her with a glass in his hand, saying as if rather doubtful of his reception:

"New milk is part of the cure: will you try it?"

For the first time, Christie looked straight up in the honest eyes that seemed to demand honesty in others, and took the glass, answering heartily:

"Yes, thank you; I drink good health to you, and better manners to me."

The newly lighted lamp shone full in her face, and though it was neither young nor blooming, it showed something better than youth and bloom to one who could read the subtle language of character as David could. He nodded as he took the glass, and went away saying quietly:

"We are plain people here, and you won't find it hard to get on with us, I think."

But he liked the candid look, and thought about it, as he chopped kindlings, whistling with a vigor which caused Christie to smile as she strained the milk.

After tea a spider-legged table was drawn out toward the hearth, where an open fire burned cheerily, and puss purred on the rug, with Bran near by. David unfolded his newspapers, Mrs. Sterling pinned on her knitting-sheath, and Christie sat a moment enjoying the comfortable little scene. She sighed without knowing it, and Mrs. Sterling asked quickly:

"Is thee tired, my dear?"

"Oh, no! only happy."

"I am glad of that: I was afraid thee would find it dull."

"It's beautiful!" then Christie checked herself, feeling that these outbursts would not suit such quiet people; and, half ashamed of showing how much she felt, she added soberly, "If you will give me something to do I shall be quite contented."

"Sewing is not good for thee. If thee likes to knit I'll set up a sock for thee to-morrow," said the old lady well pleased at the industrious turn of her new handmaid.

"I like to darn, and I see some to be done in this basket. May I do it?" and Christie laid hold of the weekly job which even the best housewives are apt to set aside for pleasanter tasks.

"As thee likes, my dear. My eyes will not let me sew much in the evening, else I should have finished that batch to-night. Thee will find the yarn and needles in the little bag."

So Christie fell to work on gray socks, and neat lavender-colored hose, while the old lady knit swiftly, and David read aloud. Christie thought she was listening to the report of a fine lecture; but her ear only caught the words, for her mind wandered away into a region of its own, and lived there till her

task was done. Then she laid the tidy pile in the basket, drew
her chair to a corner of the hearth, and quietly enjoyed herself.

The cat, feeling sure of a welcome, got up into her lap, and
went to sleep in a cosy bunch; Bran laid his nose across her
feet, and blinked at her with sleepy good-will, while her eyes
wandered round the room, from its quaint furniture and the
dreaming flowers in the windows, to the faces of its occupants,
and lingered there.

The plain border of a Quaker cap encircled that mild old
face, with bands of silver hair parted on a forehead marked
with many lines. But the eyes were clear and sweet; winter
roses bloomed in the cheeks, and an exquisite neatness pervaded the small figure, from the trim feet on the stool, to the
soft shawl folded about the shoulders, as only a Quakeress can
fold one. In Mrs. Sterling, piety and peace made old age lovely,
and the mere presence of this tranquil soul seemed to fill the
room with a reposeful charm none could resist.

The other face possessed no striking comeliness of shape or
color; but the brown, becoming beard made it manly, and the
broad arch of a benevolent brow added nobility to features
otherwise not beautiful,—a face plainly expressing resolution
and rectitude, inspiring respect as naturally as a certain protective kindliness of manner won confidence. Even in repose
wearing a vigilant look as if some hidden pain or passion lay in
wait to surprise and conquer the sober cheerfulness that softened the lines of the firm-set lips, and warmed the glance of
the thoughtful eyes.

Christie fancied she possessed the key to this, and longed to
know all the story of the cross which Mr. Power said David
had learned to bear so well. Then she began to wonder if they
could like and keep her, to hope so, and to feel that here at last
she was at home with friends. But the old sadness crept over
her, as she remembered how often she had thought this before,
and how soon the dream ended, the ties were broken, and she
adrift again.

"Ah well," she said within herself, "I won't think of the
morrow, but take the good that comes and enjoy it while I
may. I must not disappoint Rachel, since she kept her word so
nobly to me. Dear soul, when shall I see her again?"

The thought of Rachel always touched her heart, more now

than ever; and, as she leaned back in her chair with closed eyes and idle hands, these tender memories made her unconscious face most eloquent. The eyes peering over the spectacles telegraphed a meaning message to the other eyes glancing over the paper now and then; and both these friends in deed as well as name felt assured that this woman needed all the comfort they could give her. But the busy needles never stopped their click, and the sonorous voice read on without a pause, so Christie never knew what mute confidences passed between mother and son, or what helpful confessions her traitorous face had made for her.

The clock struck nine, and these primitive people prepared for rest; for their day began at dawn, and much wholesome work made sleep a luxury.

"Davy will tap at thy door as he goes down in the morning, and I will soon follow to show thee about matters. Goodnight, and good rest, my child."

So speaking, the little lady gave Christie a maternal kiss; David shook hands; and then she went away, wondering why service was so lightened by such little kindnesses.

As she lay in her narrow white bed, with the "pale light of stars" filling the quiet, cell-like room, and some one playing softly on a flute overhead, she felt as if she had left the troublous world behind her, and shutting out want, solitude, and despair, had come into some safe, secluded spot full of flowers and sunshine, kind hearts, and charitable deeds.

# Chapter XI

## IN THE STRAWBERRY BED

From that day a new life began for Christie, a happy, quiet, useful life, utterly unlike any of the brilliant futures she had planned for herself; yet indescribably pleasant to her now, for past experience had taught her its worth, and made her ready to enjoy it.

Never had spring seemed so early or so fair, never had such a crop of hopeful thoughts and happy feelings sprung up in her heart as now; and nowhere was there a brighter face, a blither voice, or more willing hands than Christie's when the apple blossoms came.

This was what she needed, the protection of a home, wholesome cares and duties; and, best of all, friends to live and labor for, loving and beloved. Her whole soul was in her work now, and as health returned, much of the old energy and cheerfulness came with it, a little sobered, but more sweet and earnest than ever. No task was too hard or humble; no day long enough to do all she longed to do; and no sacrifice would have seemed too great for those whom she regarded with steadily increasing love and gratitude.

Up at dawn, the dewy freshness of the hour, the morning rapture of the birds, the daily miracle of sunrise, set her heart in tune, and gave her Nature's most healing balm. She kept the little house in order, with Mrs. Sterling to direct and share the labor so pleasantly, that mistress and maid soon felt like mother and daughter, and Christie often said she did not care for any other wages.

The house-work of this small family was soon done, and then Christie went to tasks that she liked better. Much out-of-door life was good for her, and in garden and green-house there was plenty of light labor she could do. So she grubbed contentedly in the wholesome earth, weeding and potting, learning to prune and bud, and finding Mrs. Wilkins was quite right in her opinion of the sanitary virtues of dirt.

Trips to town to see the good woman and carry country

gifts to the little folks; afternoon drives with Mrs. Sterling in the old-fashioned chaise, drawn by the Roman-nosed horse, and Sunday pilgrimages to church to be "righted up" by one of Mr. Power's stirring sermons, were among her new pleasures. But, on the whole, the evenings were her happiest times: for then David read aloud while she worked; she sung to the old piano tuned for her use; or, better still, as spring came on, they sat in the porch, and talked as people only do talk when twilight, veiling the outer world, seems to lift the curtains of that inner world where minds go exploring, hearts learn to know one another, and souls walk together in the cool of the day.

At such times Christie seemed to catch glimpses of another David than the busy, cheerful man apparently contented with the humdrum duties of an obscure, laborious life, and the few unexciting pleasures afforded by books, music, and much silent thought. She sometimes felt with a woman's instinct that under this composed, commonplace existence another life went on; for, now and then, in the interest of conversation, or the involuntary yielding to a confidential impulse, a word, a look, a gesture, betrayed an unexpected power and passion, a secret unrest, a bitter memory that would not be ignored.

Only at rare moments did she catch these glimpses, and so brief, so indistinct, were they that she half believed her own lively fancy created them. She longed to know more; but "David's trouble" made him sacred in her eyes from any prying curiosity, and always after one of these twilight betrayals Christie found him so like his unromantic self next day, that she laughed and said:

"I never shall outgrow my foolish way of trying to make people other than they are. Gods are gone, heroes hard to find, and one should be contented with good men, even if they do wear old clothes, lead prosaic lives, and have no accomplishments but gardening, playing the flute, and keeping their temper."

She felt the influences of that friendly place at once; but for a time she wondered at the natural way in which kind things were done, the protective care extended over her, and the confiding air with which these people treated her. They asked no questions, demanded no explanations, seemed unconscious of conferring favors, and took her into their life so readily that

she marvelled, even while she rejoiced, at the good fortune
which led her there.

She understood this better when she discovered, what Mr.
Power had not mentioned, that the little cottage was a sort of
refuge for many women like herself; a half-way house where
they could rest and recover themselves after the wrongs, defeats, and weariness that come to such in the battle of life.

With a chivalry older and finer than any Spenser sung, Mr.
Power befriended these forlorn souls, and David was his faithful squire. Whoever knocked at that low door was welcomed,
warmed, and fed; comforted, and set on their way, cheered and
strengthened by the sweet good-will that made charity no
burden, and restored to the more desperate and despairing
their faith in human nature and God's love.

There are many such green spots in this world of ours, which
often seems so bad that a second Deluge could hardly wash it
clean again; and these beneficent, unostentatious asylums are the
salvation of more troubled souls than many a great institution
gilded all over with the rich bequests of men who find themselves
too heavily laden to enter in at the narrow gate of heaven.

Happy the foot-sore, heart-weary traveller who turns from
the crowded, dusty highway down the green lane that leads to
these humble inns, where the sign of the Good Samaritan is
written on the face of whomsoever opens to the stranger, and
refreshment for soul and body is freely given in the name of
Him who loved the poor.

Mr. Power came now and then, for his large parish left him
but little time to visit any but the needy. Christie enjoyed these
brief visits heartily, for her new friends soon felt that she was
one of them, and cordially took her into the large circle of
workers and believers to which they belonged.

Mr. Power's heart was truly an orphan asylum, and every
lonely creature found a welcome there. He could rebuke sin
sternly, yet comfort and uplift the sinner with fatherly compassion; righteous wrath would flash from his eyes at injustice,
and contempt sharpen his voice as he denounced hypocrisy:
yet the eyes that lightened would dim with pity for a woman's
wrong, a child's small sorrow; and the voice that thundered
would whisper consolation like a mother, or give counsel with
a wisdom books cannot teach.

He was a Moses in his day and generation, born to lead his people out of the bondage of dead superstitions, and go before them through a Red Sea of persecution into the larger liberty and love all souls hunger for, and many are just beginning to find as they come doubting, yet desiring, into the goodly land such pioneers as he have planted in the wilderness.

He was like a tonic to weak natures and wavering wills; and Christie felt a general revival going on within herself as her knowledge, honor, and affection for him grew. His strength seemed to uphold her; his integrity to rebuke all unworthiness in her own life; and the magic of his generous, genial spirit to make the hard places smooth, the bitter things sweet, and the world seem a happier, honester place than she had ever thought it since her father died.

Mr. Power had been interested in her from the first; had watched her through other eyes, and tried her by various unsuspected tests. She stood them well; showed her faults as frankly as her virtues, and tried to deserve their esteem by copying the excellencies she admired in them.

"She is made of the right stuff, and we must keep her among us; for she must not be lost or wasted by being left to drift about the world with no ties to make her safe and happy. She is doing so well here, let her stay till the restless spirit begins to stir again; then she shall come to me and learn contentment by seeing greater troubles than her own."

Mr. Power said this one day as he rose to go, after sitting an hour with Mrs. Sterling, and hearing from her a good report of his new *protégée*. The young people were out at work, and had not been called in to see him, for the interview had been a confidential one. But as he stood at the gate he saw Christie in the strawberry bed, and went toward her, glad to see how well and happy she looked.

Her hat was hanging on her shoulders, and the sun giving her cheeks a healthy color; she was humming to herself like a bee as her fingers flew, and once she paused, shaded her eyes with her hand, and took a long look at a figure down in the meadow; then she worked on silent and smiling,—a pleasant creature to see, though her hair was ruffled by the wind; her gingham gown pinned up; and her fingers deeply stained with the blood of many berries.

"I wonder if that means any thing?" thought Mr. Power, with a keen glance from the distant man to the busy woman close at hand. "It might be a helpful, happy thing for both, if poor David only could forget."

He had time for no more castle-building, for a startled robin flew away with a shrill chirp, and Christie looked up.

"Oh, I'm so glad!" she said, rising quickly. "I was picking a special box for you, and now you can have a feast beside, just as you like it, fresh from the vines. Sit here, please, and I'll hull faster than you can eat."

"This *is* luxury!" and Mr. Power sat down on the three-legged stool offered him, with a rhubarb leaf on his knee which Christie kept supplying with delicious mouthfuls.

"Well, and how goes it? Are we still happy and contented here?" he asked.

MR. POWER AND CHRISTIE IN THE STRAWBERRY BED.

"I feel as if I had been born again; as if this was a new heaven and a new earth, and every thing was as it should be," answered Christie, with a look of perfect satisfaction in her face.

"That's a pleasant hearing. Mrs. Sterling has been praising you, but I wanted to be sure you were as satisfied as she. And how does David wear? well, I hope."

"Oh, yes, he is very good to me, and is teaching me to be a gardener, so that I needn't kill myself with sewing any more. Much of this is fine work for women, and *so* healthy. Don't I look a different creature from the ghost that came here three or four months ago?" and she turned her face for inspection like a child.

"Yes, David is a good gardener. I often send my sort of plants here, and he always makes them grow and blossom sooner or later," answered Mr. Power, regarding her like a beneficent genie on a three-legged stool.

"You are the fresh air, and Mrs. Sterling is the quiet sunshine that does the work, I fancy. David only digs about the roots."

"Thank you for my share of the compliment; but why say 'only digs'? That is a most important part of the work: I'm afraid you don't appreciate David."

"Oh, yes, I do; but he rather aggravates me sometimes," said Christie, laughing, as she put a particularly big berry in the green plate to atone for her frankness.

"How?" asked Mr. Power, interested in these little revelations.

"Well, he *won't* be ambitious. I try to stir him up, for he has talents; I've found that out: but he won't seem to care for any thing but watching over his mother, reading his old books, and making flowers bloom double when they ought to be single."

"There are worse ambitions than those, Christie. I know many a man who would be far better employed in cherishing a sweet old woman, studying Plato, and doubling the beauty of a flower, than in selling principles for money, building up a cheap reputation that dies with him, or chasing pleasures that turn to ashes in his mouth."

"Yes, sir; but isn't it natural for a young man to have some personal aim or aspiration to live for? If David was a weak or dull man I could understand it; but I seem to feel a power, a possibility for something higher and better than any thing I see, and this frets me. He is so good, I want him to be great also in some way."

"A wise man says, 'The essence of greatness is the perception that virtue is enough.' *I* think David one of the most ambitious men I ever knew, because at thirty he has discovered this truth, and taken it to heart. Many men can be what the world calls great: very few men are what God calls good. This is the harder task to choose, yet the only success that satisfies, the only honor that outlives death. These faithful lives, whether seen of men or hidden in corners, are the salvation of the world, and few of us fail to acknowledge it in the hours when we are brought close to the heart of things, and see a little as God sees."

Christie did not speak for a moment: Mr. Power's voice had been so grave, and his words so earnest that she could not answer lightly, but sat turning over the new thoughts in her mind. Presently she said, in a penitent but not quite satisfied tone:

"Of course you are right, sir. I'll try not to care for the outward and visible signs of these hidden virtues; but I'm afraid I still shall have a hankering for the worldly honors that are so valued by most people."

"'Success and glory are the children of hard work and God's favor,' according to Æschylus, and you will find he was right. David got a heavy blow some years ago as I told you, I think; and he took it hard, but it did not spoil him: it made a man of him; and, if I am not much mistaken, he will yet do something to be proud of, though the world may never hear of it."

"I hope so!" and Christie's face brightened at the thought.

"Nevertheless you look as if you doubted it, O you of little faith. Every one has two sides to his nature: David has shown you the least interesting one, and you judge accordingly. I think he will show you the other side some day,—for you are one of the women who win confidence without trying,—and then you will know the real David. Don't expect too much, or quarrel with the imperfections that make him human; but take him for what he is worth, and help him if you can to make his life a brave and good one."

"I will, sir," answered Christie so meekly that Mr. Power

laughed; for this confessional in the strawberry bed amused him very much.

"You are a hero-worshipper, my dear; and if people don't come up to the mark you are so disappointed that you fail to see the fine reality which remains when the pretty romance ends. Saints walk about the world today as much as ever, but instead of haircloth and halos they now wear"—

"Broadcloth and wide-brimmed hats," added Christie, looking up as if she had already found a better St. Thomas than any the church ever canonized.

He thanked her with a smile, and went on with a glance toward the meadow.

"And knights go crusading as gallantly as ever against the giants and the dragons, though you don't discover it, because, instead of banner, lance, and shield they carry"—

"Bushel-baskets, spades, and sweet-flag for their mothers," put in Christie again, as David came up the path with the loam he had been digging.

Both began to laugh, and he joined in the merriment without knowing why, as he put down his load, took off his hat, and shook hands with his honored guest.

"What's the joke?" he asked, refreshing himself with the handful of berries Christie offered him.

"Don't tell," she whispered, looking dismayed at the idea of letting him know what she had said of him.

But Mr. Power answered tranquilly:

"We were talking about coins, and Christie was expressing her opinion of one I showed her. The face and date she understands; but the motto puzzles her, and she has not seen the reverse side yet, so does not know its value. She will some day; and then she will agree with me, I think, that it is *sterling* gold."

The emphasis on the last words enlightened David: his sunburnt cheek reddened, but he only shook his head, saying: "She will find a brass farthing I'm afraid, sir," and began to crumble a handful of loam about the roots of a carnation that seemed to have sprung up by chance at the foot of the apple-tree.

"How did that get there?" asked Christie, with sudden interest in the flower.

"It dropped when I was setting out the others, took root,

and looked so pretty and comfortable that I left it. These waifs sometimes do better than the most carefully tended ones: I only dig round them a bit and leave them to sun and air."

Mr. Power looked at Christie with so much meaning in his face that it was her turn to color now. But with feminine perversity she would not own herself mistaken, and answered with eyes as full of meaning as his own:

"I like the single ones best: double-carnations are so untidy, all bursting out of the calyx as if the petals had quarrelled and could not live together."

"The single ones are seldom perfect, and look poor and incomplete with little scent or beauty," said unconscious David propping up the thin-leaved flower, that looked like a pale solitary maiden, beside the great crimson and white carnations near by, filling the air with spicy odor.

"I suspect you will change your mind by and by, Christie, as your taste improves, and you will learn to think the double ones the handsomest," added Mr. Power, wondering in his benevolent heart if he would ever be the gardener to mix the colors of the two human plants before him.

"I must go," and David shouldered his basket as if he felt he might be in the way.

"So must I, or they will be waiting for me at the hospital. Give me a handful of flowers, David: they often do the poor souls more good than my prayers or preaching."

Then they went away, and left Christie sitting in the strawberry bed, thinking that David looked less than ever like a hero with his blue shirt, rough straw hat, and big boots; also wondering if he *would* ever show her his best side, and if she would like it when she saw it.

# *Chapter XII*

O N the fourth of September, Christie woke up, saying to herself: "It is my birthday, but no one knows it, so I shall get no presents. Ah, well, I'm too old for that now, I suppose;" but she sighed as she said it, for well she knew one never is too old to be remembered and beloved.

Just then the door opened, and Mrs. Sterling entered, carrying what looked very like a pile of snow-flakes in her arms. Laying this upon the bed, she kissed Christie, saying with a tone and gesture that made the words a benediction:

"A happy birthday, and God bless thee, my daughter!"

Before Christie could do more than hug both gift and giver, a great bouquet came flying in at the open window, aimed with such skill that it fell upon the bed, while David's voice called out from below: "A happy birthday, Christie, and many of them!"

"How sweet, how kind of you, this is! I didn't dream you knew about to-day, and never thought of such a beautiful surprise," cried Christie, touched and charmed by this unexpected celebration.

"Thee mentioned it once long ago, and we remembered. They are very humble gifts, my dear; but we could not let the day pass without some token of the thanks we owe thee for these months of faithful service and affectionate companionship."

Christie had no answer to this little address, and was about to cry as the only adequate expression of her feelings, when a hearty "Hear! Hear!" from below made her laugh, and call out:

"You conspirators! how dare you lay plots, and then exult over me when I can't find words to thank you? I always did think you were a set of angels, and now I'm quite sure of it."

"Thee may be right about Davy, but *I* am only a prudent old woman, and have taken much pleasure in privately knitting this light wrap to wear when thee sits in the porch, for the evenings will soon grow chilly. My son did not know what to get, and finally decided that flowers would suit thee best; so he made a bunch of those thee loves, and would toss it in as if he was a boy."

"I like that way, and both my presents suit me exactly," said Christie, wrapping the fleecy shawl about her, and admiring the nosegay in which her quick eye saw all her favorites, even to a plumy spray of the little wild asters which she loved so much.

"Now, child, I will step down, and see about breakfast. Take thy time; for this is to be a holiday, and we mean to make it a happy one if we can."

With that the old lady went away, and Christie soon followed, looking very fresh and blithe as she ran down smiling behind her great bouquet. David was in the porch, training up the morning-glories that bloomed late and lovely in that sheltered spot. He turned as she approached, held out his hand, and bent a little as if he was moved to add a tenderer greeting. But he did not, only held the hand she gave him for a moment, as he said with the paternal expression unusually visible:

"I wished you many happy birthdays; and, if you go on getting younger every year like this, you will surely have them."

It was the first compliment he had ever paid her, and she liked it, though she shook her head as if disclaiming it, and answered brightly:

"I used to think many years would be burdensome, and just before I came here I felt as if I could not bear another one. But now I like to live, and hope I shall a long, long time."

"I'm glad of that; and how do you mean to spend these long years of yours?" asked David, brushing back the lock of hair that was always falling into his eyes, as if he wanted to see more clearly the hopeful face before him.

"In doing what your morning-glories do,—climb up as far and as fast as I can before the frost comes," answered Christie, looking at the pretty symbols she had chosen.

"You have got on a good way already then," began David, smiling at her fancy.

"Oh no, I haven't!" she said quickly. "I'm only about half way up. See here: I'll tell how it is;" and, pointing to the different parts of the flowery wall, she added in her earnest way: "I've watched these grow, and had many thoughts about them, as I sit sewing in the porch. These variegated ones down low are my childish fancies; most of them gone to seed you see. These lovely blue ones of all shades are my girlish dreams and hopes and plans. Poor things! some are dead, some torn by the wind, and only a few pale ones left quite perfect. Here you observe they grow sombre with a tinge of purple; that means pain and gloom, and there is where I was when I came here. Now they turn from those sad colors to crimson, rose, and soft pink. That's the happiness and health I found here. You and your dear mother planted them, and you see how strong and bright they are."

She lifted up her hand, and gathering one of the great rosy cups offered it to him, as if it were brimful of the thanks she could not utter. He comprehended, took it with a quiet "Thank you," and stood looking at it for a moment, as if her little compliment pleased him very much.

"And these?" he said presently, pointing to the delicate violet bells that grew next the crimson ones.

The color deepened a shade in Christie's cheek, but she went on with no other sign of shyness; for with David she always spoke out frankly, because she could not help it.

"Those mean love to me, not passion: the deep red ones half hidden under the leaves mean that. My violet flowers are the best and purest love we can know: the sort that makes life beautiful and lasts for ever. The white ones that come next are tinged with that soft color here and there, and they mean holiness. I know there will be love in heaven; so, whether I ever find it here or not, I am sure I shall not miss it wholly."

Then, as if glad to leave the theme that never can be touched without reverent emotion by a true woman, she added, looking up to where a few spotless blossoms shone like silver in the light:

"Far away there in the sunshine are my highest aspirations. I cannot reach them: but I can look up, and see their beauty; believe in them, and try to follow where they lead; remember that frost comes latest to those that bloom the highest; and keep my beautiful white flowers as long as I can."

"The mush is ready; come to breakfast, children," called Mrs. Sterling, as she crossed the hall with a teapot in her hand.

Christie's face fell, then she exclaimed laughing: "That's

always the way; I never take a poetic flight but in comes the mush, and spoils it all."

"Not a bit; and that's where women are mistaken. Souls and bodies should go on together; and you will find that a hearty breakfast won't spoil the little hymn the morning-glories sung;" and David set her a good example by eating two bowls of hasty-pudding and milk, with the lovely flower in his button-hole.

"Now, what are we to do next?" asked Christie, when the usual morning work was finished.

"In about ten minutes thee will see, I think," answered Mrs. Sterling, glancing at the clock, and smiling at the bright expectant look in the younger woman's eyes.

She did see; for in less than ten minutes the rumble of an omnibus was heard, a sound of many voices, and then the whole Wilkins brood came whooping down the lane. It was good to see Ma Wilkins jog ponderously after in full state and festival array; her bonnet trembling with bows, red roses all over her gown, and a parasol of uncommon brilliancy brandished joyfully in her hand. It was better still to see her hug Christie, when the latter emerged, flushed and breathless, from the chaos of arms, legs, and chubby faces in which she was lost for several tumultuous moments; and it was best of all to see the good woman place her cherished "bunnit" in the middle of the parlor table as a choice and lovely ornament, administer the family pocket-handkerchief all round, and then settle down with a hearty:

"Wal, now, Mis Sterlin', you've no idee how tickled we all was when Mr. David came, and told us you was goin' to have a galy here to-day. It was so kind of providential, for 'Lisha was invited out to a day's pleasurin', so I could leave jest as wal as not. The childern's ben hankerin' to come the wust kind, and go plummin' as they did last month, though I told 'em berries was gone weeks ago. I reelly thought I'd never get 'em here whole, they trained so in that bus. Wash would go on the step, and kep fallin' off; Gusty's hat blew out a winder; them two bad boys tumbled round loose; and dear little Victory set like a lady, only I found she'd got both feet in the basket right atop of the birthday cake, I made a puppose for Christie."

"It hasn't hurt it a bit; there was a cloth over it, and I like it all the better for the marks of Totty's little feet, bless 'em!" and Christie cuddled the culprit with one hand while she revealed the damaged delicacy with the other, wondering inwardly what evil star was always in the ascendant when Mrs. Wilkins made cake.

"Now, my dear, you jest go and have a good frolic with them childern, I'm a goin' to git dinner, and you a goin' to play; so we don't want to see no more of you till the bell rings," said Mrs. Wilkins pinning up her gown, and "shooing" her brood out of the room, which they entirely filled.

Catching up her hat Christie obeyed, feeling as much like a child as any of the excited six. The revels that followed no pen can justly record, for Goths and Vandals on the rampage but feebly describes the youthful Wilkinses when their spirits effervesced after a month's bottling up in close home quarters.

David locked the greenhouse door the instant he saw them; and pervaded the premises generally like a most affable but very watchful policeman, for the ravages those innocents committed much afflicted him. Yet he never had the heart to say a word of reproof, when he saw their raptures over dandelions, the relish with which they devoured fruit, and the good it did the little souls and bodies to enjoy unlimited liberty, green grass, and country air, even for a day.

Christie usually got them into the big meadow as soon as possible, and there let them gambol at will; while she sat on the broken bough of an apple-tree, and watched her flock like an old-fashioned shepherdess. To-day she did so; and when the children were happily sailing boats, tearing to and fro like wild colts, or discovering the rustic treasures Nurse Nature lays ready to gladden little hearts and hands, Christie sat idly making a garland of green brakes, and ruddy sumach leaves ripened before the early frost had come.

David saw her there, and, feeling that he might come off guard for a time, went strolling down to lean upon the wall, and chat in the friendly fashion that had naturally grown up between these fellow-workers. She was waiting for the new supply of ferns little Adelaide was getting for her by the wall; and while she waited she sat resting her cheek upon her hand, and smiling to herself, as if she saw some pleasant picture in the green grass at her feet.

A FRIENDLY CHAT.

"Now I wonder what she's thinking about," said David's voice close by, and Christie straightway answered:

"Philip Fletcher."

"And who is he?" asked David, settling his elbow in a comfortable niche between the mossy stones, so that he could "lean and loaf" at his ease.

"The brother of the lady whose children I took care of;" and Christie wished she had thought before she answered that first question, for in telling her adventures at different times she had omitted all mention of this gentleman.

"Tell about him, as the children say: your experiences are always interesting, and you look as if this man was uncommonly entertaining in some way," said David, indolently inclined to be amused.

"Oh, dear no, not at all entertaining! invalids seldom are, and he was sick and lazy, conceited and very cross sometimes." Christie's heart rather smote her as she said this, remembering the last look poor Fletcher gave her.

"A nice man to be sure; but I don't see any thing to smile about," persisted David, who liked reasons for things; a masculine trait often very trying to feminine minds.

"I was thinking of a little quarrel we once had. He found out that I had been an actress; for I basely did not mention that fact when I took the place, and so got properly punished for my deceit. I thought he'd tell his sister of course, so I did it myself, and retired from the situation as much disgusted with Christie Devon as you are."

"Perhaps I ought to be, but I don't find that I am. Do you know I think that old Fletcher was a sneak?" and David looked as if he would rather like to mention his opinion to that gentleman.

"He probably thought he was doing his duty to the children: few people would approve of an actress for a teacher you know. He had seen me play, and remembered it all of a sudden, and told me of it: that was the way it came about," said Christie hastily, feeling that she must get out of the scrape as soon as possible, or she would be driven to tell every thing in justice to Mr. Fletcher.

"I should like to see you act."

"You a Quaker, and express such a worldly and dreadful wish?" cried Christie, much amused, and very grateful that his thoughts had taken a new direction.

"I'm not, and never have been. Mother married out of the sect, and, though she keeps many of her old ways, always left me free to believe what I chose. I wear drab because I like it, and say 'thee' to her because she likes it, and it is pleasant to have a little word all our own. I've been to theatres, but I don't care much for them. Perhaps I should if I'd had Fletcher's luck in seeing *you* play."

"You didn't lose much: I was not a good actress; though now and then when I liked my part I did pretty well they said," answered Christie, modestly.

"Why didn't you go back after the accident?" asked David, who had heard that part of the story.

"I felt that it was bad for me, and so retired to private life."

"Do you ever regret it?"

"Sometimes when the restless fit is on me: but not so often now as I used to do; for on the whole I'd rather *be* a woman than *act* a queen."

"Good!" said David, and then added persuasively: "But you *will* play for me some time: won't you? I've a curious desire to see you do it."

"Perhaps I'll try," replied Christie, flattered by his interest, and not unwilling to display her little talent.

"Who are you making that for? it's very pretty," asked David, who seemed to be in an inquiring frame of mind that day.

"Any one who wants it. I only do it for the pleasure: I always liked pretty things; but, since I have lived among flowers and natural people, I seem to care more than ever for beauty of all kinds, and love to make it if I can without stopping for any reason but the satisfaction."

> "'Tell them, dear, that if eyes were made for seeing,
> "'Then beauty is its own excuse for being,'"

observed David, who had a weakness for poetry, and, finding she liked his sort, quoted to Christie almost as freely as to himself.

"Exactly, so look at that and enjoy it," and she pointed to the child standing knee-deep in graceful ferns, looking as if she grew there, a living buttercup, with her buff frock off at one plump shoulder and her bright hair shining in the sun.

Before David could express his admiration, the little picture was spoilt; for Christie called out, "Come, Vic, bring me some more pretties!" startling baby so that she lost her balance, and disappeared with a muffled cry, leaving nothing to be seen but a pair of small convulsive shoes, soles uppermost, among the brakes. David took a leap, reversed Vic, and then let her compose her little feelings by sticking bits of green in all the button-holes of his coat, as he sat on the wall while she stood beside him in the safe shelter of his arm.

"You are very like an Englishman," said Christie, after watching the pair for a few minutes.

"How do you know?" asked David, looking surprised.

"There were several in our company, and I found them very

much alike. Blunt and honest, domestic and kind; hard to get at, but true as steel when once won; not so brilliant and original as Americans, perhaps, but more solid and steadfast. On the whole, I think them the manliest men in the world," answered Christie, in the decided way young people have of expressing their opinions.

"You speak as if you had known and studied a great variety of men," said David, feeling that he need not resent the comparison she had made.

"I have, and it has done me good. Women who stand alone in the world, and have their own way to make, have a better chance to know men truly than those who sit safe at home and only see one side of mankind. We lose something; but I think we gain a great deal that is more valuable than admiration, flattery, and the superficial service most men give to our sex. Some one says, 'Companionship teaches men and women to know, judge, and treat one another justly.' I believe it; for we who are compelled to be fellow-workers with men understand and value them more truly than many a belle who has a dozen lovers sighing at her feet. I see their faults and follies; but I also see so much to honor, love, and trust, that I feel as if the world was full of brothers. Yes, as a general rule, men have been kinder to me than women; and if I wanted a staunch friend I'd choose a man, for they wear better than women, who ask too much, and cannot see that friendship lasts longer if a little respect and reserve go with the love and confidence."

Christie had spoken soberly, with no thought of flattery or effect; for the memory of many kindnesses bestowed on her by many men, from rough Joe Butterfield to Mr. Power, gave warmth and emphasis to her words.

The man sitting on the wall appreciated the compliment to his sex, and proved that he deserved his share of it by taking it exactly as she meant it, and saying heartily:

"I like that, Christie, and wish more women thought and spoke as you do."

"If they had had my experience they would, and not be ashamed of it. I am so old now I can say these things and not be misjudged; for even some sensible people think this honest sort of fellowship impossible if not improper. I don't, and I never shall, so if I can ever do any thing for you, David, forget that I am a woman and tell me as freely as if I was a younger brother."

"I wish you were!"

"So do I; you'd make a splendid elder brother."

"No, a very bad one."

There was a sudden sharpness in David's voice that jarred on Christie's ear and made her look up quickly. She only caught a glimpse of his face, and saw that it was strangely troubled, as he swung himself over the wall with little Vic on his arm and went toward the house, saying abruptly:

"Baby's sleepy: she must go in."

Christie sat some time longer, wondering what she had said to disturb him, and when the bell rang went in still perplexed. But David looked as usual, and the only trace of disquiet was an occasional hasty shaking back of the troublesome lock, and a slight knitting of the brows; two tokens, as she had learned to know, of impatience or pain.

She was soon so absorbed in feeding the children, hungry and clamorous as young birds for their food, that she forgot every thing else. When dinner was done and cleared away, she devoted herself to Mrs. Wilkins for an hour or two, while Mrs. Sterling took her nap, the infants played riotously in the lane, and David was busy with orders.

The arrival of Mr. Power drew every one to the porch to welcome him. As he handed Christie a book, he asked with a significant smile:

"Have you found him yet?"

She glanced at the title of the new gift, read "Heroes and Hero-worship," and answered merrily:

"No, sir, but I'm looking hard."

"Success to your search," and Mr. Power turned to greet David, who approached.

"Now, what shall we play?" asked Christie, as the children gathered about her demanding to be amused.

George Washington suggested leap-frog, and the others added equally impracticable requests; but Mrs. Wilkins settled the matter by saying:

"Let's have some play-actin', Christie. That used to tickle the children amazin'ly, and I was never tired of hearin' them pieces, specially the solemn ones."

"Yes, yes! do the funny girl with the baby, and the old woman, and the lady that took pison and had fits!" shouted the children, charmed with the idea.

Christie felt ready for any thing just then, and gave them Tilly Slowboy, Miss Miggs, and Mrs. Gummage, in her best style, while the young folks rolled on the grass in ecstasies, and Mrs. Wilkins laughed till she cried.

"Now a touch of tragedy!" said Mr. Power, who sat under the elm, with David leaning on the back of his chair, both applauding heartily.

"You insatiable people! do you expect me to give you low comedy and heavy tragedy all alone? I'm equal to melodrama I think, and I'll give you Miss St. Clair as Juliet, if you wait a moment."

Christie stepped into the house, and soon reappeared with a white table-cloth draped about her, two dishevelled locks of hair on her shoulders, and the vinegar cruet in her hand, that being the first bottle she could find. She meant to burlesque the poison scene, and began in the usual ranting way; but she soon forgot St. Clair in poor Juliet, and did it as she had often longed to do it, with all the power and passion she possessed. Very faulty was her rendering, but the earnestness she put into it made it most effective to her uncritical audience, who "brought down the house," when she fell upon the grass with her best stage drop, and lay there getting her breath after the mouthful of vinegar she had taken in the excitement of the moment.

She was up again directly, and, inspired by this superb success, ran in and presently reappeared as Lady Macbeth with Mrs. Wilkins's scarlet shawl for royal robes, and the leafy chaplet of the morning for a crown. She took the stage with some difficulty, for the unevenness of the turf impaired the majesty of her tragic stride, and fixing her eyes on an invisible Thane (who cut his part shamefully, and spoke in the gruffest of gruff voices) she gave them the dagger scene.

David as the orchestra, had been performing a drum solo on the back of a chair with two of the corn-cobs Victoria had been building houses with; but, when Lady Macbeth said, "Give *me* the daggers," Christie plucked the cobs suddenly from his hands, looking so fiercely scornful, and lowering upon him so wrathfully with her corked brows that he ejaculated an involuntary, "Bless me!" as he stepped back quite daunted.

Being in the spirit of her part, Christie closed with the sleep-walking scene, using the table-cloth again, while a towel composed the tragic nightcap of her ladyship. This was an imitation, and having a fine model and being a good mimic, she did well; for the children sat staring with round eyes, the gentlemen watched the woful face and gestures intently, and Mrs. Wilkins took a long breath at the end, exclaiming: "I never did see the beat of that for gastliness! My sister Clarissy used to walk in her sleep, but she warn't half so kind of dreadful."

"If she had had the murder of a few friends on her conscience, I dare say she would have been," said Christie, going in to make herself tidy.

"Well, how do you like her as an actress?" asked Mr. Power of David, who stood looking, as if he still saw and heard the haunted lady.

"Very much; but better as a woman. I'd no idea she had it in her," answered David, in a wonder-stricken tone.

"Plenty of tragedy and comedy in all of us," began Mr. Power; but David said hastily:

"Yes, but few of us have passion and imagination enough to act Shakspeare in that way."

"Very true: Christie herself could not give a whole character in that style, and would not think of trying."

"*I* think she could; and I'd like to see her try it," said David, much impressed by the dramatic ability which Christie's usual quietude had most effectually hidden.

He was still thinking about it, when she came out again. Mr. Power beckoned to her, saying, as she came and stood before him, flushed and kindled with her efforts:

"Now, you must give me a bit from the 'Merchant of Venice.' Portia is a favorite character of mine, and I want to see if you can do any thing with it."

"No, sir, I cannot. I used to study it, but it was too sober to suit me. I am not a judicial woman, so I gave it up," answered Christie, much flattered by his request, and amused at the respectful way in which David looked at her. Then, as if it just occurred to her, she added, "I remember one little speech that

I can say to *you*, sir, with great truth, and I will, since you like that play."

Still standing before him, she bent her head a little, and with a graceful gesture of the hands, as if offering something, she delivered with heartfelt emphasis the first part of Portia's pretty speech to her fortunate suitor:

"You see me, Lord Bassanio, where I stand,
  Such as I am: though, for myself alone,
  I would not be ambitious in my wish,
  To wish myself much better; yet for you,
  I would be trebled twenty times myself;
  A thousand times more fair, ten thousand times more rich;
  That, only to stand high in your account,
  I might in virtues, beauties, livings, friends,
  Exceed account: but the full sum of me
  Is sum of something; which, to term in gross,
  Is an unlesson'd girl, unschool'd, unpractis'd:—
  Happy in this, she is not yet so old
  But she may learn; happier than this,
  She is not bred so dull but she can learn;
  Happiest of all, is that her willing spirit
  Commits itself to yours to be directed,
  As from her lord, her governor, her king."

David applauded vigorously; but Mr. Power rose silently, looking both touched and surprised; and, drawing Christie's hand through his arm, led her away into the garden for one of the quiet talks that were so much to her.

When they returned, the Wilkinses were preparing to depart; and, after repeated leave-takings, finally got under way, were packed into the omnibus, and rumbled off with hats, hands, and handkerchiefs waving from every window. Mr. Power soon followed, and peace returned to the little house in the lane.

Later in the evening, when Mrs. Sterling was engaged with a neighbor, who had come to confide some affliction to the good lady, Christie went into the porch, and found David sitting on the step, enjoying the mellow moonlight and the balmy air. As he did not speak, she sat down silently, folded her hands in her lap, and began to enjoy the beauty of the night in her own way. Presently she became conscious that David's eyes had turned from the moon to her own face. He sat in the shade, she in the light, and he was looking at her with the new expression which amused her.

"Well, what is it? You look as if you never saw me before," she said, smiling.

"I feel as if I never had," he answered, still regarding her as if she had been a picture.

"What do I look like?"

"A peaceful, pious nun, just now."

"Oh! that is owing to my pretty shawl. I put it on in honor of the day, though it is a trifle warm, I confess." And Christie stroked the soft folds about her shoulders, and settled the corner that lay lightly on her hair. "I do feel peaceful to-night, but not pious. I am afraid I never shall do that," she added soberly.

"Why not?"

"Well, it does not seem to be my nature, and I don't know how to change it. I want something to keep me steady, but I can't find it. So I whiffle about this way and that, and sometimes think I am a most degenerate creature."

"That is only human nature, so don't be troubled. We are all compasses pointing due north. We get shaken often, and the needle varies in spite of us; but the minute we are quiet, it points right, and we have only to follow it."

"The keeping quiet is just what I cannot do. Your mother shows me how lovely it is, and I try to imitate it; but this restless soul of mine will ask questions and doubt and fear, and worry me in many ways. What shall I do to keep it still?" asked Christie, smiling, yet earnest.

"Let it alone: you cannot force these things, and the best way is to wait till the attraction is strong enough to keep the needle steady. Some people get their ballast slowly, some don't need much, and some have to work hard for theirs."

"Did you?" asked Christie; for David's voice fell a little, as he uttered the last words.

"I have not got much yet."

"I think you have. Why, David, you are always cheerful and contented, good and generous. If that is not true piety, what is?"

"You are very much deceived, and I am sorry for it," said David, with the impatient gesture of the head, and a troubled look.

"Prove it!" And Christie looked at him with such sincere respect and regard, that his honest nature would not let him accept it, though it gratified him much.

He made no answer for a minute. Then he said slowly, as if feeling a modest man's hesitation to speak of himself, yet urged to it by some irresistible impulse:

"I *will* prove it if you won't mind the unavoidable egotism; for I cannot let you think me so much better than I am. Outwardly I seem to you 'cheerful, contented, generous, and good.' In reality I am sad, dissatisfied, bad, and selfish: see if I'm not. I often tire of this quiet life, hate my work, and long to break away, and follow my own wild and wilful impulses, no matter where they lead. Nothing keeps me at such times but my mother and God's patience."

David began quietly; but the latter part of this confession was made with a sudden impetuosity that startled Christie, so utterly unlike his usual self-control was it. She could only look at him with the surprise she felt. His face was in the shadow; but she saw that it was flushed, his eyes excited, and in his voice she heard an undertone that made it sternly self-accusing.

"I am not a hypocrite," he went on rapidly, as if driven to speak in spite of himself. "I try to be what I seem, but it is too hard sometimes and I despair. Especially hard is it to feel that I have learned to feign happiness so well that others are entirely deceived. Mr. Power and mother know me as I am: other friends I have not, unless you will let me call you one. Whether you do or not after this, I respect you too much to let you delude yourself about my virtues, so I tell you the truth and abide the consequences."

He looked up at her as he paused, with a curious mixture of pride and humility in his face, and squared his broad shoulders as if he had thrown off a burden that had much oppressed him.

Christie offered him her hand, saying in a tone that did his heart good: "The consequences are that I respect, admire, and trust you more than ever, and feel proud to be your friend."

David gave the hand a strong and grateful pressure, said,

"Thank you," in a moved tone, and then leaned back into the shadow, as if trying to recover from this unusual burst of confidence, won from him by the soft magic of time, place, and companionship.

Fearing he would regret the glimpse he had given her, and anxious to show how much she liked it, Christie talked on to give him time to regain composure.

"I always thought in reading the lives of saints or good men of any time, that their struggles were the most interesting and helpful things recorded. Human imperfection only seems to make real piety more possible, and to me more beautiful; for where others have conquered I can conquer, having suffered as they suffer, and seen their hard-won success. That is the sort of religion I want; something to hold by, live in, and enjoy, if I can only get it."

"I know you will." He said it heartily, and seemed quite calm again; so Christie obeyed the instinct which told her that questions would be good for David, and that he was in the mood for answering them.

"May I ask you something," she began a little timidly.

"Any thing, Christie," he answered instantly.

"That is a rash promise: I am a woman, and therefore curious; what shall you do if I take advantage of the privilege?"

"Try and see."

"I will be discreet, and only ask one thing," she replied, charmed with her success. "You said just now that you had learned to feign happiness. I wish you would tell me how you do it, for it is such an excellent imitation I shall be quite content with it till I can learn the genuine thing."

David fingered the troublesome forelock thoughtfully for a moment, then said, with something of the former impetuosity coming back into his voice and manner:

"I will tell you all about it; that's the best way: I know I shall some day because I can't help it; so I may as well have done with it now, since I have begun. It is not interesting, mind you,—only a grim little history of one man's fight with the world, the flesh, and the devil: will you have it?"

"Oh, yes!" answered Christie, so eagerly that David laughed, in spite of the bitter memories stirring at his heart.

"So like a woman, always ready to hear and forgive sinners," he said, then took a long breath, and added rapidly:

"I'll put it in as few words as possible and much good may it do you. Some years ago I was desperately miserable; never mind why: I dare say I shall tell you all about it some day if I go on at this rate. Well, being miserable, as I say, every thing looked black and bad to me: I hated all men, distrusted all women, doubted the existence of God, and was a forlorn wretch generally. Why I did not go to the devil I can't say: I did start once or twice; but the thought of that dear old woman in there sitting all alone and waiting for me dragged me back, and kept me here till the first recklessness was over. People talk about duty being sweet; I have not found it so, but there it was: I should have been a brute to shirk it; so I took it up, and held on desperately till it grew bearable."

"It *has* grown sweet now, David, I am sure," said Christie, very low.

"No, not yet," he answered with the stern honesty that would not let him deceive himself or others, cost what it might to be true. "There is a certain solid satisfaction in it that I did not use to find. It is not a mere dogged persistence now, as it once was, and that is a step towards loving it perhaps."

He spoke half to himself, and sat leaning his head on both hands propped on his knees, looking down as if the weight of the old trouble bent his shoulders again.

"What more, David?" said Christie.

"Only this. When I found I had got to live, and live manfully, I said to myself, 'I must have help or I cannot do it.' To no living soul could I tell my grief, not even to my mother, for she had her own to bear: no human being could help me, yet I *must* have help or give up shamefully. Then I did what others do when all else fails to sustain them; I turned to God: not humbly, not devoutly or trustfully, but doubtfully, bitterly, and rebelliously; for I said in my despairing heart, 'If there *is* a God, let Him help me, and I will believe.' He did help me, and I kept my word."

"Oh, David, how?" whispered Christie after a moment's silence, for the last words were solemn in their earnestness.

"The help did not come at once. No miracle answered me,

and I thought my cry had not been heard. But it had, and slowly something like submission came to me. It was not cheerful nor pious: it was only a dumb, sad sort of patience without hope or faith. It was better than desperation; so I accepted it, and bore the inevitable as well as I could. Presently, courage seemed to spring up again: I was ashamed to be beaten in the first battle, and some sort of blind instinct made me long to break away from the past and begin again. My father was dead; mother left all to me, and followed where I led. I sold the old place, bought this, and, shutting out the world as much as I could, I fell to work as if my life depended on it. That was five or six years ago: and for a long time I delved away without interest or pleasure, merely as a safety-valve for my energies, and a means of living; for I gave up all my earlier hopes and plans when the trouble came.

"I did not love my work; but it was good for me, and helped cure my sick soul. I never guessed why I felt better, but dug on with indifference first, then felt pride in my garden, then interest in the plants I tended, and by and by I saw what they had done for me, and loved them like true friends."

A broad woodbine leaf had been fluttering against David's head, as he leaned on the slender pillar of the porch where it grew. Now, as if involuntarily, he laid his cheek against it with a caressing gesture, and sat looking over the garden lying dewy and still in the moonlight, with the grateful look of a man who has learned the healing miracles of Nature and how near she is to God.

"Mr. Power helped you: didn't he?" said Christie, longing to hear more.

"So much! I never can tell you what he was to me, nor how I thank him. To him, and to my work I owe the little I have won in the way of strength and comfort after years of effort. I see now the compensation that comes out of trouble, the lovely possibilities that exist for all of us, and the infinite patience of God, which is to me one of the greatest of His divine attributes. I have only got so far, but things grow easier as one goes on; and if I keep tugging I may yet *be* the cheerful, contented man I seem. That is all, Christie, and a longer story than I meant to tell."

"Not long enough: some time you will tell me more perhaps, since you have once begun. It seems quite natural now, and I am so pleased and honored by your confidence. But I cannot help wondering what made you do it all at once," said Christie presently, after they had listened to a whippoorwill, and watched the flight of a downy owl.

"I do not think I quite know myself, unless it was because I have been on my good behavior since you came, and, being a humbug, as I tell you, was forced to unmask in spite of myself. There are limits to human endurance, and the proudest man longs to unpack his woes before a sympathizing friend now and then. I have been longing to do this for some time; but I never like to disturb mother's peace, or take Mr. Power from those who need him more. So to-day, when you so sweetly offered to help me if you could, it quite went to my heart, and seemed so friendly and comfortable, I could not resist trying it to-night, when you began about my imaginary virtues. That is the truth, I believe: now, what shall we do about it?"

"Just go on, and do it again whenever you feel like it. I know what loneliness is, and how telling worries often cures them. I meant every word I said this morning, and will prove it by doing any thing in the world I can for you. Believe this, and let me be your friend."

They had risen, as a stir within told them the guest was going; and as Christie spoke she was looking up with the moonlight full upon her face.

If there had been any hidden purpose in her mind, any false sentiment, or trace of coquetry in her manner, it would have spoiled that hearty little speech of hers.

But in her heart was nothing but a sincere desire to prove gratitude and offer sympathy; in her manner the gentle frankness of a woman speaking to a brother; and in her face the earnestness of one who felt the value of friendship, and did not ask or give it lightly.

"I will," was David's emphatic answer, and then, as if to seal the bargain, he stooped down, and gravely kissed her on the forehead.

Christie was a little startled, but neither offended nor confused; for there was no love in that quiet kiss,—only respect, affection, and much gratitude; an involuntary demonstration from the lonely man to the true-hearted woman who had dared to come and comfort him.

Out trotted neighbor Miller, and that was the end of confidences in the porch; but David played melodiously on his flute that night, and Christie fell asleep saying happily to herself:

"Now we are all right, friends for ever, and every thing will go beautifully."

# Chapter XIII

KITTY.

E VERY thing *did* "go beautifully" for a time; so much so, that Christie began to think she really *had* "got religion." A delightful peace pervaded her soul, a new interest made the dullest task agreeable, and life grew so inexpressibly sweet that she felt as if she could forgive all her enemies, love her friends more than ever, and do any thing great, good, or glorious.

She had known such moods before, but they had never lasted long, and were not so intense as this; therefore, she was sure some blessed power had come to uphold and cheer her. She sang like a lark as she swept and dusted; thought high and happy thoughts among the pots and kettles, and, when she sat sewing, smiled unconsciously as if some deep satisfaction made sunshine from within. Heart and soul seemed to wake up and rejoice as naturally and beautifully as flowers in the spring. A soft brightness shone in her eyes, a fuller tone sounded in her voice, and her face grew young and blooming with the happiness that transfigures all it touches.

"Christie's growing handsome," David would say to his mother, as if she was a flower in which he took pride.

"Thee is a good gardener, Davy," the old lady would reply, and when he was busy would watch him with a tender sort of anxiety, as if to discover a like change in him.

But no alteration appeared, except more cheerfulness and less silence; for now there was no need to hide his real self, and all the social virtues in him came out delightfully after their long solitude.

In her present uplifted state, Christie could no more help regarding David as a martyr and admiring him for it, than she could help mixing sentiment with her sympathy. By the light of the late confessions, his life and character looked very different to her now. His apparent contentment was resignation; his cheerfulness, a manly contempt for complaint; his reserve, the modest reticence of one who, having done a hard duty well, desires no praise for it. Like all enthusiastic persons, Christie had a hearty admiration for self-sacrifice and self-control; and, while she learned to see David's virtues, she also exaggerated them, and could not do enough to show the daily increasing esteem and respect she felt for him, and to atone for the injustice she once did him.

She grubbed in the garden and green-house, and learned hard botanical names that she might be able to talk intelligently upon subjects that interested her comrade. Then, as autumn ended out-of-door work, she tried to make home more comfortable and attractive than ever.

David's room was her especial care; for now to her there was something pathetic in the place and its poor furnishing. He had fought many a silent battle there; won many a secret victory; and tried to cheer his solitude with the best thoughts the minds of the bravest, wisest men could give him.

She did not smile at the dilapidated idols now, but touched them tenderly, and let no dust obscure their well-beloved faces. She set the books in order daily, taking many a sip of refreshment from them by the way, and respectfully regarded those in unknown tongues, full of admiration for David's learning. She covered the irruptive sofa neatly; saw that the little vase was always clear and freshly filled; cared for the nursery in the gable-window; and preserved an exquisite neatness everywhere, which delighted the soul of the room's order-loving occupant.

She also—alas, for romance!—cooked the dishes David loved, and liked to see him enjoy them with the appetite which once had shocked her so. She watched over his buttons with a vigilance that would have softened the heart of the crustiest bachelor: she even gave herself the complexion of a lemon by wearing blue, because David liked the pretty contrast with his mother's drabs.

After recording that last fact, it is unnecessary to explain what was the matter with Christie. She honestly thought she had got religion; but it was piety's twin-sister, who produced this wonderful revival in her soul; and though she began in all good faith she presently discovered that she was

> "Not the first maiden
>  Who came but for friendship,
>  And took away love."

After the birthnight confessions, David found it easier to go on with the humdrum life he had chosen from a sense of duty; for now he felt as if he had not only a fellow-worker, but a comrade and friend who understood, sympathized with, and encouraged him by an interest and good-will inexpressibly comfortable and inspiring. Nothing disturbed the charm of the new league in those early days; for Christie was thoroughly simple and sincere, and did her womanly work with no thought of reward or love or admiration.

David saw this, and felt it more attractive than any gift of beauty or fascination of manner would have been. He had no desire to be a lover, having forbidden himself that hope; but he found it so easy and pleasant to be a friend that he reproached himself for not trying it before; and explained his neglect by the fact that Christie was not an ordinary woman, since none of all the many he had known and helped, had ever been any thing to him but objects of pity and protection.

Mrs. Sterling saw these changes with her wise, motherly eyes, but said nothing; for she influenced others by the silent power of character. Speaking little, and unusually gifted with the meditative habits of age, she seemed to live in a more peaceful world than this. As George MacDonald somewhere says, "Her soul seemed to sit apart in a sunny little room, safe from dust and noise, serenely regarding passers-by through the clear muslin curtains of her window."

Yet, she was neither cold nor careless, stern nor selfish, but ready to share all the joys and sorrows of those about her; and when advice was asked she gave it gladly. Christie had won her heart long ago, and now was as devoted as a daughter to her; lightening her cares so skilfully that many of them slipped naturally on to the young shoulders, and left the old lady much time for rest, or the lighter tasks fitted for feeble hands. Christie often called her "Mother," and felt herself rewarded for the hardest, humblest job she ever did when the sweet old voice said gratefully, "I thank thee, daughter."

Things were in this prosperous, not to say paradisiacal, state, when one member of the family began to make discoveries of an alarming nature. The first was that the Sunday pilgrimages to church were seasons of great refreshment to soul and body when David went also, and utter failures if he did not. Next, that the restless ambitions of all sorts were quite gone; for now Christie's mission seemed to be sitting in a quiet corner and making shirts in the most exquisite manner, while thinking about—well, say botany, or any kindred subject. Thirdly, that home was woman's sphere after all, and the perfect roasting of beef, brewing of tea, and concocting of delectable puddings, an end worth living for if masculine commendation rewarded the labor.

Fourthly, and worst of all, she discovered that she was not satisfied with half confidences, and quite pined to know all about "David's trouble." The little needle-book with the faded "Letty" on it haunted her; and when, after a pleasant evening below, she heard him pace his room for hours, or play melancholy airs upon the flute, she was jealous of that unknown woman who had such power to disturb his peace, and felt a strong desire to smash the musical confidante into whose responsive breast he poured his woe.

At this point Christie paused; and, after evading any explanation of these phenomena in the most skilful manner for a time, suddenly faced the fact, saying to herself with great candor and decision:

"I know what all this means: I'm beginning to like David more than is good for me. I see this clearly, and won't dodge any longer, but put a stop to it at once. Of course I can if I choose, and now is the time to do it; for I understand myself perfectly, and if I reach a certain point it is all over with me. That point I will *not* reach: David's heart is in that Letty's grave, and he only cares for me as a friend. I promised to be one to him, and I'll keep my word like an honest woman. It may not be easy; but all the sacrifices shall not be his, and I won't be a fool."

With praiseworthy resolution Christie set about the reformation without delay; not an easy task and one that taxed all her wit and wisdom to execute without betraying the motive for it. She decided that Mrs. Sterling must not be left alone on Sunday, so the young people took turns to go to church, and such dismal trips Christie had never known; for all her Sundays were bad weather, and Mr. Power seemed to hit on unusually uninteresting texts.

She talked while she sewed instead of indulging in dangerous thoughts, and Mrs. Sterling was surprised and entertained by this new loquacity. In the evening she read and studied with a diligence that amazed and rather disgusted David; since she kept all her lively chat for his mother, and pored over her books when he wanted her for other things.

"I'm trying to brighten up my wits," she said, and went on trying to stifle her affections.

But though "the absurdity," as she called the new revelation, was stopped externally, it continued with redoubled vigor internally. Each night she said, "this *must* be conquered," yet each morning it rose fair and strong to make the light and beauty of her day, and conquer her again. She did her best and bravest, but was forced at last to own that she could not "put a stop to it," because she had already reached the point where "it was all over with her."

Just at this critical moment an event occurred which completed Christie's defeat, and made her feel that her only safety lay in flight.

One evening she sat studying ferns, and heroically saying over and over, "Andiantum, Aspidium, and Asplenium, Trichomanes," while longing to go and talk delightfully to David, who sat musing by the fire.

"I can't go on so much longer," she thought despairingly. "Polypodium aureum, a native of Florida, is all very interesting in its place; but it doesn't help me to gain self-control a bit, and I shall disgrace myself if something doesn't happen very soon."

Something did happen almost instantly; for as she shut the

cover sharply on the poor Polypods, a knock was heard, and before David could answer it the door flew open and a girl ran in. Straight to him she went, and clinging to his arm said excitedly:

"Oh, do take care of me: I've run away again!"

"Why, Kitty, what's the matter now?" asked David, putting back her hood, and looking down at her with the paternal expression Christie had not seen for a long time, and missed very much.

"Father found me, and took me home, and wanted me to marry a dreadful man, and I wouldn't, so I ran away to you. He didn't know I came here before, and I'm safe if you'll let me stay," cried Kitty, still clinging and imploring.

"Of course I will, and glad to see you back again," answered David, adding pitifully, as he put her in his easy-chair, took her cloak and hood off and stood stroking her curly hair: "Poor little girl! it is hard to have to run away so much: isn't it?"

"Not if I come here; it's so pleasant I'd like to stay all my life," and Kitty took a long breath, as if her troubles were over now. "Who's that?" she asked suddenly, as her eye fell on Christie, who sat watching her with interest:

"That is our good friend Miss Devon. She came to take your place, and we got so fond of her we could not let her go," answered David with a gesture of introduction, quite unconscious that his position just then was about as safe and pleasant as that of a man between a lighted candle and an open powder barrel.

The two young women nodded to each other, took a swift survey, and made up their minds before David had poked the fire. Christie saw a pretty face with rosy cheeks, blue eyes, and brown rings of hair lying on the smooth, low forehead; a young face, but not childlike, for it was conscious of its own prettiness, and betrayed the fact by little airs and graces that reminded one of a coquettish kitten. Short and slender, she looked more youthful than she was; while a gay dress, with gilt ear-rings, locket at the throat, and a cherry ribbon in her hair made her a bright little figure in that plain room.

Christie suddenly felt as if ten years had been added to her age, as she eyed the new-comer, who leaned back in the great chair talking to David, who stood on the rug, evidently finding it pleasanter to look at the vivacious face before him than at the fire.

"Just the pretty, lively sort of girl sensible men often marry, and then discover how silly they are," thought Christie, taking up her work and assuming an indifferent air.

"She's a lady and nice looking, but I know I shan't like her," was Kitty's decision, as she turned away and devoted herself to David, hoping he would perceive how much she had improved and admire her accordingly.

"So you don't want to marry this Miles because he is not handsome. You'd better think again before you make up your mind. He is respectable, well off, and fond of you, it seems. Why not try it, Kitty? You need some one to take care of you sadly," David said, when her story had been told.

"If father plagues me much I may take the man; but I'd rather have the other one if he wasn't poor," answered Kitty with a side-long glance of the blue eyes, and a conscious smile on the red lips.

"Oh, there's another lover, is there?"

"Lots of 'em."

David laughed and looked at Christie as if inviting her to be amused with the freaks and prattle of a child. But Christie sewed away without a sign of interest.

"That won't do, Kitty: you are too young for much of such nonsense. I shall keep you here a while, and see if we can't settle matters both wisely and pleasantly," he said, shaking his head as sagely as a grandfather.

"I'm sure I wish you would: I love to stay here, you are always so good to me. I'm in no hurry to be married; and you won't make me: will you?"

Kitty rose as she spoke, and stood before him with a beseeching little gesture, and a confiding air quite captivating to behold.

Christie was suddenly seized with a strong desire to shake the girl and call her an "artful little hussy," but crushed this unaccountable impulse, and hemmed a pocket-handkerchief with reckless rapidity, while she stole covert glances at the *tableau* by the fire.

David put his finger under Kitty's round chin, and lifting her face looked into it, trying to discover if she really cared for this suitor who seemed so providentially provided for her. Kitty smiled and blushed, and dimpled under that grave look so prettily that it soon changed, and David let her go, saying indulgently:

"You shall not be troubled, for you are only a child after all. Let the lovers go, and stay and play with me, for I've been rather lonely lately."

"That's a reproach for me," thought Christie, longing to cry out: "No, no; send the girl away and let *me* be all in all to you." But she only turned up the lamp and pretended to be looking for a spool, while her heart ached and her eyes were too dim for seeing.

"I'm too old to play, but I'll stay and tease you as I used to, if Miles don't come and carry me off as he said he would," answered Kitty, with a toss of the head which showed she was not so childlike as David fancied. But the next minute she was sitting on a stool at his feet petting the cat, while she told her adventures with girlish volubility.

Christie could not bear to sit and look on any longer, so she left the room, saying she would see if Mrs. Sterling wanted any thing, for the old lady kept her room with a touch of rheumatism. As she shut the door, Christie heard Kitty say softly:

"Now we'll be comfortable as we used to be: won't we?"

What David answered Christie did not stay to hear, but went into the kitchen, and had her first pang of jealousy out alone, while she beat up the buckwheats for breakfast with an energy that made them miracles of lightness on the morrow.

When she told Mrs. Sterling of the new arrival, the placid little lady gave a cluck of regret and said with unusual emphasis:

"I'm sorry for it."

"Why?" asked Christie, feeling as if she could embrace the speaker for the words.

"She is a giddy little thing, and much care to whoever befriends her." Mrs. Sterling would say no more, but, as Christie bade her good-night, she held her hand, saying with a kiss:

"No one will take thy place with *me*, my daughter."

For a week Christie suffered constant pin-pricks of jealousy, despising herself all the time, and trying to be friendly with the disturber of her peace. As if prompted by an evil spirit, Kitty unconsciously tried and tormented her from morning to night, and no one saw or guessed it unless Mrs. Sterling's motherly heart divined the truth. David seemed to enjoy the girl's lively chat, her openly expressed affection, and the fresh young face that always brightened when he came.

Presently, however, Christie saw a change in him, and suspected that he had discovered that Kitty was a child no longer, but a young girl with her head full of love and lovers. The blue eyes grew shy, the pretty face grew eloquent with blushes now and then, as he looked at it, and the lively tongue faltered sometimes in speaking to him. A thousand little coquetries were played off for his benefit, and frequent appeals for advice in her heart affairs kept tender subjects uppermost in their conversations.

At first all this seemed to amuse David as much as if Kitty were a small child playing at sweethearts; but soon his manner changed, growing respectful, and a little cool when Kitty was most confiding. He no longer laughed about Miles, stopped calling her "little girl," and dropped his paternal ways as he had done with Christie. By many indescribable but significant signs he showed that he considered Kitty a woman now and treated her as such, being all the more scrupulous in the respect he paid her, because she was so unprotected, and so wanting in the natural dignity and refinement which are a woman's best protection.

Christie admired him for this, but saw in it the beginning of a tenderer feeling than pity, and felt each day that she was one too many now.

Kitty was puzzled and piqued by these changes, and being a born flirt tried all her powers on David, veiled under guileless girlishness. She was very pretty, very charming, and at times most lovable and sweet when all that was best in her shallow little heart was touched. But it was evident to all that her early acquaintance with the hard and sordid side of life had brushed the bloom from her nature, and filled her mind with thoughts and feelings unfitted to her years.

Mrs. Sterling was very kind to her, but never treated her as she did Christie; and though not a word was spoken between them the elder women knew that they quite agreed in their opinion of Kitty. She evidently was rather afraid of the old lady, who said so little and saw so much. Christie also she shunned without appearing to do so, and when alone with her put on airs that half amused, half irritated the other.

"David is my friend, and I don't care for any one else," her manner said as plainly as words; and to him she devoted herself so entirely, and apparently so successfully, that Christie made up her mind he had at last begun to forget his Letty, and think of filling the void her loss had left.

A few words which she accidentally overheard confirmed this idea, and showed her what she must do. As she came quietly in one evening from a stroll in the lane, and stood taking off cloak and hood, she caught a glimpse through the half-open parlor door of David pacing to and fro with a curiously excited expression on his face, and heard Mrs. Sterling say with unusual warmth:

"Thee is too hard upon thyself, Davy. Forget the past and be happy as other men are. Thee has atoned for thy fault long ago, so let me see thee at peace before I die, my son."

"Not yet, mother, not yet. I have no right to hope or ask for any woman's love till I am worthier of it," answered David in a tone that thrilled Christie's heart: it was so full of love and longing.

Here Kitty came running in from the green-house with her hands full of flowers, and passing Christie, who was fumbling among the cloaks in the passage, she went to show David some new blossom.

He had no time to alter the expression of his face for its usual grave serenity: Kitty saw the change at once, and spoke of it with her accustomed want of tact.

"How handsome you look! What *are* you thinking about?" she said, gazing up at him with her own eyes bright with wonder, and her cheeks glowing with the delicate carmine of the frosty air.

"I am thinking that you look more like a rose than ever," answered David turning her attention from himself by a compliment, and beginning to admire the flowers, still with that flushed and kindled look on his own face.

Christie crept upstairs, and, sitting in the dark, decided with the firmness of despair to go away, lest she should betray the secret that possessed her, a dead hope now, but still too dear to be concealed.

"Mr. Power told me to come to him when I got tired of this. I'll say I *am* tired and try something else, no matter what: I can bear any thing, but to stand quietly by and see David marry that empty-hearted girl, who dares to show that she desires to win him. Out of sight of all this, I can conquer my love, at least hide it; but if I stay I know I shall betray myself in some bitter minute, and I'd rather die than do that."

Armed with this resolution, Christie went the next day to Mr. Power, and simply said: "I am not needed at the Sterlings any more: can you give me other work to do?"

Mr. Power's keen eye searched her face for a moment, as if to discover the real motive for her wish. But Christie had nerved herself to bear that look, and showed no sign of her real trouble, unless the set expression of her lips, and the un-natural steadiness of her eyes betrayed it to that experienced reader of human hearts.

Whatever he suspected or saw, Mr. Power kept to himself, and answered in his cordial way:

"Well, I've been expecting you would tire of that quiet life, and have plenty of work ready for you. One of my good Dorcases is tired out and must rest; so you shall take her place and visit my poor, report their needs, and supply them as fast as we can. Does that suit you?"

"Entirely, sir. Where shall I live?" asked Christie, with an expression of relief that said much.

"Here for the present. I want a secretary to put my papers in order, write some of my letters, and do a thousand things to help a busy man. My old housekeeper likes you, and will let you take a duster now and then if you don't find enough other work to do. When can you come?"

Christie answered with a long breath of satisfaction: "To-morrow, if you like."

"I do: can you be spared so soon?"

"Oh, yes! they don't want me now at all, or I would not leave them. Kitty can take my place: she needs protection more than I; and there is not room for two." She checked herself there, conscious that a tone of bitterness had crept into her voice. Then quite steadily she added:

"Will you be kind enough to write, and ask Mrs. Sterling if she can spare me? I shall find it hard to tell her myself, for I fear she may think me ungrateful after all her kindness."

"No: she is used to parting with those whom she has helped,

and is always glad to set them on their way toward better things. I will write to-morrow, and you can come whenever you will, sure of a welcome, my child."

Something in the tone of those last words, and the pressure of the strong, kind hand, touched Christie's sore heart, and made it impossible for her to hide the truth entirely.

She only said: "Thank you, sir. I shall be very glad to come;" but her eyes were full, and she held his hand an instant, as if she clung to it sure of succor and support.

Then she went home so pale and quiet; so helpful, patient, and affectionate, that Mrs. Sterling watched her anxiously; David looked amazed; and, even self-absorbed Kitty saw the change, and was touched by it.

On the morrow, Mr. Power's note came, and Christie fled upstairs while it was read and discussed.

"If I get through this parting without disgracing myself, I don't care what happens to me afterward," she said; and, in order that she might do so, she assumed a cheerful air, and determined to depart with all the honors of war, if she died in the attempt.

So, when Mrs. Sterling called her down, she went humming into the parlor, smiled as she read the note silently given her, and then said with an effort greater than any she had ever made in her most arduous part on the stage:

"Yes, I did say to Mr. Power that I thought I'd better be moving on. I'm a restless creature as you know; and, now that you don't need me, I've a fancy to see more of the world. If you want me back again in the spring, I'll come."

"I *shall* want thee, my dear, but will not say a word to keep thee now, for thee does need a change, and Mr. Power can give thee work better suited to thy taste than any here. We shall see thee sometimes, and spring will make thee long for the flowers, I hope," was Mrs. Sterling's answer, as Christie gave back the note at the end of her difficult speech.

"Don't think me ungrateful. I have been very happy here, and never shall forget how motherly kind you have been to me. You will believe this and love me still, though I go away and leave you for a little while?" prayed Christie, with a face full of treacherous emotion.

Mrs. Sterling laid her hand on Christie's head, as she knelt down impulsively before her, and with a soft solemnity that made the words both an assurance and a blessing, she said:

"I believe and love and honor thee, my child. My heart warmed to thee from the first: it has taken thee to itself now; and nothing can ever come between us, unless thee wills it. Remember that, and go in peace with an old friend's thanks, and good wishes in return for faithful service, which no money can repay."

Christie laid her cheek against that wrinkled one, and, for a moment, was held close to that peaceful old heart which felt so tenderly for her, yet never wounded her by a word of pity. Infinitely comforting was that little instant of time, when the venerable woman consoled the young one with a touch, and strengthened her by the mute eloquence of sympathy.

This made the hardest task of all easier to perform; and, when David met her in the evening, Christie was ready to play out her part, feeling that Mrs. Sterling would help her, if need be. But David took it very quietly; at least, he showed no very poignant regret at her departure, though he lamented it, and hoped it would not be a very long absence. This wounded Christie terribly; for all of a sudden a barrier seemed to rise between them, and the old friendliness grew chilled.

"He thinks I am ungrateful, and is offended," she said to herself. "Well, I can bear coldness better than kindness now, and it will make it easier to go."

Kitty was pleased at the prospect of reigning alone, and did not disguise her satisfaction; so Christie's last day was any thing but pleasant. Mr. Power would send for her on the morrow, and she busied herself in packing her own possessions, setting every thing in order, and making various little arrangements for Mrs. Sterling's comfort, as Kitty was a heedless creature; willing enough, but very forgetful. In the evening some neighbors came in; so that dangerous time was safely passed, and Christie escaped to her own room with her usual quiet good-night all round.

"We won't have any sentimental demonstrations; no wailing, or tender adieux. If I'm weak enough to break my heart, no one need know it,—least of all, that little fool," thought Christie, grimly, as she burnt up several long-cherished relics of her love.

She was up early, and went about her usual work with the sad pleasure with which one performs a task for the last time. Lazy little Kitty never appeared till the bell rang; and Christie was fond of that early hour, busy though it was, for David was always before her with blazing fires; and, while she got breakfast, he came and went with wood and water, milk and marketing; often stopping to talk, and always in his happiest mood.

The first snow-fall had made the world wonderfully lovely that morning; and Christie stood at the window admiring the bridal look of the earth, as it lay dazzlingly white in the early sunshine. The little parlor was fresh and clean, with no speck of dust anywhere; the fire burned on the bright andirons; the flowers were rejoicing in their morning bath; and the table was set out with dainty care. So homelike, so pleasant, so very dear to her, that Christie yearned to stay, yet dared not, and had barely time to steady face and voice, when David came in with the little posies he always had ready for his mother and Christie at breakfast time. Only a flower by their plates; but it meant much to them: for, in these lives of ours, tender little acts do more to bind hearts together than great deeds or heroic words; since the first are like the dear daily bread that none can live without; the latter but occasional feasts, beautiful and memorable, but not possible to all.

This morning David laid a sprig of sweet-scented balm at his mother's place, two or three rosy daisies at Kitty's, and a bunch of Christie's favorite violets at hers. She smiled as her eye went from the scentless daisies, so pertly pretty, to her own posy full of perfume, and the half sad, half sweet associations that haunt these blue-eyed flowers.

"I wanted pansies for you, but not one would bloom; so I did the next best, since you don't like roses," said David, as Christie stood looking at the violets with a thoughtful face, for something in the peculiarly graceful arrangement of the heart-shaped leaves recalled another nosegay to her mind.

"I like these very much, because they came to me in the beginning of this, the happiest year of my life;" and scarcely knowing why, except that it was very sweet to talk with David in the early sunshine, she told about the flowers some one had given her at church. As she finished she looked up at him; and, though his face was perfectly grave, his eyes laughed, and with a sudden conviction of the truth, Christie exclaimed!

"David, I do believe it was you!"

"I couldn't help it: you seemed so touched and troubled. I longed to speak to you, but didn't dare, so dropped the flowers and got away as fast as possible. Did you think it very rude?"

"I thought it the sweetest thing that ever happened to me. That was my first step along a road that you have strewn with flowers ever since. I can't thank you, but I never shall forget it." Christie spoke out fervently, and for an instant her heart shone in her face. Then she checked herself, and, fearing she had said too much, fell to slicing bread with an energetic rapidity which resulted in a cut finger. Dropping the knife, she tried to get her handkerchief, but the blood flowed fast, and the pain of a deep gash made her a little faint. David sprung to help her, tied up the wound, put her in the big chair, held water to her lips, and bathed her temples with a wet napkin; silently, but so tenderly, that it was almost too much for poor Christie.

For one happy moment her head lay on his arm, and his hand brushed back her hair with a touch that was a caress: she heard his heart beat fast with anxiety; felt his breath on her cheek, and wished that she might die then and there, though a bread-knife was not a romantic weapon, nor a cut finger as interesting as a broken heart. Kitty's voice made her start up, and the blissful vision of life, with David in the little house alone, vanished like a bright bubble, leaving the hard reality to be lived out with nothing but a woman's pride to conceal a woman's most passionate pain.

"It's nothing: I'm all right now. Don't say any thing to worry your mother; I'll put on a bit of court-plaster, and no one will be the wiser," she said, hastily removing all traces of the accident but her own pale face.

"Poor Christie, it's hard that you should go away with a wound like this on the hand that has done so much for us," said David, as he carefully adjusted the black strip on that forefinger, roughened by many stitches set for him.

"I loved to do it," was all Christie trusted herself to say.

"I know you did; and in your own words I can only answer: 'I don't know how to thank you, but I never shall forget it.'"

"One Happy Moment."

And David kissed the wounded hand as gratefully and reverently as if its palm was not hardened by the humblest tasks.

If he had only known—ah, if he had only known!—how easily he might repay that debt, and heal the deeper wound in Christie's heart. As it was, she could only say, "You are too kind," and begin to shovel tea into the pot, as Kitty came in, as rosy and fresh as the daisies she put in her hair.

"Ain't they becoming?" she asked, turning to David for admiration.

"No, thank you," he answered absently, looking out over her head, as he stood upon the rug in the attitude which the best men *will* assume in the bosoms of their families.

Kitty looked offended, and turned to the mirror for comfort; while Christie went on shovelling tea, quite unconscious what she was about till David said gravely:

"Won't that be rather strong?"

"How stupid of me! I always forget that Kitty does not drink tea," and Christie rectified her mistake with all speed.

Kitty laughed, and said in her pert little way:

"Getting up early don't seem to agree with either of you this morning: I wonder what you've been doing?"

"Your work. Suppose you bring in the kettle: Christie has hurt her hand."

David spoke quietly; but Kitty looked as much surprised as if he had boxed her ears, for he had never used that tone to her before. She meekly obeyed; and David added with a smile to Christie:

"Mother is coming down, and you'll have to get more color into your cheeks if you mean to hide your accident from her."

"That is easily done;" and Christie rubbed her pale cheeks till they rivalled Kitty's in their bloom.

"How well you women know how to conceal your wounds," said David, half to himself.

"It is an invaluable accomplishment for us sometimes: you forget that I have been an actress," answered Christie, with a bitter sort of smile.

"I wish I could forget what *I* have been!" muttered David, turning his back to her and kicking a log that had rolled out of place.

In came Mrs. Sterling, and every one brightened up to meet her. Kitty was silent, and wore an injured air which nobody minded; Christie was very lively; and David did his best to help her through that last meal, which was a hard one to three out of the four.

At noon a carriage came for Christie, and she said good-by, as she had drilled herself to say it, cheerfully and steadily.

"It is only for a time, else I couldn't let thee go, my dear," said Mrs. Sterling, with a close embrace.

"I shall see you at church, and Tuesday evenings, even if you don't find time to come to us, so I shall not say good-by at all;" and David shook hands warmly, as he put her into the carriage.

"I'll invite you to my wedding when I make up my mind," said Kitty, with feminine malice; for in her eyes Christie was an old maid who doubtless envied her her "lots of lovers."

"I hope you will be very happy. In the mean time try to save dear Mrs. Sterling all you can, and let her make you worthy a good husband," was Christie's answer to a speech she was too noble to resent by a sharp word, or even a contemptuous look.

Then she drove away, smiling and waving her hand to the old lady at her window; but the last thing she saw as she left the well-beloved lane, was David going slowly up the path, with Kitty close beside him, talking busily. If she had heard the short dialogue between them, the sight would have been less bitter, for Kitty said:

"She's dreadful good; but I'm glad she's gone: ain't you?"

"No."

"Had you rather have her here than me?"

"Yes."

"Then why don't you ask her to come back."

"I would if I could!"

"I never did see any thing like it; every one is so queer and cross to-day I get snubbed all round. If folks ain't good to me, I'll go and marry Miles! I declare I will."

"You'd better," and with that David left her frowning and pouting in the porch, and went to shovelling snow with unusual vigor.

# Chapter XIV

DAVID.

M R. POWER received Christie so hospitably that she felt at home at once, and took up her new duties with the energy of one anxious to repay a favor. Her friend knew well the saving power of work, and gave her plenty of it; but it was a sort that at once interested and absorbed her, so that she had little time for dangerous thoughts or vain regrets. As he once said, Mr. Power made her own troubles seem light by showing her others so terribly real and great that she was ashamed to repine at her own lot.

Her gift of sympathy served her well, past experiences gave her a quick eye to read the truth in others, and the earnest desire to help and comfort made her an excellent almoner for the rich, a welcome friend to the poor. She was in just the right mood to give herself gladly to any sort of sacrifice, and labored with a quiet energy, painful to witness had any one known the hidden suffering that would not let her rest.

If she had been a regular novel heroine at this crisis, she would have grown gray in a single night, had a dangerous illness, gone mad, or at least taken to pervading the house at unseasonable hours with her back hair down and much wringing of the hands. Being only a commonplace woman she did nothing so romantic, but instinctively tried to sustain and comfort herself with the humble, wholesome duties and affections which seldom fail to keep heads sane and hearts safe. Yet, though her days seemed to pass so busily and cheerfully, it must be confessed that there were lonely vigils in the night; and sometimes in the morning Christie's eyes were very heavy, Christie's pillow wet with tears.

But life never is all work or sorrow; and happy hours, helpful pleasures, are mercifully given like wayside springs to pilgrims trudging wearily along. Mr. Power showed Christie many such, and silently provided her with better consolation than pity or advice.

"Deeds not words," was his motto; and he lived it out most faithfully. "Books and work" he gave his new charge; and then followed up that prescription with "healthful play" of a sort she liked, and had longed for all her life. Sitting at his table Christie saw the best and bravest men and women of our times; for Mr. Power was a magnet that drew them from all parts of the world. She saw and heard, admired and loved them; felt her soul kindle with the desire to follow in their steps, share their great tasks, know their difficulties and dangers, and in the end taste the immortal satisfactions given to those who live and labor for their fellow-men. In such society all other aims seemed poor and petty; for they appeared to live in a nobler world than any she had known, and she felt as if they belonged to another race; not men nor angels, but a delightful mixture of the two; more as she imagined the gods and heroes of old; not perfect, but wonderfully strong and brave and good; each gifted with a separate virtue, and each bent on a mission that should benefit mankind.

Nor was this the only pleasure given her. One evening of each week was set apart by Mr. Power for the reception of whomsoever chose to visit him; for his parish was a large one, and his house a safe haunt for refugees from all countries, all oppressions.

Christie enjoyed these evenings heartily, for there was no ceremony; each comer brought his mission, idea, or need, and genuine hospitality made the visit profitable or memorable to all, for entire freedom prevailed, and there was stabling for every one's hobby.

Christie felt that she was now receiving the best culture, acquiring the polish that society gives, and makes truly admirable
when character adds warmth and power to its charm. The
presence of her bosom-care calmed the old unrest, softened
her manners, and at times touched her face with an expression
more beautiful than beauty. She was quite unconscious of the
changes passing over her; and if any one had told her she was
fast becoming a most attractive woman, she would have been
utterly incredulous. But others saw and felt the new charm; for
no deep experience bravely borne can fail to leave its mark,
often giving power in return for patience, and lending a subtle
loveliness to faces whose bloom it has destroyed.

This fact was made apparent to Christie one evening when
she went down to the weekly gathering in one of the melancholy
moods which sometimes oppressed her. She felt dissatisfied with
herself because her interest in all things began to flag, and a
restless longing for some new excitement to break up the monotonous pain of her inner life possessed her. Being still a little
shy in company, she slipped quietly into a recess which commanded a view of both rooms, and sat looking listlessly about
her while waiting for David, who seldom failed to come.

A curious collection of fellow-beings was before her, and at
another time she would have found much to interest and
amuse her. In one corner a newly imported German with an
Orson-like head, thumb-ring, and the fragrance of many meer-
schaums still hovering about him, was hammering away upon
some disputed point with a scientific Frenchman, whose national politeness was only equalled by his national volubility. A
prominent statesman was talking with a fugitive slave; a young
poet getting inspiration from the face and voice of a handsome
girl who had earned the right to put M. D. to her name. An
old philosopher was calming the ardor of several rampant rad-
icals, and a famous singer was comforting the heart of an Italian exile by talking politics in his own melodious tongue.

There were plenty of reformers: some as truculent as Martin
Luther; others as beaming and benevolent as if the pelting of
the world had only mellowed them, and no amount of denunci-
atory thunder could sour the milk of human kindness creaming
in their happy hearts. There were eager women just beginning
their protest against the wrongs that had wrecked their peace;

subdued women who had been worsted in the unequal conflict and given it up; resolute women with "No surrender" written all over their strong-minded countenances; and sweet, hopeful women, whose faith in God and man nothing could shake or sadden.

But to Christie there was only one face worth looking at till David came, and that was Mr. Power's; for he was a perfect host, and pervaded the rooms like a genial atmosphere, using the welcome of eye and hand which needs no language to interpret it, giving to each guest the intellectual fare he loved, and making their enjoyment his own.

"Bless the dear man! what should we all do without him?" thought Christie, following him with grateful eyes, as he led an awkward youth in rusty black to the statesman whom it had been the desire of his ambitious soul to meet.

The next minute she proved that *she* at least could do without the "dear man;" for David entered the room, and she forgot all about him. Here and at church were the only places where the friends had met during these months, except one or two short visits to the little house in the lane when Christie devoted herself to Mrs. Sterling.

David was quite unchanged, though once or twice Christie fancied he seemed ill at ease with her, and immediately tormented herself with the idea that some alteration in her own manner had perplexed or offended him. She did her best to be as frank and cordial as in the happy old days; but it was impossible, and she soon gave it up, assuming in the place of that former friendliness, a grave and quiet manner which would have led a wiser man than David to believe her busied with her own affairs and rather indifferent to every thing else.

If he had known how her heart danced in her bosom, her eyes brightened, and all the world became endurable, the moment he appeared, he would not have been so long in joining her, nor have doubted what welcome awaited him.

As it was, he stopped to speak to his host; and, before he reappeared, Christie had found the excitement she had been longing for.

"Now some bore will keep him an hour, and the evening is *so* short," she thought, with a pang of disappointment; and, turning her eyes away from the crowd which had swallowed up her heart's desire, they fell upon a gentleman just entering, and remained fixed with an expression of unutterable surprise; for there, elegant, calm, and cool as ever, stood Mr. Fletcher.

"How came he here?" was her first question; "How will he behave to me?" her second. As she could answer neither, she composed herself as fast as possible, resolving to let matters take their own course, and feeling in the mood for an encounter with a discarded lover, as she took a womanish satisfaction in remembering that the very personable gentleman before her had once been.

Mr. Fletcher and his companion passed on to find their host; and, with a glance at the mirror opposite, which showed her that the surprise of the moment had given her the color she lacked before, Christie occupied herself with a portfolio of engravings, feeling very much as she used to feel when waiting at a side scene for her cue.

She had not long to wait before Mr. Power came up, and presented the stranger; for such he fancied him, never having heard a certain episode in Christie's life. Mr. Fletcher bowed, with no sign of recognition in his face, and began to talk in the smooth, low voice she remembered so well. For the moment, through sheer surprise, Christie listened and replied as any young lady might have done to a new-made acquaintance. But very soon she felt sure that Mr. Fletcher intended to ignore the past; and, finding her on a higher round of the social ladder, to accept the fact and begin again.

At first she was angry, then amused, then interested in the somewhat dramatic turn affairs were taking, and very wisely decided to meet him on his own ground, and see what came of it.

In the midst of an apparently absorbing discussion of one of Raphael's most insipid Madonnas, she was conscious that David had approached, paused, and was scrutinizing her companion with unusual interest. Seized with a sudden desire to see the two men together, Christie beckoned; and when he obeyed, she introduced him, drew him into the conversation, and then left him in the lurch by falling silent and taking notes while they talked.

If she wished to wean her heart from David by seeing him at a disadvantage, she could have devised no better way; for, though a very feminine test, it answered the purpose excellently.

Mr. Fletcher was a handsome man, and just then looked his best. Improved health gave energy and color to his formerly sallow, listless face: the cold eyes were softer, the hard mouth suave and smiling, and about the whole man there was that indescribable something which often proves more attractive than worth or wisdom to keener-sighted women than Christie. Never had he talked better; for, as if he suspected what was in the mind of one hearer, he exerted himself to be as brilliant as possible, and succeeded admirably.

David never appeared so ill, for he had no clew to the little comedy being played before him; and long seclusion and natural reserve unfitted him to shine beside a man of the world like Mr. Fletcher. His simple English sounded harsh, after the foreign phrases that slipped so easily over the other's tongue. He had visited no galleries, seen few of the world's wonders, and could only listen when they were discussed. More than once he was right, but failed to prove it, for Mr. Fletcher skilfully changed the subject or quenched him with a politely incredulous shrug.

Even in the matter of costume, poor David was worsted; for, in a woman's eyes, dress has wonderful significance. Christie used to think his suit of sober gray the most becoming man could wear; but now it looked shapeless and shabby, beside garments which bore the stamp of Paris in the gloss and grace of broadcloth and fine linen. David wore no gloves: Mr. Fletcher's were immaculate. David's tie was so plain no one observed it: Mr. Fletcher's, elegant and faultless enough for a modern Beau Brummel. David's handkerchief was of the commonest sort (she knew that, for she hemmed it herself): Mr. Fletcher's was the finest cambric, and a delicate breath of perfume refreshed the aristocratic nose to which the article belonged.

Christie despised herself as she made these comparisons, and felt how superficial they were; but, having resolved to exalt one man at the expense of the other for her own good, she did not relent till David took advantage of a pause, and left them with a reproachful look that made her wish Mr. Fletcher at the bottom of the sea.

When they were alone a subtle change in his face and manner convinced her that he also had been taking notes, and had arrived at a favorable decision regarding herself. Women are quick at making such discoveries; and, even while she talked with him as a stranger, she felt assured that, if she chose, she might make him again her lover.

Here was a temptation! She had longed for some new excitement, and fate seemed to have put one of the most dangerous within her reach. It was natural to find comfort in the knowledge that somebody loved her, and to take pride in her power over one man, because another did not own it. In spite of her better self she felt the fascination of the hour, and yielded to it, half unconsciously assuming something of the "dash and daring" which Mr. Fletcher had once confessed to finding so captivating in the demure governess. He evidently thought so still, and played his part with spirit; for, while apparently enjoying a conversation which contained no allusion to the past, the memory of it gave piquancy to that long *tête-à-tête*.

As the first guests began to go, Mr. Fletcher's friend beckoned to him; and he rose, saying with an accent of regret which changed to one of entreaty, as he put his question:

"I, too, must go. May I come again, Miss Devon?"

"I am scarcely more than a guest myself; but Mr. Power is always glad to see whoever cares to come," replied Christie rather primly, though her eyes were dancing with amusement at the recollection of those love passages upon the beach.

"Next time, I shall come not as a stranger, but as a former—may I say friend?" he added quickly, as if emboldened by the mirthful eyes that so belied the demure lips.

"Now you forget your part," and Christie's primness vanished in a laugh. "I am glad of it, for I want to ask about Mrs. Saltonstall and the children. I've often thought of the little dears, and longed to see them."

"They are in Paris with their father."

"Mrs. Saltonstall is well, I hope?"

"She died six months ago."

An expression of genuine sorrow came over Mr. Fletcher's face as he spoke; and, remembering that the silly little woman was his sister, Christie put out her hand with a look and gesture so full of sympathy that words were unnecessary. Taking advantage of this propitious moment, he said, with an expressive glance and effective tone: "I am all alone now. You *will* let me come again?"

"Certainly, if it can give you pleasure," she answered heartily, forgetting herself in pity for his sorrow.

Mr. Fletcher pressed her hand with a grateful, "Thank you!" and wisely went away at once, leaving compassion to plead for him better than he could have done it for himself.

Leaning back in her chair, Christie was thinking over this interview so intently that she started when David's voice said close beside her:

"Shall I disturb you if I say, 'Good-night'?"

"I thought you were not going to say it at all," she answered rather sharply.

"I've been looking for a chance; but you were so absorbed with that man I had to wait."

"Considering the elegance of 'that man,' you don't treat him with much respect."

"I don't feel much. What brought him here, I wonder. A French *salon* is more in his line."

"He came to see Mr. Power, as every one else does, of course."

"Don't dodge, Christie: you know he came to see you."

"How do you like him?" she asked, with treacherous abruptness.

"Not particularly, so far. But if I knew him, I dare say I should find many good traits in him."

"I know you would!" said Christie, warmly, not thinking of Fletcher, but of David's kindly way of finding good in every one.

"He must have improved since you saw him last; for then, if I remember rightly, you found him 'lazy, cross, selfish, and conceited.'"

"Now, David, I never said any thing of the sort," began Christie, wondering what possessed him to be so satirical and short with her.

"Yes, you did, last September, sitting on the old apple-tree the morning of your birthday."

"What an inconvenient memory you have! Well, he *was* all that then; but he is not an invalid now, and so we see his real self."

"I also remember that you gave me the impression that he was an elderly man."

"Isn't forty elderly?"

"He wasn't forty when you taught his sister's children."

"No; but he looked older than he does now, being so ill. I

used to think he would be very handsome with good health; and now I see I was right," said Christie, with feigned enthusiasm; for it was a new thing to tease David, and she liked it.

But she got no more of it; for, just then, the singer began to sing to the select few who remained, and every one was silent. Leaning on the high back of Christie's chair, David watched the reflection of her face in the long mirror; for she listened to the music with downcast eyes, unconscious what eloquent expressions were passing over her countenance. She seemed a new Christie to David, in that excited mood; and, as he watched her, he thought:

"She loved this man once, or he loved her; and to-night it all comes back to her. How will it end?"

So earnestly did he try to read that altered face that Christie felt the intentness of his gaze, looked up suddenly, and met his eyes in the glass. Something in the expression of those usually serene eyes, now darkened and dilated with the intensity of that long scrutiny, surprised and troubled her; and, scarcely knowing what she said, she asked quickly:

"Who are you admiring?"

"Not myself."

"I wonder if you'd think me vain if I asked you something that I want to know?" she said, obeying a sudden impulse.

"Ask it, and I'll tell you."

"Am I much changed since you first knew me?"

"Very much."

"For the better or the worse?"

"The better, decidedly."

"Thank you, I hoped so; but one never knows how one seems to other people. I was wondering what you saw in the glass."

"A good and lovely woman, Christie."

How sweet it sounded to hear David say that! so simply and sincerely that it was far more than a mere compliment. She did not thank him, but said softly as if to herself:

"So let me seem until I be"

—and then sat silent, so full of satisfaction in the thought that David found her "good and lovely," she could not resist stealing a glance at the tell-tale mirror to see if she might believe him.

She forgot herself, however; for he was off guard now, and stood looking away with brows knit, lips tightly set, and eyes fixed, yet full of fire; his whole attitude and expression that of a man intent on subduing some strong impulse by a yet stronger will.

It startled Christie; and she leaned forward, watching him with breathless interest till the song ceased, and, with the old impatient gesture, David seemed to relapse into his accustomed quietude.

"It was the wonderful music that excited him: that was all," thought Christie; yet, when he came round to say good-night, the strange expression was not gone, and his manner was not his own.

"Shall *I* ask if I may come again," he said, imitating Mr. Fletcher's graceful bow with an odd smile.

"I let him come because he has lost his sister, and is lonely," began Christie, but got no further, for David said, "Good-night!" abruptly, and was gone without a word to Mr. Power.

"He's in a hurry to get back to his Kitty," she thought, tormenting herself with feminine skill. "Never mind," she added, with a defiant sort of smile; "*I've* got my Philip, handsomer and more in love than ever, if I'm not deceived. I wonder if he *will* come again?"

Mr. Fletcher did come again, and with flattering regularity, for several weeks, evidently finding something very attractive in those novel gatherings. Mr. Power soon saw why he came; and, as Christie seemed to enjoy his presence, the good man said nothing to disturb her, though he sometimes cast an anxious glance toward the recess where the two usually sat, apparently busy with books or pictures; yet, by their faces, showing that an under current of deeper interest than art or literature flowed through their intercourse.

Christie had not deceived herself, and it was evident that her old lover meant to try his fate again, if she continued to smile upon him as she had done of late. He showed her his sunny side now, and very pleasant she found it. The loss of his sister had touched his heart, and made him long to fill the place her death left vacant. Better health sweetened his temper, and woke the desire to do something worth the doing; and the sight of the only woman he had ever really loved, reawakened the sentiment that had not died, and made it doubly sweet.

Why he cared for Christie he could not tell, but he never had forgotten her; and, when he met her again with that new beauty in her face, he felt that time had only ripened the blithe girl into a deep-hearted woman, and he loved her with a better love than before. His whole manner showed this; for the half-careless, half-condescending air of former times was replaced by the most courteous respect, a sincere desire to win her favor, and at times the tender sort of devotion women find so charming.

Christie felt all this, enjoyed it, and tried to be grateful for it in the way he wished, thinking that hearts could be managed like children, and when one toy is unattainable, be appeased by a bigger or a brighter one of another sort.

"I must love some one," she said, as she leaned over a basket of magnificent flowers just left for her by Mr. Fletcher's servant, a thing which often happened now. "Philip has loved me with a fidelity that ought to touch my heart. Why not accept him, and enjoy a new life of luxury, novelty, and pleasure? All these things he can give me: all these things are valued, admired, and sought for; and who would appreciate them more than I? I could travel, cultivate myself in many delightful ways, and do so much good. No matter if I was not very happy: I should make Philip so, and have it in my power to comfort many poor souls. That ought to satisfy me; for what is nobler than to live for others?"

This idea attracted her, as it does all generous natures; she became enamoured of self-sacrifice, and almost persuaded herself that it was her duty to marry Mr. Fletcher, whether she loved him or not, in order that she might dedicate her life to the service of poorer, sadder creatures than herself.

But in spite of this amiable delusion, in spite of the desire to forget the love she would have in the love she might have, and in spite of the great improvement in her faithful Philip, Christie could not blind herself to the fact that her head, rather than her heart, advised the match; she could not conquer a suspicion that, however much Mr. Fletcher might love his wife, he would be something of a tyrant, and she was very sure she never would make a good slave. In her cooler moments she remembered that men are not puppets, to be moved as a woman's will commands, and the uncertainty of being able to carry out her charitable plans made her pause to consider whether she would not be selling her liberty too cheaply, if in return she got only dependence and bondage along with fortune and a home.

So tempted and perplexed, self-deluded and self-warned, attracted and repelled, was poor Christie, that she began to feel as if she had got into a labyrinth without any clew to bring her safely out. She longed to ask advice of some one, but could not turn to Mrs. Sterling; and what other woman friend had she except Rachel, from whom she had not heard for months?

As she asked herself this question one day, feeling sure that Mr. Fletcher would come in the evening, and would soon put his fortune to the touch again, the thought of Mrs. Wilkins seemed to answer her.

"Why not?" said Christie: "she is sensible, kind, and discreet; she may put me right, for I'm all in a tangle now with doubts and fears, feelings and fancies. I'll go and see her: that will do me good, even if I don't say a word about my 'werryments,' as the dear soul would call them."

Away she went, and fortunately found her friend alone in the "settin'-room," darning away at a perfect stack of socks, as she creaked comfortably to and fro in her old rocking-chair.

"I was jest wishin' somebody would drop in: it's so kinder lonesome with the children to school and Adelaide asleep. How be you, dear?" said Mrs. Wilkins, with a hospitable hug and a beaming smile.

"I'm worried in my mind, so I came to see you," answered Christie, sitting down with a sigh.

"Bless your dear heart, what *is* to pay. Free your mind, and I'll do my best to lend a hand."

The mere sound of that hearty voice comforted Christie, and gave her courage to introduce the little fiction under which she had decided to defraud Mrs. Wilkins of her advice. So she helped herself to a very fragmentary blue sock and a big needle, that she might have employment for her eyes, as they were not so obedient as her tongue, and then began in as easy a tone as she could assume.

"Well, you see a friend of mine wants my advice on a very serious matter, and I really don't know what to give her. It is strictly confidential, you know, so I won't mention any names, but just set the case before you and get your opinion, for I've great faith in your sensible way of looking at things."

"Thanky, dear, you'r welcome to my 'pinion ef it's wuth any thing. Be these folks you tell of young?" asked Mrs. Wilkins, with evident relish for the mystery.

"No, the woman is past thirty, and the man 'most forty, I believe," said Christie, darning away in some trepidation at having taken the first plunge.

"My patience! ain't the creater old enough to know her own mind? for I s'pose she's the one in the quanderry?" exclaimed Mrs. Wilkins, looking over her spectacles with dangerously keen eyes.

"The case is this," said Christie, in guilty haste. "The 'creature' is poor and nobody, the man rich and of good family, so you see it's rather hard for her to decide."

"No, I don't see nothin' of the sort," returned blunt Mrs. Wilkins. "Ef she loves the man, take him: ef she don't, give him the mittin and done with it. Money and friends and family ain't much to do with the matter accordin' to my view. It's jest a plain question betwixt them two. Ef it takes much settlin' they'd better let it alone."

"She doesn't love him as much as she might, I fancy, but she is tired of grubbing along alone. He is very fond of her, and very rich; and it would be a fine thing for her in a worldly way, I'm sure."

"Oh, she's goin' to marry for a livin' is she? Wal, now I'd ruther one of my girls should grub the wust kind all their days than do that. Hows'ever, it may suit some folks ef they ain't got much heart, and is contented with fine clothes, nice vittles, and handsome furnitoor. Selfish, cold, silly kinder women might git on, I dare say; but I shouldn't think any friend of your'n would be one of that sort."

"But she might do a great deal of good, and make others happy even if she was not so herself."

"She might, but I doubt it, for money got that way wouldn't prosper wal. Mis'able folks ain't half so charitable as happy ones; and I don't believe five dollars from one of 'em would go half so fur, or be half so comfortin' as a kind word straight out of a cheerful heart. I know some thinks that is a dreadful smart thing to do; but *I* don't, and ef any one wants to go a sacrificin' herself for the good of others, there's better ways of doin' it than startin' with a lie in her mouth."

Mrs. Wilkins spoke warmly; for Christie's face made her fiction perfectly transparent, though the good woman with true delicacy showed no sign of intelligence on that point.

"Then you wouldn't advise my friend to say yes?"

"Sakes alive, no! I'd say to her as I did to my younger sisters when their courtin' time come: 'Jest be sure you're right as to there bein' love enough, then go ahead, and the Lord will bless you.'"

"Did they follow your advice?"

"They did, and both is prosperin' in different ways. Gusty, she found she was well on't for love, so she married, though Samuel Buck was poor, and they're happy as can be a workin' up together, same as Lisha and me did. Addy, she calc'lated she wan't satisfied somehow, so she *didn't* marry, though James Miller was wal off; and she's kep stiddy to her trade, and ain't never repented. There's a sight said and writ about such things," continued Mrs. Wilkins, rambling on to give Christie time to think; "but I've an idee that women's hearts is to be trusted ef they ain't been taught all wrong. Jest let 'em remember that they take a husband for wuss as well as better (and there's a sight of wuss in this tryin' world for some on us), and be ready to do their part patient and faithful, and I ain't a grain afraid but what they'll be fetched through, always pervidin' they love the man and not his money."

There was a pause after that last speech, and Christie felt as if her perplexity was clearing away very fast; for Mrs. Wilkins's plain talk seemed to show her things in their true light, with all the illusions of false sentiment and false reasoning stripped away. She felt clearer and stronger already, and as if she could make up her mind very soon when one other point had been discussed.

"I fancy my friend is somewhat influenced by the fact that this man loved and asked her to marry him some years ago. He has not forgotten her, and this touches her heart more than any thing else. It seems as if his love must be genuine to last so long, and not to mind her poverty, want of beauty, and accomplishments; for he is a proud and fastidious man."

"I think wal of him for that!" said Mrs. Wilkins, approvingly; "but I guess she's wuth all he gives her, for there must be somethin' pretty gennywin' in her to make him overlook her lacks and hold on so stiddy. It don't alter *her* side of the case one mite though; for love is love, and ef she ain't got it, he'd better not take gratitude instid, but sheer off and leave her for somebody else."

"Nobody else wants her!" broke from Christie like an involuntary cry of pain; then she hid her face by stooping to gather up the avalanche of hosiery which fell from her lap to the floor.

"She can't be sure of that," said Mrs. Wilkins cheerily, though her spectacles were dim with sudden mist. "I know there's a mate for her somewheres, so she'd better wait a spell and trust in Providence. It wouldn't be so pleasant to see the right one come along after she'd went and took the wrong one in a hurry: would it? Waitin' is always safe, and time needn't be wasted in frettin' or bewailin'; for the Lord knows there's a sight of good works sufferin' to be done, and single women has the best chance at 'em."

"I've accomplished one good work at any rate; and, small as it is, I feel better for it. Give this sock to your husband, and tell him his wife sets a good example both by precept and practice to other women, married or single. Thank you very much, both for myself and my friend, who shall profit by your advice," said Christie, feeling that she had better go before she told every thing.

"I hope she will," returned Mrs. Wilkins, as her guest went away with a much happier face than the one she brought. "And ef I know her, which I think I do, she'll find that Cinthy Wilkins ain't fur from right, ef her experience is good for any thing," added the matron with a sigh, and a glance at a dingy photograph of her Lisha on the wall, a sigh that seemed to say there had been a good deal of "*wuss*" in her bargain, though she was too loyal to confess it.

Something in Christie's face struck Mr. Fletcher at once when he appeared that evening. He had sometimes found her cold and quiet, often gay and capricious, usually earnest and cordial, with a wistful look that searched his face and both won and checked him by its mute appeal, seeming to say, "Wait a little till I have taught my heart to answer as you wish."

To-night her eyes shunned his, and when he caught a glimpse of them they were full of a soft trouble; her manner was kinder than ever before, and yet it made him anxious, for there was a resolute expression about her lips even when she smiled, and though he ventured upon allusions to the past hitherto tacitly avoided, she listened as if it had no tender charm for her.

Being thoroughly in earnest now, Mr. Fletcher resolved to ask the momentous question again without delay. David was not there, and had not been for several weeks, another thorn in Christie's heart, though she showed no sign of regret, and said to herself, "It is better so." His absence left Fletcher master of the field, and he seized the propitious moment.

"Will you show me the new picture? Mr. Power spoke of it, but I do not like to trouble him."

"With pleasure," and Christie led the way to a little room where the newly arrived gift was placed. She knew what was coming, but was ready, and felt a tragic sort of satisfaction in the thought of all she was relinquishing for love of David.

No one was in the room, but a fine copy of Michael Angelo's Fates hung on the wall, looking down at them with weird significance.

"They look as if they would give a stern answer to any questioning of ours," Mr. Fletcher said, after a glance of affected interest.

"They would give a true one I fancy," answered Christie, shading her eyes as if to see the better.

"I'd rather question a younger, fairer Fate, hoping that she will give me an answer both true and kind. May I, Christie?"

"I will be true but—I cannot be kind." It cost her much to say that; yet she did it steadily, though he held her hand in both his own, and waited for her words with ardent expectation.

"Not yet perhaps,—but in time, when I have proved how sincere my love is, how entire my repentance for the ungenerous words you have not forgotten. I wanted you then for my own sake, now I want you for yourself, because I love and honor you above all women. I tried to forget you, but I could not; and all these years have carried in my heart a very tender memory of the girl who dared to tell me that all I could offer her was not worth her love."

"I was mistaken," began Christie, finding this wooing much harder to withstand than the other.

"No, you were right: I felt it then and resented it, but I owned it later, and regretted it more bitterly than I can tell. I'm not worthy of you; I never shall be: but I've loved you for five years without hope, and I'll wait five more if in the end you will come to me. Christie, I need you very much!"

If Mr. Fletcher had gone down upon his knees and poured out the most ardent protestations that ever left a lover's lips, it would not have touched her as did that last little appeal, uttered with a break in the voice that once was so proud and was so humble now.

"Forgive me!" she cried, looking up at him with real respect in her face, and real remorse smiting her conscience. "Forgive me! I have misled you and myself. I tried to love you: I was grateful for your regard, touched by your fidelity, and I hoped I might repay it; but I cannot! I cannot!"

"Why?"

Such a hard question! She owed him all the truth, yet how could she tell it? She could not in words, but her face did, for the color rose and burned on cheeks and forehead with painful fervor; her eyes fell, and her lips trembled as if endeavoring to keep down the secret that was escaping against her will. A moment of silence as Mr. Fletcher searched for the truth and found it; then he said with such sharp pain in his voice that Christie's heart ached at the sound:

"I see: I am too late?"

"Yes."

"And there is no hope?"

"None."

"Then there is nothing more for me to say but good-by. May you be happy."

"I shall not be;—I have no hope;—I only try to be true to you and to myself. Oh, believe it, and pity me as I do you!"

As the words broke from Christie, she covered up her face, bowed down with the weight of remorse that made her long to atone for what she had done by any self-humiliation.

Mr. Fletcher was at his best at that moment; for real love ennobles the worst and weakest while it lasts: but he could not resist the temptation that confession offered him. He tried to be generous, but the genuine virtue was not in him; he did want Christie very much, and the knowledge of a rival in her heart only made her the dearer.

"I'm not content with your pity, sweet as it is: I want your love, and I believe that I might earn it if you would let me try. You are all alone, and life is hard to you: come to me and let me make it happier. I'll be satisfied with friendship till you can give me more."

He said this very tenderly, caressing the bent head while he spoke, and trying to express by tone and gesture how eagerly he longed to receive and cherish what that other man neglected.

Christie felt this to her heart's core, and for a moment longed to end the struggle, say, "Take me," and accept the shadow for the substance. But those last words of his vividly recalled the compact made with David that happy birthday night. How could she be his friend if she was Mr. Fletcher's wife? She knew she could not be true to both, while her heart reversed the sentiment she then would owe them: David's friendship was dearer than Philip's love, and she would keep it at all costs. These thoughts flashed through her mind in the drawing of a breath, and she looked up, saying steadily in spite of wet eyes and still burning cheeks:

"Hope nothing; wait for nothing from me. I will have no more delusions for either of us: it is weak and wicked, for I know I shall not change. Some time we may venture to be friends perhaps, but not now. Forgive me, and be sure I shall suffer more than you for this mistake of mine."

When she had denied his suit before he had been ungenerous and angry; for his pride was hurt and his will thwarted: now his heart bled and hope died hard; but all that was manliest in him rose to help him bear the loss, for *this* love was genuine, and made him both just and kind. His face was pale with the pain of that fruitless passion, and his voice betrayed how hard he strove for self-control, as he said hurriedly:

"*You* need not suffer: this mistake has given me the happiest hours of my life, and I am better for having known so sweet and true a woman. God bless you, Christie!" and with a quick embrace that startled her by its suddenness and strength he left her, standing there alone before the three grim Fates.

# Chapter XV

## MIDSUMMER

"Now it is all over. I shall never have another chance like that, and must make up my mind to be a lonely and laborious spinster all my life. Youth is going fast, and I have little in myself to attract or win, though David did call me 'good and lovely.' Ah, well, I'll try to deserve his praise, and not let disappointment sour or sadden me. Better to hope and wait all my life than marry without love."

Christie often said this to herself during the hard days that followed Mr. Fletcher's disappearance; a disappearance, by the way, which caused Mr. Power much satisfaction, though he only betrayed it by added kindness to Christie, and in his manner an increased respect very comforting to her.

But she missed her lover, for nothing now broke up the monotony of a useful life. She had enjoyed that little episode; for it had lent romance to every thing while it lasted, even the charity basket with which she went her rounds; for Mr. Fletcher often met her by accident apparently, and carried it as if to prove the sincerity of his devotion. No bouquets came now; no graceful little notes with books or invitations to some coveted pleasure; no dangerously delightful evenings in the recess, where, for a time, she felt and used the power which to a woman is so full of subtle satisfaction; no bitter-sweet hopes; no exciting dreams of what might be with the utterance of a word; no soft uncertainty to give a charm to every hour that passed. Nothing but daily duties, a little leisure that hung heavy on her hands with no hope to stimulate, no lover to lighten it, and a sore, sad heart that would clamor for its right; and even when pride silenced it ached on with the dull pain which only time and patience have the power to heal.

But as those weeks went slowly by, she began to discover some of the miracles true love can work. She thought she had laid it in its grave; but an angel rolled the stone away, and the lost passion rose stronger, purer, and more beautiful than when she buried it with bitter tears. A spirit now, fed by no hope, warmed by no tenderness, clothed in no fond delusion; the vital soul of love which outlives the fairest, noblest form humanity can give it, and sits among the ruins singing the immortal hymn of consolation the Great Musician taught.

Christie felt this strange comfort resting like a baby in her lonely bosom, cherished and blessed it; wondering while she rejoiced, and soon perceiving with the swift instinct of a woman, that this was a lesson, hard to learn, but infinitely precious, helpful, and sustaining when once gained. She was not happy, only patient; not hopeful, but trusting; and when life looked dark and barren without, she went away into that inner world of deep feeling, high thought, and earnest aspiration; which is a never-failing refuge to those whose experience has built within them

"The nunnery of a chaste heart and quiet mind."

Some women live fast; and Christie fought her battle, won her victory, and found peace declared during that winter: for her loyalty to love brought its own reward in time, giving her the tranquil steadfastness which comes to those who submit and ask nothing but fortitude.

She had seen little of David, except at church, and began to regard him almost as one might a statue on a tomb, the marble effigy of the beloved dead below; for the sweet old friendship was only a pale shadow now. He always found her out, gave her the posy she best liked, said cheerfully, "How goes it, Christie?" and she always answered, "Good-morning, David. I am well and busy, thank you." Then they sat together listening to Mr. Power, sung from the same book, walked a little way together, and parted for another week with a hand-shake for good-by.

Christie often wondered what prayers David prayed when he sat so still with his face hidden by his hand, and looked up with such a clear and steady look when he had done. She tried to do the same; but her thoughts would wander to the motionless gray figure beside her, and she felt as if peace and strength unconsciously flowed from it to sustain and comfort her. Some of her happiest moments were those she spent sitting there, pale and silent, with absent eyes, and lips that trembled now and then, hidden by the flowers held before them, kissed covertly, and kept like relics long after they were dead.

One bitter drop always marred the pleasure of that hour; for when she had asked for Mrs. Sterling, and sent her love, she forced herself to say kindly:

"And Kitty, is she doing well?"

"Capitally; come and see how she has improved; we are quite proud of her."

"I will if I can find time. It's a hard winter and we have so much to do," she would answer smiling, and then go home to struggle back into the patient mood she tried to make habitual.

But she seldom made time to go and see Kitty's improvement; and, when she did run out for an hour she failed to discover any thing, except that the girl was prettier and more coquettish than ever, and assumed airs of superiority that tried Christie very much.

"I am ready for any thing," she always said with a resolute air after one of these visits; but, when the time seemed to have come she was not so ready as she fancied.

Passing out of a store one day, she saw Kitty all in her best, buying white gloves with a most important air. "That looks suspicious," she thought, and could not resist speaking.

"All well at home?" she asked.

"Grandma and I have been alone for nearly a week; David went off on business; but he's back now and—oh, my goodness! I forgot: I'm not to tell a soul yet;" and Kitty pursed up her lips, looking quite oppressed with some great secret.

"Bless me, how mysterious! Well, I won't ask any dangerous questions, only tell me if the dear old lady is well," said Christie, desperately curious, but too proud to show it.

"She's well, but dreadfully upset by what's happened; well she may be." And Kitty shook her head with a look of mingled mystery and malicious merriment.

"Mr. Sterling is all right I hope?" Christie never called him David to Kitty; so that impertinent little person took especial pains to speak familiarly, sometimes even fondly of him to Christie.

"Dear fellow! he's so happy he don't know what to do with himself. I just wish you could see him go round smiling, and singing, and looking as if he'd like to dance."

"That looks as if he was going to get a chance to do it," said Christie, with a glance at the gloves, as Kitty turned from the counter.

"So he is!" laughed Kitty, patting the little parcel with a joyful face.

"I do believe you are going to be married!" exclaimed Christie, half distracted with curiosity.

"I am, but not to Miles. Now don't you say another word, for I'm dying to tell, and I promised I wouldn't. David wants to do it himself. By-by." And Kitty hurried away, leaving Christie as pale as if she had seen a ghost at noonday.

She had; for the thought of David's marrying Kitty had haunted her all those months, and now she was quite sure the blow had come.

"If she was only a nobler woman I could bear it better; but I am sure he will regret it when the first illusion is past. I fancy she reminds him of his lost Letty, and so he thinks he loves her. I pray he may be happy, and I hope it will be over soon," thought Christie, with a groan, as she trudged away to carry comfort to those whose woes could be relieved by tea and sugar, flannel petticoats, and orders for a ton of coal.

It *was* over soon, but not as Christie had expected.

That evening Mr. Power was called away, and she sat alone, bravely trying to forget suspense and grief in copying the record of her last month's labor. But she made sad work of it; for her mind was full of David and his wife, so happy in the little home which had grown doubly dear to her since she left it. No wonder then that she put down "two dozen children" to Mrs. Flanagan, and "four knit hoods" with the measles; or that a great blot fell upon "twenty yards red flannel," as the pen dropped from the hands she clasped together; saying with all the fervor of true self-abnegation: "I hope he will be happy; oh, I hope he will be happy!"

If ever woman deserved reward for patient endeavor, hard-won submission, and unselfish love, Christie did then. And she received it in full measure; for the dear Lord requites some faithful hearts, blesses some lives that seem set apart for silent pain and solitary labor.

Snow was falling fast, and a bitter wind moaned without; the house was very still, and nothing stirred in the room but the flames dancing on the hearth, and the thin hand moving to and fro among the records of a useful life.

Suddenly the bell rang loudly and repeatedly, as if the new-comer was impatient of delay. Christie paused to listen. It was not Mr. Power's ring, not his voice in the hall below, not his step that came leaping up the stairs, nor his hand that threw wide the door. She knew them all, and her heart stood still an instant; then she gathered up her strength, said low to herself, "Now it is coming," and was ready for the truth, with a color-less face; eyes unnaturally bright and fixed; and one hand on her breast, as if to hold in check the rebellious heart that would throb so fast.

It was David who came in with such impetuosity. Snow-flakes shone in his hair; the glow of the keen wind was on his cheek, a smile on his lips, and in his eyes an expression she had never seen before. Happiness, touched with the shadow of some past pain; doubt and desire; gratitude and love,—all seemed to meet and mingle in it; while, about the whole man, was the free and ardent air of one relieved from some heavy burden, released from some long captivity.

"O David, what is it?" cried Christie, as he stood looking at her with this strange look.

"News, Christie! such happy news I can't find words to tell them," he answered, coming nearer, but too absorbed in his own emotion to heed hers.

She drew a long breath and pressed her hand a little heavier on her breast, as she said, with the ghost of a smile, more pa-thetic than the saddest tears:

"I guess it, David."

"How?" he demanded, as if defrauded of a joy he had set his heart upon.

"I met Kitty,—she told me nothing,—but her face betrayed what I have long suspected."

David laughed, such a glad yet scornful laugh, and, snatch-ing a little miniature from his pocket, offered it, saying, with the new impetuosity that changed him so:

"*That* is the daughter I have found for my mother. You know her,—you love her; and you will not be ashamed to welcome her, I think."

Christie took it; saw a faded, time-worn likeness of a young girl's happy face; a face strangely familiar, yet, for a moment, she groped to find the name belonging to it. Then memory helped her; and she said, half incredulously, half joyfully:

"Is it my Rachel?"

"It is *my* Letty!" cried David, with an accent of such mingled love and sorrow, remorse and joy, that Christie seemed to hear in it the death-knell of her faith in him. The picture fell from the hands she put up, as if to ward off some heavy blow, and her voice was sharp with reproachful anguish, as she cried:

"O David, David, any thing but that!"

An instant he seemed bewildered, then the meaning of the grief in her face flashed on him, and his own grew white with indignant repudiation of the thought that daunted her; but he only said with the stern brevity of truth:

"Letty is my sister."

"Forgive me,—how could I know? Oh, thank God! thank God!" and, dropping down upon a chair, Christie broke into a passion of the happiest tears she ever shed.

David stood beside her silent, till the first irrepressible paroxysm was over; then, while she sat weeping softly, quite bowed down by emotion, he said, sadly now, not sternly:

"You could *not* know, because we hid the truth so carefully. I have no right to resent that belief of yours, for I did wrong my poor Letty, almost as much as that lover of hers, who, being dead, I do not curse. Let me tell you every thing, Christie, before I ask your respect and confidence again. I never deserved them, but I tried to; for they were very precious to me."

He paused a moment, then went on rapidly, as if anxious to accomplish a hard task; and Christie forgot to weep while listening breathlessly.

"Letty was the pride of my heart; and I loved her very dearly, for she was all I had. Such a pretty child; such a gay, sweet girl; how could I help it, when she was so fond of me? We were poor then,—poorer than now,—and she grew restless; tired of hard work; longed for a little pleasure, and could not bear to waste her youth and beauty in that dull town. I did not blame my little girl; but I could not help her, for I was tugging away to fill father's place, he being broken down and helpless. She wanted to go away and support herself. *You* know the feeling;

and I need not tell you how the proud, high-hearted creature hated dependence, even on a brother who would have worked his soul out for her. She *would* go, and we had faith in her. For a time she did bravely; but life was too hard for her; pleasure too alluring, and, when temptation came in the guise of love, she could not resist. One dreadful day, news came that she was gone, never to come back, my innocent little Letty, any more."

His voice failed there, and he walked fast through the room, as if the memory of that bitter day was still unbearable. Christie could not speak for very pity; and he soon continued, pacing restlessly before her, as he had often done when she sat by, wondering what unquiet spirit drove him to and fro:

"That was the beginning of my trouble; but not the worst of it: God forgive me, not the worst! Father was very feeble, and the shock killed him; mother's heart was nearly broken, and all the happiness was taken out of life for me. But I could bear it, heavy as the blow was, for I had no part in that sin and sorrow. A year later, there came a letter from Letty,—a penitent, imploring, little letter, asking to be forgiven and taken home, for her lover was dead, and she alone in a foreign land. How would you answer such a letter, Christie?"

"As you did; saying: 'Come home and let us comfort you.'"

"I said: 'You have killed your father; broken your mother's heart; ruined your brother's hopes, and disgraced your family. You no longer have a home with us; and we never want to see your face again.'"

"O David, that was cruel!"

"I said you did not know me; now you see how deceived you have been. A stern, resentful devil possessed me then, and I obeyed it. I was very proud; full of ambitious plans and jealous love for the few I took into my heart. Letty had brought a stain upon our honest name that time could never wash away; had quenched my hopes in despair and shame; had made home desolate, and destroyed my faith in every thing; for whom could I trust, when she, the nearest and dearest creature in the world, deceived and deserted me. I could *not* forgive; wrath burned hot within me, and the desire for retribution would not be appeased till those cruel words were said. The retribution and remorse came swift and sure; but they came most heavily to me."

Still standing where he had paused abruptly as he asked his question, David wrung his strong hands together with a gesture of passionate regret, while his face grew sharp with the remembered suffering of the years he had given to the atonement of that wrong.

Christie put her own hand on those clenched ones, and whispered softly:

"Don't tell me any more now: I can wait."

"I *must*, and you must listen! I've longed to tell you, but I was afraid; now, you shall know every thing, and then decide if you can forgive me for Letty's sake," he said, so resolutely that she listened with a face full of mute compassion.

"That little letter came to me; I never told my mother, but answered it, and kept silent till news arrived that the ship in which Letty had taken passage was lost. Remorse had been tugging at my heart; and, when I knew that she was dead, I forgave her with a vain forgiveness, and mourned for my darling, as if she had never left me. I told my mother then, and she did not utter one reproach; but age seemed to fall upon her all at once, and the pathetic quietude you see.

"Then, but for her, I should have been desperate; for day and night Letty's face haunted me; Letty's voice cried: 'Take me home!' and every word of that imploring letter burned before my eyes as if written in fire. Do you wonder now that I hid myself; that I had no heart to try for any honorable place in the world, and only struggled to forget, only hoped to expiate my sin?"

With his head bowed down upon his breast, David stood silent, asking himself if he had even now done enough to win the reward he coveted. Christie's voice seemed to answer him; for she said, with heartfelt gratitude and respect:

"Surely you have atoned for that harshness to one woman by years of devotion to many. Was it this that made you 'a brother of girls,' as Mr. Power once called you? And, when I asked what he meant, he said the Arabs call a man that who has 'a clean heart to love all women as his sisters, and strength and courage to fight for their protection!'"

She hoped to lighten his trouble a little, and spoke with a smile that was like cordial to poor David.

"Yes," he said, lifting his head again. "I tried to be that, and, for Letty's sake, had pity on the most forlorn, patience with the most abandoned; always remembering that she might have been what they were, if death had not been more merciful than I."

"But she was *not* dead: she was alive and working as bravely as you. Ah, how little I thought, when I loved Rachel, and she loved me, that we should ever meet so happily as we soon shall. Tell me how you found her? Does she know I am the woman she once saved? Tell me all about her; and tell it fast," prayed Christie, getting excited, as she more fully grasped the happy fact that Rachel and Letty were one.

David came nearer, and his face kindled as he spoke.

"The ship sailed without her; she came later; and, finding that her name was among the lost, she did not deny it, for she *was* dead to us, and decided to remain so till she had earned the right to be forgiven. You know how she lived and worked, stood firm with no one to befriend her till you came, and, by years of patient well-doing, washed away her single sin. If any one dares think I am ashamed to own her now, let him know what cause I have to be proud of her; let him come and see how tenderly I love her; how devoutly I thank God for permitting me to find and bring my little Letty home."

Only the snow-flakes drifting against the windowpane, and the wailing of the wind, was heard for a moment; then David added, with brightening eyes and a glad voice:

"I went into a hospital while away, to look after one of my poor girls who had been doing well till illness brought her there. As I was passing out I saw a sleeping face, and stopped involuntarily: it was so like Letty's. I never doubted she was dead; the name over the bed was not hers; the face was sadly altered from the happy, rosy one I knew, but it held me fast; and as I paused the eyes opened,—Letty's own soft eyes,—they saw me, and, as if I was the figure of a dream, she smiled, put up her arms and said, just as she used to say, a child, when I woke her in her little bed—'Why, Davy!'—I can't tell any more,—only that when I brought her home and put her in mother's arms, I felt as if I was forgiven at last."

He broke down there, and went and stood behind the window curtains, letting no one see the grateful tears that washed away the bitterness of those long years.

Christie had taken up the miniature and was looking at it,

while her heart sang for joy that the lost was found, when David came back to her, wearing the same look she had seen the night she listened among the cloaks. Moved and happy, with eager eyes and ardent manner, yet behind it all a pale expectancy as if some great crisis was at hand:

"Christie, I never can forget that when all others, even I, cast Letty off, you comforted and saved her. What can I do to thank you for it?"

"Be my friend, and let me be hers again," she answered, too deeply moved to think of any private hope or pain.

"Then the past, now that you know it all, does not change your heart to us?"

"It only makes you dearer."

"And if I asked you to come back to the home that has been desolate since you went, would you come?"

"Gladly, David."

"And if I dared to say I loved you?"

She only looked at him with a quick rising light and warmth over her whole face; he stretched both arms to her, and, going to him, Christie gave her answer silently.

Lovers usually ascend straight into the seventh heaven for a time: unfortunately they cannot stay long; the air is too rarefied, the light too brilliant, the fare too ethereal, and they are forced to come down to mundane things, as larks drop from heaven's gate into their grassy nests. David was summoned from that blissful region, after a brief enjoyment of its divine delights, by Christie, who looked up from her new refuge with the abrupt question:

"What becomes of Kitty?"

He regarded her with a dazed expression for an instant, for she had been speaking the delightful language of lips and eyes that lovers use, and the old tongue sounded harsh to him.

"She is safe with her father, and is to marry the 'other one' next week."

"Heaven be praised!" ejaculated Christie, so fervently that David looked suddenly enlightened and much amused, as he said quickly:

"What becomes of Fletcher?"

"He's safely out of the way, and I sincerely hope *he* will marry some 'other one' as soon as possible."

"Christie, you were jealous of that girl."

"David, you were jealous of that man."

Then they both burst out laughing like two children, for heavy burdens had been lifted off their hearts and they were bubbling over with happiness.

"But truly, David, weren't you a little jealous of P. F.?" persisted Christie, feeling an intense desire to ask all manner of harassing questions, with the agreeable certainty that they would be fully answered.

"Desperately jealous. You were so kind, so gay, so altogether charming when with him, that I could not stand by and see it, so I kept away. Why were you never so to me?"

"Because you never showed that you cared for me, and *he* did. But it was wrong in me to do it, and I repent of it heartily; for it hurt him more than I thought it would when the experiment failed. I truly tried to love him, but I couldn't."

"Yet he had so much to offer, and could give you all you most enjoy. It is very singular that you failed to care for him, and preferred a poor old fellow like me," said David, beaming at her like a beatified man.

"I do love luxury and pleasure, but I love independence more. I'm happier poking in the dirt with you than I should be driving in a fine carriage with 'that piece of elegance' as Mr. Power called him; prouder of being your wife than his; and none of the costly things he offered me were half so precious in my sight as your little nosegays, now mouldering away in my treasure-box upstairs. Why, Davy, I've longed more intensely for the right to push up the curly lock that is always tumbling into your eyes, than for Philip's whole fortune. *May* I do it now?"

"You may," and Christie did it with a tender satisfaction that made David love her the more, though he laughed like a boy at the womanly whim.

"And so you thought I cared for Kitty?" he said presently, taking his turn at the new game.

"How could I help it when she was so young and pretty and fond of you?"

"Was she?" innocently.

"Didn't you see it? How blind men are!"

"Not always."

"David, did you see that *I* cared for you?" asked Christie, turning crimson under the significant glance he gave her.

"I wish I had; I confess I once or twice fancied that I caught glimpses of bliss round the corner, as it were; but, before I could decide, the glimpses vanished, and I was very sure I was a conceited coxcomb to think it for a moment. It was very hard, and yet I was glad."

"Glad!"

"Yes, because I had made a sort of vow that I'd never love or marry as a punishment for my cruelty to Letty."

"That was wrong, David."

"I see it now; but it was not hard to keep that foolish vow till you came; and you see I've broken it without a shadow of regret to-night."

"You might have done it months ago and saved me so much woe if you had not been a dear, modest, morbidly conscientious bat," sighed Christie, pleased and proud to learn her power, yet sorry for the long delay.

"Thank you, love. You see I didn't find out why I liked my friend so well till I lost her. I had just begun to feel that you were very dear,—for after the birthday you were like an angel in the house, Christie,—when you changed all at once, and I thought you suspected me, and didn't like it. Your running away when Kitty came confirmed my fear; then in came that— would you mind if I said—confounded Fletcher?"

"Not in the least."

"Well, as he didn't win, I won't be hard on him; but I gave up then and had a tough time of it; especially that first night when this splendid lover appeared and received such a kind welcome."

Christie saw the strong hand that lay on David's knee clenched slowly, as he knit his brows with a grim look, plainly showing that he was not what she was inclined to think him, a perfect saint.

"Oh, my heart! and there I was loving you so dearly all the time, and you wouldn't see or speak or understand, but went away, left me to torment all three of us," cried Christie with a tragic gesture.

"My dearest girl, did you ever know a man in love do, say, or think the right thing at the right time? *I* never did," said David, so penitently that she forgave him on the spot.

"Never mind, dear. It has taught us the worth of love, and perhaps we are the better for the seeming waste of precious time. Now I've not only got you but Letty also, and your mother is mine in very truth. Ah, how rich I am!"

"But I thought it was all over with me when I found Letty, because, seeing no more of Fletcher, I had begun to hope again, and when she came back to me I knew my home must be hers, yet feared you would refuse to share it if you knew all. You are very proud, and the purest-hearted woman I ever knew."

"And if I *had* refused, you would have let me go and held fast to Letty?"

"Yes, for I owe her every thing."

"You should have known me better, David. But I don't refuse, and there is no need to choose between us."

"No, thank heaven, and you, my Christie! Imagine what I felt when Letty told me all you had been to her. If any thing *could* make me love you more than I now do, it would be that! No, don't hide your face; I like to see it blush and smile and turn to me confidingly, as it has not done all these long months."

"Did Letty tell you what she had done for me?" asked Christie, looking more like a rose than ever Kitty did.

"She told me every thing, and wished me to tell you all her story, even the saddest part of it. I'd better do it now before you meet again."

He paused as if the tale was hard to tell; but Christie put her hand on his lips saying softly:

"Never tell it; let her past be as sacred as if she were dead. She was my friend when I had no other: she is my dear sister now, and nothing can ever change the love between us."

If she had thought David's face beautiful with gratitude when he told the happier portions of that history, she found it doubly so when she spared him the recital of its darkest chapter, and bade him "leave the rest to silence."

"Now you will come home? Mother wants you, Letty longs for you, and I have got and mean to keep you all my life, God willing!"

"I'd better die to-night and make a blessed end, for so much happiness is hardly possible in a world of woe," answered Christie to that fervent invitation.

"We shall be married very soon, take a wedding trip to any part of the world you like, and our honeymoon will last for ever, Mrs. Sterling, Jr.," said David, soaring away into the future with sublime disregard of obstacles.

Before Christie could get her breath after that somewhat startling announcement, Mr. Power appeared, took in the situation at a glance, gave them a smile that was a benediction, and said heartily as he offered a hand to each:

"Now I'm satisfied; I've watched and waited patiently, and after many tribulations you have found each other in good time;" then with a meaning look at Christie he added slyly: "But David is 'no hero' you know."

She remembered the chat in the strawberry bed, laughed, and colored brightly, as she answered with her hand trustfully in David's, her eyes full of loving pride and reverence lifted to his face:

"I've seen both sides of the medal now, and found it 'sterling gold.' Hero or not I'm content; for, though he 'loves his mother much,' there is room in his heart for me too; his 'old books' have given him something better than learning, and he has convinced me that 'double flowers' *are* loveliest and best."

# Chapter XVI

MUSTERED IN

C HRISTIE'S return was a very happy one, and could not well
be otherwise with a mother, sister, and lover to welcome
her back. Her meeting with Letty was indescribably tender,
and the days that followed were pretty equally divided between
her and her brother, in nursing the one and loving the other.
There was no cloud now in Christie's sky, and all the world
seemed in bloom. But even while she enjoyed every hour of
life, and begrudged the time given to sleep, she felt as if the
dream was too beautiful to last, and often said:

"Something will happen: such perfect happiness is not possible in this world."

"Then let us make the most of it," David would reply, wisely
bent on getting his honey while he could, and not borrowing
trouble for the morrow.

So Christie turned a deaf ear to her "prophetic soul," and
gave herself up to the blissful holiday that had come at last.
Even while March winds were howling outside, she blissfully
"poked in the dirt" with David in the green-house, put up the
curly lock as often as she liked, and told him she loved him a
dozen times a day, not in words, but in silent ways, that
touched him to the heart, and made his future look so bright
he hardly dared believe in it.

A happier man it would have been difficult to find just then;
all his burdens seemed to have fallen off, and his spirits rose
again with an elasticity which surprised even those who knew
him best. Christie often stopped to watch and wonder if the
blithe young man who went whistling and singing about the
house, often stopping to kiss somebody, to joke, or to exclaim
with a beaming face like a child at a party: "Isn't every thing
beautiful?" could be the sober, steady David, who used to plod
to and fro with his shoulders a little bent, and the absent look
in his eyes that told of thoughts above or beyond the daily
task.

It was good to see his mother rejoice over him with an

exceeding great joy; it was better still to see Letty's eyes follow him with unspeakable love and gratitude in their soft depths; but it was best of all to see Christie marvel and exult over the discoveries she made: for, though she had known David for a year, she had never seen the real man till now.

"Davy, you are a humbug," she said one day when they were making up a bridal order in the green-house.

"I told you so, but you wouldn't believe it," he answered, using long stemmed rose-buds with as prodigal a hand as if the wedding was to be his own.

"I thought I was going to marry a quiet, studious, steady-going man; and here I find myself engaged to a romantic youth who flies about in the most undignified manner, em-braces people behind doors, sings opera airs,—very much out of tune by the way,—and conducts himself more like an infat-uated Claude Melnotte, than a respectable gentleman on the awful verge of matrimony. Nothing can surprise me now: I'm prepared for any thing, even the sight of my Quakerish lover dancing a jig."

"Just what I've been longing to do! Come and take a turn: it will do you good;" and, to Christie's utter amazement, David caught her round the waist and waltzed her down the boarded walk with a speed and skill that caused less havoc among the flower-pots than one would imagine, and seemed to delight the plants, who rustled and nodded as if applauding the dance of the finest double flower that had ever blossomed in their midst.

"I can't help it, Christie," he said, when he had landed her breathless and laughing at the other end. "I feel like a boy out of school, or rather a man out of prison, and *must* enjoy my liberty in some way. I'm not a talker, you know; and, as the laws of gravitation forbid my soaring aloft anywhere, I can only express my joyfully uplifted state of mind by 'prancing,' as you call it. Never mind dignity: let's be happy, and by and by I'll sober down."

"I don't want you to; I love to see you so young and happy, only you are not the old David, and I've got to get acquainted with the new one."

"I hope you'll like him better than the frost-bitten 'old David' you first knew and were kind enough to love. Mother says I've gone back to the time before we lost Letty, and I sometimes feel as if I had. In that case you will find me a proud, impetuous, ambitious fellow, Christie, and how will that suit?"

"Excellently; I like pride of your sort; impetuosity becomes you, for you have learned to control it if need be; and the ambition is best of all. I always wondered at your want of it, and longed to stir you up; for you did not seem the sort of man to be contented with mere creature comforts when there are so many fine things men may do. What shall you choose, Davy?"

"I shall wait for time to show. The sap is all astir in me, and I'm ready for my chance. I don't know what it is, but I feel very sure that some work will be given me into which I can put my whole heart and soul and strength. I spoilt my first chance; but I know I shall have another, and, whatever it is, I am ready to do my best, and live or die for it as God wills."

"So am I," answered Christie, with a voice as earnest and a face as full of hopeful resolution as his own.

Then they went back to their work, little dreaming as they tied roses and twined smilax wreaths, how near that other chance was; how soon they were to be called upon to keep their promise, and how well each was to perform the part given them in life and death.

The gun fired one April morning at Fort Sumter told many men like David what their work was to be, and showed many women like Christie a new right to claim and bravely prove their fitness to possess.

No need to repeat the story of the war begun that day; it has been so often told that it will only be touched upon here as one of the experiences of Christie's life, an experience which did for her what it did for all who took a share in it, and loyally acted their part.

The North woke up from its prosperous lethargy, and began to stir with the ominous hum of bees when rude hands shake the hive. Rich and poor were proud to prove that they loved their liberty better than their money or their lives, and the descendants of the brave old Puritans were worthy of their race. Many said: "It will soon be over;" but the wise men, who had warned in vain, shook their heads, as that first disastrous summer showed that the time for compromise was past, and the stern reckoning day of eternal justice was at hand.

To no home in the land did the great trouble bring a more sudden change than the little cottage in the lane. All its happy peace was broken; excitement and anxiety, grief and indignation, banished the sweet home joys and darkened the future that had seemed so clear. David was sober enough now, and went about his work with a grim set to his lips, and a spark in his eyes that made the three women look at one another pale with unspoken apprehension. As they sat together, picking lint or rolling bandages while David read aloud some dismal tale of a lost battle that chilled their blood and made their hearts ache with pity, each woman, listening to the voice that stirred her like martial music, said within herself: "Sooner or later he will go, and I have no right to keep him." Each tried to be ready to make her sacrifice bravely when the time came, and each prayed that it might not be required of her.

David said little, but they knew by the way he neglected his garden and worked for the soldiers, that his heart was in the war. Day after day he left Christie and his sister to fill the orders that came so often now for flowers to lay on the grave of some dear, dead boy brought home to his mother in a shroud. Day after day he hurried away to help Mr. Power in the sanitary work that soon claimed all hearts and hands; and, day after day, he came home with what Christie called the "heroic look" more plainly written on his face. All that first summer, so short and strange; all that first winter, so long and hard to those who went and those who stayed, David worked and waited, and the women waxed strong in the new atmosphere of self-sacrifice which pervaded the air, bringing out the sturdy virtues of the North.

"How terrible! Oh, when will it be over!" sighed Letty one day, after hearing a long list of the dead and wounded in one of the great battles of that second summer.

"Never till we have beaten!" cried David, throwing down the paper and walking about the room with his head up like a war-horse who smells powder. "It *is* terrible and yet glorious. I thank heaven I live to see this great wrong righted, and only wish I could do my share like a man."

"That is natural; but there are plenty of men who have fewer ties than you, who can fight better, and whose places are easier to fill than yours if they die," said Christie, hastily.

"But the men who have most to lose fight best they say; and to my thinking a soldier needs a principle as well as a weapon, if he is to do real service."

"As the only son of a widow, you can't be drafted: that's one comfort," said Letty, who could not bear to give up the brother lost to her for so many years.

"I should not wait for that, and I know mother would give her widow's mite if she saw that it was needed."

"Yes, Davy." The soft, old voice answered steadily; but the feeble hand closed instinctively on the arm of this only son, who was so dear to her. David held it close in both of his, saying gratefully: "Thank you, mother;" then, fixing his eyes on the younger yet not dearer women, he added with a ring in his voice that made their hearts answer with a prompt "Ay, ay!" in spite of love or fear:

"Now listen, you dear souls, and understand that, if I do this thing, I shall not do it hastily, nor without counting well the cost. My first and most natural impulse was to go in the beginning; but I stayed for your sakes. I saw I was not really needed: I thought the war would soon be over, and those who went then could do the work. You see how mistaken we were, and God only knows when the end will come. The boys—bless their brave hearts!—have done nobly, but older men are needed now. We cannot sacrifice all the gallant lads; and we who have more to lose than they must take our turn and try to do as well. You own this; I see it in your faces: then don't hold me back when the time comes for me to go. I *must* do my part, however small it is, or I shall never feel as if I deserved the love you give me. You will let me go, I am sure, and not regret that I did what seemed to me a solemn duty, leaving the consequences to the Lord!"

"Yes, David," sister and sweetheart answered, bravely forgetting in the fervor of the moment what heavy consequences God might see fit to send.

"Good! I knew my Spartans would be ready, and I won't disgrace them. I've waited more than a year, and done what I could. But all the while I felt that I was going to get a chance at the hard work, and I've been preparing for it. Bennet will take the garden and green-house off my hands this autumn for a year or longer, if I like. He's a kind, neighborly man, and his boy will take my place about the house and protect you faithfully. Mr. Power cannot be spared to go as chaplain, though he longs to desperately; so he is near in case of need, and with your two devoted daughters by you, mother, I surely can be spared for a little while."

"Only one daughter near her, David: I shall enlist when you do," said Christie, resolutely.

"You mean it?"

"I mean it as honestly as you do. I knew you would go: I saw you getting ready, and I made up my mind to follow. I, too, have prepared for it, and even spoken to Mrs. Amory. She has gone as matron of a hospital, and promised to find a place for me when I was ready. The day you enlist I shall write and tell her I *am* ready."

There was fire in Christie's eyes and a flush on her cheek now, as she stood up with the look of a woman bent on doing well her part. David caught her hands in his, regardless of the ominous bandages they held, and said, with tender admiration and reproach in his voice:

"You wouldn't marry me when I asked you this summer, fearing you would be a burden to me; but now you want to share hardship and danger with me, and support me by the knowledge of your nearness. Dear, ought I to let you do it?"

"You *will* let me do it, and in return I will marry you whenever you ask me," answered Christie, sealing the promise with a kiss that silenced him.

He had been anxious to be married long ago, but when he asked Mr. Power to make him happy, a month after his engagement, that wise friend said to them:

"I don't advise it yet. You have tried and proved one another as friends, now try and prove one another as lovers; then, if you feel that all is safe and happy, you will be ready for the greatest of the three experiments, and then in God's name marry."

"We will," they said, and for a year had been content, studying one another, finding much to love, and something to learn in the art of bearing and forbearing.

David had begun to think they had waited long enough, but Christie still delayed, fearing she was not worthy, and secretly afflicted by the thought of her poverty. She had so little to give in return for all she received that it troubled her, and she was sometimes tempted to ask Uncle Enos for a modest marriage portion. She never had yet, and now resolved to ask nothing, but to earn her blessing by doing her share in the great work.

"I shall remember that," was all David answered to that last promise of hers, and three months later he took her at her word.

For a week or two they went on in the old way; Christie did her housework with her head full of new plans, read books on nursing, made gruel, plasters, and poultices, till Mrs. Sterling pronounced her perfect; and dreamed dreams of a happy time to come when peace had returned, and David was safe at home with all the stars and bars a man could win without dying for them.

David set things in order, conferred with Bennet, petted his womankind, and then hurried away to pack boxes of stores, visit camps, and watch departing regiments with a daily increasing certainty that his time had come.

One September day he went slowly home, and, seeing Christie in the garden, joined her, helped her finish matting up some delicate shrubs, put by the tools, and when all was done said with unusual gentleness:

"Come and walk a little in the lane."

She put her arm in his, and answered quickly:

"You've something to tell me: I see it in your face."

"Dear, I must go."

"Yes, David."

"And you?"

"I go too."

"Yes, Christie."

That was all: she did not offer to detain him now; he did not deny her right to follow. They looked each other bravely in the face a moment, seeing, acknowledging the duty and the danger, yet ready to do the one and dare the other, since they went together. Then shoulder to shoulder, as if already mustered in, these faithful comrades marched to and fro, planning their campaign.

Next evening, as Mrs. Sterling sat alone in the twilight, a tall man in army blue entered quietly, stood watching the tranquil figure for a moment, then went and knelt down beside it, saying, with a most unsoldierly choke in the voice:

"I've done it, mother: tell me you're not sorry."

But the little Quaker cap went down on the broad shoulder, and the only answer he heard was a sob that stirred the soft folds over the tender old heart that clung so closely to the son who had lived for her so long. What happened in the twilight no one ever knew; but David received promotion for bravery in a harder battle than any he was going to, and from his mother's breast a decoration more precious to him than the cross of the Legion of Honor from a royal hand.

When Mr. Power presently came in, followed by the others, they found their soldier standing very erect in his old place on the rug, with the firelight gleaming on his bright buttons, and Bran staring at him with a perplexed aspect; for the uniform, shorn hair, trimmed beard, and a certain lofty carriage of the head so changed his master that the sagacious beast was disturbed.

Letty smiled at him approvingly, then went to comfort her mother who could not recover her tranquillity so soon. But Christie stood aloof, looking at her lover with something more than admiration in the face that kindled beautifully as she exclaimed:

"O David, you are splendid! Once I was so blind I thought you plain; but now my 'boy in blue' is the noblest looking man I ever saw. Yes, Mr. Power, I've found my hero at last! Here he is, my knight without reproach or fear, going out to take his part in the grandest battle ever fought. I wouldn't keep him if I could; I'm glad and proud to have him go; and if he never should come back to me I can bear it better for knowing that he dutifully did his best, and left the consequences to the Lord."

Then, having poured out the love and pride and confidence that enriched her sacrifice, she broke down and clung to him, weeping as so many clung and wept in those hard days when men and women gave their dearest, and those who prayed and waited suffered almost as much as those who fought and died.

When the deed was once done, it was astonishing what satisfaction they all took in it, how soon they got accustomed to the change, and what pride they felt in "our soldier." The loyal frenzy fell upon the three quiet women, and they could not do too much for their country. Mrs. Sterling cut up her treasured old linen without a murmur; Letty made "comfort bags" by the dozen, put up jelly, and sewed on blue jackets with tireless industry; while Christie proclaimed that if she had twenty lovers she would send them all; and then made preparations enough to nurse the entire party.

David meantime was in camp, getting his first taste of martial life, and not liking it any better than he thought he should; but no one heard a complaint, and he never regretted his "love among the roses," for he was one of the men who had a "principle as well as a weapon," and meant to do good service with both.

It would have taken many knapsacks to hold all the gifts showered upon him by his friends and neighbors. He accepted all that came, and furnished forth those of his company who were less favored. Among these was Elisha Wilkins, and how he got there should be told.

Elisha had not the slightest intention of enlisting, but Mrs. Wilkins was a loyal soul, and could not rest till she had sent a substitute, since she could not go herself. Finding that Lisha showed little enthusiasm on the subject, she tried to rouse him by patriotic appeals of various sorts. She read stirring accounts of battles, carefully omitting the dead and wounded; she turned out, baby and all if possible, to cheer every regiment that left; and was never tired of telling Wash how she wished she could add ten years to his age and send him off to fight for his country like a man.

But nothing seemed to rouse the supine Elisha, who chewed his quid like a placid beast of the field, and showed no sign of a proper spirit.

"Very well," said Mrs. Wilkins resolutely to herself, "ef I can't make no impression on his soul I will on his stommick, and see how that'll work."

Which threat she carried out with such skill and force that Lisha was effectually waked up, for he *was* "partial to good vittles," and Cynthy was a capital cook. Poor rations did not suit him, and he demanded why his favorite dishes were not forthcoming.

"We can't afford no nice vittles now when our men are

sufferin' so. I should be ashamed to cook 'em, and expect to
choke tryin' to eat 'em. Every one is sacrificin' somethin', and
we mustn't be slack in doin' our part,—the Lord knows it's
precious little,—and there won't be no stuffin' in this house for
a consid'able spell. Ef I *could* save up enough to send a man to
do my share of the fightin', I should be proud to do it. Anyway
I shall stint the family and send them dear brave fellers every
cent I can git without starvin' the children."

"Now, Cynthy, don't be ferce. Things will come out all
right, and it ain't no use upsettin' every thing and bein' so
darned uncomfortable," answered Mr. Wilkins with unusual
energy.

"Yes it is, Lisha. No one has a right to be comfortable in
such times as these, and *this* family ain't goin' to be ef I can
help it," and Mrs. Wilkins set down her flat-iron with a slam
which plainly told her Lisha war was declared.

He said no more but fell a thinking. He was not as unmoved
as he seemed by the general excitement, and had felt sundry
manly impulses to "up and at 'em," when his comrades in the
shop discussed the crisis with ireful brandishing of awls, and
vengeful pounding of sole leather, as if the rebels were under
the hammer. But the selfish, slothful little man could not make
up his mind to brave hardship and danger, and fell back on his
duty to his family as a reason for keeping safe at home.

But now that home was no longer comfortable, now that
Cynthy had sharpened her tongue, and turned "ferce," and
now—hardest blow of all—that he was kept on short com-
mons, he began to think he might as well be on the tented
field, and get a little glory along with the discomfort if that
was inevitable. Nature abhors a vacuum, and when food fell
short patriotism had a chance to fill the aching void. Lisha had
about made up his mind, for he knew the value of peace and
quietness; and, though his wife was no scold, she was the ruling power, and in his secret soul he considered her a very remarkable woman. He knew what she wanted, but was not
going to be hurried for anybody; so he still kept silent, and
Mrs. Wilkins began to think she must give it up. An unexpected ally appeared however, and the good woman took advantage of it to strike one last blow.

Lisha sat eating a late breakfast one morning, with a small

son at either elbow, waiting for stray mouthfuls and committing petty larcenies right and left, for Pa was in a brown study. Mrs. Wilkins was frying flapjacks, and though this is not considered an heroical employment she made it so that day. This was a favorite dish of Lisha's, and she had prepared it as a bait for this cautious fish. To say that the fish rose at once and swallowed the bait, hook and all, but feebly expresses the justice done to the cakes by that long-suffering man. Waiting till he had a tempting pile of the lightest, brownest flapjacks ever seen upon his plate, and was watching an extra big bit of butter melt luxuriously into the warm bosom of the upper one, with a face as benign as if some of the molasses he was trickling over them had been absorbed into his nature, Mrs. Wilkins seized the propitious moment to say impressively:

"David Sterlin' has enlisted!"

"Sho! has he, though?"

"Of course he has! any man with the spirit of a muskeeter would."

"Well, he ain't got a family, you see."

"He's got his old mother, that sister home from furrin' parts somewheres, and Christie just going to be married. I should like to know who's got a harder family to leave than that?"

"Six young children is harder: ef I went fifin' and drummin' off, who'd take care of them I'd like to know?"

"I guess *I* could support the family ef I give my mind to it;" and Mrs. Wilkins turned a flapjack with an emphasis that caused her lord to bolt a hot triangle with dangerous rapidity; for well he knew very little of *his* money went into the common purse. She never reproached him, but the fact nettled him now; and something in the tone of her voice made that sweet morsel hard to swallow.

"'Pears to me you're in ruther a hurry to be a widder, Cynthy, shovin' me off to git shot in this kind of a way," growled Lisha, ill at ease.

"I'd ruther be a brave man's widder than a coward's wife, any day!" cried the rebellious Cynthy: then she relented, and softly slid two hot cakes into his plate; adding, with her hand upon his shoulder, "Lisha, dear, I want to be proud of my husband as other women be of theirs. Every one gives somethin', I've only got you, and I want to do my share, and do it hearty."

She went back to her work, and Mr. Wilkins sat thoughtfully stroking the curly heads beside him, while the boys ravaged his plate, with no reproof, but a half audible, "My little chaps, my little chaps!"

She thought she had got him, and smiled to herself, even while a great tear sputtered on the griddle at those last words of his.

Imagine her dismay, when, having consumed the bait, her fish gave signs of breaking the line, and escaping after all; for Mr. Wilkins pushed back his chair, and said slowly, as he filled his pipe:

"I'm blest ef I can see the sense of a lot of decent men going off to be froze, and starved, and blowed up jest for them confounded niggers."

He got no further, for his wife's patience gave out; and, leaving her cakes to burn black, she turned to him with a face glowing like her stove, and cried out:

"Lisha, ain't you got no heart? can you remember what Hepsey told us, and call them poor, long-sufferin' creeters names? Can you think of them wretched wives sold from their husbands; them children as dear as ourn tore from their mothers; and old folks kep slavin eighty long, hard years with no pay, no help, no pity, when they git past work? Lisha Wilkins, look at *that*, and say no ef you darst!"

Mrs. Wilkins was a homely woman in an old calico gown, but her face, her voice, her attitude were grand, as she flung wide the door of the little back bedroom, and pointed with her tin spatula to the sight beyond.

Only Hepsey sitting by a bed where lay what looked more like a shrivelled mummy than a woman. Ah! but it was that old mother worked and waited for so long: blind now, and deaf; childish, and half dead with many hardships, but safe and free at last; and Hepsey's black face was full of a pride, a peace, and happiness more eloquent and touching than any speech or sermon ever uttered.

Mr. Wilkins had heard her story, and been more affected by it than he would confess: now it came home to him with sudden force; the thought of his own mother, wife, or babies torn from him stirred him to the heart, and the manliest emotion he had ever known caused him to cast his pipe at his feet, put on his hat with an energetic slap, and walk out of the house, wearing an expression on his usually wooden face that caused his wife to clap her hands and cry exultingly:

"I thought that would fetch him!"

Then she fell to work like an inspired woman; and at noon a sumptuous dinner "smoked upon the board;" the children were scrubbed till their faces shone; and the room was as fresh and neat as any apartment could be with the penetrating perfume of burnt flapjacks still pervading the air, and three dozen ruffled nightcaps decorating the clothes-line overhead.

"Tell me the instant minute you see Pa a comin', and I'll dish up the gravy," was Mrs. Wilkins's command, as she stepped in with a cup of tea for old "Marm," as she called Hepsey's mother.

"He's a comin', Ma!" called Gusty, presently.

"No, he ain't: it's a trainer," added Ann Lizy.

"Yes, 'tis Pa! oh, my eye! ain't he stunnin'!" cried Wash, stricken for the first time with admiration of his sire.

Before Mrs. Wilkins could reply to these conflicting rumors her husband walked in, looking as martial as his hollow chest and thin legs permitted, and, turning his cap nervously in his hands, said half-proudly, half-reproachfully:

"Now, Cynthy, *be* you satisfied?"

"Oh, my Lisha! I be, I be!" and the inconsistent woman fell upon his buttony breast weeping copiously.

If ever a man was praised and petted, admired and caressed, it was Elisha Wilkins that day. His wife fed him with the fat of the land, regardless of consequences; his children revolved about him with tireless curiosity and wonder; his neighbors flocked in to applaud, advise, and admire; every one treated him with a respect most grateful to his feelings; he was an object of interest, and with every hour his importance increased, so that by night he felt like a Commander-in-Chief, and bore himself accordingly. He had enlisted in David's regiment, which was a great comfort to his wife; for though her stout heart never failed her, it grew very heavy at times; and when Lisha was gone, she often dropped a private tear over the broken pipe that always lay in its old place, and vented her emotions by sending baskets of nourishment to Private Wilkins, which caused that bandy-legged warrior to be much envied and cherished by his mates.

"I'm glad I done it; for it will make a man of Lisha; and, if I've sent him to his death, God knows he'll be fitter to die than if he stayed here idlin' his life away."

Then the good soul openly shouldered the burden she had borne so long in secret, and bravely trudged on alone.

"Another great battle!" screamed the excited newsboys in the streets. "Another great battle!" read Letty in the cottage parlor. "Another great battle!" cried David, coming in with the war-horse expression on his face a month or two after he enlisted.

The women dropped their work to look and listen; for his visits were few and short, and every instant was precious. When the first greetings were over, David stood silent an instant, and a sudden mist came over his eyes as he glanced from one be-loved face to another; then he threw back his head with the old impatient gesture, squared his shoulders, and said in a loud, cheerful voice, with a suspicious undertone of emotion in it, however:

"My precious people, I've got something to tell you: are you ready?"

They knew what it was without a word. Mrs. Sterling clasped her hands and bowed her head. Letty turned pale and dropped her work; but Christie's eyes kindled, as she answered with a salute:

"Ready, my General."

"We are ordered off at once, and go at four this afternoon. I've got a three hours' leave to say good-by in. Now, let's be brave and enjoy every minute of it."

"We will: what can I do for you, Davy?" asked Christie, wonderfully supported by the thought that she was going too.

"Keep your promise, dear," he answered, while the warlike expression changed to one of infinite tenderness.

"What promise?"

"This;" and he held out his hand with a little paper in it. She saw it was a marriage license, and on it lay a wedding-ring. She did not hesitate an instant, but laid her own hand in his, and answered with her heart in her face:

"I'll keep it, David."

"I knew you would!" then holding her close he said in a tone that made it very hard for her to keep steady, as she had vowed she would do to the last: "I know it is much to ask, but I want to feel that you are mine before I go. Not only that, but it will be a help and protection to you, dear, when you follow. As a married woman you will get on better, as my wife you will be allowed to come to me if I need you, and as my"—he stopped there, for he could not add—"as my widow you will have my pension to support you."

She understood, put both arms about his neck as if to keep him safe, and whispered fervently:

"Nothing can part us any more, not even death; for love like ours will last for ever."

"Then you are quite willing to try the third great experiment?"

"Glad and proud to do it."

"With no doubt, no fear, to mar your consent."

"Not one, David."

"That's true love, Christie!"

Then they stood quite still for a time, and in the silence the two hearts talked together in the sweet language no tongue can utter. Presently David said regretfully:

"I meant it should be so different. I always planned that we'd be married some bright summer day, with many friends about us; then take a happy little journey somewhere together, and come back to settle down at home in the dear old way. Now it's all so hurried, sorrowful, and strange. A dull November day; no friends but Mr. Power, who will be here soon; no journey but my march to Washington alone; and no happy coming home together in this world perhaps. Can you bear it, love?"

"Have no fear for me: I feel as if I could bear any thing just now; for I've got into a heroic mood and I mean to keep so as long as I can. I've always wanted to live in stirring times, to have a part in great deeds, to sacrifice and suffer something for a principle or a person; and now I have my wish. I like it, David: it's a grand time to live, a splendid chance to do and suffer; and I want to be in it heart and soul, and earn a little of the glory or the martyrdom that will come in the end. Surely I shall if I give you and myself to the cause; and I do it gladly, though I know that my heart has got to ache as it never has ached yet, when my courage fails, as it will by and by, and my selfish soul counts the cost of my offering after the excitement is over. Help me to be brave and strong, David: don't let me complain or regret, but show me what lies beyond, and teach me to believe that simply doing the right is reward and happiness enough."

Christie was lifted out of herself for the moment, and looked inspired by the high mood which was but the beginning of a nobler life for her. David caught the exaltation, and gave no further thought to any thing but the duty of the hour, finding himself stronger and braver for that long look into the illuminated face of the woman he loved.

"I'll try," was all his answer to her appeal; then proved that he meant it by adding, with his lips against her cheek: "I must go to mother and Letty. We leave them behind, and they must be comforted."

He went, and Christie vanished to make ready for her wedding, conscious, in spite of her exalted state of mind, that every thing *was* very hurried, sad, and strange, and very different from the happy day she had so often planned.

"No matter, we are 'well on' for love,' and that is all we really need," she thought, recalling with a smile Mrs. Wilkins's advice.

"David sends you these, dear. Can I help in any way?" asked Letty, coming with a cluster of lovely white roses in her hand, and a world of affection in her eyes.

"I thought he'd give me violets," and a shadow came over Christie's face.

"But they are mourning flowers, you know."

"Not to me. The roses are, for they remind me of poor Helen, and the first work I did with David was arranging flowers like these for a dead baby's little coffin."

"My dearest Christie, don't be superstitious: all brides wear roses, and Davy thought you'd like them," said Letty, troubled at her words.

"Then I'll wear them, and I won't have fancies if I can help it. But I think few brides dress with a braver, happier heart than mine, though I do choose a sober wedding-gown," answered Christie, smiling again, as she took from a half-packed trunk her new hospital suit of soft, gray, woollen stuff.

"Won't you wear the pretty silvery silk we like so well?"

asked Letty timidly, for something in Christie's face and manner impressed her very much.

"No, I will be married in my uniform as David is," she answered with a look Letty long remembered.

"Mr. Power has come," she said softly a few minutes later, with an anxious glance at the clock.

"Go dear, I'll come directly. But first"—and Christie held her friend close a moment, kissed her tenderly, and whispered in a broken voice: "Remember, I don't take his heart from you, I only share it with my sister and my mother."

"I'm glad to give him to you, Christie; for now I feel as if I had partly paid the great debt I've owed so long," answered Letty through her tears.

Then she went away, and Christie soon followed, looking very like a Quaker bride in her gray gown with no ornament but delicate frills at neck and wrist, and the roses in her bosom.

"No bridal white, dear?" said David, going to her.

"Only this," and she touched the flowers, adding with her hand on the blue coat sleeve that embraced her: "I want to consecrate my uniform as you do yours by being married in it. Isn't it fitter for a soldier's wife than lace and silk at such a time as this?"

"Much fitter: I like it; and I find you beautiful, my Christie," whispered David, as she put one of her roses in his button-hole.

"Then I'm satisfied."

"Mr. Power is waiting: are you ready, love?"

"Quite ready."

Then they were married, with Letty and her mother standing beside them, Bennet and his wife dimly visible in the doorway, and poor Bran at his master's feet, looking up with wistful eyes, half human in the anxious affection they expressed.

Christie never forgot that service, so simple, sweet, and solemn; nor the look her husband gave her at the end, when he kissed her on lips and forehead, saying fervently, "God bless my wife!"

A tender little scene followed that can better be imagined than described; then Mr. Power said cheerily:

"One hour more is all you have, so make the most of it, dearly beloved. You young folks take a wedding-trip to the greenhouse, while we see how well we can get on without you."

"THEN THEY WERE MARRIED."

David and Christie went smiling away together, and if they shed any tears over the brief happiness no one saw them but the flowers, and they loyally kept the secret folded up in their tender hearts.

Mr. Power cheered the old lady, while Letty, always glad to serve, made ready the last meal David might ever take at home.

A very simple little marriage feast, but more love, good-will, and tender wishes adorned the plain table than is often found at wedding breakfasts; and better than any speech or song was Letty's broken whisper, as she folded her arms round David's empty chair when no one saw her, "Heaven bless and keep and bring him back to us."

How time went that day! The inexorable clock *would* strike

twelve so soon, and then the minutes flew till one was at hand, and the last words were still half said, the last good-byes still unuttered.

"I *must* go!" cried David with a sort of desperation, as Letty clung to one arm, Christie to the other.

"I shall see you soon: good-by, my husband," whispered Christie, setting him free.

"Give the last kiss to mother," added Letty, following her example, and in another minute David was gone.

At the turn of the lane, he looked back and swung his cap; all waved their hands to him; and then he marched away to the great work before him, leaving those loving hearts to ask the unanswerable question: "How will he come home?"

Christie was going to town to see the regiment off, and soon followed with Mr. Power. They went early to a certain favorable spot, and there found Mrs. Wilkins, with her entire family perched upon a fence, on the spikes of which they impaled themselves at intervals, and had to be plucked off by the stout girl engaged to assist in this memorable expedition.

"Yes, Lisha's goin', and I was bound he should see every one of his blessed children the last thing, ef I took 'em all on my back. He knows where to look, and he's a goin' to see seven cheerful faces as he goes by. Time enough to cry byme by; so set stiddy, boys, and cheer loud when you see Pa," said Mrs. Wilkins, fanning her hot face, and utterly forgetting her cherished bonnet in the excitement of the moment.

"I hear drums! They're comin'!" cried Wash, after a long half hour's waiting had nearly driven him frantic.

The two younger boys immediately tumbled off the fence, and were with difficulty restored to their perches. Gusty began to cry, Ann Elizy to wave a minute red cotton handkerchief, and Adelaide to kick delightedly in her mother's arms.

"Jane Carter, take this child for massy sake: my legs do tremble so I can't h'ist her another minute. Hold on to me behind, somebody, for I *must* see ef I do pitch into the gutter," cried Mrs. Wilkins, with a gasp, as she wiped her eyes on her shawl, clutched the railing, and stood ready to cheer bravely when her conquering hero came.

Wash had heard drums every five minutes since he arrived,

but this time he was right, and began to cheer the instant a red cockade appeared at the other end of the long street.

It was a different scene now than in the first enthusiastic, hopeful days. Young men and ardent boys filled the ranks then, brave by instinct, burning with loyal zeal, and blissfully ignorant of all that lay before them.

Now the blue coats were worn by mature men, some gray, all grave and resolute; husbands and fathers with the memory of wives and children tugging at their heart-strings; homes left desolate behind them, and before them the grim certainty of danger, hardship, and perhaps a captivity worse than death. Little of the glamour of romance about the war now: they saw what it was, a long, hard task; and here were the men to do it well.

Even the lookers-on were different. Once all was wild enthusiasm and glad uproar; now men's lips were set, and women's smileless even as they cheered; fewer handkerchiefs whitened the air, for wet eyes needed them; and sudden lulls, almost solemn in their stillness, followed the acclamations of the crowd. All watched with quickened breath and proud souls that living wave, blue below, and bright with a steely glitter above, as it flowed down the street and away to join the sea of dauntless hearts that for months had rolled up against the South, and ebbed back reddened with the blood of men like these.

As the inspiring music, the grand tramp drew near, Christie felt the old thrill and longed to fall in and follow the flag anywhere. Then she saw David, and the regiment became one man to her. He was pale, but his eyes shone, and his whole face expressed that two of the best and bravest emotions of a man, love and loyalty, were at their height as he gave his new-made wife a long, lingering look that seemed to say:

> "I could not love thee, dear, so much,
> Loved I not honor more."

Christie smiled and waved her hand to him, showed him his wedding roses still on her breast, and bore up as gallantly as he, resolved that his last impression of her should be a cheerful one. But when it was all over, and nothing remained but the trampled street, the hurrying crowd, the bleak November sky, when Mrs. Wilkins sat sobbing on the steps like Niobe with her children scattered about her, then Christie's heart gave way, and she hid her face on Mr. Power's shoulder for a moment, all her ardor quenched in tears as she cried within herself:

"No, I could *not* bear it if I was not going too!"

# Chapter XVII

## THE COLONEL

TEN years earlier Christie made her *début* as an Amazon, now she had a braver part to play on a larger stage, with a nation for audience, martial music and the boom of cannon for orchestra; the glare of battle-fields was the "red light;" danger, disease, and death, the foes she was to contend against; and the *troupe* she joined, not timid girls, but high-hearted women, who fought gallantly till the "demon" lay dead, and sang their song of exultation with bleeding hearts, for this great spectacle was a dire tragedy to them.

Christie followed David in a week, and soon proved herself so capable that Mrs. Amory rapidly promoted her from one important post to another, and bestowed upon her the only honors left the women, hard work, responsibility, and the gratitude of many men.

"You are a treasure, my dear, for you can turn your hand to any thing and do well whatever you undertake. So many come with plenty of good-will, but not a particle of practical ability, and are offended because I decline their help. The boys don't want to be cried over, or have their brows 'everlastingly swabbed,' as old Watkins calls it: they want to be well fed and nursed, and cheered up with creature comforts. Your nice beef-tea and cheery ways are worth oceans of tears and cart-loads of tracts."

Mrs. Amory said this, as Christie stood waiting while she wrote an order for some extra delicacy for a very sick patient. Mrs. Sterling, Jr., certainly did look like an efficient nurse, who thought more of "the boys" than of herself; for one hand bore a pitcher of gruel, the other a bag of oranges, clean shirts hung over the right arm, a rubber cushion under the left, and every pocket in the big apron was full of bottles and bandages, papers and letters.

"I never discovered what an accomplished woman I was till I came here," answered Christie, laughing. "I'm getting vain with so much praise, but I like it immensely, and never was so

pleased in my life as I was yesterday when Dr. Harvey came for
me to take care of poor Dunbar, because no one else could
manage him."

"It's your firm yet pitiful way the men like so well. I can't
describe it better than in big Ben's words: 'Mis Sterlin' is the
nuss for me, marm. She takes care of me as ef she was my own
mother, and it's a comfort jest to see her round.' It's a gift, my
dear, and you may thank heaven you have got it, for it works
wonders in a place like this."

"I only treat the poor fellows as I would have other women
treat my David if he should be in their care. He may be any
hour, you know."

"And my boys, God keep them!"

The pen lay idle, and the gruel cooled, as young wife and
gray-haired mother forgot their duty for a moment in tender
thoughts of the absent. Only a moment, for in came an atten-
dant with a troubled face, and an important young surgeon
with the well-worn little case under his arm.

"Bartlett's dying, marm: could you come and see to him?"
says the man to Mrs. Amory.

"We have got to amputate Porter's arm this morning, and
he won't consent unless you are with him. You will come, of
course?" added the surgeon to Christie, having tried and found
her a woman with no "confounded nerves" to impair her usefulness.

So matron and nurse go back to their duty, and dying Bartlett and suffering Porter are all the more tenderly served for
that wasted minute.

Like David, Christie had enlisted for the war, and in the two
years that followed, she saw all sorts of service; for Mrs. Amory
had influence, and her right-hand woman, after a few months'
apprenticeship, was ready for any post. The gray gown and
comforting face were known in many hospitals, seen on
crowded transports, among the ambulances at the front, invalid cars, relief tents, and food depots up and down the land,
and many men went out of life like tired children holding the
hand that did its work so well.

David meanwhile was doing his part manfully, not only in
some of the great battles of those years, but among the hardships, temptations, and sacrifices of soldiers' life. Spite of his

Quaker ancestors, he was a good fighter, and, better still, a magnanimous enemy, hating slavery, but not the slave-holder, and often spared the master while he saved the chattel. He was soon promoted, and might have risen rapidly, but was content to remain as captain of his company; for his men loved him, and he was prouder of his influence over them than of any decoration he could win.

His was the sort of courage that keeps a man faithful to death, and though he made no brilliant charge, uttered few protestations of loyalty, and was never heard to "damn the rebs," his comrades felt that his brave example had often kept them steady till a forlorn hope turned into a victory, knew that all the wealth of the world could not bribe him from his duty, and learned of him to treat with respect an enemy as brave and less fortunate than themselves. A noble nature soon takes its proper rank and exerts its purifying influence, and Private Sterling won confidence, affection, and respect, long before promotion came; for, though he had tended his flowers like a woman and loved his books like a student, he now proved that he could also do his duty and keep his honor stainless as a soldier and a gentleman.

He and Christie met as often as the one could get a brief furlough, or the other be spared from hospital duty; but when these meetings did come, they were wonderfully beautiful and rich, for into them was distilled a concentration of the love, happiness, and communion which many men and women only know through years of wedded life.

Christie liked romance, and now she had it, with a very sombre reality to give it an added charm. No Juliet ever welcomed her Romeo more joyfully than she welcomed David when he paid her a flying visit unexpectedly; no Bayard ever had a more devoted lady in his tent than David, when his wife came through every obstacle to bring him comforts or to nurse the few wounds he received. Love-letters, written beside watch-fires and sick-beds, flew to and fro like carrier-doves with wondrous speed; and nowhere in all the brave and busy land was there a fonder pair than this, although their honeymoon was spent apart in camp and hospital, and well they knew that there might never be for them a happy going home together.

In her wanderings to and fro, Christie not only made many
new friends, but met some old ones; and among these one
whose unexpected appearance much surprised and touched
her.

She was "scrabbling" eggs in a tin basin on board a crowded
transport, going up the river with the echoes of a battle dying
away behind her, and before her the prospect of passing the
next day on a wharf serving out food to the wounded in an
easterly storm.

"O Mrs. Sterling, do go up and see what's to be done! We
are all full below, and more poor fellows are lying about on
deck in a dreadful state. I'll take your place here, but I can't
stand that any longer," said one of her aids, coming in heart-
sick and exhausted by the ghastly sights and terrible confusion
of the day.

"I'll go: keep scrabbling while the eggs last, then knock out
the head of that barrel and make gruel till I pass the word to
stop."

Forgetting her bonnet, and tying the ends of her shawl behind her, Christie caught up a bottle of brandy and a canteen
of water, and ran on deck. There a sight to daunt most any
woman, met her eyes; for all about her, so thick that she could
hardly step without treading on them, lay the sad wrecks of
men: some moaning for help; some silent, with set, white faces
turned up to the gray sky; all shelterless from the cold wind
that blew, and the fog rising from the river. Surgeons and
nurses were doing their best; but the boat was loaded, and
greater suffering reigned below.

"Heaven help us all!" sighed Christie, and then she fell to
work.

Bottle and canteen were both nearly empty by the time she
came to the end of the long line, where lay a silent figure with
a hidden face. "Poor fellow, is he dead?" she said, kneeling
down to lift a corner of the blanket lent by a neighbor.

A familiar face looked up at her, and a well remembered
voice said courteously, but feebly:

"Thanks, not yet. Excuse my left hand. I'm very glad to see
you."

"Mr. Fletcher, can it be you!" she cried, looking at him with
pitiful amazement. Well she might ask, for any thing more

unlike his former self can hardly be imagined. Unshaven, haggard, and begrimed with powder, mud to the knees, coat half on, and, worst of all, the right arm gone, there lay the "piece of elegance" she had known, and answered with a smile she never saw before:

"All that's left of me, and very much at your service. I must apologize for the dirt, but I've laid in a mud-puddle for two days; and, though it was much easier than a board, it doesn't improve one's appearance."

"What can I do for you? Where can I put you? I can't bear to see you here!" said Christie, much afflicted by the spectacle before her.

"Why not? we are all alike when it comes to this pass. I shall do very well if I might trouble you for a draught of water."

She poured her last drop into his parched mouth and hurried off for more. She was detained by the way, and, when she returned, fancied he was asleep, but soon discovered that he had fainted quietly away, utterly spent with two days of hunger, suffering, and exposure. He was himself again directly, and lay contentedly looking up at her as she fed him with hot soup, longing to talk, but refusing to listen to a word till he was refreshed.

"That's very nice," he said gratefully, as he finished, adding with a pathetic sort of gayety, as he groped about with his one hand: "I don't expect napkins, but I *should* like a handkerchief. They took my coat off when they did my arm, and the gentleman who kindly lent me this doesn't seem to have possessed such an article."

Christie wiped his lips with the clean towel at her side, and smiled as she did it, at the idea of Mr. Fletcher's praising burnt soup, and her feeding him like a baby out of a tin cup.

"I think it would comfort you if I washed your face: can you bear to have it done?" she asked.

"If you can bear to do it," he answered, with an apologetic look, evidently troubled at receiving such services from her.

Yet as her hands moved gently about his face, he shut his eyes, and there was a little quiver of the lips now and then, as if he was remembering a time when he had hoped to have her near him in a tenderer capacity than that of nurse. She guessed the thought, and tried to banish it by saying cheerfully as she finished:

"There, you look more like yourself after that. Now the hands."

"Fortunately for you, there is but one," and he rather reluctantly surrendered a very dirty member.

"Forgive me, I forgot. It is a brave hand, and I am proud to wash it!"

"How do you know that?" he asked, surprised at her little burst of enthusiasm, for as she spoke she pressed the grimy hand in both her own.

"While I was recovering you from your faint, that man over there informed me that you were his Colonel; that you 'fit like a tiger,' and when your right arm was disabled, you took your sword in the left and cheered them on as if you 'were bound to beat the whole rebel army.'"

"That's Drake's story," and Mr. Fletcher tried to give the old shrug, but gave an irrepressible groan instead, then endeavored to cover it, by saying in a careless tone, "I thought I might get a little excitement out of it, so I went soldiering like all the rest of you. I'm not good for much, but I *can* lead the way for the brave fellows who do the work. Officers make good targets, and a rebel bullet would cause no sorrow in taking me out of the world."

"Don't say that! *I* should grieve sincerely; and yet I'm very glad you came, for it will always be a satisfaction to you in spite of your great loss."

"There are greater losses than right arms," muttered Mr. Fletcher gloomily, then checked himself, and added with a pleasant change in voice and face, as he glanced at the wedding-ring she wore:

"This is not exactly the place for congratulations, but I can't help offering mine; for if I'm not mistaken *your* left hand also has grown doubly precious since we met?"

Christie had been wondering if he knew, and was much relieved to find he took it so well. Her face said more than her words, as she answered briefly:

"Thank you. Yes, we were married the day David left, and have both been in the ranks ever since."

"Not wounded yet? your husband, I mean," he said, getting over the hard words bravely.

"Three times, but not badly. I think a special angel stands before him with a shield;" and Christie smiled as she spoke.

"I think a special angel stands behind him with prayers that avail much," added Mr. Fletcher, looking up at her with an expression of reverence that touched her heart.

"Now I must go to my work, and you to sleep: you need all the rest you can get before you have to knock about in the ambulances again," she said, marking the feverish color in his face, and knowing well that excitement was his only strength.

"How can I sleep in such an *Inferno* as this?"

"Try, you are so weak, you'll soon drop off;" and, laying the cool tips of her fingers on his eyelids, she kept them shut till he yielded with a long sigh of mingled weariness and pleasure, and was asleep before he knew it.

When he woke it was late at night; but little of night's blessed rest was known on board that boat laden with a freight of suffering. Cries still came up from below, and moans of pain still sounded from the deck, where shadowy figures with lanterns went to and fro among the beds that in the darkness looked like graves.

Weak with pain and fever, the poor man gazed about him half bewildered, and, conscious only of one desire, feebly called "Christie!"

"Here I am;" and the dull light of a lantern showed him her face very worn and tired, but full of friendliest compassion.

"What can I do for you?" she asked, as he clutched her gown, and peered up at her with mingled doubt and satisfaction in his haggard eyes.

"Just speak to me; let me touch you: I thought it was a dream; thank God it isn't. How much longer will this last?" he added, falling back on the softest pillows she could find for him.

"We shall soon land now; I believe there is an officers' hospital in the town, and you will be quite comfortable there."

"I want to go to your hospital: where is it?"

"I have none; and, unless the old hotel is ready, I shall stay on the wharf with the boys until it is."

"Then I shall stay also. Don't send me away, Christie: I shall not be a trouble long; surely David will let you help me die?"

and poor Fletcher stretched his one hand imploringly to her in the first terror of the delirium that was coming on.

"I will not leave you: I'll take care of you, and no one can forbid it. Drink this, Philip, and trust to Christie."

He obeyed like a child, and soon fell again into a troubled sleep while she sat by him thinking about David.

The old hotel *was* ready; but by the time he got there Mr. Fletcher was past caring where he went, and for a week was too ill to know any thing, except that Christie nursed him. Then he turned the corner and began to recover. She wanted him to go into more comfortable quarters; but he would not stir as long as she remained; so she put him in a little room by himself, got a man to wait on him, and gave him as much of her care and time as she could spare from her many duties. He was not an agreeable patient, I regret to say; he tried to bear his woes heroically, but did not succeed very well, not being used to any exertion of that sort; and, though in Christie's presence he did his best, his man confided to her that the Colonel was "as fractious as a teething baby, and the domineeringest party he ever nussed."

Some of Mr. Fletcher's attempts were comical, and some pathetic, for though the sacred circle of her wedding-ring was an effectual barrier against a look or word of love, Christie knew that the old affection was not dead, and it showed itself in his desire to win her respect by all sorts of small sacrifices and efforts at self-control. He would not use many of the comforts sent him, but insisted on wearing an army dressing-gown, and slippers that cost him a secret pang every time his eye was affronted by their ugliness. Always after an angry scene with his servant, he would be found going round among the men bestowing little luxuries and kind words; not condescendingly, but humbly, as if it was an atonement for his own shortcomings, and a tribute due to the brave fellows who bore their pains with a fortitude he could not imitate.

"Poor Philip, he tries so hard I must pity, not despise him; for he was never taught the manly virtues that make David what he is," thought Christie, as she went to him one day with an unusually happy heart.

She found him sitting with a newly opened package before him, and a gloomy look upon his face.

"See what rubbish one of my men has sent me, thinking I might value it," he said, pointing to a broken sword-hilt and offering her a badly written letter.

She read it, and was touched by its affectionate respect and manly sympathy; for the good fellow had been one of those who saved the Colonel when he fell, and had kept the broken sword as a trophy of his bravery, "thinking it might be precious in the eyes of them that loved him."

"Poor Burny might have spared himself the trouble, for I've no one to give it to, and in my eyes it's nothing but a bit of old metal," said Fletcher, pushing the parcel away with a half-irritated, half-melancholy look.

"Give it to me as a parting keepsake. I have a fine collection of relics of the brave men I have known; and this shall have a high place in my museum when I go home," said Christie, taking up the "bit of old metal" with more interest than she had ever felt in the brightest blade.

"Parting keepsake! are you going away?" asked Fletcher, catching at the words in anxious haste, yet looking pleased at her desire to keep the relic.

"Yes, I'm ordered to report in Washington, and start to-morrow."

"Then I'll go as escort. The doctor has been wanting me to leave for a week, and now I've no desire to stay," he said eagerly.

But Christie shook her head, and began to fold up paper and string with nervous industry as she answered:

"I am not going directly to Washington: I have a week's furlough first."

"And what is to become of me?" asked Mr. Fletcher, as fretfully as a sick child; for he knew where her short holiday would be passed, and his temper got the upper-hand for a minute.

"You should go home and be comfortably nursed: you'll need care for some time; and your friends will be glad of a chance to give it I've no doubt."

"I have no home, as you know; and I don't believe I've got a friend in the world who cares whether I live or die."

"This looks as if you were mistaken;" and Christie glanced about the little room, which was full of comforts and luxuries accumulated during his stay.

His face changed instantly, and he answered with the honest look and tone never given to any one but her.

"I beg your pardon: I'm an ungrateful brute. But you see I'd just made up my mind to do something worth the doing, and now it is made impossible in a way that renders it hard to bear. You are very patient with me, and I owe my life to your care: I never can thank you for it; but I will take myself out of your way as soon as I can, and leave you free to enjoy your happy holiday. Heaven knows you have earned it!"

He said those last words so heartily that all the bitterness went out of his voice, and Christie found it easy to reply with a cordial smile:

"I shall stay and see you comfortably off before I go myself. As for thanks and reward I have had both; for you *have* done something worth the doing, and you give me this."

She took up the broken blade as she spoke, and carried it away, looking proud of her new trophy.

Fletcher left next day, saying, while he pressed her hand as warmly as if the vigor of two had gone into his one:

"You will let me come and see you by and by when you too get your discharge: won't you?"

"So gladly that you shall never again say you have no home. But you must take care of yourself, or you will get the long discharge, and we can't spare you yet," she answered warmly.

"No danger of that: the worthless ones are too often left to cumber the earth; it is the precious ones who are taken," he said, thinking of her as he looked into her tired face, and remembered all she had done for him.

Christie shivered involuntarily at those ominous words, but only said, "Good-by, Philip," as he went feebly away, leaning on his servant's arm, while all the men touched their caps and wished the Colonel a pleasant journey.

# *Chapter XVIII*

## SUNRISE

---

THREE months later the war seemed drawing toward an end, and Christie was dreaming happy dreams of home and rest with David, when, as she sat one day writing a letter full of good news to the wife of a patient, a telegram was handed to her, and tearing it open she read:

> "Captain Sterling dangerously wounded. Tell his wife to come at once.          E. WILKINS."

"No bad news I hope, ma'am?" said the young fellow anxiously, as his half-written letter fluttered to the ground, and Christie sat looking at that fateful strip of paper with all the strength and color stricken out of her face by the fear that fell upon her.

"It might be worse. They told me he was dying once, and when I got to him he met me at the door. I'll hope for the best now as I did then, but I never felt like this before," and she hid her face as if daunted by ominous forebodings too strong to be controlled.

In a moment she was up and doing as calm and steady as if her heart was not torn by an anxiety too keen for words. By the time the news had flown through the house, she was ready; and, coming down with no luggage but a basket of comforts on her arm, she found the hall full of wan and crippled creatures gathered there to see her off, for no nurse in the hospital was more beloved than Mrs. Sterling. Many eyes followed her,—many lips blessed her, many hands were outstretched for a sympathetic grasp: and, as the ambulance went clattering away, many hearts echoed the words of one grateful ghost of a man, "The Lord go with her and stand by her as she's stood by us."

It was not a long journey that lay before her; but to Christie it seemed interminable, for all the way one unanswerable question haunted her, "Surely God will not be so cruel as to take

287

David now when he has done his part so well and the reward is so near."

It was dark when she arrived at the appointed spot; but Elisha Wilkins was there to receive her, and to her first breathless question, "How is David?" answered briskly:

"Asleep and doin' well, ma'am. At least I should say so, and I peeked at him the last thing before I started."

"Where is he?"

"In the little hospital over yonder. Camp warn't no place for him, and I fetched him here as the nighest, and the best thing I could do for him."

"How is he wounded?"

"Shot in the shoulder, side, and arm."

"Dangerously you said?"

"No, ma'am, that warn't and ain't my opinion. The sergeant sent that telegram, and I think he done wrong. The Captain is hit pretty bad; but it ain't by no means desperate accordin' to my way of thinkin'," replied the hopeful Wilkins, who seemed mercifully gifted with an unusual flow of language.

"Thank heaven! Now go on and tell me all about it as fast as you can," commanded Christie, walking along the rough road so rapidly that Private Wilkins would have been distressed both in wind and limb if discipline and hardship had not done much for him.

"Well, you see we've been skirmishin' round here for a week, for the woods are full of rebs waitin' to surprise some commissary stores that's expected along. Contrabands is always comin' into camp, and we do the best we can for the poor devils, and send 'em along where they'll be safe. Yesterday four women and a boy come: about as desperate a lot as I ever see; for they'd been two days and a night in the big swamp, wadin' up to their waists in mud and water, with nothin' to eat, and babies on their backs all the way. Every woman had a child, one dead, but she'd fetched it, 'so it might be buried free,' the poor soul said."

Mr. Wilkins stopped an instant as if for breath, but the thought of his own "little chaps" filled his heart with pity for that bereaved mother; and he understood now why decent men were willing to be shot and starved for "the confounded niggers," as he once called them.

"Go on," said Christie, and he made haste to tell the little story that was so full of intense interest to his listener.

"I never saw the Captain so worked up as he was by the sight of them wretched women. He fed and warmed 'em, comforted their poor scared souls, give what clothes we could find, buried the dead baby with his own hands, and nussed the other little creeters as if they were his own. It warn't safe to keep 'em more'n a day, so when night come the Captain got 'em off down the river as quiet as he could. Me and another man helped him, for he wouldn't trust no one but himself to boss the job. A boat was ready,—blest if I know how he got it,—and about midnight we led them women down to it. The boy was a strong lad, and any of 'em could help row, for the current would take 'em along rapid. This way, ma'am; be we goin' too fast for you?"

"Not fast enough. Finish quick."

"We got down the bank all right, the Captain standing in the little path that led to the river to keep guard, while Bates held the boat stiddy and I put the women in. Things was goin' lovely when the poor gal who'd lost her baby must needs jump out and run up to thank the Captain agin for all he'd done for her. Some of them sly rascals was watchin' the river: they see her, heard Bates call out, 'Come back, wench; come back!' and they fired. She did come back like a shot, and we give that boat a push that sent it into the middle of the stream. Then we run along below the bank, and come out further down to draw off the rebs. Some followed us and we give it to 'em handsome. But some warn't deceived, and we heard 'em firin' away at the Captain; so we got back to him as fast as we could, but it warn't soon enough.—Take my arm, Mis' Sterlin': it's kinder rough here."

"And you found him?"—

"Lyin' right acrost the path with two dead men in front of him; for he'd kep 'em off like a lion till the firin' brought up a lot of our fellers and the rebs skedaddled. I thought he was dead, for by the starlight I see he was bleedin' awful,—hold on, my dear, hold on to me,—he warn't, thank God, and looked up at me and sez, sez he, 'Are they safe?' 'They be, Captain,' sez I. 'Then it's all right,' sez he, smilin' in that bright way of his, and then dropped off as quiet as a lamb. We got him back to camp double quick, and when the surgeon see them three wounds he shook his head, and I mistrusted that it warn't no joke. So when the Captain come to I asked him what I could do or git for him, and he answered in a whisper, 'My wife.'"

For an instant Christie did "hold on" to Mr. Wilkins's arm, for those two words seemed to take all her strength away. Then the thought that David was waiting for her strung her nerves and gave her courage to bear any thing.

"Is he here?" she asked of her guide a moment later, as he stopped before a large, half-ruined house, through whose windows dim lights and figures were seen moving to and fro.

"Yes, ma'am; we've made a hospital of this; the Captain's got the best room in it, and now he's got the best nuss that's goin' anywheres. Won't you have a drop of something jest as a stand-by before you see him?"

"Nothing; take me to him at once."

"Here we be then. Still sleepin': that looks well."

Mr. Wilkins softly led the way down a long hall, opened a door, and after one look fell back and saluted as the Captain's wife passed in.

A surgeon was bending over the low bed, and when a hoarse voice at his elbow asked:

"How is he?" The doctor answered without looking up:

"Done for: this shot through the lungs will finish him before morning I'm afraid."

"Then leave him to me: I am his wife," said the voice, clear and sharp now with the anguish those hard words had brought.

"Good God, why did no one tell me! My dear lady, I thought you were a nurse!" cried the poor surgeon rent with remorse for what now seemed the brutal frankness of his answer, as he saw the white face of the woman at his side, with a look in her eyes harder to see than the bitterest tears that ever fell.

"I *am* a nurse. If you can do nothing, please go and leave him to me the little while he has to live."

Without a word the surgeon vanished, and Christie was alone with David.

The instant she saw him she felt that there was no hope, for she had seen too many faces wear the look his wore to be deceived even by her love. Lying with closed eyes already sunken by keen suffering, hair damp with the cold dew on his forehead, a scarlet spot on either cheek, gray lines about the mouth, and pale lips parted by the painful breaths that came in heavy gasps or fluttered fitfully. This was what Christie saw, and after that long look she knew the truth, and sunk down beside the bed, crying with an exceeding bitter cry:

"O David, O my husband, must I give you up so soon?"

His eyes opened then, and he turned his cheek to hers, whispering with a look that tried to be a smile, but ended in a sigh of satisfaction:

"I knew you'd come;" then, as a tearless sob shook her from head to foot, he added steadily, though each breath cost a pang, "Yes, dear, I must go first, but it won't be hard with you to help me do it bravely."

In that supremely bitter moment there returned to Christie's memory certain words of the marriage service that had seemed so beautiful when she took part in it: "For better for worse, till death us do part." She had known the better, so short, so sweet! This was the worse, and till death came she must keep faithfully the promise made with such a happy heart. The thought brought with it unexpected strength, and gave her courage to crush down her grief, seal up her tears, and show a brave and tender face as she took that feeble hand in hers ready to help her husband die.

He saw and thanked her for the effort, felt the sustaining power of a true wife's heart, and seemed to have no other care, since she was by him steadfast to the end. He lay looking at her with such serene and happy eyes that she would not let a tear, a murmur, mar his peace; and for a little while she felt as if she had gone out of this turbulent world into a heavenly one, where love reigned supreme.

But such hours are as brief as beautiful, and at midnight mortal suffering proved that immortal joy had not yet begun.

Christie had sat by many death-beds, but never one like this; for, through all the bitter pangs that tried his flesh, David's soul remained patient and strong, upheld by the faith that conquers pain and makes even Death a friend. In the quiet time that went before, he had told his last wishes, given his last messages of love, and now had but one desire,—to go soon that Christie might be spared the trial of seeing suffering she could neither lighten nor share.

"Go and rest, dear; go and rest," he whispered more than once. "Let Wilkins come: this is too much for you. I thought it would be easier, but I am so strong life fights for me inch by inch."

But Christie would not go, and for her sake David made haste to die.

Hour after hour the tide ebbed fast, hour after hour the man's patient soul sat waiting for release, and hour after hour the woman's passionate heart clung to the love that seemed drifting away leaving her alone upon the shore. Once or twice she could not bear it, and cried out in her despair:

"No, it is not just that you should suffer this for a creature whose whole life is not worth a day of your brave, useful, precious one! Why did you pay such a price for that girl's liberty?" she said, as the thought of her own wrecked future fell upon her dark and heavy.

"Because I owed it;—she suffered more than this seeing her baby die;—I thought of *you* in her place, and I could not help doing it."

The broken answer, the reproachful look, wrung Christie's heart, and she was silent: for, in all the knightly tales she loved so well, what Sir Galahad had rescued a more wretched, wronged, and helpless woman than the poor soul whose dead baby David buried tenderly before he bought the mother's freedom with his life?

Only one regret escaped him as the end drew very near, and mortal weakness brought relief from mortal pain. The first red streaks of dawn shone in the east, and his dim eyes brightened at the sight;

"Such a beautiful world!" he whispered with the ghost of a smile, "and so much good work to do in it, I wish I could stay and help a little longer," he added, while the shadow deepened on his face. But soon he said, trying to press Christie's hand, still holding his: "You will do my part, and do it better than I could. Don't mourn, dear heart, but work; and by and by you will be comforted."

"I will try; but I think I shall soon follow you, and need no comfort here," answered Christie, already finding consolation in the thought. "What is it, David?" she asked a little later, as

"DON'T MOURN, DEAR HEART, BUT WORK."

she saw his eyes turn wistfully toward the window where the rosy glow was slowly creeping up the sky.

"I want to see the sun rise;—that used to be our happy time;—turn my face toward the light, Christie, and we'll wait for it together."

An hour later when the first pale ray crept in at the low window, two faces lay upon the pillow; one full of the despairing grief for which there seems no balm; the other with lips and eyes of solemn peace, and that mysterious expression, lovelier than any smile, which death leaves as a tender token that all is well with the new-born soul.

To Christie that was the darkest hour of the dawn, but for David sunrise had already come.

# Chapter XIX

### LITTLE HEART'S-EASE

WHEN it was all over, the long journey home, the quiet funeral, the first sad excitement, then came the bitter moment when life says to the bereaved: "Take up your burden and go on alone." Christie's had been the still, tearless grief hardest to bear, most impossible to comfort; and, while Mrs. Sterling bore her loss with the sweet patience of a pious heart, and Letty mourned her brother with the tender sorrow that finds relief in natural ways, the widow sat among them as tranquil, colorless, and mute, as if her soul had followed David, leaving the shadow of her former self behind.

"He will not come to me, but I shall go to him," seemed to be the thought that sustained her, and those who loved her said despairingly to one another: "Her heart is broken: she will not linger long."

But one woman wise in her own motherliness always answered hopefully: "Don't you be troubled; Nater knows what's good for us, and works in her own way. Hearts like this don't break, and sorrer only makes 'em stronger. You mark my words: the blessed baby that's a comin' in the summer will work a merrycle, and you'll see this poor dear a happy woman yet."

Few believed in the prophecy; but Mrs. Wilkins stoutly repeated it and watched over Christie like a mother; often trudging up the lane in spite of wind or weather to bring some dainty mess, some remarkable puzzle in red or yellow calico to be used as a pattern for the little garments the three women sewed with such tender interest, consecrated with such tender tears; or news of the war fresh from Lisha who "was goin' to see it through ef he come home without a leg to stand on." A cheery, hopeful, wholesome influence she brought with her, and all the house seemed to brighten as she sat there freeing her mind upon every subject that came up, from the delicate little shirts Mrs. Sterling knit in spite of failing eyesight, to the fall of Richmond, which, the prophetic spirit being strong within her, Mrs. Wilkins foretold with sibylline precision.

She alone could win a faint smile from Christie with some odd saying, some shrewd opinion, and she alone brought tears to the melancholy eyes that sorely needed such healing dew; for she carried little Adelaide, and without a word put her into Christie's arms, there to cling and smile and babble till she had soothed the bitter pain and hunger of a suffering heart.

She and Mr. Power held Christie up through that hard time, ministering to soul and body with their hope and faith till life grew possible again, and from the dust of a great affliction rose the sustaining power she had sought so long.

As spring came on, and victory after victory proclaimed that the war was drawing to an end, Christie's sad resignation was broken by gusts of grief so stormy, so inconsolable, that those about her trembled for her life. It was so hard to see the regiments come home proudly bearing the torn battle-flags, weary, wounded, but victorious, to be rapturously welcomed, thanked, and honored by the grateful country they had served so well; to see all this and think of David in his grave unknown, unrewarded, and forgotten by all but a faithful few.

"I used to dream of a time like this, to hope and plan for it, and cheer myself with the assurance that, after all our hard work, our long separation, and the dangers we had faced, David would get some honor, receive some reward, at least be kept for me to love and serve and live with for a little while. But these men who have merely saved a banner, led a charge, or lost an arm, get all the glory, while he gave his life so nobly; yet few know it, no one thanked him, and I am left desolate when so many useless ones might have been taken in his place. Oh, it is not just! I cannot forgive God for robbing him of all his honors, and me of all my happiness."

So lamented Christie with the rebellious protest of a strong nature learning submission through the stern discipline of grief. In vain Mr. Power told her that David *had* received a better reward than any human hand could give him, in the gratitude of many women, the respect of many men. That to do bravely the daily duties of an upright life was more heroic in God's sight, than to achieve in an enthusiastic moment a single deed that won the world's applause; and that the seeming incompleteness of his life was beautifully rounded by the act that caused his death, although no eulogy recorded it, no song embalmed it, and few knew it but those he saved, those he loved, and the Great Commander who promoted him to the higher rank he had won.

Christie could not be content with this invisible, intangible recompense for her hero: she wanted to see, to know beyond a doubt, that justice had been done; and beat herself against the barrier that baffles bereaved humanity till impatient despair was wearied out, and passionate heart gave up the struggle.

Then, when no help seemed possible, she found it where she least expected it, in herself. Searching for religion, she had found love: now seeking to follow love she found religion. The desire for it had never left her, and, while serving others, she was earning this reward; for when her life seemed to lie in ashes, from their midst, this slender spire of flame, purifying while it burned, rose trembling toward heaven; showing her how great sacrifices turn to greater compensations; giving her light, warmth, and consolation, and teaching her the lesson all must learn.

God was very patient with her, sending much help, and letting her climb up to Him by all the tender ways in which aspiring souls can lead unhappy hearts.

David's room had been her refuge when those dark hours came, and sitting there one day trying to understand the great mystery that parted her from David, she seemed to receive an answer to her many prayers for some sign that death had not estranged them. The house was very still, the window open, and a soft south wind was wandering through the room with hints of May-flowers on its wings. Suddenly a breath of music startled her, so airy, sweet, and short-lived that no human voice or hand could have produced it. Again and again it came, a fitful and melodious sigh, that to one made superstitious by much sorrow, seemed like a spirit's voice delivering some message from another world.

Christie looked and listened with hushed breath and expectant heart, believing that some special answer was to be given her. But in a moment she saw it was no supernatural sound, only the south wind whispering in David's flute that hung beside the window. Disappointment came first, then warm over her sore heart flowed the tender recollection that she used to call the old flute "David's voice," for into it he poured the joy and sorrow, unrest and pain, he told no living soul. How often it had been her lullaby, before she learned to read its language; how gaily it had piped for others; how plaintively it had sung for him, alone and in the night; and now how full of pathetic music was that hymn of consolation fitfully whispered by the wind's soft breath.

Ah, yes! this was a better answer than any supernatural voice could have given her; a more helpful sign than any phantom face or hand; a surer confirmation of her hope than subtle argument or sacred promise: for it brought back the memory of the living, loving man so vividly, so tenderly, that Christie felt as if the barrier was down, and welcomed a new sense of David's nearness with the softest tears that had flowed since she closed the serene eyes whose last look had been for her.

After that hour she spent the long spring days lying on the old couch in his room, reading his books, thinking of his love and life, and listening to "David's voice." She always heard it now, whether the wind touched the flute with airy fingers or it hung mute; and it sung to her songs of patience, hope, and cheer, till a mysterious peace came to her, and she discovered in herself the strength she had asked, yet never thought to find. Under the snow, herbs of grace had been growing silently; and, when the heavy rains had melted all the frost away, they sprung up to blossom beautifully in the sun that shines for every spire of grass, and makes it perfect in its time and place.

Mrs. Wilkins was right; for one June morning, when she laid "that blessed baby" in its mother's arms, Christie's first words were:

"Don't let me die: I must live for baby now," and gathered David's little daughter to her breast, as if the soft touch of the fumbling hands had healed every wound and brightened all the world.

"I told you so; God bless 'em both!" and Mrs. Wilkins retired precipitately to the hall, where she sat down upon the stairs and cried most comfortable tears; for her maternal heart was full of a thanksgiving too deep for words.

A sweet, secluded time to Christie, as she brooded over her little treasure and forgot there was a world outside. A fond and jealous mother, but a very happy one, for after the bitterest came the tenderest experience of her life. She felt its sacredness, its beauty, and its high responsibilities; accepted them prayerfully, and found unspeakable delight in fitting herself to bear them worthily, always remembering that she had a double duty to perform toward the fatherless little creature given to her care.

It is hardly necessary to mention the changes one small individual made in that feminine household. The purring and clucking that went on; the panics over a pin-prick; the consultations over a pellet of chamomilla; the raptures at the dawn of a first smile; the solemn prophecies of future beauty, wit, and wisdom in the bud of a woman; the general adoration of the entire family at the wicker shrine wherein lay the idol, a mass of flannel and cambric with a bald head at one end, and a pair of microscopic blue socks at the other. Mysterious little porringers sat unreproved upon the parlor fire, small garments aired at every window, lights burned at unholy hours, and three agitated nightcaps congregated at the faintest chirp of the restless bird in the maternal nest.

Of course Grandma grew young again, and produced nursery reminiscences on every occasion; Aunt Letty trotted day and night to gratify the imaginary wants of the idol, and Christie was so entirely absorbed that the whole South might have been swallowed up by an earthquake without causing her as much consternation as the appearance of a slight rash upon the baby.

No flower in David's garden throve like his little June rose, for no wind was allowed to visit her too roughly; and when rain fell without, she took her daily airing in the green-house, where from her mother's arms she soon regarded the gay sight with such sprightly satisfaction that she seemed a little flower herself dancing on its stem.

She was named Ruth for grandma, but Christie always called her "Little Heart's-ease," or "Pansy," and those who smiled at first at the mother's fancy, came in time to see that there was an unusual fitness in the name. All the bitterness seemed taken out of Christie's sorrow by the soft magic of the child: there was so much to live for now she spoke no more of dying; and, holding that little hand in hers, it grew easier to go on along the way that led to David.

A prouder mother never lived; and, as baby waxed in beauty and in strength, Christie longed for all the world to see her. A sweet, peculiar, little face she had, sunny and fair; but, under the broad forehead where the bright hair fell as David's used to do, there shone a pair of dark and solemn eyes, so large, so deep, and often so unchildlike, that her mother wondered where she got them. Even when she smiled the shadow lingered in these eyes, and when she wept they filled and overflowed with great, quiet tears like flowers too full of dew. Christie often said remorsefully:

"My little Pansy! I put my own sorrow into your baby soul, and now it looks back at me with this strange wistfulness, and these great drops are the unsubmissive tears I locked up in my heart because I would not be grateful for the good gift God gave me, even while he took that other one away. O Baby, forgive your mother; and don't let her find that she has given you clouds instead of sunshine."

This fear helped Christie to keep her own face cheerful, her own heart tranquil, her own life as sunny, healthful, and hopeful as she wished her child's to be. For this reason she took garden and green-house into her own hands when Bennet gave them up, and, with a stout lad to help her, did well this part of the work that David bequeathed to her. It was a pretty sight to see the mother with her year-old daughter out among the fresh, green things: the little golden head bobbing here and there like a stray sunbeam; the baby voice telling sweet, unintelligible stories to bird and bee and butterfly; or the small creature fast asleep in a basket under a rose-bush, swinging in a hammock from a tree, or in Bran's keeping, rosy, vigorous, and sweet with sun and air, and the wholesome influence of a wise and tender love.

While Christie worked she planned her daughter's future, as mothers will, and had but one care concerning it. She did not fear poverty, but the thought of being straitened for the means of educating little Ruth afflicted her. She meant to teach her to labor heartily and see no degradation in it, but she could not bear to feel that her child should be denied the harmless pleasures that make youth sweet, the opportunities that educate, the society that ripens character and gives a rank which money cannot buy. A little sum to put away for Baby, safe from all risk, ready to draw from as each need came, and sacredly devoted to this end, was now Christie's sole ambition.

With this purpose at her heart, she watched her fruit and nursed her flowers; found no task too hard, no sun too hot, no weed too unconquerable; and soon the garden David planted when his life seemed barren, yielded lovely harvests to swell his little daughter's portion.

One day Christie received a letter from Uncle Enos expressing a wish to see her if she cared to come so far and "stop a spell." It both surprised and pleased her, and she resolved to go, glad that the old man remembered her, and proud to show him the great success of her life, as she considered Baby.

So she went, was hospitably received by the ancient cousin five times removed who kept house, and greeted with as much cordiality as Uncle Enos ever showed to any one. He looked askance at Baby, as if he had not bargained for the honor of her presence; but he said nothing, and Christie wisely refrained from mentioning that Ruth was the most remarkable child ever born.

She soon felt at home, and went about the old house visiting familiar nooks with the bitter, sweet satisfaction of such returns. It was sad to miss Aunt Betsey in the big kitchen, strange to see Uncle Enos sit all day in his arm-chair too helpless now to plod about the farm and carry terror to the souls of those who served him. He was still a crabbed, gruff, old man; but the narrow, hard, old heart was a little softer than it used to be; and he sometimes betrayed the longing for his kindred that the aged often feel when infirmity makes them desire tenderer props than any they can hire.

Christie saw this wish, and tried to gratify it with a dutiful affection which could not fail to win its way. Baby unconsciously lent a hand, for Uncle Enos could not long withstand the sweet enticements of this little kinswoman. He did not own the conquest in words, but was seen to cuddle his small captivator in private; allowed all sorts of liberties with his spectacles, his pockets, and bald pate; and never seemed more comfortable than when she confiscated his newspaper, and sitting on his knee read it to him in a pretty language of her own.

"She's a good little gal; looks consid'able like you; but you warn't never such a quiet puss as she is," he said one day, as the child was toddling about the room with an old doll of her mother's lately disinterred from its tomb in the garret.

"She is like her father in that. But I get quieter as I grow old, uncle," answered Christie, who sat sewing near him.

"You be growing old, that's a fact; but somehow it's kind of becomin'. I never thought you'd be so much of a lady, and look so well after all you've ben through," added Uncle Enos, vainly trying to discover what made Christie's manners so agreeable in spite of her plain dress, and her face so pleasant in spite of the gray hair at her temples and the lines about her mouth.

It grew still pleasanter to see as she smiled and looked up at him with the soft yet bright expression that always made him think of her mother.

"I'm glad you don't consider me an entire failure, uncle. You know you predicted it. But though I have gone through a good deal, I don't regret my attempt, and when I look at Pansy I feel as if I'd made a grand success."

"You haven't made much money, I guess. If you don't mind tellin', what *have* you got to live on?' asked the old man, unwilling to acknowledge any life a success, if dollars and cents were left out of it.

"Only David's pension and what I can make by my garden."

"The old lady has to have some on't, don't she?"

"She has a little money of her own; but I see that she and Letty have two-thirds of all I make."

"That ain't a fair bargain if you do all the work."

"Ah, but we don't make bargains, sir: we work for one another and share every thing together."

"So like women!" grumbled Uncle Enos, longing to see that "the property was fixed up square."

"How are you goin' to eddicate the little gal? I s'pose you think as much of culter and so on as ever you did," he presently added with a gruff laugh.

"More," answered Christie, smiling too, as she remembered the old quarrels. "I shall earn the money, sir. If the garden fails I can teach, nurse, sew, write, cook even, for I've half a dozen useful accomplishments at my fingers' ends, thanks to the education you and dear Aunt Betsey gave me, and I may have to use them all for Pansy's sake."

"SHE'S A GOOD LITTLE GAL; LOOKS CONSID'ABLE LIKE YOU."

Pleased by the compliment, yet a little conscience-stricken at the small share he deserved of it, Uncle Enos sat rubbing up his glasses a minute, before he led to the subject he had in his mind.

"Ef you fall sick or die, what then?"

"I've thought of that," and Christie caught up the child as if her love could keep even death at bay. But Pansy soon struggled down again, for the dirty-faced doll was taking a walk and could not be detained. "If I am taken from her, then my little girl must do as her mother did. God has orphans in His special care, and He won't forget her I am sure."

Uncle Enos had a coughing spell just then; and, when he got over it, he said with an effort, for even to talk of giving away his substance cost him a pang:

"I'm gettin' into years now, and it's about time I fixed up matters in case I'm took suddin'. I always meant to give you a little suthing, but as you didn't ask for't, I took good care on't, and it ain't none the worse for waitin' a spell. I jest speak on't, so you needn't be anxious about the little gal. It ain't much, but it will make things easy I reckon."

"You are very kind, uncle; and I am more grateful than I can tell. I don't want a penny for myself, but I should love to know that my daughter was to have an easier life than mine."

"I s'pose you thought of that when you come so quick?" said the old man, with a suspicious look, that made Christie's eyes kindle as they used to years ago, but she answered honestly:

"I did think of it and hope it, yet I should have come quicker if you had been in the poor-house."

Neither spoke for a minute; for, in spite of generosity and gratitude, the two natures struck fire when they met as inevitably as flint and steel.

"What's your opinion of missionaries," asked Uncle Enos, after a spell of meditation.

"If I had any money to leave them, I should bequeath it to those who help the heathen here at home, and should let the innocent Feejee Islanders worship their idols a little longer in benighted peace," answered Christie, in her usual decided way.

"That's my idee exactly; but it's uncommon hard to settle *which* of them that stays at home you'll trust your money to. You see Betsey was always pesterin' me to give to charity things; but I told her it was better to save up and give it in a handsome lump that looked well, and was a credit to you. When she was dyin' she reminded me on't, and I promised I'd do suthing before I follered. I've been turnin' on't over in my mind for a number of months, and I don't seem to find any thing that's jest right. You've ben round among the charity folks lately accordin' to your tell, now what would you do if you had a tidy little sum to dispose on?"

"Help the Freed people."

The answer came so quick that it nearly took the old gentleman's breath away, and he looked at his niece with his mouth open after an involuntary, "Sho!" had escaped him.

"David helped give them their liberty, and I would so gladly

help them to enjoy it!" cried Christie, all the old enthusiasm
blazing up, but with a clearer, steadier flame than in the days
when she dreamed splendid dreams by the kitchen fire.

"Well, no, that wouldn't meet my views. What else is there?"
asked the old man quite unwarmed by her benevolent ardor.

"Wounded soldiers, destitute children, ill-paid women, young
people struggling for independence, homes, hospitals, schools,
churches, and God's charity all over the world."

"That's the pesky part on't: there's such a lot to choose
from; I don't know much about any of 'em," began Uncle
Enos, looking like a perplexed raven with a treasure which it
cannot decide where to hide.

"Whose fault is that, sir?"

The question hit the old man full in the conscience, and he
winced, remembering how many of Betsey's charitable impulses he had nipped in the bud, and now all the accumulated
alms she would have been so glad to scatter weighed upon him
heavily. He rubbed his bald head with a yellow bandana, and
moved uneasily in his chair, as if he wanted to get up and finish
the neglected job that made his helplessness so burdensome.

"I'll ponder on't a spell, and make up my mind," was all he
said, and never renewed the subject again.

But he had very little time to ponder, and he never did make
up his mind; for a few months after Christie's long visit ended,
Uncle Enos "was took suddin'," and left all he had to her.

Not an immense fortune, but far larger than she expected,
and great was her anxiety to use wisely this unlooked-for bene-
faction. She was very grateful, but she kept nothing for herself,
feeling that David's pension was enough, and preferring the
small sum he earned so dearly to the thousands the old man
had hoarded up for years. A good portion was put by for Ruth,
something for "mother and Letty" that want might never
touch them, and the rest she kept for David's work, believing
that, so spent, the money would be blest.

# Chapter XX

"NEARLY twenty years since I set out to seek my fortune. It has been a long search, but I think I have found it at last. I only asked to be a useful, happy woman, and my wish is granted: for, I believe I *am* useful; I *know* I am happy."

Christie looked so as she sat alone in the flowery parlor one September afternoon, thinking over her life with a grateful, cheerful spirit. Forty to-day, and pausing at that half-way house between youth and age, she looked back into the past without bitter regret or unsubmissive grief, and forward into the future with courageous patience; for three good angels attended her, and with faith, hope, and charity to brighten life, no woman need lament lost youth or fear approaching age. Christie did not, and though her eyes filled with quiet tears as they were raised to the faded cap and sheathed sword hanging on the wall, none fell; and in a moment tender sorrow changed to still tenderer joy as her glance wandered to rosy little Ruth playing hospital with her dollies in the porch. Then they shone with genuine satisfaction as they went from the letters and papers on her table to the garden, where several young women were at work with a healthful color in the cheeks that had been very pale and thin in the spring.

"I think David is satisfied with me; for I have given all my heart and strength to his work, and it prospers well," she said to herself, and then her face grew thoughtful, as she recalled a late event which seemed to have opened a new field of labor for her if she chose to enter it.

A few evenings before she had gone to one of the many meetings of working-women, which had made some stir of late. Not a first visit, for she was much interested in the subject and full of sympathy for this class of workers.

There were speeches of course, and of the most unparliamentary sort, for the meeting was composed almost entirely of women, each eager to tell her special grievance or theory. Any one who chose got up and spoke; and whether wisely or foolishly each proved how great was the ferment now going on, and how difficult it was for the two classes to meet and help one another in spite of the utmost need on one side and the sincerest good-will on the other. The workers poured out their wrongs and hardships passionately or plaintively, demanding or imploring justice, sympathy, and help; displaying the ignorance, incapacity, and prejudice, which make their need all the more pitiful, their relief all the more imperative.

The ladies did their part with kindliness, patience, and often unconscious condescension, showing in their turn how little they knew of the real trials of the women whom they longed to serve, how very narrow a sphere of usefulness they were fitted for in spite of culture and intelligence, and how rich they were in generous theories, how poor in practical methods of relief.

One accomplished creature with learning radiating from every pore, delivered a charming little essay on the strong-minded women of antiquity; then, taking labor into the region of art, painted delightful pictures of the time when all would work harmoniously together in an Ideal Republic, where each did the task she liked, and was paid for it in liberty, equality, and fraternity.

Unfortunately she talked over the heads of her audience, and it was like telling fairy tales to hungry children to describe Aspasia discussing Greek politics with Pericles and Plato reposing upon ivory couches; or Hypatia modestly delivering philosophical lectures to young men behind a Tyrian purple curtain; and the Ideal Republic met with little favor from anxious seamstresses, type-setters, and shop-girls, who said ungratefully among themselves, "That's all very pretty, but I don't see how it's going to better wages among us *now*."

Another eloquent sister gave them a political oration which fired the revolutionary blood in their veins, and made them eager to rush to the State-house *en masse*, and demand the ballot before one-half of them were quite clear what it meant, and the other half were as unfit for it as any ignorant Patrick bribed with a dollar and a sup of whiskey.

A third well-wisher quenched their ardor like a wet blanket, by reading reports of sundry labor reforms in foreign parts; most interesting, but made entirely futile by differences of climate, needs, and customs. She closed with a cheerful budget of statistics, giving the exact number of needle-women who had starved, gone mad, or committed suicide during the past year; the enormous profits wrung by capitalists from the blood and muscles of their employés; and the alarming increase in the cost of living, which was about to plunge the nation into debt and famine, if not destruction generally.

When she sat down despair was visible on many countenances, and immediate starvation seemed to be waiting at the door to clutch them as they went out; for the impressible creatures believed every word and saw no salvation anywhere.

Christie had listened intently to all this; had admired, regretted, or condemned as each spoke; and felt a steadily increasing sympathy for all, and a strong desire to bring the helpers and the helped into truer relations with each other.

The dear ladies were so earnest, so hopeful, and so unpractically benevolent, that it grieved her to see so much breath wasted, so much good-will astray; while the expectant, despondent, or excited faces of the work-women touched her heart; for well she knew how much they needed help, how eager they were for light, how ready to be led if some one would only show a possible way.

As the statistical extinguisher retired, beaming with satisfaction at having added her mite to the good cause, a sudden and uncontrollable impulse moved Christie to rise in her place and ask leave to speak. It was readily granted, and a little stir of interest greeted her; for she was known to many as Mr. Power's friend, David Sterling's wife, or an army nurse who had done well. Whispers circulated quickly, and faces brightened as they turned toward her; for she had a helpful look, and her first words pleased them. When the president invited her to the platform she paused on the lowest step, saying with an expressive look and gesture:

"I am better here, thank you; for I have been and mean to be a working-woman all my life."

"Hear! hear!" cried a stout matron in a gay bonnet, and the rest indorsed the sentiment with a hearty round. Then they were very still, and then in a clear, steady voice, with the sympathetic undertone to it that is so magical in its effect, Christie made her first speech in public since she left the stage.

That early training stood her in good stead now, giving her

self-possession, power of voice, and ease of gesture; while the purpose at her heart lent her the sort of simple eloquence that touches, persuades, and convinces better than logic, flattery, or oratory.

What she said she hardly knew: words came faster than she could utter them, thoughts pressed upon her, and all the lessons of her life rose vividly before her to give weight to her arguments, value to her counsel, and the force of truth to every sentence she uttered. She had known so many of the same trials, troubles, and temptations that she could speak understandingly of them; and, better still, she had conquered or outlived so many of them, that she could not only pity but help others to do as she had done. Having found in labor her best teacher, comforter, and friend, she could tell those who listened that, no matter how hard or humble the task at the beginning, if faithfully and bravely performed, it would surely prove a stepping-stone to something better, and with each honest effort they were fitting themselves for the nobler labor, and larger liberty God meant them to enjoy.

The women felt that this speaker was one of them; for the same lines were on her face that they saw on their own, her hands were no fine lady's hands, her dress plainer than some of theirs, her speech simple enough for all to understand; cheerful, comforting, and full of practical suggestion, illustrations out of their own experience, and a spirit of companionship that uplifted their despondent hearts.

Yet more impressive than any thing she said was the subtle magnetism of character, for that has a universal language which all can understand. They saw and felt that a genuine woman stood down there among them like a sister, ready with head, heart, and hand to help them help themselves; not offering pity as an alms, but justice as a right. Hardship and sorrow, long effort and late-won reward had been hers they knew; wifehood, motherhood, and widowhood brought her very near to them; and behind her was the background of an earnest life, against which this figure with health on the cheeks, hope in the eyes, courage on the lips, and the ardor of a wide benevolence warming the whole countenance stood out full of unconscious dignity and beauty; an example to comfort, touch, and inspire them.

It was not a long speech, and in it there was no learning, no statistics, and no politics; yet it was the speech of the evening, and when it was over no one else seemed to have any thing to say. As the meeting broke up Christie's hand was shaken by many roughened by the needle, stained with printer's ink, or hard with humbler toil; many faces smiled gratefully at her, and many voices thanked her heartily. But sweeter than any applause were the words of one woman who grasped her hand, and whispered with wet eyes:

"I knew your blessed husband; he was very good to me, and I've been thanking the Lord he had such a wife for his reward!"

Christie was thinking of all this as she sat alone that day, and asking herself if she should go on; for the ladies had been as grateful as the women; had begged her to come and speak again, saying they needed just such a mediator to bridge across the space that now divided them from those they wished to serve. She certainly seemed fitted to act as interpreter between the two classes; for, from the gentleman her father she had inherited the fine instincts, gracious manners, and unblemished name of an old and honorable race; from the farmer's daughter, her mother, came the equally valuable dower of practical virtues, a sturdy love of independence, and great respect for the skill and courage that can win it.

Such women were much needed and are not always easy to find; for even in democratic America the hand that earns its daily bread must wear some talent, name, or honor as an ornament, before it is very cordially shaken by those that wear white gloves.

"Perhaps this is the task my life has been fitting me for," she said. "A great and noble one which I should be proud to accept and help accomplish if I can. Others have finished the emancipation work and done it splendidly, even at the cost of all this blood and sorrow. I came too late to do any thing but give my husband and behold the glorious end. This new task seems to offer me the chance of being among the pioneers, to do the hard work, share the persecution, and help lay the foundation of a new emancipation whose happy success I may never see. Yet I had rather be remembered as those brave beginners are, though many of them missed the triumph, than as the late comers will be, who only beat the drums and wave the banners when the victory is won."

Just then the gate creaked on its hinges, a step sounded in the porch, and little Ruth ran in to say in an audible whisper:

"It's a lady, mamma, a very pretty lady: can you see her?"

"Yes, dear, ask her in."

There was a rustle of sweeping silks through the narrow hall, a vision of a very lovely woman in the door-way, and two daintily gloved hands were extended as an eager voice asked: "Dearest Christie, don't you remember Bella Carrol?"

Christie did remember, and had her in her arms directly, utterly regardless of the imminent destruction of a marvellous hat, or the bad effect of tears on violet ribbons. Presently they were sitting close together, talking with April faces, and telling their stories as women must when they meet after the lapse of years. A few letters had passed between them, but Bella had been abroad, and Christie too busy living her life to have much time to write about it.

"Your mother, Bella? how is she, and where?"

"Still with Augustine, and he you know is melancholy mad: very quiet, very patient, and very kind to every one but himself. His penances for the sins of his race would soon kill him if mother was not there to watch over him. And her penance is never to leave him."

"Dear child, don't tell me any more; it is too sad. Talk of yourself and Harry. Now you smile, so I'm sure all is well with him."

"Yes, thank heaven! Christie, I do believe fate means to spare us as dear old Dr. Shirley said. I never can be gay again, but I keep as cheerful and busy as I can, for Harry's sake, and he does the same for mine. We shall always be together, and all in all to one another, for we can never marry and have homes apart you know. We have wandered over the face of the earth for several years, and now we mean to settle down and be as happy and as useful as we can."

"That's brave! I am so glad to hear it, and so truly thankful it is possible. But tell me, Bella, what Harry means to do? You spoke in one of your first letters of his being hard at work studying medicine. Is that to be his profession?"

"Yes; I don't know what made him choose it, unless it was the hope that he might spare other families from a curse like ours, or lighten it if it came. After Helen's death he was a

changed creature; no longer a wild boy, but a man. I told him
what you said to me, and it gave him hope. Dr. Shirley confirmed it as far as he dared; and Hal resolved to make the most
of his one chance by interesting himself in some absorbing
study, and leaving no room for fear, no time for dangerous
recollections. I was so glad, and mother so comforted, for we
both feared that sad trouble would destroy him. He studied
hard, got on splendidly, and then went abroad to finish off. I
went with him; for poor August was past hope, and mamma
would not let me help her. The doctor said it was best for me
to be away, and excellent for Hal to have me with him, to
cheer him up, and keep him steady with a little responsibility.
We have been happy together in spite of our trouble, he in his
profession, and I in him; now he is ready, so we have come
home, and now the hardest part begins for me."

"How, Bella?"

"He has his work and loves it: I have nothing after my duty
to him is done. I find I've lost my taste for the old pleasures
and pursuits, and though I have tried more sober, solid ones,
there still remains much time to hang heavy on my hands, and
such an empty place in my heart, that even Harry's love cannot
fill it. I'm afraid I shall get melancholy,—that is the beginning
of the end for us, you know."

As Bella spoke the light died out of her eyes, and they grew
despairing with the gloom of a tragic memory. Christie drew
the beautiful, pathetic face down upon her bosom, longing to
comfort, yet feeling very powerless to lighten Bella's burden.

But Christie's little daughter did it for her. Ruth had been
standing near regarding the "pretty lady," with as much wonder and admiration as if she thought her a fairy princess, who
might vanish before she got a good look at her. Divining with
a child's quick instinct that the princess was in trouble, Ruth
flew into the porch, caught up her latest and dearest treasure,
and presented it as a sure consolation, with such sweet good-
will, that Bella could not refuse, although it was only a fuzzy
caterpillar in a little box.

"I give it to you because it is my nicest one and just ready to
spin up. Do you like pussy-pillars, and know how they do it?"
asked Ruth, emboldened by the kiss she got in return for her
offering.

"Tell me all about it, darling," and Bella could not help smiling, as the child fixed her great eyes upon her, and told her little story with such earnestness, that she was breathless by the time she ended.

"At first they are only grubs you know, and stay down in the earth; then they are like this, nice and downy and humpy, when they walk; and when it's time they spin up and go to sleep. It's all dark in their little beds, and they don't know what may happen to 'em; but they are not afraid 'cause God takes care of 'em. So they wait and don't fret, and when it's right for 'em they come out splendid butterflies, all beautiful and shining like your gown. They are happy then, and fly away to eat honey, and live in the air, and never be creeping worms any more."

"That's a pretty lesson for me," said Bella softly, "I accept and thank you for it, little teacher; I'll try to be a patient 'pussy-pillar' though it *is* dark, and I don't know what may happen to me; and I'll wait hopefully till it's time to float away a happy butterfly."

"Go and get the friend some flowers, the gayest and sweetest you can find, Pansy," said Christie, and, as the child ran off, she added to her friend:

"Now we must think of something pleasant for you to do. It may take a little time, but I know we shall find your niche if we give our minds to it."

"That's one reason why I came. I heard some friends of mine talking about you yesterday, and they seemed to think you were equal to any thing in the way of good works. Charity is the usual refuge for people like me, so I wish to try it. I don't mind doing or seeing sad or disagreeable things, if it only fills up my life and helps me to forget."

"You will help more by giving of your abundance to those who know how to dispense it wisely, than by trying to do it yourself, my dear. I never advise pretty creatures like you to tuck up their silk gowns and go down into the sloughs with alms for the poor, who don't like it any better than you do, and so much pity and money are wasted in sentimental charity."

"Then what shall I do?"

"If you choose you can find plenty of work in your own

class; for, if you will allow me to say it, they need help quite as much as the paupers, though in a very different way."

"Oh, you mean I'm to be strong-minded, to cry aloud and spare not, to denounce their iniquities, and demand their money or their lives?"

"Now, Bella, that's personal; for I made my first speech a night or two ago."

"I know you did, and I wish I'd heard it. I'd make mine to-night if I could do it half as well as I'm told you did," interrupted Bella, clapping her hands with a face full of approval.

But Christie was in earnest, and produced her new project with all speed.

"I want you to try a little experiment for me, and if it succeeds you shall have all the glory; I've been waiting for some one to undertake it, and I fancy you are the woman. Not every one could attempt it; for it needs wealth and position, beauty and accomplishments, much tact, and more than all a heart that has not been spoilt by the world, but taught through sorrow how to value and use life well."

"Christie, what is it? this experiment that needs so much, and yet which you think me capable of trying?" asked Bella, interested and flattered by this opening.

"I want you to set a new fashion: you know you can set almost any you choose in your own circle; for people are very like sheep, and will follow their leader if it happens to be one they fancy. I don't ask you to be a De Staël, and have a brilliant *salon*: I only want you to provide employment and pleasure for others like yourself, who now are dying of frivolity or *ennui*."

"I should love to do that if I could. Tell me how."

"Well, dear, I want you to make Harry's home as beautiful and attractive as you can; to keep all the elegance and refinement of former times, and to add to it a new charm by setting the fashion of common sense. Invite all the old friends, and as many new ones as you choose; but have it understood that they are to come as intelligent men and women, not as pleasure-hunting beaux and belles; give them conversation instead of gossip; less food for the body and more for the mind; the healthy stimulus of the nobler pleasures they can command, instead of the harmful excitements of present dissipation. In short, show them the sort of society we need more of, and might so easily have if those who possess the means of culture cared for the best sort, and took pride in acquiring it. Do you understand, Bella?"

"Yes, but it's a great undertaking, and you could do it better than I."

"Bless you, no! I haven't a single qualification for it but the will to have it done. I'm 'strong-minded,' a radical, and a reformer. I've done all sorts of dreadful things to get my living, and I have neither youth, beauty, talent, or position to back me up; so I should only be politely ignored if I tried the experiment myself. I don't want you to break out and announce your purpose with a flourish; or try to reform society at large, but I *do* want you to devote yourself and your advantages to quietly insinuating a better state of things into one little circle. The very fact of your own want, your own weariness, proves how much such a reform is needed. There are so many fine young women longing for something to fill up the empty places that come when the first flush of youth is over, and the serious side of life appears; so many promising young men learning to conceal or condemn the high ideals and the noble purposes they started with, because they find no welcome for them. You might help both by simply creating a purer atmosphere for them to breathe, sunshine to foster instead of frost to nip their good aspirations, and so, even if you planted no seed, you might encourage a timid sprout or two that would one day be a lovely flower or a grand tree all would admire and enjoy."

As Christie ended with the figure suggested by her favorite work, Bella said after a thoughtful pause:

"But few of the women I know can talk about any thing but servants, dress, and gossip. Here and there one knows something of music, art, or literature; but the superior ones are not favorites with the larger class of gentlemen."

"Then let the superior women cultivate the smaller class of men who do admire intelligence as well as beauty. There are plenty of them, and you had better introduce a few as samples, though their coats may not be of the finest broadcloth, nor their fathers 'solid men.' Women lead in society, and when men find that they can not only dress with taste, but talk with sense, the lords of creation will be glad to drop mere twaddle and converse as with their equals. Bless my heart!" cried Christie, walking about the room as if she had mounted her hobby, and was off for a canter, "how people can go on in such an idiotic fashion passes my understanding. Why keep up an endless clatter about gowns and dinners, your neighbors' affairs, and your own aches, when there is a world full of grand questions to settle, lovely things to see, wise things to study, and noble things to imitate. Bella, you *must* try the experiment, and be the queen of a better society than any you can reign over now."

"It looks inviting, and I *will* try it with you to help me. I know Harry would like it, and I'll get him to recommend it to his patients. If he is as successful here as elsewhere they will swallow any dose he orders; for he knows how to manage people wonderfully well. He prescribed a silk dress to a despondent, dowdy patient once, telling her the electricity of silk was good for her nerves: she obeyed, and when well dressed felt so much better that she bestirred herself generally and recovered; but to this day she sings the praises of Dr. Carrol's electric cure."

Bella was laughing gaily as she spoke, and so was Christie as she replied:

"That's just what I want you to do with *your* patients. Dress up their minds in their best; get them out into the air; and cure their ills by the magnetism of more active, earnest lives."

They talked over the new plan with increasing interest; for Christie did not mean that Bella should be one of the brilliant women who shine for a little while, and then go out like a firework. And Bella felt as if she had found something to do in her own sphere, a sort of charity she was fitted for, and with it a pleasant sense of power to give it zest.

When Letty and her mother came in, they found a much happier looking guest than the one Christie had welcomed an hour before. Scarcely had she introduced them when voices in the lane made all look up to see old Hepsey and Mrs. Wilkins approaching.

"Two more of my dear friends, Bella: a fugitive slave and a laundress. One has saved scores of her own people, and is my pet heroine. The other has the bravest, cheeriest soul I know, and is my private oracle."

The words were hardly out of Christie's mouth when in they came; Hepsey's black face shining with affection, and Mrs. Wilkins as usual running over with kind words.

"My dear creeter, the best of wishes and no end of happy birthdays. There's a triflin' keepsake; tuck it away, and look at it byme by. Mis' Sterlin', I'm proper glad to see you lookin' so well. Aunt Letty, how's that darlin' child? I ain't the pleasure of your acquaintance, Miss, but I'm pleased to see you. The children all sent love, likewise Lisha, whose bones is better sense I tried the camfire and red flannel."

Then they settled down like a flock of birds of various plumage and power of song, but all amicably disposed, and ready to peck socially at any topic which might turn up.

Mrs. Wilkins started one by exclaiming as she "laid off" her bonnet:

"Sakes alive, there's a new picter! Ain't it beautiful?"

"Colonel Fletcher brought it this morning. A great artist painted it for him, and he gave it to me in a way that added much to its value," answered Christie, with both gratitude and affection in her face; for she was a woman who could change a lover to a friend, and keep him all her life.

It was a quaint and lovely picture of Mr. Greatheart, leading the fugitives from the City of Destruction. A dark wood lay behind; a wide river rolled before; Mercy and Christiana pressed close to their faithful guide, who went down the rough and narrow path bearing a cross-hilted sword in his right hand, and holding a sleeping baby with the left. The sun was just rising, and a long ray made a bright path athwart the river, turned Greatheart's dinted armor to gold, and shone into the brave and tender face that seemed to look beyond the sunrise.

"There's just a hint of Davy in it that is very comforting to me," said Mrs. Sterling, as she laid her old hands softly together, and looked up with her devout eyes full of love.

"Dem women oughter bin black," murmured Hepsey, tearfully; for she considered David worthy of a place with old John Brown and Colonel Shaw.

"The child looks like Pansy, we all think," added Letty, as the little girl brought her nosegay for Aunty to tie up prettily.

Christie said nothing, because she felt too much; and Bella was also silent because she knew too little. But Mrs. Wilkins with her kindly tact changed the subject before it grew painful, and asked with sudden interest:

"When be you a goin' to hold forth agin, Christie? Jest let me know beforehand, and I'll wear my old gloves: I tore my best ones all to rags clappin' of you; it was so extra good."

"I don't deserve any credit for the speech, because it spoke itself, and I couldn't help it. I had no thought of such a thing till it came over me all at once, and I was up before I knew it. I'm truly glad you liked it, but I shall never make another, unless you think I'd better. You know I always ask your advice, and what is more remarkable usually take it," said Christie, glad to consult her oracle.

"Hadn't you better rest a little before you begin any new task, my daughter? You have done so much these last years you must be tired," interrupted Mrs. Sterling, with a look of tender anxiety.

"You know I work for two, mother," answered Christie, with the clear, sweet expression her face always wore when she spoke of David. "I am not tired yet: I hope I never shall be, for without my work I should fall into despair or *ennui*. There is so much to be done, and it is so delightful to help do it, that I never mean to fold my hands till they are useless. I owe all I can do, for in labor, and the efforts and experiences that grew out of it, I have found independence, education, happiness, and religion."

"Then, my dear, you are ready to help other folks into the same blessed state, and it's your duty to do it!" cried Mrs. Wilkins, her keen eyes full of sympathy and commendation as they rested on Christie's cheerful, earnest face. "Ef the sperrit moves you to speak, up and do it without no misgivin's. *I* think it was a special leadin' that night, and I hope you'll foller, for it ain't every one that can make folks laugh and cry with a few plain words that go right to a body's heart and stop there real comfortable and fillin'. I guess this is your next job, my dear, and you'd better ketch hold and give it the right turn; for it's goin' to take time, and women ain't stood alone for so long they'll need a sight of boostin'.'"

There was a general laugh at the close of Mrs. Wilkins's remarks; but Christie answered seriously: "I accept the task, and will do my share faithfully with words or work, as shall seem best. We all need much preparation for the good time that is coming to us, and can get it best by trying to know and help, love and educate one another,—as we do here."

With an impulsive gesture Christie stretched her hands to the friends about her, and with one accord they laid theirs on hers, a loving league of sisters, old and young, black and white, rich and poor, each ready to do her part to hasten the coming of the happy end.

"Me too!" cried little Ruth, and spread her chubby hand above the rest: a hopeful omen, seeming to promise that the coming generation of women will not only receive but deserve their liberty, by learning that the greatest of God's gifts to us is the privilege of sharing His great work.

"EACH READY TO DO HER PART TO HASTEN THE
COMING OF THE HAPPY END."

# EIGHT COUSINS;

OR,

## THE AUNT-HILL

*WITH ILLUSTRATIONS*

To

The many boys & girls
whose letters it has been
impossible to answer,
this book is dedicated
as a peace offering
by their friend

L. M. Alcott

# PREFACE.

THE Author is quite aware of the defects of this little story, many of which were unavoidable, as it first appeared serially. But, as Uncle Alec's experiment was intended to amuse the young folks, rather than suggest educational improvements for the consideration of the elders, she trusts that these short-comings will be overlooked by the friends of the EIGHT COUSINS, and she will try to make amends in a second volume, which shall attempt to show THE ROSE IN BLOOM.

L. M. A.

# CONTENTS

# *Chapter I*

## TWO GIRLS

Rose sat all alone in the big best parlor, with her little hand-kerchief laid ready to catch the first tear, for she was thinking of her troubles, and a shower was expected. She had retired to this room as a good place in which to be miserable; for it was dark and still, full of ancient furniture, sombre curtains, and hung all round with portraits of solemn old gentlemen in wigs, severe-nosed ladies in top-heavy caps, and staring children in little bob-tailed coats or short-waisted frocks. It *was* an excellent place for woe; and the fitful spring rain that pattered on the window-pane seemed to sob, "Cry away: I'm with you."

Rose really did have some cause to be sad; for she had no mother, and had lately lost her father also, which left her no home but this with her great-aunts. She had been with them only a week, and, though the dear old ladies had tried their best to make her happy, they had not succeeded very well, for she was unlike any child they had ever seen, and they felt very much as if they had the care of a low-spirited butterfly.

They had given her the freedom of the house, and for a day or two she had amused herself roaming all over it, for it was a capital old mansion, and was full of all manner of odd nooks, charming rooms, and mysterious passages. Windows broke out in unexpected places, little balconies overhung the garden most romantically, and there was a long upper hall full of curiosities from all parts of the world; for the Campbells had been sea-captains for generations.

Aunt Plenty had even allowed Rose to rummage in her great china closet,—a spicy retreat, rich in all the "goodies" that children love; but Rose seemed to care little for these toothsome temptations; and when that hope failed, Aunt Plenty gave up in despair.

Gentle Aunt Peace had tried all sorts of pretty needle-work, and planned a doll's wardrobe that would have won the heart of even an older child. But Rose took little interest in pink satin hats and tiny hose, though she sewed dutifully till her aunt caught her wiping tears away with the train of a wedding-dress, and that discovery put an end to the sewing society.

Then both old ladies put their heads together and picked out the model child of the neighborhood to come and play with their niece. But Ariadne Blish was the worst failure of all, for Rose could not bear the sight of her, and said she was so like a wax doll she longed to give her a pinch and see if she would squeak. So prim little Ariadne was sent home, and the exhausted aunties left Rose to her own devices for a day or two.

Bad weather and a cold kept her in-doors, and she spent most of her time in the library where her father's books were stored. Here she read a great deal, cried a little, and dreamed many of the innocent bright dreams in which imaginative children find such comfort and delight. This suited her better than any thing else, but it was not good for her, and she grew pale, heavy-eyed, and listless, though Aunt Plenty gave her iron enough to make a cooking-stove, and Aunt Peace petted her like a poodle.

Seeing this, the poor aunties racked their brains for a new amusement, and determined to venture a bold stroke, though not very hopeful of its success. They said nothing to Rose about their plan for this Saturday afternoon, but let her alone till the time came for the grand surprise, little dreaming that the odd child would find pleasure for herself in a most unexpected quarter.

Before she had time to squeeze out a single tear a sound broke the stillness, making her prick up her ears. It was only the soft twitter of a bird, but it seemed to be a peculiarly gifted bird, for while she listened the soft twitter changed to a lively whistle, then a trill, a coo, a chirp, and ended in a musical mixture of all the notes, as if the bird burst out laughing. Rose laughed also, and, forgetting her woes, jumped up, saying eagerly,—

"It is a mocking-bird. Where is it?"

Running down the long hall, she peeped out at both doors, but saw nothing feathered except a draggle-tailed chicken under a burdock leaf. She listened again, and the sound seemed to be in the house. Away she went, much excited by the chase, and following the changeful song it led her to the china-closet door.

"In there? How funny!" she said. But when she entered, not a bird appeared except the everlastingly kissing swallows on the Canton china that lined the shelves. All of a sudden Rose's face brightened, and, softly opening the slide, she peered into the kitchen. But the music had stopped, and all she saw was a girl in a blue apron scrubbing the hearth. Rose stared about her for a minute, and then asked abruptly,—

"Did you hear that mocking-bird?"

"I should call it a phebe-bird," answered the girl, looking up with a twinkle in her black eyes.

"Where did it go?"

"It is here still."

"Where?"

"In my throat. Do you want to hear it?"

"Oh, yes! I'll come in." And Rose crept through the slide to the wide shelf on the other side, being too hurried and puzzled to go round by the door.

The girl wiped her hands, crossed her feet on the little island of carpet where she was stranded in a sea of soap-suds, and then, sure enough, out of her slender throat came the swallow's twitter, the robin's whistle, the blue-jay's call, the thrush's song, the wood-dove's coo, and many another familiar note, all ending as before with the musical ecstasy of a bobolink singing and swinging among the meadow grass on a bright June day.

Rose was so astonished that she nearly fell off her perch, and when the little concert was over clapped her hands delightedly.

"Oh, it was lovely! Who taught you?"

"The birds," answered the girl, with a smile, as she fell to work again.

"It is very wonderful! I can sing, but nothing half so fine as that. What is your name, please?"

"Phebe Moore."

"I've heard of phebe-birds; but I don't believe the real ones could do that," laughed Rose, adding, as she watched with interest the scattering of dabs of soft soap over the bricks, "May I stay and see you work? It is very lonely in the parlor."

"Yes, indeed, if you want to," answered Phebe, wringing out

her cloth in a capable sort of way that impressed Rose very much.

"It must be fun to swash the water round and dig out the soap. I'd love to do it, only aunt wouldn't like it, I suppose," said Rose, quite taken with the new employment.

"You'd soon get tired, so you'd better keep tidy and look on."

"I suppose you help your mother a good deal?"

"I haven't got any folks."

"Why, where do you live, then?"

"I'm going to live here, I hope. Debby wants some one to help round, and I've come to try for a week."

"I hope you *will* stay, for it is very dull," said Rose, who had taken a sudden fancy to this girl, who sung like a bird and worked like a woman.

"Hope I shall; for I'm fifteen now, and old enough to earn my own living. You have come to stay a spell, haven't you?" asked Phebe, looking up at her guest and wondering how life *could* be dull to a girl who wore a silk frock, a daintily frilled apron, a pretty locket, and had her hair tied up with a velvet snood.

"Yes, I shall stay till my uncle comes. He is my guardian now, and I don't know what he will do with me. Have you a guardian?"

"My sakes, no! I was left on the poor-house steps a little mite of a baby, and Miss Rogers took a liking to me, so I've been there ever since. But she is dead now, and I take care of myself."

"How interesting! It is like Arabella Montgomery in the 'Gypsy's Child.' Did you ever read that sweet story?" asked Rose, who was fond of tales of foundlings, and had read many.

"I don't have any books to read, and all the spare time I get I run off into the woods; that rests me better than stories," answered Phebe, as she finished one job and began on another.

Rose watched her as she got out a great pan of beans to look over, and wondered how it would seem to have life all work and no play. Presently Phebe seemed to think it was her turn to ask questions, and said, wistfully,—

"You've had lots of schooling, I suppose?"

"Oh, dear me, yes! I've been at boarding-school nearly a year, and I'm almost dead with lessons. The more I got, the more Miss Power gave me, and I was so miserable I 'most cried my eyes out. Papa never gave me hard things to do, and he always taught me so pleasantly I loved to study. Oh, we were *so* happy and so fond of one another! But now he is gone, and I am left all alone."

The tear that would not come when Rose sat waiting for it came now of its own accord,—two of them in fact,—and rolled down her cheeks, telling the tale of love and sorrow better than any words could do it.

For a minute there was no sound in the kitchen but the little daughter's sobbing and the sympathetic patter of the rain. Phebe stopped rattling her beans from one pan to the other, and her eyes were full of pity as they rested on the curly head bent down on Rose's knee, for she saw that the heart under the pretty locket ached with its loss, and the dainty apron was used to dry sadder tears than any she had ever shed.

Somehow, she felt more contented with her brown calico gown and blue-checked pinafore; envy changed to compassion; and if she had dared she would have gone and hugged her afflicted guest.

Fearing that might not be considered proper, she said, in her cheery voice,—

"I'm sure you ain't all alone with such a lot of folks belonging to you, and all so rich and clever. You'll be petted to pieces, Debby says, because you are the only girl in the family."

Phebe's last words made Rose smile in spite of her tears, and she looked out from behind her apron with an April face, saying in a tone of comic distress,—

"That's one of my troubles! I've got six aunts, and they all want me, and I don't know any of them very well. Papa named this place the Aunt-hill, and now I see why."

Phebe laughed with her as she said encouragingly,—

"Every one calls it so, and it's a real good name, for all the Mrs. Campbells live handy by, and keep coming up to see the old ladies."

"I could stand the aunts, but there are dozens of cousins, dreadful boys all of them, and I detest boys! Some of them came to see me last Wednesday, but I was lying down, and when auntie came to call me I went under the quilt and pretended to be asleep. I shall *have* to see them some time, but I do dread it so." And Rose gave a shudder, for, having lived alone with her invalid father, she knew nothing of boys, and considered them a species of wild animal.

"Oh! I guess you'll like 'em. I've seen 'em flying round when they come over from the Point, sometimes in their boats and sometimes on horseback. If you like boats and horses, you'll enjoy yourself first-rate."

"But I don't! I'm afraid of horses, and boats make me ill, and I *hate* boys!" And poor Rose wrung her hands at the awful prospect before her. One of these horrors alone she could have borne, but all together were too much for her, and she began to think of a speedy return to the detested school.

Phebe laughed at her woe till the beans danced in the pan, but tried to comfort her by suggesting a means of relief.

"Perhaps your uncle will take you away where there ain't any boys. Debby says he is a real kind man, and always brings heaps of nice things when he comes."

"Yes, but you see that is another trouble, for I don't know Uncle Alec at all. He hardly ever came to see us, though he sent me pretty things very often. Now I belong to him, and shall have to mind him, till I am eighteen. I may not like him a bit, and I fret about it all the time."

"Well, I wouldn't borrow trouble, but have a real good time. I'm sure I should think I was in clover if I had folks and money, and nothing to do but enjoy myself," began Phebe, but got no further, for a sudden rush and rumble outside made them both jump.

"It's thunder," said Phebe.

"It's a circus!" cried Rose, who from her elevated perch had caught glimpses of a gay cart of some sort and several ponies with flying manes and tails.

The sound died away, and the girls were about to continue their confidences when old Debby appeared, looking rather cross and sleepy after her nap.

"You are wanted in the parlor, Miss Rose."

"Has anybody come?"

"Little girls shouldn't ask questions, but do as they are bid," was all Debby would answer.

"I do hope it isn't Aunt Myra; she always scares me out of my wits asking how my cough is, and groaning over me as if I was going to die," said Rose, preparing to retire the way she came, for the slide, being cut for the admission of bouncing Christmas turkeys and puddings, was plenty large enough for a slender girl.

"Guess you'll wish it *was* Aunt Myra when you see who has come. Don't never let me catch you coming into my kitchen that way again, or I'll shut you up in the big biler," growled Debby, who thought it her duty to snub children on all occasions.

# *Chapter II*

## THE CLAN

R OSE scrambled into the china-closet as rapidly as possible, and there refreshed herself by making faces at Debby, while she settled her plumage and screwed up her courage. Then she crept softly down the hall and peeped into the parlor. No one appeared, and all was so still she felt sure the company was upstairs. So she skipped boldly through the half-open folding-doors, to behold on the other side a sight that nearly took her breath away.

Seven boys stood in a row,—all ages, all sizes, all yellow-haired and blue-eyed, all in full Scotch costume, and all smiling, nodding, and saying as with one voice, "How are you, cousin?"

Rose gave a little gasp and looked wildly about her as if ready to fly, for fear magnified the seven and the room seemed full of boys. Before she could run, however, the tallest lad stepped out of the line, saying pleasantly,—

"Don't be frightened. This is the clan come to welcome you; and I'm the chief, Archie, at your service."

He held out his hand as he spoke, and Rose timidly put her own into a brown paw, which closed over the white morsel and held it as the chief continued his introductions.

"We came in full rig, for we always turn out in style on grand occasions. Hope you like it. Now I'll tell you who these chaps are, and then we shall be all right. This big one is Prince Charlie, Aunt Clara's boy. She has but one, so he is an extra good one. This old fellow is Mac, the bookworm, called Worm for short. This sweet creature is Steve the Dandy. Look at his gloves and top-knot, if you please. They are Aunt Jane's lads, and a precious pair you'd better believe. These are the Brats, my brothers, Geordie and Will, and Jamie the Baby. Now, my men, step out and show your manners."

At this command, to Rose's great dismay, six more hands were offered, and it was evident that she was expected to shake them *all*. It was a trying moment to the bashful child; but,

The Eight Cousins.

remembering that they were her kinsmen come to welcome her, she tried her best to return the greeting cordially.

This impressive ceremony being over, the clan broke ranks, and both rooms instantly appeared to be pervaded with boys. Rose hastily retired to the shelter of a big chair and sat there watching the invaders and wondering when her aunt would come and rescue her.

As if bound to do their duty manfully, yet rather oppressed by it, each lad paused beside her chair in his wanderings, made a brief remark, received a still briefer answer, and then sheered off with a relieved expression.

Archie came first, and, leaning over the chair-back, observed in a paternal tone,—

"I'm glad you've come, cousin, and I hope you'll find the Aunt-hill pretty jolly."

"I think I shall."

Mac shook his hair out of his eyes, stumbled over a stool, and asked abruptly,—

"Did you bring any books with you?"

"Four boxes full. They are in the library."

Mac vanished from the room, and Steve, striking an attitude which displayed his costume effectively, said with an affable smile,—

"We were sorry not to see you last Wednesday. I hope your cold is better."

"Yes, thank you." And a smile began to dimple about Rose's mouth as she remembered her retreat under the bed-cover.

Feeling that he had been received with distinguished marks of attention, Steve strolled away with his top-knot higher than ever, and Prince Charlie pranced across the room, saying in a free and easy tone,—

"Mamma sent her love and hopes you will be well enough to come over for a day next week. It must be desperately dull here for a little thing like you."

"I'm thirteen and a half, though I *do* look small," cried Rose, forgetting her shyness in indignation at this insult to her newly acquired teens.

"Beg pardon, ma'am; never should have guessed it." And Charlie went off with a laugh, glad to have struck a spark out of his meek cousin.

Geordie and Will came together, two sturdy eleven and twelve year olders, and, fixing their round blue eyes on Rose, fired off a question apiece as if it was a shooting match and she the target.

"Did you bring your monkey?"

"No; he is dead."

"Are you going to have a boat?"

"I hope not."

Here the two, with a right-about-face movement, abruptly marched away, and little Jamie demanded with childish frankness,—

"Did you bring me any thing nice?"

"Yes, lots of candy," answered Rose, whereupon Jamie ascended into her lap with a sounding kiss and the announcement that he liked her very much.

This proceeding rather startled Rose, for the other lads looked and laughed, and in her confusion she said hastily to the young usurper,—

"Did you see the circus go by?"

"When? Where?" cried all the boys in great excitement at once.

"Just before you came. At least I thought it was a circus, for I saw a red and black sort of cart and ever so many little ponies, and—"

She got no farther, for a general shout made her pause suddenly, as Archie explained the joke by saying in the middle of his laugh,—

"It was our new dog-cart and the Shetland ponies. You'll never hear the last of your circus, cousin."

"But there were so many, and they went so fast, and the cart was so very red," began Rose, trying to explain her mistake.

"Come and see them all!" cried the Prince. And before she knew what was happening she was borne away to the barn and tumultuously introduced to three shaggy ponies and the gay new dog-cart.

She had never visited these regions before, and had her doubts as to the propriety of her being there now, but when she suggested that "Auntie might not like it," there was a general cry of,—

"She told us to amuse you, and we can do it ever so much better out here than poking round in the house."

"I'm afraid I shall get cold without my sacque," began Rose, who wanted to stay, but felt rather out of her element.

"No, you won't! We'll fix you," cried the lads, as one clapped his cap on her head, another tied a rough jacket round her neck by the sleeves, a third nearly smothered her in a carriage blanket, and a fourth threw open the door of the old barouche that stood there, saying with a flourish,—

"Step in, ma'am, and make yourself comfortable while we show you some fun."

So Rose sat in state enjoying herself very much, for the lads proceeded to dance a Highland Fling with a spirit and skill that made her clap her hands and laugh as she had not done for weeks.

"How is that, my lassie?" asked the Prince, coming up all flushed and breathless when the ballet was over.

"It was splendid! I never went to the theatre but once, and the dancing was not half so pretty as this. What clever boys you must be!" said Rose, smiling upon her kinsmen like a little queen upon her subjects.

"Ah, we're a fine lot, and that is only the beginning of our larks. We haven't got the pipes here or we'd

> 'Sing for you, play for you
> A dulcy melody,'"

answered Charlie, looking much elated at her praise.

"I did not know we were Scotch; papa never said any thing about it, or seemed to care about Scotland, except to have me sing the old ballads," said Rose, beginning to feel as if she had left America behind her somewhere.

"Neither did we till lately. We've been reading Scott's novels, and all of a sudden we remembered that our grandfather was a Scotchman. So we hunted up the old stories, got a bagpipe, put on our plaids, and went in, heart and soul, for the glory of the clan. We've been at it some time now, and it's great fun. Our people like it, and I think we are a pretty canny set."

Archie said this from the other coach-step, where he had perched, while the rest climbed up before and behind to join in the chat as they rested.

"I'm Fitzjames and he's Roderick Dhu, and we'll give you

the broadsword combat some day. It's a great thing, you'd better believe," added the Prince.

"Yes, and you should hear Steve play the pipes. He makes 'em skirl like a good one," cried Will from the box, eager to air the accomplishments of his race.

"Mac's the fellow to hunt up the old stories and tell us how to dress right, and pick out rousing bits for us to speak and sing," put in Geordie, saying a good word for the absent Worm.

"And what do you and Will do?" asked Rose of Jamie, who sat beside her as if bound to keep her in sight till the promised gift had been handed over.

"Oh, I'm the little foot-page, and do errands, and Will and Geordie are the troops when we march, and the stags when we hunt, and the traitors when we want to cut any heads off."

"They are very obliging, I'm sure," said Rose, whereat the "utility men" beamed with modest pride, and resolved to enact Wallace and Montrose as soon as possible for their cousin's special benefit.

"Let's have a game of tag," cried the Prince, swinging himself up to a beam with a sounding slap on Stevie's shoulder.

Regardless of his gloves, Dandy tore after him, and the rest swarmed in every direction as if bent on breaking their necks and dislocating their joints as rapidly as possible.

It was a new and astonishing spectacle to Rose, fresh from a prim boarding-school, and she watched the active lads with breathless interest, thinking their antics far superior to those of Mops, the dear departed monkey.

Will had just covered himself with glory by pitching off of a high loft head first and coming up all right, when Phebe appeared with a cloak, hood, and rubbers, also a message from Aunt Plenty that "Miss Rose was to come in directly."

"All right; we'll bring her!" answered Archie, issuing some mysterious order, which was so promptly obeyed that, before Rose could get out of the carriage, the boys had caught hold of the pole and rattled her out of the barn, round the oval and up to the front door with a cheer that brought two caps to an upper window, and caused Debby to cry aloud from the back porch,—

"Them harum-scarum boys will certainly be the death of that delicate little creter!"

But the "delicate little creter" seemed all the better for her trip, and ran up the steps looking rosy, gay, and dishevelled, to be received with lamentation by Aunt Plenty, who begged her to go and lie down at once.

"Oh, please don't! We have come to tea with our cousin, and we'll be as good as gold if you'll let us stay, auntie," clamored the boys, who not only approved of "our cousin," but had no mind to lose their tea, for Aunt Plenty's name but feebly expressed her bountiful nature.

"Well, dears, you can; only be quiet, and let Rose go and take her iron and be made tidy, and then we will see what we can find for supper," said the old lady as she trotted away, followed by a volley of directions for the approaching feast.

"Marmalade for me, auntie."

"Plenty of plum-cake, please."

"Tell Debby to trot out the baked pears."

"I'm your man for lemon-pie, ma'am."

"Do have fritters; Rose will like 'em."

"She'd rather have tarts, I know."

When Rose came down, fifteen minutes later, with every curl smoothed and her most beruffled apron on, she found the boys loafing about the long hall, and paused on the half-way landing to take an observation, for till now she had not really examined her new-found cousins.

There was a strong family resemblance among them, though some of the yellow heads were darker than others, some of the cheeks brown instead of rosy, and the ages varied all the way from sixteen-year-old Archie to Jamie, who was ten years younger. None of them were especially comely but the Prince, yet all were hearty, happy-looking lads, and Rose decided that boys were not as dreadful as she had expected to find them.

They were all so characteristically employed that she could not help smiling as she looked. Archie and Charlie, evidently great cronies, were pacing up and down, shoulder to shoulder, whistling "Bonnie Dundee;" Mac was reading in a corner, with his book close to his near-sighted eyes; Dandy was arranging his hair before the oval glass in the hat-stand; Geordie and Will investigating the internal economy of the moon-faced clock; and Jamie lay kicking up his heels on the mat at the foot of the stairs, bent on demanding his sweeties the instant Rose appeared.

She guessed his intention, and forestalled his demand by dropping a handful of sugar-plums down upon him.

At his cry of rapture the other lads looked up and smiled involuntarily, for the little kinswoman standing there above was a winsome sight with her shy, soft eyes, bright hair, and laughing face. The black frock reminded them of her loss, and filled the boyish hearts with a kindly desire to be good to "our cousin," who had no longer any home but this.

"There she is, as fine as you please," cried Steve, kissing his hand to her.

"Come on, Missy; tea is ready," added the Prince encouragingly.

"*I* shall take her in." And Archie offered his arm with great dignity, an honor that made Rose turn as red as a cherry and long to run upstairs again.

It was a merry supper, and the two elder boys added much to the fun by tormenting the rest with dark hints of some interesting event which was about to occur. Something uncommonly fine they declared it was, but enveloped in the deepest mystery for the present.

"Did I ever see it?" asked Jamie.

"Not to remember it; but Mac and Steve have, and liked it immensely," answered Archie, thereby causing the two mentioned to neglect Debby's delectable fritters for several minutes, while they cudgelled their brains.

"Who will have it first?" asked Will, with his mouth full of marmalade.

"Aunt Plenty, I guess."

"When will she have it?" demanded Geordie, bouncing in his seat with impatience.

"Sometime on Monday."

"Heart alive! what is the boy talking about?" cried the old lady from behind the tall urn, which left little to be seen but the topmost bow of her cap.

"Doesn't auntie know?" asked a chorus of voices.

"No; and that's the best of the joke, for she is desperately fond of it."

"What color is it?" asked Rose, joining in the fun.

"Blue and brown."

"Is it good to eat?" asked Jamie.

"Some people think so, but I shouldn't like to try it," answered Charlie, laughing so he spilt his tea.

"Who does it belong to?" put in Steve.

Archie and the Prince stared at one another rather blankly for a minute, then Archie answered with a twinkle of the eye that made Charlie explode again,—

"To Grandfather Campbell."

This was a poser, and they gave up the puzzle, though Jamie confided to Rose that he did not think he could live till Monday without knowing what this remarkable thing was.

Soon after tea the Clan departed, singing "All the blue bonnets are over the border" at the tops of their voices.

"Well, dear, how do you like your cousins?" asked Aunt Plenty, as the last pony frisked round the corner and the din died away.

"Pretty well, ma'am; but I like Phebe better." An answer which caused Aunt Plenty to hold up her hands in despair and trot away to tell sister Peace that she never *should* understand that child, and it was a mercy Alec was coming soon to take the responsibility off their hands.

Fatigued by the unusual exertions of the afternoon, Rose curled herself up in the sofa corner to rest and think about the great mystery, little guessing that she was to know it first of all.

Right in the middle of her meditations, she fell asleep and dreamed she was at home again in her own little bed. She seemed to wake and see her father bending over her; to hear him say, "My little Rose;" to answer, "Yes, papa;" and then to feel him take her in his arms and kiss her tenderly. So sweet, so real was the dream, that she started up with a cry of joy to find herself in the arms of a brown, bearded man, who held her close, and whispered in a voice so like her father's that she clung to him involuntarily,—

"This is my little girl, and I am Uncle Alec."

# *Chapter III*

### UNCLES

WHEN Rose woke next morning, she was not sure whether she had dreamed what occurred the night before, or it had actually happened. So she hopped up and dressed, although it was an hour earlier than she usually rose, for she could not sleep any more, being possessed with a strong desire to slip down and see if the big portmanteau and packing-cases were really in the hall. She seemed to remember tumbling over them when she went to bed, for the aunts had sent her off very punctually, because they wanted their pet nephew all to themselves.

The sun was shining, and Rose opened her window to let in the soft May air fresh from the sea. As she leaned over her little balcony, watching an early bird get the worm, and wondering how she should like Uncle Alec, she saw a man leap the garden wall and come whistling up the path. At first she thought it was some trespasser, but a second look showed her that it was her uncle returning from an early dip into the sea. She had hardly dared to look at him the night before, because whenever she tried to do so she always found a pair of keen blue eyes looking at her. Now she could take a good stare at him as he lingered along, looking about him as if glad to see the old place again.

A brown, breezy man, in a blue jacket, with no hat on the curly head which he shook now and then like a water-dog; broad-shouldered, alert in his motions, and with a general air of strength and stability about him which pleased Rose, though she could not explain the feeling of comfort it gave her. She had just said to herself, with a sense of relief, "I guess I *shall* like him, though he looks as if he made people mind," when he lifted his eyes to examine the budding horse-chestnut overhead, and saw the eager face peering down at him. He waved his hand to her, nodded, and called out in a bluff, cheery voice,—

"You are on deck early, little niece."

"I got up to see if you had really come, uncle."

"Did you? Well, come down here and make sure of it."

"I'm not allowed to go out before breakfast, sir."

"Oh, indeed!" with a shrug. "Then I'll come aboard and salute," he added; and, to Rose's great amazement, Uncle Alec went up one of the pillars of the back piazza hand over hand, stepped across the roof, and swung himself into her balcony, saying, as he landed on the wide balustrade: "Have you any doubts about me now, ma'am?"

Rose was so taken aback, she could only answer with a smile as she went to meet him.

"How does my girl do this morning?" he asked, taking the little cold hand she gave him in both his big warm ones.

"Pretty well, thank you, sir."

"Ah, but it should be *very well*. Why isn't it?"

"I always wake up with a headache, and feel tired."

"Don't you sleep well?"

"I lie awake a long time, and then I dream, and my sleep does not seem to rest me much."

"What do you do all day?"

"Oh, I read, and sew a little, and take naps, and sit with auntie."

"No running about out of doors, or house-work, or riding, hey?"

"Aunt Plenty says I'm not strong enough for much exercise. I drive out with her sometimes, but I don't care for it."

"I'm not surprised at that," said Uncle Alec, half to himself, adding, in his quick way: "Who have you had to play with?"

"No one but Ariadne Blish, and she was *such* a goose I couldn't bear her. The boys came yesterday, and seemed rather nice; but, of course, I couldn't play with them."

"Why not?"

"I'm too old to play with boys."

"Not a bit of it: that's just what you need, for you've been molly-coddled too much. They are good lads, and you'll be mixed up with them more or less for years to come, so you may as well be friends and playmates at once. I will look you up some girls also, if I can find a sensible one who is not spoilt by her nonsensical education."

"Phebe is sensible, I'm sure, and I like her, though I only saw her yesterday," cried Rose, waking up suddenly.

"And who is Phebe, if you please?"

Rose eagerly told all she knew, and Uncle Alec listened, with an odd smile lurking about his mouth, though his eyes were quite sober as he watched the face before him.

"I'm glad to see that you are not aristocratic in your tastes, but I don't quite make out why you like this young lady from the poor-house."

"You may laugh at me, but I do. I can't tell why, only she seems so happy and busy, and sings so beautifully, and is strong enough to scrub and sweep, and hasn't any troubles to plague her," said Rose, making a funny jumble of reasons in her efforts to explain.

"How do you know that?"

"Oh, I was telling her about mine, and asked if she had any, and she said, 'No, only I'd like to go to school, and I mean to some day.'"

"So she doesn't call desertion, poverty, and hard work, troubles? She's a brave little girl, and I shall be proud to know her." And Uncle Alec gave an approving nod, that made Rose wish she had been the one to earn it.

"But what are these troubles of yours, child?" he asked, after a minute of silence.

"Please don't ask me, uncle."

"Can't you tell them to me as well as to Phebe?"

Something in his tone made Rose feel that it would be better to speak out and be done with it, so she answered, with sudden color and averted eyes,—

"The greatest one was losing dear papa."

As she said that, Uncle Alec's arm came gently round her, and he drew her to him, saying, in the voice so like papa's,—

"That *is* a trouble which I cannot cure, my child; but I shall try to make you feel it less. What else, dear?"

"I am so tired and poorly all the time, I can't do any thing I want to, and it makes me cross," sighed Rose, rubbing the aching head like a fretful child.

"That we *can* cure and we *will*," said her uncle, with a decided nod that made the curls bob on his head, so that Rose saw the gray ones underneath the brown.

"Aunt Myra says I have no constitution, and never shall be strong," observed Rose, in a pensive tone, as if it was rather a nice thing to be an invalid.

"Aunt Myra is a—ahem!—an excellent woman, but it is her hobby to believe that every one is tottering on the brink of the grave; and, upon my life, I believe she is offended if people don't fall into it! We will show her how to make constitutions and turn pale-faced little ghosts into rosy, hearty girls. That's my business, you know," he added, more quietly, for his sudden outburst had rather startled Rose.

"I had forgotten you were a doctor. I'm glad of it, for I do want to be well, only I hope you won't give me much medicine, for I've taken quarts already, and it does me no good."

As she spoke, Rose pointed to a little table just inside the window, on which appeared a regiment of bottles.

"Ah, ha! Now we'll see what mischief these blessed women have been at." And, making a long arm, Dr. Alec set the bottles on the wide railing before him, examined each carefully, smiled over some, frowned over others, and said, as he put down the last: "Now I'll show you the best way to take these messes." And, as quick as a flash, he sent one after another smashing down into the posy-beds below.

"But Aunt Plenty won't like it; and Aunt Myra will be angry, for she sent most of them!" cried Rose, half frightened and half pleased at such energetic measures.

"You are my patient now, and I'll take the responsibility. My way of giving physic is evidently the best, for you look better already," he said, laughing so infectiously that Rose followed suit, saying saucily,—

"If I don't like your medicines any better than those, I shall throw them into the garden, and then what will you do?"

"When I prescribe such rubbish, I'll give you leave to pitch it overboard as soon as you like. Now what is the next trouble?"

"I hoped you would forget to ask."

"But how can I help you if I don't know them? Come, let us have No. 3."

"It is very wrong, I suppose, but I do sometimes wish I had not *quite* so many aunts. They are all very good to me, and I want to please them; but they are so different, I feel sort of pulled to pieces among them," said Rose, trying to express the emotions of a stray chicken with six hens all clucking over it at once.

Uncle Alec threw back his head and laughed like a boy, for he could entirely understand how the good ladies had each put in her oar and tried to paddle her own way, to the great disturbance of the waters and the entire bewilderment of poor Rose.

"I intend to try a course of uncles now, and see how that suits your constitution. I'm going to have you all to myself, and no one is to give a word of advice unless I ask it. There is no other way to keep order aboard, and I am captain of this little craft, for a time at least. What comes next?"

But Rose stuck there, and grew so red, her uncle guessed what that trouble was.

"I don't think I *can* tell this one. It wouldn't be polite, and I feel pretty sure that it isn't going to be a trouble any more."

As she blushed and stammered over these words, Dr. Alec turned his eyes away to the distant sea, and said so seriously, so tenderly, that she felt every word and long remembered them,—

"My child, I don't expect you to love and trust me all at once, but I do want you to believe that I shall give my whole heart to this new duty; and if I make mistakes, as I probably shall, no one will grieve over them more bitterly than I. It is my fault that I am a stranger to you, when I want to be your best friend. That is one of my mistakes, and I never repented it more deeply than I do now. Your father and I had a trouble once, and I thought I never could forgive him; so I kept away for years. Thank God, we made it all up the last time I saw him, and he told me then, that if he was forced to leave her he should bequeath his little girl to me as a token of his love. I can't fill his place, but I shall try to be a father to her; and if she learns to love me half as well as she did the good one she has lost, I shall be a proud and happy man. Will she believe this and try?"

Something in Uncle Alec's face touched Rose to the heart, and when he held out his hand with that anxious, troubled look in his eyes, she was moved to put up her innocent lips and seal the contract with a confiding kiss. The strong arm held her close a minute, and she felt the broad chest heave once as if with a great sigh of relief; but not a word was spoken till a tap at the door made both start.

Rose popped her head through the window to say "come in," while Dr. Alec hastily rubbed the sleeve of his jacket across his eyes and began to whistle again.

Phebe appeared with a cup of coffee.

"Debby told me to bring this and help you get up," she said, opening her black eyes wide, as if she wondered how on earth "the sailor man" got there.

"I'm all dressed, so I don't need any help. I hope that is good and strong," added Rose, eying the steaming cup with an eager look.

But she did not get it, for a brown hand took possession of it as her uncle said quickly,—

"Hold hard, my lass, and let me overhaul that dose before you take it. Do you drink all this strong coffee every morning, Rose?"

"Yes, sir, and I like it. Auntie says it 'tones' me up, and I always feel better after it."

"This accounts for the sleepless nights, the flutter your heart gets into at the least start, and this is why that cheek of yours is pale yellow instead of rosy red. No more coffee for you, my dear, and by and by you'll see that I am right. Any new milk downstairs, Phebe?"

"Yes, sir, plenty,—right in from the barn."

"That's the drink for my patient. Go bring me a pitcherful, and another cup; I want a draught myself. This won't hurt the honeysuckles, for they have no nerves to speak of." And, to Rose's great discomfort, the coffee went after the medicine.

Dr. Alec saw the injured look she put on, but took no notice, and presently banished it by saying pleasantly,—

"I've got a capital little cup among my traps, and I'll give it to you to drink your milk in, as it is made of wood that is supposed to improve whatever is put into it,—something like a quassia cup. That reminds me; one of the boxes Phebe wanted to lug upstairs last night is for you. Knowing that I was coming home to find a ready-made daughter, I picked up all sorts of odd and pretty trifles along the way, hoping she would be able to find something she liked among them all. Early to-morrow we'll have a grand rummage. Here's our milk! I propose the health of Miss Rose Campbell—and drink it with all my heart."

It was impossible for Rose to pout with the prospect of a delightful boxful of gifts dancing before her eyes; so, in spite of herself, she smiled as she drank her own health, and found that fresh milk was not a hard dose to take.

"Now I must be off, before I am caught again with my wig in a toss," said Dr. Alec, preparing to descend the way he came.

"Do you always go in and out like a cat, uncle?" asked Rose, much amused at his odd ways.

"I used to sneak out of my window when I was a boy, so I need not disturb the aunts, and now I rather like it, for it's the shortest road, and it keeps me limber when I have no rigging to climb. Good-by till breakfast." And away he went down the water-spout, over the roof, and vanished among the budding honeysuckles below.

"Ain't he a funny guardeen?" exclaimed Phebe, as she went off with the cups.

"He is a very kind one, I think," answered Rose, following, to prowl round the big boxes and try to guess which was hers.

When her uncle appeared at the sound of the bell, he found her surveying with an anxious face a new dish that smoked upon the table.

"Got a fresh trouble, Rosy?" he asked, stroking her smooth head.

"Uncle, *are* you going to make me eat oatmeal?" asked Rose, in a tragic tone.

"Don't you like it?"

"I de-test it!" answered Rose, with all the emphasis which a turned-up nose, a shudder, and a groan could give to the three words.

"You are not a true Scotchwoman, if you don't like the 'parritch.' It's a pity, for I made it myself, and thought we'd have such a good time with all that cream to float it in. Well, never mind." And he sat down with a disappointed air.

Rose had made up her mind to be obstinate about it, because she did heartily "detest" the dish; but as Uncle Alec did not attempt to make her obey, she suddenly changed her mind and thought she would.

"I'll try to eat it to please you, uncle; but people are always saying how wholesome it is, and that makes me hate it," she said, half ashamed at her silly excuse.

"I do want you to like it, because I wish my girl to be as well and strong as Jessie's boys, who are brought up on this in the good old fashion. No hot bread and fried stuff for them, and they are the biggest and bonniest lads of the lot. Bless you, auntie, and good morning!"

Dr. Alec turned to greet the old lady, and, with a firm resolve to eat or die in the attempt, Rose sat down.

In five minutes she forgot what she was eating, so interested was she in the chat that went on. It amused her very much to hear Aunt Plenty call her forty-year-old nephew "my dear boy;" and Uncle Alec was so full of lively gossip about all creation in general, and the Aunt-hill in particular, that the detested porridge vanished without a murmur.

"You will go to church with us, I hope, Alec, if you are not too tired," said the old lady, when breakfast was over.

"I came all the way from Calcutta for that express purpose, ma'am. Only I must send the sisters word of my arrival, for they don't expect me till to-morrow, you know, and there will be a row in church if those boys see me without warning."

"I'll send Ben up the hill, and you can step over to Myra's yourself; it will please her, and you will have plenty of time."

Dr. Alec was off at once, and they saw no more of him till the old barouche was at the door, and Aunt Plenty just rustling downstairs in her Sunday best, with Rose like a little black shadow behind her.

Away they drove in state, and all the way Uncle Alec's hat was more off his head than on, for every one they met smiled and bowed, and gave him as blithe a greeting as the day permitted.

It was evident that the warning had been a wise one, for, in spite of time and place, the lads were in such a ferment that their elders sat in momentary dread of an unseemly outbreak somewhere. It was simply impossible to keep those fourteen eyes off Uncle Alec, and the dreadful things that were done during sermon-time will hardly be believed.

Rose dared not look up after a while, for these bad boys

vented their emotions upon her till she was ready to laugh and cry with mingled amusement and vexation. Charlie winked rapturously at her behind his mother's fan; Mac openly pointed to the tall figure beside her; Jamie stared fixedly over the back of his pew, till Rose thought his round eyes would drop out of his head; George fell over a stool and dropped three books in his excitement; Will drew sailors and Chinamen on his clean cuffs, and displayed them, to Rose's great tribulation; Steve nearly upset the whole party by burning his nose with salts, as he pretended to be overcome by his joy; even dignified Archie disgraced himself by writing in his hymn-book, "Isn't he *blue* and *brown?*" and passing it politely to Rose.

Her only salvation was trying to fix her attention upon Uncle Mac,—a portly, placid gentleman, who seemed entirely unconscious of the iniquities of the Clan, and dozed peacefully in his pew corner. This was the only uncle Rose had met for years, for Uncle Jem and Uncle Steve, the husbands of Aunt Jessie and Aunt Clara, were at sea, and Aunt Myra was a widow. Uncle Mac was a merchant, very rich and busy, and as quiet as a mouse at home, for he was in such a minority among the women folk he dared not open his lips, and let his wife rule undisturbed.

Rose liked the big, kindly, silent man who came to her when papa died, was always sending her splendid boxes of goodies at school, and often invited her into his great warehouse, full of teas and spices, wines and all sorts of foreign fruits, there to eat and carry away whatever she liked. She had secretly regretted that he was not to be her guardian; but since she had seen Uncle Alec she felt better about it, for she did not particularly admire Aunt Jane.

When church was over, Dr. Alec got into the porch as quickly as possible, and there the young bears had a hug all round, while the sisters shook hands and welcomed him with bright faces and glad hearts. Rose was nearly crushed flat behind a door in that dangerous passage from pew to porch; but Uncle Mac rescued her, and put her into the carriage for safe keeping.

"Now, girls, I want you all to come and dine with Alec; Mac also, of course. But I cannot ask the boys, for we did not expect this dear fellow till to-morrow, you know, so I made no preparations. Send the lads home, and let them wait till Monday, for really I was shocked at their behavior in church," said Aunt Plenty, as she followed Rose.

In any other place the defrauded boys would have set up a howl; as it was, they growled and protested till Dr. Alec settled the matter by saying,—

"Never mind, old chaps, I'll make it up to you to-morrow, if you sheer off quietly; if you don't, not a blessed thing shall you have out of my big boxes."

Rose and Her Aunts.

# Chapter IV

## AUNTS

A<small>LL</small> dinner-time Rose felt that she was going to be talked about, and afterward she was sure of it, for Aunt Plenty whispered to her as they went into the parlor,—

"Run up and sit awhile with Sister Peace, my dear. She likes to have you read while she rests, and we are going to be busy."

Rose obeyed, and the quiet rooms above were so like a church that she soon composed her ruffled feelings, and was unconsciously a little minister of happiness to the sweet old lady, who for years had sat there patiently waiting to be set free from pain.

Rose knew the sad romance of her life, and it gave a certain tender charm to this great-aunt of hers, whom she already loved. When Peace was twenty, she was about to be married; all was done, the wedding-dress lay ready, the flowers were waiting to be put on, the happy hour at hand, when word came that the lover was dead. They thought that gentle Peace would die too; but she bore it bravely, put away her bridal gear, took up her life afresh, and lived on,—a beautiful, meek woman, with hair as white as snow and cheeks that never bloomed again. She wore no black, but soft, pale colors, as if always ready for the marriage that had never come.

For thirty years she had lived on, fading slowly, but cheerful, busy, and full of interest in all that went on in the family; especially the joys and sorrows of the young girls growing up about her, and to them she was adviser, confidante, and friend in all their tender trials and delights. A truly beautiful old maiden, with her silvery hair, tranquil face, and an atmosphere of repose about her that soothed whoever came to her!

Aunt Plenty was utterly dissimilar, being a stout, brisk old lady, with a sharp eye, a lively tongue, and a face like a winter-apple. Always trotting, chatting, and bustling, she was a regular Martha, cumbered with the cares of this world and quite happy in them.

Rose was right; and while she softly read psalms to Aunt

Peace, the other ladies were talking about her little self in the frankest manner.

"Well, Alec, how do you like your ward?" began Aunt Jane, as they all settled down, and Uncle Mac deposited himself in a corner to finish his doze.

"I should like her better if I could have begun at the beginning, and so got a fair start. Poor George led such a solitary life that the child has suffered in many ways, and since he died she has been going on worse than ever, judging from the state I find her in."

"My dear boy, we did what we thought best while waiting for you to wind up your affairs and get home. I always told George he was wrong to bring her up as he did; but he never took my advice, and now here we are with this poor dear child upon our hands. I, for one, freely confess that I don't know what to do with her any more than if she was one of those strange, outlandish birds you used to bring home from foreign parts." And Aunt Plenty gave a perplexed shake of the head which caused great commotion among the stiff loops of purple ribbon that bristled all over her cap like crocus buds.

"If *my* advice had been taken, she would have remained at the excellent school where I placed her. But our aunt thought best to remove her because she complained, and she has been dawdling about ever since she came. A most ruinous state of things for a morbid, spoilt girl like Rose," said Mrs. Jane, severely.

She had never forgiven the old ladies for yielding to Rose's pathetic petition that she might wait her guardian's arrival before beginning another term at the school, which was a regular Blimber hot-bed, and turned out many a feminine Toots.

"*I* never thought it the proper school for a child in good circumstances,—an heiress, in fact, as Rose is. It is all very well for girls who are to get their own living by teaching, and that sort of thing; but all *she* needs is a year or two at a fashionable finishing-school, so that at eighteen she can come out with *éclat*," put in Aunt Clara, who had been a beauty and a belle, and was still a handsome woman.

"Dear, dear! how short-sighted you all are to be discussing education and plans for the future, when this unhappy child is so plainly marked for the tomb," sighed Aunt Myra, with a lugubrious sniff and a solemn wag of the funereal bonnet, which she refused to remove, being afflicted with a chronic catarrh.

"Now, it is my opinion that the dear thing only wants freedom, rest, and care. There is a look in her eyes that goes to my heart, for it shows that she feels the need of what none of us can give her,—a mother," said Aunt Jessie, with tears in her own bright eyes at the thought of her boys being left, as Rose was, to the care of others.

Uncle Alec, who had listened silently as each spoke, turned quickly toward the last sister, and said, with a decided nod of approval,—

"You've got it, Jessie; and, with you to help me, I hope to make the child feel that she is not quite fatherless and motherless."

"I'll do my best, Alec; and I think you *will* need me, for, wise as you are, you cannot understand a tender, timid little creature like Rose as a woman can," said Mrs. Jessie, smiling back at him with a heart full of motherly good-will.

"I cannot help feeling that *I*, who have had a daughter of my own, can best bring up a girl; and I am *very* much surprised that George did not intrust her to me," observed Aunt Myra, with an air of melancholy importance, for she was the only one who had given a daughter to the family, and she felt that she had distinguished herself, though ill-natured people said that she had dosed her darling to death.

"I never blamed him in the least, when I remember the perilous experiments you tried with poor Carrie," began Mrs. Jane, in her hard voice.

"Jane Campbell, I will *not* hear a word! My sainted Caroline is a sacred subject," cried Aunt Myra, rising as if to leave the room.

Dr. Alec detained her, feeling that he must define his position at once, and maintain it manfully if he hoped to have any success in his new undertaking.

"Now, my dear souls, don't let us quarrel and make Rose a bone of contention,—though, upon my word, she *is* almost a bone, poor little lass! You have had her among you for a year, and done what you liked. I cannot say that your success is great, but that is owing to too many fingers in the pie. Now, I intend to try my way for a year, and if at the end of it she is not in better trim than now, I'll give up the case, and hand her over to some one else. That's fair, I think."

"She will not be here a year hence, poor darling, so no one need dread future responsibility," said Aunt Myra, folding her black gloves as if all ready for the funeral.

"By Jupiter, Myra, you are enough to damp the ardor of a saint!" cried Dr. Alec, with a sudden spark in his eyes. "Your croaking will worry that child out of her wits, for she is an imaginative puss, and will fret and fancy untold horrors. You have put it into her head that she has no constitution, and she rather likes the idea. If she had not had a pretty good one, she *would* have been 'marked for the tomb' by this time, at the rate you have been going on with her. I will not have any interference,—please understand that; so just wash your hands of her, and let me manage till I want help, then I'll ask for it."

"Hear, hear!" came from the corner where Uncle Mac was apparently wrapt in slumber.

"You were appointed guardian, so we can do nothing. But I predict that the girl will be spoilt, utterly spoilt," answered Mrs. Jane, grimly.

"Thank you, sister. I have an idea that if a woman can bring up two boys as perfectly as you do yours, a man, if he devotes his whole mind to it, may at least attempt as much with one girl," replied Dr. Alec, with a humorous look that tickled the others immensely, for it was a well-known fact in the family that Jane's boys were more indulged than all the other lads put together.

"*I* am quite easy, for I really do think that Alec will improve the child's health; and by the time his year is out, it will be quite soon enough for her to go to Madame Roccabella's and be finished off," said Aunt Clara, settling her rings, and thinking, with languid satisfaction, of the time when she could bring out a pretty and accomplished niece.

"I suppose you will stay here in the old place, unless you think of marrying, and it's high time you did," put in Mrs. Jane, much nettled at her brother's last hit.

"No, thank you. Come and have a cigar, Mac," said Dr. Alec, abruptly.

"Don't marry; women enough in the family already," muttered Uncle Mac; and then the gentlemen hastily fled.

"Aunt Peace would like to see you all, she says," was the message Rose brought before the ladies could begin again.

"Hectic, hectic!—dear me, dear me!" murmured Aunt Myra, as the shadow of her gloomy bonnet fell upon Rose, and the stiff tips of a black glove touched the cheek where the color deepened under so many eyes.

"I am glad these pretty curls are natural; they will be invaluable by and by," said Aunt Clara, taking an observation with her head on one side.

"Now that your uncle has come, I no longer expect you to review the studies of the past year. I trust your time will not be *entirely* wasted in frivolous sports, however," added Aunt Jane, sailing out of the room with the air of a martyr.

Aunt Jessie said not a word, but kissed her little niece, with a look of tender sympathy that made Rose cling to her a minute, and follow her with grateful eyes as the door closed behind her.

After everybody had gone home, Dr. Alec paced up and down the lower hall in the twilight for an hour, thinking so intently that sometimes he frowned, sometimes he smiled, and more than once he stood still in a brown study. All of a sudden he said, half aloud, as if he had made up his mind,—

"I might as well begin at once, and give the child something new to think about, for Myra's dismals and Jane's lectures have made her as blue as a little indigo bag."

Diving into one of the trunks that stood in a corner, he brought up, after a brisk rummage, a silken cushion, prettily embroidered, and a quaint cup of dark carved wood.

"This will do for a start," he said, as he plumped up the cushion and dusted the cup. "It won't do to begin too energetically, or Rose will be frightened. I must beguile her gently and pleasantly along till I've won her confidence, and then she will be ready for any thing."

Just then Phebe came out of the dining-room with a plate of brown bread, for Rose had been allowed no hot biscuit for tea.

"I'll relieve you of some of that," said Dr. Alec, and, helping himself to a generous slice, he retired to the study, leaving Phebe to wonder at his appetite.

She would have wondered still more if she had seen him making that brown bread into neat little pills, which he packed into an attractive ivory box, out of which he emptied his own bits of lovage.

"There! if they insist on medicine, I'll order these, and no harm will be done. I *will* have my own way, but I'll keep the peace, if possible, and confess the joke when my experiment has succeeded," he said to himself, looking very much like a mischievous boy, as he went off with his innocent prescriptions.

Rose was playing softly on the small organ that stood in the upper hall, so that Aunt Peace could enjoy it; and all the while he talked with the old ladies Uncle Alec was listening to the fitful music of the child, and thinking of another Rose who used to play for him.

As the clock struck eight, he called out,—

"Time for my girl to be abed, else she won't be up early, and I'm full of jolly plans for to-morrow. Come and see what I have found for you to begin upon."

Rose ran in and listened with bright, attentive face, while Dr. Alec said, impressively,—

"In my wanderings over the face of the earth, I have picked up some excellent remedies, and, as they are rather agreeable ones, I think you and I will try them. This is an herb-pillow, given to me by a wise old woman when I was ill in India. It is filled with saffron, poppies, and other soothing plants; so lay your little head on it to-night, sleep sweetly without a dream, and wake to-morrow without a pain."

"Shall I really? How nice it smells." And Rose willingly received the pretty pillow, and stood enjoying its faint, sweet odor, as she listened to the doctor's next remedy.

"This is the cup I told you of. Its virtue depends, they say, on the drinker filling it himself; so you must learn to milk. I'll teach you."

"I'm afraid I never can," said Rose; but she surveyed the cup with favor, for a funny little imp danced on the handle, as if all ready to take a header into the white sea below.

"Don't you think she ought to have something more strengthening than milk, Alec? I really shall feel anxious if she does not have a tonic of some sort," said Aunt Plenty, eying the new remedies suspiciously, for she had more faith in her old-fashioned doses than all the magic cups and poppy pillows of the East.

"Well, ma'am, I'm willing to give her a pill, if you think best. It is a very simple one, and very large quantities may be taken without harm. You know hasheesh is the extract of hemp? Well, this is a preparation of corn and rye, much used in old times, and I hope it will be again."

"Dear me, how singular!" said Aunt Plenty, bringing her spectacles to bear upon the pills, with a face so full of respectful interest that it was almost too much for Dr. Alec's gravity.

"Take one in the morning, and a good-night to you, my dear," he said, dismissing his patient with a hearty kiss.

Then, as she vanished, he put both hands into his hair, exclaiming, with a comical mixture of anxiety and amusement,—

"When I think what I have undertaken, I declare to you, aunt, I feel like running away and not coming back till Rose is eighteen!"

# *Chapter V*

### A BELT AND A BOX

WHEN Rose came out of her chamber, cup in hand, next morning, the first person she saw was Uncle Alec standing on the threshold of the room opposite, which he appeared to be examining with care. When he heard her step, he turned about and began to sing,—

"Where are you going, my pretty maid?"

"I'm going a-milking, sir, she said," answered Rose, waving the cup; and then they finished the verse together in fine style.

Before either spoke, a head, in a nightcap so large and beruffled that it looked like a cabbage, popped out of a room farther down the hall, and an astonished voice exclaimed,—

"What in the world are you about so early?"

"Clearing our pipes for the day, ma'am. Look here, auntie, can I have this room?" said Dr. Alec, making her a sailor's bow.

"Any room you like, except sister's."

"Thanks. And may I go rummaging round in the garrets and glory-holes to furnish it as I like?"

"My dear boy, you may turn the house upside down if you will only stay in it."

"That's a handsome offer, I'm sure. I'll stay, ma'am; here's my little anchor, so you will get more than you want of me this time."

"That's impossible! Put on your jacket, Rose. Don't tire her out with antics, Alec. Yes, sister, I'm coming!" and the cabbage vanished suddenly.

The first milking lesson was a droll one; but after several scares and many vain attempts, Rose at last managed to fill her cup, while Ben held Clover's tail so that it could not flap, and Dr. Alec kept her from turning to stare at the new milk-maid, who objected to both these proceedings very much.

"You look chilly in spite of all this laughing. Take a smart run round the garden and get up a glow," said the doctor, as they left the barn.

"I'm too old for running, uncle; Miss Power said it was not lady-like for girls in their teens," answered Rose primly.

"I take the liberty of differing from Madame Prunes and Prisms, and, as your physician, I *order* you to run. Off with you!" said Uncle Alec, with a look and a gesture that made Rose scurry away as fast as she could go.

Anxious to please him, she raced round the beds till she came back to the porch where he stood, and, dropping down upon the steps, she sat panting, with cheeks as rosy as the rigolette on her shoulders.

"Very well done, child; I see you have not lost the use of your limbs though you *are* in your teens. That belt is too tight; unfasten it, then you can take a long breath without panting so."

"It isn't tight, sir; I can breathe perfectly well," began Rose, trying to compose herself.

Her uncle's only answer was to lift her up and unhook the new belt of which she was so proud. The moment the clasp was open the belt flew apart several inches, for it was impossible to restrain the involuntary sigh of relief that flatly contradicted her words.

"Why, I didn't know it was tight! it didn't feel so a bit. Of course it would open if I puff like this, but I never do, because I hardly ever run," explained Rose, rather discomfited by this discovery.

"I see you don't half fill your lungs, and so you can wear this absurd thing without feeling it. The idea of cramping a tender little waist in a stiff band of leather and steel just when it ought to be growing," said Dr. Alec, surveying the belt with great disfavor as he put the clasp forward several holes, to Rose's secret dismay, for she was proud of her slender figure, and daily rejoiced that she wasn't as stout as Luly Miller, a former schoolmate, who vainly tried to repress her plumpness.

"It will fall off if it is so loose," she said anxiously, as she stood watching him pull her precious belt about.

"Not if you keep taking long breaths to hold it on. That is what I want you to do, and when you have filled this out we will go on enlarging it till your waist is more like that of Hebe, goddess of health, and less like that of a fashion-plate,—the ugliest thing imaginable."

"How it does look!" and Rose gave a glance of scorn at the loose belt hanging round her trim little waist. "It will be lost, and then I shall feel badly, for it cost ever so much, and is real steel and Russia leather. Just smell how nice."

"If it is lost I'll give you a better one. A soft silken sash is much fitter for a pretty child like you than a plated harness like this; and I've got no end of Italian scarfs and Turkish sashes among my traps. Ah! that makes you feel better, doesn't it?" and he pinched the cheek that had suddenly dimpled with a smile.

"It is very silly of me, but I can't help liking to know that"—here she stopped and blushed and held down her head, ashamed to add, "you think I am pretty."

Dr. Alec's eyes twinkled, but he said very soberly,—

"Rose, are you vain?"

"I'm afraid I am," answered a very meek voice from behind the veil of hair that hid the red face.

"That is a sad fault." And he sighed as if grieved at the confession.

"I know it is, and I try not to be; but people praise me, and I can't help liking it, for I really don't think I am repulsive."

The last word and the funny tone in which it was uttered were too much for Dr. Alec, and he laughed in spite of himself, to Rose's great relief.

"I quite agree with you; and in order that you may be still less repulsive, I want you to grow as fine a girl as Phebe."

"Phebe!" and Rose looked so amazed that her uncle nearly went off again.

"Yes, Phebe; for she has what you need,—health. If you dear little girls would only learn what real beauty is, and not pinch and starve and bleach yourselves out so, you'd save an immense deal of time and money and pain. A happy soul in a healthy body makes the best sort of beauty for man or woman. Do you understand that, my dear?"

"Yes, sir," answered Rose, much taken down by this comparison with the girl from the poor-house. It nettled her sadly, and she showed that it did by saying quickly,—

"I suppose you would like to have me sweep and scrub, and wear an old brown dress, and go round with my sleeves rolled up, as Phebe does?"

"I should very much, if you could work as well as she does, and show as strong a pair of arms as she can. I haven't seen a prettier picture for some time than she made of herself this morning, up to the elbows in suds, singing like a blackbird while she scrubbed on the back stoop."

"Well, I do think you are the queerest man that ever lived!" was all Rose could find to say after this display of bad taste.

"I haven't begun to show my oddities yet, so you must make up your mind to worse shocks than this," he said, with such a whimsical look that she was glad the sound of a bell prevented her showing more plainly what a blow her little vanities had already received.

"You will find your box all open up in auntie's parlor, and there you can amuse her and yourself by rummaging to your heart's content; I've got to be cruising round all the morning getting my room to rights," said Dr. Alec, as they rose from breakfast.

"Can't I help you, uncle?" asked Rose, quite burning to be useful.

"No, thank you. I'm going to borrow Phebe for a while, if Aunt Plenty can spare her."

"Anybody,—any thing, Alec. You will want me, I know, so I'll give orders about dinner and be all ready to lend a hand;" and the old lady bustled away full of interest and good-will.

"Uncle will find that *I* can do some things that Phebe can't; so now!" thought Rose, with a toss of the head as she flew to Aunt Peace and the long-desired box.

Every little girl can easily imagine what an extra good time she had diving into a sea of treasures and fishing up one pretty thing after another, till the air was full of the mingled odors of musk and sandal-wood, the room gay with bright colors, and Rose in a rapture of delight. She began to forgive Dr. Alec for the oatmeal diet when she saw a lovely ivory work-box; became resigned to the state of her belt when she found a pile of rainbow-colored sashes; and when she came to some distractingly pretty bottles of attar of rose, she felt that they almost atoned for the great sin of thinking Phebe the finer girl of the two.

Dr. Alec meanwhile had apparently taken Aunt Plenty at her word, and *was* turning the house upside down. A general revolution was evidently going on in the green-room, for the dark damask curtains were seen bundling away in Phebe's arms; the air-tight stove retiring to the cellar on Ben's shoulder; and the great bedstead going up garret in a fragmentary state, escorted by three bearers. Aunt Plenty was constantly on the trot among her store-rooms, camphor-chests, and linen-closets, looking as if the new order of things both amazed and amused her.

Half the peculiar performances of Dr. Alec cannot be revealed; but as Rose glanced up from her box now and then she caught glimpses of him striding by, bearing a bamboo chair, a pair of ancient andirons, a queer Japanese screen, a rug or two, and finally a large bathing-pan upon his head.

"What a curious room it will be," she said, as she sat resting and refreshing herself with "Lumps of Delight," all the way from Cairo.

"I fancy *you* will like it, deary," answered Aunt Peace, looking up with a smile from some pretty trifle she was making with blue silk and white muslin.

Rose did not see the smile, for just at that moment her uncle paused at the door, and she sprang up to dance before him, saying, with a face full of childish happiness,—

"Look at me! look at me! I'm so splendid I don't know myself. I haven't put these things on right, I dare say, but I do like them *so* much!"

"You look as gay as a parrot in your fez and cabaja, and it does my heart good to see the little black shadow turned into a rainbow," said Uncle Alec, surveying the bright figure before him with great approbation.

He did not say it, but he thought she made a much prettier picture than Phebe at the wash-tub, for she had stuck a purple fez on her blonde head, tied several brilliant scarfs about her waist, and put on a truly gorgeous scarlet jacket with a golden sun embroidered on the back, a silver moon on the front, and stars of all sizes on the sleeves. A pair of Turkish slippers adorned her feet, and necklaces of amber, coral, and filigree hung about her neck, while one hand held a smelling-bottle, and the other the spicy box of oriental sweetmeats.

"I feel like a girl in the 'Arabian Nights,' and expect to find a magic carpet or a wonderful talisman somewhere. Only I don't see how I ever *can* thank you for all these lovely things," she said, stopping her dance, as if suddenly oppressed with gratitude.

"I'll tell you how,—by leaving off the black clothes, that never should have been kept so long on such a child, and wearing the gay ones I've brought. It will do your spirits good, and cheer up this sober old house. Won't it, auntie?"

"I think you are right, Alec, and it is fortunate that we have not begun on her spring clothes yet, for Myra thought she ought not to wear any thing brighter than violet, and she is too pale for that."

"You just let me direct Miss Hemming how to make some of these things. You will be surprised to see how much I know about piping hems and gathering arm-holes and shirring biases," began Dr. Alec, patting a pile of muslin, cloth, and silk with a knowing air.

Aunt Peace and Rose laughed so that he could not display his knowledge any farther till they stopped, when he said good-naturedly,—

"That will go a great way toward filling out the belt, so laugh away, Morgiana, and I'll go back to my work, or I never shall be done."

"I couldn't help it, 'shirred biases' were so very funny!" Rose said, as she turned to her box after the splendid laugh. "But really, auntie," she added soberly, "I feel as if I ought not to have so many nice things. I suppose it wouldn't do to give Phebe some of them? Uncle might not like it."

"He would not mind; but they are not suitable for Phebe. Some of the dresses you are done with would be more useful, if they can be made over to fit her," answered Aunt Peace in the prudent, moderate tone which is so trying to our feelings when we indulge in little fits of charitable enthusiasm.

"I'd rather give her new ones, for I think she is a little bit proud and might not like old things. If she was my sister it would do, because sisters don't mind, but she isn't, and that makes it bad, you see. I know how I can manage beautifully; I'll adopt her!" and Rose looked quite radiant with this new idea.

"I'm afraid you could not do it legally till you are older, but you might see if she likes the plan, and at any rate you can be very kind to her, for in one sense we are all sisters, and should help one another."

The sweet old face looked at her so kindly that Rose was

fired with a desire to settle the matter at once, and rushed away to the kitchen just as she was. Phebe was there, polishing up the antique andirons so busily that she started when a voice cried out: "Smell that, taste this, and look at me!"

Phebe sniffed attar of rose, crunched the "Lump of Delight" tucked into her mouth, and stared with all her eyes at little Morgiana prancing about the room like a brilliant paroquet.

"My stars, ain't you splendid!" was all she could say, holding up two dusty hands.

"I've got heaps of lovely things upstairs, and I'll show them all to you, and I'd go halves, only auntie thinks they wouldn't

ROSE AND PHEBE.

be useful, so I shall give you something else; and you won't mind, will you? because I want to adopt you as Arabella was in the story. Won't that be nice?"

"Why, Miss Rose, have you lost your wits?"

No wonder Phebe asked, for Rose talked very fast, and looked so odd in her new costume, and was so eager she could not stop to explain. Seeing Phebe's bewilderment, she quieted down and said, with a pretty air of earnestness,—

"It isn't fair that I should have so much and you so little, and I want to be as good to you as if you were my sister, for Aunt Peace says we are all sisters really. I thought if I adopted you as much as I can now, it would be nicer. Will you let me, please?"

To Rose's great surprise, Phebe sat down on the floor and hid her face in her apron for a minute without answering a word.

"Oh dear, now she's offended, and I don't know what to do," thought Rose, much discouraged by this reception of her offer.

"Please, forgive me; I didn't mean to hurt your feelings, and hope you won't think—" she faltered presently, feeling that she must undo the mischief if possible.

But Phebe gave her another surprise, by dropping the apron and showing a face all smiles, in spite of tears in the eyes, as she put both arms round Rose and said, with a laugh and sob,—

"I think you are the dearest girl in the world, and I'll let you do any thing you like with me."

"Then you do like the plan? You didn't cry because I seemed to be kind of patronizing? I truly didn't mean to be," cried Rose, delighted.

"I guess I do like it! and cried because no one was ever so good to me before, and I couldn't help it. As for patronizing, you may walk on me if you want to, and I won't mind," said Phebe, in a burst of gratitude, for the words, "we are all sisters," went straight to her lonely heart and nestled there.

"Well, now, we can play I'm a good sprite out of the box, or, what is better, a fairy godmother come down the chimney, and you are Cinderella, and must say what you want," said Rose, trying to put the question delicately.

Phebe understood that, for she had a good deal of natural refinement, though she did come from the poor-house.

"I don't feel as if I wanted any thing now, Miss Rose, but to find some way of thanking you for all you've done," she said, rubbing off a tear that went rolling down the bridge of her nose in the most unromantic way.

"Why, I haven't done any thing but given you a bit of candy! Here, have some more, and eat 'em while you work, and think what I *can* do. I must go and clear up, so good-by, and don't forget I've adopted you."

"You've given me sweeter things than candy, and I'm not likely to forget it." And carefully wiping off the brick-dust, Phebe pressed the little hand Rose offered warmly in both her hard ones, while the black eyes followed the departing visitor with a grateful look that made them very soft and bright.

# *Chapter VI*

SOON after dinner, and before she had got acquainted with half her new possessions, Dr. Alec proposed a drive, to carry round the first instalment of gifts to the aunts and cousins. Rose was quite ready to go, being anxious to try a certain soft burnous from the box, which not only possessed a most engaging little hood, but had funny tassels bobbing in all directions.

The big carriage was full of parcels, and even Ben's seat was loaded with Indian war-clubs, a Chinese kite of immense size, and a pair of polished ox-horns from Africa. Uncle Alec, very blue as to his clothes, and very brown as to his face, sat bolt upright, surveying well-known places with interest, while Rose, feeling unusually elegant and comfortable, leaned back folded in her soft mantle, and played she was an Eastern princess making a royal progress among her subjects.

At three of the places their calls were brief, for Aunt Myra's catarrh was unusually bad; Aunt Clara had a room full of company; and Aunt Jane showed such a tendency to discuss the population, productions, and politics of Europe, Asia, and Africa, that even Dr. Alec was dismayed, and got away as soon as possible.

"Now we will have a good time! I do hope the boys will be at home," said Rose, with a sigh of relief, as they wound yet higher up the hill to Aunt Jessie's.

"I left this for the last call, so that we might find the lads just in from school. Yes, there is Jamie on the gate watching for us; now you'll see the Clan gather; they are always swarming about together."

The instant Jamie saw the approaching guests he gave a shrill whistle, which was answered by echoes from meadow, house, and barn, as the cousins came running from all directions, shouting, "Hooray for Uncle Alec!" They went at the carriage like highwaymen, robbed it of every parcel, took the occupants prisoners, and marched them into the house with great exultation.

"Little Mum! little Mum! here they are with lots of goodies! Come down and see the fun right away! quick!" bawled Will and Geordie amidst a general ripping off of papers and a reckless cutting of strings that soon turned the tidy room into a chaos.

Down came Aunt Jessie with her pretty cap half on, but such a beaming face below it that one rather thought the fly-away head-gear an improvement than otherwise. She had hardly time to greet Rose and the doctor before the boys were about her, each clamoring for her to see his gift and rejoice over it with him, for "little Mum" went halves in every thing. The great horns skirmished about her as if to toss her to the ceiling; the war-clubs hurtled over her head as if to annihilate her; an amazing medley from the four quarters of the globe filled her lap, and seven excited boys all talked to her at once.

But she liked it; oh dear, yes! and sat smiling, admiring, and explaining, quite untroubled by the din, which made Rose cover up her ears and Dr. Alec threaten instant flight if the riot was not quelled. That threat produced a lull, and while the uncle received thanks in one corner, the aunt had some little confidences made to her in the other.

"Well, dear, and how are things going with you now? Better, I hope, than they were a week ago."

"Aunt Jessie, I think I'm going to be very happy, now uncle has come. He does the queerest things, but he is *so* good to me I can't help loving him;" and, nestling closer to little Mum, Rose told all that had happened, ending with a rapturous account of the splendid box.

"I am very glad, dear. But, Rose, I must warn you of one thing; don't let uncle spoil you."

"But I like to be spoilt, auntie."

"I don't doubt it; but if you turn out badly when the year is over he will be blamed, and his experiment prove a failure. That would be a pity, wouldn't it? when he wants to do so much for you, and can do it if his kind heart does not get in the way of his good judgment."

"I never thought of that, and I'll try not to be spoilt. But how *can* I help it?" asked Rose anxiously.

"By not complaining of the wholesome things he wants you to do; by giving him cheerful obedience as well as love; and even making some small sacrifices for his sake."

"I will, I truly will! and when I get in a worry about things may I come to you? Uncle told me to, and I feel as if I shouldn't be afraid."

"You may, darling; this is the place where little troubles are best cured, and this is what mothers are for, I fancy;" and Aunt Jessie drew the curly head to her shoulder with a tender look that proved how well she knew what medicine the child most needed.

It was so sweet and comfortable that Rose sat still enjoying it till a little voice said,—

"Mamma, don't you think Pokey would like some of my shells? Rose gave Phebe some of her nice things, and it was very good of her. Can I?"

"Who is Pokey?" asked Rose, popping up her head, attracted by the odd name.

"My dolly; do you want to see her?" asked Jamie, who had been much impressed by the tale of adoption he had over-heard.

"Yes; I'm fond of dollies, only don't tell the boys or they will laugh at me."

"They don't laugh at me, and they play with my dolly a great deal; but she likes me best;" and Jamie ran away to produce his pet.

"I brought my old doll, but I keep her hidden because I am too big to play with her, and yet I can't bear to throw her away, I'm so fond of her," said Rose, continuing her confidences in a whisper.

"You can come and play with Jamie's whenever you like, for we believe in dollies up here," began Aunt Jessie, smiling to herself as if something amused her.

Just then Jamie came back, and Rose understood the smile, for his dolly proved to be a pretty four-year-old little girl, who trotted in as fast as her fat legs would carry her, and, making straight for the shells, scrambled up an armful, saying, with a laugh that showed her little white teeth,—

"All for Dimmy and me, for Dimmy and me!"

"That's my dolly; isn't she a nice one?" asked Jamie, proudly surveying his pet with his hands behind him and his short legs rather far apart,—a manly attitude copied from his brothers.

JAMIE AND HIS DOLLY.

"She is a dear dolly. But why call her Pokey?" asked Rose, charmed with the new plaything.

"She is such an inquisitive little body she is always poking that mite of a nose into every thing; and as Paul Pry did not suit, the boys fell to calling her Pokey. Not a pretty name, but very expressive."

It certainly was, for, having examined the shells, the busy tot laid hold of every thing she could find, and continued her researches till Archie caught her sucking his carved ivory chessmen to see if they were not barley-sugar. Rice-paper pictures were also discovered crumpled up in her tiny pocket, and she nearly smashed Will's ostrich egg by trying to sit upon it.

"Here, Jim, take her away; she's worse than the puppies, and we can't have her round," commanded the elder brother, picking her up and handing her over to the little fellow, who received her with open arms and the warning remark,—

"You'd better mind what you do, for I'm going to 'dopt Pokey like Rose did Phebe, and then you'll have to be very good to her, you big fellows."

"'Dopt away, baby, and I'll give you a cage to keep her in, or you won't have her long, for she is getting worse than a monkey;" and Archie went back to his mates, while Aunt Jessie, foreseeing a crisis, proposed that Jamie should take his dolly home, as she was borrowed, and it was time her visit ended.

"*My* dolly is better than yours, isn't she? 'cause she can walk and talk and sing and dance, and yours can't do any thing, can she?" asked Jamie with pride, as he regarded his Pokey, who just then had been moved to execute a funny little jig and warble the well-known couplet,—

> "'Puss-tat, puss-tat, where you been?'
> 'I been Lunnin, to saw a Tween.'"

After which superb display she retired, escorted by Jamie, both making a fearful din blowing on conch shells.

"We must tear ourselves away, Rose, because I want to get you home before sunset. Will you come for a drive, Jessie?" said Dr. Alec, as the music died away in the distance.

"No, thank you; but I see the boys want a scamper, so, if you don't mind, they may escort you home, but not go in. That is only allowed on holidays."

The words were hardly out of Aunt Jessie's mouth when Archie said, in a tone of command,—

"Pass the word, lads. Boot and saddle, and be quick about it."

"All right!" And in a moment not a vestige of boy remained but the litter on the floor.

The cavalcade went down the hill at a pace that made Rose cling to her uncle's arm, for the fat old horses got excited by the antics of the ponies careering all about them, and went as fast as they could pelt, with the gay dog-cart rattling in front, for Archie and Charlie scorned shelties since this magnificent equipage had been set up. Ben enjoyed the fun, and the lads cut up capers till Rose declared that "circus" was the proper name for them after all.

When they reached the house they dismounted, and stood, three on each side the steps, in martial attitudes, while her ladyship was handed out with great elegance by Uncle Alec. Then the clan saluted, mounted at word of command, and with a wild whoop tore down the avenue in what they considered the true Arab style.

"That was splendid, now it is safely ended," said Rose, skipping up the steps with her head over her shoulder to watch the
dear tassels bob about.

"I shall get you a pony as soon as you are a little stronger,"
said Dr. Alec, watching her with a smile.

"Oh, I couldn't ride one of those horrid, frisky little beasts!
They roll their eyes and bounce about so, I should die of
fright," cried Rose, clasping her hands tragically.

"Are you a coward?"

"About horses I am."

"Never mind, then; come and see my new room;" and he
led the way upstairs without another word.

As Rose followed she remembered her promise to Aunt
Jessie, and was sorry she had objected so decidedly. She was a
great deal more sorry five minutes later, and well she might be.

"Now take a good look, and tell me what you think of it,"
said Dr. Alec, opening the door and letting her enter before
him, while Phebe was seen whisking down the backstairs with
a dust-pan.

Rose walked to the middle of the room, stood still, and
gazed about her with eyes that brightened as they looked, for
all was changed.

This chamber had been built out over the library to suit
some fancy, and had been unused for years, except at Christmas
times, when the old house overflowed. It had three windows,—
one to the east, that overlooked the bay; one to the south,
where the horse-chestnuts waved their green fans; and one to
the west, toward the hills and the evening sky. A ruddy sunset
burned there now, filling the room with an enchanted glow;
the soft murmur of the sea was heard, and a robin chirped
"Good night!" among the budding trees.

Rose saw and heard these things first, and felt their beauty
with a child's quick instinct; then her eye took in the altered
aspect of the room, once so shrouded, still and solitary, now so
full of light and warmth and simple luxury.

India matting covered the floor, with a gay rug here and
there; the antique andirons shone on the wide hearth, where a
cheery blaze dispelled the dampness of the long-closed room.
Bamboo lounges and chairs stood about, and quaint little tables in cosey corners; one bearing a pretty basket, one a desk,

and on a third lay several familiar-looking books. In a recess stood a narrow white bed, with a lovely Madonna hanging over it. The Japanese screen half folded back showed a delicate toilet-service of blue and white set forth on a marble slab, and near by was the great bath-pan, with Turkish towels and a sponge as big as Rose's head.

"Uncle must love cold water like a duck," she thought, with a shiver.

Then her eye went on to the tall cabinet, where a half-open door revealed a tempting array of the drawers, shelves, and "cubby holes," which so delight the hearts of children.

"What a grand place for my new things," she thought, wondering what her uncle kept in that cedar retreat.

"Oh me, what a sweet toilet-table!" was her next mental exclamation, as she approached this inviting spot.

A round old-fashioned mirror hung over it, with a gilt eagle a-top, holding in his beak the knot of blue ribbon that tied up a curtain of muslin falling on either side of the table, where appeared little ivory-handled brushes, two slender silver candlesticks, a porcelain match-box, several pretty trays for small matters, and, most imposing of all, a plump blue silk cushion, coquettishly trimmed with lace, and pink rose-buds at the corners.

That cushion rather astonished Rose; in fact, the whole table did, and she was just thinking, with a sly smile,—

"Uncle is a dandy, but I never should have guessed it," when he opened the door of a large closet, saying, with a careless wave of the hand,—

"Men like plenty of room for their rattle-traps; don't you think that ought to satisfy me?"

Rose peeped in and gave a start, though all she saw was what one usually finds in closets,—clothes and boots, boxes and bags. Ah! but you see these clothes were small black and white frocks; the row of little boots that stood below had never been on Dr. Alec's feet; the green bandbox had a gray veil straying out of it, and,—yes! the bag hanging on the door was certainly her own piece-bag, with a hole in one corner. She gave a quick look round the room and understood now why it had seemed too dainty for a man, why *her* Testament and Prayer-book were on the table by the bed, and what those rose-buds meant on the blue cushion. It came upon her in one delicious burst that this little paradise was all for her, and, not knowing how else to express her gratitude, she caught Dr. Alec round the neck, saying impetuously,—

"O uncle, you are *too* good to me! I'll do any thing you ask me; ride wild horses and take freezing baths and eat bad-tasting messes, and let my clothes hang on me, to show how much I thank you for this dear, sweet, lovely room!"

"You like it, then? But why do you think it is yours, my lass?" asked Dr. Alec, as he sat down looking well pleased, and drew his excited little niece to his knee.

"I don't *think*, I *know* it is for me; I see it in your face, and I feel as if I didn't half deserve it. Aunt Jessie said you would spoil me, and I must not let you. I'm afraid this looks like it, and perhaps,—oh me!—perhaps I ought not to have this beautiful room after all!" and Rose tried to look as if she could be heroic enough to give it up if it was best.

"I owe Mrs. Jessie one for that," said Dr. Alec, trying to frown, though in his secret soul he felt that she was quite right. Then he smiled that cordial smile, which was like sunshine on his brown face, as he said,—

"This is part of the cure, Rose, and I put you here that you might take my three great remedies in the best and easiest way. Plenty of sun, fresh air, and cold water; also cheerful surroundings and some work; for Phebe is to show you how to take care of this room, and be your little maid as well as friend and teacher. Does that sound hard and disagreeable to you, dear?"

"No, sir; very, very pleasant, and I'll do my best to be a good patient. But I really don't think any one *could* be sick in this delightful room," she said, with a long sigh of happiness as her eye went from one pleasant object to another.

"Then you like my sort of medicine better than Aunt Myra's, and don't want to throw it out of the window, hey?"

# Chapter VII

A TRIP TO CHINA

---

"COME, little girl, I've got another dose for you. I fancy you won't take it as well as you did the last, but you will like it better after a while," said Dr. Alec, about a week after the grand surprise.

Rose was sitting in her pretty room, where she would gladly have spent all her time if it had been allowed; but she looked up with a smile, for she had ceased to fear her uncle's remedies, and was always ready to try a new one. The last had been a set of light gardening tools, with which she had helped him put the flower-beds in order, learning all sorts of new and pleasant things about the plants as she worked, for, though she had studied botany at school, it seemed very dry stuff compared with Uncle Alec's lively lesson.

"What is it now?" she asked, shutting her work box without a murmur.

"Salt-water."

"How must I take it?"

"Put on the new suit Miss Hemming sent home yesterday, and come down to the beach; then I'll show you."

"Yes, sir," answered Rose obediently, adding to herself, with a shiver, as he went off: "It is too early for bathing, so I *know* it is something to do with a dreadful boat."

Putting on the new suit of blue flannel, prettily trimmed with white, and the little sailor-hat with long streamers, diverted her mind from the approaching trial, till a shrill whistle reminded her that her uncle was waiting. Away she ran through the garden, down the sandy path, out upon the strip of beach that belonged to the house, and here she found Dr. Alec busy with a slender red and white boat that lay rocking on the rising tide.

"That is a dear little boat; and 'Bonnie Belle' is a pretty name," she said, trying not to show how nervous she felt.

"It is for you; so sit in the stern and learn to steer, till you are ready to learn to row."

"Do all boats wiggle about in that way?" she asked, lingering as if to tie her hat more firmly.

"Oh, yes, pitch about like nut-shells when the sea is a bit rough," answered her sailor uncle, never guessing her secret woe.

"Is it rough to-day?"

"Not very; it looks a trifle squally to the eastward, but we are all right till the wind changes. Come."

"Can you swim, uncle?" asked Rose, clutching at his arm as he took her hand.

"Like a fish. Now then."

"Oh, please hold me *very* tight till I get there! Why *do* you have the stern so far away?" and, stifling several squeaks of alarm in her passage, Rose crept to the distant seat, and sat there holding on with both hands and looking as if she expected every wave to bring a sudden shipwreck.

Uncle Alec took no notice of her fear, but patiently instructed her in the art of steering, till she was so absorbed in remembering which was starboard and which larboard, that she forgot to say "Ow!" every time a big wave slapped against the boat.

"Now where shall we go?" she asked, as the wind blew freshly in her face, and a few long, swift strokes sent them half across the little bay.

"Suppose we go to China?"

"Isn't that rather a long voyage?"

"Not as I go. Steer round the Point into the harbor, and I'll give you a glimpse of China in twenty minutes or so."

"I should like that!" and Rose sat wondering what he meant, while she enjoyed the new sights all about her.

Behind them the green Aunt-hill sloped gently upward to the grove at the top, and all along the seaward side stood familiar houses, stately, cosey, or picturesque. As they rounded the Point, the great bay opened before them full of shipping, and the city lay beyond, its spires rising above the tall masts with their gay streamers.

"Are we going there?" she asked, for she had never seen this aspect of the rich and busy old city before.

"Yes. Uncle Mac has a ship just in from Hong Kong, and I thought you would like to go and see it."

"Suppose we go to China."

"Oh, I should! I love dearly to go poking about in the warehouses with Uncle Mac; every thing is so curious and new to me; and I'm specially interested in China because you have been there."

"I'll show you two genuine Chinamen who have just arrived. You will like to welcome Whang Lo and Fun See, I'm sure."

"Don't ask me to speak to them, uncle; I shall be sure to laugh at the odd names and the pig-tails and the slanting eyes. Please let me just trot round after you; I like that best."

"Very well; now steer toward the wharf where the big ship with the queer flag is. That's the 'Rajah,' and we will go aboard if we can."

In among the ships they went, by the wharves where the water was green and still, and queer barnacles grew on the slippery piles. Odd smells saluted her nose, and odd sights met her eyes, but Rose liked it all, and played she was really landing in Hong Kong when they glided up to the steps in the shadow of the tall "Rajah." Boxes and bales were rising out of the hold and being carried into the warehouse by stout porters, who tugged and bawled and clattered about with small trucks, or worked cranes with iron claws that came down and clutched heavy weights, whisking them aloft to where wide doors like mouths swallowed them up.

Dr. Alec took her aboard the ship, and she had the satisfaction of poking her inquisitive little nose into every available corner, at the risk of being crushed, lost, or drowned.

"Well, child, how would you like to take a voyage round the world with me in a jolly old craft like this?" asked her uncle, as they rested a minute in the captain's cabin.

"I should like to see the world, but not in such a small, untidy, smelly place as this. We would go in a yacht all clean and comfortable; Charlie says that is the proper way," answered Rose, surveying the close quarters with little favor.

"You are not a true Campbell if you don't like the smell of tar and salt-water, nor Charlie either, with his luxurious yacht. Now come ashore and chin-chin with the Celestials."

After a delightful progress through the great warehouse, peeping and picking as they went, they found Uncle Mac and the yellow gentlemen in his private room, where samples, gifts, curiosities, and newly arrived treasures of all sorts were piled up in pleasing pro-fusion and con-fusion.

As soon as possible Rose retired to a corner, with a porcelain god on one side, a green dragon on the other, and, what was still more embarrassing, Fun See sat on a tea-chest in front, and stared at her with his beady black eyes till she did not know where to look.

Mr. Whang Lo was an elderly gentleman in American costume, with his pig-tail neatly wound round his head. He spoke English, and was talking busily with Uncle Mac in the most commonplace way,—so Rose considered *him* a failure. But Fun See was delightfully Chinese from his junk-like shoes to the button on his pagoda hat; for he had got himself up in style, and was a mass of silk jackets and slouchy trousers. He was short and fat, and waddled comically; his eyes were very "slanting," as Rose said; his queue was long, so were his nails; his yellow face was plump and shiny, and he was altogether a highly satisfactory Chinaman.

Uncle Alec told her that Fun See had come out to be educated, and could only speak a little pigeon English; so she must be kind to the poor fellow, for he was only a lad, though he looked nearly as old as Mr. Whang Lo. Rose said she would be kind; but had not the least idea how to entertain the queer guest, who looked as if he had walked out of one of the rice-paper landscapes on the wall, and sat nodding at her so like a toy Mandarin that she could hardly keep sober.

In the midst of her polite perplexity, Uncle Mac saw the two young people gazing wistfully at one another, and seemed to enjoy the joke of this making acquaintance under difficulties. Taking a box from his table, he gave it to Fun See with an order that seemed to please him very much.

Descending from his perch, he fell to unpacking it with great neatness and despatch, while Rose watched him, wondering what was going to happen. Presently, out from the wrappings came a teapot, which caused her to clasp her hands with delight, for it was made in the likeness of a plump little Chinaman. His hat was the cover, his queue the handle, and his pipe the nose. It stood upon feet in shoes turned up at the toes, and the smile on the fat, sleepy face was so like that on

Fun's when he displayed the teapot, that Rose couldn't help laughing, which pleased him much.

Two pretty cups with covers, and a fine scarlet tray, completed the set, and made one long to have a "dish of tea," even in Chinese style, without cream or sugar.

When he had arranged them on a little table before her, Fun signified in pantomime that they were hers, from her uncle.

Fun signified in pantomime that they were hers.

She returned her thanks in the same way, whereupon he returned to his tea-chest, and, having no other means of communication, they sat smiling and nodding at one another in an
absurd sort of way till a new idea seemed to strike Fun. Tumbling off his seat, he waddled away as fast as his petticoats
permitted, leaving Rose hoping that he had not gone to get a
roasted rat, a stewed puppy, or any other foreign mess which
civility would oblige her to eat.

While she waited for her funny new friend, she improved her
mind in a way that would have charmed Aunt Jane. The gentlemen were talking over all sorts of things, and she listened
attentively, storing up much of what she heard, for she had an
excellent memory, and longed to distinguish herself by being
able to produce some useful information when reproached
with her ignorance.

She was just trying to impress upon her mind that Amoy
was two hundred and eighty miles from Hong Kong, when
Fun came scuffling back, bearing what she thought was a small
sword, till he unfurled an immense fan, and presented it with a
string of Chinese compliments, the meaning of which would
have amused her even more than the sound if she could have
understood it.

She had never seen such an astonishing fan, and at once became absorbed in examining it. Of course, there was no per-
spective whatever, which only gave it a peculiar charm to Rose,
for in one place a lovely lady, with blue knitting-needles in her
hair, sat directly upon the spire of a stately pagoda. In another
charming view a brook appeared to flow in at the front door of
a stout gentleman's house, and out at his chimney. In a third a
zigzag wall went up into the sky like a flash of lightning, and a
bird with two tails was apparently brooding over a fisherman
whose boat was just going aground upon the moon.

It was altogether a fascinating thing, and she would have sat
wafting it to and fro all the afternoon, to Fun's great satisfaction, if Dr. Alec's attention had not suddenly been called to her
by a breeze from the big fan that blew his hair into his eyes,
and reminded him that they must go. So the pretty china was
repacked, Rose furled her fan, and with several parcels of
choice teas for the old ladies stowed away in Dr. Alec's pockets,
they took their leave, after Fun had saluted them with the

"three bendings and the nine knockings," as they salute the Emperor, or "Son of Heaven," at home.

"I feel as if I had really been to China, and I'm sure I look so," said Rose, as they glided out of the shadow of the "Rajah."

She certainly did, for Mr. Whang Lo had given her a Chinese umbrella; Uncle Alec had got some lanterns to light up her balcony; the great fan lay in her lap, and the tea-set reposed at her feet.

"This is not a bad way to study geography, is it?" asked her uncle, who had observed her attention to the talk.

"It is a very pleasant way, and I really think I have learned more about China to-day than in all the lessons I had at school, though I used to rattle off the answers as fast as I could go. No one explained any thing to us, so all I remember is that tea and silk come from there, and the women have little bits of feet. I saw Fun looking at mine, and he must have thought them perfectly immense," answered Rose, surveying her stout boots with sudden contempt.

"We will have out the maps and the globe, and I'll show you some of my journeys, telling stories as we go. That will be next best to doing it actually."

"You are so fond of travelling, I should think it would be very dull for you here, uncle. Do you know, Aunt Plenty says she is sure you will be off in a year or two."

"Very likely."

"Oh me! what *shall* I do then?" sighed Rose, in a tone of despair that made Uncle Alec's face brighten with a look of genuine pleasure as he said significantly,—

"Next time I go I shall take my little anchor with me. How will that suit?"

"Really, uncle?"

"Really, niece."

Rose gave a little bounce of rapture which caused the boat to "wiggle" in a way that speedily quieted her down. But she sat beaming joyfully and trying to think which of some hundred questions she would ask first, when Dr. Alec said, pointing to a boat that was coming up behind them in great style,—

"How well those fellows row! Look at them, and take notes for your own use by and by."

The "Stormy Petrel" was manned by half a dozen jaunty-

looking sailors, who made a fine display of blue shirts and
shiny hats, with stars and anchors in every direction.

"How beautifully they go, and they are only boys. Why, I do
believe they are *our* boys! Yes, I see Charlie laughing over his
shoulder. Row, uncle, row! oh, please do, and not let them
catch up with us!" cried Rose, in such a state of excitement
that the new umbrella nearly went overboard.

"All right, here we go!" and away they did go with a long
steady sweep of the oars that carried the "Bonnie Belle"
through the water with a rush.

The lads pulled their prettiest, but Dr. Alec would have
reached the Point first, if Rose, in her flurry, had not retarded
him by jerking the rudder ropes in a most unseamanlike way,
and just as she got right again her hat blew off. That put an
end to the race, and while they were still fishing for the hat the
other boat came alongside, with all the oars in the air, and the
jolly young tars ready for a frolic.

"Did you catch a crab, uncle?"

"No, a blue-fish," he answered, as the dripping hat was
landed on a seat to dry.

"What have you been doing?"

"Seeing Fun."

"Good for you, Rose! I know what you mean. We are going
to have him up to show us how to fly the big kite, for we can't
get the hang of it. Isn't he great fun, though?"

"No, little Fun."

"Come, stop joking, and show us what you've got."

"You'd better hoist that fan for a sail."

"Lend Dandy your umbrella; he hates to burn his pretty
nose."

"I say, uncle, are you going to have a Feast of Lanterns?"

"No, I'm going to have a feast of bread and butter, for it's
tea-time. If that black cloud doesn't lie, we shall have a gust
before long, so you had better get home as soon as you can, or
your mother will be anxious, Archie."

"Ay, ay, skipper. Good-night, Rose; come out often, and
we'll teach you all there is to know about rowing," was Charlie's modest invitation.

Then the boats parted company, and across the water from

the "Petrel's" crew came a verse from one of the Nonsense
Songs in which the boys delighted.

> "Oh, Timballoo! how happy we are,
>   We live in a sieve and a crockery jar!
>   And all night long, in the starlight pale,
>   We sail away, with a pea-green sail,
>   And whistle and warble a moony song
>   To the echoing sound of a coppery gong.
>       Far and few, far and few
>   Are the lands where the Jumblies live;
>   Their heads are green, and their hands are blue,
>       And they went to sea in a sieve."

# *Chapter VIII*

## AND WHAT CAME OF IT

"UNCLE, could you lend me a ninepence? I'll return it as soon as I get my pocket-money," said Rose, coming into the library in a great hurry that evening.

"I think I could, and I won't charge any interest for it, so you need not be in any hurry to repay me. Come back here and help me settle these books if you have nothing pleasanter to do," answered Dr. Alec, handing out the money with that readiness which is so delightful when we ask small loans.

"I'll come in a minute; I've been longing to fix my books, but didn't dare to touch them, because you always shake your head when I read."

"I shall shake my head when you write, if you don't do it better than you did in making out this catalogue."

"I know it's bad, but I was in a hurry when I did it, and I am in one now." And away went Rose, glad to escape a lecture.

But she got it when she came back, for Uncle Alec was still knitting his brows over the list of books, and sternly demanded, pointing to a tipsy-looking title staggering down the page,—

"Is that meant for 'Pulverized Bones,' ma'am?"

"No, sir; it's 'Paradise Lost.'"

"Well, I'm glad to know it, for I began to think you were planning to study surgery or farming. And what is this, if you please? 'Babies' Aprons' is all *I* can make of it."

Rose looked hard at the scrawl, and presently announced, with an air of superior wisdom,—

"Oh, that's 'Bacon's Essays.'"

"Miss Power did not teach any thing so old-fashioned as writing, I see. Now look at this little memorandum Aunt Plenty gave me, and see what a handsome plain hand that is. She went to a dame-school and learnt a few useful things well; that is better than a smattering of half a dozen so-called higher branches, I take the liberty of thinking."

"Well, I'm sure I was considered a bright girl at school, and learned every thing I was taught. Luly and me were the first in all our classes, and 'specially praised for our French and music and those sort of things," said Rose, rather offended at Uncle Alec's criticism.

"I dare say; but if your French grammar was no better than your English, I think the praise was not deserved, my dear."

"Why, uncle, we *did* study English grammar, and I could parse beautifully. Miss Power used to have us up to show off when people came. I don't see but I talk as right as most girls."

"I dare say you do, but we are all too careless about our English. Now, think a minute and tell me if these expressions are correct,—'Luly and me,' 'those sort of things,' and 'as right as most girls.'"

Rose pulled her pet curl and put up her lip, but had to own that she was wrong, and said meekly, after a pause which threatened to be sulky,—

"I suppose I should have said 'Luly and I,' in that case, and 'that sort of things' and 'rightly,' though 'correctly' would have been a better word, I guess."

"Thank you; and if you will kindly drop 'I guess,' I shall like my little Yankee all the better. Now, see here, Rosy, I don't pretend to set myself up for a model in any thing, and you may come down on my grammar, manners, or morals as often as you think I'm wrong, and I'll thank you. I've been knocking about the world for years, and have got careless, but I want my girl to be what *I* call well educated, even if she studies nothing but the 'three Rs' for a year to come. Let us be thorough, no matter how slowly we go."

He spoke so earnestly and looked so sorry to have ruffled her that Rose went and sat on the arm of his chair, saying, with a pretty air of penitence,—

"I'm sorry I was cross, uncle, when I ought to thank you for taking so much interest in me. I guess,—no, I think you are right about being thorough, for I used to understand a great deal better when papa taught me a few lessons than when Miss Power hurried me through so many. I declare my head used to be such a jumble of French and German, history and arithmetic, grammar and music, I used to feel sometimes as if it would split. I'm sure I don't wonder it ached." And she held on to it as if the mere memory of the "jumble" made it swim.

"Yet that is considered an excellent school, I find, and I dare say it would be if the benighted lady did not think it necessary to cram her pupils like Thanksgiving turkeys, instead of feeding them in a natural and wholesome way. It is the fault with most American schools, and the poor little heads will go on aching till we learn better."

This was one of Dr. Alec's hobbies, and Rose was afraid he was off for a gallop, but he reined himself in and gave her thoughts a new turn by saying suddenly, as he pulled out a fat pocket-book,—

"Uncle Mac has put all your affairs into my hands now, and here is your month's pocket-money. You keep your own little accounts, I suppose?"

"Thank you. Yes, Uncle Mac gave me an account-book when I went to school, and I used to put down my expenses, but I couldn't make them go very well, for figures are the one thing I am not at all clever about," said Rose, rummaging in her desk for a dilapidated little book, which she was ashamed to show when she found it.

"Well, as figures are rather important things to most of us, and you may have a good many accounts to keep some day, wouldn't it be wise to begin at once and learn to manage your pennies before the pounds come to perplex you?"

"I thought you would do all that fussy part and take care of the pounds, as you call them. Need I worry about it? I do hate sums so!"

"I shall take care of things till you are of age, but I mean that you shall know how your property is managed and do as much of it as you can by and by; then you won't be dependent on the honesty of other people."

"Gracious me! as if I wouldn't trust you with millions of billions if I had them," cried Rose, scandalized at the mere suggestion.

"Ah, but I might be tempted; guardians are sometimes; so you'd better keep your eye on me, and in order to do that you must learn all about these affairs," answered Dr. Alec, as he made an entry in his own very neat account-book.

Rose peeped over his shoulder at it, and then turned to the arithmetical puzzle in her hand with a sigh of despair.

"Uncle, when you add up your expenses do you ever find you have got more money than you had in the beginning?"

"No; I usually find that I have a good deal less than I had in the beginning. Are you troubled in the peculiar way you mention?"

"Yes; it is very curious, but I never *can* make things come out square."

"Perhaps I can help you," began Uncle Alec, in the most respectful tone.

"I think you had better, for if I have got to keep accounts I may as well begin in the right way. But please don't laugh! I know I'm very stupid, and my book is a disgrace, but I never *could* get it straight." And with great trepidation Rose gave up her funny little accounts.

It really *was* good in Dr. Alec not to laugh, and Rose felt deeply grateful when he said, in a mildly suggestive tone,—

"The dollars and cents seem to be rather mixed; perhaps if I just straightened them out a bit we should find things all right."

"Please do, and then show me on a fresh leaf how to make mine look nice and ship-shape as yours do."

As Rose stood by him watching the ease with which he quickly brought order out of chaos, she privately resolved to hunt up her old arithmetic and perfect herself in the four first rules, with a good tug at fractions, before she read any more fairy tales.

"Am I a rich girl, uncle?" she asked suddenly, as he was copying a column of figures.

"Rather a poor one, I should say, since you had to borrow a ninepence."

"That was your fault, because you forgot my pocket-money. But, really, shall I be rich by and by?"

"I am afraid you will."

"Why afraid, uncle?"

"Too much money is a bad thing."

"But I can give it away, you know; that is always the pleasantest part of having it, *I* think."

"I'm glad you feel so, for you *can* do much good with your fortune if you know how to use it well."

"You shall teach me, and when I am a woman we will set up a school where nothing but the three Rs shall be taught, and all the children live on oatmeal, and the girls have waists a yard round," said Rose, with a sudden saucy smile dimpling her cheeks.

"You are an impertinent little baggage, to turn on me in that way right in the midst of my first attempt at teaching. Never mind, I'll have an extra bitter dose for you next time, miss."

"I knew you wanted to laugh, so I gave you a chance. Now I will be good, master, and do my lesson nicely."

So Dr. Alec had his laugh, and then Rose sat down and took a lesson in accounts which she never forgot.

"Now come and read aloud to me; my eyes are tired, and it is pleasant to sit here by the fire while the rain pours outside and Aunt Jane lectures upstairs," said Uncle Alec, when last month's accounts had been put in good order and a fresh page neatly begun.

Rose liked to read aloud, and gladly gave him the chapter in "Nicholas Nickleby" where the Miss Kenwigses take their French lesson. She did her very best, feeling that she was being criticised, and hoping that she might not be found wanting in this as in other things.

"Shall I go on, sir?" she asked very meekly when the chapter ended.

"If you are not tired, dear. It is a pleasure to hear you, for you read remarkably well," was the answer that filled her heart with pride and pleasure.

"Do you really think so, uncle? I'm so glad! papa taught me, and I read for hours to him, but I thought, perhaps, he liked it because he was fond of me."

"So am I; but you really do read unusually well, and I am very glad of it, for it is a rare accomplishment, and one I value highly. Come here in this cosey, low chair; the light is better, and I can pull these curls if you go too fast. I see you are going to be a great comfort as well as a great credit to your old uncle, Rosy." And Dr. Alec drew her close beside him with such a fatherly look and tone that she felt it would be very easy to love and obey him since he knew how to mix praise and blame so pleasantly together.

Another chapter was just finished, when the sound of a carriage warned them that Aunt Jane was about to depart. Before they could go to meet her, however, she appeared in the door-way looking like an unusually tall mummy in her waterproof, with her glasses shining like cat's eyes from the depths of the hood.

"Just as I thought! petting that child to death and letting her sit up late reading trash. I do hope you feel the weight of the responsibility you have taken upon yourself, Alec," she said, with a certain grim sort of satisfaction at seeing things go wrong.

"I think I have a very realizing sense of it, sister Jane," answered Dr. Alec, with a comical shrug of the shoulders and a glance at Rose's bright face.

"It is sad to see a great girl wasting these precious hours so. Now, my boys have studied all day, and Mac is still at his books, I've no doubt, while you have not had a lesson since you came, I suspect."

"I have had five to-day, ma'am," was Rose's very unexpected answer.

"I'm glad to hear it; and what were they, pray?"

Rose looked very demure as she replied,—

"Navigation, geography, grammar, arithmetic, and keeping my temper."

"Queer lessons, I fancy; and what have you learned from this remarkable mixture, I should like to know?"

A naughty sparkle came into Rose's eyes as she answered, with a droll look at her uncle,—

"I can't tell you all, ma'am, but I have collected some useful information about China, which you may like, especially the teas. The best are Lapsing Souchong, Assam Pekoe, rare Ankoe, Flowery Pekoe, Howqua's mixture, Scented Caper, Padral tea, black Congou, and green Twankey. Shanghai is on the Woosung River. Hong Kong means 'Island of sweet waters.' Singapore is 'Lion's Town.' 'Chops' are the boats they live in; and they drink tea out of little saucers. Principal productions are porcelain, tea, cinnamon, shawls, tin, tamarinds, and opium. They have beautiful temples and queer gods; and in Canton is the Dwelling of the Holy Pigs, fourteen of them, very big, and all blind."

The effect of this remarkable burst was immense, especially the fact last mentioned. It entirely took the wind out of Aunt Jane's sails; it was so sudden, so varied and unexpected, that she had not a word to say. The glasses remained fixed full upon

Rose for a moment, and then, with a hasty "Oh, indeed!" the excellent lady bundled into her carriage and drove away, somewhat bewildered and very much disturbed.

She would have been more so if she had seen her reprehensible brother-in-law dancing a triumphal polka down the hall with Rose in honor of having silenced the enemy's battery for once.

# Chapter IX

## PHEBE'S SECRET

"WHY do you keep smiling to yourself, Phebe?" asked Rose, as they were working together one morning, for Dr. Alec considered house-work the best sort of gymnastics for girls; so Rose took lessons of Phebe in sweeping, dusting, and bed-making.

"I was thinking about a nice little secret I know, and couldn't help smiling."

"Shall I know it sometime?"

"Guess you will."

"Shall I like it?"

"Oh, won't you, though!"

"Will it happen soon?"

"Sometime this week."

"I know what it is! The boys are going to have fire-works on the Fourth, and have got some surprise for me. Haven't they?"

"That's telling."

"Well, I can wait; only tell me one thing,—is uncle in it?"

"Of course he is; there's never any fun without him."

"Then it is all right, and sure to be nice."

Rose went out on the balcony to shake the rugs, and, having given them a vigorous beating, hung them on the balustrade to air, while she took a look at her plants. Several tall vases and jars stood there, and a month of June sun and rain had worked wonders with the seeds and slips she had planted. Morning-glories and nasturtiums ran all over the bars, making haste to bloom. Scarlet beans and honeysuckles were climbing up from below to meet their pretty neighbors, and the woodbine was hanging its green festoons wherever it could cling.

The waters of the bay were dancing in the sunshine, a fresh wind stirred the chestnut-trees with a pleasant sound, and the garden below was full of roses, butterflies, and bees. A great chirping and twittering went on among the birds, busy with their summer housekeeping, and, far away, the white-winged gulls were dipping and diving in the sea, where ships, like larger birds, went sailing to and fro.

"Oh, Phebe, it's such a lovely day, I do wish your fine secret was going to happen right away! I feel just like having a good time; don't you?" said Rose, waving her arms as if she was going to fly.

"I often feel that way, but I have to wait for my good times, and don't stop working to wish for 'em. There, now you can finish as soon as the dust settles; I must go do my stairs," and Phebe trudged away with the broom, singing as she went.

Rose leaned where she was, and fell to thinking how many good times she had had lately, for the gardening had prospered finely, and she was learning to swim and row, and there were drives and walks, and quiet hours of reading and talk with Uncle Alec, and, best of all, the old pain and *ennui* seldom troubled her now. She could work and play all day, sleep sweetly all night, and enjoy life with the zest of a healthy, happy child. She was far from being as strong and hearty as Phebe, but she was getting on; the once pale cheeks had color in them now, the hands were growing plump and brown, and the belt was not much too loose. No one talked to her about her health, and she forgot that she had "no constitution." She took no medicine but Dr. Alec's three great remedies, and they seemed to suit her excellently. Aunt Plenty said it was the pills; but, as no second batch ever followed the first, I think the old lady was mistaken.

Rose looked worthy of her name as she stood smiling to herself over a happier secret than any Phebe had,—a secret which she did not know herself till she found out, some years later, the magic of good health.

> "'Look only,' said the brownie,
>     'At the pretty gown of blue,
>   At the kerchief pinned about her head,
>     And at her little shoe,'"

said a voice from below, as a great cabbage-rose came flying against her cheek.

"What is the princess dreaming about up there in her hanging-garden?" added Dr. Alec as she flung back a morning-glory.

"I was wishing I could do something pleasant this fine day;

something very new and interesting, for the wind makes me feel frisky and gay."

"Suppose we take a pull over to the Island? I intended to go this afternoon; but if you feel more like it now, we can be off at once."

"I do! I do! I'll come in fifteen minutes, uncle. I *must* just scrabble my room to rights, for Phebe has got a great deal to do."

Rose caught up the rugs and vanished as she spoke, while Dr. Alec went in, saying to himself, with an indulgent smile,—

"It may upset things a trifle, but half a child's pleasure consists in having their fun *when* they want it."

Never did duster flap more briskly than the one Rose used that day, and never was a room "scrabbled" to rights in such haste as hers. Tables and chairs flew into their places as if alive; curtains shook as if a gale was blowing; china rattled and small articles tumbled about as if a young earthquake was playing with them. The boating suit went on in a twinkling, and Rose was off with a hop and a skip, little dreaming how many hours it would be before she saw her pretty room again.

Uncle Alec was putting a large basket into the boat when she arrived, and before they were off Phebe came running down with a queer, knobby bundle done up in a water-proof.

"We can't eat half that luncheon, and I know we shall not need so many wraps. I wouldn't lumber the boat up so," said Rose, who still had secret scares when on the water.

"Couldn't you make a smaller parcel, Phebe?" asked Dr. Alec, eying the bundle suspiciously.

"No, sir, not in such a hurry," and Phebe laughed as she gave a particularly large knob a good poke.

"Well, it will do for ballast. Don't forget the note to Mrs. Jessie, I beg of you."

"No, sir. I'll send it right off," and Phebe ran up the bank as if she had wings to her feet.

"We'll take a look at the light-house first, for you have not been there yet, and it is worth seeing. By the time we have done that it will be pretty warm, and we will have lunch under the trees on the Island."

Rose was ready for any thing, and enjoyed her visit to the light-house on the Point very much, especially climbing up the narrow stairs and going inside the great lantern. They made a long stay, for Dr. Alec seemed in no hurry to go, and kept looking through his spy-glass as if he expected to discover something remarkable on sea or land. It was past twelve before they reached the Island, and Rose was ready for her lunch long before she got it.

"Now this *is* lovely! I do wish the boys were here. Won't it be nice to have them with us all their vacation? Why, it begins to-day, doesn't it? Oh, I wish I'd remembered it sooner, and perhaps they would have come with us," she said, as they lay luxuriously eating sandwiches under the old apple-tree.

"So we might. Next time we won't be in such a hurry. I expect the lads will take our heads off when they find us out," answered Dr. Alec, placidly drinking cold tea.

"Uncle, I smell a frying sort of a smell," Rose said, pausing suddenly as she was putting away the remains of the lunch half an hour later.

"So do I; it is fish, I think."

For a moment they both sat with their noses in the air, sniffing like hounds; then Dr. Alec sprang up, saying with great decision,—

"Now this won't do! No one is permitted on this island without asking leave. I must see who dares to fry fish on my private property."

Taking the basket on one arm and the bundle on the other, he strode away toward the traitorous smell, looking as fierce as a lion, while Rose marched behind under her umbrella.

"We are Robinson Crusoe and his man Friday going to see if the savages have come," she said presently, for her fancy was full of the dear old stories that all children love so well.

"And there they are! Two tents and two boats, as I live! These rascals mean to enjoy themselves, that's evident."

"There ought to be more boats and no tents. I wonder where the prisoners are?"

"There are traces of them," and Dr. Alec pointed to the heads and tails of fishes strewn on the grass.

"And there are more," said Rose, laughing, as she pointed to a scarlet heap of what looked like lobsters.

"The savages are probably eating their victims now; don't you hear the knives rattle in that tent?"

"We ought to creep up and peep; Crusoe was cautious, you know, and Friday scared out of his wits," added Rose, still keeping up the joke.

"But this Crusoe is going to pounce upon them regardless of consequences. If I am killed and eaten, you seize the basket and run for the boat; there are provisions enough for your voyage home."

With that Uncle Alec slipped round to the front of the tent, and, casting in the big bundle like a bombshell, roared out, in a voice of thunder,—

"Pirates, surrender!"

A crash, a shout, a laugh, and out came the savages, brandishing knives and forks, chicken bones, and tin mugs, and all fell upon the intruder, pommelling him unmercifully as they cried,—

"You came too soon! We are not half ready! You've spoilt it all! Where is Rose?"

"Here I am," answered a half-stifled voice, and Rose was discovered sitting on the pile of red flannel bathing-clothes, which she had mistaken for lobsters, and where she had fallen in a fit of merriment when she discovered that the cannibals were her merry cousins.

"You good-for-nothing boys! You are always bursting out upon me in some ridiculous way, and I always get taken in because I'm not used to such pranks. Uncle is as bad as the rest, and it's great fun," she said, as the lads came round her, half scolding, half welcoming, and wholly enjoying the double surprise.

"You were not to come till afternoon, and mamma was to be here to receive you. Every thing is in a mess now, except your tent; we got that in order the first thing, and you can sit there and see us work," said Archie, doing the honors as usual.

"Rose felt it in her bones, as Dolly says, that something was in the wind, and wanted to be off at once. So I let her come, and should have kept her away an hour longer if your fish had not betrayed you," explained Uncle Alec, subsiding from a ferocious Crusoe into his good-natured self again.

"As this seat is rather damp, I think I'll rise," said Rose, as the excitement lessened a little.

Several fishy hands helped her up, and Charlie said, as he scattered the scarlet garments over the grass with an oar,—

A CRASH, A SHOUT, A LAUGH, AND OUT CAME THE SAVAGES.

"We had a jolly good swim before dinner, and I told the Brats to spread these to dry. Hope you brought *your* things, Rose, for you belong to the Lobsters, you know, and we can have no end of fun teaching you to dive and float and tread water."

"I didn't bring any thing—" began Rose, but was interrupted by the Brats (otherwise Will and Geordie), who appeared bearing the big bundle, so much demoralized by its fall that a red flannel tunic trailed out at one end and a little blue dressing-gown at the other, while the knobs proved to be a toilet-case, rubbers, and a silver mug.

"Oh, that sly Phebe! This was the secret, and she bundled up those things after I went down to the boat," cried Rose, with sparkling eyes.

"Guess something is smashed inside, for a bit of glass fell out," observed Will, as they deposited the bundle at her feet.

"Catch a girl going anywhere without a looking-glass. We haven't got one among the whole lot of us," added Mac, with masculine scorn.

"Dandy has; I caught him touching up his wig behind the trees after our swim," cut in Geordie, wagging a derisive finger at Steve, who promptly silenced him by a smart rap on the head with the drum-stick he had just polished off.

"Come, come, you lazy lubbers, fall to work, or we shall not be ready for mamma. Take Rose's things to her tent, and tell her all about it, Prince. Mac and Steve, you cut away and bring up the rest of the straw; and you small chaps clear off the table, if you have stuffed all you can. Please, uncle, I'd like your advice about the boundary lines and the best place for the kitchen."

Every one obeyed the Chief, and Rose was escorted to her tent by Charlie, who devoted himself to her service. She was charmed with her quarters, and still more so with the programme which he unfolded before her as they worked.

"We always camp out somewhere in vacation, and this year we thought we'd try the Island. It is handy, and our fire-works will show off well from here."

"Shall we stay over the Fourth? Three whole days! Oh, me! what a frolic it will be!"

"Bless your heart, we often camp for a week, we big fellows; but this year the small chaps wanted to come, so we let them.

We have great larks, as you'll see; for we have a cave and play
Captain Kidd, and have shipwrecks, and races, and all sorts of
games. Arch and I are rather past that kind of thing now, but
we do it to please the children," added Charlie, with a sudden
recollection of his sixteen years.

"I had no idea boys had such good times. Their plays never
seemed a bit interesting before. But I suppose that was because
I never knew any boys very well, or perhaps you are unusually
nice ones," observed Rose, with an artless air of appreciation
that was very flattering.

"We are a pretty clever set, I fancy; but we have a good
many advantages, you see. There are a tribe of us, to begin
with; then our family has been here for ages, and we have
plenty of 'spondulics,' so we can rather lord it over the other
fellows and do as we like. There, ma'am, you can hang your
smashed glass on that nail and do up your back hair as fine as
you please. You can have a blue blanket or a red one, and a
straw pillow or an air cushion for your head, whichever you
like. You can trim up to any extent, and be as free and easy as
squaws in a wigwam, for this corner is set apart for you ladies,
and we never cross the line uncle is drawing until we ask leave.
Any thing more I can do for you, cousin?"

"No, thank you. I think I'll leave the rest till auntie comes,
and go and help you somewhere else, if I may."

"Yes, indeed, come on and see to the kitchen. Can you
cook?" asked Charlie, as he led the way to the rocky nook
where Archie was putting up a sail-cloth awning.

"I can make tea and toast bread."

"Well, we'll show you how to fry fish and make chowder.
Now you just set these pots and pans round tastefully, and sort
of tidy up a bit, for Aunt Jessie insists on doing some of the
work, and I want it to be decent here."

By four o'clock the camp was in order, and the weary workers settled down on Lookout Rock to watch for Mrs. Jessie
and Jamie, who was never far from mamma's apron-string.
They looked like a flock of blue-birds, all being in sailor rig,
with blue ribbon enough flying from the seven hats to have set
up a milliner. Very tuneful blue-birds they were, too, for all the
lads sang, and the echo of their happy voices reached Mrs.
Jessie long before she saw them.

The moment the boat hove in sight up went the Island flag, and the blue-jackets cheered lustily, as they did on every possible occasion, like true young Americans. This welcome was answered by the flapping of a handkerchief and the shrill "Rah! Rah! Rah!" of the one small tar who stood in the stern waving his hat manfully, while a maternal hand clutched him firmly in the rear.

Cleopatra landing from her golden galley never received a heartier greeting than "Little Mum" as she was borne to her tent by the young folk, for love of whom she smilingly resigned herself to three days of discomfort; while Jamie immediately attached himself to Rose, assuring her of his protection from the manifold perils which might assail them.

Taught by long experience that boys are *always* hungry, Aunt Jessie soon proposed supper, and proceeded to get it, enveloped in an immense apron, with an old hat of Archie's stuck atop of her cap. Rose helped, and tried to be as handy as Phebe, though the peculiar style of table she had to set made it no easy task. It was accomplished at last, and a very happy party lay about under the trees, eating and drinking out of any one's plate and cup, and quite untroubled by the frequent appearance of ants and spiders in places which these interesting insects are not expected to adorn.

"I never thought I should like to wash dishes, but I do," said Rose, as she sat in a boat after supper lazily rinsing plates in the sea, and rocking luxuriously as she wiped them.

"Mum is mighty particular; *we* just give 'em a scrub with sand, and dust 'em off with a bit of paper. It's much the best way, *I* think," replied Geordie, who reposed in another boat alongside.

"How Phebe would like this! I wonder uncle did not have her come."

"I believe he tried to, but Dolly was as cross as two sticks, and said she couldn't spare her. I'm sorry, for we all like the Phebe bird, and she'd chirp like a good one out here, wouldn't she?"

"She ought to have a holiday like the rest of us. It's too bad to leave her out."

This thought came back to Rose several times that evening, for Phebe would have added much to the little concert they had in the moonlight, would have enjoyed the stories told, been quick at guessing the conundrums, and laughed with all her heart at the fun. The merry going to bed would have been best of all, for Rose wanted some one to cuddle under the blue blanket with her, there to whisper and giggle and tell secrets, as girls delight to do.

Long after the rest were asleep, Rose lay wide awake, excited by the novelty of all about her, and a thought that had come into her mind. Far away she heard a city clock strike twelve; a large star like a mild eye peeped in at the opening of the tent, and the soft plash of the waves seemed calling her to come out. Aunt Jessie lay fast asleep, with Jamie rolled up like a kitten at her feet, and neither stirred as Rose in her wrapper crept out to see how the world looked at midnight.

She found it very lovely, and sat down on a cracker keg to enjoy it with a heart full of the innocent sentiment of her years. Fortunately, Dr. Alec saw her before she had time to catch cold, for coming out to tie back the door-flap of his tent for more air, he beheld the small figure perched in the moonlight. Having no fear of ghosts, he quietly approached, and, seeing that she was wide awake, said, with a hand on her shining hair,—

"What is my girl doing here?"

"Having a good time," answered Rose, not at all startled.

"I wonder what she was thinking about with such a sober look?"

"The story you told of the brave sailor who gave up his place on the raft to the woman, and the last drop of water to the poor baby. People who make sacrifices are very much loved and admired, aren't they?" she asked, earnestly.

"If the sacrifice is a true one. But many of the bravest never are known, and get no praise. That does not lessen their beauty, though perhaps it makes them harder, for we all like sympathy," and Dr. Alec sighed a patient sort of sigh.

"I suppose you have made a great many? Would you mind telling me one of them?" asked Rose, arrested by the sigh.

"My last was to give up smoking," was the very unromantic answer to her pensive question.

"Why did you?"

"Bad example for the boys."

"That was very good of you, uncle! Was it hard?"

"I'm ashamed to say it was. But as a wise old fellow once said, 'It is necessary to do right; it is not necessary to be happy.'"

Rose pondered over the saying as if it pleased her, and then said, with a clear, bright look,—

"A real sacrifice is giving up something you want or enjoy very much, isn't it?"

"Yes."

"Doing it one's own self because one loves another person very much and wants her to be happy?"

"Yes."

"And doing it pleasantly, and being glad about it, and not minding the praise if it doesn't come?"

"Yes, dear, that is the true spirit of self-sacrifice; you seem to understand it, and I dare say you will have many chances in your life to try the real thing. I hope they won't be very hard ones."

"I think they will," began Rose, and there stopped short.

"Well, make one now, and go to sleep, or my girl will be ill to-morrow, and then the aunts will say camping out was bad for her."

"I'll go,—good night!" and throwing him a kiss, the little ghost vanished, leaving Uncle Alec to pace the shore and think about some of the unsuspected sacrifices that had made him what he was.

# Chapter X

ROSE'S SACRIFICE

THERE certainly were "larks" on Campbell's Island next day, as Charlie had foretold, and Rose took her part in them like one intent on enjoying every minute to the utmost. There was a merry breakfast, a successful fishing expedition, and then the lobsters came out in full force, for even Aunt Jessie appeared in red flannel. There was nothing Uncle Alec could not do in the water, and the boys tried their best to equal him in strength and skill, so there was a great diving and ducking, for every one was bent on distinguishing himself.

Rose swam far out beyond her depth, with uncle to float her back; Aunt Jessie splashed placidly in the shallow pools, with Jamie paddling near by like a little whale beside its mother; while the lads careered about, looking like a flock of distracted flamingoes, and acting like the famous dancing party in "Alice's Adventures in Wonderland."

Nothing but chowder would have lured them from their gambols in the briny deep; that time-honored dish demanded the concentrated action of several mighty minds; so the "Water Babies" came ashore and fell to cooking.

It is unnecessary to say that, when done, it was the most remarkable chowder ever cooked, and the quantity eaten would have amazed the world if the secret had been divulged. After this exertion a *siesta* was considered the thing, and people lay about in tents or out as they pleased, the boys looking like warriors slumbering where they fell.

The elders had just settled to a comfortable nap when the youngsters rose, refreshed and ready for further exploits. A hint sent them all off to the cave, and there were discovered bows and arrows, battle clubs, old swords, and various relics of an interesting nature. Perched upon a commanding rock, with Jamie to "splain" things to her, Rose beheld a series of stirring scenes enacted with great vigor and historical accuracy by her gifted relatives.

Captain Cook was murdered by the natives of Owhyhee in

the most thrilling manner. Captain Kidd buried untold wealth in the chowder kettle at the dead of night, and shot both the trusting villains who shared the secret of the hiding-place. Sinbad came ashore there and had manifold adventures, and numberless wrecks bestrewed the sands.

Rose considered them by far the most exciting dramas she had ever witnessed; and when the performance closed with a grand ballet of Feejee Islanders, whose barbaric yells alarmed the gulls, she had no words in which to express her gratification.

Another swim at sunset, another merry evening on the rocks watching the lighted steamers pass seaward and the pleasure-boats come into port, ended the second day of the camping out, and sent every one to bed early that they might be ready for the festivities of the morrow.

"Archie, didn't I hear uncle ask you to row home in the morning for fresh milk and things?"

"Yes; why?"

"Please, may I go too? I have something of *great* importance to arrange; you know I was carried off in a hurry," Rose said in a confidential whisper as she was bidding her cousins good-night.

"I'm willing, and I guess Charlie won't mind."

"Thank you; be you stand by me when I ask leave in the morning, and don't say any thing till then, except to Charlie. Promise," urged Rose, so eagerly that Archie struck an attitude, and cried dramatically,—

"By yonder moon I swear!"

"Hush! it's all right, go along;" and Rose departed as if satisfied.

"She's a queer little thing, isn't she, Prince?"

"Rather a nice little thing, *I* think. I'm quite fond of her."

Rose's quick ears caught both remarks, and she retired to her tent, saying to herself with sleepy dignity,—

"Little thing, indeed! Those boys talk as if I was a baby. They will treat me with more respect after to-morrow, I guess."

Archie did stand by her in the morning, and her request was readily granted, as the lads were coming directly back. Off they went, and Rose waved her hand to the islanders with a somewhat pensive air, for an heroic purpose glowed within her, and the spirit of self-sacrifice was about to be illustrated in a new and touching manner.

While the boys got the milk Rose ran to Phebe, ordered her to leave her dishes, to put on her hat and take a note back to Uncle Alec, which would explain this somewhat mysterious performance. Phebe obeyed, and when she went to the boat Rose accompanied her, telling the boys she was not ready to go yet, but they could some of them come for her when she hung a white signal on her balcony.

"But why not come now? What are you about, miss? Uncle won't like it," protested Charlie, in great amazement.

"Just do as I tell you, little boy; uncle will understand and explain. Obey, as Phebe does, and ask no questions. *I* can have secrets as well as other people;" and Rose walked off with an air of lofty independence that impressed her friends immensely.

"It's some plot between uncle and herself, so we won't meddle. All right, Phebe? Pull away, Prince;" and off they went, to be received with much surprise by the islanders.

This was the note Phebe bore:—

> "DEAR UNCLE,—I am going to take Phebe's place to-day, and let her have all the fun she can. Please don't mind what she says, but keep her, and tell the boys to be very good to her for my sake. Don't think it is easy to do this; it is very hard to give up the best day of all, but I feel so selfish to have all the pleasure, and Phebe none, that I wish to make this sacrifice. Do let me, and don't laugh at it; I truly do not wish to be praised, and I truly want to do it. Love to all from          ROSE."

"Bless the little dear, what a generous heart she has! Shall we go after her, Jessie, or let her have her way?" said Dr. Alec, after the first mingled amusement and astonishment had subsided.

"Let her alone, and don't spoil her little sacrifice. She means it, I know, and the best way in which we can show our respect for her effort is to give Phebe a pleasant day. I'm sure she has earned it;" and Mrs. Jessie made a sign to the boys to suppress their disappointment and exert themselves to please Rose's guest.

Phebe was with difficulty kept from going straight home,

and declared that she should not enjoy herself one bit without Miss Rose.

"She won't hold out all day, and we shall see her paddling back before noon, I'll wager any thing," said Charlie; and the rest so strongly inclined to his opinion that they resigned themselves to the loss of the little queen of the revels, sure that it would be only a temporary one.

But hour after hour passed, and no signal appeared on the balcony, though Phebe watched it hopefully. No passing boat brought the truant back, though more than one pair of eyes looked out for the bright hair under the round hat; and sunset came, bringing no Rose but the lovely color in the western sky.

"I really did not think the child had it in her. I fancied it was a bit of sentiment, but I see she *was* in earnest, and means that her sacrifice shall be a true one. Dear little soul! I'll make it up to her a thousand times over, and beg her pardon for thinking it might be done for effect," Dr. Alec said remorsefully, as he strained his eyes through the dusk, fancying he saw a small figure sitting in the garden as it had sat on the keg two nights before, laying the generous little plot that had cost more than he could guess.

"Well, she can't help seeing the fire-works any way, unless she is goose enough to think she must hide in a dark closet and not look," said Archie, who was rather disgusted at Rose's seeming ingratitude.

"She will see ours capitally, but miss the big ones on the hill, unless papa has forgotten all about them," added Steve, cutting short the harangue Mac had begun upon the festivals of the ancients.

"I'm sure the sight of her will be better than the finest fire-works that ever went off," said Phebe, meditating an elopement with one of the boats if she could get a chance.

"Let things work; if she resists the brilliant invitation we give her she will be a heroine," added Uncle Alec, secretly hoping that she would not.

Meanwhile Rose had spent a quiet, busy day helping Dolly, waiting on Aunt Peace, and steadily resisting Aunt Plenty's attempts to send her back to the happy island. It had been hard in the morning to come in from the bright world outside, with flags flying, cannon booming, crackers popping, and every one making ready for a holiday, and go to washing cups, while Dolly grumbled and the aunts lamented. It was very hard to see the day go by, knowing how gay each hour must have been across the water, and how a word from her would take her where she longed to be with all her heart. But it was hardest of all when evening came and Aunt Peace was asleep, Aunt Plenty seeing a gossip in the parlor, Dolly established in the porch to enjoy the show, and nothing left for the little maid to do but sit alone in her balcony and watch the gay rockets whizz up from island, hill, and city, while bands played and boats laden with happy people went to and fro in the fitful light.

Then it must be confessed that a tear or two dimmed the blue eyes, and once, when a very brilliant display illuminated the island for a moment, and she fancied she saw the tents, the curly head went down on the railing, and a wide-awake nasturtium heard a little whisper,—

"I hope some one wishes I was there!"

The tears were all gone, however, and she was watching the hill and island answer each other with what Jamie called "whizzers, whirligigs, and busters," and smiling as she thought how hard the boys must be working to keep up such a steady fire, when Uncle Mac came walking in upon her, saying hurriedly,—

"Come, child, put on your tippet, pelisse, or whatever you call it, and run off with me. I came to get Phebe, but aunt says she is gone, so I want you. I've got Fun down in the boat, and I want you to go with us and see my fire-works. Got them up for you, and you mustn't miss them, or I shall be disappointed."

"But, uncle," began Rose, feeling as if she ought to refuse even a glimpse of bliss, "perhaps—"

"I know, my dear, I know; aunt told me; but no one needs you now so much as I do, and I insist on your coming," said Uncle Mac, who seemed in a great hurry to be off, yet was unusually kind.

So Rose went and found the little Chinaman with a funny lantern waiting to help her in and convulse her with laughter trying to express his emotions in pigeon English. The city clocks were striking nine as they got out into the bay, and the island fire-works seemed to be over, for no rocket answered the last Roman candle that shone on the Aunt-hill.

"That was rather a neat thing, I flatter myself," said Uncle Mac.

"Ours are done, I see, but they are going up all round the city, and how pretty they are," said Rose, folding her mantle about her and surveying the scene with a pensive interest.

"Hope my fellows have not got into trouble up there," muttered Uncle Mac, adding, with a satisfied chuckle, as a spark shone out, "No; there it goes! Look, Rosy, and see how you like this one; it was ordered especially in honor of your coming."

Rose looked with all her eyes, and saw the spark grow into the likeness of a golden vase, then green leaves came out, and then a crimson flower glowing on the darkness with a splendid lustre.

"Is it a rose, uncle?" she asked, clasping her hands with delight as she recognized the handsome flower.

"Of course it is! Look again, and guess what those are," answered Uncle Mac, chuckling and enjoying it all like a boy.

A wreath of what looked at first like purple brooms appeared below the vase, but Rose guessed what they were meant for and stood straight up, holding by his shoulder, and crying excitedly,—

"Thistles, uncle, Scotch thistles! There are seven of them,— one for each boy! Oh, what a joke!" and she laughed so that she plumped into the bottom of the boat and stayed there till the brilliant spectacle was quite gone.

"That was rather a neat thing, I flatter myself," said Uncle Mac in high glee at the success of his illumination. "Now, shall I leave you on the Island or take you home again, my good little girl?" he added, lifting her up with such a tone of approbation in his voice that Rose kissed him on the spot.

"Home, please, uncle; and I thank you very, very much for the beautiful fire-work you got up for me. I'm so glad I saw it; and I know I shall dream about it," answered Rose steadily, though a wistful glance went toward the Island, now so near that she could smell powder and see shadowy figures flitting about.

Home they went; and Rose fell asleep saying to herself, "It was harder than I thought, but I'm glad I did it, and I truly don't want any reward but Phebe's pleasure."

# Chapter XI

## POOR MAC

Rose's sacrifice was a failure in one respect, for, though the elders loved her the better for it, and showed that they did, the boys were not inspired with the sudden respect which she had hoped for. In fact, her feelings were much hurt by overhearing Archie say that he couldn't see any sense in it; and the Prince added another blow by pronouncing her "the queerest chicken ever seen."

It is apt to be so, and it is hard to bear; for, though we do not want trumpets blown, we do like to have our little virtues appreciated, and cannot help feeling disappointed if they are not.

A time soon came, however, when Rose, quite unconsciously, won not only the respect of her cousins, but their gratitude and affection likewise.

Soon after the Island episode, Mac had a sun-stroke, and was very ill for some time. It was so sudden that every one was startled, and for some days the boy's life was in danger. He pulled through, however; and then, just as the family were rejoicing, a new trouble appeared which cast a gloom over them all.

Poor Mac's eyes gave out; and well they might, for he had abused them, and never being very strong, they suffered doubly now.

No one dared to tell him the dark predictions of the great oculist who came to look at them, and the boy tried to be patient, thinking that a few weeks of rest would repair the overwork of several years.

He was forbidden to look at a book, and as that was the one thing he most delighted in, it was a terrible affliction to the Worm. Every one was very ready to read to him, and at first the lads contended for this honor. But as week after week went by, and Mac was still condemned to idleness and a darkened room, their zeal abated, and one after the other fell off. It *was* hard for the active fellows, right in the midst of their vacation;

and nobody blamed them when they contented themselves with brief calls, running of errands, and warm expressions of sympathy.

The elders did their best, but Uncle Mac was a busy man, Aunt Jane's reading was of a funereal sort, impossible to listen to long, and the other aunties were all absorbed in their own cares, though they supplied the boy with every delicacy they could invent.

Uncle Alec was a host in himself, but he could not give all his time to the invalid; and if it had not been for Rose, the afflicted Worm would have fared ill. Her pleasant voice suited him, her patience was unfailing, her time of no apparent value, and her eager good-will was very comforting.

The womanly power of self-devotion was strong in the child, and she remained faithfully at her post when all the rest dropped away. Hour after hour she sat in the dusky room, with one ray of light on her book, reading to the boy, who lay with shaded eyes silently enjoying the only pleasure that lightened the weary days. Sometimes he was peevish and hard to please, sometimes he growled because his reader could not manage the dry books he wished to hear, and sometimes he was so despondent that her heart ached to see him. Through all these trials Rose persevered, using all her little arts to please him. When he fretted, she was patient; when he growled, she ploughed bravely through the hard pages,—not dry to her in one sense, for quiet tears dropped on them now and then; and when Mac fell into a despairing mood, she comforted him with every hopeful word she dared to offer.

He said little, but she knew he was grateful, for she suited him better than any one else. If she was late, he was impatient; when she had to go, he seemed forlorn; and when the tired head ached worst, she could always soothe him to sleep, crooning the old songs her father used to love.

"I don't know what I *should* do without that child," Aunt Jane often said.

"She's worth all those racketing fellows put together," Mac would add, fumbling about to discover if the little chair was ready for her coming.

That was the sort of reward Rose liked, the thanks that cheered her; and whenever she grew very tired, one look at the green shade, the curly head so restless on the pillow, and the poor groping hands, touched her tender heart and put new spirit into the weary voice.

She did not know how much she was learning, both from the books she read and the daily sacrifices she made. Stories and poetry were her delight, but Mac did not care for them; and since his favorite Greeks and Romans were forbidden, he satisfied himself with travels, biographies, and the history of great inventions or discoveries. Rose despised this taste at first, but soon got interested in Livingstone's adventures, Hobson's stirring life in India, and the brave trials and triumphs of Watt and Arkwright, Fulton, and "Palissy, the Potter." The true, strong books helped the dreamy girl; her faithful service and sweet patience touched and won the boy; and long afterward both learned to see how useful those seemingly hard and weary hours had been to them.

One bright morning, as Rose sat down to begin a fat volume entitled "History of the French Revolution," expecting to come to great grief over the long names, Mac, who was lumbering about the room like a blind bear, stopped her by asking abruptly,—

"What day of the month is it?"

"The seventh of August, I believe."

"More than half my vacation gone, and I've only had a week of it! I call that hard," and he groaned dismally.

"So it is; but there is more to come, and you may be able to enjoy that."

"*May* be able! I *will* be able! Does that old noodle think I'm going to stay stived up here much longer?"

"I guess he does, unless your eyes get on faster than they have yet."

"Has he said any thing more lately?"

"I haven't seen him, you know. Shall I begin?—this looks rather nice."

"Read away; it's all one to me." And Mac cast himself down upon the old lounge, where his heavy head felt easiest.

Rose began with great spirit, and kept on gallantly for a couple of chapters, getting over the unpronounceable names with unexpected success, she thought, for her listener did not correct her once, and lay so still she fancied he was deeply interested. All of a sudden she was arrested in the middle of a fine paragraph by Mac, who sat bolt upright, brought both feet down with a thump, and said, in a rough, excited tone,—

"Stop! I don't hear a word, and you may as well save your breath to answer my question."

"What is it?" asked Rose, looking uneasy, for she had something on her mind, and feared that he suspected what it was. His next words proved that she was right.

"Now look here, I want to know something, and you've *got* to tell me."

"Please, don't—" began Rose, beseechingly.

"You *must*, or I'll pull off this shade and stare at the sun as hard as ever I can stare. Come now!" and he half rose, as if ready to execute the threat.

"I will! oh, I will tell, if I know! But don't be reckless and do any thing so crazy as that," cried Rose, in great distress.

"Very well; then listen, and don't dodge, as every one else does. Didn't the doctor think my eyes worse the last time he came? Mother won't say, but you *shall*."

"I believe he did," faltered Rose.

"I thought so! Did he say I should be able to go to school when it begins?"

"No, Mac," very low.

"Ah!"

That was all, but Rose saw her cousin set his lips together and take a long breath, as if she had hit him hard. He bore the disappointment bravely, however, and asked quite steadily in a minute,—

"How soon does he think I *can* study again?"

It was so hard to answer that! Yet Rose knew she must, for Aunt Jane had declared she *could* not do it, and Uncle Mac had begged her to break the truth to the poor lad.

"Not for a good many months."

"How many?" he asked with a pathetic sort of gruffness.

"A year, perhaps."

"A whole year! Why, I expected to be ready for college by that time." And, pushing up the shade, Mac stared at her with startled eyes, that soon blinked and fell before the one ray of light.

"Plenty of time for that; you must be patient now, and get them thoroughly well, or they will trouble you again when it will be harder to spare them," she said, with tears in her own eyes.

"I won't do it! I *will* study and get through somehow. It's all humbug about taking care so long. These doctors like to keep hold of a fellow if they can. But I won't stand it,—I vow I won't!" and he banged his fist down on the unoffending pillow as if he were pommelling the hard-hearted doctor.

"Now, Mac, listen to me," Rose said very earnestly, though her voice shook a little and her heart ached. "You know you have hurt your eyes reading by firelight and in the dusk, and sitting up late, and now you'll have to pay for it; the doctor said so. You *must* be careful, and do as he tells you, or you will be—blind."

"No!"

"Yes, it is true, and he wanted us to tell you that nothing but entire rest would cure you. I know it's dreadfully hard, but we'll all help you; I'll read all day long, and lead you, and wait upon you, and try to make it easier—"

She stopped there, for it was evident that he did not hear a sound; the word "blind" seemed to have knocked him down, for he had buried his face in the pillow, and lay so still that Rose was frightened. She sat motionless for many minutes, longing to comfort him, but not knowing how, and wishing Uncle Alec would come, for he had promised to tell Mac.

Presently, a sort of choking sound came out of the pillow, and went straight to her heart,—the most pathetic sob she ever heard, for, though it was the most natural means of relief, the poor fellow must not indulge in it because of the afflicted eyes. The "French Revolution" tumbled out of her lap, and, running to the sofa, she knelt down by it, saying, with the motherly sort of tenderness girls feel for any sorrowing creature,—

"Oh, my dear, you mustn't cry! It is so bad for your poor eyes. Take your head out of that hot pillow, and let me cool it. I don't wonder you feel so, but please don't cry. I'll cry for you; it won't hurt *me*."

As she spoke, she pulled away the cushion with gentle force, and saw the green shade all crushed and stained with the few hot tears that told how bitter the disappointment had been. Mac felt her sympathy, but, being a boy, did not thank her for

J.P.DAVIS·S·

"RUNNING TO THE SOFA, SHE KNELT DOWN BY IT."

it; only sat up with a jerk, saying, as he tried to rub away the tell-tale drops with the sleeve of his jacket: "Don't bother; weak eyes always water. I'm all right."

But Rose cried out, and caught his arm: "Don't touch them with that rough woollen stuff! Lie down and let me bathe them, there's a dear boy; then there will be no harm done."

"They do smart confoundedly. I say, don't you tell the other fellows that I made a baby of myself, will you?" he added, yielding with a sigh to the orders of his nurse, who had flown for the eye-wash and linen cambric handkerchief.

"Of course I won't; but any one would be upset at the idea of being—well—troubled in this way. I'm sure you bear it splendidly, and you know it isn't half so bad when you get used to it. Besides, it is only for a time, and you can do lots of pleasant things if you can't study. You'll have to wear blue goggles, perhaps; won't that be funny?"

And while she was pouring out all the comfortable words she could think of, Rose was softly bathing the eyes and dabbing the hot forehead with lavender-water, as her patient lay quiet with a look on his face that grieved her sadly.

"Homer was blind, and so was Milton, and they did something to be remembered by, in spite of it," he said, as if to himself, in a solemn tone, for even the blue goggles did not bring a smile.

"Papa had a picture of Milton and his daughters writing for him. It was a very sweet picture, I thought," observed Rose in a serious voice, trying to meet the sufferer on his own ground.

"Perhaps I could study if some one read and did the eye part. Do you suppose I could, by and by?" he asked, with a sudden ray of hope.

"I dare say, if your head is strong enough. This sun-stroke, you know, is what upset you, and your brains need rest, the doctor says."

"I'll have a talk with the old fellow next time he comes, and find out just what I *may* do; then I shall know where I am. What a fool I was that day to be stewing my brains and letting the sun glare on my book till the letters danced before me! I see 'em now when I shut my eyes; black balls bobbing round, and stars and all sorts of queer things. Wonder if all blind people do?"

"Don't think about them; I'll go on reading, shall I? We shall come to the exciting part soon, and then you'll forget all this," suggested Rose.

"No, I never shall forget. Hang the old 'Revolution!' I don't want to hear another word of it. My head aches, and I'm hot. Oh, wouldn't I like to go for a pull in the 'Stormy Petrel!'" and poor Mac tossed about as if he did not know what to do with himself.

"Let me sing, and perhaps you'll drop off; then the day will seem shorter," said Rose, taking up a fan and sitting down beside him.

"Perhaps I shall; I didn't sleep much last night, and when I did I dreamed like fun. See here, you tell the people that I know, and it's all right, and I don't want them to talk about it or howl over me. That's all; now drone away, and I'll try to sleep. Wish I could for a year, and wake up cured."

"Oh, I wish, I wish you could!"

Rose said it so fervently, that Mac was moved to grope for her apron and hold on to a corner of it, as if it was comfortable to feel her near him. But all he said was,—

"You are a good little soul, Rosy. Give us 'The Birks;' that is a drowsy one that always sends me off."

Quite contented with this small return for all her sympathy, Rose waved her fan and sang, in a dreamy tone, the pretty Scotch air, the burden of which is,—

> "Bonny lassie, will ye gang, will ye gang
> To the Birks of Aberfeldie?"

Whether the lassie went or not I cannot say, but the laddie was off to the land of Nod in about ten minutes, quite worn out with hearing the bad tidings and the effort to bear them manfully.

# Chapter XII

## "THE OTHER FELLOWS"

---

Rose did tell "the people" what had passed, and no one "howled" over Mac, or said a word to trouble him. He had his talk with the doctor, and got very little comfort out of it, for he found that "just what he might do" was nothing at all; though the prospect of some study by and by, if all went well, gave him courage to bear the woes of the present. Having made up his mind to this, he behaved so well that every one was astonished, never having suspected so much manliness in the quiet Worm.

The boys were much impressed, both by the greatness of the affliction which hung over him and by his way of bearing it. They were very good to him, but not always particularly wise in their attempts to cheer and amuse; and Rose often found him much downcast after a visit of condolence from the Clan. She still kept her place as head-nurse and chief-reader, though the boys did their best in an irregular sort of way. They were rather taken aback sometimes at finding Rose's services preferred to theirs, and privately confided to one another that "Old Mac was getting fond of being molly-coddled." But they could not help seeing how useful she was, and owning that she alone had remained faithful,—a fact which caused some of them much secret compunction now and then.

Rose felt that she ruled in that room, if nowhere else, for Aunt Jane left a great deal to her, finding that her experience with her invalid father fitted her for a nurse, and in a case like this her youth was an advantage rather than a drawback. Mac soon came to think that no one could take care of him so well as Rose, and Rose soon grew fond of her patient, though at first she had considered this cousin the least attractive of the seven. He was not polite and sensible like Archie, nor gay and handsome like Prince Charlie, nor neat and obliging like Steve, nor amusing like the "Brats," nor confiding and affectionate like little Jamie. He was rough, absent-minded, careless, and awkward, rather priggish, and not at all agreeable to a dainty, beauty-loving girl like Rose.

But when his trouble came upon him, she discovered many good things in this cousin of hers, and learned not only to pity but to respect and love the poor Worm, who tried to be patient, brave, and cheerful, and found it a harder task than any one guessed, except the little nurse, who saw him in his gloomiest moods. She soon came to think that his friends did not appreciate him, and upon one occasion was moved to free her mind in a way that made a deep impression on the boys.

Vacation was almost over, and the time drawing near when Mac would be left outside the happy school-world which he so much enjoyed. This made him rather low in his mind, and his cousins exerted themselves to cheer him up, especially one afternoon when a spasm of devotion seemed to seize them all. Jamie trudged down the hill with a basket of blackberries which he had "picked all his ownself," as his scratched fingers and stained lips plainly testified. Will and Geordie brought their puppies to beguile the weary hours, and the three elder lads called to discuss base-ball, cricket, and kindred subjects, eminently fitted to remind the invalid of his privations.

Rose had gone to drive with Uncle Alec, who declared she was getting as pale as a potato sprout, living so much in a dark room. But her thoughts were with her boy all the while, and she ran up to him the moment she returned, to find things in a fine state of confusion.

With the best intentions in life, the lads had done more harm than good, and the spectacle that met Nurse Rose's eye was a trying one. The puppies were yelping, the small boys romping, and the big boys all talking at once; the curtains were up, the room close, berries scattered freely about, Mac's shade half off, his cheeks flushed, his temper ruffled, and his voice loudest of all as he disputed hotly with Steve about lending certain treasured books which he could no longer use.

Now Rose considered this her special kingdom, and came down upon the invaders with an energy which amazed them and quelled the riot at once. They had never seen her roused before, and the effect was tremendous; also comical, for she drove the whole flock of boys out of the room like an indignant little hen defending her brood. They all went as meekly as sheep; the small lads fled from the house precipitately, but the three elder ones only retired to the next room, and remained

"THE SPECTACLE THAT MET NURSE ROSE'S EYE WAS A TRYING ONE."

there hoping for a chance to explain and apologize, and so appease the irate young lady, who had suddenly turned the tables and clattered them about their ears.

As they waited, they observed her proceedings through the half-open door, and commented upon them briefly but expressively, feeling quite bowed down with remorse at the harm they had innocently done.

"She's put the room to rights in a jiffy. What jacks we were to let those dogs in and kick up such a row," observed Steve, after a prolonged peep.

"The poor old Worm turns as if she was treading on him instead of cuddling him like a pussy cat. Isn't he cross, though?" added Charlie, as Mac was heard growling about his "confounded head."

"She will manage him; but it's mean in us to rumple him up and then leave her to smooth him down. I'd go and help, but I don't know how," said Archie, looking much depressed, for he was a conscientious fellow, and blamed himself for his want of thought.

"No more do I. Odd, isn't it, what a knack women have for taking care of sick folks?" and Charlie fell a-musing over this undeniable fact.

"She has been ever so good to Mac," began Steve, in a self-reproachful tone.

"Better than his own brother, hey?" cut in Archie, finding relief for his own regret in the delinquencies of another.

"Well, you needn't preach; you didn't any of you do any more, and you might have, for Mac likes you better than he does me. I always fret him, he says, and it isn't my fault if I am a quiddle," protested Steve, in self-defence.

"We have all been selfish and neglected him, so we won't fight about it, but try and do better," said Archie, generously taking more than his share of blame, for he had been less inattentive than either of the others.

"Rose has stood by him like a good one, and it's no wonder he likes to have her round best. I should myself if I was down on my luck as he is," put in Charlie, feeling that he really had not done "the little thing" justice.

"I'll tell you what it is, boys,—we haven't been half good enough to Rose, and we've got to make it up to her somehow," said Archie, who had a very manly sense of honor about paying his debts, even to a girl.

"I'm awfully sorry I made fun of her doll when Jamie lugged it out; and I called her 'baby bunting' when she cried over the dead kitten. Girls *are* such geese sometimes, I can't help it," said Steve, confessing his transgressions handsomely, and feeling quite ready to atone for them if he only knew how.

"I'll go down on my knees and beg her pardon for treating her as if she was a child. Don't it make her mad, though? Come to think of it, she's only two years or so younger than I am. But she is so small and pretty, she always seems like a dolly to me," and the Prince looked down from his lofty height of five feet five as if Rose was indeed a pygmy beside him.

"That dolly has got a real good little heart, and a bright mind of her own, you'd better believe. Mac says she understands some things quicker than he can, and mother thinks she is an uncommonly nice girl, though she don't know all creation. You needn't put on airs, Charlie, though you *are* a tall one, for Rose likes Archie better than you; she said she did because he treated her respectfully."

"Steve looks as fierce as a game-cock; but don't you get excited, my son, for it won't do a bit of good. Of course, everybody likes the Chief best; they ought to, and I'll punch their heads if they don't. So calm yourself, Dandy, and mend your own manners before you come down on other people's."

Thus the Prince with great dignity and perfect good nature, while Archie looked modestly gratified with the flattering opinions of his kinsfolk, and Steve subsided, feeling he had done his duty as a cousin and a brother. A pause ensued, during which Aunt Jane appeared in the other room, accompanied by a tea-tray sumptuously spread, and prepared to feed her big nestling, as that was a task she allowed no one to share with her.

"If you have a minute to spare before you go, child, I wish you'd just make Mac a fresh shade; this has got a berry stain on it, and he must be tidy, for he is to go out to-morrow if it is a cloudy day," said Mrs. Jane, spreading toast in a stately manner, while Mac slopped his tea about without receiving a word of reproof.

"Yes, aunt," answered Rose, so meekly that the boys could

hardly believe it could be the same voice which had issued the stern command, "Out of this room, every one of you!" not very long ago.

They had not time to retire, without unseemly haste, before she walked into the parlor and sat down at the work-table without a word. It was funny to see the look the three tall lads cast at the little person sedately threading a needle with green silk. They all wanted to say something expressive of repentance, but no one knew how to begin, and it was evident, from the prim expression of Rose's face, that she intended to stand upon her dignity till they had properly abased themselves. The pause was becoming very awkward, when Charlie, who possessed all the persuasive arts of a born scapegrace, went slowly down upon his knees before her, beat his breast, and said, in a heart-broken tone,—

"Please forgive me this time, and I'll never do so any more."

It was very hard to keep sober, but Rose managed it, and answered gravely,—

"It is Mac's pardon you should ask, not mine, for you haven't hurt me, and I shouldn't wonder if you had him a great deal, with all that light and racket, and talk about things that only worry him."

"Do you really think we've hurt him, cousin?" asked Archie, with a troubled look, while Charlie settled down in a remorseful heap among the table legs.

"Yes, I do, for he has got a raging headache, and his eyes are as red as—as this emery bag," answered Rose, solemnly plunging her needle into a fat flannel strawberry.

Steve tore his hair, metaphorically speaking, for he clutched his cherished top-knot and wildly dishevelled it, as if that was the heaviest penance he could inflict upon himself at such short notice. Charlie laid himself out flat, melodramatically begging some one to take him away and hang him; but Archie, who felt worst of all, said nothing except to vow within himself that he would read to Mac till his own eyes were as red as a dozen emery bags combined.

Seeing the wholesome effects of her treatment upon these culprits, Rose felt that she might relent and allow them a gleam of hope. She found it impossible to help trampling upon the prostrate Prince a little, in words at least, for he had hurt her feelings oftener than he knew; so she gave him a thimble-pie on the top of his head, and said, with the air of an infinitely superior being,—

"Don't be silly, but get up, and I'll tell you something much better to do than sprawling on the floor and getting all over lint."

Charlie obediently sat himself upon a hassock at her feet; the other sinners drew near to catch the words of wisdom about to fall from her lips, and Rose, softened by this gratifying humility, addressed them in her most maternal tone.

"Now, boys, if you really want to be good to Mac, you can do it in this way. Don't keep talking about things he can't do, or go and tell what fun you have had batting your ridiculous balls about. Get some nice book and read quietly; cheer him up about school, and offer to help him study by and by; *you* can do that better than I, because I'm only a girl, and don't learn Greek and Latin and all sorts of headachy stuff."

"Yes, but you can do heaps of things better than we can; you've proved that," said Archie, with an approving look that delighted Rose, though she could not resist giving Charlie one more rebuke, by saying, with a little bridling up of the head, and a curl of the lip that wanted to smile instead,—

"I'm glad you think so, though I *am* a 'queer chicken.'"

This scathing remark caused the Prince to hide his face for shame, and Steve to erect his head in the proud consciousness that this shot was not meant for him. Archie laughed, and Rose, seeing a merry blue eye winking at her from behind two brown hands, gave Charlie's ear a friendly tweak, and extended the olive-branch of peace.

"Now we'll all be good, and plan nice things for poor Mac," she said, smiling so graciously that the boys felt as if the sun had suddenly burst out from behind a heavy cloud and was shining with great brilliancy.

The storm had cleared the air, and quite a heavenly calm succeeded, during which plans of a most varied and surprising sort were laid, for every one burned to make noble sacrifices upon the shrine of "poor Mac," and Rose was the guiding star to whom the others looked with most gratifying submission. Of course, this elevated state of things could not endure long, but it was *very* nice while it lasted, and left an excellent effect upon the minds of all when the first ardor had subsided.

"There, that's ready for to-morrow, and I do hope it will be cloudy," said Rose, as she finished off the new shade, the progress of which the boys had watched with interest.

"I'd bespoken an extra sunny day, but I'll tell the clerk of the weather to change it. He's an obliging fellow, and he'll attend to it; so make yourself easy," said Charlie, who had become quite perky again.

"It is very easy for you to joke, but how would you like to wear a blinder like that for weeks and weeks, sir?" and Rose quenched his rising spirits by slipping the shade over his eyes, as he still sat on the cushion at her feet.

"It's horrid! Take it off, take it off! I don't wonder the poor old boy has the blues with a thing like that on;" and Charlie sat looking at what seemed to him an instrument of torture, with such a sober face that Rose took it gently away, and went in to bid Mac good-night.

"I shall go home with her, for it is getting darkish, and she is rather timid," said Archie, forgetting that he had often laughed at this very timidity.

"I think *I* might, for she's taking care of my brother," put in Steve, asserting his rights.

"Let's all go; that will please her," proposed Charlie, with a burst of gallantry which electrified his mates.

"We will!" they said with one voice, and they did, to Rose's great surprise and secret contentment; though Archie had all the care of her, for the other two were leaping fences, running races, and having wrestling matches all the way down.

They composed themselves on reaching the door, however; shook hands cordially all round, made their best bows, and retired with great elegance and dignity, leaving Rose to say to herself, with girlish satisfaction, as she went in,—

"Now, *that* is the way I like to be treated."

# Chapter XIII

COSEY CORNER

VACATION was over, the boys went back to school, and poor Mac was left lamenting. He was out of the darkened room now, and promoted to blue goggles, through which he took a gloomy view of life, as might have been expected; for there was nothing he could do but wander about, and try to amuse himself without using his eyes. Any one who has ever been condemned to that sort of idleness knows how irksome it is, and can understand the state of mind which caused Mac to say to Rose in a desperate tone one day,—

"Look here, if you don't invent some new employment or amusement for me, I shall knock myself on the head as sure as you live."

Rose flew to Uncle Alec for advice, and he ordered both patient and nurse to the mountains for a month, with Aunt Jessie and Jamie as escort. Pokey and her mother joined the party, and one bright September morning six very happy-looking people were aboard the express train for Portland,—two smiling mammas, laden with luncheon baskets and wraps; a pretty young girl with a bag of books on her arm; a tall, thin lad with his hat over his eyes; and two small children, who sat with their short legs straight out before them, and their chubby faces beaming with the first speechless delight of "truly travelling."

An especially splendid sunset seemed to have been prepared to welcome them when, after a long day's journey, they drove into a wide, green door-yard, where a white colt, a red cow, two cats, four kittens, many hens, and a dozen people, old and young, were gayly disporting themselves. Every one nodded and smiled in the friendliest manner, and a lively old lady kissed the new-comers all round, as she said heartily,—

"Well, now, I'm proper glad to see you! Come right in and rest, and we'll have tea in less than no time, for you must be tired. Lizzie, you show the folks upstairs; Kitty, you fly round and help father in with the trunks; and Jenny and I will have

425

the table all ready by the time you come down. Bless the dears, they want to go see the pussies, and so they shall!"

The three pretty daughters did "fly round," and every one felt at home at once, all were so hospitable and kind. Aunt Jessie had raptures over the homemade carpets, quilts, and quaint furniture; Rose could not keep away from the windows, for each framed a lovely picture; and the little folks made friends at once with the other children, who filled their arms with chickens and kittens, and did the honors handsomely.

The toot of a horn called all to supper, and a goodly party, including six children besides the Campbells, assembled in the long dining-room, armed with mountain appetites and the gayest spirits. It was impossible for any one to be shy or sober, for such gales of merriment arose they blew the starch out of the stiffest, and made the saddest jolly. Mother Atkinson, as all called their hostess, was the merriest there, and the busiest; for she kept flying up to wait on the children, to bring out some new dish, or to banish the live stock, who were of such a social turn that the colt came into the entry and demanded sugar; the cats sat about in people's laps, winking suggestively at the food; and speckled hens cleared the kitchen floor of crumbs, as they joined in the chat with a cheerful clucking.

Everybody turned out after tea to watch the sunset till all the lovely red was gone, and mosquitoes wound their shrill horns to sound the retreat. The music of an organ surprised the new-comers, and in the parlor they found Father Atkinson playing sweetly on the little instrument made by himself. All the children gathered about him, and, led by the tuneful sisters, sang prettily till Pokey fell asleep behind the door, and Jamie gaped audibly right in the middle of his favorite,—

> "Coo," said the little doves: "Coo," said she,
> "All in the top of the old pine-tree."

The older travellers, being tired, went to "bye low" at the same time, and slept like tops in home-spun sheets, on husk mattresses made by Mother Atkinson, who seemed to have put some soothing powder among them, so deep and sweet was the slumber that came.

Next day began the wholesome out-of-door life, which works such wonders with tired minds and feeble bodies. The weather was perfect, and the mountain air made the children as frisky as young lambs; while the elders went about smiling at one another, and saying, "Isn't it splendid?" Even Mac, the "slow coach," was seen to leap over a fence as if he really could not help it; and when Rose ran after him with his broad-brimmed hat, he made the spirited proposal to go into the woods and hunt for a catamount.

Jamie and Pokey were at once enrolled in the Cosey Corner Light Infantry,—a truly superb company, composed entirely of officers, all wearing cocked hats, carrying flags, waving swords, or beating drums. It was a spectacle to stir the dullest soul when this gallant band marched out of the yard in full regimentals, with Captain Dove—a solemn, big-headed boy of eleven—issuing his orders with the gravity of a general, and his Falstaffian regiment obeying them with more docility than skill. The little Snow children did very well, and Lieutenant Jack Dove was fine to see; so was Drummer Frank, the errand-boy of the house, as he rub-a-dub-dubbed with all his heart and drumsticks. Jamie had "trained" before, and was made a colonel at once; but Pokey was the best of all, and called forth a spontaneous burst of applause from the spectators as she brought up the rear, her cocked hat all over one eye, her flag trailing over her shoulder, and her wooden sword straight up in the air; her face beaming and every curl bobbing with delight as her fat legs tottered in the vain attempt to keep step manfully.

Mac and Rose were picking blackberries in the bushes beside the road when the soldiers passed without seeing them, and they witnessed a sight that was both pretty and comical. A little farther on was one of the family burial spots so common in those parts, and just this side of it Captain Fred Dove ordered his company to halt, explaining his reason for so doing in the following words:—

"That's a graveyard, and it's proper to muffle the drums and lower the flags as we go by, and we'd better take off our hats, too; it's more respectable, I think."

"Isn't that cunning of the dears?" whispered Rose, as the little troop marched slowly by to the muffled roll of the drums, every flag and sword held low, all the little heads uncovered, and the childish faces very sober as the leafy shadows flickered over them.

"Let's follow and see what they are after," proposed Mac, who found sitting on a wall and being fed with blackberries luxurious but tiresome.

So they followed and heard the music grow lively, saw the banners wave in the breeze again when the graveyard was passed, and watched the company file into the dilapidated old church that stood at the corner of three woodland roads. Presently the sound of singing made the outsiders quicken their steps, and, stealing up, they peeped in at one of the broken windows.

Captain Dove was up in the old wooden pulpit, gazing solemnly down upon his company, who, having stacked their arms in the porch, now sat in the bare pews singing a Sunday-school hymn with great vigor and relish.

"Let us pray," said Captain Dove, with as much reverence as an army chaplain; and, folding his hands, he repeated a prayer which he thought all would know,—an excellent little prayer, but not exactly appropriate to the morning, for it was,—

> "Now I lay me down to sleep."

Every one joined in saying it, and it was a pretty sight to see the little creatures bowing their curly heads and lisping out the words they knew so well. Tears came into Rose's eyes as she looked; Mac took his hat off involuntarily, and then clapped it on again as if ashamed of showing any feeling.

"Now I shall preach you a short sermon, and my text is, 'Little children, love one another.' I asked mamma to give me one, and she thought that would be good; so you all sit still and I'll preach it. You mustn't whisper, Marion, but hear *me*. It means that we should be good to each other, and play fair, and not quarrel as we did this very day about the wagon. Jack can't always drive, and needn't be mad because I like to go with Frank. Annette ought to be horse sometimes and not always driver; and Willie may as well make up his mind to let Marion build her house by his, for she *will* do it, and he needn't fuss about it. Jamie seems to be a good boy, but I shall preach to him if he isn't. No, Pokey, people don't kiss in church or put their hats on. Now you must all remember what I tell you, because I'm the captain, and you should mind me."

Here Lieutenant Jack spoke right out in meeting with the rebellious remark,—

"Don't care if you are; you'd better mind yourself, and tell how you took away my strap, and kept the biggest doughnut, and didn't draw fair when we had the truck."

"Yes, and you slapped Frank; I saw you," bawled Willie Snow, bobbing up in his pew.

"And you took my book away and hid it 'cause I wouldn't go and swing when you wanted me to," added Annette, the oldest of the Snow trio.

"I *shan't* build my house by Willie's if he don't want me to, so now!" put in little Marion, joining the mutiny.

"I *will* tiss Dimmy! and I tored up my hat 'tause a pin picked me," shouted Pokey, regardless of Jamie's efforts to restrain her.

Captain Dove looked rather taken aback at this outbreak in the ranks; but, being a dignified and calm personage, he quelled the rising rebellion with great tact and skill by saying, briefly,—

"We will sing the last hymn; 'Sweet, sweet good-by,'—you all know that, so do it nicely, and then we will go and have luncheon."

Peace was instantly restored, and a burst of melody drowned the suppressed giggles of Rose and Mac, who found it impossible to keep sober during the latter part of this somewhat remarkable service. Fifteen minutes of repose rendered it a physical impossibility for the company to march out as quietly as they had marched in. I grieve to state that the entire troop raced home as hard as they could pelt, and were soon skirmishing briskly over their lunch, utterly oblivious of what Jamie (who had been much impressed by the sermon) called "the captain's beautiful teek."

It was astonishing how much they all found to do at Cosey Corner; and Mac, instead of lying in a hammock and being read to, as he had expected, was busiest of all. He was invited to survey and lay out Skeeterville, a town which the children were getting up in a huckleberry pasture; and he found much amusement in planning little roads, staking off house-lots, attending to the water-works, and consulting with the "selectmen" about the best sites for public buildings; for Mac was a boy still, in spite of his fifteen years and his love of books.

Then he went fishing with a certain jovial gentleman from the West; and though they seldom caught any thing but colds, they had great fun and exercise chasing the phantom trout they were bound to have. Mac also developed a geological mania, and went tapping about at rocks and stones, discoursing wisely of "strata, periods, and fossil remains;" while Rose picked up leaves and lichens, and gave him lessons in botany, in return for his lectures on geology.

They led a very merry life; for the Atkinson girls kept up a sort of perpetual picnic; and did it so capitally, that one was never tired of it. So their visitors throve finely, and long before the month was out it was evident that Dr. Alec had prescribed the right medicine for his patients.

# Chapter XIV

THE twelfth of October was Rose's birthday, but no one seemed to remember that interesting fact, and she felt delicate about mentioning it, so fell asleep the night before wondering if she would have any presents. That question was settled early the next morning, for she was awakened by a soft tap on her face, and opening her eyes she beheld a little black and white figure sitting on her pillow, staring at her with a pair of round eyes very like blueberries, while one downy paw patted her nose to attract her notice. It was Kitty Comet, the prettiest of all the pussies, and Comet evidently had a mission to perform, for a pink bow adorned her neck, and a bit of paper was pinned to it bearing the words, "For Miss Rose, from Frank."

That pleased her extremely, and that was only the beginning of the fun, for surprises and presents kept popping out in the most delightful manner all through the day, the Atkinson girls being famous jokers and Rose a favorite. But the best gift of all came on the way to Mount Windy-top, where it was decided to picnic in honor of the great occasion. Three jolly loads set off soon after breakfast, for everybody went, and everybody seemed bound to have an extra good time, especially Mother Atkinson, who wore a hat as broad-brimmed as an umbrella, and took the dinner-horn to keep her flock from straying away.

"I'm going to drive aunty and a lot of the babies, so you must ride the pony. And please stay behind us a good bit when we go to the station, for a parcel is coming, and you are not to see it till dinner-time. You won't mind, will you?" said Mac in a confidential aside during the wild flurry of the start.

"Not a bit," answered Rose. "It hurts my feelings *very* much to be told to keep out of the way at any other time, but birthdays and Christmas it is part of the fun to be blind and stupid, and poked into corners. I'll be ready as soon as you are, Giglamps."

"Stop under the big maple till I call,—then you can't possibly see any thing," added Mac, as he mounted her on the pony his father had sent up for his use. "Barkis" was so gentle and so "willin," however, that Rose was ashamed to be afraid to ride him; so she had learned, that she might surprise Dr. Alec when she got home; meantime she had many a fine canter "over the hills and far away" with Mac, who preferred Mr. Atkinson's old Sorrel.

Away they went, and, coming to the red maple, Rose obediently paused; but could not help stealing a glance in the forbidden direction before the call came. Yes, there was a hamper going under the seat, and then she caught sight of a tall man whom Mac seemed to be hustling into the carriage in a great

"WHICH CAUSED BARKIS TO SHY."

hurry. One look was enough, and, with a cry of delight, Rose was off down the road as fast as Barkis could go.

"Now I'll astonish uncle," she thought. "I'll dash up in grand style, and show him that I am not a coward, after all."

Fired by this ambition, she startled Barkis by a sharp cut, and still more bewildered him by leaving him to his own guidance down the steep, stony road. The approach would have been a fine success if, just as Rose was about to pull up and salute, two or three distracted hens had not scuttled across the road with a great squawking, which caused Barkis to shy and stop so suddenly that his careless rider landed in an ignominious heap just under old Sorrel's astonished nose.

Rose was up again before Dr. Alec was out of the carryall, and threw two dusty arms about his neck, crying with a breathless voice,—

"O uncle, I'm *so* glad to see you! It is better than a cart-load of goodies, and so dear of you to come!"

"But aren't you hurt, child? That was a rough tumble, and I'm afraid you must be damaged somewhere," answered the Doctor, full of fond anxiety, as he surveyed his girl with pride.

"My feelings are hurt, but my bones are all safe. It's too bad! I was going to do it so nicely, and those stupid hens spoilt it all," said Rose, quite crest-fallen, as well as much shaken.

"I couldn't believe my eyes when I asked 'Where is Rose?' and Mac pointed to the little Amazon pelting down the hill at such a rate. You couldn't have done any thing that would please me more, and I'm delighted to see how well you ride. Now, will you mount again, or shall we turn Mac out and take you in?" asked Dr. Alec, as Aunt Jessie proposed a start, for the others were beckoning them to follow.

"Pride goeth before a fall,—better not try to show off again, ma'am," said Mac, who would have been more than mortal if he had refrained from teasing when so good a chance offered.

"Pride does go before a fall, but I wonder if a sprained ankle always comes after it?" thought Rose, bravely concealing her pain, as she answered, with great dignity,—

"I *prefer* to ride. Come on, and see who will catch up first."

She was up and away as she spoke, doing her best to efface the memory of her downfall by sitting very erect, elbows down, head well up, and taking the motion of the pony as Barkis cantered along as easily as a rocking-chair.

"You ought to see her go over a fence and race when we ride together. She can scud, too, like a deer when we play 'Follow the leader,' and skip stones and bat balls almost as well as I can," said Mac, in reply to his uncle's praise of his pupil.

"I'm afraid you will think her a sad tomboy, Alec; but really she seems so well and happy, I have not the heart to check her. She has broken out in the most unexpected way, and frisks like a colt; for she says she feels so full of spirits she *must* run and shout whether it is proper or not," added Mrs. Jessie, who had been a pretty hoyden years ago herself.

"Good,—good! that's the best news you could tell me;" and Dr. Alec rubbed his hands heartily. "Let the girl run and shout as much as she will,—it is a sure sign of health, and as natural to a happy child as frisking is to any young animal full of life. Tomboys make strong women usually, and I had far rather find Rose playing foot-ball with Mac than puttering over bead-work like that affected midget, Ariadne Blish."

"But she cannot go on playing foot-ball very long; and we must not forget that she has a woman's work to do by and by," began Mrs. Jessie.

"Neither will Mac play foot-ball much longer, but he will be all the better fitted for business, because of the health it gives him. Polish is easily added, if the foundations are strong; but no amount of gilding will be of use if your timber is not sound. I'm sure I'm right, Jessie; and if I can do as well by my girl during the next six months as I have the last, my experiment *will* succeed."

"It certainly will; for when I contrast that bright, blooming face with the pale, listless one that made my heart ache a while ago, I can believe in almost any miracle," said Mrs. Jessie, as Rose looked round to point out a lovely view, with cheeks like the ruddy apples in the orchard near by, eyes clear as the autumn sky overhead, and vigor in every line of her girlish figure.

A general scramble among the rocks was followed by a regular gypsy lunch, which the young folks had the rapture of helping to prepare. Mother Atkinson put on her apron, turned up her sleeves, and fell to work as gayly as if in her own kitchen, boiling the kettle slung on three sticks over a fire of cones and fir-boughs; while the girls spread the mossy table with a feast of country goodies, and the children tumbled about in every one's way till the toot of the horn made them settle down like a flock of hungry birds.

As soon as the merry meal and a brief interval of repose were over, it was unanimously voted to have some charades. A smooth, green spot between two stately pines was chosen for the stage; shawls hung up, properties collected, audience and actors separated, and a word quickly chosen.

The first scene discovered Mac in a despondent attitude and shabby dress, evidently much troubled in mind. To him entered a remarkable creature with a brown-paper bag over its head. A little pink nose peeped through one hole in the middle, white teeth through another, and above two eyes glared fiercely. Spires of grass stuck in each side of the mouth seemed meant to represent whiskers; the upper corners of the bag were twisted like ears, and no one could doubt for a moment that the black scarf pinned on behind was a tail.

This singular animal seemed in pantomime to be comforting his master and offering advice, which was finally acted upon, for Mac pulled off his boots, helped the little beast into them, and gave him a bag; then, kissing his paw with a hopeful gesture, the creature retired, purring so successfully that there was a general cry of "Cat, puss, boots!"

"Cat is the word," replied a voice, and the curtain fell.

The next scene was a puzzler, for in came another animal, on all-fours this time, with a new sort of tail and long ears. A gray shawl concealed its face, but an inquisitive sunbeam betrayed the glitter as of goggles under the fringe. On its back rode a small gentleman in Eastern costume, who appeared to find some difficulty in keeping his seat as his steed jogged along. Suddenly a spirit appeared, all in white, with long newspaper wings upon its back and golden locks about its face. Singularly enough, the beast beheld this apparition and backed instantly, but the rider evidently saw nothing and whipped up unmercifully, also unsuccessfully, for the spirit stood directly in the path, and the amiable beast would not budge a foot. A lively skirmish followed, which ended in the Eastern gentleman's being upset into a sweet-fern bush, while the better-bred animal abased itself before the shining one.

The children were all in the dark till Mother Atkinson said, in an inquiring tone,—

"If that isn't Balaam and the ass, I'd like to know what it is. Rose makes a sweet angel, don't she?"

"Ass" was evidently the word, and the angel retired, smiling with mundane satisfaction over the compliment that reached her ears.

The next was a pretty little scene from the immortal story of "Babes in the Wood." Jamie and Pokey came trotting in, hand-in-hand, and, having been through the parts many times before, acted with great ease and much fluency, audibly directing each other from time to time as they went along. The berries were picked, the way lost, tears shed, baby consolation administered, and then the little pair lay down among the brakes and died with their eyes wide open and the toes of their four little boots turned up to the daisies in the most pathetic manner.

"Now the wobins tum. You be twite dead, Dimmy, and I'll peep and see 'em," one defunct innocent was heard to say.

"I hope they'll be quick, for I'm lying on a stone, and ants are walking up my leg like fury," murmured the other.

Here the robins came flapping in with red scarfs over their breasts and leaves in their mouths, which they carefully laid upon the babes wherever they would show best. A prickly blackberry-leaf placed directly over Pokey's nose caused her to sneeze so violently that her little legs flew into the air; Jamie gave a startled "Ow!" and the pitying fowls fled giggling.

After some discussion it was decided that the syllable must be "strew or strow," and then they waited to see if it was a good guess.

This scene discovered Annette Snow in bed, evidently very ill; Miss Jenny was her anxious mamma, and her merry conversation amused the audience till Mac came in as a physician, and made great fun with his big watch, pompous manner, and absurd questions. He prescribed one pellet with an unpronounceable name, and left after demanding twenty dollars for his brief visit.

The pellet was administered, and such awful agonies immediately set in that the distracted mamma bade a sympathetic neighbor run for Mother Know-all. The neighbor ran, and in came a brisk little old lady in cap and specs, with a bundle of herbs under her arm, which she at once applied in all sorts of funny ways, explaining their virtues as she clapped a plantain poultice here, put a pounded catnip plaster there, or tied a couple of mullein leaves round the sufferer's throat. Instant relief ensued, the dying child sat up and demanded baked beans, the grateful parent offered fifty dollars; but Mother Know-all indignantly refused it and went smiling away, declaring that a neighborly turn needed no reward, and a doctor's *fee* was all a humbug.

The audience were in fits of laughter over this scene, for Rose imitated Mrs. Atkinson capitally, and the herb-cure was a good hit at the excellent lady's belief that "yarbs" would save mankind if properly applied. No one enjoyed it more than herself, and the saucy children prepared for the grand *finale* in high feather.

This closing scene was brief but striking, for two trains of cars whizzed in from opposite sides, met with a terrible collision in the middle of the stage, and a general smash-up completed the word *catastrophe*.

"Now let us act a proverb. I've got one all ready," said Rose, who was dying to distinguish herself in some way before Uncle Alec.

So every one but Mac, the gay Westerner, and Rose, took their places on the rocky seats and discussed the late beautiful and varied charade, in which Pokey frankly pronounced her own scene the "bestest of all."

In five minutes the curtain was lifted; nothing appeared but a very large sheet of brown paper pinned to a tree, and on it was drawn a clock-face, the hands pointing to four. A small note below informed the public that 4 A.M. was the time. Hardly had the audience grasped this important fact when a long water-proof serpent was seen uncoiling itself from behind a stump. An inch-worm, perhaps, would be a better description, for it travelled in the same humpy way as that pleasing reptile. Suddenly a very wide-awake and active fowl advanced, pecking, chirping, and scratching vigorously. A tuft of green leaves waved upon his crest, a larger tuft of brakes made an umbrageous tail, and a shawl of many colors formed his flapping wings. A truly noble bird, whose legs had the genuine strut, whose eyes shone watchfully, and whose voice had a ring that evidently struck terror into the caterpillar's soul, if it was a caterpillar. He squirmed, he wriggled, he humped as fast as he could, trying to escape; but all in vain. The tufted bird espied him, gave one warbling sort of crow, pounced upon him, and flapped triumphantly away.

"That early bird got such a big worm he could hardly carry him off," laughed Aunt Jessie, as the children shouted over the joke suggested by Mac's nickname.

"That is one of uncle's favorite proverbs, so I got it up for his especial benefit," said Rose, coming up with the two-legged worm beside her.

"Very clever; what next?" asked Dr. Alec as she sat down beside him.

"The Dove boys are going to give us an 'Incident in the Life of Napoleon,' as they call it; the children think it very splendid, and the little fellows do it rather nicely," answered Mac with condescension.

A tent appeared, and pacing to and fro before it was a little sentinel, who, in a brief soliloquy, informed the observers that the elements were in a great state of confusion, that he had marched some hundred miles or so that day, and that he was dying for want of sleep. Then he paused, leaned upon his gun, and seemed to doze; dropped slowly down, overpowered with slumber, and finally lay flat, with his gun beside him, a faithless little sentinel. Enter Napoleon, cocked hat, gray coat, high boots, folded arms, grim mouth, and a melodramatic stride. Freddy Dove always covered himself with glory in this part, and "took the stage" with a Napoleonic attitude that brought down the house; for the big-headed boy, with solemn, dark eyes and square brow, was "the very moral of that rascal, Boneyparty," Mother Atkinson said.

Some great scheme was evidently brewing in his mighty mind,—a trip across the Alps, a bonfire at Moscow, or a little skirmish at Waterloo, perhaps, for he marched in silent majesty till suddenly a gentle snore disturbed the imperial reverie. He saw the sleeping soldier and glared upon him, saying in an awful tone,—

"Ha! asleep at his post! Death is the penalty,—he must die!"

Picking up the musket, he is about to execute summary justice, as emperors are in the habit of doing, when something in the face of the weary sentinel appears to touch him. And well it might, for a most engaging little warrior was Jack as he lay with his shako half off, his childish face trying to keep sober, and a great black moustache over his rosy mouth. It would have softened the heart of any Napoleon, and the Little Corporal proved himself a man by relenting, and saying, with a lofty gesture of forgiveness,—

"Brave fellow, he is worn out; I will let him sleep, and mount guard in his place."

Then, shouldering the gun, this noble being strode to and fro with a dignity which thrilled the younger spectators. The sentinel awakes, sees what has happened, and gives himself up for lost. But the Emperor restores his weapon, and, with that smile which won all hearts, says, pointing to a high rock whereon a crow happens to be sitting: "Be brave, be vigilant, and remember that from yonder Pyramid generations are beholding you," and with these memorable words he vanishes, leaving the grateful soldier bolt upright, with his hand at his temple and deathless devotion stamped upon his youthful countenance.

The applause which followed this superb piece had hardly subsided, when a sudden splash and a shrill cry caused a general rush toward the waterfall that went gambolling down the rocks, singing sweetly as it ran. Pokey had tried to gambol also, and had tumbled into a shallow pool, whither Jamie had gallantly followed, in a vain attempt to fish her out, and both were paddling about half frightened, half pleased with the unexpected bath.

This mishap made it necessary to get the dripping infants home as soon as possible; so the wagons were loaded up, and away they went, as merry as if the mountain air had really been "Oxygenated Sweets not Bitters," as Dr. Alec suggested when Mac said he felt as jolly as if he had been drinking champagne instead of the currant wine that came with a great frosted cake wreathed with sugar roses in Aunt Plenty's hamper of goodies.

Rose took part in all the fun, and never betrayed by look or word the twinges of pain she suffered in her ankle. She excused herself from the games in the evening, however, and sat talking to Uncle Alec in a lively way, that both amazed and delighted him; for she confided to him that she played horse with the children, drilled with the light infantry, climbed trees, and did other dreadful things that would have caused the aunts to cry aloud if they knew of them.

"I don't care a pin what they say if you don't mind, uncle," she answered, when he pictured the dismay of the good ladies.

"Ah, it's all very well to defy *them*, but you are getting so rampant, I'm afraid you will defy me next, and then where are we?"

"No, I won't! I shouldn't dare; because you are my guardian, and can put me in a strait-jacket if you like;" and Rose laughed in his face, even while she nestled closer with a confiding gesture pleasant to see.

"Upon my word, Rosy, I begin to feel like the man who bought an elephant, and then didn't know what to do with him. I thought I had got a pet and plaything for years to come; but here you are growing up like a bean-stalk, and I shall find I've got a strong-minded little woman on my hands before I can turn round. There's a predicament for a man and an uncle!"

Dr. Alec's comic distress was mercifully relieved for the time being by a dance of goblins on the lawn, where the children, with pumpkin lanterns on their heads, frisked about like will-o'-the-wisps, as a parting surprise.

When Rose went to bed, she found that Uncle Alec had not forgotten her; for on the table stood a delicate little easel, holding two miniatures set in velvet. She knew them both, and stood looking at them till her eyes brimmed over with tears that were both sweet and sad; for they were the faces of her father and mother, beautifully copied from portraits fast fading away.

Presently she knelt down, and, putting her arms round the little shrine, kissed one after the other, saying with an earnest voice, "I'll truly try to make them glad to see me by and by."

And that was Rose's little prayer on the night of her fourteenth birthday.

Two days later, the Campbells went home, a larger party than when they came; for Dr. Alec was escort, and Kitty Comet was borne in state in a basket, with a bottle of milk, some tiny sandwiches, and a doll's dish to drink out of, as well as a bit of carpet to lie on in her palace car, out of which she kept popping her head in the most fascinating manner.

There was a great kissing and cuddling, waving of handkerchiefs, and last good-bys, as they went; and when they had started, Mother Atkinson came running after them, to tuck in some little pies, hot from the oven, "for the dears, who might get tired of bread and butter during that long day's travel."

Another start, and another halt; for the Snow children came shrieking up to demand the three kittens that Pokey was coolly carrying off in a travelling-bag. The unhappy kits were rescued, half smothered, and restored to their lawful owners, amid dire lamentation from the little kidnapper, who declared that she only "tooked um 'cause they'd want to go wid their sister Tomit."

Start number three and stoppage number three, as Frank hailed them with the luncheon-basket, which had been forgotten, after every one had protested that it was safely in.

All went well after that, and the long journey was pleasantly beguiled by Pokey and Pussy, who played together so prettily that they were considered public benefactors.

"Rose doesn't want to go home, for she knows the aunts won't let her rampage as she did up at Cosey Corner," said Mac, as they approached the old house.

"I *can't* rampage if I want to,—for a time, at least; and I'll tell you why. I sprained my ankle when I tumbled off of Barkis, and it gets worse and worse; though I've done all I know to cure it and hide it, so it shouldn't trouble any one," whispered Rose, knitting her brows with pain, as she prepared to descend, wishing her uncle would take her instead of her bundles.

How he did it, she never knew; but Mac had her up the steps and on the parlor sofa before she could put her foot to the ground.

"There you are,—right side up with care; and mind, now, if your ankle bothers you, and you are laid up with it, *I* am to be your footman. It's only fair, you know; for I don't forget how good you have been to me." And Mac went to call Phebe, so full of gratitude and good-will that his very goggles shone.

Rose's sprain proved to be a serious one, owing to neglect, and Dr. Alec ordered her to lie on the sofa for a fortnight at least; whereat she groaned dismally, but dared not openly complain, lest the boys turn upon her with some of the wise little sermons on patience which she had delivered for their benefit.

It was Mac's turn now, and honorably did he repay his debt; for, as school was still forbidden, he had plenty of leisure, and devoted most of it to Rose. He took many steps for her, and even allowed her to teach him to knit, after assuring himself that many a brave Scotchman knew how to "click the pricks." She was obliged to take a solemn vow of secrecy, however, before he would consent; for, though he did not mind being called "Giglamps," "Granny" was more than his boyish soul could bear, and at the approach of any of the clan his knitting vanished as if by magic, which frequent "chucking" out of sight did not improve the stripe he was doing for Rose's new afghan.

She was busy with this pretty work one bright October afternoon, all nicely established on her sofa in the upper hall, while Jamie and Pokey (lent for her amusement) were keeping house in a corner, with Comet and Rose's old doll for their "childerns."

Presently, Phebe appeared with a card. Rose read it, made a grimace, then laughed and said,—

"I'll see Miss Blish," and immediately put on her company face, pulled out her locket, and settled her curls.

"You dear thing, how *do* you do? I've been trying to call every day since you got back, but I have so many engagements, I really couldn't manage it till to-day. So glad you are alone, for mamma said I could sit awhile, and I brought my lace-work to show you, for it's perfectly lovely," cried Miss Blish, greeting Rose with a kiss, which was not very warmly returned, though

Rose politely thanked her for coming, and bid Phebe roll up the easy chair.

"How nice to have a maid!" said Ariadne, as she settled herself with much commotion. "Still, dear, you must be very lonely, and feel the need of a bosom friend."

"I have my cousins," began Rose, with dignity, for her visitor's patronizing manner ruffled her temper.

"Gracious, child! you don't make friends of those great boys, do you? Mamma says she really doesn't think it's proper for you to be with them so much."

"They are like brothers, and my aunts *do* think it's proper," replied Rose, rather sharply, for it struck her that this was none of Miss Blish's business.

"I was merely going to say I should be glad to have you for *my* bosom friend, for Hatty Mason and I have had an awful quarrel, and don't speak. She is too mean to live, so I gave her up. Just think, she never paid back one of the caramels I've given her, and never invited me to her party. I could have forgiven the caramels, but to be left out in that rude way was more than I could bear, and I told her never to look at me again as long as she lived."

"You are very kind, but I don't think I want a bosom friend, thank you," said Rose, as Ariadne stopped to bridle and shake her flaxen head over the delinquent Hatty Mason.

Now, in her heart Miss Blish thought Rose "a stuck-up puss," but the other girls wanted to know her and couldn't, the old house was a charming place to visit, the lads were considered fine fellows, and the Campbells "are one of our first families," mamma said. So Ariadne concealed her vexation at Rose's coolness, and changed the subject as fast as possible.

"Studying French, I see; who is your teacher?" she asked, flirting over the leaves of "Paul and Virginia," that lay on the table.

"I don't *study* it, for I read French as well as English, and uncle and I often speak it for hours. He talks like a native, and says I have a remarkably good accent."

Rose really could not help this small display of superiority, for French was one of her strong points, and she was vain of it, though she usually managed to hide this weakness. She felt that Ariadne would be the better for a little crushing, and could not resist the temptation to patronize in her turn.

"Oh, indeed!" said Miss Blish, rather blankly, for French was not *her* strong point by any means.

"I am to go abroad with uncle in a year or two, and he knows how important it is to understand the languages. Half the girls who leave school can't speak decent French, and when they go abroad they are *so* mortified. I shall be very glad to help you, if you like, for of course *you* have no one to talk with at home."

Now Ariadne, though she *looked* like a wax doll, had feelings within her instead of sawdust, and these feelings were hurt by Rose's lofty tone. She thought her more "stuck up" than ever, but did not know how to bring her down, yet longed to do it, for she felt as if she had received a box on the ear, and involuntarily put her hand up to it. The touch of an ear-ring consoled her, and suggested a way of returning tit for tat in a telling manner.

"Thank you, dear; I don't need any help, for our teacher is from Paris, and of course *he* speaks better French than your uncle." Then she added, with a gesture of her head that set the little bells on her ears to tingling: "How do you like my new ear-rings? Papa gave them to me last week, and every one says they are lovely."

Rose came down from her high horse with a rapidity that was comical, for Ariadne had the upper hand now. Rose adored pretty things, longed to wear them, and the desire of her girlish soul was to have her ears bored, only Dr. Alec thought it foolish, so she never had done it. She would gladly have given all the French she could jabber for a pair of golden bells with pearl-tipped tongues, like those Ariadne wore; and, clasping her hands, she answered, in a tone that went to the hearer's heart,—

"They are *too* sweet for any thing! If uncle would only let me wear some, I should be *perfectly* happy."

"I wouldn't mind what he says. Papa laughed at me at first, but he likes them now, and says I shall have diamond solitaires when I am eighteen," said Ariadne, quite satisfied with her shot.

"I've got a pair now that were mamma's, and a beautiful

little pair of pearl and turquoise ones, that I am dying to wear," sighed Rose.

"Then do it. I'll pierce your ears, and you must wear a bit of silk in them till they are well; your curls will hide them nicely; then, some day, slip in your smallest ear-rings, and see if your uncle don't like them."

"I asked him if it wouldn't do my eyes good once when they were red, and he only laughed. People do cure weak eyes that way, don't they?"

"Yes, indeed, and yours *are* sort of red. Let me see. Yes, I really think you ought to do it before they get worse," said Ariadne, peering into the large clear eye offered for inspection.

"Does it hurt much?" asked Rose, wavering.

"Oh dear, no! just a prick and a pull, and it's all over. I've done lots of ears, and know just how. Come, push up your hair and get a big needle."

"I don't quite like to do it without asking uncle's leave," faltered Rose, when all was ready for the operation.

"Did he ever forbid it?" demanded Ariadne, hovering over her prey like a vampire.

"No, never!"

"Then do it, unless you are *afraid*," cried Miss Blish, bent on accomplishing the deed.

That last word settled the matter, and, closing her eyes, Rose said "Punch!" in the tone of one giving the fatal order "Fire!"

Ariadne punched, and the victim bore it in heroic silence, though she turned pale and her eyes were full of tears of anguish.

"There! Now pull the bits of silk often, and cold-cream your ears every night, and you'll soon be ready for the rings," said Ariadne, well pleased with her job, for the girl who spoke French with "a fine accent" lay flat upon the sofa, looking as exhausted as if she had had both ears cut off.

"It does hurt dreadfully, and I know uncle won't like it," sighed Rose, as remorse began to gnaw. "Promise not to tell, or I shall be teased to death," she added, anxiously, entirely forgetting the two little pitchers gifted with eyes as well as ears, who had been watching the whole performance from afar.

"Never. Mercy me, what's that?" and Ariadne started as a sudden sound of steps and voices came up from below.

"Punch!" said Rose, in the tone of one giving the order "Fire!"

"It's the boys! Hide the needle. Do my ears show? Don't breathe a word!" whispered Rose, scrambling about to conceal all traces of their iniquity from the sharp eyes of the clan.

Up they came, all in good order, laden with the proceeds of a nutting expedition, for they always reported to Rose and paid tribute to their queen in the handsomest manner.

"How many, and how big! We'll have a grand roasting frolic after tea, won't we?" said Rose, plunging both hands into a bag of glossy brown nuts, while the clan "stood at ease" and nodded to Ariadne.

"That lot was picked especially for you, Rosy. I got every one myself, and they are extra whackers," said Mac, presenting a bushel or so.

"You should have seen Giglamps when he was after them. He pitched out of the tree, and would have broken his blessed old neck if Arch had not caught him," observed Steve, as he lounged gracefully in the window seat.

"You needn't talk, Dandy, when you didn't know a chestnut from a beech, and kept on thrashing till I told you of it," retorted Mac, festooning himself over the back of the sofa, being a privileged boy.

"I don't make mistakes when I thrash you, old Worm, so you'd better mind what you are about," answered Steve, without a ray of proper respect for his elder brother.

"It is getting dark, and I must go, or mamma will be alarmed," said Ariadne, rising in sudden haste, though she hoped to be asked to remain to the nut-party.

No one invited her; and all the while she was putting on her things and chatting to Rose the boys were telegraphing to one another the sad fact that some one ought to escort the young lady home. Not a boy felt heroic enough to cast himself into the breach, however; even polite Archie shirked the duty, saying to Charlie, as they quietly slipped into an adjoining room,—

"I'm not going to do all the gallivanting. Let Steve take that chit home and show his manners."

"I'll be hanged if I do!" answered Prince, who disliked Miss Blish because she tried to be coquettish with him.

"Then I will," and, to the dismay of both recreant lads, Dr. Alec walked out of the room to offer his services to the "chit."

He was too late, however, for Mac, obeying a look from Rose, had already made a victim of himself, and trudged meekly away, wishing the gentle Ariadne at the bottom of the Red Sea.

"Then I will take this lady down to tea, as the other one has found a *gentleman* to go home with her. I see the lamps are lighted below, and I smell a smell which tells me that aunty has something extra nice for us to-night."

As he spoke, Dr. Alec was preparing to carry Rose downstairs as usual; but Archie and Prince rushed forward, begging with penitent eagerness for the honor of carrying her in an arm-chair. Rose consented, fearing that her uncle's keen eye would discover the fatal bits of silk; so the boys crossed hands, and, taking a good grip of each curly pate, she was borne down in state, while the others followed by way of the banisters.

Tea was ordered earlier than usual, so that Jamie and his dolly could have a taste, at least, of the holiday fun, for they were to stay till seven, and be allowed twelve roasted chestnuts apiece, which they were under bonds not to eat till next day.

Tea was despatched rapidly, therefore, and the party gathered round the wide hearth in the dining-room, where the nuts were soon dancing gayly on hot shovels or bouncing out among the company, thereby causing delightful panics among the little ones.

"Come, Rosy, tell us a story while we work, for you can't help much, and must amuse us as your share," proposed Mac, who sat in the shade pricking nuts, and who knew by experience what a capital little Scheherazade his cousin was.

"Yes, we poor monkeys can't burn our paws for nothing, so tell away, Pussy," added Charlie, as he threw several hot nuts into her lap and shook his fingers afterward.

"Well, I happen to have a little story with a moral to it in my mind, and I will tell it, though it is intended for younger children than you," answered Rose, who was rather fond of telling instructive tales.

"Fire away," said Geordie, and she obeyed, little thinking what a disastrous story it would prove to herself.

"Well, once upon a time, a little girl went to see a young lady who was very fond of her. Now, the young lady happened to be lame, and had to have her foot bandaged up every day;

so she kept a basketful of bandages, all nicely rolled and ready. The little girl liked to play with this basket, and one day, when she thought no one saw her, she took one of the rolls without asking leave, and put it in her pocket."

Here Pokey, who had been peering lovingly down at the five warm nuts that lay at the bottom of her tiny pocket, suddenly looked up and said, "Oh!" in a startled tone, as if the moral tale had become intensely interesting all at once.

Rose heard and saw the innocent betrayal of the small sinner, and went on in a most impressive manner, while the boys nudged one another and winked as they caught the joke.

"But an eye did see this naughty little girl, and whose eye do you think it was?"

"Eye of Dod," murmured conscience-stricken Pokey, spreading two chubby little hands before the round face, which they were not half big enough to hide.

Rose was rather taken aback by this reply, but, feeling that she was producing a good effect, she added, seriously,—

"Yes, God saw her, and so did the young lady, but she did not say any thing; she waited to see what the little girl would do about it. She had been very happy before she took the bandage, but when it was in her pocket she seemed troubled, and pretty soon stopped playing and sat down in a corner, looking very sober. She thought a few minutes, and then went and put back the roll very softly, and her face cleared up, and she was a happy child again. The young lady was glad to see that, and wondered what made the little girl put it back."

"Tonscience p'icked her," murmured a contrite voice from behind the small hands pressed tightly over Pokey's red face.

"And why did she take it, do you suppose?" asked Rose, in a school-marmish tone, feeling that all the listeners were interested in her tale and its unexpected application.

"It was *so* nice and wound, and she wanted it deffly," answered the little voice.

"Well, I'm glad she had such a good conscience. The moral is that people who steal don't enjoy what they take, and are not happy till they put it back. What makes that little girl hide her face?" asked Rose, as she concluded.

"Me's so 'shamed of Pokey," sobbed the small culprit, quite overcome by remorse and confusion at this awful disclosure.

"Come, Rose, it's too bad to tell her little tricks before every one, and preach at her in that way; you wouldn't like it yourself," began Dr. Alec, taking the weeper on his knee and administering consolation in the shape of kisses and nuts.

Before Rose could express her regret, Jamie, who had been reddening and ruffling like a little turkey-cock for several minutes, burst out indignantly, bent on avenging the wound given to his beloved dolly.

"*I* know something bad that *you* did, and I'm going to tell right out. You thought we didn't see you, but we did, and you said uncle wouldn't like it, and the boys would tease, and you made Ariadne promise not to tell, and she punched holes in your ears to put ear-rings in. So now! and that's much badder than to take an old piece of rag; and I hate you for making my Pokey cry."

Jamie's somewhat incoherent explosion produced such an effect that Pokey's small sin was instantly forgotten, and Rose felt that her hour had come.

"What! what! what!" cried the boys in a chorus, dropping their shovels and knives to gather round Rose, for a guilty clutching at her ears betrayed her, and with a feeble cry of "Ariadne made me!" she hid her head among the pillows like an absurd little ostrich.

"Now she'll go prancing round with bird-cages and baskets and carts and pigs, for all I know, in her ears, as the other girls do, and won't she look like a goose?" asked one tormentor, tweaking a curl that strayed out from the cushions.

"I didn't think she'd be so silly," said Mac, in a tone of disappointment that told Rose she had sunk in the esteem of her wise cousin.

"That Blish girl is a nuisance, and ought not to be allowed to come here with her nonsensical notions," said the Prince, feeling a strong desire to shake that young person as an angry dog might shake a mischievous kitten.

"How do *you* like it, uncle?" asked Archie, who, being the head of a family himself, believed in preserving discipline at all costs.

"I am very much surprised; but I see she is a girl, after all, and must have her vanities like all the rest of them," answered

Dr. Alec, with a sigh, as if he had expected to find Rose a sort of angel, above all earthly temptation.

"What shall you do about it, sir?" inquired Geordie, wondering what punishment would be inflicted on a feminine culprit.

"As she is fond of ornaments, perhaps we had better give her a nose-ring also. I have one somewhere that a Fiji belle once wore; I'll look it up," and, leaving Pokey to Jamie's care, Dr. Alec rose as if to carry out his suggestion in earnest.

"Good! good! We'll do it right away! Here's a gimlet, so you hold her, boys, while I get her dear little nose all ready," cried Charlie, whisking away the pillows as the other boys danced about the sofa in true Fiji style.

It was a dreadful moment, for Rose could not run away,— she could only grasp her precious nose with one hand and extend the other, crying distractedly,—

"O uncle, save me, save me!"

Of course he saved her; and when she was securely barricaded by his strong arm, she confessed her folly in such humiliation of spirit that the lads, after a good laugh at her, decided to forgive her and lay all the blame on the tempter, Ariadne. Even Dr. Alec relented so far as to propose two gold rings for the ears instead of one copper one for the nose; a proceeding which proved that if Rose had all the weakness of her sex for jewellery, he had all the inconsistency of his in giving a pretty penitent exactly what she wanted, spite of his better judgment.

# Chapter XVI

## BREAD AND BUTTON-HOLES

"WHAT in the world is my girl thinking about all alone here, with such a solemn face?" asked Dr. Alec, coming into the study, one November day, to find Rose sitting there with folded hands and a very thoughtful aspect.

"Uncle, I want to have some serious conversation with you, if you have time," she said, coming out of a brown study, as if she had not heard his question.

"I'm entirely at your service, and most happy to listen," he answered, in his politest manner, for when Rose put on her womanly little airs he always treated her with a playful sort of respect that pleased her very much.

Now, as he sat down beside her, she said, very soberly,—

"I've been trying to decide what trade I would learn, and I want you to advise me."

"Trade, my dear?" and Dr. Alec looked so astonished that she hastened to explain.

"I forgot that you didn't hear the talk about it up at Cosey Corner. You see we used to sit under the pines and sew, and talk a great deal,—all the ladies, I mean,—and I liked it very much. Mother Atkinson thought that every one should have a trade, or something to make a living out of, for rich people may grow poor, you know, and poor people have to work. Her girls were very clever, and could do ever so many things, and Aunt Jessie thought the old lady was right; so when I saw how happy and independent those young ladies were, I wanted to have a trade, and then it wouldn't matter about money, though I like to have it well enough."

Dr. Alec listened to this explanation with a curious mixture of surprise, pleasure, and amusement in his face, and looked at his little niece as if she had suddenly changed into a young woman. She had grown a good deal in the last six months, and an amount of thinking had gone on in that young head which would have astonished him greatly could he have known it all, for Rose was one of the children who observe and meditate much, and now and then nonplus their friends by a wise or curious remark.

"I quite agree with the ladies, and shall be glad to help you decide on something if I can," said the Doctor seriously. "What do you incline to? A natural taste or talent is a great help in choosing, you know."

"I haven't any talent, or any especial taste that I can see, and that is why I can't decide, uncle. So, I think it would be a good plan to pick out some very *useful* business and learn it, because I don't do it for pleasure, you see, but as a part of my education, and to be ready in case I'm ever poor," answered Rose, looking as if she rather longed for a little poverty so that her useful gift might be exercised.

"Well, now, there is one very excellent, necessary, and womanly accomplishment that no girl should be without, for it is a help to rich and poor, and the comfort of families depends upon it. This fine talent is neglected nowadays, and considered old-fashioned, which is a sad mistake, and one that I don't mean to make in bringing up my girl. It should be a part of every girl's education, and I know of a most accomplished lady who will teach you in the best and pleasantest manner."

"Oh, what is it?" cried Rose eagerly, charmed to be met in this helpful and cordial way.

"Housekeeping!" answered Dr. Alec.

"Is that an accomplishment?" asked Rose, while her face fell, for she had indulged in all sorts of vague, delightful dreams.

"Yes; it is one of the most beautiful as well as useful of all the arts a woman can learn. Not so romantic, perhaps, as singing, painting, writing, or teaching, even; but one that makes many happy and comfortable, and home the sweetest place in the world. Yes, you may open your big eyes; but it is a fact that I had rather see you a good housekeeper than the greatest belle in the city. It need not interfere with any talent you may possess, but it *is* a necessary part of your training, and I hope that you will set about it at once, now that you are well and strong."

"Who is the lady?" asked Rose, rather impressed by her uncle's earnest speech.

"Aunt Plenty."

"Is *she* accomplished?" began Rose in a wondering tone, for this great-aunt of hers had seemed the least cultivated of them all.

"In the good old-fashioned way she is very accomplished, and has made this house a happy home to us all, ever since we can remember. She is not elegant, but genuinely good, and so beloved and respected that there will be universal mourning for her when her place is empty. No one can fill it, for the solid, homely virtues of the dear soul have gone out of fashion, as I say, and nothing new can be half so satisfactory, to me at least."

"I should like to have people feel so about me. Can she teach me to do what she does, and to grow as good?" asked Rose, with a little prick of remorse for even thinking that Aunt Plenty was a commonplace old lady.

"Yes, if you don't despise such simple lessons as she can give. I know it would fill her dear old heart with pride and pleasure to feel that any one cared to learn of her, for she fancies her day gone by. Let her teach you how to be what she has been,—a skilful, frugal, cheerful housewife; the maker and the keeper of a happy home, and by and by you will see what a valuable lesson it is."

"I will, uncle. But how shall I begin?"

"I'll speak to her about it, and she will make it all right with Dolly, for cooking is one of the main things, you know."

"So it is! I don't mind that a bit, for I like to mess, and used to try at home; but I had no one to tell me, so I never did much but spoil my aprons. Pies are great fun, only Dolly is *so* cross, I don't believe she will ever let me do a thing in the kitchen."

"Then we'll cook in the parlor. I fancy Aunt Plenty will manage her, so don't be troubled. Only mind this, I'd rather you learned how to make good bread than the best pies ever baked. When you bring me a handsome, wholesome loaf, entirely made by yourself, I shall be more pleased than if you offered me a pair of slippers embroidered in the very latest style. I don't wish to bribe you, but I'll give you my heartiest kiss, and promise to eat every crumb of the loaf myself."

"It's a bargain! it's a bargain! Come and tell aunty all about it, for I'm in a hurry to begin," cried Rose, dancing before him toward the parlor, where Miss Plenty sat alone knitting contentedly, yet ready to run at the first call for help of any sort, from any quarter.

No need to tell how surprised and gratified she was at the

invitation she received to teach the child the domestic arts which were her only accomplishments, nor to relate how energetically she set about her pleasant task. Dolly dared not grumble, for Miss Plenty was the one person whom she obeyed, and Phebe openly rejoiced, for these new lessons brought Rose nearer to her, and glorified the kitchen in the good girl's eyes.

To tell the truth, the elder aunts had sometimes felt that they did not have quite their share of the little niece who had won their hearts long ago, and was the sunshine of the house. They talked it over together sometimes, but always ended by saying that as Alec had all the responsibility, he should have the larger share of the dear girl's love and time, and they would be contented with such crumbs of comfort as they could get.

Dr. Alec had found out this little secret, and, after reproaching himself for being blind and selfish, was trying to devise some way of mending matters without troubling any one, when Rose's new whim suggested an excellent method of weaning her a little from himself. He did not know how fond he was of her till he gave her up to the new teacher, and often could not resist peeping in at the door, to see how she got on, or stealing sly looks through the slide when she was deep in dough, or listening intently to some impressive lecture from Aunt Plenty. They caught him at it now and then, and ordered him off the premises at the point of the rolling-pin; or, if unusually successful, and, therefore, in a milder mood, they lured him away with bribes of gingerbread, a stray pickle, or a tart that was not quite symmetrical enough to suit their critical eyes.

Of course he made a point of partaking copiously of all the delectable messes that now appeared at table, for both the cooks were on their mettle, and he fared sumptuously every day. But an especial relish was given to any dish when, in reply to his honest praise of it, Rose colored up with innocent pride, and said modestly,—

"I made that, uncle, and I'm glad you like it."

It was some time before the perfect loaf appeared, for bread-making is an art not easily learned, and Aunt Plenty was very thorough in her teaching; so Rose studied yeast first, and through various stages of cake and biscuit came at last to the

UNCLE ALEC COULD NOT RESIST PEEPING IN AT THE DOOR.

crowning glory of the "handsome, wholesome loaf." It appeared at tea-time, on a silver salver, proudly borne in by Phebe, who could not refrain from whispering, with a beaming face, as she set it down before Dr. Alec,—

"Ain't it just lovely, sir?"

"It is a regularly splendid loaf! Did my girl make it all herself?" he asked, surveying the shapely, sweet-smelling object, with real interest and pleasure.

"Every particle herself, and never asked a bit of help or advice from any one," answered Aunt Plenty, folding her hands with an air of unmitigated satisfaction, for her pupil certainly did her great credit.

"I've had so many failures and troubles that I really thought

I never should be able to do it alone. Dolly let one splendid batch burn up because I forgot it. She was there and smelt it, but never did a thing, for she said, when I undertook to bake bread I must give my whole mind to it. Wasn't it hard? She might have called me at least," said Rose, recollecting, with a sigh, the anguish of that moment.

"She meant you should learn by experience, as Rosamond did in that little affair of the purple jar, you remember."

"I always thought it very unfair in her mother not to warn the poor thing a little bit; and she was regularly mean when Rosamond asked for a bowl to put the purple stuff in, and she said, in such a provoking way, 'I did not agree to lend you a bowl, but I will, my dear.' Ugh! I always want to shake that hateful woman, though she *was* a moral mamma."

"Never mind her now, but tell me all about my loaf," said Dr. Alec, much amused at Rose's burst of indignation.

"There's nothing to tell, uncle, except that I did my best, gave my mind to it, and sat watching over it all the while it was in the oven till I was quite baked myself. Every thing went right this time, and it came out a nice, round, crusty loaf, as you see. Now taste it, and tell me if it is good as well as handsome."

"Must I cut it? Can't I put it under a glass cover and keep it in the parlor as they do wax flowers and fine works of that sort?"

"What an idea, uncle! It would mould and be spoilt. Besides, people would laugh at us, and make fun of my old-fashioned accomplishment. You promised to eat it, and you must; not all at once, but as soon as you can, so I can make you some more."

Dr. Alec solemnly cut off his favorite crusty slice, and solemnly ate it; then wiped his lips, and brushing back Rose's hair, solemnly kissed her on the forehead, saying heartily,—

"My dear, it is perfect bread, and you are an honor to your teacher. When we have our model school I shall offer a prize for the best bread, and *you* will get it."

"I've got it already, and I'm quite satisfied," said Rose, slipping into her seat, and trying to hide her right hand which had a burn on it.

But Dr. Alec saw it, guessed how it came there, and after tea insisted on easing the pain which she would hardly confess.

"Aunt Clara says I am spoiling my hands, but I don't care, for I've had *such* good times with Aunt Plenty, and I think she has enjoyed it as much as I have. Only one thing troubles me, uncle, and I want to ask you about it," said Rose, as they paced up and down the hall in the twilight, the bandaged hand very carefully laid on Dr. Alec's arm.

"More little confidences? I like them immensely, so tell away, my dear."

"Well, you see I feel as if Aunt Peace would like to do something for me, and I've found out what it can be. You know she can't go about like Aunty Plen, and we are so busy nowadays that she is rather lonely, I'm afraid. So I want to take lessons in sewing of her. She works so beautifully, and it is a useful thing, you know, and I ought to be a good needlewoman as well as housekeeper, oughtn't I?"

"Bless your kind little heart, that is what I was thinking of the other day when Aunt Peace said she saw you very seldom now, you were so busy, I wanted to speak of it, but fancied you had as much on your hands as you could manage. It would delight the dear woman to teach you all her delicate handicraft, especially button-holes, for I believe that is where young ladies fail; at least I've heard them say so. So, do you devote your mind to button-holes; make 'em all over my clothes if you want something to practice on. I'll wear any quantity."

Rose laughed at this reckless offer, but promised to attend to that important branch, though she confessed that darning was her weak point. Whereupon Uncle Alec engaged to supply her with socks in all stages of dilapidation, and to have a new set at once, so that she could run the heels for him as a pleasant beginning.

Then they went up to make their request in due form, to the great delight of gentle Aunt Peace, who got quite excited with the fun that went on while they wound yarn, looked up darning-needles, and fitted out a nice little mending basket for her pupil.

Very busy and very happy were Rose's days now, for in the morning she went about the house with Aunt Plenty attending to linen-closets and store-rooms, pickling and preserving, exploring garret and cellar to see that all was right, and learning, in the good old-fashioned manner, to look well after the ways of the household.

In the afternoon, after her walk or drive, she sat with Aunt Peace plying her needle, while Aunt Plenty, whose eyes were failing, knit and chatted briskly, telling many a pleasant story of old times, till the three were moved to laugh and cry together, for the busy needles were embroidering all sorts of bright patterns on the lives of the workers, though they seemed to be only stitching cotton and darning hose.

It was a pretty sight to see the rosy-faced little maid sitting between the two old ladies, listening dutifully to their instructions, and cheering the lessons with her lively chatter and blithe laugh. If the kitchen had proved attractive to Dr. Alec when Rose was there at work, the sewing-room was quite irresistible, and he made himself so agreeable that no one had the heart to drive him away, especially when he read aloud or spun yarns.

"There! I've made you a new set of warm nightgowns with four button-holes in each. See if they are not neatly done," said Rose, one day, some weeks after the new lessons began.

"Even to a thread, and nice little bars across the end so I can't tear them when I twitch the buttons out. Most superior work, ma'am, and I'm deeply grateful; so much so, that I'll sew on these buttons myself, and save those tired fingers from another prick."

"You sew them on?" cried Rose, with her eyes wide open in amazement.

"Wait a bit till I get my sewing tackle, and then you shall see what *I* can do."

"Can he, really?" asked Rose of Aunt Peace, as Uncle Alec marched off with a comical air of importance.

"Oh, yes, I taught him years ago, before he went to sea; and I suppose he has had to do things for himself, more or less, ever since; so he has kept his hand in."

He evidently had, for he was soon back with a funny little work-bag, out of which he produced a thimble without a top; and, having threaded his needle, he proceeded to sew on the buttons so handily that Rose was much impressed and amused.

"I wonder if there is any thing in the world that *you* cannot do," she said, in a tone of respectful admiration.

"There are one or two things that I am not up to yet," he answered, with a laugh in the corner of his eye, as he waxed his thread with a flourish.

"I should like to know what?"

"Bread and button-holes, ma'am."

# Chapter XVII

## GOOD BARGAINS

---

$I$T was a rainy Sunday afternoon, and four boys were trying to spend it quietly in the "liberry," as Jamie called the room devoted to books and boys, at Aunt Jessie's. Will and Geordie were sprawling on the sofa, deep in the adventures of the scapegraces and ragamuffins whose histories are now the fashion. Archie lounged in the easy chair surrounded by newspapers; Charlie stood upon the rug, in an Englishman's favorite attitude, and, I regret to say, both were smoking cigars.

"It is my opinion that this day will *never* come to an end," said Prince, with a yawn that nearly rent him asunder.

"Read and improve your mind, my son," answered Archie, peering solemnly over the paper behind which he had been dozing.

"Don't you preach, parson; but put on your boots and come out for a tramp, instead of mulling over the fire like a granny."

"No, thank you, tramps in an easterly storm don't strike me as amusing." There Archie stopped and held up his hand, for a pleasant voice was heard saying outside,—

"Are the boys in the library, auntie?"

"Yes, dear, and longing for sunshine; so run in and make it for them," answered Mrs. Jessie.

"It's Rose," and Archie threw his cigar into the fire.

"What's that for?" asked Charlie.

"Gentlemen don't smoke before ladies."

"True; but I'm not going to waste *my* weed," and Prince poked his into the empty inkstand that served them for an ash tray.

A gentle tap at the door was answered by a chorus of "Come in," and Rose appeared, looking blooming and breezy with the chilly air.

"If I disturb you, say so, and I'll go away," she began, pausing on the threshold with modest hesitation, for something in the elder boys' faces excited her curiosity.

"You never disturb us, cousin," said the smokers, while the

461

readers tore themselves from the heroes of the bar-room and gutter long enough to nod affably to their guest.

As Rose bent to warm her hands, one end of Archie's cigar stuck out of the ashes, smoking furiously and smelling strongly.

"Oh, you bad boys, how could you do it, to-day of all days?" she said reproachfully.

"Where's the harm?" asked Archie.

"You know as well as I do; your mother doesn't like it, and it's a bad habit, for it wastes money and does you no good."

"Fiddle-sticks! every man smokes, even Uncle Alec, whom you think so perfect," began Charlie, in his teasing way.

"No, he doesn't! He has given it up, and I know why," cried Rose eagerly.

"Now I think of it, I haven't seen the old meerschaum

since he came home. Did he stop it on our account?" asked Archie.

"Yes," and Rose told the little scene on the sea-shore in the camping-out time.

Archie seemed much impressed, and said manfully,—"He won't have done that in vain so far as I'm concerned. I don't care a pin about smoking, so can give it up as easy as not, and I promise you I will. I only do it now and then for fun."

"You too?" and Rose looked up at the bonny Prince, who never looked less bonny than at that moment, for he had resumed his cigar, just to torment her.

Now Charlie cared as little as Archie about smoking, but it would not do to yield too soon; so he shook his head, gave a great puff, and said loftily,—

"You women are always asking us to give up harmless little things, just because *you* don't approve of them. How would you like it if we did the same by you, Miss?"

"If I did harmful or silly things, I'd thank you for telling me of them, and I'd try to mend my ways," answered Rose heartily.

"Well, now, we'll see if you mean what you say. I'll give up smoking to please you, if you will give up something to please me," said Prince, seeing a good chance to lord it over the weaker vessel at small cost to himself.

"I'll agree if it is as foolish as cigars."

"Oh, it's ever so much sillier."

"Then I promise; what is it?" and Rose quite trembled with anxiety to know which of her pet habits or possessions she must lose.

"Give up your ear-rings," and Charlie laughed wickedly, sure that she would never hold to that bargain.

Rose uttered a cry and clapped both hands to her ears where the gold rings hung.

"O Charlie, wouldn't any thing else do as well? I've been through so much teasing and trouble, I do want to enjoy my pretty ear-rings, for I can wear them now."

"Wear as many as you like, and I'll smoke in peace," returned this bad boy.

"Will *nothing* else satisfy you?" imploringly.

"Nothing," sternly.

Rose stood silent for a minute, thinking of something Aunt Jessie once said,—"You have more influence over the boys than you know; use it for their good, and I shall thank you all my life." Here was a chance to do some good by sacrificing a little vanity of her own. She felt it was right to do it, yet found it very hard, and asked wistfully,—

"Do you mean *never* wear them, Charlie?"

"*Never*, unless you want me to smoke."

"I never do."

"Then clinch the bargain."

He had no idea she would do it, and was much surprised when she took the dear rings from her ears, with a quick gesture, and held them out to him, saying, in a tone that made the color come up to his brown cheek, it was so full of sweet good will,—

"I care more for my cousins than for my ear-rings, so I promise, and I'll keep my word."

"For shame, Prince! let her wear her little danglers if she likes, and don't bargain about doing what you know is right," cried Archie, coming out of his grove of newspapers with an indignant bounce.

But Rose was bent on showing her aunt that she *could* use her influence for the boys' good, and said steadily,—

"It is fair, and I want it to be so, then you will believe I'm in earnest. Here, each of you wear one of these on your watch-guard to remind you. *I* shall not forget, because very soon I cannot wear ear-rings if I want to."

As she spoke, Rose offered a little ring to each cousin, and the boys, seeing how sincere she was, obeyed her. When the pledges were safe, Rose stretched a hand to each, and the lads gave hers a hearty grip, half pleased and half ashamed of their part in the compact.

Just at that moment Dr. Alec and Mrs. Jessie came in.

"What's this? Dancing Ladies Triumph on Sunday?" exclaimed Uncle Alec, surveying the trio with surprise.

"No, sir, it is the Anti-Tobacco League. Will you join?" said Charlie, while Rose slipped away to her aunt, and Archie buried both cigars behind the back log.

When the mystery was explained, the elders were well pleased, and Rose received a vote of thanks, which made her feel as if she had done a service to her country, as she had, for every boy who grows up free from bad habits bids fair to make a good citizen.

"I wish Rose would drive a bargain with Will and Geordie also, for I think these books are as bad for the small boys as cigars for the large ones," said Mrs. Jessie, sitting down on the sofa between the readers, who politely curled up their legs to make room for her.

"I thought they were all the fashion," answered Dr. Alec, settling in the big chair with Rose.

"So is smoking, but it is harmful. The writers of these popular stories intend to do good, I have no doubt, but it seems to me they fail because their motto is, 'Be smart, and you will be rich,' instead of 'Be honest, and you will be happy.' I do not judge hastily, Alec, for I have read a dozen, at least, of these stories, and, with much that is attractive to boys, I find a great deal to condemn in them, and other parents say the same when I ask them."

"Now, Mum, that's too bad! I like 'em tip-top. This one is a regular screamer," cried Will.

"They're bully books, and I'd like to know where's the harm," added Geordie.

"You have just shown us one of the chief evils, and that is slang," answered their mother quickly.

"Must have it, ma'am. If these chaps talked all right, there'd be no fun in 'em," protested Will.

"A boot-black *mustn't* use good grammar, and a newsboy *must* swear a little, or he wouldn't be natural," explained Geordie, both boys ready to fight gallantly for their favorites.

"But my sons are neither boot-blacks nor newsboys, and I object to hearing them use such words as 'screamer,' 'bully,' and 'buster.' In fact, I fail to see the advantage of writing books about such people unless it is done in a very different way. I cannot think they will help to refine the ragamuffins, if they read them, and I'm sure they can do no good to the better class of boys, who through these books are introduced to police courts, counterfeiters' dens, gambling houses, drinking saloons, and all sorts of low life."

"Some of them are about first-rate boys, mother; and they go to sea and study, and sail round the world, having great larks all the way."

"I have read about them, Geordie, and though they *are* better than the others, I am not satisfied with these *optical* delusions, as I call them. Now, I put it to you, boys, is it natural for lads from fifteen to eighteen to command ships, defeat pirates, outwit smugglers, and so cover themselves with glory, that Admiral Farragut invites them to dinner, saying: 'Noble boy, you are an honor to your country!' Or, if the hero is in the army, he has hair-breadth escapes and adventures enough in one small volume to turn his hair white, and in the end he goes to Washington at the express desire of the President or Commander-in-Chief to be promoted to no end of stars and bars. Even if the hero is merely an honest boy trying to get his living, he is not permitted to do so in a natural way, by hard work and years of patient effort, but is suddenly adopted by a millionaire whose pocket-book he has returned; or a rich uncle appears from sea, just in the nick of time; or the remarkable boy earns a few dollars, speculates in pea-nuts or neckties, and grows rich so rapidly that Sinbad in the diamond valley is a pauper compared to him. Isn't it so, boys?"

"Well, the fellows in these books *are* mighty lucky, and very smart, I must say," answered Will, surveying an illustration on the open page before him, where a small but virtuous youth is upsetting a tipsy giant in a bar-room, and under it the elegant inscription: "Dick Dauntless punches the head of Sam Soaker."

"It gives boys such wrong ideas of life and business; shows them so much evil and vulgarity that they need not know about, and makes the one success worth having a fortune, a lord's daughter, or some worldly honor, often not worth the time it takes to win. It does seem to me that some one might write stories that should be lively, natural, and helpful,—tales in which the English should be good, the morals pure, and the characters such as we can love in spite of the faults that all may have. I can't bear to see such crowds of eager little fellows at the libraries reading such trash; weak, when it is not wicked, and totally unfit to feed the hungry minds that feast on it for want of something better. There! my lecture is done; now I should like to hear what you gentlemen have to say," and Aunt Jessie subsided with a pretty flush on the face that was full of motherly anxiety for her boys.

"Tom Brown just suits mother, and me too, so I wish Mr. Hughes would write another story as good," said Archie.

"You don't find things of this sort in Tom Brown; yet these books are all in the Sunday-school libraries"—and Mrs. Jessie read the following paragraph from the book she had taken from Will's hand:—

"'In this place we saw a tooth of John the Baptist. Ben said he could see locust and wild honey sticking to it. I couldn't. Perhaps John used a piece of the true cross for a toothpick.'"

"A larky sort of a boy says that, Mum, and we skip the parts where they describe what they saw in the different countries," cried Will.

"And those descriptions, taken mostly from guidebooks, I fancy, are the only parts of any real worth. The scrapes of the bad boys make up the rest of the story, and it is for those you read these books, I think," answered his mother, stroking back the hair off the honest little face that looked rather abashed at this true statement of the case.

"Any way, mother, the ship part is useful, for we learn how to sail her, and by and by that will all come handy when we go to sea," put in Geordie.

"Indeed; then you can explain this manœuvre to me, of course—" and Mrs. Jessie read from another page the following nautical paragraph:—

"The wind is south-south-west, and we can have her up four points closer to the wind, and still be six points off the wind. As she luffs up we shall man the fore and main sheets, slack on the weather, and haul on the lee braces."

"I guess I could, if I wasn't afraid of uncle. He knows so much more than I do, he'd laugh," began Geordie, evidently puzzled by the question.

"Ho, you know you can't, so why make believe? We don't understand half of the sea lingo, Mum, and I dare say it's all wrong," cried Will, suddenly going over to the enemy, to Geordie's great disgust.

"I do wish the boys wouldn't talk to me as if *I* was a ship," said Rose, bringing forward a private grievance. "Coming home from church, this morning, the wind blew me about, and Will called out, right in the street, 'Brail up the foresail, and take in the flying-jib, that will ease her.'"

The boys shouted at the plaintive tone in which Rose repeated the words that offended her, and Will vainly endeavored to explain that he only meant to tell her to wrap her cloak closer, and tie a veil over the tempest-tossed feathers in her hat.

"To tell the truth, if the boys *must* have slang, I can bear the 'sea lingo,' as Will calls it, better than the other. It afflicts me less to hear my sons talk about 'brailing up the foresail' than doing as they 'darn please,' and 'cut your cable' is decidedly preferable to 'let her rip.' I once made a rule that I would have no slang in the house. I give it up now, for I cannot keep it; but I will *not* have rubbishy books; so, Archie, please send these two after your cigars."

Mrs. Jessie held both the small boys fast with an arm round each neck, and when she took this base advantage of them they could only squirm with dismay. "Yes, right behind the back log," she continued, energetically. "There, my hearties—(you like sea slang, so I'll give you a bit)—now, I want you to promise not to read any more stuff for a month, and I'll agree to supply you with wholesome fare."

"O mother! not a single one?" cried Will.

"Couldn't we just finish those?" pleaded Geordie.

"The boys threw away half-smoked cigars; and your books must go after them. Surely you would not be outdone by the 'old fellows,' as you call them, or be less obedient to little Mum than they were to Rose."

"Course not! Come on, Geordie," and Will took the vow like a hero. His brother sighed, and obeyed, but privately resolved to finish his story the minute the month was over.

"You have laid out a hard task for yourself, Jessie, in trying to provide good reading for boys who have been living on sensation stories. It will be like going from raspberry tarts to plain bread and butter; but you will probably save them from a bilious fever," said Dr. Alec, much amused at the proceedings.

"I remember hearing grandpa say that a love for good books was one of the best safeguards a man could have," began Archie, staring thoughtfully at the fine library before him.

"Yes, but there's no time to read nowadays; a fellow has to keep scratching round to make money or he's nobody," cut in Charlie, trying to look worldly-wise.

"This love of money is the curse of America, and for the sake of it men will sell honor and honesty, till we don't know whom to trust, and it is only a genius like Agassiz who dares to say, 'I cannot waste my time in getting rich,'" said Mrs. Jessie sadly.

"Do you want us to be poor, mother?" asked Archie, wondering.

"No, dear, and you never need be, while you can use your hands; but I *am* afraid of this thirst for wealth, and the temptations it brings. O my boys! I tremble for the time when I must let you go, because I think it would break my heart to have you fail as so many fail. It would be far easier to see you dead if it could be said of you as of Sumner,—'No man dared offer him a bribe.'"

Mrs. Jessie was so earnest in her motherly anxiety that her voice faltered over the last words, and she hugged the yellow heads closer in her arms, as if she feared to let them leave that safe harbor for the great sea where so many little boats go down. The younger lads nestled closer to her, and Archie said, in his quiet, resolute way,—

"I cannot promise to be an Agassiz or a Sumner, mother; but I do promise to be an honest man, please God."

"Then I'm satisfied!" and holding fast the hand he gave her, she sealed his promise with a kiss that had all a mother's hope and faith in it.

"I don't see how they ever *can* be bad, she is so fond and proud of them," whispered Rose, quite touched by the little scene.

"You must help her make them what they should be. You have begun already, and when I see those rings where they are, my girl is prettier in my sight than if the biggest diamonds that ever twinkled shone in her ears," answered Dr. Alec, looking at her with approving eyes.

"I'm so glad you think I can do any thing, for I perfectly *ache* to be useful, every one is *so* good to me, especially Aunt Jessie."

"I think you are in a fair way to pay your debts, Rosy, for when girls give up their little vanities, and boys their small vices, and try to strengthen each other in well-doing, matters are going as they ought. Work away, my dear, and help their mother keep these sons fit friends for an innocent creature like yourself; they will be the manlier men for it, I can assure you."

# Chapter XVIII

## FASHION AND PHYSIOLOGY

"PLEASE, sir, I guess you'd better step up right away, or it will be too late, for I heard Miss Rose say she knew you wouldn't like it, and she'd never dare to let you see her."

Phebe said this as she popped her head into the study, where Dr. Alec sat reading a new book.

"They are at it, are they?" he said, looking up quickly, and giving himself a shake, as if ready for a battle of some sort.

"Yes, sir, as hard as they can talk, and Miss Rose don't seem to know what to do, for the things are ever so stylish, and she looks elegant in 'em; though I like her best in the old ones," answered Phebe.

"You are a girl of sense. I'll settle matters for Rosy, and you'll lend a hand. Is every thing ready in her room, and are you sure you understand how they go?"

"Oh, yes, sir; but they are so funny! I know Miss Rose will think it's a joke," and Phebe laughed as if something tickled her immensely.

"Never mind what she thinks so long as she obeys. Tell her to do it for my sake, and she will find it the best joke she ever saw. I expect to have a tough time of it, but we'll win yet," said the Doctor, as he marched upstairs with the book in his hand, and an odd smile on his face.

There was such a clatter of tongues in the sewing-room that no one heard his tap at the door, so he pushed it open and took an observation. Aunt Plenty, Aunt Clara, and Aunt Jessie were all absorbed in gazing at Rose, who slowly revolved between them and the great mirror, in a full winter costume of the latest fashion.

"Bless my heart! worse even than I expected," thought the Doctor, with an inward groan, for, to his benighted eyes, the girl looked like a trussed fowl, and the fine new dress had neither grace, beauty, nor fitness to recommend it.

The suit was of two peculiar shades of blue, so arranged that patches of light and dark distracted the eye. The upper skirt was tied so tightly back that it was impossible to take a long step, and the under one was so loaded with plaited frills that it "wobbled"—no other word will express it—ungracefully, both fore and aft. A bunch of folds was gathered up just below the waist behind, and a great bow rode a-top. A small jacket of the same material was adorned with a high ruff at the back, and laid well open over the breast, to display some lace and a locket. Heavy fringes, bows, puffs, ruffles, and *revers* finished off the dress, making one's head ache to think of the amount of work wasted, for not a single graceful line struck the eye, and the beauty of the material was quite lost in the profusion of ornament.

A high velvet hat, audaciously turned up in front, with a bunch of pink roses and a sweeping plume, was cocked over one ear, and, with her curls braided into a club at the back of her neck, Rose's head looked more like that of a dashing young cavalier than a modest little girl's. High-heeled boots tilted her well forward, a tiny muff pinioned her arms, and a spotted veil tied so closely over her face that her eyelashes were rumpled by it, gave the last touch of absurdity to her appearance.

"Now she looks like other girls, and as *I* like to see her," Mrs. Clara was saying, with an air of great satisfaction.

"She does look like a fashionable young lady, but somehow I miss my little Rose, for children dressed like children in my day," answered Aunt Plenty, peering through her glasses with a troubled look, for she could not imagine the creature before her ever sitting in her lap, running to wait upon her, or making the house gay with a child's blithe presence.

"Things have changed since your day, Aunt, and it takes time to get used to new ways. But you, Jessie, surely like this costume better than the dowdy things Rose has been wearing all summer. Now, be honest, and own you do," said Mrs. Clara, bent on being praised for her work.

"Well, dear, to be *quite* honest, then, I think it is frightful," answered Mrs. Jessie with a candor that caused revolving Rose to stop in dismay.

"Hear, hear," cried a deep voice, and with a general start the ladies became aware that the enemy was among them.

Rose blushed up to her hat brim, and stood, looking, as she felt, like a fool, while Mrs. Clara hastened to explain.

"Of course I don't expect *you* to like it, Alec, but I don't consider you a judge of what is proper and becoming for a young lady. Therefore I have taken the liberty of providing a pretty street suit for Rose. She need not wear it if you object, for I know we promised to let you do what you liked with the poor dear for a year."

"It is a street costume, is it?" asked the Doctor, mildly. "Do you know, I never should have guessed that it was meant for winter weather and brisk locomotion. Take a turn, Rosy, and let me see all its beauties and advantages."

Rose tried to walk off with her usual free tread, but the under-skirt got in her way, the over-skirt was so tight she could not take a long step, and her boots made it impossible to carry herself perfectly erect.

"I haven't got used to it yet," she said, petulantly, kicking at her train, as she turned to toddle back again.

"Suppose a mad dog or a runaway horse was after you, could you get out of the way without upsetting, Colonel?" asked the Doctor, with a twinkle in the eyes that were fixed on the rakish hat.

"Don't think I could, but I'll try," and Rose made a rush across the room. Her boot-heels caught on a rug, several strings broke, her hat tipped over her eyes, and she plunged promiscuously into a chair, where she sat laughing so infectiously that all but Mrs. Clara joined in her mirth.

"I should say that a walking suit in which one could not walk, and a winter suit which exposes the throat, head, and feet to cold and damp, was rather a failure, Clara; especially as it has no beauty to reconcile one to its utter unfitness," said Dr. Alec, as he helped Rose undo her veil, adding, in a low tone, "Nice thing for the eyes; you'll soon see spots when it is off as well as when it is on, and, by and by, be a case for an oculist."

"No beauty!" cried Mrs. Clara, warmly. "Now that is just a man's blindness. This is the best of silk and camel's hair, real ostrich feathers, and an expensive ermine muff. What *could* be in better taste, or more proper for a young girl?"

"I'll show you, if Rose will go to her room and oblige me by putting on what she finds there," answered the Doctor, with unexpected readiness.

"Alec, if it is a Bloomer, I shall protest. I've been expecting it, but I know I *cannot* bear to see that pretty child sacrificed to your wild ideas of health. Tell me it *isn't* a Bloomer!" and Mrs. Clara clasped her hands imploringly.

"It is not."

"Thank Heaven!" and she resigned herself with a sigh of relief, adding plaintively, "I did hope you'd accept my suit, for poor Rose has been afflicted with frightful clothes long enough to spoil the taste of any girl."

"You talk of *my* afflicting the child, and then make a helpless guy like that of her!" answered the Doctor, pointing to the little fashion plate that was scuttling out of sight as fast as it could go.

He closed the door with a shrug, but before any one could speak, his quick eye fell upon an object which caused him to frown, and demand in an indignant tone,—

"After all I have said, were you really going to tempt my girl with those abominable things?"

"I thought we put them away when she wouldn't wear them," murmured Mrs. Clara, whisking a little pair of corsets out of sight, with guilty haste. "I only brought them to try, for Rose is growing stout, and will have no figure if it is not attended to soon," she added, with an air of calm conviction that roused the Doctor still more, for this was one of his especial abominations.

"Growing stout! Yes, thank Heaven, she is, and shall continue to do it, for Nature knows how to mould a woman better than any corset-maker, and I won't have her interfered with. My dear Clara, *have* you lost your senses that you can for a moment dream of putting a growing girl into an instrument of torture like this?" and with a sudden gesture he plucked forth the offending corsets from under the sofa cushion, and held them out with the expression one would wear on beholding the thumbscrews or the rack of ancient times.

"Don't be absurd, Alec. There is no torture about it, for tight lacing is out of fashion, and we have nice, sensible things nowadays. Every one wears them; even babies have stiffened waists to support their weak little backs," began Mrs. Clara, rushing to the defence of the pet delusion of most women.

"I know it, and so the poor little souls have weak backs all their days, as their mothers had before them. It is vain to argue the matter, and I won't try, but I wish to state, once for all, that if I ever see a pair of corsets near Rose, I'll put them in the fire, and you may send the bill to me."

As he spoke, the corsets were on their way to destruction, but Mrs. Jessie caught his arm, exclaiming merrily, "Don't burn them, for mercy sake, Alec; they are full of whalebones, and will make a dreadful odor. Give them to me. I'll see that they do no harm."

"Whalebones indeed! A regular fence of them, and metal gate-posts in front. As if our own bones were not enough, if we'd give them a chance to do their duty," growled the Doctor, yielding up the bone of contention with a last shake of contempt. Then his face cleared suddenly, and he held up his finger, saying, with a smile, "Hear those girls laugh; cramped lungs could not make hearty music like that."

Peals of laughter issued from Rose's room, and smiles involuntarily touched the lips of those who listened to the happy sound.

"Some new prank of yours, Alec?" asked Aunt Plenty, indulgently, for she had come to believe in most of her nephew's odd notions, because they seemed to work so well.

"Yes, ma'am, my last, and I hope you will like it. I discovered what Clara was at, and got my rival suit ready for to-day. I'm not going to 'afflict' Rose, but let her choose, and if I'm not entirely mistaken, she will like my rig best. While we wait I'll explain, and then you will appreciate the general effect better. I got hold of this little book, and was struck with its good sense and good taste, for it suggests a way to clothe women both healthfully and handsomely, and that is a great point. It begins at the foundations, as you will see if you will look at these pictures, and I should think women would rejoice at this lightening of their burdens."

As he spoke, the Doctor laid the book before Aunt Plenty, who obediently brought her spectacles to bear upon the illustrations, and after a long look exclaimed with a scandalized face,—

"Mercy on us, these things are like the night-drawers Jamie wears! You don't mean to say you want Rose to come out in this costume? It's not proper, and I won't consent to it!"

"I do mean it, and I'm sure my sensible aunt *will* consent when she understands that these,—well,—I'll call them by an Indian name, and say,—pajamas,—are for underwear, and Rose can have as pretty frocks as she likes outside. These two suits of flannel, each in one piece from head to foot, with a skirt or so hung on this easily fitting waist, will keep the child warm without burdening her with belts, and gathers, and buckles, and bunches round the waist, and leave free the muscles that need plenty of room to work in. She shall never have the back-ache if *I* can help it, nor the long list of ills you dear women think you cannot escape."

"*I* don't consider it modest, and I'm sure Rose will be shocked at it," began Mrs. Clara, but stopped suddenly as Rose appeared in the door-way, not looking shocked a bit.

"Come on, my hygienic model, and let us see you," said her uncle, with an approving glance, as she walked in looking so mischievously merry, that it was evident she enjoyed the joke.

"Well, I don't see any thing remarkable. That is a neat, plain suit; the materials are good, and it's not unbecoming, if you want her to look like a little schoolgirl; but it has not a particle of style, and no one would ever give it a second glance," said Mrs. Clara, feeling that her last remark condemned the whole thing.

"Exactly what I want," answered the provoking Doctor, rubbing his hands with a satisfied air. "Rosy looks now like what she is, a modest little girl, who does not want to be stared at. I think she would get a glance of approval, though, from people who like sense and simplicity, rather than fuss and feathers. Revolve, my Hebe, and let me refresh my eyes by the sight of you."

There was very little to see, however, only a pretty Gabrielle dress, of a soft, warm shade of brown, coming to the tops of a trim pair of boots with low heels. A seal-skin sack, cap, and mittens, with a glimpse of scarlet at the throat, and the pretty curls tied up with a bright velvet of the same color, completed the external adornment, making her look like a robin red-breast,—wintry, yet warm.

"How do you like it, Rosy?" asked the Doctor, feeling that *her* opinion was more important to the success of his new idea than that of all the aunts on the hill.

"I feel very odd and light, but I'm warm as a toast, and nothing seems to be in my way," answered Rose, with a skip which displayed shapely gaiters on legs that now might be as free and active as a boy's under the modest skirts of the girl.

"You can run away from the mad dogs, and walk off at a smart pace without tumbling on your nose, now, I fancy?"

"Yes, uncle! suppose the dog coming, I just hop over a wall so—and when I walk of a cold day, I go like this—"

Entering fully into the spirit of the thing, Rose swung herself over the high back of the sofa as easily as one of her cousins, and then went down the long hall as if her stout boots were related to the famous seven-leaguers.

"There! you see how it will be; dress her in that boyish way and she will act like a boy. I do hate all these inventions of strong-minded women!" exclaimed Mrs. Clara, as Rose came back at a run.

"Ah, but you see some of these sensible inventions come from the brain of a fashionable *modiste*, who will make you lovely, or what you value more,—'stylish' outside and comfortable within. Mrs. Van Tassel has been to Madame Stone, and is wearing a full suit of this sort. Van himself told me, when I asked how she was, that she had given up lying on the sofa, and was going about in a most astonishing way, considering her feeble health."

"You don't say so! Let me see that book a moment," and Aunt Clara examined the new patterns with a more respectful air, for if the elegant Mrs. Van Tassel wore these "dreadful things" it would never do to be left behind, in spite of her prejudices.

Dr. Alec looked at Mrs. Jessie, and both smiled, for "little Mum" had been in the secret, and enjoyed it mightily.

"I thought that would settle it," he said with a nod.

"I didn't wait for Mrs. Van to lead the way, and for once in my life I have adopted a new fashion before Clara. My freedom suit is ordered, and you *may* see me playing tag with Rose and the boys before long," answered Mrs. Jessie, nodding back at him.

Meantime Aunt Plenty was examining Rose's costume, for the hat and sack were off, and the girl was eagerly explaining the new under-garments.

"See, auntie, all nice scarlet flannel, and a gay little petticoat, and long stockings, oh, so warm! Phebe and I nearly died laughing when I put this rig on, but I like it ever so much. The dress is so comfortable, and doesn't need any belt or sash, and I can sit without rumpling any trimming, that's *such* a comfort! I like to be tidy, and so, when I wear fussed-up things, I'm thinking of my clothes all the time, and that's tiresome. Do say you like it. I resolved *I* would, just to please uncle, for he does know more about health than any one else, I'm sure, and I'd wear a bag if he asked me to do it."

"I don't ask that, Rose, but I wish you'd weigh and compare the two suits, and then choose which seems best. I leave it to your own common-sense," answered Dr. Alec, feeling pretty sure he had won.

"Why, I take this one, of course, uncle. The other is fashionable, and—yes—I must say I think it's pretty—but it's very heavy, and I should have to go round like a walking doll if I wore it. I'm much obliged to auntie, but I'll keep this, please."

Rose spoke gently but decidedly, though there was a look of regret when her eye fell on the other suit which Phebe had brought in; and it was very natural to like to look as other girls did. Aunt Clara sighed; Uncle Alec smiled, and said heartily,—

"Thank you, dear; now read this book and you will understand why I ask it of you. Then, if you like, I'll give you a new lesson; you asked for one yesterday, and this is more necessary than French or housekeeping."

"Oh, what?" and Rose caught up the book which Mrs. Clara had thrown down with a disgusted look.

Though Dr. Alec was forty, the boyish love of teasing was not yet dead in him, and, being much elated at his victory, he could not resist the temptation of shocking Mrs. Clara by suggesting dreadful possibilities, so he answered, half in earnest half in jest: "Physiology, Rose. Wouldn't you like to be a little medical student with Uncle Doctor for teacher, and be ready to take up his practice when he has to stop? If you agree, I'll hunt up my old skeleton to-morrow."

That was *too* much for Aunt Clara, and she hastily departed with her mind in a sad state of perturbation about Mrs. Van Tassel's new costume, and Rose's new study.

# Chapter XIX

## BROTHER BONES

ROSE accepted her uncle's offer, as Aunt Myra discovered two or three days later. Coming in for an early call, and hearing voices in the study, she opened the door, gave a cry and shut it quickly, looking a good deal startled. The Doctor appeared in a moment, and begged to know what the matter was.

"How *can* you ask when that long box looks so like a coffin I thought it was one, and that dreadful thing stared me in the face as I opened the door," answered Mrs. Myra, pointing to the skeleton that hung from the chandelier cheerfully grinning at all beholders.

"This is a medical college where women are freely admitted, so walk in, madam, and join the class if you'll do me the honor," said the Doctor, waving her forward with his politest bow.

"Do, auntie; it's perfectly splendid," cried Rose's voice, and Rose's blooming face was seen behind the ribs of the skeleton, smiling and nodding in the gayest possible manner.

"What *are* you doing, child?" demanded Aunt Myra, dropping into a chair and staring about her.

"Oh, I'm learning bones to-day, and I like it so much. There are twelve ribs, you know, and the two lower ones are called floating ribs, because they are not fastened to the breast bone. That's why they go in so easily if you lace tight and squeeze the lungs and heart in the—let me see, what was that big word—oh, I know—thoracic cavity," and Rose beamed with pride as she aired her little bit of knowledge.

"Do you think that is a good sort of thing for her to be poking over? She is a nervous child, and I'm afraid it will be bad for her," said Aunt Myra, watching Rose as she counted vertebræ, and waggled a hip-joint in its socket with an inquiring expression.

"An excellent study, for she enjoys it, and I mean to teach her how to manage her nerves so that they won't be a curse to her, as many a woman's become through ignorance or want of thought. To make a mystery or a terror of these things is a mistake, and I mean Rose shall understand and respect her body so well that she won't dare to trifle with it as most women do."

"And she really likes it?"

"Very much, auntie! It's all so wonderful, and so nicely planned, you can hardly believe what you see. Just think, there are 600,000,000 air cells in one pair of lungs, and 2,000 pores to a square inch of surface; so you see what quantities of air we *must* have, and what care we should take of our skin so all the little doors will open and shut right. And brains, auntie, you've no idea how curious they are; I haven't got to them yet, but I long to, and uncle is going to show me a manikin that you can take to pieces. Just think how nice it will be to see all the organs in their places; I only wish they could be made to work as ours do."

It was funny to see Aunt Myra's face as Rose stood before her talking rapidly with one hand laid in the friendliest manner on the skeleton's shoulder. Every word both the Doctor and Rose uttered hit the good lady in her weakest spot, and as she looked and listened a long array of bottles and pill-boxes rose up before her, reproaching her with the "ignorance and want of thought" that made her what she was, a nervous, dyspeptic, unhappy old woman.

"Well, I don't know but you may be right, Alec, only I wouldn't carry it too far. Women don't need much of this sort of knowledge, and are not fit for it. I couldn't bear to touch that ugly thing, and it gives me the creeps to hear about 'organs,'" said Aunt Myra, with a sigh and her hand on her side.

"Wouldn't it be a comfort to know that your liver was on the right side, auntie, and not on the left?" asked Rose with a naughty laugh in her eyes, for she had lately learned that Aunt Myra's liver complaint was not in the proper place.

"It's a dying world, child, and it don't much matter where the pain is, for sooner or later we all drop off and are seen no more," was Aunt Myra's cheerful reply.

"Well, I intend to know what kills me if I can, and meantime I'm going to enjoy myself in spite of a dying world. I wish you'd do so too, and come and study with uncle, it would do you good I'm sure," and Rose went back to counting vertebræ with such a happy face that Aunt Myra had not the heart to say a word to dampen her ardor.

"Perhaps it's as well to let her do what she likes the little while she is with us. But pray be careful of her, Alec, and not allow her to overwork," she whispered as she went out.

"That's exactly what I'm trying to do, ma'am, and rather a hard job I find it," he added, as he shut the door, for the dear aunts were dreadfully in his way sometimes.

Half an hour later came another interruption in the shape of Mac, who announced his arrival by the brief but elegant remark,—

"Hullo! what new game is this?"

Rose explained, Mac gave a long whistle of surprise, and then took a promenade round the skeleton, observing gravely,—

"Brother Bones looks very jolly, but I can't say much for his beauty."

"You mustn't make fun of him, for he's a good old fellow, and you'd be just as ugly if your flesh was off," said Rose, defending her new friend with warmth.

"I dare say, so I'll keep my flesh on, thank you. You are so busy you can't read to a fellow, I suppose?" asked Mac, whose eyes were better, but still too weak for books.

"Don't you want to come and join my class? uncle explains it all to us, and you can take a look at the plates as they come along. We'll give up bones to-day and have eyes instead; that will be more interesting to *you*," added Rose, seeing no ardent thirst for physiological information in his face.

"Rose, we must not fly about from one thing to another in this way," began Dr. Alec; but she whispered quickly, with a nod towards Mac, whose goggles were turned wistfully in the direction of the forbidden books,—

"He's blue to-day, and we must amuse him; give a little lecture on eyes, and it will do him good. No matter about me, uncle."

"Very well; the class will please be seated," and the Doctor gave a sounding rap on the table.

"Come, sit by me, dear, then we can both see the pictures; and if your head gets tired you can lie down," said Rose, generously opening her little college to a brother, and kindly providing for the weaknesses that all humanity is subject to.

Side by side they sat and listened to a very simple explanation of the mechanism of the eye, finding it as wonderful as a fairy tale, for fine plates illustrated it, and a very willing teacher did his best to make the lesson pleasant.

"Jove! if I'd known what mischief I was doing to that mighty delicate machine of mine, you wouldn't have caught me reading by fire light, or studying with a glare of sunshine on my book," said Mac, peering solemnly at a magnified eyeball; then, pushing it away, he added indignantly: "Why isn't a fellow taught all about his works, and how to manage 'em, and not left to go blundering into all sorts of worries? Telling him after he's down isn't much use, for then he's found it out himself and won't thank you."

"Ah, Mac, that's just what I keep lecturing about, and people *won't* listen. You lads need that sort of knowledge so much, and fathers and mothers ought to be able to give it to you. Few of them *are* able, and so we all go blundering, as you say. Less Greek and Latin and more knowledge of the laws of health for *my* boys, if I had them. Mathematics are all very well, but morals are better, and I wish, *how* I wish that I could help teachers and parents to feel it as they ought."

"Some do; Aunt Jessie and her boys have capital talks, and I wish we could; but mother's so busy with her housekeeping, and father with his business, there never seems to be any time for that sort of thing; even if there was, it don't seem as if it would be easy to talk to them, because we've never got into the way of it, you know."

Poor Mac was right there, and expressed a want that many a boy and girl feels. Fathers and mothers *are* too absorbed in business and housekeeping to study their children, and cherish that sweet and natural confidence which is a child's surest safeguard, and a parent's subtlest power. So the young hearts hide trouble or temptation till the harm is done, and mutual regret comes too late. Happy the boys and girls who tell all things freely to father or mother, sure of pity, help, and pardon; and thrice happy the parents who, out of their own experience, and by their own virtues, can teach and uplift the souls for which they are responsible.

This longing stirred in the hearts of Rose and Mac, and by a natural impulse both turned to Dr. Alec, for in this queer world of ours, fatherly and motherly hearts often beat warm and wise in the breasts of bachelor uncles and maiden aunts; and it is my private opinion that these worthy creatures are a beautiful provision of nature for the cherishing of other people's children. They certainly get great comfort out of it, and receive much innocent affection that otherwise would be lost.

Dr. Alec was one of these, and his big heart had room for every one of the eight cousins, especially orphaned Rose and afflicted Mac; so, when the boy uttered that unconscious reproach to his parents, and Rose added with a sigh, "It must be beautiful to have a mother!"—the good Doctor yearned over them, and, shutting his book with a decided slam, said in that cordial voice of his,—

"Now, look here, children, you just come and tell *me* all your worries, and with God's help I'll settle them for you. That is what I'm here for, I believe, and it will be a great happiness to me if you can trust me."

"We can, uncle, and we will!" both answered with a heartiness that gratified him much.

"Good! now school is dismissed, and I advise you to go and refresh your 600,000,000 air cells by a brisk run in the garden. Come again whenever you like, Mac, and we'll teach you all we can about your 'works,' as you call them, so you can keep them running smoothly."

"We'll come, sir, much obliged," and the class in physiology went out to walk.

Mac did come again, glad to find something he could study in spite of his weak eyes, and learned much that was of more value than any thing his school had ever taught him.

Of course, the other lads made great fun of the whole thing, and plagued Dr. Alec's students half out of their lives. But they kept on persistently, and one day something happened which made the other fellows behave themselves for ever after.

It was a holiday, and Rose up in her room thought she heard the voices of her cousins, so she ran down to welcome them, but found no one there.

"Never mind, they will be here soon, and then we'll have a frolic," she said to herself, and thinking she had been mistaken she went into the study to wait. She was lounging over the table looking at a map when an odd noise caught her ear. A gentle tapping somewhere, and following the sound it seemed to come from the inside of the long case in which the skeleton lived when not professionally engaged. This case stood upright in a niche between two book-cases at the back of the room, a darkish corner, where Brother Bones, as the boys *would* call him, was out of the way.

As Rose stood looking in that direction, and wondering if a rat had got shut in, the door of the case swung slowly open, and with a great start she saw a bony arm lifted, and a bony finger beckon to her. For a minute she was frightened, and ran to the study door with a fluttering heart, but just as she touched the handle a queer, stifled sort of giggle made her stop short and turn red with anger. She paused an instant to collect herself, and then went softly toward the bony beckoner. A nearer look revealed black threads tied to the arm and fingers, the ends of threads disappearing through holes bored in the back of the case. Peeping into the deep recess, she also caught sight of the tip of an elbow covered with a rough gray cloth which she knew very well.

Quick as a flash she understood the joke, her fear vanished, and with a wicked smile, she whipped out her scissors, cut the threads, and the bony arm dropped with a rattle. Before she could say, "Come out, Charlie, and let my skeleton alone," a sudden irruption of boys all in a high state of tickle proclaimed to the hidden rogue that his joke was a failure.

"I told him not to do it, because it might give you a start," explained Archie, emerging from the closet.

"I had a smelling-bottle all ready if she fainted away," added Steve, popping up from behind the great chair.

"It's too bad of you not to squawk and run; we depended on it, it's such fun to howl after you," said Will and Geordie, rolling out from under the sofa in a promiscuous heap.

"You are getting altogether too strong-minded, Rose; most girls would have been in a jolly twitter to see this old fellow waggling his finger at them," complained Charlie, squeezing out from his tight quarters, dusty and disgusted.

"I'm used to your pranks now, so I'm always on the watch and prepared. But I won't have Brother Bones made fun of. I know uncle wouldn't like it, so please don't," began Rose just as Dr. Alec came in, and, seeing the state of the case at a glance, he said quietly,—

"Hear how I got that skeleton, and then I'm sure you will treat it with respect."

The boys settled down at once on any article of furniture that was nearest and listened dutifully.

"Years ago, when I was in the hospital, a poor fellow was brought there with a rare and very painful disease. There was no hope for him, but we did our best, and he was so grateful that when he died he left us his body that we might discover the mysteries of his complaint, and so be able to help others afflicted in the same way. It did do good, and his brave patience made us remember him long after he was gone. He thought I had been kind to him, and said to a fellow-student of mine: 'Tell the Doctor I lave him me bones for I've nothing else in the wide world, and I'll not be wanting 'em at all, at all, when the great pain has kilt me entirely.' So that is how they came to be mine, and why I've kept them carefully; for, though only a poor, ignorant fellow, Mike Nolan did what he could to help others, and prove his gratitude to those who tried to help him."

As Dr. Alec paused, Archie closed the door of the case as respectfully as if the mummy of an Egyptian king was inside; Will and Geordie looked solemnly at one another, evidently much impressed, and Charlie pensively remarked from the coal-hod where he sat,—

"I've often heard of a skeleton in the house, but I think few people have one as useful and as interesting as ours."

# Chapter XX

UNDER THE MISTLETOE

Rose made Phebe promise that she would bring her stocking into the "Bower," as she called her pretty room, on Christmas morning, because that first delicious rummage loses half its charm if two little night-caps at least do not meet over the treasures, and two happy voices Oh and Ah together.

So when Rose opened her eyes that day they fell upon faithful Phebe, rolled up in a shawl, sitting on the rug before a blazing fire, with her untouched stocking laid beside her.

"Merry Christmas!" cried the little mistress, smiling gayly.

"Merry Christmas!" answered the little maid, so heartily that it did one good to hear her.

"Bring the stockings right away, Phebe, and let's see what we've got," said Rose, sitting up among the pillows, and looking as eager as a child.

A pair of long knobby hose were laid out upon the coverlet and their contents examined with delight, though each knew every blessed thing that had been put into the other's stocking.

Never mind what they were; it is evident that they were quite satisfactory, for as Rose leaned back, she said, with a luxurious sigh of satisfaction: "Now, I believe I've got every thing in the world that I want," and Phebe answered, smiling over a lapful of treasures: "This is the most splendid Christmas I ever had since I was born." Then, she added with an important air,—

"Do wish for something else, because I happen to know of two more presents outside the door this minute."

"Oh, me, what richness!" cried Rose, much excited. "I used to wish for a pair of glass slippers like Cinderella's, but as I can't have them, I really don't know what to ask for."

Phebe clapped her hands as she skipped off the bed and ran to the door, saying merrily: "One of them *is* for your feet any way. I don't know what you'll say to the other, but *I* think it's elegant."

So did Rose, when a shining pair of skates and a fine sled appeared.

"Uncle sent those; I know he did; and, now I see them, I remember that I did want to skate and coast. Isn't it a beauty? See! they fit nicely," and, sitting on the new sled, Rose tried a skate on her little bare foot, while Phebe stood by admiring the pretty *tableau*.

"Now we must hurry and get dressed, for there is a deal to do to-day, and I want to get through in time to try my sled before dinner."

"Gracious me, and I ought to be dusting my parlors this blessed minute!" and mistress and maid separated with such happy faces that any one would have known what day it was without being told.

"Birnam Wood has come to Dunsinane, Rosy," said Dr. Alec, as he left the breakfast table to open the door for a procession of holly, hemlock, and cedar boughs that came marching up the steps.

Snowballs and "Merry Christmases!" flew about pretty briskly for several minutes; then all fell to work trimming up the old house, for the family always dined together there on that day.

"I rode miles and mileses, as Ben says, to get this fine bit, and I'm going to hang it there as the last touch to the rig-a-madooning," said Charlie, as he fastened a dull green branch to the chandelier in the front parlor.

"It isn't very pretty," said Rose, who was trimming the chimney-piece with glossy holly sprays.

"Never mind that, it's mistletoe, and any one who stands under it will get kissed whether they like it or not. Now's your time, ladies," answered the saucy Prince, keeping his place and looking sentimentally at the girls, who retired precipitately from the dangerous spot.

"You won't catch me," said Rose, with great dignity.

"See if I don't!"

"I've got my eye on Phebe," observed Will, in a patronizing tone that made them all laugh.

"Bless the dear; I sha'n't mind it a bit," answered Phebe, with such a maternal air that Will's budding gallantry was chilled to death.

"Oh, the mistletoe bough!" sang Rose.

"Oh, the mistletoe bough!" echoed all the boys, and the teasing ended in the plaintive ballad they all liked so well.

There was plenty of time to try the new skates before dinner, and then Rose took her first lesson on the little bay, which seemed to have frozen over for that express purpose. She found tumbling down and getting up again warm work for a time, but, with six boys to teach her, she managed at last to stand alone; and, satisfied with that success, she refreshed herself with a dozen grand coasts on the Amazon, as her sled was called.

"Ah, that fatal color! it breaks my heart to see it," croaked Aunt Myra, as Rose came down a little late, with cheeks almost as ruddy as the holly berries on the wall, and every curl as smooth as Phebe's careful hands could make it.

"I'm glad to see that Alec allows the poor child to make herself pretty in spite of his absurd notions," added Aunt Clara, taking infinite satisfaction in the fact that Rose's blue silk dress had three frills on it.

"She is a very intelligent child, and has a nice little manner of her own," observed Aunt Jane, with unusual affability; for Rose had just handed Mac a screen to guard his eyes from the brilliant fire.

"If I had a daughter like that to show my Jem when he gets home, I should be a very proud and happy woman," thought Aunt Jessie, and then reproached herself for not being perfectly satisfied with her four brave lads.

Aunt Plenty was too absorbed in the dinner to have an eye for any thing else; if she had not been, she would have seen what an effect her new cap produced upon the boys. The good lady owned that she did "love a dressy cap," and on this occasion her headgear was magnificent; for the towering structure of lace was adorned with buff ribbons to such an extent that it looked as if a flock of yellow butterflies had settled on her dear old head. When she trotted about the rooms the ruches quivered, the little bows all stood erect, and the streamers waved in the breeze so comically that it was absolutely necessary for Archie to smother the Brats in the curtains till they had had their first laugh out.

Uncle Mac had brought Fun See to dinner, and it was a

mercy he did, for the elder lads found a vent for their merriment in joking the young Chinaman on his improved appearance. He was in American costume now, with a cropped head, and spoke remarkably good English after six months at school; but, for all that, his yellow face and beady eyes made a curious contrast to the blonde Campbells all about him. Will called him the "Typhoon," meaning Tycoon, and the name stuck to him to his great disgust.

Aunt Peace was brought down and set in the chair of state at table, for she never failed to join the family on this day, and sat smiling at them all "like an embodiment of Peace on earth," Uncle Alec said, as he took his place beside her, while Uncle Mac supported Aunt Plenty at the other end.

"I ate hardly any breakfast, and I've done every thing I know to make myself extra hungry, but I really don't think I *can* eat straight through, unless I burst my buttons off," whispered Geordie to Will, as he surveyed the bounteous stores before him with a hopeless sigh.

"A fellow never knows what he can do till he tries," answered Will, attacking his heaped-up plate with the evident intention of doing his duty like a man.

Everybody knows what a Christmas dinner is, so we need waste no words in describing this one, but hasten at once to tell what happened at the end of it. The end, by the way, was so long in coming that the gas was lighted before dessert was over, for a snow flurry had come on and the wintry daylight faded fast. But that only made it all the jollier in the warm, bright rooms, full of happy souls. Every one was very merry, but Archie seemed particularly uplifted,—so much so, that Charlie confided to Rose that he was afraid the Chief had been at the decanters.

Rose indignantly denied the insinuation, for when healths were drunk in the good old-fashioned way to suit the elders, she had observed that Aunt Jessie's boys filled their glasses with water, and had done the same herself in spite of the Prince's jokes about "the rosy."

But Archie certainly *was* unusually excited, and when some one remembered that it was the anniversary of Uncle Jem's wedding, and wished he was there to make a speech, his son electrified the family by trying to do it for him. It was rather incoherent and flowery, as maiden speeches are apt to be, but the end was considered superb; for, turning to his mother with a queer little choke in his voice, he said that she "deserved to be blessed with peace and plenty, to be crowned with roses and lads-love, and to receive the cargo of happiness sailing home to her in spite of wind or tide to add another Jem to the family jewels."

That allusion to the Captain, now on his return trip, made Mrs. Jessie sob in her napkin, and set the boys cheering. Then, as if that was not sensation enough, Archie suddenly dashed out of the room as if he had lost his wits.

"Too bashful to stay and be praised," began Charlie, excusing the peculiarities of his chief as in duty bound.

"Phebe beckoned to him; I saw her," cried Rose, staring hard at the door.

"Is it more presents coming?" asked Jamie, just as his brother re-appeared looking more excited than ever.

"Yes; a present for mother, and here it is!" roared Archie, flinging wide the door to let in a tall man who cried out,—

"Where's my little woman? The first kiss for her, then the rest may come on as fast as they like."

Before the words were out of his mouth, Mrs. Jessie was half hidden under his rough great-coat, and four boys were prancing about him clamoring for their turn.

Of course, there was a joyful tumult for a time, during which Rose slipped into the window recess and watched what went on, as if it were a chapter in a Christmas story. It was good to see bluff Uncle Jem look proudly at his tall son, and fondly hug the little ones. It was better still to see him shake his brothers' hands as if he would never leave off, and kiss all the sisters in a way that made even solemn Aunt Myra brighten up for a minute. But it was best of all to see him finally established in grandfather's chair, with his "little woman" beside him, his three youngest boys in his lap, and Archie hovering over him like a large-sized cherub. That really was, as Charlie said, "A landscape to do one's heart good."

"All hearty and all here, thank God!" said Captain Jem in the first pause that came, as he looked about him with a grateful face.

"All but Rose," answered loyal little Jamie, remembering the absent.

"Faith, I forgot the child! Where is George's little girl?" asked the Captain, who had not seen her since she was a baby.

"You'd better say Alec's great girl," said Uncle Mac, who professed to be madly jealous of his brother.

"Here I am, sir," and Rose appeared from behind the curtains, looking as if she had rather have staid there.

"Saint George Germain, how the mite has grown!" cried Captain Jem, as he tumbled the boys out of his lap, and rose to greet the tall girl, like a gentleman as he was. But, somehow, when he shook her hand it looked so small in his big one, and her face reminded him so strongly of his dead brother, that he was not satisfied with so cold a welcome, and with a sudden softening of the keen eyes he took her up in his arms, whispering, with a rough cheek against her smooth one,—

"God bless you, child! forgive me if I forgot you for a minute, and be sure that not one of your kinsfolk is happier to see you here than Uncle Jem."

That made it all right; and when he set her down, Rose's face was so bright it was evident that some spell had been used to banish the feeling of neglect that had kept her moping behind the curtain so long.

Then every one sat round and heard all about the voyage home,—how the Captain had set his heart on getting there in time to keep Christmas; how every thing had conspired to thwart his plan; and how, at the very last minute, he had managed to do it, and had sent a telegram to Archie, bidding him keep the secret, and be ready for his father at any moment, for the ship got into another port, and he might be late.

Then Archie told how that telegram had burnt in his pocket all dinner-time; how he had to take Phebe into his confidence, and how clever she was to keep the Captain back till the speech was over, and he could come in with effect.

The elders would have sat and talked all the evening, but the young folks were bent on having their usual Christmas frolic; so, after an hour of pleasant chat, they began to get restless, and having consulted together in dumb show, they devised a way to very effectually break up the family council.

Steve vanished, and, sooner than the boys imagined Dandy could get himself up, the skirl of the bag-pipe was heard in the hall, and the bonny piper came to lead Clan Campbell to the revel.

"Draw it mild, Stenie, my man; ye play unco weel, but ye mak a most infernal din," cried Uncle Jem, with his hands over his ears, for this accomplishment was new to him, and "took him all aback," as he expressed it.

So Steve droned out a Highland reel as softly as he could, and the boys danced it to a circle of admiring relations. Captain Jem was a true sailor, however, and could not stand idle while any thing lively was going on; so, when the piper's breath gave out, he cut a splendid pigeon-wing into the middle of the hall, saying, "Who can dance a Fore and After?" and, waiting for no reply, began to whistle the air so invitingly that Mrs. Jessie "set" to him laughing like a girl; Rose and Charlie took their places behind, and away went the four with a spirit and skill that inspired all the rest to "cut in" as fast as they could.

That was a grand beginning, and they had many another dance before any one would own they were tired. Even Fun See distinguished himself with Aunt Plenty, whom he greatly admired as the stoutest lady in the company; plumpness being considered a beauty in his country. The merry old soul professed herself immensely flattered by his admiration, and the boys declared she "set her cap at him," else he would never have dared to catch her under the mistletoe, and, rising on the tips of his own toes, gallantly salute her fat cheek.

How they all laughed at her astonishment, and how Fun's little black eyes twinkled over this exploit! Charlie put him up to it, and Charlie was so bent on catching Rose, that he laid all sorts of pitfalls for her, and bribed the other lads to help him. But Rose was wide-awake, and escaped all his snares, professing great contempt for such foolish customs. Poor Phebe did not fare so well, and Archie was the one who took a base advantage of her as she stood innocently offering tea to Aunt Myra, whom she happened to meet just under the fatal bough. If his father's arrival had not rather upset him, I doubt if the dignified Chief would have done it, for he apologized at once in the handsomest manner, and caught the tray that nearly dropped from Phebe's hands.

Jamie boldly invited *all* the ladies to come and salute him;

and as for Uncle Jem, he behaved as if the entire room was a grove of mistletoe. Uncle Alec slyly laid a bit of it on Aunt Peace's cap, and then softly kissed her; which little joke seemed to please her very much, for she liked to have part in all the home pastimes, and Alec was her favorite nephew.

Charlie alone failed to catch his shy bird, and the oftener she escaped the more determined he was to ensnare her. When every other wile had been tried in vain, he got Archie to propose a game with forfeits.

"I understand that dodge," thought Rose, and was on her guard so carefully that not one among the pile soon collected belonged to her.

"Now let us redeem them and play something else," said Will, quite unconscious of the deeply laid plots all about him.

"One more round and then we will," answered the Prince, who had now baited his trap anew.

Just as the question came to Rose, Jamie's voice was heard in the hall crying distressfully, "Oh, come quick, quick!" Rose started up, missed the question, and was greeted with a general cry of "Forfeit! forfeit!" in which the little traitor came to join.

"Now I've got her," thought the young rascal, exulting in his fun-loving soul.

"Now I'm lost," thought Rose, as she gave up her pin-cushion with a sternly defiant look that would have daunted any one but the reckless Prince. In fact, it made even him think twice, and resolve to "let Rose off easy," she had been so clever.

"Here's a very pretty pawn, and what shall be done to redeem it?" asked Steve, holding the pin-cushion over Charlie's head, for he had insisted on being judge, and kept that for the last.

"Fine or superfine?"

"Super."

"Hum, well, she shall take old Mac under the mistletoe and kiss him prettily. Won't he be mad, though?"—and this bad boy chuckled over the discomfort he had caused two harmless beings.

There was an impressive pause among the young folks in their corner, for they all knew that Mac *would* "be mad," since he hated nonsense of this sort, and had gone to talk with the elders when the game began. At this moment he was standing before the fire, listening to a discussion between his uncles and his father, looking as wise as a young owl, and blissfully unconscious of the plots against him.

Charlie expected that Rose would say, "I won't!" therefore he was rather astonished, not to say gratified, when, after a look at the victim, she laughed suddenly, and, going up to the group of gentlemen, drew her *uncle* Mac under the mistletoe and surprised him with a hearty kiss.

"Thank you, my dear," said the innocent gentleman, looking much pleased at the unexpected honor.

"Oh, come; that's not fair," began Charlie. But Rose cut him short by saying, as she made him a fine courtesy,—

"You said 'Old Mac,' and though it was very disrespectful, I did it. That was your last chance, sir, and you've lost it."

He certainly had, for, as she spoke, Rose pulled down the mistletoe and threw it into the fire, while the boys jeered at the crest-fallen Prince, and exalted quick-witted Rose to the skies.

"What's the joke?" asked young Mac, waked out of a brown study by the laughter, in which the elders joined.

But there was a regular shout when, the matter having been explained to him, Mac took a meditative stare at Rose through his goggles, and said in a philosophical tone, "Well, I don't think I should have minded much if she *had* done it."

That tickled the lads immensely, and nothing but the appearance of a slight refection would have induced them to stop chaffing the poor Worm, who could not see any thing funny in the beautiful resignation he had shown on this trying occasion.

Soon after this, the discovery of Jamie curled up in the sofa corner, as sound asleep as a dormouse, suggested the propriety of going home, and a general move was made.

They were all standing about the hall lingering over the good-nights, when the sound of a voice softly singing "Sweet Home," made them pause and listen. It was Phebe, poor little Phebe, who never had a home, never knew the love of father or mother, brother or sister; who stood all alone in the wide world, yet was not sad nor afraid, but took her bits of happiness gratefully, and sung over her work without a thought of discontent.

I fancy the happy family standing there together remembered this and felt the beauty of it, for when the solitary voice came to the burden of its song, other voices took it up and finished it so sweetly, that the old house seemed to echo the word "Home" in the ears of both the orphan girls, who had just spent their first Christmas under its hospitable roof.

# Chapter XXI

## A SCARE

"BROTHER ALEC, you surely don't mean to allow that child to go out such a bitter cold day as this," said Mrs. Myra, looking into the study, where the Doctor sat reading his paper, one February morning.

"Why not? If a delicate invalid like yourself can bear it, surely my hearty girl can, especially as *she* is dressed for cold weather," answered Dr. Alec with provoking confidence.

"But you have no idea how sharp the wind is. I am chilled to the very marrow of my bones," answered Aunt Myra, chafing the end of her purple nose with her sombre glove.

"I don't doubt it, ma'am, if you *will* wear crape and silk instead of fur and flannel. Rosy goes out in all weathers, and will be none the worse for an hour's brisk skating."

"Well, I warn you that you are trifling with the child's health, and depending too much on the seeming improvement she has made this year. She is a delicate creature for all that, and will drop away suddenly at the first serious attack, as her poor mother did," croaked Aunt Myra, with a despondent wag of the big bonnet.

"I'll risk it," answered Dr. Alec, knitting his brows, as he always did when any allusion was made to that other Rose.

"Mark my words, you will repent it," and, with that awful prophecy, Aunt Myra departed like a black shadow.

Now it must be confessed that among the Doctor's failings—and he had his share—was a very masculine dislike of advice which was thrust upon him unasked. He always listened with respect to the great-aunts, and often consulted Mrs. Jessie; but the other three ladies tried his patience sorely, by constant warnings, complaints, and counsels. Aunt Myra was an especial trial, and he always turned contrary the moment she began to talk. He could not help it, and often laughed about it with comic frankness. Here now was a sample of it, for he had just been thinking that Rose had better defer her run till the wind went down and the sun was warmer. But Aunt Myra spoke, and he could not resist the temptation to make light of her advice, and let Rose brave the cold. He had no fear of its harming her, for she went out every day, and it was a great satisfaction to him to see her run down the avenue a minute afterward, with her skates on her arm, looking like a rosy-faced Esquimaux in her seal-skin suit, as she smiled at Aunt Myra stalking along as solemnly as a crow.

"I hope the child won't stay out long, for this wind *is* enough to chill the marrow in younger bones than Myra's," thought Dr. Alec, half an hour later, as he drove toward the city to see the few patients he had consented to take for old acquaintance' sake.

The thought returned several times that morning, for it *was* truly a bitter day, and, in spite of his bear-skin coat, the Doctor shivered. But he had great faith in Rose's good sense, and it never occurred to him that she was making a little Casabianca of herself, with the difference of freezing instead of burning at her post.

You see, Mac had made an appointment to meet her at a certain spot, and have a grand skating bout as soon as the few lessons he was allowed were over. She had promised to wait for him, and did so with a faithfulness that cost her dear, because Mac forgot his appointment when the lessons were done, and became absorbed in a chemical experiment, till a general combustion of gases drove him out of his laboratory. Then he suddenly remembered Rose, and would gladly have hurried away to her, but his mother forbade his going out, for the sharp wind would hurt his eyes.

"She will wait and wait, mother, for she always keeps her word, and I told her to hold on till I came," explained Mac, with visions of a shivering little figure watching on the windy hill-top.

"Of course, your uncle won't let her go out such a day as this. If he does, she will have the sense to come here for you, or to go home again when you don't appear," said Aunt Jane, returning to her "Watts on the Mind."

"I wish Steve would just cut up and see if she's there, since I can't go," began Mac, anxiously.

"Steve won't stir a peg, thank you. He's got his own toes to thaw out, and wants his dinner," answered Dandy, just in from school, and wrestling impatiently with his boots.

So Mac resigned himself, and Rose waited dutifully till dinner-time assured her that her waiting was in vain. She had done her best to keep warm, had skated till she was tired and hot, then stood watching others till she was chilled; tried to get up a glow again by trotting up and down the road, but failed to do so, and finally cuddled disconsolately under a pine-tree to wait and watch. When she at length started for home, she was benumbed with the cold, and could hardly make her way against the wind that buffeted the frost-bitten rose most unmercifully.

Dr. Alec was basking in the warmth of the study fire, after his drive, when the sound of a stifled sob made him hurry to the door and look anxiously into the hall. Rose lay in a shivering bunch near the register, with her things half off, wringing her hands, and trying not to cry with the pain returning warmth brought to her half-frozen fingers.

"My darling, what is it?" and Uncle Alec had her in his arms in a minute.

"Mac didn't come—I can't get warm—the fire makes me ache!" and with a long shiver Rose burst out crying, while her teeth chattered, and her poor little nose was so blue, it made one's heart ache to see it.

In less time than it takes to tell it, Dr. Alec had her on the sofa rolled up in the bear-skin coat, with Phebe rubbing her cold feet while he rubbed the aching hands, and Aunt Plenty made a comfortable hot drink, and Aunt Peace sent down her own foot-warmer and embroidered blanket "for the dear."

Full of remorseful tenderness, Uncle Alec worked over his new patient till she declared she was all right again. He would not let her get up to dinner, but fed her himself, and then forgot his own while he sat watching her fall into a drowse, for Aunt Plenty's cordial made her sleepy.

She lay so several hours, for the drowse deepened into a heavy sleep, and Uncle Alec, still at his post, saw with growing anxiety that a feverish color began to burn in her cheeks, that her breathing was quick and uneven, and now and then she gave a little moan, as if in pain. Suddenly she woke up with a start, and seeing Aunt Plenty bending over her, put out her arms like a sick child, saying wearily,—

"Please, could I go to bed?"

"The best place for you, deary. Take her right up, Alec; I've got the hot water ready, and after a nice bath, she shall have a cup of my sage tea, and be rolled up in blankets to sleep off her cold," answered the old lady, cheerily, as she bustled away to give orders.

"Are you in pain, darling?" asked Uncle Alec, as he carried her up.

"My side aches when I breathe, and I feel stiff and queer; but it isn't bad, so don't be troubled, uncle," whispered Rose, with a little hot hand against his cheek.

But the poor Doctor did look troubled, and had cause to do so, for just then Rose tried to laugh at Dolly charging into the room with a warming-pan, but could not, for the sharp pain that took her breath away, and made her cry out.

"Pleurisy," sighed Aunt Plenty, from the depths of the bath-tub.

"Pewmonia!" groaned Dolly, burrowing among the bed-clothes with the long-handled pan, as if bent on fishing up that treacherous disease.

"Oh, is it bad?" asked Phebe, nearly dropping a pail of hot water in her dismay, for she knew nothing of sickness, and Dolly's suggestion had a peculiarly dreadful sound to her.

"Hush!" ordered the Doctor, in a tone that silenced all fur-ther predictions, and made every one work with a will.

"Make her as comfortable as you can, and when she is in her little bed I'll come and say good-night," he added, when the bath was ready and the blankets browning nicely before the fire.

Then he went away to talk quite cheerfully to Aunt Peace about its being "only a chill;" after which he tramped up and down the hall, pulling his beard and knitting his brows, sure signs of great inward perturbation.

"I thought it would be too good luck to get through the year without a downfall. Confound my perversity! why couldn't I take Myra's advice and keep Rose at home. It's not fair that the poor child should suffer for my sinful over-confidence. She shall *not* suffer for it! Pneumonia, indeed! I defy it!" and he shook his fist in the ugly face of an Indian idol that happened to be before him, as if that particularly hideous god had some spite against his own little goddess.

In spite of his defiance his heart sunk when he saw Rose again, for the pain was worse, and the bath and blankets, the warming-pan and piping-hot sage tea, were all in vain. For several hours there was no rest for the poor child, and all man-ner of gloomy forebodings haunted the minds of those who hovered about her with faces full of the tenderest anxiety.

In the midst of the worst paroxysm Charlie came to leave a message from his mother, and was met by Phebe coming de-spondently downstairs with a mustard plaster that had brought no relief.

"What the dickens is the matter? You look as dismal as a tombstone," he said, as she held up her hand to stop his lively whistling.

"Miss Rose is dreadful sick."

"The deuce she is!"

"Don't swear, Mr. Charlie; she really is, and it's Mr. Mac's fault," and Phebe told the sad tale in a few sharp words, for she felt at war with the entire race of boys at that moment.

"I'll give it to him, make your mind easy about that," said Charlie, with an ominous doubling up of his fist. "But Rose isn't dangerously ill, is she?" he added anxiously, as Aunt Plenty was seen to trot across the upper hall, shaking a bottle violently as she went.

"Oh, but she is, though. The Doctor don't say much, but he don't call it a 'chill' any more. It's 'pleurisy' now, and I'm *so* afraid it will be *pewmonia* to-morrow," answered Phebe, with a despairing glance at the plaster.

Charlie exploded into a stifled laugh at the new pronunciation of pneumonia, to Phebe's great indignation.

"How can you have the heart to do it, and she in such horrid pain? Hark to that, and then laugh if you darst," she said with a tragic gesture, and her black eyes full of fire.

Charlie listened and heard little moans that went to his heart and made his face as sober as Phebe's. "O uncle, please stop the pain and let me rest a minute! Don't tell the boys I wasn't brave. I try to bear it, but it's so sharp I can't help crying."

Neither could Charlie, when he heard the broken voice say that; but, boy-like, he wouldn't own it, and said pettishly, as he rubbed his sleeve across his eyes,—

"Don't hold that confounded thing right under my nose; the mustard makes my eyes smart."

"Don't see how it can, when it hasn't any more strength in it than meal. The Doctor said so, and I'm going to get some better," began Phebe, not a bit ashamed of the great tears that were bedewing the condemned plaster.

"I'll go!" and Charlie was off like a shot, glad of an excuse to get out of sight for a few minutes.

When he came back all inconvenient emotion had been disposed of, and, having delivered a box of the hottest mustard procurable for money, he departed to "blow up" Mac, that being his next duty in his opinion. He did it so energetically and thoroughly, that the poor Worm was cast into the depths of remorseful despair, and went to bed that evening feeling that he was an outcast from among men, and bore the mark of Cain upon his brow.

Thanks to the skill of the Doctor, and the devotion of his

helpers, Rose grew easier about midnight, and all hoped that the worst was over. Phebe was making tea by the study fire, for the Doctor had forgotten to eat and drink since Rose was ill, and Aunt Plenty insisted on his having a "good, cordial dish of tea" after his exertions. A tap on the window startled Phebe, and, looking up, she saw a face peering in. She was not afraid, for a second look showed her that it was neither ghost nor burglar, but Mac, looking pale and wild in the wintry moonlight.

"Come and let a fellow in," he said in a low tone, and when he stood in the hall he clutched Phebe's arm, whispering gruffly, "How is Rose?"

"Thanks be to goodness, she's better," answered Phebe, with a smile that was like broad sunshine to the poor lad's anxious heart.

"And she will be all right again to-morrow?"

"Oh, dear, no. Dolly says she's sure to have rheumatic fever, if she don't have noo-monia!" answered Phebe, careful to pronounce the word rightly this time.

Down went Mac's face, and remorse began to gnaw at him again as he gave a great sigh and said doubtfully,—

"I suppose I couldn't see her?"

"Of course not at this time of night, when we want her to go to sleep!"

Mac opened his mouth to say something more, when a sneeze came upon him unawares, and a loud "Ah rash hoo!" awoke the echoes of the quiet house.

"Why didn't you stop it?" said Phebe reproachfully. "I dare say you've waked her up."

"Didn't know it was coming. Just my luck!" groaned Mac, turning to go before his unfortunate presence did more harm.

But a voice from the stair-head called softly, "Mac, come up; Rose wants to see you."

Up he went, and found his uncle waiting for him.

"What brings you here, at this hour, my boy?" asked the Doctor in a whisper.

"Charlie said it was all my fault, and if she died I'd killed her. I couldn't sleep, so I came to see how she was, and no one knows it but Steve," he said with such a troubled face and voice that the Doctor had not the heart to blame him.

Before he could say any thing more a feeble voice called "Mac!" and with a hasty "Stay a minute just to please her, and then slip away, for I want her to sleep," the Doctor led him into the room.

The face on the pillow looked very pale and childish, and the smile that welcomed Mac was very faint, for Rose was spent with pain, yet could not rest till she had said a word of comfort to her cousin.

"I knew your funny sneeze, and I guessed that you came to see how I did, though it is very late. Don't be worried. I'm better now, and it is my fault I was ill, not yours; for I needn't have been so silly as to wait in the cold just because I said I would."

Mac hastened to explain, to load himself with reproaches, and to beg her not to die on any account, for Charlie's lecture had made a deep impression on the poor boy's mind.

"I didn't know there was any danger of my dying," and Rose looked up at him with a solemn expression in her great eyes.

"Oh, I hope not; but people do sometimes go suddenly, you know, and I couldn't rest till I'd asked you to forgive me," faltered Mac, thinking that Rose looked very like an angel already, with the golden hair loose on the pillow, and the meekness of suffering on her little white face.

"I don't think I shall die; uncle won't let me; but if I do, remember I forgave you."

She looked at him with a tender light in her eyes, and, seeing how pathetic his dumb grief was, she added softly, drawing his head down: "I wouldn't kiss you under the mistletoe, but I will now, for I want you to be sure I do forgive and love you just the same."

That quite upset poor Mac; he could only murmur his thanks and get out of the room as fast as possible, to grope his way to the couch at the far end of the hall, and lie there till he fell asleep, worn out with trying not to "make a baby" of himself.

# Chapter XXII

## SOMETHING TO DO

WHATEVER danger there might have been from the effects of that sudden chill, it was soon over, though of course Aunt Myra refused to believe it, and Dr. Alec cherished his girl with redoubled vigilance and tenderness for months afterward. Rose quite enjoyed being sick, because as soon as the pain ended the fun began, and for a week or two she led the life of a little princess secluded in the Bower, while every one served, amused, and watched over her in the most delightful manner. But the Doctor was called away to see an old friend who was dangerously ill, and then Rose felt like a young bird deprived of its mother's sheltering wing; especially on one afternoon when the aunts were taking their naps, and the house was very still within while snow fell softly without.

"I'll go and hunt up Phebe, she is always nice and busy, and likes to have me help her. If Dolly is out of the way we can make caramels and surprise the boys when they come," Rose said to herself, as she threw down her book and felt ready for society of some sort.

She took the precaution to peep through the slide before she entered the kitchen, for Dolly allowed no messing when she was round. But the coast was clear, and no one but Phebe appeared, sitting at the table with her head on her arms apparently asleep. Rose was just about to wake her with a "Boo!" when she lifted her head, dried her wet eyes with her blue apron, and fell to work with a resolute face on something she was evidently much interested in. Rose could not make out what it was, and her curiosity was greatly excited, for Phebe was writing with a sputtering pen on some bits of brown paper, apparently copying something from a little book.

"I *must* know what the dear thing is about, and why she cried, and then set her lips tight and went to work with all her might," thought Rose, forgetting all about the caramels, and, going round to the door, she entered the kitchen, saying pleasantly,—

"Phebe, I want something to do. Can't you let me help you about any thing? or shall I be in the way?"

"Oh, dear, no, miss; I always love to have you round when things are tidy. What would you like to do?" answered Phebe, opening a drawer as if about to sweep her own affairs out of sight: but Rose stopped her, exclaiming, like a curious child,—

"Let me see! What is it? I won't tell if you'd rather not have Dolly know."

"I'm only trying to study a bit; but I'm so stupid I don't get on much," answered the girl reluctantly, permitting her little mistress to examine the poor contrivances she was trying to work with.

A broken slate that had blown off the roof, an inch or two of pencil, an old almanac for a reader, several bits of brown or yellow paper ironed smoothly and sewed together for a copy-book, and the copies sundry receipts written in Aunt Plenty's neat hand. These, with a small bottle of ink and a rusty pen, made up Phebe's outfit, and it was little wonder that she did not "get on" in spite of the patient persistence that dried the desponding tears and drove along the sputtering pen with a will.

"You may laugh if you want to, Miss Rose, I know my things are queer, and that's why I hide 'em; but I don't mind since you've found me out, and I ain't a bit ashamed except of being so backward at my age," said Phebe humbly, though her cheeks grew redder as she washed out some crooked capitals with a tear or two not yet dried upon the slate.

"Laugh at you! I feel more like crying to think what a selfish girl I am, to have loads of books and things and never remember to give you some. Why didn't you come and ask me, and not go struggling along alone in this way? It was very wrong of you, Phebe, and I'll never forgive you if you do so again," answered Rose, with one hand on Phebe's shoulder while the other gently turned the leaves of the poor little copy-book.

"I didn't like to ask for any thing more when you are so good to me all the time, miss, dear," began Phebe, looking up with grateful eyes.

"O you proud thing! just as if it wasn't fun to give away, and I had the best of it. Now, see here, I've got a plan and you mustn't say no, or I shall scold. I want something to do, and

I'm going to teach you all I know; it won't take long," and Rose laughed as she put her arm around Phebe's neck, and patted the smooth dark head with the kind little hand that so loved to give.

"It would be just heavenly!" and Phebe's face shone at the mere idea; but fell again as she added wistfully, "Only I'm afraid I ought not to let you do it, Miss Rose. It will take time, and maybe the Doctor wouldn't like it."

"He didn't want me to study much, but he never said a word about teaching, and I don't believe he will mind a bit. Any way, we can try it till he comes, so pack up your things and go right to my room and we'll begin this very day; I'd truly like to do it, and we'll have nice times, see if we don't!" cried Rose eagerly.

It was a pretty sight to see Phebe bundle her humble outfit into her apron, and spring up as if the desire of her heart had suddenly been made a happy fact to her; it was a still prettier sight to see Rose run gayly on before, smiling like a good fairy as she beckoned to the other, singing as she went,—

"The way into my parlor is up a winding stair,
    And many are the curious things I'll show you when you're
        there.
            Will you, will you walk in, Phebe dear?"

"Oh, won't I!" answered Phebe fervently, adding, as they entered the Bower, "You are the dearest spider that ever was, and I'm the happiest fly."

"I'm going to be very strict, so sit down in that chair and don't say a word till school is ready to open," ordered Rose, delighted with the prospect of such a useful and pleasant "something to do."

So Phebe sat demurely in her place while her new teacher laid forth books and slates, a pretty inkstand and a little globe; hastily tore a bit off her big sponge, sharpened pencils with more energy than skill, and when all was ready gave a prance of satisfaction that set the pupil laughing.

"Now the school is open, and I shall hear you read, so that I may know in which class to put you, Miss Moore," began Rose with great dignity, as she laid a book before her scholar, and sat down in the easy chair with a long rule in her hand.

Phebe did pretty well, only tripping now and then over a hard word, and pronouncing identical "identickle," in a sober way that tickled Rose, though never a smile betrayed her. The spelling lesson which followed was rather discouraging; Phebe's ideas of geography were very vague, and grammar was nowhere, though the pupil protested that she tried so hard to "talk nice like educated folks" that Dolly called her "a stuck-up piece who didn't know her place."

"Dolly's an old goose, so don't you mind her, for she will say 'nater,' 'vittles,' and 'doos' as long as she lives, and insist that they are right. You do talk very nicely, Phebe, I've observed it, and grammar will help you, and show why some things are right and others ain't,—are not, I mean," added Rose, correcting herself, and feeling that she must mind her own parts of speech if she was to serve as an example for Phebe.

When the arithmetic came the little teacher was surprised to find her scholar quicker in some things than herself, for Phebe had worked away at the columns in the butcher's and baker's books till she could add so quickly and correctly that Rose was amazed, and felt that in this branch the pupil would soon excel the teacher if she kept on at the same pace. Her praise cheered Phebe immensely, and they went bravely on, both getting so interested that time flew unheeded till Aunt Plenty appeared, exclaiming, as she stared at the two heads bent over one slate,—

"Bless my heart, what is going on now?"

"School, aunty. I'm teaching Phebe, and it's great fun!" cried Rose, looking up with a bright face.

But Phebe's was brighter, though she added, with a wistful look,—

"Maybe I ought to have asked leave first; only when Miss Rose proposed this, I was so happy I forgot to. Shall I stop, ma'am?"

"Of course not, child; I'm glad to see you fond of your book, and to find Rose helping you along. My blessed mother used to sit at work with her maids about her, teaching them many a useful thing in the good old fashion that's gone by now. Only don't neglect your work, dear, or let the books interfere with the duties."

As Aunt Plenty spoke, with her kind old face beaming approvingly upon the girls, Phebe glanced at the clock, saw that it pointed to five, knew that Dolly would soon be down, expecting to find preparations for supper under way, and, hastily dropping her pencil, she jumped up, saying,—

"Please, can I go? I'll clear up after I've done my chores."

"School is dismissed," answered Rose, and with a grateful "Thank you, heaps and heaps!" Phebe ran away singing the multiplication table as she set the tea ditto.

That was the way it began, and for a week the class of one went on with great pleasure and profit to all concerned; for the pupil proved a bright one, and came to her lessons as to a feast, while the young teacher did her best to be worthy the high opinion held of her, for Phebe firmly believed that Miss Rose knew *every thing* in the way of learning.

Of course the lads found out what was going on, and chaffed the girls about the "Seminary," as they called the new enterprise; but they thought it a good thing on the whole, kindly offered to give lessons in Greek and Latin gratis, and decided among themselves that "Rose was a little trump to give the Phebe-bird such a capital boost."

Rose herself had some doubts as to how it would strike her uncle, and concocted a wheedlesome speech which should at once convince him that it was the most useful, wholesome, and delightful plan ever devised. But she got no chance to deliver her address, for Dr. Alec came upon her so unexpectedly that it went out of her head entirely. She was sitting on the floor in the library, poring over a big book laid open in her lap, and knew nothing of the long-desired arrival till two large, warm hands met under her chin and gently turned her head back, so that some one could kiss her heartily on either cheek, while a fatherly voice said, half reproachfully, "Why is my girl brooding over a dusty Encyclopedia when she ought to be running to meet the old gentleman who couldn't get on another minute without her?"

"O uncle! I'm so glad! and so sorry! Why didn't you let us know what time you'd be here, or call out the minute you came? Haven't I been homesick for you? and now I'm so happy to have you back I could hug your dear old curly head off," cried Rose, as the Encyclopedia went down with a bang, and she up with a spring that carried her into Dr. Alec's arms, to be kept there in the sort of embrace a man gives to the dearest creature the world holds for him.

Presently he was in his easy chair with Rose upon his knee smiling up in his face and talking as fast as her tongue could go, while he watched her with an expression of supreme content, as he stroked the smooth round cheek, or held the little hand in his, rejoicing to see how rosy was the one, how plump and strong the other.

"*Have* you had a good time? *Did* you save the poor lady? *Aren't* you glad to be home again with your girl to torment you?"

"Yes, to all those questions. Now tell me what you've been at, little sinner? Aunty Plen says you want to consult me about some new and remarkable project which you have dared to start in my absence."

"She didn't tell you, I hope?"

"Not a word more except that you were rather doubtful how I'd take it, and so wanted to 'fess' yourself and get round me as you always try to do, though you don't often succeed. Now, then, own up and take the consequences."

So Rose told about her school in her pretty, earnest way, dwelling on Phebe's hunger for knowledge, and the delight it was to help her, adding, with a wise nod,—

"And it helps me too, uncle, for she is so quick and eager I have to do my best or she will get ahead of me in some things. To-day, now, she had the word 'cotton' in a lesson and asked all about it, and I was ashamed to find I really knew so little that I could only say that it was a plant that grew down South in a kind of a pod, and was made into cloth. That's what I was reading up when you came, and to-morrow I shall tell her all about it, and indigo too. So you see it teaches me also, and is as good as a general review of what I've learned, in a pleasanter way than going over it alone."

"You artful little baggage! that's the way you expect to get round me, is it? That's not studying, I suppose?"

"No, sir, it's teaching; and please, I like it much better than having a good time all by myself. Besides, you know, I adopted Phebe and promised to be a sister to her, so I am bound to keep my word, am I not?" answered Rose, looking both anxious and resolute as she waited for her sentence.

Dr. Alec was evidently already won, for Rose had described

the old slate and brown paper copy-book with pathetic effect, and the excellent man had not only decided to send Phebe to school long before the story was done, but reproached himself for forgetting his duty to one little girl in his love for another. So when Rose tried to look meek and failed utterly, he laughed and pinched her cheek, and answered in that genial way which adds such warmth and grace to any favor,—

"I haven't the slightest objection in the world. In fact, I was beginning to think I might let you go at your books again, moderately, since you are so well; and this is an excellent way to try your powers. Phebe is a brave, bright lass, and shall have a fair chance in the world, if we can give it to her, so that if she ever finds her friends they need not be ashamed of her."

"I think she has found some already," began Rose eagerly.

"Hey? what? has any one turned up since I've been gone?" asked Dr. Alec quickly, for it was a firm belief in the family that Phebe would prove to be "somebody" sooner or later.

"No, her best friend turned up when *you* came home, uncle," answered Rose with an approving pat, adding gratefully, "I can't half thank you for being so good to my girl, but she will, because I know she is going to make a woman to be proud of, she's so strong and true, and loving."

"Bless your dear heart, I haven't begun to do any thing yet, more shame to me! But I'm going at it now, and as soon as she gets on a bit, she shall go to school as long as she likes. How will that do for a beginning?"

"It will be 'just heavenly,' as Phebe says, for it is the wish of her life to 'get lots of schooling,' and she will be *too* happy when I tell her. May I, please?—it will be so lovely to see the dear thing open her big eyes and clap her hands at the splendid news."

"No one shall have a finger in this nice little pie; you shall do it all yourself, only don't go too fast, or make too many castles in the air, my dear; for time and patience must go into this pie of ours if it is to turn out well."

"Yes, uncle, only when it *is* opened won't 'the birds begin to sing?'" laughed Rose, taking a turn about the room as a vent for the joyful emotions that made her eyes shine. All of a sudden she stopped and asked soberly,—

"If Phebe goes to school who will do her work? I'm willing, if I can."

"Come here and I'll tell you a secret. Dolly's 'bones' are getting so troublesome, and her dear old temper so bad, that the aunts have decided to pension her off and let her go and live with her daughter, who has married very well. I saw her this week, and she'd like to have her mother come, so in the spring we shall have a grand change, and get a new cook and chambergirl if any can be found to suit our honored relatives."

"Oh, me! how can I ever get on without Phebe? Couldn't she stay, just so I could see her? I'd pay her board rather than have her go, I'm *so* fond of her."

How Dr. Alec laughed at that proposal, and how satisfied Rose was when he explained that Phebe was still to be her maid, with no duties except such as she could easily perform between school-hours.

"She is a proud creature, for all her humble ways, and even from us would not take a favor if she did not earn it somehow. So this arrangement makes it all square and comfortable, you see, and she will pay for the schooling by curling these goldilocks a dozen times a day if you let her."

"Your plans are always *so* wise and kind! That's why they work so well, I suppose, and why people let you do what you like with them. I really don't see how other girls get along without an Uncle Alec!" answered Rose, with a sigh of pity for those who had missed so great a blessing.

When Phebe was told the splendid news, she did not "stand on her head with rapture," as Charlie prophesied she would, but took it quietly, because it was such a happy thing she had no words "big and beautiful enough to thank them in," she said; but every hour of her day was brightened by this granted wish, and dedicated to the service of those who gave it.

Her heart was so full of content that it overflowed in music, and the sweet voice singing all about the house gave thanks so blithely that no other words were needed. Her willing feet were never tired of taking steps for those who had smoothed her way; her skilful hands were always busy in some labor of love for them, and on the face fast growing in comeliness there was an almost womanly expression of devotion, which proved how well Phebe had already learned one of life's great lessons, —gratitude.

# Chapter XXIII

## PEACE-MAKING

"STEVE, I want you to tell me something," said Rose to Dandy, who was making faces at himself in the glass, while he waited for an answer to the note he brought from his mother to Aunt Plenty.

"P'raps I will, and p'raps I won't. What is it?"

"Haven't Arch and Charlie quarrelled?"

"Dare say; we fellows are always having little rows, you know. I do believe a sty is coming on my starboard eye," and Steve affected to be absorbed in a survey of his yellow lashes.

"No, that won't do; I want to know all about it; for I'm sure something more serious than a 'little row' is the matter. Come, please tell me, Stenie, there's a dear."

"Botheration! you don't want me to turn telltale, do you?" growled Steve, pulling his top-knot, as he always did when perplexed.

"Yes, I do," was Rose's decided answer,—for she saw from his manner that she was right, and determined to have the secret out of him if coaxing would do it. "I don't wish you to tell things to every one, of course, but to me you may, and you must, because I have a right to know. You boys need somebody to look after you, and I'm going to do it, for girls are nice peace-makers, and know how to manage people. Uncle said so, and he is never wrong."

Steve was about to indulge in a derisive hoot at the idea of her looking after them, but a sudden thought restrained him, and suggested a way in which he could satisfy Rose, and better himself at the same time.

"What will you give me if I'll tell you every bit about it?" he asked, with a sudden red in his cheeks, and an uneasy look in his eyes, for he was half ashamed of the proposition.

"What do you want?" and Rose looked up rather surprised at his question.

"I'd like to borrow some money. I shouldn't think of asking you, only Mac never has a cent since he's set up his old chemical shop, where he'll blow himself to bits some day, and you and uncle will have the fun of putting him together again," and Steve tried to look as if the idea amused him.

"I'll lend it to you with pleasure, so tell away," said Rose, bound to get at the secret.

Evidently much relieved by the promise, Steve set his top-knot cheerfully erect again, and briefly stated the case.

"As you say, it's all right to tell *you*, but don't let the boys know I blabbed, or Prince will take my head off. You see, Archie don't like some of the fellows Charlie goes with, and cuts 'em. That makes Prince mad, and he holds on just to plague Arch, so they don't speak to one another, if they can help it, and that's the row."

"Are those boys bad?" asked Rose, anxiously.

"Guess not, only rather wild. They are older than our fellows, but they like Prince, he's such a jolly boy; sings so well, dances jigs and breakdowns, you know, and plays any game that's going. He beat Morse at billiards, and that's something to brag of, for Morse thinks he knows every thing. I saw the match, and it was great fun!"

Steve got quite excited over the prowess of Charlie, whom he admired immensely, and tried to imitate. Rose did not know half the danger of such gifts and tastes as Charlie's, but felt instinctively that something must be wrong if Archie disapproved.

"If Prince likes any billiard-playing boy better than Archie, I don't think much of his sense," she said severely.

"Of course he doesn't; but, you see, Charlie and Arch are both as proud as they can be, and won't give in. I suppose Arch *is* right, but I don't blame Charlie a bit for liking to be with the others sometimes, they are such a jolly set," and Steve shook his head morally, even while his eye twinkled over the memory of some of the exploits of the "jolly set."

"Oh, dear me!" sighed Rose, "I don't see what I can do about it, but I wish the boys would make up, for Prince can't come to any harm with Archie, he's so good and sensible."

"That's the trouble; Arch preaches, and Prince won't stand it. He told Arch he was a prig and a parson, and Arch told him he wasn't a gentleman. My boots! weren't they both mad though! I thought for a minute they'd pitch into one another and have it out. Wish they had, and not gone stalking round stiff and glum ever since. Mac and I settle our rows with a bat or so over the head, and then we are all right."

Rose couldn't help laughing as Steve sparred away at a fat sofa-pillow, to illustrate his meaning; and, having given it several scientific whacks, he pulled down his cuffs and smiled upon her with benign pity for her feminine ignorance of this summary way of settling a quarrel.

"What droll things boys are!" she said, with a mixture of admiration and perplexity in her face, which Steve accepted as a compliment to his sex.

"We are a pretty clever invention, miss, and you can't get on without us," he answered, with his nose in the air. Then, taking a sudden plunge into business, he added, "How about that bit of money you were going to lend me? I've told, now you pay up."

"Of course I will! How much do you want?" and Rose pulled out her purse.

"*Could* you spare five dollars? I want to pay a little debt of honor that is rather pressing," and Steve put on a mannish air that was comical to see.

"Aren't all debts honorable?" asked innocent Rose.

"Yes, of course; but this is a bet I made, and it ought to be settled up at once," began Steve, finding it awkward to explain.

"Oh, don't bet, it's not right, and I know your father wouldn't like it. Promise you won't do so again, please promise!" and Rose held fast the hand into which she had just put the money.

"Well, I won't. It's worried me a good deal, but I was joked into it. Much obliged, cousin, I'm all right now," and Steve departed hastily.

Having decided to be a peace-maker, Rose waited for an opportunity, and very soon it came.

She was spending the day with Aunt Clara, who had been entertaining some young guests, and invited Rose to meet them, for she thought it high time her niece conquered her bashfulness, and saw a little of society. Dinner was over, and every one had gone. Aunt Clara was resting before going out to an evening party, and Rose was waiting for Charlie to come and take her home.

She sat alone in the elegant drawing-room, feeling particularly nice and pretty, for she had her best frock on, a pair of gold bands her aunt had just given her, and a tea-rose bud in her sash, like the beautiful Miss Van Tassel, whom every one admired. She had spread out her little skirts to the best advantage, and, leaning back in a luxurious chair, sat admiring her own feet in new slippers with rosettes almost as big as dahlias. Presently Charlie came lounging in, looking rather sleepy and queer, Rose thought. On seeing her, however, he roused up and said with a smile that ended in a gape,—

"I thought you were with mother, so I took forty winks after I got those girls off. Now, I'm at your service, Rosamunda, whenever you like."

"You look as if your head ached. If it does, don't mind me. I'm not afraid to run home alone, it's so early," answered Rose, observing the flushed cheeks and heavy eyes of her cousin.

"I think I see myself letting you do it. Champagne always makes my head ache, but the air will set me up."

"Why do you drink it, then?" asked Rose, anxiously.

"Can't help it, when I'm host. Now, don't *you* begin to lecture; I've had enough of Archie's old-fashioned notions, and I don't want any more."

Charlie's tone was decidedly cross, and his whole manner so unlike his usual merry good-nature, that Rose felt crushed, and answered meekly,—

"I wasn't going to lecture, only when people like other people, they can't bear to see them suffer pain."

That brought Charlie round at once, for Rose's lips trembled a little, though she tried to hide it by smelling the flower she pulled from her sash.

"I'm a regular bear, and I beg your pardon for being so cross, Rosy," he said in the old frank way that was so winning.

"I wish you'd beg Archie's too, and be good friends again. You never were cross when *he* was your chum," Rose said, looking up at him as he bent toward her from the low chimney-piece, where he had been leaning his elbows.

In an instant he stood as stiff and straight as a ramrod, and the heavy eyes kindled with an angry spark as he said, in his high and mighty manner,—

"You'd better not meddle with what you don't understand, cousin."

"But I do understand, and it troubles me very much to see you so cold and stiff to one another. You always used to be together, and now you hardly speak. You are so ready to beg my pardon I don't see why you can't beg Archie's, if you are in the wrong."

"I'm not!" this was so short and sharp that Rose started, and Charlie added in a calmer but still very haughty tone: "A gentleman always begs pardon when he has been rude to a lady, but one man doesn't apologize to another man who has insulted him."

"Oh, my heart, what a pepperpot!" thought Rose, and, hoping to make him laugh, she added slyly: "I was not talking about men, but boys, and one of them a Prince, who ought to set a good example to his subjects."

But Charlie would not relent, and tried to turn the subject by saying gravely, as he unfastened the little gold ring from his watch-guard,—

"I've broken my word, so I want to give this back and free you from the bargain. I'm sorry, but I think it a foolish promise, and don't intend to keep it. Choose a pair of ear-rings to suit yourself, as my forfeit. You have a right to wear them now."

"No, I can only wear one, and that is no use, for Archie will keep *his* word I'm sure!" Rose was so mortified and grieved at this downfall of her hopes that she spoke sharply, and would not take the ring the deserter offered her.

He shrugged his shoulders, and threw it into her lap, trying to look cool and careless, but failing entirely, for he was ashamed of himself, and out of sorts generally. Rose wanted to cry, but pride would not let her, and, being very angry, she relieved herself by talk instead of tears. Looking pale and excited, she rose out of her chair, cast away the ring, and said in a voice that she vainly tried to keep steady,—

"You are not at all the boy I thought you were, and I don't respect you one bit. I've tried to help you be good, but you won't let me, and I shall not try any more. You talk a great deal about being a gentleman, but you are not, for you've broken your word, and I can never trust you again. I don't wish you to go home with me. I'd rather have Mary. Good-night."

And with that last dreadful blow, Rose walked out of the room, leaving Charlie as much astonished as if one of his pet pigeons had flown in his face and pecked at him. She was so seldom angry, that when her temper did get the better of her it made a deep impression on the lads, for it was generally a righteous sort of indignation at some injustice or wrong-doing, not childish passion.

Her little thunder-storm cleared off in a sob or two as she put on her things in the entry-closet, and when she emerged she looked the brighter for the shower. A hasty good-night to Aunt Clara,—now under the hands of the hair-dresser,—and then she crept down to find Mary the maid. But Mary was out, so was the man, and Rose slipped away by the back-door, flattering herself that she had escaped the awkwardness of having Charlie for escort.

There she was mistaken, however, for the gate had hardly closed behind her when a well-known tramp was heard, and the Prince was beside her, saying in a tone of penitent politeness that banished Rose's wrath like magic,—

"You needn't speak to me if you don't choose, but I must see you safely home, cousin."

She turned at once, put out her hand, and answered heartily,—

"*I* was the cross one. Please forgive me, and let's be friends again."

Now that was better than a dozen sermons on the beauty of forgiveness, and did Charlie more good, for it showed him how sweet humility was, and proved that Rose practised as she preached.

He shook the hand warmly, then drew it through his arm and said, as if anxious to recover the good opinion with the loss of which he had been threatened,—

"Look here, Rosy, I've put the ring back, and I'm going to try again. But you don't know how hard it is to stand being laughed at."

"Yes, I do! Ariadne plagues me every time I see her, because I don't wear ear-rings after all the trouble I had getting ready for them."

"Ah, but her twaddle isn't half as bad as the chaffing *I* get. It takes a deal of pluck to hold out when you are told you are tied to an apron-string, and all that sort of thing," sighed Charlie.

"I thought you had a 'deal of pluck,' as you call it. The boys all say you are the bravest of the seven," said Rose.

"So I am about some things, but I *cannot* bear to be laughed at."

"It is hard, but if one is right won't that make it easier?"

"Not to me; it might to a pious parson like Arch."

"Please don't call him names! I guess *he* has what is called moral courage, and *you* physical courage. Uncle explained the difference to me, and moral is the best, though often it doesn't look so," said Rose thoughtfully.

Charlie didn't like that, and answered quickly, "I don't believe he'd stand it any better than I do, if he had those fellows at him."

"Perhaps that's why he keeps out of their way, and wants you to."

Rose had him there, and Charlie felt it, but would not give in just yet, though he was going fast, for, somehow, in the dark he seemed to see things clearer than in the light, and found it very easy to be confidential when it was "only Rose."

"If he was my brother, now, he'd have some right to interfere," began Charlie, in an injured tone.

"I wish he was!" cried Rose.

"So do I," answered Charlie, and then they both laughed at his inconsistency.

The laugh did them good, and when Prince spoke again, it was in a different tone,—pensive, not proud nor perverse.

"You see, it's hard upon me that I have no brothers and sisters. The others are better off and needn't go abroad for chums if they don't like. *I* am all alone, and I'd be thankful even for a little sister."

Rose thought that very pathetic, and, overlooking the uncomplimentary word "even" in that last sentence, she said, with a timid sort of earnestness that conquered her cousin at once,—

"Play I was a little sister. I know I'm silly, but perhaps I'm better than nothing, and I'd dearly love to do it."

"So should I! and we will, for you are not silly, my dear, but a very sensible girl, we all think, and I'm proud to have you for a sister. There, now!" and Charlie looked down at the curly head bobbing along beside him, with real affection in his face.

Rose gave a skip of pleasure, and laid one seal-skin mitten over the other on his arm, as she said happily,—

"That's so nice of you! Now, you needn't be lonely any more, and I'll try to fill Archie's place till he comes back, for I know he will, as soon as you let him."

"Well, I don't mind telling *you* that while he was my mate I never missed brothers and sisters, or wanted any one else; but since he cast me off, I'll be hanged if I don't feel as forlorn as old Crusoe before Friday turned up."

This burst of confidence confirmed Rose in her purpose of winning Charlie's Mentor back to him, but she said no more, contented to have done so well. They parted excellent friends, and Prince went home, wondering why "a fellow didn't mind saying things to a girl or woman which they would die before they'd own to another fellow."

Rose also had some sage reflections upon the subject, and fell asleep thinking that there were a great many curious things in this world, and feeling that she was beginning to find out some of them.

Next day she trudged up the hill to see Archie, and having told him as much as she thought best about her talk with Charlie, begged him to forget and forgive.

"I've been thinking that perhaps I ought to, though I *am* in the right. I'm no end fond of Charlie, and he's the best-hearted lad alive; but he can't say No, and that will play the mischief with him, if he does not take care," said Archie in his grave, kind way. "While father was home, I was very busy with him, so Prince got into a set I don't like. They try to be fast, and think it's manly, and they flatter him, and lead him on to do all sorts of things,—play for money, and bet, and loaf about. I hate to have him do so, and tried to stop it, but went to work the wrong way, so we got into a mess."

"He is all ready to make up if you don't say much, for he owned to me he *was* wrong; but I don't think he will own it to you, in words," began Rose.

"I don't care for that; if he'll just drop those rowdies and come back, I'll hold my tongue and not preach. I wonder if he owes those fellows money, and so doesn't like to break off till he can pay it. I hope not, but don't dare to ask; though, perhaps, Steve knows, he's always after Prince, more's the pity," and Archie looked anxious.

"I think Steve does know, for he talked about debts of honor the day I gave him—" There Rose stopped short and turned scarlet.

But Archie ordered her to "fess," and had the whole story in five minutes, for none dared disobey the Chief. He completed her affliction by putting a five-dollar bill into her pocket by main force, looking both indignant and resolute as he said,—

"Never do so, again; but send Steve to me, if he is afraid to go to his father. Charlie had nothing to do with that; *he* wouldn't borrow a penny of a girl, don't think it. But that's the harm he does Steve, who adores him, and tries to be like him in all things. Don't say a word; I'll make it all right, and no one shall blame you."

"Oh, me! I always make trouble by trying to help, and then letting out the wrong thing," sighed Rose, much depressed by her slip of the tongue.

Archie comforted her with the novel remark that it was always best to tell the truth, and made her quite cheerful by promising to heal the breach with Charlie, as soon as possible.

He kept his word so well that the very next afternoon, as Rose looked out of the window, she beheld the joyful spectacle of Archie and Prince coming up the avenue, arm-in-arm, as of old, talking away as if to make up for the unhappy silence of the past weeks.

Rose dropped her work, hurried to the door, and, opening it wide, stood there smiling down upon them so happily, that the faces of the lads brightened as they ran up the steps eager to show that all was well with them.

"Here's our little peace-maker!" said Archie, shaking hands with vigor.

But Charlie added, with a look that made Rose very proud and happy, "And *my* little sister."

# *Chapter XXIV*

## WHICH?

"UNCLE, I have discovered what girls are made for," said Rose, the day after the reconciliation of Archie and the Prince.

"Well, my dear, what is it?" asked Dr. Alec, who was "planking the deck," as he called his daily promenade up and down the hall.

"To take care of boys," answered Rose, quite beaming with satisfaction as she spoke. "Phebe laughed when I told her, and said she thought girls had better learn to take care of themselves first. But that's because *she* hasn't got seven boy-cousins as I have."

"She is right, nevertheless, Rosy, and so are you, for the two things go together, and in helping seven lads you are unconsciously doing much to improve one lass," said Dr. Alec, stopping to nod and smile at the bright-faced figure resting on the old bamboo chair, after a lively game of battledore and shuttlecock, in place of a run which a storm prevented.

"Am I? I'm glad of that, but really, uncle, I do feel as if I *must* take care of the boys, for they come to me in all sorts of troubles, and ask advice, and I like it *so* much. Only I don't always know what to do, and I'm going to consult you privately and then surprise them with my wisdom."

"All right, my dear; what's the first worry? I see you have something on your little mind, so come and tell uncle."

Rose put her arm in his, and, pacing to and fro, told him all about Charlie, asking what she could do to keep him straight, and be a real sister to him.

"Could you make up your mind to go and stay with Aunt Clara a month?" asked the Doctor, when she ended.

"Yes, sir; but I shouldn't like it. Do you really want me to go?"

"The best cure for Charlie is a daily dose of Rose water, or Rose and water; will you go and see that he takes it?" laughed Dr. Alec.

"You mean that if I'm there and try to make it pleasant, he will stay at home and keep out of mischief?"

"Exactly."

"But *could* I make it pleasant? He would want the boys."

"No danger but he'd have the boys, for they swarm after you like bees after their queen. Haven't you found that out?"

"Aunt Plen often says they never used to be here half so much before I came, but I never thought *I* made the difference, it seemed so natural to have them round."

"Little Modesty doesn't know what a magnet she is; but she will find it out some day," and the Doctor softly stroked the cheek that had grown rosy with pleasure at the thought of being so much loved. "Now, you see, if I move the magnet to Aunt Clara's, the lads will go there as sure as iron to steel, and Charlie will be so happy at home he won't care for these mischievous mates of his; I hope," added the Doctor, well knowing how hard it was to wean a seventeen-year-old boy from his first taste of what is called "seeing life," which, alas! often ends in seeing death.

"I'll go, uncle, right away! Aunt Clara is always asking me, and will be glad to get me. I shall have to dress and dine late, and see lots of company, and be very fashionable, but I'll try not to let it hurt me; and if I get in a puzzle or worried about any thing I can run to you," answered Rose, good-will conquering timidity.

So it was decided, and without saying much about the real reason for this visit, Rose was transplanted to Aunt Clara's, feeling that she had a work to do, and very eager to do it well.

Dr. Alec was right about the bees, for the boys did follow their queen, and astonished Mrs. Clara by their sudden assiduity in making calls, dropping in to dinner, and getting up evening frolics. Charlie was a devoted host, and tried to show his gratitude by being very kind to his "little sister," for he guessed why she came, and his heart was touched by her artless endeavors to "help him be good."

Rose often longed to be back in the old house, with the simpler pleasures and more useful duties of the life there; but, having made up her mind, in spite of Phebe, that "girls were made to take care of boys," her motherly little soul found much to enjoy in the new task she had undertaken.

It was a pretty sight to see the one earnest, sweet-faced girl among the flock of tall lads, trying to understand, to help and please them with a patient affection that worked many a small miracle unperceived. Slang, rough manners, and careless habits were banished or bettered by the presence of a little gentle-woman; and all the manly virtues cropping up were encour-aged by the hearty admiration bestowed upon them by one whose good opinion all valued more than they confessed; while Rose tried to imitate the good qualities she praised in them, to put away her girlish vanities and fears, to be strong and just and frank and brave as well as modest, kind, and beautiful.

This trial worked so well that when the month was over, Mac and Steve demanded a visit in their turn, and Rose went, feeling that she would like to hear grim Aunt Jane say, as Aunt Clara did at parting, "I wish I could keep you all my life, dear."

After Mac and Steve had had their turn, Archie and Com-pany bore her away for some weeks; and with them she was so happy, she felt as if she would like to stay for ever, if she could have Uncle Alec also.

Of course, Aunt Myra could not be neglected, and, with se-cret despair, Rose went to the "Mausoleum," as the boys called her gloomy abode. Fortunately, she was very near home, and Dr. Alec dropped in so often that her visit was far less dismal than she expected. Between them, they actually made Aunt Myra laugh heartily more than once; and Rose did her so much good by letting in the sunshine, singing about the silent house, cooking wholesome messes, and amusing the old lady with funny little lectures on physiology, that she forgot to take her pills and gave up "Mum's Elixir," because she slept so well, after the long walks and drives she was beguiled into taking, that she needed no narcotic.

So the winter flew rapidly away, and it was May before Rose was fairly settled again at home. They called her the "Monthly Rose," because she had spent a month with each of the aunts, and left such pleasant memories of bloom and fragrance be-hind her, that all wanted the family flower back again.

Dr. Alec rejoiced greatly over his recovered treasure; but as the time drew near when his year of experiment ended, he had many a secret fear that Rose might like to make her home for the next twelvemonth with Aunt Jessie, or even Aunt Clara, for Charlie's sake. He said nothing, but waited with much anxiety for the day when the matter should be decided; and while he waited he did his best to finish as far as possible the task he had begun so well.

Rose was very happy now, being out nearly all day enjoying the beautiful awakening of the world, for spring came bright and early, as if anxious to do its part. The old horse-chestnuts budded round her windows, green things sprung up like magic in the garden under her hands, hardy flowers bloomed as fast as they could, the birds sang blithely overhead, and every day a chorus of pleasant voices cried, "Good morning, cousin, isn't it jolly weather?"

No one remembered the date of the eventful conversation which resulted in the Doctor's experiment (no one but himself at least); so when the aunts were invited to tea one Saturday they came quite unsuspiciously, and were all sitting together having a social chat, when Brother Alec entered with two photographs in his hand.

"Do you remember that?" he said, showing one to Aunt Clara, who happened to be nearest.

"Yes, indeed; it is very like her when she came. Quite her sad, unchildlike expression, and thin little face, with the big dark eyes."

The picture was passed round, and all agreed that "it was very like Rose a year ago." This point being settled, the Doctor showed the second picture, which was received with great approbation, and pronounced a "charming likeness."

It certainly was, and a striking contrast to the first one, for it was a blooming, smiling face, full of girlish spirit and health, with no sign of melancholy, though the soft eyes were thoughtful, and the lines about the lips betrayed a sensitive nature.

Dr. Alec set both photographs on the chimney-piece, and, falling back a step or two, surveyed them with infinite satisfaction for several minutes, then wheeled round, saying briefly, as he pointed to the two faces,—

"Time is up; how do you think my experiment has succeeded, ladies?"

"Bless me, so it is!" cried Aunt Plenty, dropping a stitch in her surprise.

"Beautifully, dear," answered Aunt Peace, smiling entire approval.

"She certainly *has* improved, but appearances are deceitful, and she had no constitution to build upon," croaked Aunt Myra.

"I am willing to allow that, as far as mere health goes, the experiment *is* a success," graciously observed Aunt Jane, unable to forget Rose's kindness to her Mac.

"So am I; and I'll go farther, for I really do believe Alec has done wonders for the child; she will be a beauty in two or three years," added Aunt Clara, feeling that she could say nothing better than that.

"I always knew he would succeed, and I'm so glad you all allow it, for he deserves more credit than you know, and more praise than he will ever get," cried Aunt Jessie, clapping her hands with an enthusiasm that caused Jamie's little red stocking to wave like a triumphal banner in the air.

Dr. Alec made them a splendid bow, looking much gratified, and then said soberly,—

"Thank you; now the question is, shall I go on?—for this is only the beginning. None of you know the hinderances I've had, the mistakes I've made, the study I've given the case, and the anxiety I've often felt. Sister Myra is right in one thing,—Rose *is* a delicate creature, quick to flourish in the sunshine, and as quick to droop without it. She has no special weakness, but inherits her mother's sensitive nature, and needs the wisest, tenderest care to keep a very ardent little soul from wearing out a finely organized little body. I think I have found the right treatment, and, with you to help me, I believe we may build up a lovely and a noble woman, who will be a pride and comfort to us all."

There Dr. Alec stopped to get his breath, for he had spoken very earnestly, and his voice got a little husky over the last words. A gentle murmur from the aunts seemed to encourage him, and he went on with an engaging smile, for the good man was slyly trying to win all the ladies to vote for him when the time came.

"Now, I don't wish to be selfish or arbitrary, because I am her guardian, and I shall leave Rose free to choose for herself. We all want her, and if she likes to make her home with any of you rather than with me, she shall do so. In fact, I encouraged her visits last winter, that she might see what we can all offer her, and judge where she will be happiest. Is not that the fairest way? Will you agree to abide by her choice, as I do?"

"Yes, we will," said all the aunts, in quite a flutter of excitement, at the prospect of having Rose for a whole year.

"Good! she will be here directly, and then we will settle the question for another year. A most important year, mind you, for she has got a good start, and will blossom rapidly now if all goes well with her. So I beg of you don't undo my work, but deal very wisely and gently with my little girl, for if any harm come to her, I think it would break my heart."

As he spoke, Dr. Alec turned his back abruptly and affected to be examining the pictures again; but the aunts understood how dear the child was to the solitary man who had loved her mother years ago, and who now found his happiness in cherishing the little Rose who was so like her. The good ladies nodded and sighed, and telegraphed to one another that none of them would complain if not chosen, or ever try to rob Brother Alec of his "Heart's Delight," as the boys called Rose.

Just then a pleasant sound of happy voices came up from the garden, and smiles broke out on all serious faces. Dr. Alec turned at once, saying, as he threw back his head, "There she is; now for it!"

The cousins had been a-Maying, and soon came flocking in laden with the spoils.

"Here is our bonny Scotch rose with all her thorns about her," said Dr. Alec, surveying her with unusual pride and tenderness, as she went to show Aunt Peace her basket full of early flowers, fresh leaves, and curious lichens.

"Leave your clutter in the hall, boys, and sit quietly down if you choose to stop here, for we are busy," said Aunt Plenty, shaking her finger at the turbulent clan, who were bubbling over with the jollity born of spring sunshine and healthy exercise.

"Of course, we choose to stay! Wouldn't miss our Saturday high tea for any thing," said the Chief, as he restored order among his men with a nod, a word, and an occasional shake.

"What is up? a court-martial?" asked Charlie, looking at the

"THE COUSINS HAD BEEN A-MAYING."

assembled ladies with affected awe and real curiosity, for their faces betrayed that some interesting business was afloat.

Dr. Alec explained in a few words, which he made as brief and calm as he could; but the effect was exciting, nevertheless, for each of the lads began at once to bribe, entice, and wheedle "our cousin" to choose his home.

"You really ought to come to us for mother's sake, as a relish, you know, for she must be perfectly satiated with boys," began Archie, using the strongest argument he could think of at the moment.

"Ah! yes," she thought, "*he* wants me most! I've often

longed to give him something that he wished for very much, and now I can."

So, when, at a sudden gesture from Aunt Peace, silence fell, Rose said slowly, with a pretty color in her cheeks, and a beseeching look about the room, as if asking pardon of the boys,—

"It's very hard to choose when everybody is so fond of me; therefore I think I'd better go to the one who seems to need me most."

"No, dear, the one you love the best and will be happiest with," said Dr. Alec quickly, as a doleful sniff from Aunt Myra, and a murmur of "My sainted Caroline," made Rose pause and look that way.

"Take time, cousin; don't be in a hurry to make up your mind, and remember, 'Codlin's your friend,'" added Charlie, hopeful still.

"I don't want any time! I *know* who I love best, who I'm happiest with, and I choose uncle. Will he have me?" cried Rose, in a tone that produced a sympathetic thrill among the hearers, it was so full of tender confidence and love.

If she really had any doubt, the look in Dr. Alec's face banished it without a word, as he opened wide his arms, and she ran into them, feeling that home was there.

No one spoke for a minute, but there were signs of emotion among the aunts, which warned the boys to bestir themselves before the water-works began to play. So they took hands and began to prance about uncle and niece, singing, with sudden inspiration, the nursery rhyme,—

"Ring around a Rosy!"

Of course that put an end to all sentiment, and Rose emerged laughing from Dr. Alec's bosom, with the mark of a waistcoat button nicely imprinted on her left cheek. He saw it, and said with a merry kiss that half effaced it, "This is my ewe lamb, and I have set my mark on her, so no one can steal her away."

That tickled the boys, and they set up a shout of

"Uncle had a little lamb!"

But Rose hushed the noise by slipping into the circle, and

making them dance prettily,—like lads and lasses round a May-pole; while Phebe, coming in with fresh water for the flowers, began to twitter, chirp, and coo, as if all the birds of the air had come to join in the spring revel of the eight cousins.

END OF PART FIRST.

# ROSE IN BLOOM

## A SEQUEL TO
## "EIGHT COUSINS"

*WITH ILLUSTRATIONS*

# PREFACE

As authors may be supposed to know better than any one else what they intended to do when writing a book, I beg leave to say that there is no moral to this story. Rose is not designed for a model girl: and the Sequel was simply written in fulfilment of a promise; hoping to afford some amusement, and perhaps here and there a helpful hint, to other roses getting ready to bloom.

L. M. ALCOTT.

SEPTEMBER, 1876.

# CONTENTS

# Chapter I

## COMING HOME

---

Three young men stood together on a wharf one bright October day, awaiting the arrival of an ocean steamer with an impatience which found a vent in lively skirmishes with a small lad, who pervaded the premises like a will-o'-the-wisp, and afforded much amusement to the other groups assembled there.

"They are the Campbells, waiting for their cousin, who has been abroad several years with her uncle, the Doctor," whispered one lady to another, as the handsomest of the young men touched his hat to her as he passed, lugging the boy, whom he had just rescued from a little expedition down among the piles.

"Which is that?" asked the stranger.

"Prince Charlie, as he's called,—a fine fellow, the most promising of the seven; but a little fast, people say," answered the first speaker, with a shake of the head.

"Are the others his brothers?"

"No, cousins. The elder is Archie, a most exemplary young man. He has just gone into business with the merchant uncle, and bids fair to be an honor to his family. The other, with the eye-glasses and no gloves, is Mac, the odd one, just out of college."

"And the boy?"

"Oh, he is Jamie, the youngest brother of Archibald, and the pet of the whole family. Mercy on us! he'll be in if they don't hold on to him."

The ladies' chat came to a sudden end just there; for, by the time Jamie had been fished out of a hogshead, the steamer hove in sight and every thing else was forgotten. As it swung slowly round to enter the dock, a boyish voice shouted,—

"There she is! I see her and uncle and Phebe! Hooray for Cousin Rose!" and three small cheers were given with a will by Jamie, as he stood on a post waving his arms like a windmill, while his brother held on to the tail of his jacket.

Yes, there they were,—Uncle Alec swinging his hat like a boy, with Phebe smiling and nodding on one side, and Rose kissing both hands delightedly on the other, as she recognized familiar faces and heard familiar voices welcoming her home.

"Bless her dear heart, she's bonnier than ever! Looks like a Madonna,—doesn't she?—with that blue cloak round her, and her bright hair flying in the wind!" said Charlie excitedly, as they watched the group upon the deck with eager eyes.

"Madonnas don't wear hats like that. Rose hasn't changed much, but Phebe has. Why, she's a regular beauty!" answered Archie, staring with all his might at the dark-eyed young woman, with the brilliant color and glossy, black braids shining in the sun.

"Dear old uncle! doesn't it seem good to have him back?" was all Mac said; but he was not looking at "dear old uncle," as he made the fervent remark, for he saw only the slender blonde girl near by, and stretched out his hands to meet hers, forgetful of the green water tumbling between them.

During the confusion that reigned for a moment as the steamer settled to her moorings, Rose looked down into the three faces upturned to hers, and seemed to read in them something that both pleased and pained her. It was only a glance, and her own eyes were full; but through the mist of happy tears she received the impression that Archie was about the same, that Mac had decidedly improved, and that something was amiss with Charlie. There was no time for observation, however; for in a moment the shoreward rush began, and, before she could grasp her travelling bag, Jamie was clinging to her like an ecstatic young bear. She was with difficulty released from his embrace, to fall into the gentler ones of the elder cousins, who took advantage of the general excitement to welcome both blooming girls with affectionate impartiality. Then the wanderers were borne ashore in a triumphal procession, while Jamie danced rapturous jigs before them even on the gangway.

Archie remained to help his uncle get the luggage through the Custom House, and the others escorted the damsels home. No sooner were they shut up in a carriage, however, than a new and curious constraint seemed to fall upon the young people; for they realized, all at once, that their former playmates were men and women now. Fortunately, Jamie was quite free from this feeling of restraint, and, sitting bodkin-wise between the ladies, took all sorts of liberties with them and their belongings.

"Well, my mannikin, what do you think of us?" asked Rose, to break an awkward pause.

"You've both grown so pretty, I can't decide which I like best. Phebe is the biggest and brightest looking, and I was always fond of Phebe; but, somehow you are so kind of sweet and precious, I really think I *must* hug you again," and the small youth did it tempestuously.

"If you love me best, I shall not mind a bit about your thinking Phebe the handsomest, because she *is.* Isn't she, boys?" asked Rose, with a mischievous look at the gentlemen opposite, whose faces expressed a respectful admiration which much amused her.

"I'm so dazzled by the brilliancy and beauty that has suddenly burst upon me, I have no words to express my emotions," answered Charlie, gallantly dodging the dangerous question.

"I can't say yet, for I have not had time to look at any one. I will now, if you don't mind;" and, to the great amusement of the rest, Mac gravely adjusted his eye-glasses and took an observation.

"Well?" said Phebe, smiling and blushing under his honest stare, yet seeming not to resent it as she did the lordly sort of approval which made her answer the glance of Charlie's audacious blue eyes with a flash of her black ones.

"I think if you were my sister, I should be very proud of you, because your face shows what I admire more than its beauty,—truth and courage, Phebe," answered Mac, with a little bow, full of such genuine respect that surprise and pleasure brought a sudden dew to quench the fire of the girl's eyes, and soothe the sensitive pride of the girl's heart.

Rose clapped her hands just as she used to do when any thing delighted her, and beamed at Mac approvingly, as she said,—

"Now that's a criticism worth having, and we are much obliged. I was sure *you'd* admire my Phebe when you knew her: but I didn't believe you would be wise enough to see it at once; and you have gone up many pegs in my estimation, I assure you."

"I was always fond of mineralogy you remember, and I've been tapping round a good deal lately, so I've learned to know precious metals when I see them," Mac said with his shrewd smile.

"That is the last hobby, then? Your letters have amused us immensely; for each one had a new theory or experiment, and the latest was always the best. I thought uncle would have died of laughing over the vegetarian mania: it was so funny to imagine you living on bread and milk, baked apples, and potatoes roasted in your own fire," continued Rose, changing the subject again.

"This old chap was the laughing-stock of his class. They called him Don Quixote; and the way he went at windmills of all sorts was a sight to see," put in Charlie, evidently feeling that Mac had been patted on the head quite as much as was good for him.

"But in spite of that the Don got through college with all the honors. Oh, wasn't I proud when Aunt Jane wrote us about it! and didn't she rejoice that her boy kept at the head of his class, and won the medal!" cried Rose, shaking Mac by both hands in a way that caused Charlie to wish "the old chap" had been left behind with Dr. Alec.

"Oh come, that's all mother's nonsense. I began earlier than the other fellows and liked it better: so I don't deserve any praise. Prince is right, though: I did make a regular jack of myself; but, on the whole, I'm not sure that my wild oats weren't better than some I've seen sowed. Anyway, they didn't cost much, and I'm none the worse for them," said Mac, placidly.

"I know what 'wild oats' mean. I heard Uncle Mac say Charlie was sowing 'em too fast, and I asked mamma, so she told me. And I know that he was suspelled or expended, I don't remember which, but it was something bad, and Aunt Clara cried," added Jamie, all in one breath; for he possessed a fatal gift of making *malapropos* remarks, which caused him to be a terror to his family.

"Do you want to go on the box again?" demanded Prince, with a warning frown.

"No, I don't."

"Then hold your tongue."

"Well, Mac needn't kick me; for I was only"—began the culprit, innocently trying to make a bad matter worse.

"That will do," interrupted Charlie, sternly, and James subsided a crushed boy, consoling himself with Rose's new watch for the indignities he suffered at the hands of the "old fellows" as he vengefully called his elders.

Mac and Charlie immediately began to talk as hard as their tongues could wag, bringing up all sorts of pleasant subjects so successfully that peals of laughter made passers-by look after the merry load with sympathetic smiles.

An avalanche of aunts fell upon Rose as soon as she reached home, and for the rest of the day the old house buzzed like a beehive. Evening found the whole tribe collected in the drawing-rooms, with the exception of Aunt Peace, whose place was empty now.

Naturally enough, the elders settled into one group after a while, and the young fellows clustered about the girls, like butterflies around two attractive flowers. Dr. Alec was the central figure in one room and Rose in the other; for the little girl, whom they had all loved and petted, had bloomed into a woman; and two years of absence had wrought a curious change in the relative positions of the cousins, especially the three elder ones, who eyed her with a mixture of boyish affection and manly admiration that was both new and pleasant.

Something sweet yet spirited about her charmed them and piqued their curiosity; for she was not quite like other girls, and rather startled them now and then by some independent little speech or act, which made them look at one another with a sly smile, as if reminded that Rose was "uncle's girl."

Let us listen, as in duty bound, to what the elders are saying first; for they are already building castles in the air for the boys and girls to inhabit.

"Dear child! how nice it is to see her safely back, so well and happy and like her sweet little self!" said Aunt Plenty, folding her hands as if giving thanks for a great happiness.

"I shouldn't wonder if you found that you'd brought a fire-brand into the family, Alec. Two, in fact; for Phebe is a fine girl, and the lads have found it out already, if I'm not mistaken," added Uncle Mac, with a nod toward the other room.

All eyes followed his, and a highly suggestive tableau presented itself to the paternal and maternal audience in the back parlor.

Rose and Phebe, sitting side by side on the sofa, had evidently assumed at once the places which they were destined to fill by right of youth, sex, and beauty; for Phebe had long since ceased to be the maid and become the friend, and Rose meant to have that fact established at once.

Jamie occupied the rug, on which Will and Geordie stood at ease, showing their uniforms to the best advantage; for they were now in a great school, where military drill was the delight of their souls. Steve posed gracefully in an arm-chair, with Mac lounging over the back of it; while Archie leaned on one corner of the low chimney-piece, looking down at Phebe as she listened to his chat with smiling lips, and cheeks almost as rich in color as the carnations in her belt.

But Charlie was particularly effective, although he sat upon a music-stool, that most trying position for any man not gifted with grace in the management of his legs. Fortunately Prince was, and had fallen into an easy attitude, with one arm over the back of the sofa, his handsome head bent a little, as he monopolized Rose, with a devoted air and a very becoming expression of contentment on his face.

Aunt Clara smiled as if well pleased; Aunt Jessie looked thoughtful; Aunt Jane's keen eyes went from dapper Steve to broad-shouldered Mac with an anxious glance; Mrs. Myra murmured something about her "blessed Caroline;" and Aunt Plenty said warmly,—

"Bless the dears! any one might be proud of such a bonny flock of bairns as that."

"I am all ready to play chaperon as soon as you please, Alec; for I suppose the dear girl will come out at once, as she did not before you went away. My services won't be wanted long, I fancy; for with her many advantages she will be carried off in her first season or I'm much mistaken," said Mrs. Clara, with significant nods and smiles.

"You must settle all those matters with Rose: I am no longer captain, only first mate now, you know," answered Dr. Alec, adding soberly, half to himself, half to his brother,—"I wonder people are in such haste to 'bring out' their daughters, as it's called. To me there is something almost pathetic in the sight of a young girl standing on the threshold of the world, so innocent and hopeful, so ignorant of all that lies before her, and usually so ill prepared to meet the ups and downs of life. We do our duty better by the boys; but the poor little women are seldom provided with any armor worth having; and, sooner or later, they are sure to need it, for every one must fight her own battle, and only the brave and strong can win."

"You can't reproach yourself with neglect of that sort, Alec, for you have done your duty faithfully by George's girl; and I envy you the pride and happiness of having such a daughter, for she is that to you," answered old Mac, unexpectedly betraying the paternal sort of tenderness men seldom feel for their sons.

"I've tried, Mac, and I *am* both proud and happy; but with every year my anxiety seems to increase. I've done my best to fit Rose for what may come, as far as I can foresee it; but now she must stand alone, and all my care is powerless to keep her heart from aching, her life from being saddened by mistakes, or thwarted by the acts of others. I can only stand by, ready to share her joy and sorrow, and watch her shape her life."

"Why, Alec, what is the child going to do, that you need look so solemn?" exclaimed Mrs. Clara, who seemed to have assumed a sort of right to Rose already.

"Hark! and let her tell you herself," answered Dr. Alec, as Rose's voice was heard saying very earnestly,—

"Now you have all told your plans for the future, why don't you ask us ours?"

"Because we know that there is only one thing for a pretty girl to do,—break a dozen or so of hearts before she finds one to suit, then marry and settle," answered Charlie, as if no other reply was possible.

"That may be the case with many, but not with us; for Phebe and I believe that it is as much a right and a duty for women to do something with their lives as for men; and we are not going to be satisfied with such frivolous parts as you give us," cried Rose, with kindling eyes. "I mean what I say, and you cannot laugh me down. Would *you* be contented to be told to enjoy yourself for a little while, then marry and do nothing more till you die?" she added, turning to Archie.

"Of course not: that is only a part of a man's life," he answered decidedly.

"A very precious and lovely part, but not *all*," continued Rose; "neither should it be for a woman: for we've got minds and souls as well as hearts; ambition and talents, as well as beauty and accomplishments; and we want to live and learn as well as love and be loved. I'm sick of being told that is all a woman is fit for! I won't have anything to do with love till I prove that I am something beside a housekeeper and baby-tender!"

"Heaven preserve us! here's woman's rights with a vengeance!" cried Charlie, starting up with mock horror, while the others regarded Rose with mingled surprise and amusement, evidently fancying it all a girlish outbreak.

"Ah, you needn't pretend to be shocked: you will be in earnest presently; for this is only the beginning of my strong-mindedness," continued Rose, nothing daunted by the smiles of good-natured incredulity or derision on the faces of her cousins. "I have made up my mind not to be cheated out of the real things that make one good and happy; and, just because I'm a rich girl, fold my hands and drift as so many do. I haven't lived with Phebe all these years in vain: I know what courage and self-reliance can do for one; and I sometimes wish I hadn't a penny in the world so that I could go and earn my bread with her, and be as brave and independent as she will be pretty soon."

It was evident that Rose was in earnest now; for, as she spoke, she turned to her friend with such respect as well as love in her face that the look told better than any words how heartily the rich girl appreciated the virtues hard experience had given the poor girl, and how eagerly she desired to earn what all her fortune could not buy for her.

Something in the glance exchanged between the friends impressed the young men in spite of their prejudices; and it was in a perfectly serious tone that Archie said,—

"I fancy you'll find your hands full, cousin, if you want work; for I've heard people say that wealth has its troubles and trials as well as poverty."

"I know it, and I'm going to try and fill my place well. I've got some capital little plans all made, and have begun to study my profession already," answered Rose, with an energetic nod.

"Could I ask what it is to be?" inquired Charlie, in a tone of awe.

"Guess!" and Rose looked up at him with an expression half-earnest, half-merry.

"Well, I should say that you were fitted for a beauty and a belle; but, as that is evidently not to your taste, I am afraid you are going to study medicine and be a doctor. Won't your patients have a heavenly time though? It will be easy dying with an angel to poison them."

"Now, Charlie, that's base of you, when you know how well women have succeeded in this profession, and what a comfort Dr. Mary Kirk was to dear Aunt Peace. I did want to study medicine; but uncle thought it wouldn't do to have so many M.D.'s in one family, since Mac thinks of trying it. Besides, I seem to have other work put into my hands that I am better fitted for."

"You are fitted for any thing that is generous and good; and I'll stand by you, no matter what you've chosen," cried Mac heartily; for this was a new style of talk from a girl's lips, and he liked it immensely.

"Philanthropy is a generous, good, and beautiful profession; and I've chosen it for mine because I have much to give. I'm only the steward of the fortune papa left me; and I think, if I use it wisely for the happiness of others, it will be more blest than if I keep it all for myself."

Very sweetly and simply was this said, but it was curious to see how differently the various hearers received it.

Charlie shot a quick look at his mother, who exclaimed, as if in spite of herself,—

"Now, Alec, *are* you going to let that girl squander a fine fortune on all sorts of charitable nonsense and wild schemes, for the prevention of pauperism and crime?"

"'They who give to the poor lend to the Lord,' and practical Christianity is the kind He loves the best," was all Dr. Alec answered; but it silenced the aunts, and caused even prudent Uncle Mac to think with sudden satisfaction of certain secret investments he had made, which paid him no interest but the thanks of the poor.

Archie and Mac looked well pleased, and promised their advice and assistance with the enthusiasm of generous young hearts. Steve shook his head, but said nothing; and the lads on the rug at once proposed founding a hospital for invalid dogs and horses, white mice, and wounded heroes.

"Don't you think that will be a better way for a woman to spend her life, than in dancing, dressing, and husband-hunting, Charlie?" asked Rose, observing his silence and anxious for his approval.

"Very pretty for a little while, and very effective too; for I don't know any thing more captivating than a sweet girl in a meek little bonnet, going on charitable errands and glorifying poor people's houses with a delightful mixture of beauty and benevolence. Fortunately, the dear souls soon tire of it, but it's heavenly while it lasts."

Charlie spoke in a tone of mingled admiration and contempt, and smiled a superior sort of smile, as if he understood all the innocent delusions as well as the artful devices of the sex, and expected nothing more from them. It both surprised and grieved Rose, for it did not sound like the Charlie she had left two years ago. But she only said, with a reproachful look and a proud little gesture of head and hand, as if she put the subject aside since it was not treated with respect,—

"I am sorry you have so low an opinion of women: there *was* a time when you believed in them sincerely."

"I do still, upon my word I do! They haven't a more devoted admirer and slave in the world than I am. Just try me and see," cried Charlie, gallantly kissing his hand to the sex in general.

But Rose was not appeased, and gave a disdainful shrug, as she answered with a look in her eyes that his lordship did not like,—

"Thank you: I don't want admirers or slaves, but friends and helpers. I've lived so long with a wise, good man that I am rather hard to suit, perhaps; but I don't intend to lower my standard, and any one who cares for my regard must at least try to live up to it."

"Whew! here's a wrathful dove! Come and smooth her ruffled plumage, Mac. I'll dodge before I do further mischief," and Charlie strolled away into the other room, privately lamenting that Uncle Alec had spoiled a fine girl by making her strong-minded.

He wished himself back again in five minutes; for Mac said

something that produced a gale of laughter, and when he took a look over his shoulder the "wrathful dove" was cooing so peacefully and pleasantly he was sorely tempted to return and share the fun. But Charlie had been spoiled by too much indulgence, and it was hard for him to own himself in the wrong even when he knew it. He always got what he wanted sooner or later; and, having long ago made up his mind that Rose and her fortune were to be his, he was secretly displeased at the new plans and beliefs of the young lady, but flattered himself that they would soon be changed when she saw how unfashionable and inconvenient they were.

Musing over the delightful future he had laid out, he made himself comfortable in the sofa corner near his mother, till the appearance of a slight refection caused both groups to melt into one. Aunt Plenty believed in eating and drinking; so the slightest excuse for festivity delighted her hospitable soul, and on this joyful occasion she surpassed herself.

It was during this informal banquet that Rose, roaming about from one admiring relative to another, came upon the three younger lads, who were having a quiet little scuffle in a secluded corner.

"Come out here and let me have a look at you," she said enticingly; for she predicted an explosion and public disgrace if peace was not speedily restored.

Hastily smoothing themselves down, the young gentlemen presented three flushed and merry countenances for inspection, feeling highly honored by the command.

"Dear me, how you two have grown! You big things! how dare you get ahead of me in this way?" she said, standing on tiptoe to pat the curly pates before her; for Will and Geordie had shot up like weeds, and now grinned cheerfully down upon her as she surveyed them in comic amazement.

"The Campbells are all fine, tall fellows; and we mean to be the best of the lot. Shouldn't wonder if we were six-footers, like Grandpa," observed Will proudly, looking so like a young Shanghae rooster, all legs and an insignificant head, that Rose kept her countenance with difficulty.

"We shall broaden out when we get our growth. We are taller than Steve now, a half a head, both of us," added Geordie, with his nose in the air.

Rose turned to look at Steve, and, with a sudden smile, beckoned to him. He dropped his napkin, and flew to obey the summons; for she was queen of the hour, and he had openly announced his deathless loyalty.

"Tell the other boys to come here. I've a fancy to stand you all in a row and look you over, as you did me that dreadful day when you nearly frightened me out of my wits," she said, laughing at the memory of it as she spoke.

They came in a body, and, standing shoulder to shoulder, made such an imposing array that the young commander was rather daunted for a moment. But she had seen too much of the world lately to be abashed by a trifle; and the desire to try a girlish test gave her courage to face the line of smiling cousins with dignity and spirit.

"Now I'm going to stare at you as you stared at me. It is my revenge on you seven bad boys for entrapping one poor little girl, and enjoying her alarm. I'm not a bit afraid of you now; so tremble and beware!"

As she spoke, Rose looked up into Archie's face and nodded approvingly; for the steady gray eyes met hers fairly, and softened as they did so,—a becoming change, for naturally they were rather keen than kind.

"A true Campbell, bless you!" she said, and shook his hand heartily as she passed on.

Charlie came next, and here she felt less satisfied, though scarcely conscious why; for, as she looked, there came a defiant sort of flash, changing suddenly to something warmer than anger, stronger than pride, making her shrink a little and say, hastily,—

"I don't find the Charlie I left; but the Prince is there still, I see."

Turning to Mac with a sense of relief, she gently took off his "winkers," as Jamie called them, and looked straight into the honest blue eyes that looked straight back at her, full of a frank and friendly affection that warmed her heart, and made her own eyes brighten as she gave back the glasses, saying, with a look and tone of cordial satisfaction,—

"*You* are not changed, my dear old Mac; and I'm so glad of that!"

"Now say something extra sweet to me, because I'm the

flower of the family," said Steve, twirling the blond moustache, which was evidently the pride of his life.

Rose saw at a glance that Dandy deserved his name more than ever, and promptly quenched his vanities by answering, with a provoking laugh,—

"Then the name of the flower of the family is Cock's-comb."

"Ah, ha! who's got it now?" jeered Will.

"Let us off easy, please," whispered Geordie, mindful that their turn came next.

"You blessed beanstalks! I'm proud of you: only don't grow quite out of sight, or ever be ashamed to look a woman in the face," answered Rose, with a gentle pat on the cheek of either bashful young giant; for both were as red as peonies, though their boyish eyes were as clear and calm as summer lakes.

"Now me!" And Jamie assumed his manliest air, feeling that he did not appear to advantage among his tall kinsmen. But he went to the head of the class in every one's opinion when Rose put her arms round him, saying, with a kiss,—

"You must be my boy now; for all the others are too old, and I want a faithful little page to do my errands for me."

"I will, I will! and I'll marry you too, if you'll just hold on till I grow up!" cried Jamie, rather losing his head at this sudden promotion.

"Bless the baby, what is he talking about?" laughed Rose, looking down at her little knight, as he clung about her with grateful ardor.

"Oh, I heard the aunts say that you'd better marry one of us, and keep the property in the family; so I speak first, because you are very fond of me, and I *do* love curls."

Alas for Jamie! this awful speech had hardly left his innocent lips when Will and Geordie swept him out of the room like a whirlwind; and the howls of that hapless boy were heard from the torture-hall, where being shut into the skeleton-case was one of the mildest punishments inflicted upon him.

Dismay fell upon the unfortunates who remained: but their confusion was soon ended; for Rose, with a look which they had never seen upon her face before, dismissed them with the brief command, "Break ranks,—the review is over," and walked away to Phebe.

"Confound that boy! You ought to shut him up, or gag him!" fumed Charlie, irritably.

"He shall be attended to," answered poor Archie, who was trying to bring up the little marplot with the success of most parents and guardians.

"The whole thing was deuced disagreeable," growled Steve, who felt that he had not distinguished himself in the late engagement.

"Truth generally is," observed Mac dryly, as he strolled away with his odd smile.

As if he suspected discord somewhere, Dr. Alec proposed music at this crisis; and the young people felt that it was a happy thought.

"I want you to hear both my birds; for they have improved immensely, and I am very proud of them," said the Doctor, twirling up the stool and pulling out the old music-books.

"I had better come first, for after you have heard the nightingale you won't care for the canary," added Rose, wishing to put Phebe at her ease; for she sat among them looking like a picture, but rather shy and silent, remembering the days when her place was in the kitchen.

"I'll give you some of the dear old songs you used to like so much. This was a favorite, I think;" and sitting down she sang the first familiar air that came, and sang it well in a pleasant, but by no means finished, manner.

It chanced to be "The Birks of Aberfeldie," and vividly recalled the time when Mac was ill, and she took care of him. The memory was sweet to her, and involuntarily her eye wandered in search of him. He was not far away, sitting just as he used to sit when she soothed his most despondent moods,— astride of a chair with his head down on his arms, as if the song suggested the attitude. Her heart quite softened to him as she looked, and she decided to forgive *him* if no one else; for she was sure that he had no mercenary plans about her tiresome money.

Charlie had assumed a pensive air, and fixed his fine eyes upon her with an expression of tender admiration, which made her laugh in spite of all her efforts to seem unconscious of it. She was both amused and annoyed at his very evident desire to remind her of certain sentimental passages in the last year of their girl and boyhood, and to change what she had considered a childish joke into romantic earnest. This did not suit her; for, young as she was, Rose had very serious ideas of love, and had no intention of being beguiled into even a flirtation with her handsome cousin.

So Charlie attitudinized unnoticed, and was getting rather out of temper when Phebe began to sing; and he forgot all about himself in admiration of her. It took every one by surprise: for two years of foreign training added to several at home had worked wonders; and the beautiful voice that used to warble cheerily over pots and kettles, now rang out melodiously or melted to a mellow music that woke a sympathetic thrill in those who listened. Rose glowed with pride as she accompanied her friend; for Phebe was in her own world now,—a lovely world where no depressing memory of poor-house or kitchen, ignorance or loneliness, came to trouble her; a happy world where she could be herself, and rule others by the magic of her sweet gift.

Yes, Phebe was herself now, and showed it in the change that came over her at the first note of music. No longer shy and silent, no longer the image of a handsome girl, but a blooming woman, alive and full of the eloquence her art gave her, as she laid her hands softly together, fixed her eye on the light, and just poured out her song as simply and joyfully as the lark does soaring toward the sun.

"My faith, Alec! that's the sort of voice that wins a man's heart out of his breast!" exclaimed Uncle Mac, wiping his eyes after one of the plaintive ballads that never grow old.

"So it would!" answered Dr. Alec, delightedly.

"So it has," added Archie to himself; and he was right: for, just at that moment, he fell in love with Phebe. He actually did, and could fix the time almost to a second: for, at a quarter past nine, he merely thought her a very charming young person; at twenty minutes past, he considered her the loveliest woman he ever beheld; at five and twenty minutes past, she was an angel singing his soul away; and at half after nine he was a lost man, floating over a delicious sea to that temporary heaven on earth where lovers usually land after the first rapturous plunge.

If any one had mentioned this astonishing fact, nobody

"Phebe began to sing."

would have believed it; nevertheless, it was quite true: and sober, business-like Archie suddenly discovered a fund of romance at the bottom of his hitherto well-conducted heart that amazed him. He was not quite clear what had happened to him at first, and sat about in a dazed sort of way; seeing, hearing, knowing nothing but Phebe: while the unconscious idol found something wanting in the cordial praise so modestly received, because Mr. Archie never said a word.

This was one of the remarkable things which occurred that evening; another was that Mac paid Rose a compliment, which was such an unprecedented fact, it produced a great sensation, though only one person heard it.

Everybody had gone but Mac and his father, who was busy with the Doctor. Aunt Plenty was counting the teaspoons in the dining-room, and Phebe was helping her as of old. Mac and Rose were alone,—he apparently in a brown study, leaning his elbows on the chimney-piece; and she lying back in a low chair, looking thoughtfully at the fire. She was tired; and the quiet was grateful to her: so she kept silence and Mac respectfully held his tongue. Presently, however, she became conscious that he was looking at her as intently as eyes and glasses could do it; and, without stirring from her comfortable attitude, she said, smiling up at him,—

"He looks as wise as an owl: I wonder what he's thinking about?"

"You, cousin."

"Something good, I hope?"

"I was thinking Leigh Hunt was about right when he said, 'A girl is the sweetest thing God ever made.'"

"Why, Mac!" and Rose sat bolt upright with an astonished face: this was such an entirely unexpected sort of remark for the philosopher to make.

Evidently interested in the new discovery, Mac placidly continued, "Do you know, it seems as if I never really saw a girl before, or had any idea what agreeable creatures they could be. I fancy you are a remarkably good specimen, Rose."

"No, indeed! I'm only hearty and happy; and being safe at home again may make me look better than usual perhaps: but I'm no beauty except to uncle."

"'Hearty and happy,'—that must be it," echoed Mac, soberly

investigating the problem. "Most girls are sickly or silly, I think I have observed; and that is probably why I am so struck with you."

"Of all queer boys you are the queerest! Do you really mean that you don't like or notice girls?" asked Rose, much amused at this new peculiarity of her studious cousin.

"Well, no: I am only conscious of two sorts,—noisy and quiet ones. I prefer the latter: but, as a general thing, I don't notice any of them much more than I do flies, unless they bother me; then I'd like to flap them away; but, as that won't do, I hide."

Rose leaned back and laughed till her eyes were full: it was so comical to hear Mac sink his voice to a confidential whisper at the last words, and see him smile with sinful satisfaction at the memory of the tormentors he had eluded.

"You needn't laugh: it's a fact, I assure you. Charlie likes the creatures, and they spoil him; Steve follows suit, of course. Archie is a respectful slave when he can't help himself. As for me, I don't often give them a chance; and, when I get caught, I talk science and dead languages till they run for their lives. Now and then I find a sensible one, and then we get on excellently."

"A sad prospect for Phebe and me," sighed Rose, trying to keep sober.

"Phebe is evidently a quiet one. I know she is sensible, or you wouldn't care for her. I can see that she is pleasant to look at, so I fancy I shall like her. As for you, I helped bring you up; therefore I am a little anxious to see how you turn out. I was afraid your foreign polish might spoil you, but I think it has not. In fact, I find you quite satisfactory so far, if you don't mind my saying it. I don't quite know what the charm is, though. Must be the power of inward graces, since you insist that you have no outward ones."

Mac was peering at her with a shrewd smile on his lips, but such a kindly look behind the glasses, that she found both words and glance very pleasant, and answered merrily,—

"I am glad you approve of me, and much obliged for your care of my early youth. I hope to be a credit to you, and depend on your keeping me straight; for I'm afraid I shall be spoilt among you all."

"I'll keep my eye on you upon one condition," replied the youthful Mentor.

"Name it."

"If you are going to have a lot of lovers round, I wash my hands of you. If not, I'm your man."

"You must be sheep-dog, and help keep them away; for I don't want any yet awhile; and, between ourselves, I don't believe I shall have any if it is known that I am strong-minded. That fact will scare most men away like a yellow flag," said Rose: for, thanks to Dr. Alec's guardianship, she had wasted neither heart nor time in the foolish flirtations so many girls fritter away their youth upon.

"Hum! I rather doubt that," muttered Mac, as he surveyed the damsel before him.

She certainly did not look unpleasantly strong-minded, for she *was* beautiful in spite of her modest denials. Beautiful with the truest sort of beauty; for nobility of character lent its subtle charm to the bloom of youth, the freshness of health, the innocence of a nature whose sweet maidenliness Mac felt but could not describe. Gentle yet full of spirit, and all aglow with the earnestness that suggests lovely possibilities, and makes one hope that such human flowers may have heaven's purest air and warmest sunshine to blossom in.

"Wait and see," answered Rose; then, as her uncle's voice was heard in the hall, she held out her hand, adding pleasantly, "The old times are to begin again, so come soon and tell me all your doings, and help me with mine just as you used to do."

"You really mean it?" and Mac looked much pleased.

"I really do. You are so little altered, except to grow big, that I don't feel at all strange with you, and want to begin where we left off."

"That will be capital. Good-night, cousin," and to her great amazement he gave her a hearty kiss.

"Oh, but that is not the old way at all!" cried Rose, stepping back in merry confusion; while the audacious youth assumed an air of mild surprise, as he innocently asked,—

"Didn't we always say good-night in that way? I had an impression that we did, and were to begin just as we left off."

"Of course not; no power on earth would have bribed you

to do it, as you know well enough. I don't mind the first night, but we are too old for that sort of thing now."

"I'll remember. It was the force of habit, I suppose; for I'm sure I must have done it in former times, it seemed so natural. Coming, father!" and Mac retired, evidently convinced he was right.

"Dear old thing! he is as much a boy as ever, and that is such a comfort; for some of the others have grown up very fast," said Rose to herself, recalling Charlie's sentimental airs, and Archie's beatified expression while Phebe sang.

# *Chapter II*

## OLD FRIENDS WITH NEW FACES

"IT is *so* good to be at home again! I wonder how we ever made up our minds to go away!" exclaimed Rose, as she went roaming about the old house next morning, full of the satisfaction one feels at revisiting familiar nooks and corners, and finding them unchanged.

"That we might have the pleasure of coming back again," answered Phebe, walking down the hall beside her little mistress, as happy as she.

"Every thing seems just as we left it, even to the rose-leaves we used to tuck in here," continued the younger girl, peeping into one of the tall India jars that stood about the hall.

"Don't you remember how Jamie and Pokey used to play Forty Thieves with them, and how you tried to get into that blue one and got stuck, and the other boys found us before I could pull you out?" asked Phebe, laughing.

"Yes, indeed; and speaking of angels one is apt to hear the rustling of their wings," added Rose, as a shrill whistle came up the avenue, accompanied by the clatter of hoofs.

"It is the circus!" cried Phebe, gaily, as they both recalled the red cart and the charge of the Clan.

There was only one boy now, alas! but he made noise enough for half a dozen; and, before Rose could run to the door, Jamie came bouncing in with a "shining morning face," a bat over his shoulder, a red and white jockey cap on his head, one pocket bulging with a big ball, the other overflowing with cookies, and his mouth full of the apple he was just finishing off in hot haste.

"Morning! I just looked in to make sure you'd really come, and see that you were all right," he observed, saluting with the bat and doffing the gay cap with one effective twitch.

"Good-morning, dear. Yes, we are really here, and getting to rights as fast as possible. But it seems to me you are rather gorgeous, Jamie. What do you belong to,—a fire company or a jockey club?" asked Rose, turning up the once chubby face, which now was getting brown, and square about the chin.

"No, *ma'am!* Why, don't you know? I'm captain of the Base Ball Star Club. Look at that, will you?" and, as if the fact was one of national importance, Jamie flung open his jacket to display upon his proudly swelling chest a heart-shaped red-flannel shield, decorated with a white cotton star the size of a tea-plate.

"Superb! I've been away so long I forgot there was such a game. And *you* are the captain?" cried Rose, deeply impressed by the high honor to which her kinsman had arrived.

"I just am, and it's no joke you'd better believe; for we knock our teeth out, black our eyes, and split our fingers almost as well as the big fellows. You come down to the Common between one and two and see us play a match; then you'll understand what hard work it is. I'll teach you to bat now if you'll come out on the lawn," added Jamie, fired with a wish to exhibit his prowess.

"No, thank you, captain. The grass is wet, and you'll be late at school if you stay for us."

"I'm not afraid. Girls are not good for much generally; but you never used to mind a little wet, and played cricket like a good one. Can't you ever do that sort of thing now?" asked the boy, with a pitying look at these hapless creatures, debarred from the joys and perils of manly sports.

"I can run still: and I'll get to the gate before you; see if I don't;" and, yielding to the impulse of the moment, Rose darted down the steps before astonished Jamie could mount and follow.

He was off in a moment: but Rose had the start; and, though old Sheltie did his best, she reached the goal just ahead, and stood there laughing and panting, all rosy with the fresh October air, a pretty picture for several gentlemen who were driving by.

"Good for you, Rose!" said Archie, jumping out to shake hands, while Will and Geordie saluted, and Uncle Mac laughed at Jamie, who looked as if girls had risen slightly in his opinion.

"I'm glad it is you, because you won't be shocked. But I'm so happy to be back I forgot I was not little Rose still," said Atalanta, smoothing down her flying hair.

"You look very like her, with the curls on your shoulders in the old way. I missed them last night, and wondered what it was. How is uncle and Phebe?" asked Archie, whose eyes had been looking over Rose's head while he spoke toward the piazza, where a female figure was visible among the reddening woodbines.

"All well, thanks. Won't you come up and see for your-selves?"

"Can't, my dear, can't possibly. Business, you know, business. This fellow is my right-hand man, and I can't spare him a minute. Come, Arch, we must be off, or these boys will miss their train," answered Uncle Mac, pulling out his watch.

With a last look from the light-haired figure at the gate to the dark-haired one among the vines, Archie drove away, and Jamie cantered after, consoling himself for his defeat with apple number two.

Rose lingered a moment, feeling much inclined to continue her run, and pop in upon all the aunts in succession; but, re-membering her uncovered head, was about to turn back, when a cheerful "Ahoy! ahoy!" made her look up, to see Mac ap-proaching at a great pace, waving his hat as he came.

"The Campbells are coming thick and fast this morning, and the more the merrier," she said, running to meet him. "You look like a good boy going to school, and virtuously conning your lesson by the way," she added, smiling to see him take his finger out of the book he had evidently been reading, and tuck it under his arm, just as he used to do years ago.

"I *am* a school-boy going to the school I like best," he an-swered, waving a plumy spray of asters, as if pointing out the lovely autumn world about them, full of gay hues, fresh airs, and mellow sunshine.

"That reminds me that I didn't get a chance to hear much about your plans last night: the other boys all talked at once, and you only got in a word now and then. What have you decided to be, Mac?" asked Rose, as they went up the avenue side by side.

"A man first, and a good one if possible; after that, what God pleases."

Something in the tone, as well as the words, made Rose look up quickly into Mac's face, to see a new expression there. It was indescribable; but she felt as she had often done when watching the mists part suddenly, giving glimpses of some mountain-top, shining serene and high against the blue.

"I think you *will* be something splendid; for you really look quite glorified, walking under this arch of yellow leaves with the sunshine on your face," she exclaimed, conscious of a sudden admiration never felt before; for Mac was the plainest of all the cousins.

"I don't know about that; but I have my dreams and aspirations, and some of them are pretty high ones. Aim at the best, you know, and keep climbing if you want to get on," he said, looking at the asters with an inward sort of smile, as if he and they had some sweet secret between them.

"You are queerer than ever. But I like your ambition, and hope you will get on. Only mustn't you begin at something soon? I fancied you would study medicine with uncle: that used to be our plan, you know."

"I shall, for the present at least, because I quite agree with you that it is necessary to have an anchor somewhere, and not go floating off into the world of imagination without ballast of the right sort. Uncle and I had some talk about it last night, and I'm going up to begin as soon as possible; for I've mooned long enough," and giving himself a shake, Mac threw down the pretty spray, adding half aloud,—

> "Chide me not, laborious band,
>     For the idle flowers I brought;
> Every aster in my hand
>     Goes home laden with a thought."

Rose caught the words and smiled, thinking to herself, "Oh, that's it: he is getting into the sentimental age, and Aunt Jane has been lecturing him. Dear me, how we *are* growing up!"

"You look as if you didn't like the prospect very well," she said aloud; for Mac had rammed the volume of Shelley into his pocket, and the glorified expression was so entirely gone Rose fancied that she had been mistaken about the mountain-top behind the mists.

"Yes, well enough: I always thought the profession a grand one; and where could I find a better teacher than uncle? I've got into lazy ways lately, and it is high time I went at something useful; so here I go," and Mac abruptly vanished into the study, while Rose joined Phebe in Aunt Plenty's room.

The dear old lady had just decided, after long and earnest

discussion, which of six favorite puddings should be served for dinner, and thus had a few moments to devote to sentiment; so, when Rose came in, she held out her arms, saying fondly,—

"I shall not feel as if I'd got my child back again, until I have her in my lap a minute. No, you're not a bit too heavy; my rheumatism doesn't begin much before November: so sit here, darling, and put your two arms round my neck."

Rose obeyed, and neither spoke for a moment, as the old woman held the young one close, and appeased the two years' longing of a motherly heart by the caresses women give the creatures dearest to them. Right in the middle of a kiss, however, she stopped suddenly; and, holding out one arm, caught Phebe, who was trying to steal away unobserved.

"Don't go: there's room for both in my love, though there isn't in my lap. I'm so grateful to get my dear girls safely home again, that I hardly know what I'm about," said Aunt Plenty, embracing Phebe so heartily that she could not feel left out in the cold, and stood there with her black eyes shining through the happiest tears.

"There, now I've had a good hug, and feel as if I was all right again. I wish you'd set that cap in order, Rose: I went to bed in such a hurry I pulled the strings off and left it all in a heap. Phebe, dear, you shall dust round a mite, just as you used to; for I haven't had any one to do it as I like since you've been gone, and it will do me good to see all my knickknacks straightened out in your tidy way," said the elder lady, getting up with a refreshed expression on her rosy old face.

"Shall I dust in here too?" asked Phebe, glancing toward an inner room which used to be her care.

"No, dear, I'd rather do that myself. Go in if you like: nothing is changed. I *must* go and see to my pudding;" and Aunt Plenty trotted abruptly away, with a quiver of emotion in her voice which made even her last words pathetic.

Pausing on the threshold as if it was a sacred place, the girls looked in with eyes soon dimmed by tender tears; for it seemed as if the gentle occupant was still there. Sunshine shone on the old geraniums by the window; the cushioned chair stood in its accustomed place, with the white wrapper hung across it, and the faded slippers lying ready. Books and basket, knitting and spectacles, were all just as she had left them; and the beautiful tranquillity that always filled the room seemed so natural both lookers turned involuntarily toward the bed where Aunt Peace used to greet them with a smile. There was no sweet old face upon the pillow now, yet the tears that wet the blooming cheeks were not for her who had gone, but for her who was left; because they saw something which spoke eloquently of the love which outlives death and makes the humblest things beautiful and sacred.

A well-worn footstool stood beside the bed, and in the high-piled whiteness of the empty couch there was a little hollow where a gray head nightly rested, while Aunt Plenty said the prayers her mother taught her seventy years ago.

Without a word, the girls softly shut the door: and, while Phebe put the room in the most exquisite order, Rose re-trimmed the plain white cap, where pink and yellow ribbons never rustled now; both feeling honored by their tasks, and better for their knowledge of the faithful love and piety which sanctified a good old woman's life.

"You darling creature, I'm *so* glad to get you back! I know it's shamefully early; but I really couldn't keep away another minute. Let me help you: I'm dying to see all your splendid things; for I saw the trunks pass, and I know you've quantities of treasures," cried Annabel Bliss, all in one breath as she embraced Rose an hour later, and glanced about the room bestrewn with a variety of agreeable objects.

"How well you are looking! Sit down and I'll show you my lovely photographs. Uncle chose all the best for me, and it's a treat to see them," answered Rose, putting a roll on the table and looking about for more.

"Oh, thanks! I haven't time now: one needs hours to study such things. Show me your Paris dresses, there's a dear: I'm perfectly aching to see the last styles," and Annabel cast a hungry eye toward certain large boxes delightfully suggestive of French finery.

"I haven't got any," said Rose, fondly surveying the fine photographs as she laid them away.

"Rose Campbell! you don't mean to say that you didn't get one Paris dress at least?" cried Annabel, scandalized at the bare idea of such neglect.

"Not one for myself: Aunt Clara ordered several, and will be charmed to show them when her box comes."

"Such a chance! right there and plenty of money! How *could* you love your uncle after such cruelty?" sighed Annabel, with a face full of sympathy.

Rose looked puzzled for a minute, then seemed to understand, and assumed a superior air which became her very well, as she said, good-naturedly opening a box of laces, "Uncle did not forbid my doing it, and I had money enough; but I chose not to spend it on things of that sort."

"Could and didn't! I can't believe it!" And Annabel sunk into a chair, as if the thought was too much for her.

"I did rather want to at first, just for the fun of the thing; in fact, I went and looked at some amazing gowns. But they were very expensive, very much trimmed, and not my style at all; so I gave them up, and kept what I valued more than all the gowns Worth ever made."

"What in the world was it?" cried Annabel, hoping she would say diamonds.

"Uncle's good opinion," answered Rose, looking thoughtfully into the depths of a packing case, where lay the lovely picture that would always remind her of the little triumph over girlish vanity, which not only kept but increased "Uncle's good opinion."

"Oh, indeed!" said Annabel, blankly, and fell to examining Aunt Plenty's lace; while Rose went on with a happy smile in her eyes as she dived into another trunk.

"Uncle thinks one has no right to waste money on such things; but he is very generous, and loves to give useful, beautiful, or curious gifts. See, all these pretty ornaments are for presents; and you shall choose first whatever you like."

"He's a perfect dear!" cried Annabel, revelling in the crystal, filigree, coral, and mosaic trinkets spread before her; while Rose completed her rapture by adding sundry tasteful trifles fresh from Paris.

"Now tell me, when do you mean to have your coming-out party? I ask because I've nothing ready, and want plenty of time; for, I suppose, it will be *the* event of the season," asked Annabel, a few minutes later, as she wavered between a pink coral and a blue lava set.

"I came out when I went to Europe; but I suppose Aunty Plen will want to have some sort of merrymaking to celebrate our return. I shall begin as I mean to go on, and have a simple, sociable sort of party, and invite every one whom I like, no matter in what 'set' they happen to belong. No one shall ever say *I* am aristocratic and exclusive: so prepare yourself to be shocked; for old friends and young, rich and poor, will be asked to all my parties."

"Oh, my heart! you *are* going to be odd just as mamma predicted!" sighed Annabel, clasping her hands in despair, and studying the effect of three bracelets on her chubby arm in the midst of her woe.

"In my own house I'm going to do as I think best; and, if people call me odd, I can't help it. I shall endeavor not to do any thing very dreadful; but I seem to inherit uncle's love for experiments, and mean to try some. I dare say they will fail and I shall get laughed at; I intend to do it nevertheless, so you had better drop me now before I begin," said Rose, with an air of resolution that was rather alarming.

"What shall you wear at this new sort of party of yours?" asked Annabel, wisely turning a deaf ear to all delicate or dangerous topics and keeping to matters she understood.

"That white thing over there. It is fresh and pretty, and Phebe has one like it. I never want to dress more than she does; and gowns of that sort are always most appropriate and becoming to girls of our age."

"Phebe! you don't mean to say you are going to make a lady of *her!*" gasped Annabel, upsetting her treasures, as she fell back with a gesture that made the little chair creak again; for Miss Bliss was as plump as a partridge.

"She *is* one already, and anybody who slights her slights me; for she is the best girl I know and the dearest," cried Rose, warmly.

"Yes, of course,—I was only surprised,—you are quite right; for she *may* turn out to be somebody, and then how glad you'll feel that you were so good to her!" said Annabel, veering round at once, seeing which way the wind blew.

Before Rose could speak again, a cheery voice called from the hall,—

"Little mistress, where are you?"

"In my room, Phebe, dear," and up came the girl Rose was going to "make a lady of," looking so like one that Annabel opened her china-blue eyes, and smiled involuntarily as Phebe dropped a little courtesy in playful imitation of her old manner, and said quietly,—

"How do you do, Miss Bliss?"

"Glad to see you back, Miss Moore," answered Annabel, shaking hands in a way that settled the question of Phebe's place in *her* mind for ever; for the stout damsel had a kind heart in spite of a weak head, and was really fond of Rose. It was evidently, "Love me, love my Phebe;" so she made up her mind on the spot that Phebe *was* somebody, and that gave an air of romance even to the poor-house.

She could not help staring a little, as she watched the two friends work together, and listened to their happy talk over each new treasure as it came to light; for every look and word plainly showed that years of close companionship had made them very dear to one another. It was pretty to see Rose try to do the hardest part of any little job herself: still prettier to see Phebe circumvent her, and untie the hard knots, fold the stiff papers, or lift the heavy trays with her own strong hands; and prettiest of all to hear her say in a motherly tone, as she put Rose into an easy chair,—

"Now, my deary, sit and rest; for you will have to see company all day, and I can't let you get tired out so early."

"That is no reason why I should let you either. Call Jane to help or I'll bob up again directly," answered Rose, with a very bad assumption of authority.

"Jane may take my place downstairs; but no one shall wait on you here except me, as long as I'm with you," said stately Phebe, stooping to put a hassock under the feet of her little mistress.

"It is very nice and pretty to see; but I don't know what people *will* say when she goes into society with the rest of us. I do hope Rose won't be *very* odd," said Annabel to herself as she went away to circulate the depressing news that there was to be no grand ball; and, saddest disappointment of all, that Rose had not a single Paris costume with which to refresh the eyes and rouse the envy of her amiable friends.

"Now I've seen or heard from all the boys but Charlie, and I suppose he is too busy. I wonder what he is about," thought

Rose, turning from the hall door, whither she had courteously accompanied her guest.

The wish was granted a moment after; for, going into the parlor to decide where some of her pictures should hang, she saw a pair of boots at one end of the sofa, a tawny-brown head at the other, and discovered that Charlie was busily occupied in doing nothing.

"The voice of the Bliss was heard in the land, so I dodged till she went upstairs, and then took a brief *siesta* while waiting to pay my respects to the distinguished traveller, Lady Hester Stanhope," he said, leaping up to make his best bow.

"The voice of the sluggard would be a more appropriate quotation, I think. Does Annabel still pine for you?" asked Rose, recalling certain youthful jokes upon the subject of un-requited affections.

"Not a bit of it. Fun has cut me out, and the fair Annabella will be Mrs. Tokio before the winter is over, if I'm not much mistaken."

"What, little Fun See? How droll it seems to think of him grown up and married to Annabel of all people! She never said a word about him; but this accounts for her admiring my pretty Chinese things, and being so interested in Canton."

"Little Fun is a great swell now, and much enamoured of our fat friend, who will take to chopsticks whenever he says the word. I needn't ask how you do, cousin; for you beat that Au-rora all hollow in the way of color. I should have been up be-fore, but I thought you'd like a good rest after your voyage."

"I was running a race with Jamie before nine o'clock. What were you doing, young man?"

"'Sleeping I dreamed, love, dreamed, love, of thee,'"

began Charlie; but Rose cut him short by saying as reproach-fully as she could, while the culprit stood regarding her with placid satisfaction,—

"You ought to have been up and at work like the rest of the boys. I felt like a drone in a hive of very busy bees, when I saw them all hurrying off to their business."

"But, my dear girl, I've got no business. I'm making up my mind, you see, and do the ornamental while I'm deciding. There always ought to be one gentleman in a family, and that seems to be rather my line," answered Charlie, posing for the character, with an assumption of languid elegance which would have been very effective if his twinkling eyes had not spoilt it.

"There are none *but* gentlemen in our family, I hope," answered Rose, with the proud air she always wore when any thing was said derogatory to the name of Campbell.

"Of course, of course. I should have said gentleman of leisure. You see it is against my principles to slave as Archie does. What's the use? Don't need the money, got plenty; so why not enjoy it, and keep jolly as long as possible? I'm sure cheerful people are public benefactors in this world of woe."

It was not easy to object to this proposition, especially when made by a comely young man, who looked the picture of health and happiness as he sat on the arm of the sofa, smiling at his cousin in the most engaging manner. Rose knew very well that the Epicurean philosophy was not the true one to begin life upon; but it was difficult to reason with Charlie, because he always dodged sober subjects, and was so full of cheery spirits, one hated to lessen the sort of sunshine which certainly is a public benefactor.

"You have such a clever way of putting things that I don't know how to contradict you, though I still think I'm right," she said gravely. "Mac likes to idle as well as you; but he is not going to do it, because he knows it's bad for him to fritter away his time. He is going to study a profession like a wise boy; though he would much prefer to live among his beloved books, or ride his hobbies in peace."

"That's all very well for *him*, because *he* doesn't care for society, and may as well be studying medicine as philandering about the woods with his pockets full of musty philosophers and old-fashioned poets," answered Charlie, with a shrug which plainly expressed his opinion of Mac.

"I wonder if musty philosophers, like Socrates and Aristotle, and old-fashioned poets, like Shakespeare and Milton, are not safer company for him to keep than some of the more modern friends you have?" said Rose, remembering Jamie's hints about wild oats; for she could be a little sharp sometimes, and had not lectured "the boys" for so long it seemed unusually pleasant.

But Charlie changed the subject skilfully by exclaiming with an anxious expression,—

"I do believe you are going to be like Aunt Jane; for that's just the way she comes down on me whenever she gets a chance! Don't take her for a model, I beg: she is a good woman, but a mighty disagreeable one, in my humble opinion."

The fear of being disagreeable is a great bugbear to a girl, as this artful young man well knew, and Rose fell into the trap at once; for Aunt Jane was far from being her model, though she could not help respecting her worth.

"Have you given up your painting?" she asked rather abruptly, turning to a gilded Fra Angelico angel which leaned in the sofa corner.

"Sweetest face I ever saw, and very like you about the eyes, isn't it?" said Charlie, who seemed to have a Yankee trick of replying to one question with another.

"I want an answer, not a compliment," and Rose tried to look severe, as she put away the picture more quickly than she took it up.

"Have I given up painting? Oh, no! I daub a little in oils, slop a little in water-colors, sketch now and then, and poke about the studios when the artistic fit comes on."

"How is the music?"

"More flourishing. I don't practise much, but sing a good deal in company. Set up a guitar last summer, and went troubadouring round in great style. The girls like it, and it's jolly among the fellows."

"Are you studying any thing?"

"Well, I have some law books on my table,—good, big, wise-looking chaps,—and I take a turn at them semi-occasionally, when pleasure palls or parents chide. But I doubt if I do more than learn what 'a allybi' is this year," and a sly laugh in Charlie's eye suggested that he sometimes availed himself of this bit of legal knowledge.

"What *do* you do then?"

"Fair catechist, I enjoy myself. Private theatricals have been the rage of late, and I have won such laurels that I seriously think of adopting the stage as my profession."

"Really!" cried Rose, alarmed.

"Why not? if I *must* go to work, isn't that as good as any thing?"

"Not without more talent than I think you possess. With

genius one can do any thing: without it one had better let the stage alone."

"There's a quencher for the 'star of the goodlie companie' to which I belong. Mac hasn't a ray of genius for any thing, yet you admire him for trying to be an M.D.," cried Charlie, rather nettled by her words.

"It is respectable, at all events; and I'd rather be a second-rate doctor than a second-rate actor. But I know you don't mean it, and only say so to frighten me."

"Exactly. I always bring it up when any one begins to lecture, and it works wonders. Uncle Mac turns pale, the aunts hold up their hands in holy horror, and a general panic ensues. Then I magnanimously promise not to disgrace the family; and in the first burst of gratitude the dear souls agree to every thing I ask; so peace is restored, and I go on my way rejoicing."

"Just the way you used to threaten to run off to sea, if your mother objected to any of your whims. You are not changed in that respect, though you are in others. You had great plans and projects once, Charlie; and now you seem to be contented with being a 'jack of all trades and master of none.'"

"Boyish nonsense! Time has brought wisdom; and I don't see the sense of tying myself down to one particular thing, and grinding away at it year after year. People of one idea get so deucedly narrow and tame, I've no patience with them. Culture is the thing; and the sort one gets by ranging over a wide field is the easiest to acquire, the handiest to have, and the most successful in the end. At any rate, it is the kind I like, and the only kind I intend to bother myself about."

With this declaration, Charlie smoothed his brow, clasped his hands over his head, and, leaning back, gently warbled the chorus of a college song, as if it expressed his views of life better than he could:—

> "While our rosy fillets shed
>  Blushes o'er each fervid head,
>  With many a cup and many a smile
>  The festal moments we beguile."

"Some of my saints here were people of one idea; and, though they were not very successful in a worldly point of view while alive, they were loved and canonized when dead," said

Rose, who had been turning over a pile of photographs upon the table, and, just then, found her favorite, St. Francis, among them.

"This is more to my taste. Those worn-out, cadaverous fellows give me the blues; but here's a gentlemanly saint, who takes things easy, and does good as he goes along, without howling over his own sins, or making other people miserable by telling them of theirs." And Charlie laid a handsome St. Martin beside the brown-frocked monk.

Rose looked at both, and understood why her cousin preferred the soldierly figure with the sword to the ascetic with his crucifix. One was riding bravely through the world in purple and fine linen, with horse and hound, and squires at his back; the other was in a lazar-house, praying over the dead and dying. The contrast was a strong one; and the girl's eyes lingered longest on the knight, though she said thoughtfully,—

"Yours is certainly the pleasantest: and yet I never heard of any good deed he did, except divide his cloak with a beggar; while my St. Francis gave himself to charity just when life was most tempting, and spent years working for God without reward. He's old and poor, and in a dreadful place, but I won't give him up; and you may have your gay St. Martin, if you want him."

"No, thank you; saints are not in my line: but I'd like the golden-haired angel in the blue gown, if you'll let me have her. She shall be my little Madonna, and I'll pray to her like a good Catholic," answered Charlie, turning to the delicate, deep-eyed figure, with the lilies in its hand.

"With all my heart, and any others that you like. Choose some for your mother, and give them to her with my love."

So Charlie sat down beside Rose to turn and talk over the pictures for a long and pleasant hour. But when they went away to lunch, if there had been any one to observe so small but significant a trifle, good St. Francis lay face downward behind the sofa, while gallant St. Martin stood erect upon the chimney-piece.

# Chapter III

MISS CAMPBELL

WHILE the travellers unpack their trunks, we will pick up, as briefly as possible, the dropped stitches in the little romance we are weaving.

Rose's life had been a very busy and quiet one for the four years following the May-day when she made her choice. Study, exercise, house-work, and many wholesome pleasures, kept her a happy, hearty creature, yearly growing in womanly graces, yet always preserving the innocent freshness girls lose so soon when too early sent upon the world's stage, and given a part to play.

Not a remarkably gifted girl in any way, and far from perfect; full of all manner of youthful whims and fancies; a little spoiled by much love; rather apt to think all lives as safe and sweet as her own; and, when want or pain appealed to her, the tender heart overflowed with a remorseful charity, which gave of its abundance recklessly. Yet, with all her human imperfections, the upright nature of the child kept her desires climbing toward the just and pure and true, as flowers struggle to the light; and the woman's soul was budding beautifully under the green leaves behind the little thorns.

At seventeen, Dr. Alec pronounced her ready for the voyage round the world, which he considered a better finishing off than any school could give her. But just then Aunt Peace began to fail, and soon slipped quietly away to rejoin the lover she had waited for so long. Youth seemed to come back in a mysterious way to touch the dead face with lost loveliness, and all the romance of her past to gather round her memory. Unlike most aged women, her friends were among the young; and, at her funeral, the gray heads gave place to the band of loving girls who made the sweet old maiden ready for her rest, bore her pall, and covered her grave with the white flowers she had never worn.

When this was over, poor Aunt Plenty seemed so lost without her life-long charge that Dr. Alec would not leave her; and

Rose gladly paid the debt she owed by the tender service which comforts without words. But Aunt Plenty, having lived for others all her days, soon rebelled against this willing sacrifice, soon found strength in her own sincere piety, solace in cheerful occupation, and amusement in nursing Aunt Myra, who was a capital patient, as she never died and never got well.

So, at last, the moment came when, with free minds, the travellers could set out; and on Rose's eighteenth birthday, with Uncle Alec and the faithful Phebe, she sailed away to see and study the big, beautiful world, which lies ready for us all, if we only know how to use and to enjoy it.

Phebe was set to studying music in the best schools; and, while she trained her lovely voice with happy industry, Rose and her uncle roamed about in the most delightful way, till two years were gone like a dream, and those at home clamored for their return.

Back they came, and now the heiress must make ready to take her place; for at twenty-one she came into possession of the fortune she had been trying to learn how to use well. Great plans fermented in her brain; for, though the heart was as generous as ever, time had taught her prudence, and observation shown her that the wisest charity is that which helps the poor to help themselves.

Dr. Alec found it a little difficult to restrain the ardor of this young philanthropist, who wanted to begin at once to endow hospitals, build homes, adopt children, and befriend all mankind.

"Take a little time to look about you and get your bearings, child; for the world you have been living in is a much simpler, honester one than that you are now to enter. Test yourself a bit, and see if the old ways seem best after all; for you are old enough to decide, and wise enough to discover, what is for your truest good, I hope," he said, trying to feel ready to let the bird escape from under his wing, and make little flights alone.

"Now, uncle, I'm very much afraid you are going to be disappointed in me," answered Rose, with unusual hesitation, yet a very strong desire visible in her eyes. "You like to have me quite honest, and I've learned to tell you all my foolish thoughts: so I'll speak out, and if you find my wish very wrong

and silly, please say so; for I don't want you to cast me off entirely, though I am grown up. You say, wait a little, test myself,
and try if the old ways are best. I should like to do that; and
can I in a better way than by leading the life other girls lead,
just for a little while," she added, as her uncle's face grew grave.

He *was* disappointed; yet acknowledged that the desire was
natural, and in a moment saw that a trial of this sort might
have its advantages. Nevertheless, he dreaded it; for he had
intended to choose her society carefully, and try to keep her
unspoiled by the world as long as possible, like many another
fond parent and guardian. But the spirit of Eve is strong in all
her daughters: forbidden fruit will look rosier to them than
any in their own orchards, and the temptation to take just one
little bite proves irresistible to the wisest. So Rose, looking out
from the safe seclusion of her girlhood into the woman's kingdom which she was about to take possession of, felt a sudden
wish to try its pleasures before assuming its responsibilities,
and was too sincere to hide the longing.

"Very well, my dear, try it if you like, only take care of your
health: be temperate in your gayety, and don't lose more than
you gain; if that is possible," he added under his breath, endeavoring to speak cheerfully and not look anxious.

"I know it is foolish; but I do want to be a regular butterfly
for a little while and see what it is like. You know I couldn't
help seeing a good deal of fashionable life abroad, though we
were not in it; and here at home the girls tell me about all sorts
of pleasant things that are to happen this winter; so, if you
won't despise me *very* much, I should like to try it."

"For how long?"

"Would three months be too long? New Year is a good time
to take a fresh start. Every one is going to welcome me; so I
must be gay in spite of myself, unless I'm willing to seem very
ungrateful and morose," said Rose, glad to have so good a
reason to offer for her new experiment.

"You may like it so well that the three months may become
years. Pleasure is very sweet when we are young."

"Do you think it will intoxicate me?"

"We shall see, my dear."

"We shall!" and Rose marched away; looking as if she had
taken a pledge of some sort, and meant to keep it.

It was a great relief to the public mind when it became known that Miss Campbell was really coming out at last; and invitations to Aunt Plenty's party were promptly accepted. Aunt Clara was much disappointed about the grand ball she had planned; but Rose stood firm, and the dear old lady had her way about every thing.

The consequence was a delightfully informal gathering of friends to welcome the travellers home. Just a good, old-fashioned, hospitable house-warming; so simple, cordial, and genuine that those who came to criticise remained to enjoy, and many owned the charm they could neither describe nor imitate.

Much curiosity was felt about Phebe, and much gossip went on behind fans that evening; for those who had known her years ago found it hard to recognize the little house-maid in the handsome young woman who bore herself with such quiet dignity, and charmed them all with her fine voice. "Cinderella has turned out a princess," was the general verdict: and Rose enjoyed the little sensation immensely; for she had had many battles to fight for her Phebe since she came among them, and now her faith was vindicated.

Miss Campbell herself was in great demand, and did the honors so prettily that even Miss Bliss forgave her for her sad neglect of Worth; though she shook her head over the white gowns, just alike except that Phebe wore crimson and Rose blue trimmings.

The girls swarmed eagerly round their recovered friend; for Rose had been a favorite before she went away, and found her throne waiting for her now. The young men privately pronounced Phebe the handsomest,—"But then you know there's neither family nor money; so it's no use." Phebe, therefore, was admired as one of the ornamental properties belonging to the house, and let respectfully alone.

But bonny Rose was "all right," as these amiable youths expressed it; and many a wistful eye followed the bright head as it flitted about the rooms, as if it were a second Golden Fleece to be won with difficulty; for stalwart kinsmen hedged it round, and watchful aunts kept guard.

Little wonder that the girl found her new world an enchanting one, and that her first sip of pleasure rather went to her head; for everybody welcomed and smiled on her, flattered and praised, whispered agreeable prophecies in her ear, and looked the compliments and congratulations they dared not utter, till she felt as if she must have left her old self somewhere abroad, and suddenly become a new and wonderfully gifted being.

"It is very nice, uncle; and I'm not sure that I mayn't want another three months of it when the first are gone," she whispered to Dr. Alec, as he stood watching the dance she was leading with Charlie in the long hall after supper.

"Steady, my lass, steady; and remember that you are not really a butterfly, but a mortal girl with a head that will ache to-morrow," he answered, watching the flushed and smiling face before him.

"I almost wish there wasn't any to-morrow, but that to-night would last for ever: it is so pleasant, and every one so kind," she said with a little sigh of happiness, as she gathered up her fleecy skirts like a white bird pluming itself for flight.

"I'll ask your opinion about that at two A.M.," began her uncle, with a warning nod.

"I'll give it honestly," was all Rose had time to say before Charlie swept her away into the parti-colored cloud before them.

"It's no use, Alec: train a girl as wisely as you choose, she will break loose when the time comes, and go in for pleasure as eagerly as the most frivolous; for ''tis their nature to,'" said Uncle Mac, keeping time to the music as if he would not mind "going in" for a bit of pleasure himself.

"My girl shall taste and try; but, unless I'm much mistaken, a little of it will satisfy her. I want to see if she will stand the test; for, if not, all my work is a failure, and I'd like to know it," answered the doctor, with a hopeful smile on his lips, but an anxious look in his eyes.

"She will come out all right,—bless her heart! so let her sow her innocent wild oats and enjoy herself till she is ready to settle down. I wish all our young folks were likely to have as small a crop, and get through as safely as she will," added Uncle Mac, with a shake of the head, as he glanced at some of the young men revolving before him.

"Nothing amiss with your lads, I hope?"

"No, thank heaven! So far I've had little trouble with either;

though Mac is an odd stick, and Steve a puppy. I don't complain; for both will outgrow that sort of thing, and are good fellows at heart, thanks to their mother. But Clara's boy is in a bad way; and she will spoil him as a man as she has as a boy, if his father doesn't interfere."

"I told brother Stephen all about him when I was in Calcutta last year, and he wrote to the boy; but Clara has got no end of plans in her head, and so she insisted on keeping Charlie a year longer when his father ordered him off to India," replied the doctor, as they walked away.

"It is too late to 'order:' Charlie is a man now, and Stephen will find that he has been too easy with him all these years. Poor fellow, it has been hard lines for him, and is likely to be harder, I fancy, unless he comes home and straightens things out."

"He won't do that if he can help it; for he has lost all his energy living in that climate, and hates worry more than ever: so you can imagine what an effort it would be to manage a foolish woman and a headstrong boy. We must lend a hand, Mac, and do our best for poor old Steve."

"The best we can do for the lad is to marry and settle him as soon as possible."

"My dear fellow, he is only three and twenty," began the doctor, as if the idea was preposterous: then a sudden change came over him, as he added with a melancholy smile, "I forget how much one can hope and suffer, even at twenty-three."

"And be all the better for, if bravely outlived," said Uncle Mac, with his hand on his brother's shoulder, and the sincerest approval in his voice. Then, kindly returning to the younger people, he went on inquiringly, "You don't incline to Clara's view of a certain matter, I fancy?"

"Decidedly not. My girl must have the best, and Clara's training would spoil an angel," answered Dr. Alec, quickly.

"But we shall find it hard to let our little Rose go out of the family. How would Archie do? He has been well brought up, and is a thoroughly excellent lad."

The brothers had retired to the study by this time, and were alone; yet Dr. Alec lowered his voice as he said with a tender sort of anxiety pleasant to see,—

"You know I do not approve of cousins marrying, so I'm in a quandary, Mac; for I love the child as if she were my own, and feel as if I could not give her up to any man whom I did not know and trust entirely. It is of no use for us to plan; for she must choose for herself: yet I do wish we could keep her among us, and give one of our boys a wife worth having."

"We must; so never mind your theories, but devote yourself to testing our elder lads, and making one of them a happy fellow. All are heart-whole, I believe, and, though young still for this sort of thing, we can be gently shaping matters for them, since no one knows how soon the moment may come. My faith! it is like living in a powder-mill to be among a lot of young folks now-a-days. All looks as calm as possible, till a sudden spark produces an explosion, and heaven only knows where we find ourselves after it is over."

And Uncle Mac sat himself comfortably down to settle Rose's fate; while the doctor paced the room, plucking at his beard and knitting his brows, as if he found it hard to see his way.

"Yes, Archie is a good fellow," he said, answering the question he had ignored before. "An upright, steady, intelligent lad, who will make an excellent husband, if he ever finds out that he has a heart. I suppose I'm an old fool, but I do like a little more romance in a young man than he seems to have; more warmth and enthusiasm, you know. Bless the boy! he might be forty instead of three or four and twenty: he's so sober, calm, and cool. I'm younger now than he is, and could go a-wooing like a Romeo if I had any heart to offer a woman."

The doctor looked rather shamefaced as he spoke, and his brother burst out laughing,—

"See here, Alec, it's a pity so much romance and excellence as yours should be lost; so why don't you set these young fellows an example, and go a-wooing yourself? Jessie has been wondering how you have managed to keep from falling in love with Phebe all this time; and Clara is quite sure that you only waited till she was safe under Aunt Plenty's wing to offer yourself in the good old-fashioned style."

"I!" and the doctor stood aghast at the mere idea; then he gave a resigned sort of sigh and added like a martyr, "If those dear women would let me alone, I'd thank them for ever. Put the idea out of their minds for heaven's sake, Mac, or I shall be having that poor girl flung at my head, and her comfort destroyed. She is a fine creature, and I'm proud of her; but she deserves a better lot than to be tied to an old fellow like me, whose only merit is his fidelity."

"As you please, I was only joking," and Uncle Mac dropped the subject with secret relief; for the excellent man thought a good deal of family, and had been rather worried at the hints of the ladies. After a moment's silence, he returned to a former topic, which was rather a pet plan of his. "I don't think you do Archie justice, Alec. You don't know him as well as I do; but you'll find that he has heart enough under his cool, quiet manner. I've grown very fond of him, think highly of him, and don't see how you could do better for Rose than to give her to him."

"If she will go," said the doctor, smiling at his brother's business-like way of disposing of the young people.

"She'll do any thing to please you," began Uncle Mac, in perfect good faith; for twenty-five years in the society of a very prosaic wife had taken nearly all the romance out of him.

"It is of no use for us to plan, and I shall never interfere except to advise; but, if I *were* to choose one of the boys, I should incline to my godson," answered the doctor, gravely.

"What, my Ugly Duckling!" exclaimed Uncle Mac, in great surprise.

"The Ugly Duckling turned out a swan, you remember. I've always been fond of the boy, because he's so genuine and original. Crude as a green apple now, but sound at the core, and only needs time to ripen. I'm sure he'll turn out a capital specimen of the Campbell variety."

"Much obliged, Alec; but it will never do at all. He's a good fellow, and may do something to be proud of by and by; but he's not the mate for our Rose. She needs some one who can manage her property when we are gone; and Archie is the man for that, depend upon it."

"Confound the property!" cried Dr. Alec, impetuously. "I want her to be *happy*; and I don't care how soon she gets rid of her money if it is going to be a millstone round her neck. I declare to you, I dreaded the thought of this time so much that I've kept her away as long as I could, and trembled whenever a young fellow joined us while we were abroad. Had one or two narrow escapes, and now I'm in for it, as you can see by to-night's 'success,' as Clara calls it. Thank heaven, I haven't *many* daughters to look after!"

"Come, come, don't be anxious: take Archie, and settle it right up safely and happily. That's my advice, and you'll find it sound," replied the elder conspirator, like one having experience.

"I'll think of it; but mind you, Mac, not a word of this to the sisters. We are a couple of old fools to be match-making so soon; but I see what is before me, and it's a comfort to free my mind to some one."

"So it is. Depend on me; not a breath even to Jane," answered Uncle Mac, with a hearty shake and a sympathetic slap on the shoulder.

"Why, what dark and awful secrets are going on here? Is it a Freemasons' Lodge, and those the mystic signs?" asked a gay voice at the door; and there stood Rose, full of smiling wonder at the sight of her two uncles hand in hand, whispering and nodding to one another mysteriously.

They started, like school-boys caught plotting mischief, and looked so guilty that she took pity on them, innocently imagining that the brothers were indulging in a little sentiment on this joyful occasion; so she added quickly, as she beckoned, without crossing the threshold,—

"Women not allowed, of course: but both of you dear Odd Fellows are wanted; for Aunt Plenty begs we will have an old-fashioned contra dance, and I'm to lead off with Uncle Mac. I chose you, sir, because you do it in style, pigeon-wings and all. So, please come; and Phebe is waiting for you, Uncle Alec. She is rather shy you know, but will enjoy it with you to take care of her."

"Thank you, thank you!" cried both gentlemen, following with great alacrity.

Unconscious Rose enjoyed that Virginia reel immensely; for the pigeon-wings were superb, and her partner conducted her through the convolutions of the dance without a fault, going down the middle in his most gallant style. Landing safely at the bottom, she stood aside to let him get his breath; for stout Uncle Mac was bound to do or die on that occasion, and would have danced his pumps through without a murmur if she had desired it.

Leaning against the wall with his hair in his eyes, and a

decidedly bored expression of countenance, was Mac, Jr., who had been surveying the gymnastics of his parent with respectful astonishment.

"Come and take a turn, my lad. Rose is as fresh as a daisy; but we old fellows soon get enough of it, so you shall have my place," said his father, wiping his face, which glowed like a cheerful peony.

"No, thank you, sir: I can't stand that sort of thing. I'll race you round the piazza with pleasure, cousin; but this oven is too much for me," was Mac's uncivil reply, as he backed toward the open window, as if glad of an excuse to escape.

"Fragile creature, don't stay on my account, I beg. *I* can't leave my guests for a moonlight run, even if I dared to take it on a frosty night in a thin dress," said Rose, fanning herself, and not a bit ruffled by Mac's refusal; for she knew his ways, and they amused her.

"Not half so bad as all this dust, gas, heat, and noise. What do you suppose lungs are made of?" demanded Mac, ready for a discussion then and there.

"I used to know, but I've forgotten now. Been so busy with other things that I've neglected the hobbies I used to ride five or six years ago," she said, laughing.

"Ah, those were times worth having! Are you going in for much of this sort of thing, Rose?" he asked, with a disapproving glance at the dancers.

"About three months of it, I think."

"Then good-by till New Year," and Mac vanished behind the curtains.

"Rose, my dear, you really must take that fellow in hand before he gets to be quite a bear. Since you have been gone, he has lived in his books, and got on so finely that we have let him alone, though his mother groans over his manners. Polish him up a bit, I beg of you; for it is high time he mended his odd ways and did justice to the fine gifts he hides behind them," said Uncle Mac, scandalized at the bluntness of his son.

"I know my chestnut-burr too well to mind his prickles. But others do not; so I *will* take him in hand and make him a credit to the family," answered Rose, readily.

"Take Archie for your model: he's one of a thousand; and the girl who gets him gets a prize I do assure you," added

Uncle Mac, who found match-making to his taste, and thought that closing remark a deep one.

"Oh me, how tired I am!" cried Rose, dropping into a chair as the last carriage rolled away, somewhere between one and two.

"What is your opinion now, Miss Campbell?" asked the doctor, addressing her for the first time by the name which had been uttered so often that night.

"My opinion is that Miss Campbell is likely to have a gay life if she goes on as she has begun; and that she finds it very delightful so far," answered the girl, with lips still smiling from their first taste of what the world calls pleasure.

# Chapter IV

## THORNS AMONG THE ROSES

For a time every thing went smoothly, and Rose was a happy girl; for the world seemed a beautiful and friendly place, and the fulfilment of her brightest dreams appeared to be a possibility. Of course, this could not last, and disappointment was inevitable; because young eyes look for a Paradise, and weep when they find a work-a-day world, which seems full of care and trouble, till one learns to gladden and glorify it with high thoughts and holy living.

Those who loved her waited anxiously for the disillusion which must come in spite of all their cherishing; for, till now, Rose had been so busy with her studies, travels, and home duties, that she knew very little of the triumphs, trials, and temptations of fashionable life. Birth and fortune placed her where she could not well escape some of them; and Doctor Alec, knowing that experience is the best teacher, wisely left her to learn this lesson as she must many another, devoutly hoping that it would not be a hard one.

October and November passed rapidly; and Christmas was at hand, with all its merry mysteries, home-gatherings, and good wishes.

Rose sat in her own little sanctum, opening from the parlor, busily preparing gifts for the dear five hundred friends who seemed to grow fonder and fonder as the holidays drew near. The drawers of her commode stood open, giving glimpses of dainty trifles, which she was tying up with bright ribbons.

A young girl's face at such moments is apt to be a happy one; but Rose's was very grave as she worked, and now and then she threw a parcel into the drawer with a careless toss, as if no love made the gift precious. So unusual was this expression that it struck Dr. Alec as he came in, and brought an anxious look to his eyes; for any cloud on that other countenance dropped its shadow over his.

"Can you spare a minute from your pretty work to take a

stitch in my old glove?" he asked, coming up to the table strewn with ribbon, lace, and colored papers.

"Yes, uncle, as many as you please."

The face brightened with sudden sunshine; both hands were put out to receive the shabby driving-glove; and the voice was full of that affectionate alacrity which makes the smallest service sweet.

"My Lady Bountiful is hard at work, I see. Can I help in any way?" he asked, glancing at the display before him.

"No, thank you; unless you can make me as full of interest and pleasure in these things as I used to be. Don't you think preparing presents a great bore, except for those you love, and who love you?" she added, in a tone which had a slight tremor in it as she uttered the last words.

"I don't give to people whom I care nothing for. Can't do it; especially at Christmas, when good-will should go into every thing one does. If all these 'pretties' are for dear friends, you must have a great many."

"I thought they were friends; but I find many of them are not, and that's the trouble, sir."

"Tell me all about it, dear, and let the old glove go," he said, sitting down beside her with his most sympathetic air.

But she held the glove fast, saying eagerly, "No, no, I love to do this! I don't feel as if I could look at you while I tell what a bad, suspicious girl I am," she added, keeping her eyes upon her work.

"Very well, I'm ready for confessions of any iniquity, and glad to get them; for sometimes lately I've seen a cloud in my girl's eyes, and caught a worried tone in her voice. Is there a bitter drop in the cup that promised to be so sweet, Rose?"

"Yes, uncle. I've tried to think there was not; but it *is* there, and I don't like it. I'm ashamed to tell; and yet I want to, because you will show me how to make it sweet, or assure me that I shall be the better for it, as you used to do when I took medicine."

She paused a minute, sewing swiftly; then out came the trouble all in one burst of girlish grief and chagrin.

"Uncle, half the people who are so kind to me don't care a bit for me, but for what I can give them; and that makes me unhappy, because I was so glad and proud to be liked. I do

"CAN YOU SPARE A MINUTE FROM YOUR PRETTY WORK?"

wish I hadn't a penny in the world, then I should know who my true friends were."

"Poor little lass! she has found out that all that glitters is not gold, and the dis-illusion has begun," said the doctor to himself, adding aloud, smiling yet pitiful, "And so all the pleasure is gone out of the pretty gifts, and Christmas is a failure?"

"Oh, no! not for those whom nothing can make me doubt. It is sweeter than ever to make *these* things, because my heart is in every stitch; and I know that, poor as they are, they will be dear to you, Aunty Plen, Aunt Jessie, Phebe, and the boys."

She opened a drawer where lay a pile of pretty gifts, wrought with loving care by her own hands; touching them tenderly as she spoke, and patting the sailor's knot of blue ribbon on one fat parcel with a smile that told how unshakable her faith in some one was. "But *these*," she said, pulling open another drawer, and tossing over its gay contents with an air half sad, half scornful, "these I *bought* and give because they are expected. *These* people only care for a rich gift, not one bit for the giver, whom they will secretly abuse if she is not as generous as they expect. How *can* I enjoy that sort of thing, uncle?"

"You cannot; but perhaps you do some of them injustice, my dear. Don't let the envy or selfishness of a few poison your faith in all. Are you sure that none of these girls care for you?" he asked, reading a name here and there on the parcels scattered about.

"I'm afraid I am. You see I heard several talking together the other evening at Annabel's, only a few words, but it hurt me very much; for nearly every one was speculating on what I would give them, and hoping it would be something fine. 'She's so rich she ought to be generous,' said one. 'I've been perfectly devoted to her for weeks, and hope she won't forget it,' said another. 'If she doesn't give me some of her gloves, I shall think she's very mean; for she has heaps, and I tried on a pair in fun so she could see they fitted and take a hint,' added a third. I did take the hint, you see;" and Rose opened a handsome box in which lay several pairs of her best gloves, with buttons enough to satisfy the heart of the most covetous.

"Plenty of silver paper and perfume, but not much love went into *that* bundle, I fancy?" and Dr. Alec could not help smiling at the disdainful little gesture with which Rose pushed away the box.

"Not a particle, nor in most of these. I have given them what they wanted, and taken back the confidence and respect they didn't care for. It is wrong, I know; but I can't bear to think all the seeming good-will and friendliness I've been enjoying was insincere and for a purpose. That's not the way *I* treat people."

"I am sure of it. Take things for what they are worth, dear, and try to find the wheat among the tares; for there is plenty if one knows how to look. Is that all the trouble?"

"No, sir, that is the lightest part of it. I shall soon get over my disappointment in those girls, and take them for what they are worth as you advise; but being deceived in them makes me suspicious of others, and that is hateful. If I cannot trust people, I'd rather keep by myself and be happy. I do detest manœuvring and underhand plots and plans!"

Rose spoke petulantly, and twitched her silk till it broke; while regret seemed to give place to anger as she spoke.

"There is evidently another thorn pricking. Let us have it out, and then 'I'll kiss the place to make it well,' as I used to do when I took the splinters from the fingers you are pricking so unmercifully," said the doctor, anxious to relieve his pet patient as soon as possible.

Rose laughed, but the color deepened in her cheeks, as she answered with a pretty mixture of maidenly shyness and natural candor.

"Aunt Clara worries me by warning me against half the young men I meet, and insisting that they only want my money. Now that is dreadful, and I won't listen: but I can't help thinking of it sometimes; for they *are* very kind to me, and I'm not vain enough to think it is my beauty. I suppose I am foolish, but I do like to feel that I am something beside an heiress."

The little quiver was in Rose's voice again as she ended; and Dr. Alec gave a quick sigh as he looked at the downcast face so full of the perplexity ingenuous spirits feel when doubt first mars their faith, and dims the innocent beliefs still left from childhood. He had been expecting this, and knew that what the girl just began to perceive and try modestly to tell, had long ago been plain to worldlier eyes. The heiress *was* the attraction to most of the young men whom she met. Good fellows enough, but educated, as nearly all are now-a-days, to believe that girls with beauty or money are brought to market to sell or buy as the case may be.

Rose could purchase any thing she liked, as she combined both advantages; and was soon surrounded by many admirers, each striving to secure the prize. Not being trained to believe that the only end and aim of a woman's life was a good match, she was a little disturbed, when the first pleasing excitement was over, to discover that her fortune was her chief attraction.

It was impossible for her to help seeing, hearing, guessing this from a significant glance, a stray word, a slight hint here and there; and the quick instinct of a woman felt even before it understood the self-interest which chilled for her so many opening friendships. In her eyes love was a very sacred thing, hardly to be thought of till it came, reverently received, and cherished faithfully to the end. Therefore, it is not strange that she shrunk from hearing it flippantly discussed, and marriage treated as a bargain to be haggled over, with little thought of its high duties, great responsibilities, and tender joys. Many things perplexed her, and sometimes a doubt of all that till now she had believed and trusted made her feel as if at sea without a compass; for the new world was so unlike the one she had been living in that it bewildered while it charmed the novice.

Dr. Alec understood the mood in which he found her, and did his best to warn without saddening by too much worldly wisdom.

"You are something besides an heiress to those who know and love you; so take heart, my girl, and hold fast to the faith that is in you. There is a touchstone for all these things, and whatever does not ring true doubt and avoid. Test and try men and women as they come along; and I am sure conscience, instinct, and experience will keep you from any dire mistake," he said, with a protecting arm about her, and a trustful look that was very comforting.

After a moment's pause she answered, while a sudden smile dimpled round her mouth, and the big glove went up to half hide her tell-tale cheeks,—

"Uncle, if I must have lovers, I do wish they'd be more

interesting. How can I like or respect men who go on as some of them do, and then imagine women *can* feel honored by the offer of their hands? Hearts are out of fashion, so they don't say much about them."

"Ah, ha! that is the trouble is it? and we begin to have delicate distresses do we?" said Dr. Alec, glad to see her brightening, and full of interest in the new topic; for he *was* a romantic old fellow, as he confessed to his brother.

Rose put down the glove, and looked up with a droll mixture of amusement and disgust in her face. "Uncle, it is perfectly disgraceful! I've wanted to tell you, but I was ashamed, because I never could boast of such things as some girls do; and they were so absurd I couldn't feel as if they were worth repeating even to you. Perhaps I ought, though; for you may think proper to command me to make a good match, and of course I should have to obey," she added, trying to look meek.

"Tell, by all means. Don't I always keep your secrets, and give you the best advice, like a model guardian? You must have a confidant, and where find a better one than here?" he asked, tapping his waistcoat with an inviting gesture.

"Nowhere: so I'll tell all but the names. I'd best be prudent; for I'm afraid you may get a little fierce: you do sometimes when people vex me," began Rose, rather liking the prospect of a confidential chat with uncle; for he had kept himself a good deal in the background lately.

"You know our ideas are old-fashioned; so I was not prepared to have men propose at all times and places, with no warning but a few smiles and soft speeches. I expected things of that sort would be very interesting and proper, not to say thrilling, on my part: but they are not; and I find myself laughing instead of crying, feeling angry instead of glad, and forgetting all about it very soon. Why, uncle, one absurd boy proposed when we'd only met half a dozen times. But he was dreadfully in debt, so that accounted for it perhaps," and Rose dusted her fingers, as if she had soiled them.

"I know him, and I thought he'd do it," observed the doctor with a shrug.

"You see and know every thing; so there's no need of going on, is there?"

"Do, do! who else? I won't even guess."

"Well, another went down upon his knees in Mrs. Van's greenhouse and poured forth his passion manfully, with a great cactus pricking his poor legs all the while. Kitty found him there, and it was impossible to keep sober; so he has hated me ever since."

The doctor's "Ha! ha!" was good to hear, and Rose joined him; for it was impossible to regard these episodes seriously, since no true sentiment redeemed them from absurdity.

"Another one sent me reams of poetry, and went on so Byronically, that I began to wish I had red hair and my name was Betsey Ann. I burnt all the verses: so don't expect to see them; and he, poor fellow, is consoling himself with Emma. But the worst of all was the one who would make love in public, and insisted on proposing in the middle of a dance. I seldom dance round dances except with our boys; but that night I did, because the girls laughed at me for being so 'prudish,' as they called it. I don't mind them now; for I found I *was* right, and felt that I deserved my fate."

"Is that all?" asked her uncle, looking "fierce," as she predicted, at the idea of his beloved girl obliged to listen to a declaration, twirling about on the arm of a lover.

"One more: but him I shall not tell about; for I know *he* was in earnest and really suffered, though I was as kind as I knew how to be. I'm young in these things yet, so I grieved for him, and treat his love with the tenderest respect."

Rose's voice sunk almost to a whisper as she ended; and Dr. Alec bent his head, as if involuntarily saluting a comrade in misfortune. Then he got up, saying with a keen look into the face he lifted by a finger under the chin,—

"Do you want another three months of this?"

"I'll tell you on New Year's day, uncle."

"Very well: try to keep a straight course, my little captain; and, if you see dirty weather ahead, call on your first mate."

"Ay, ay, sir; I'll remember."

# *Chapter V*

## PRINCE CHARMING

---

THE old glove lay upon the floor forgotten, while Rose sat musing, till a quick step sounded in the hall, and a voice drew near tunefully humming.

> "As he was walkin' doun the street
>  The city for to view,
> Oh, there he spied a bonny lass,
>  The window lookin' through."

> "Sae licht he jumpèd up the stair,
>  And tirled at the pin;
> Oh, wha sae ready as hersel'
>  To let the laddie in?"

sung Rose, as the voice paused and a tap came at the door.

"Good morning, Rosamunda; here are your letters, and your most devoted ready to execute any commissions you may have for him," was Charlie's greeting, as he came in looking comely, gay, and debonair as usual.

"Thanks: I've no errands unless you mail my replies, if these need answering; so by your leave, Prince," and Rose began to open the handful of notes he threw into her lap.

"Ha! what sight is this to blast mine eyes?" ejaculated Charlie, as he pointed to the glove with a melodramatic start; for, like most accomplished amateur actors, he was fond of introducing private theatricals into his "daily walk and conversation."

"Uncle left it."

"'Tis well; methought perchance a rival had been here," and, picking it up, Charlie amused himself with putting it on the head of a little Psyche, which ornamented the mantle-piece, humming, as he did so, another verse of the old song,—

> "He set his Jenny on his knee,
>  All in his Highland dress;
> For brawly well he kenned the way
>  To please a bonny lass."

Rose went on reading her letters, but all the while was thinking of her conversation with her uncle, and something else, suggested by the newcomer and his ditty.

During the three months since her return, she had seen more of this cousin than any of the others; for he seemed to be the only one who had leisure to "play with Rose," as they used to say years ago. The other boys were all at work, even little Jamie, many of whose play hours were devoted to manful struggles with Latin grammar, the evil genius of his boyish life. Dr. Alec had many affairs to arrange after his long absence; Phebe was busy with her music; and Aunt Plenty still actively superintended her housekeeping. Thus it fell out, quite naturally, that Charlie should form the habit of lounging in at all hours with letters, messages, bits of news, and agreeable plans for Rose. He helped her with her sketching, rode with her, sung with her, and took her to parties, as a matter of course; for Aunt Clara, being the gayest of the sisters, played chaperon on all occasions.

For a time it was very pleasant; but, by and by, Rose began to wish Charlie would find something to do like the rest, and not make dawdling after her the business of his life. The family were used to his self-indulgent ways: and there was an amiable delusion in the minds of the boys that he had a right to the best of every thing; for to them he was still the Prince, the flower of the flock, and in time to be an honor to the name. No one exactly knew how: for, though full of talent, he seemed to have no especial gift or bias; and the elders began to shake their heads, because, in spite of many grand promises and projects, the moment for decisive action never came.

Rose saw all this, and longed to inspire her brilliant cousin with some manful purpose, which should win for him respect as well as admiration. But she found it very hard: for, though he listened with imperturbable good humor, and owned his shortcomings with delightful frankness, he always had some argument, reason, or excuse to offer, and out-talked her in five minutes; leaving her silenced, but unconvinced.

Of late she had observed that he seemed to feel as if her time and thoughts belonged exclusively to him, and rather resented the approach of any other claimant. This annoyed her, and suggested the idea that her affectionate interest and efforts were misunderstood by him, misrepresented and taken advantage of by Aunt Clara, who had been most urgent that she should "use her influence with the dear boy," though the fond mother resented all other interference. This troubled Rose, and made her feel as if caught in a snare; for, while she owned to herself that Charlie was the most attractive of her cousins, she was not ready to be taken possession of in this masterful way, especially since other and sometimes better men sought her favor more humbly.

These thoughts were floating vaguely in her mind as she read her letters, and unconsciously influenced her in the chat that followed.

"Only invitations, and I can't stop to answer them now, or I shall never get through this job," she said, returning to her work.

"Let me help. You do up, and I'll direct. Have a secretary; do now, and see what a comfort it will be," proposed Charlie, who could turn his hand to any thing, and had made himself quite at home in the sanctum.

"I'd rather finish this myself, but you may answer the notes if you will. Just regrets to all but two or three. Read the names as you go along, and I'll tell you which."

"To hear is to obey. Who says I'm a 'frivolous idler' now?" and Charlie sat down at the writing table with alacrity; for these hours in the little room were his best and happiest.

"Order is heaven's first law, and the view a lovely one, but I *don't* see any note-paper," he added, opening the desk and surveying its contents with interest.

"Right-hand drawer: violet monogram for the notes; plain paper for the business letter. I'll see to that, though," answered Rose, trying to decide whether Annabel or Emma should have the laced handkerchief.

"Confiding creature! Suppose I open the wrong drawer, and come upon the tender secrets of your soul?" continued the new secretary, rummaging out the delicate note-paper with masculine disregard of order.

"I haven't got any," answered Rose, demurely.

"What, not one despairing scrawl, one cherished miniature, one faded floweret, etc., etc.? I can't believe it, cousin," and he shook his head incredulously.

"If I had, I certainly should not show them to you, impertinent person! There *are* a few little souvenirs in that desk, but nothing very sentimental or interesting."

"How I'd like to see 'em! But I should never dare to ask," observed Charlie, peering over the top of the half-open lid with a most persuasive pair of eyes.

"You may if you want to, but you'll be disappointed, Paul Pry. Lower left-hand drawer with the key in it."

"'Angel of goodness, how shall I requite thee? Interesting moment, with what palpitating emotions art thou fraught!'" and, quoting from the "Mysteries of Udolpho," he unlocked and opened the drawer with a tragic gesture.

"Seven locks of hair in a box, all light; for 'here's your straw color, your orange tawny, your French crown color, and your perfect yellow' Shakspeare. They look very familiar, and I fancy I know the heads they thatched."

"Yes, you all gave me one when I went away, you know; and I carried them round the world with me in that very box."

"I wish the heads had gone too. Here's a jolly little amber god, with a gold ring in his back and a most balmy breath," continued Charlie, taking a long sniff at the scent-bottle.

"Uncle brought me that long ago, and I'm very fond of it."

"This now looks suspicious,—a man's ring with a lotus cut on the stone and a note attached. I tremble as I ask, Who, when, and where?"

"A gentleman, on my birthday, in Calcutta."

"I breathe again: it was my sire?"

"Don't be absurd. Of course it was, and he did every thing to make my visit pleasant. I wish you'd go and see him like a dutiful son, instead of idling here."

"That's what Uncle Mac is eternally telling me; but I don't intend to be lectured into the tread-mill till I've had my fling first," muttered Charlie, rebelliously.

"If you fling yourself in the wrong direction, you may find it hard to get back again," began Rose, gravely.

"No fear, if you look after me as you seem to have promised to do, judging by the thanks you get in this note. Poor old governor! I *should* like to see him; for it's almost four years since he came home last, and he must be getting on."

Charlie was the only one of the boys who ever called his

father "governor:" perhaps because the others knew and loved their fathers, while he had seen so little of his that the less respectful name came more readily to his lips; since the elder man seemed in truth a governor issuing requests or commands, which the younger too often neglected or resented.

Long ago Rose had discovered that Uncle Stephen found home made so distasteful by his wife's devotion to society, that he preferred to exile himself, taking business as an excuse for his protracted absences.

The girl was thinking of this, as she watched her cousin turn the ring about with a sudden sobriety which became him well; and, believing that the moment was propitious, she said earnestly,—

"He *is* getting on. Dear Charlie, do think of duty more than pleasure in this case, and I'm sure you never will regret it."

"Do *you* want me to go?" he asked quickly.

"I think you ought."

"And I think you'd be much more charming if you wouldn't always be worrying about right and wrong! Uncle Alec taught you that along with the rest of his queer notions."

"I'm glad he did!" cried Rose, warmly; then checked herself, and said with a patient sort of sigh, "You know women always want the men they care for to be good, and can't help trying to make them so."

"So they do; and we ought to be a set of angels: but I've a strong conviction that, if we were, the dear souls wouldn't like us half as well. Would they now?" asked Charlie, with an insinuating smile.

"Perhaps not; but that is dodging the point. Will you go?" persisted Rose, unwisely.

"No, I will not."

That was sufficiently decided; and an uncomfortable pause followed, during which Rose tied a knot unnecessarily tight, and Charlie went on exploring the drawer with more energy than interest.

"Why, here's an old thing I gave you ages ago!" he suddenly exclaimed in a pleased tone, holding up a little agate heart on a faded blue ribbon. "Will you let me take away the heart of stone and give you a heart of flesh?" he asked, half in earnest, half in jest, touched by the little trinket and the recollections it awakened.

"No, I will not," answered Rose, bluntly, much displeased by the irreverent and audacious question.

Charlie looked rather abashed for a moment; but his natural light-heartedness made it easy for him to get the better of his own brief fits of waywardness, and put others in good humor with him and themselves.

"Now we are even: let's drop the subject and start afresh," he said with irresistible affability, as he coolly put the little heart in his pocket, and prepared to shut the drawer. But something caught his eye, and exclaiming, "What's this? what's this?" he snatched up a photograph which lay half under a pile of letters with foreign post-marks.

"Oh! I forgot that was there," said Rose, hastily.

"Who is the man?" demanded Charlie, eying the good-looking countenance before him with a frown.

"That is the Honorable Gilbert Murry, who went up the Nile with us, and shot crocodiles and other small deer, being a mighty hunter, as I told you in my letters," answered Rose gayly, though ill-pleased at the little discovery just then; for this had been one of the narrow escapes her uncle spoke of.

"And they haven't eaten him yet, I infer from that pile of letters?" said Charlie, jealously.

"I hope not. His sister did not mention it when she wrote last."

"Ah! then she is your correspondent? Sisters are dangerous things sometimes." And Charlie eyed the packet suspiciously.

"In this case, a very convenient thing; for she tells me all about her brother's wedding as no one else would take the trouble to do."

"Oh! well, if he's married, I don't care a straw about him. I fancied I'd found out why you are such a hard-hearted charmer. But, if there is no secret idol, I'm all at sea again." And Charlie tossed the photograph into the drawer, as if it no longer interested him.

"I'm hard-hearted because I'm particular, and, as yet, do not find any one at all to my taste."

"No one?" with a tender glance.

"No one," with a rebellious blush, and the truthful addition, "I see much to admire and like in many persons, but none quite strong and good enough to suit me. My heroes are old-fashioned, you know."

"Prigs, like Guy Carleton, Count Altenberg, and John Halifax: I know the pattern you goody girls like," sneered Charlie, who preferred the Guy Livingston, Beauclerc, and Rochester style.

"Then I'm not a 'goody girl,' for I don't like prigs. I want a gentleman in the best sense of the word, and I can wait; for I've seen one, and know there are more in the world."

"The deuce you have! Do I know him?" asked Charlie, much alarmed.

"You think you do," answered Rose, with a mischievous sparkle in her eye.

"If it isn't Pem, I give it up. He is the best-bred fellow I know."

"Oh, dear, no! far superior to Mr. Pemberton, and many years older," said Rose, with so much respect that Charlie looked perplexed as well as anxious.

"Some apostolic minister, I fancy. You pious creatures always like to adore a parson. But all we know are married."

"He isn't."

"Give a name, for pity's sake: I'm suffering tortures of suspense," begged Charlie.

"Alexander Campbell."

"Uncle? Well, upon my word, that's a relief, but mighty absurd all the same. So, when you find a young saint of that sort, you intend to marry him, do you?" demanded Charlie, much amused and rather disappointed.

"When I find any man half as honest, good, and noble as uncle, I shall be proud to marry him, if he asks me," answered Rose, decidedly.

"What odd tastes women have!" And Charlie leaned his chin on his hand, to muse pensively for a moment over the blindness of one woman who could admire an excellent old uncle more than a dashing young cousin.

Rose, meanwhile, tied up her parcels industriously, hoping she had not been too severe; for it was very hard to lecture Charlie, though he seemed to like it sometimes, and came to confession voluntarily, knowing that women love to forgive when the sinners are of his sort.

"It will be mail-time before you are done," she said presently; for silence was less pleasant than his rattle.

Charlie took the hint, and dashed off several notes in his best manner. Coming to the business-letter, he glanced at it, and asked, with a puzzled expression,—

"What is all this? Cost of repairs, &c., from a man named Buffum?"

"Never mind that: I'll see to it by and by."

"But I do mind, for I'm interested in all your affairs; and, though you think I've no head for business, you'll find I have, if you'll try me."

"This is only about my two old houses in the city, which are being repaired and altered so that the rooms can be let singly."

"Going to make tenement-houses of them? Well, that's not a bad idea: such places pay well, I've heard."

"That is just what I'm *not* going to do. I wouldn't have a tenement-house on my conscience for a million of dollars,— not as they are now," said Rose, decidedly.

"Why, what do *you* know about it, except that poor people live in them, and the owners turn a penny on the rents?"

"I know a good deal about them; for I've seen many such, both here and abroad. It was not all pleasure with us, I assure you. Uncle was interested in hospitals and prisons, and I sometimes went with him: but they made me sad; so he suggested other charities, that I could help about when we came home. I visited Infant Schools, Working-women's Homes, Orphan Asylums, and places of that sort. You don't know how much good it did me, and how glad I am that I have the means of lightening a little some of the misery in the world."

"But, my dear girl, you needn't make ducks and drakes of your fortune trying to feed and cure and clothe all the poor wretches you see. Give, of course: every one should do something in that line, and no one likes it better than I. But don't, for mercy's sake, go at it as some women do, and get so desperately earnest, practical, and charity-mad that there is no living in peace with you," protested Charlie, looking alarmed at the prospect.

"You can do as you please. *I* intend to do all the good I can

by asking the advice and following the example of the most
'earnest,' 'practical,' and 'charitable' people I know: so, if you
don't approve, you can drop my acquaintance," answered Rose,
emphasizing the obnoxious words, and assuming the resolute
air she always wore when defending her hobbies.

"You'll be laughed at."

"I'm used to that."

"And criticised and shunned."

"Not by people whose opinion I value."

"Women shouldn't go poking into such places."

"I've been taught that they should."

"Well, you'll get some dreadful disease and lose your beauty,
and then where are you?" added Charlie, thinking that might
daunt the young philanthropist.

But it did not; for Rose answered, with a sudden kindling of
the eyes as she remembered her talk with Uncle Alec,—

"I shouldn't like it: but there would be one satisfaction in it;
for, when I'd lost my beauty and given away my money, I
should know who really cared for me."

Charlie nibbled his pen in silence for a moment, then asked,
meekly,—

"Could I respectfully inquire what great reform is to be
carried on in the old houses which their amiable owner is re-
pairing?"

"I am merely going to make them comfortable homes for poor
but respectable women to live in. There is a class who cannot afford to pay much, yet suffer a great deal from being obliged to
stay in noisy, dirty, crowded places like tenement-houses and
cheap lodgings. I can help a few of them, and I'm going to try."

"May I humbly ask if these decayed gentlewomen are to inhabit their palatial retreat rent-free?"

"That was my first plan; but uncle showed me that it was
wiser not to make genteel paupers of them, but let them pay a
small rent and feel independent. I don't want the money of
course, and shall use it in keeping the houses tidy, or helping
other women in like case," said Rose, entirely ignoring her
cousin's covert ridicule.

"Don't expect any gratitude, for you won't get it; nor much
comfort with a lot of forlornities on your hands; and be sure

that when it is too late you will tire of it all, and wish you had done as other people do."

"Thanks for your cheerful prophecies; but I think I'll venture."

She looked so undaunted that Charlie was a little nettled, and fired his last shot rather recklessly,—

"Well, one thing I do know: you'll never get a husband if you go on in this absurd way; and, by Jove! you need one to take care of you and keep the property together!"

Rose had a temper, but seldom let it get the better of her; now, however, it flashed up for a moment. Those last words were peculiarly unfortunate, because Aunt Clara had used them more than once, when warning her against impecunious suitors and generous projects. She was disappointed in her cousin, annoyed at having her little plans laughed at, and indignant with him for his final suggestion.

"I'll never have one, if I must give up the liberty of doing what I know is right; and I'd rather go into the poor-house to-morrow than 'keep the property together' in the selfish way you mean!"

That was all: but Charlie saw that he had gone too far, and hastened to make his peace with the skill of a lover; for, turning to the little cabinet piano behind him, he sung in his best style the sweet old song,—

"Oh were thou in the cauld blast,"

dwelling with great effect, not only upon the tender assurance that

"My plaid should shelter thee,"

but also that, even if a king,

"The brightest jewel in my crown
    Wad be my queen, wad be my queen."

It was very evident that Prince Charming had not gone troubadouring in vain; for Orpheus himself could not have restored harmony more successfully. The tuneful apology was accepted with a forgiving smile, and a frank,—

"I'm sorry I was cross; but you haven't forgotten how to

tease, and I'm rather out of sorts to-day. Late hours don't agree with me."

"Then you won't feel like going to Mrs. Hope's to-morrow night, I'm afraid," and Charlie took up the last note with an expression of regret which was very flattering.

"I must go, because it is made for me; but I can come away early, and make up lost sleep. I do hate to be so fractious," and Rose rubbed the forehead that ached with too much racketing.

"But the German does not begin till late: I'm to lead, and depend upon you. Just stay this once to oblige me," pleaded Charlie; for he had set his heart on distinguishing himself.

"No: I promised uncle to be temperate in my pleasures, and I must keep my word. I'm so well now, it would be very foolish to get ill and make him anxious: not to mention losing my beauty, as you are good enough to call it; for that depends on health, you know."

"But the fun doesn't begin till after supper. Every thing will be delightful, I assure you; and we'll have a gay old time as we did last week at Emma's."

"Then I certainly will not; for I'm ashamed of myself when I remember what a romp that was, and how sober uncle looked, as he let me in at three in the morning, all fagged out; my dress in rags, my head aching, my feet so tired that I could hardly stand, and nothing to show for five hours' hard work but a pocketful of bonbons, artificial flowers, and tissue-paper fool's-caps. Uncle said I'd better put one on and go to bed; for I looked as if I'd been to a French Bal Masqué. I never want to hear him say so again, and I'll never let dawn catch me out in such a plight any more."

"You were all right enough; for mother didn't object, and I got you both home before daylight. Uncle is notional about such things, so I shouldn't mind; for we had a jolly time, and we were none the worse for it."

"Indeed we were, every one of us! Aunt Clara hasn't got over her cold yet; I slept all the next day; and you looked like a ghost, for you'd been out every night for weeks, I think."

"Oh, nonsense! every one does it during the season, and you'll get used to the pace very soon," began Charlie, bent on making her go; for he was in his element in a ballroom, and never happier than when he had his pretty cousin on his arm.

"Ah! but I don't want to get used to it; for it costs too much in the end. I don't wish to get used to being whisked about a hot room by men who have taken too much wine; to turn day into night, wasting time that might be better spent; and grow into a fashionable fast girl who can't get on without excitement. I don't deny that much of it is pleasant, but don't try to make me too fond of gayety. Help me to resist what I know is hurtful, and please don't laugh me out of the good habits uncle has tried so hard to give me."

Rose was quite sincere in her appeal, and Charlie knew she was right: but he always found it hard to give up any thing he had set his heart upon, no matter how trivial; for the maternal indulgence which had harmed the boy had fostered the habit of self-indulgence which was ruining the man. So when Rose looked up at him, with a very honest desire to save him as well as herself from being swept into the giddy vortex which keeps so many young people revolving aimlessly, till they go down or are cast upon the shore wrecks of what they might have been, he gave a shrug and answered briefly,—

"As you please. I'll bring you home as early as you like, and Effie Waring can take your place in the German. What flowers shall I send you?"

Now, that was an artful speech of Charlie's; for Miss Waring was a fast and fashionable damsel, who openly admired Prince Charming, and had given him the name. Rose disliked her, and was sure her influence was bad; for youth made frivolity forgivable, wit hid want of refinement, and beauty always covers a multitude of sins in a man's eyes. At the sound of Effie's name, Rose wavered, and would have yielded but for the memory of the "first mate's" last words. She did desire to "keep a straight course;" so, though the current of impulse set strongly in a southerly direction, principle, the only compass worth having, pointed due north, and she tried to obey it like a wise young navigator, saying steadily, while she directed to Annabel the parcel containing a capacious pair of slippers intended for Uncle Mac,—

"Don't trouble yourself about me. I can go with uncle, and slip away without disturbing anybody."

"I don't believe you'll have the heart to do it," said Charlie, incredulously, as he sealed the last note.

"Wait and see."

"I will, but shall hope to the last," and, kissing his hand to her, he departed to post her letters, quite sure that Miss Waring would not lead the German.

It certainly looked for a moment as if Miss Campbell *would,* because she ran to the door with the words "I'll go" upon her lips. But she did not open it till she had stood a minute staring hard at the old glove on Psyche's head; then, like one who had suddenly got a bright idea, she gave a decided nod and walked slowly out of the room.

# Chapter VI

### POLISHING MAC

"PLEASE could I say one word?" was the question three times repeated before a rough head bobbed out from the grotto of books in which Mac usually sat when he studied.

"Did any one speak?" he asked, blinking in the flood of sunshine that entered with Rose.

"Only three times, thank you. Don't disturb yourself, I beg; for I merely want to say a word," answered Rose, as she prevented him from offering the easy-chair in which he sat.

"I was rather deep in a compound fracture, and didn't hear. What can I do for you, cousin?" and Mac shoved a stack of pamphlets off the chair near him, with a hospitable wave of the hand that sent his papers flying in all directions.

Rose sat down, but did not seem to find her "word" an easy one to utter; for she twisted her handkerchief about her fingers in embarrassed silence, till Mac put on his glasses, and, after a keen look, asked soberly,—

"Is it a splinter, a cut, or a whitlow, ma'am?"

"It is neither; do forget your tiresome surgery for a minute, and be the kindest cousin that ever was," answered Rose, beginning rather sharply and ending with her most engaging smile.

"Can't promise in the dark," said the wary youth.

"It is a favor, a great favor, and one I don't choose to ask any of the other boys," answered the artful damsel.

Mac looked pleased, and leaned forward, saying more affably,—

"Name it, and be sure I'll grant it if I can."

"Go with me to Mrs. Hope's party to-morrow night."

"What!" and Mac recoiled as if she had put a pistol to his head.

"I've left you in peace a long time: but it is your turn now; so do your duty like a man and a cousin."

"But I never go to parties!" cried the unhappy victim in great dismay.

"High time you began, sir."

"But I don't dance fit to be seen."

"I'll teach you."

"My dress-coat isn't decent, I know."

"Archie will lend you one: he isn't going."

"I'm afraid there's a lecture that I ought not to cut."

"No, there isn't: I asked uncle."

"I'm always so tired and dull in the evening."

"This sort of thing is just what you want to rest and freshen up your spirits."

Mac gave a groan and fell back vanquished; for it was evident that escape was impossible.

"What put such a perfectly wild idea into your head?" he demanded, rather roughly; for hitherto he *had* been "left in peace," and this sudden attack decidedly amazed him.

"Sheer necessity; but don't do it if it is so very dreadful to you. I must go to several more parties, because they are made for me; but after that I'll refuse, and then no one need be troubled with me."

Something in Rose's voice made Mac answer penitently, even while he knit his brows in perplexity,—

"I didn't mean to be rude; and of course I'll go anywhere if I'm really needed. But I don't understand where the sudden necessity is, with three other fellows at command, all better dancers and beaux than I am."

"I don't want them, and I do want you; for I haven't the heart to drag uncle out any more, and you know I never go with any gentleman but those of my own family."

"Now look here, Rose: if Steve has been doing any thing to tease you just mention it, and I'll attend to him," cried Mac, plainly seeing that something was amiss, and fancying that Dandy was at the bottom of it, as he had done escort duty several times lately.

"No, Steve has been very good: but I know he had rather be with Kitty Van; so of course I feel like a marplot, though he is too polite to hint it."

"What a noodle that boy is! But there's Archie: he's as steady as a church, and has no sweetheart to interfere," continued Mac, bound to get at the truth, and half suspecting what it was.

"He is on his feet all day, and Aunt Jessie wants him in the evening. He does not care for dancing as he used, and I suppose he really does prefer to rest and read." Rose might have added, "and hear Phebe sing;" for Phebe did not go out as much as Rose did, and Aunt Jessie often came in to sit with the old lady when the young folks were away; and, of course, dutiful Archie came with her; so willingly of late!

"What's amiss with Charlie? I thought *he* was the prince of cavaliers. Annabel says he dances 'like an angel,' and I know a dozen mothers couldn't keep him at home of an evening. Have you had a tiff with Adonis, and so fall back on poor me?" asked Mac, coming last to the person of whom he thought first, but did not mention, feeling shy about alluding to a subject often discussed behind her back.

"Yes, we have; and I don't intend to go with him any more for some time. His ways do not suit me, and mine do not suit him; so I want to be quite independent, and you can help me if you will," said Rose, rather nervously spinning the big globe close by.

Mac gave a low whistle, looking wide awake all in a minute, as he said with a gesture, as if he brushed a cobweb off his face,—

"Now, see here, cousin: I'm not good at mysteries, and shall only blunder if you put me blindfold into any nice manœuvre. Just tell me straight out what you want, and I'll do it if I can. Play I'm uncle, and free your mind; come now."

He spoke so kindly, and the honest eyes were so full of merry good-will, that Rose felt she might confide in him, and answered as frankly as he could desire,—

"You are right, Mac; and I don't mind talking to you almost as freely as to uncle, because you are such a reliable fellow, and won't think me silly for trying to do what I believe to be right. Charlie does, and so makes it hard for me to hold to my resolutions. I want to keep early hours, dress simply, and behave properly; no matter what fashionable people do. You will agree to that, I'm sure; and stand by me through thick and thin for principle's sake."

"I will; and begin by showing you that I understand the case. I don't wonder you are not pleased; for Charlie is too presuming, and you do need some one to help you head him off a bit. Hey, cousin?"

"What a way to put it!" and Rose laughed in spite of herself, adding with an air of relief, "That *is* it; and I do want some one to help me make him understand that I don't choose to be taken possession of in that lordly way, as if I belonged to him more than to the rest of the family. I don't like it; for people begin to talk, and Charlie won't see how disagreeable it is to me."

"Tell him so," was Mac's blunt advice.

"I have; but he only laughs and promises to behave, and then he does it again, when I am so placed that I can't say any thing. You will never understand, and I cannot explain; for it is only a look, or a word, or some little thing: but I won't have it, and the best way to cure him is to put it out of his power to annoy me so."

"He is a great flirt, and wants to teach you how, I suppose. I'll speak to him if you like, and tell him you don't want to learn. Shall I?" asked Mac, finding the case rather an interesting one.

"No, thank you: that would only make trouble. If you will kindly play escort a few times, it will show Charlie that I am in earnest without more words, and put a stop to the gossip," said Rose, coloring like a poppy at the recollection of what she heard one young man whisper to another, as Charlie led her through a crowded supper-room with his most devoted air, "Lucky dog! he is sure to get the heiress, and we are nowhere."

"There's no danger of people's gossiping about us, is there?" and Mac looked up, with the oddest of all his odd expressions.

"Of course not: you're only a boy."

"I'm twenty-one, thank you; and Prince is but a couple of years older," said Mac, promptly resenting the slight put upon his manhood.

"Yes; but he is like other young men, while you are a dear old bookworm. No one would ever mind what *you* did; so you may go to parties with me every night, and not a word would be said; or, if there was, I shouldn't mind since it is 'only Mac,'" answered Rose, smiling as she quoted a household word often used to excuse his vagaries.

"Then *I* am nobody?" lifting his brows, as if the discovery surprised and rather nettled him.

"Nobody in society as yet; but my very best cousin in

private, and I've just proved my regard by making you my confidant, and choosing you for my knight," said Rose, hastening to soothe the feelings her careless words seemed to have ruffled slightly.

"Much good *that* is likely to do me," grumbled Mac.

"You ungrateful boy, not to appreciate the honor I've conferred upon you! I know a dozen who would be proud of the place: but you only care for compound fractures; so I won't detain you any longer, except to ask if I may consider myself provided with an escort for to-morrow night?" said Rose, a trifle hurt at his indifference; for she was not used to refusals.

"If I may hope for the honor," and, rising, he made her a bow which was such a capital imitation of Charlie's grand manner that she forgave him at once, exclaiming with amused surprise,—

"Why, Mac! I didn't know you *could* be so elegant!"

"A fellow can be almost any thing he likes, if he tries hard enough," he answered, standing very straight, and looking so tall and dignified that Rose was quite impressed, and with a stately courtesy she retired, saying graciously,—

"I accept with thanks. Good-morning, Doctor Alexander Mackenzie Campbell."

When Friday evening came, and word was sent up that her escort had arrived, Rose ran down, devoutly hoping that he had not come in a velveteen jacket, top-boots, black gloves, or made any trifling mistake of that sort. A young gentleman was standing before the long mirror, apparently intent on the arrangement of his hair; and Rose paused suddenly as her eye went from the glossy broadcloth to the white-gloved hands, busy with an unruly lock that would not stay in place.

"Why, Charlie, I thought—" she began with an accent of surprise in her voice, but got no further; for the gentleman turned and she beheld Mac in immaculate evening costume, with his hair parted sweetly on his brow, a superior posy at his button-hole, and the expression of a martyr upon his face.

"Ah, don't you wish it was? No one but yourself to thank that it isn't he. Am I right? Dandy got me up, and he ought to know what is what," demanded Mac, folding his hands and standing as stiff as a ramrod.

"You are so regularly splendid that I don't know you."

"Neither do I."

"I really had no idea you could look so like a gentleman," added Rose, surveying him with great approval.

"Nor I that I could feel so like a fool."

"Poor boy! he does look rather miserable. What can I do to cheer him up, in return for the sacrifice he is making?"

"Stop calling me a boy. It will soothe my agony immensely, and give me courage to appear in a low-necked coat and a curl on my forehead; for I'm not used to such elegancies, and find them no end of a trial."

Mac spoke in such a pathetic tone, and gave such a gloomy glare at the aforesaid curl, that Rose laughed in his face, and added to his woe by handing him her cloak. He surveyed it gravely for a minute, then carefully put it on wrong side out, and gave the swan's-down hood a good pull over her head, to the utter destruction of all smoothness to the curls inside.

Rose uttered a cry and cast off the cloak, bidding him learn to do it properly, which he meekly did, and then led her down the hall without walking on her skirts more than three times by the way. But at the door she discovered that she had forgotten her furred overshoes, and bade Mac get them.

"Never mind: it's not wet," he said, pulling his cap over his eyes and plunging into his coat, regardless of the "elegancies" that afflicted him.

"But I can't walk on cold stones with thin slippers, can I?" began Rose, showing a little white foot.

"You needn't, for—there you are, my lady;" and, unceremoniously picking her up, Mac landed her in the carriage before she could say a word.

"What an escort!" she exclaimed in comic dismay, as she rescued her delicate dress from the rug in which he was about to tuck her up like a mummy.

"It's 'only Mac,' so don't mind," and he cast himself into an opposite corner, with the air of a man who had nerved himself to the accomplishment of many painful duties, and was bound to do them or die.

"But gentlemen don't catch up ladies like bags of meal, and poke them into carriages in this way. It is evident that you need looking after, and it is high time I undertook your society manners. Now, do mind what you are about, and don't get yourself or me into a scrape if you can help it," besought Rose, feeling that on many accounts she had gone farther and fared worse.

"I'll behave like a Turveydrop: see if I don't."

Mac's idea of the immortal Turveydrop's behavior seemed to be a peculiar one; for, after dancing once with his cousin, he left her to her own devices, and soon forgot all about her in a long conversation with Professor Stumph, the learned geologist. Rose did not care; for one dance proved to her that that branch of Mac's education *had* been sadly neglected, and she was glad to glide smoothly about with Steve, though he was only an inch or two taller than herself. She had plenty of partners, however, and plenty of chaperons; for all the young men were her most devoted, and all the matrons beamed upon her with maternal benignity.

Charlie was not there; for when he found that Rose stood firm, and had moreover engaged Mac as a permanency, he would not go at all, and retired in high dudgeon to console himself with more dangerous pastimes. Rose feared it would be so; and, even in the midst of the gayety about her, an anxious mood came over her now and then, and made her thoughtful for a moment. She felt her power, and wanted to use it wisely; but did not know how to be kind to Charlie without being untrue to herself and giving him false hopes.

"I wish we were all children again, with no hearts to perplex us and no great temptations to try us," she said to herself, as she rested a moment in a quiet nook while her partner went to get a glass of water. Right in the midst of this half-sad, half-sentimental reverie, she heard a familiar voice behind her say earnestly,—

"And allophite is the new hydrous silicate of alumina and magnesia, much resembling pseudophite, which Websky found in Silesia."

"What *is* Mac talking about!" she thought: and, peeping behind a great azalea in full bloom, she saw her cousin in deep converse with the professor, evidently having a capital time; for his face had lost its melancholy expression and was all alive with interest, while the elder man was listening as if his remarks were both intelligent and agreeable.

"What is it?" asked Steve, coming up with the water, and seeing a smile on Rose's face.

She pointed out the scientific *tête-à-tête* going on behind the azalea, and Steve grinned as he peeped, then grew sober and said in a tone of despair,—

"If you had seen the pains I took with that fellow, the patience with which I brushed his wig, the time I spent trying to convince him that he must wear thin boots, and the fight I had to get him into that coat; you'd understand my feelings when I see him now."

"Why, what is the matter with him?" asked Rose.

"Will you take a look, and see what a spectacle he has made of himself. He'd better be sent home at once, or he will disgrace the family by looking as if he'd been in a row."

Steve spoke in such a tragic tone that Rose took another peep and did sympathize with Dandy; for Mac's elegance was quite gone. His tie was under one ear, his posy hung upside down, his gloves were rolled into a ball, which he absently squeezed and pounded as he talked, and his hair looked as if a whirlwind had passed over it; for his ten fingers set it on end now and then, as they had a habit of doing when he studied or talked earnestly. But he looked so happy and wide awake, in spite of his dishevelment, that Rose gave an approving nod, and said behind her fan,—

"It *is* a trying spectacle, Steve: yet, on the whole, I think his own odd ways suit him best; and I fancy we shall yet be proud of him, for he knows more than all the rest of us put together. Hear that now," and Rose paused, that they might listen to the following burst of eloquence from Mac's lips:—

"You know Frenzel has shown that the globular forms of silicate of bismuth at Schneeburg and Johanngeorgenstadt are not isometric, but monoclinic in crystalline form; and consequently he separates them from the old eulytite, and gives them the new name Agricolite."

"Isn't it awful? Let us get out of this before there's another avalanche, or we shall be globular silicates and isometric crystals in spite of ourselves," whispered Steve with a panic-stricken air; and they fled from the hail-storm of hard words that rattled about their ears, leaving Mac to enjoy himself in his own way.

But when Rose was ready to go home, and looked about for her escort, he was nowhere to be seen; for the professor had departed, and Mac with him, so absorbed in some new topic that he entirely forgot his cousin, and went placidly home, still pondering on the charms of geology. When this pleasing fact dawned upon Rose, her feelings may be imagined. She was both angry and amused: it was so like Mac to go mooning off and leave her to her fate. Not a hard one, however; for, though Steve was gone with Kitty before her flight was discovered, Mrs. Bliss was only too glad to take the deserted damsel under her wing, and bear her safely home.

Rose was warming her feet, and sipping the chocolate which Phebe always had ready for her, as she never ate suppers; when a hurried tap came at the long window whence the light streamed, and Mac's voice was heard softly asking to be let in "just for one minute."

Curious to know what had befallen him, Rose bade Phebe obey his call; and the delinquent cavalier appeared, breathless, anxious, and more dilapidated than ever: for he had forgotten his overcoat; his tie was at the back of his neck now; and his hair as rampantly erect as if all the winds of heaven had been blowing freely through it, as they had; for he had been tearing to and fro the last half-hour trying to undo the dreadful deed he had so innocently committed.

"Don't take any notice of me; for I don't deserve it: I only came to see that you were safe, cousin, and then go hang myself, as Steve advised," he began, in a remorseful tone, that would have been very effective, if he had not been obliged to catch his breath with a comical gasp now and then.

"I never thought *you* would be the one to desert me," said Rose, with a reproachful look; thinking it best not to relent too soon, though she was quite ready to do it when she saw how sincerely distressed he was.

"It was that confounded man! He was a regular walking encyclopædia; and, finding I could get a good deal out of him, I went in for general information, as the time was short. You know I always forget every thing else when I get hold of such a fellow."

"That is evident. I wonder how you came to remember me at all," answered Rose, on the brink of a laugh: it was so absurd.

"I didn't till Steve said something that reminded me: then it burst upon me, in one awful shock, that I'd gone and left you;

and you might have knocked me down with a feather," said honest Mac, hiding none of his iniquity.

"What did you do then?"

"Do! I went off like a shot, and never stopped till I reached the Hopes"—

"You didn't walk all that way?" cried Rose.

"Bless you, no: I ran. But you were gone with Mrs. Bliss: so I pelted back again to see with my own eyes that you were safe at home," answered Mac, wiping his hot forehead, with a sigh of relief.

"But it is three miles at least each way; and twelve o'clock, and dark and cold. O Mac! how could you!" exclaimed Rose, suddenly realizing what he had done, as she heard his labored breathing, saw the state of the thin boots, and detected the absence of an overcoat.

"Couldn't do less, could I?" asked Mac, leaning up against the door and trying not to pant.

"There was no need of half-killing yourself for such a trifle. You might have known I could take care of myself for once, at least, with so many friends about. Sit down this minute. Bring another cup, please, Phebe: this boy isn't going home till he is rested and refreshed after such a run as that," commanded Rose.

"Don't be good to me: I'd rather take a scolding than a chair, and drink hemlock instead of chocolate if you happen to have any ready," answered Mac, with a pathetic puff, as he subsided on to the sofa, and meekly took the draught Phebe brought him.

"If you had any thing the matter with your heart, sir, a race of this sort might be the death of you: so never do it again," said Rose, offering her fan to cool his heated countenance.

"Haven't got any heart."

"Yes, you have, for I hear it beating like a trip-hammer, and it is my fault: I ought to have stopped as we went by, and told you I was all right."

"It's the mortification, not the miles, that upsets me. I often take that run for exercise, and think nothing of it; but to-night I was so mad I made extra good time, I fancy. Now don't you worry, but compose your mind, and 'sip your dish of tea,' as

Evelina says," answered Mac, artfully turning the conversation from himself.

"What do you know about Evelina?" asked Rose, in great surprise.

"All about her. Do you suppose I never read a novel?"

"I thought you read nothing but Greek and Latin, with an occasional glance at Websky's pseudophites and the monoclinics of Johanngeorgenstadt."

Mac opened his eyes wide at this reply, then seemed to see the joke, and joined in the laugh with such heartiness that Aunt Plenty's voice was heard demanding from above, with sleepy anxiety,—

"*Is* the house afire?"

"No, ma'am, every thing is safe, and I'm only saying good-night," answered Mac, diving for his cap.

"Then go at once, and let that child have her sleep," added the old lady, retiring to her bed.

Rose ran into the hall, and, catching up her uncle's fur coat, met Mac as he came out of the study, absently looking about for his own.

"You haven't got any, you benighted boy! so take this, and have your wits about you next time, or I won't let you off so easily," she said, holding up the heavy garment, and peeping over it, with no sign of displeasure in her laughing eyes.

"Next time! Then you do forgive me? You will try me again, and give me a chance to prove that I'm not a fool?" cried Mac, embracing the big coat with emotion.

"Of course I will; and, so far from thinking you a fool, I was much impressed with your learning to-night, and told Steve that we ought to be proud of our philosopher."

"Learning be hanged! I'll show you that I'm *not* a book-worm, but as much a man as any of them; and then you may be proud or not, as you like!" cried Mac, with a defiant nod, that caused the glasses to leap wildly off his nose, as he caught up his hat and departed as he came.

A day or two later, Rose went to call upon Aunt Jane, as she dutifully did once or twice a week. On her way upstairs, she heard a singular sound in the drawing-room, and involuntarily stopped to listen.

"One, two, three, slide! One, two, three, turn! Now then, come on!" said one voice, impatiently.

"It's very easy to say 'come on;' but what the dickens do I do with my left leg while I'm turning and sliding with my right?" demanded another voice, in a breathless and mournful tone.

Then the whistling and thumping went on more vigorously than before; and Rose, recognizing the voices, peeped through the half-open door to behold a sight which made her shake with suppressed laughter. Steve, with a red table-cloth tied round his waist, languished upon Mac's shoulder, dancing in perfect time to the air he whistled; for Dandy was a proficient in the graceful art, and plumed himself upon his skill. Mac, with a flushed face and dizzy eye, clutched his brother by the small of his back, vainly endeavoring to steer him down the long room without entangling his own legs in the table-cloth, treading on his partner's toes, or colliding with the furniture. It was very droll; and Rose enjoyed the spectacle, till Mac, in a frantic attempt to swing round, dashed himself against the wall, and landed Steve upon the floor. Then it was impossible to restrain her laughter any longer; and she walked in upon them, saying merrily,—

"It was splendid! Do it again, and I'll play for you."

Steve sprung up, and tore off the table-cloth in great confusion; while Mac, still rubbing his head, dropped into a chair, trying to look quite calm and cheerful as he gasped out,—

"How are you, cousin? When did you come? John should have told us."

"I'm glad he didn't, for then I should have missed this touching tableau of cousinly devotion and brotherly love. Getting ready for our next party, I see."

"Trying to; but there are so many things to remember all at once,—keep time, steer straight, dodge the petticoats, and manage my confounded legs,—that it isn't easy to get on at first," answered Mac, wiping his hot forehead, with a sigh of exhaustion.

"Hardest job *I* ever undertook; and, as I'm not a battering-ram, I decline to be knocked round any longer," growled Steve, dusting his knees, and ruefully surveying the feet that had been trampled on till they tingled; for his boots and broadcloth were dear to the heart of the dapper youth.

"Very good of you, and I'm much obliged. I've got the pace, I think, and can practise with a chair to keep my hand in," said Mac, with such a comic mixture of gratitude and resignation that Rose went off again so irresistibly that her cousins joined her with a hearty roar.

"As you are making a martyr of yourself in my service, the least I can do is lend a hand. Play for us, Steve, and I'll give Mac a lesson, unless he prefers the chair." And, throwing off hat and cloak, Rose beckoned so invitingly that the gravest philosopher would have yielded.

"A thousand thanks, but I'm afraid I shall hurt you," began Mac, much gratified, but mindful of past mishaps.

"I'm not. Steve didn't manage his train well, for good dancers always loop theirs up. I have none at all: so that trouble is gone; and the music will make it much easier to keep step. Just do as I tell you, and you'll go beautifully after a few turns."

"I will, I will! Pipe up, Steve! Now, Rose!" And, brushing his hair out of his eyes with an air of stern determination, Mac grasped Rose, and returned to the charge, bent on distinguishing himself if he died in the attempt.

The second lesson prospered: for Steve marked the time by a series of emphatic bangs; Mac obeyed orders as promptly as if his life depended on it; and, after several narrow escapes at exciting moments, Rose had the satisfaction of being steered safely down the room, and landed with a grand pirouette at the bottom. Steve applauded, and Mac, much elated, exclaimed with artless candor,—

"There really is a sort of inspiration about you, Rose. I always detested dancing before; but now, do you know, I rather like it."

"I knew you would; only you mustn't stand with your arm round your partner in this way when you are done. You must seat and fan her, if she likes it," said Rose, anxious to perfect a pupil who seemed so lamentably in need of a teacher.

"Yes, of course, I know how they do it;" and, releasing his cousin, Mac raised a small whirlwind round her with a folded newspaper, so full of grateful zeal that she had not the heart to chide him again.

"Well done, old fellow. I begin to have hopes of you, and will order you a new dress-coat at once, since you are really going in for the proprieties of life," said Steve from the music-stool, with the approving nod of one who was a judge of said proprieties. "Now, Rose, if you will just coach him a little in his small-talk, he won't make a laughing-stock of himself as he did the other night," added Steve. "I don't mean his geological gabble: that was bad enough, but his chat with Emma Curtis was much worse. Tell her, Mac, and see if she doesn't think poor Emma had a right to think you a first-class bore."

"I don't see why, when I merely tried to have a little sensible conversation," began Mac, with reluctance; for he had been unmercifully chaffed by his cousins, to whom his brother had betrayed him.

"What did you say? I won't laugh if I can help it," said Rose, curious to hear; for Steve's eyes were twinkling with fun.

"Well, I knew she was fond of theatres; so I tried that first, and got on pretty well till I began to tell her how they managed those things in Greece. Most interesting subject, you know?"

"Very. Did you give her one of the choruses or a bit of Agamemnon, as you did when you described it to me?" asked Rose, keeping sober with difficulty as she recalled that serio-comic scene.

"Of course not; but I was advising her to read Prometheus, when she gaped behind her fan, and began to talk about Phebe. What a 'nice creature' she was, 'kept her place,' 'dressed according to her station,' and that sort of twaddle. I suppose it *was* rather rude, but being pulled up so short confused me a bit, and I said the first thing that came into my head, which was that I thought Phebe the best-dressed woman in the room, because she wasn't all fuss and feathers like most of the girls."

"O Mac! that to Emma, who makes it the labor of her life to be always in the height of the fashion, and was particularly splendid that night. What *did* she say?" cried Rose, full of sympathy for both parties.

"She bridled and looked daggers at me."

"And what did you do?"

"I bit my tongue, and tumbled out of one scrape into another. Following her example, I changed the subject by talking about the Charity Concert for the orphans; and, when she gushed about the 'little darlings,' I advised her to adopt one, and wondered why young ladies didn't do that sort of thing, instead of cuddling cats and lapdogs."

"Unhappy boy! her pug is the idol of her life, and she hates babies," said Rose.

"More fool she! Well, she got my opinion on the subject, anyway, and she's very welcome; for I went on to say that I thought it would not only be a lovely charity, but excellent training for the time when they had little darlings of their own. No end of poor things die through the ignorance of mothers, you know," added Mac, so seriously that Rose dared not smile at what went before.

"Imagine Emma trotting round with a pauper baby under her arm instead of her cherished Toto," said Steve, with an ecstatic twirl on the stool.

"Did she seem to like your advice, Monsieur Malapropos?" asked Rose, wishing she had been there.

"No, she gave a little shriek, and said, 'Good gracious, Mr. Campbell, how droll you are! Take me to mamma, please,' which I did with a thankful heart. Catch me setting her pug's leg again," ended Mac, with a grim shake of the head.

"Never mind. You were unfortunate in your listener that time. Don't think all girls are so foolish. I can show you a dozen sensible ones, who would discuss dress reform and charity with you, and enjoy Greek tragedy if you did the chorus for them as you did for me," said Rose, consolingly; for Steve would only jeer.

"Give me a list of them, please; and I'll cultivate their acquaintance. A fellow must have some reward for making a teetotum of himself."

"I will with pleasure; and if you dance well they will make it very pleasant for you, and you'll enjoy parties in spite of yourself."

"I cannot be a 'glass of fashion and a mould of form' like Dandy here, but I'll do my best: only, if I had my choice, I'd much rather go round the streets with an organ and a monkey," answered Mac, despondently.

"Thank you kindly for the compliment," and Rose made him a low courtesy, while Steve cried,—

"Now you *have* done it!" in a tone of reproach which reminded the culprit, all too late, that he was Rose's chosen escort.

"By the gods, so I have!" and, casting away the newspaper with a gesture of comic despair, Mac strode from the room, chanting tragically the words of Cassandra,—

"'Woe! woe! O Earth! O Apollo! I will dare to die; I will accost the gates of Hades, and make my prayer that I may receive a mortal blow!'"

# Chapter VII

PHEBE

WHILE Rose was making discoveries and having experiences, Phebe was doing the same in a quieter way: but, though they usually compared notes during the bedtime *tête-à-tête* which always ended their day, certain topics were never mentioned; so each had a little world of her own into which even the eye of friendship did not peep.

Rose's life just now was the gayest, but Phebe's the happiest. Both went out a good deal; for the beautiful voice was welcomed everywhere, and many were ready to patronize the singer who would have been slow to recognize the woman. Phebe knew this, and made no attempt to assert herself; content to know that those whose regard she valued felt her worth, and hopeful of a time when she could gracefully take the place she was meant to fill.

Proud as a princess was Phebe about some things, though in most as humble as a child; therefore, when each year lessened the service she loved to give, and increased the obligations she would have refused from any other source, dependence became a burden which even the most fervent gratitude could not lighten. Hitherto the children had gone on together, finding no obstacles to their companionship in the secluded world in which they lived: now that they were women their paths inevitably diverged, and both reluctantly felt that they must part before long.

It had been settled, when they were abroad, that on their return Phebe should take her one gift in her hand, and try her fortunes. On no other terms would she accept the teaching which was to fit her for the independence she desired. Faithfully had she used the facilities so generously afforded both at home and abroad, and now was ready to prove that they had not been in vain. Much encouraged by the small successes she won in drawing-rooms, and the praise bestowed by interested friends, she began to feel that she might venture on a larger field, and begin her career as a concert singer; for she aimed no higher.

Just at this time, much interest was felt in a new asylum for orphan girls, which could not be completed for want of funds. The Campbells "well had borne their part," and still labored to accomplish the much-needed charity. Several fairs had been given for this purpose, followed by a series of concerts. Rose had thrown herself into the work with all her heart, and now proposed that Phebe should make her *début* at the last concert which was to be a peculiarly interesting one, as all the orphans were to be present, and were expected to plead their own cause by the sight of their innocent helplessness, as well as touch hearts by the simple airs they were to sing.

Some of the family thought Phebe would object to so humble a beginning: but Rose knew her better, and was not disappointed; for, when she made her proposal, Phebe answered readily,—

"Where could I find a fitter time and place to come before the public than here among my little sisters in misfortune? I'll sing for them with all my heart: only I must be one of them, and have no flourish made about me."

"You shall arrange it as you like; and, as there is to be little vocal music but yours and the children's, I'll see that you have every thing as you please," promised Rose.

It was well she did; for the family got much excited over the prospect of "our Phebe's *début*," and *would* have made a flourish if the girls had not resisted. Aunt Clara was in despair about the dress; because Phebe decided to wear a plain claret-colored merino with frills at neck and wrists, so that she might look as much as possible, like the other orphans in their stuff gowns and white aprons. Aunt Plenty wanted to have a little supper afterward in honor of the occasion; but Phebe begged her to change it to a Christmas dinner for the poor children. The boys planned to throw bushels of flowers, and Charlie claimed the honor of leading the singer in. But Phebe, with tears in her eyes, declined their kindly offers, saying earnestly,—

"I had better begin as I am to go on, and depend upon myself entirely. Indeed, Mr. Charlie, I'd rather walk in alone; for you'd be out of place among us, and spoil the pathetic effect we wish to produce," and a smile sparkled through the tears, as Phebe looked at the piece of elegance before her, and thought of the brown gowns and pinafores.

So, after much discussion, it was decided that she should have her way in all things, and the family content themselves with applauding from the front.

"We'll blister our hands every man of us, and carry you home in a chariot and four: see if we don't, you perverse prima donna!" threatened Steve, not at all satisfied with the simplicity of the affair.

"A chariot and two will be very acceptable as soon as I'm done. I shall be quite steady till my part is all over, and then I may feel a little upset; so I'd like to get away before the confusion begins. Indeed I don't mean to be perverse: but you are all so kind to me, my heart is full whenever I think of it; and that wouldn't do if I'm to sing," said Phebe, dropping one of the tears on the little frill she was making.

No diamond could have adorned it better Archie thought, as he watched it shine there for a moment; and felt like shaking Steve for daring to pat the dark head with an encouraging,—

"All right. I'll be on hand, and whisk you away while the rest are splitting their gloves. No fear of your breaking down. If you feel the least bit like it, though, just look at me; and I'll glare at you and shake my fist, since kindness upsets you."

"I wish you would, because one of my ballads is rather touching, and I always want to cry when I sing it. The sight of you trying to glare will make me want to laugh, and that will steady me nicely: so sit in front, please, ready to slip out when I come off the last time."

"Depend upon me!" And the little man departed, taking great credit to himself for his influence over tall, handsome Phebe.

If he had known what was going on in the mind of the silent young gentleman behind the newspaper, Steve would have been much astonished; for Archie, though apparently engrossed by business, was fathoms deep in love by this time. No one suspected this but Rose; for he did his wooing with his eyes, and only Phebe knew how eloquent they could be. He had discovered what the matter was long ago,—had made many attempts to reason himself out of it; but, finding it a hopeless task, had given up trying, and let himself drift deliciously. The knowledge that the family would not approve only seemed to add ardor to his love and strength to his purpose: for the same energy and persistence which he brought to business went into every thing he did; and, having once made up his mind to marry Phebe, nothing could change his plan except a word from her.

He watched and waited for three months, so that he might not be accused of precipitation, though it did not take him one to decide that this was the woman to make him happy. Her steadfast nature; quiet, busy ways; and the reserved power and passion betrayed sometimes by a flash of the black eyes, a quiver of the firm lips,—suited Archie, who possessed many of the same attributes himself: while the obscurity of her birth and isolation of her lot, which would have deterred some lovers, not only appealed to his kindly heart, but touched the hidden romance which ran like a vein of gold through his strong common-sense, and made practical, steady-going Archie a poet when he fell in love. If Uncle Mac had guessed what dreams and fancies went on in the head bent over his ledgers, and what emotions were fermenting in the bosom of his staid "right-hand man," he would have tapped his forehead, and suggested a lunatic asylum. The boys thought Archie had sobered down too soon. His mother began to fear that the air of the counting-room did not suit him: and Dr. Alec was deluded into the belief that the fellow really began to "think of Rose;" he came so often in the evening, seeming quite contented to sit beside her work-table, and snip tape, or draw patterns, while they chatted.

No one observed that, though he talked to Rose on these occasions, he looked at Phebe, in her low chair close by, busy but silent; for she always tried to efface herself when Rose was near, and often mourned that she was too big to keep out of sight. No matter what he talked about, Archie always saw the glossy black braids on the other side of the table, the damask cheek curving down into the firm white throat, and the dark lashes, lifted now and then, showing eyes so deep and soft he dared not look into them long. Even the swift needle charmed him, the little brooch which rose and fell with her quiet breath, the plain work she did, and the tidy way she gathered her bits of thread into a tiny bag. He seldom spoke to her; never

touched her basket, though he ravaged Rose's if he wanted
string or scissors; very rarely ventured to bring her some curious or pretty thing when ships came in from China: only sat
and thought of her; imagined that this was *his* parlor, this *her*
work-table, and they two sitting there alone a happy man and
wife.

At this stage of the little evening drama, he would be conscious of such a strong desire to do something rash that he
took refuge in a new form of intoxication, and proposed music,
sometimes so abruptly that Rose would pause in the middle of
a sentence and look at him, surprised to meet a curiously excited look in the usually cool, gray eyes.

Then Phebe, folding up her work, would go to the piano, as
if glad to find a vent for the inner life which she seemed to
have no power of expressing except in song. Rose would follow to accompany her; and Archie, moving to a certain shady
corner whence he could see Phebe's face as she sang, would
give himself up to unmitigated rapture for half an hour. Phebe
never sang so well as at such times: for the kindly atmosphere
was like sunshine to a bird, criticisms were few and gentle,
praises hearty and abundant; and she poured out her soul as
freely as a spring gushes up when its hidden source is full.

Always comely, with a large and wholesome growth, in moments such as these Phebe was beautiful with the beauty that
makes a man's eye brighten with honest admiration, and thrills
his heart with a sense of womanly nobility and sweetness. Little
wonder, then, that the chief spectator of this agreeable tableau
grew nightly more enamoured; and, while the elders were deep
in whist, the young people were playing that still more absorbing game in which hearts are always trumps.

Rose, having Dummy for a partner, soon discovered the
fact, and lately had begun to feel as she fancied Wall must have
done when Pyramus wooed Thisbe through its chinks. She
was a little startled at first, then amused, then anxious, then
heartily interested, as every woman is in such affairs, and willingly continued to be a medium, though sometimes she quite
tingled with the electricity which seemed to pervade the air.
She said nothing, waiting for Phebe to speak; but Phebe was
silent, seeming to doubt the truth, till doubt became impossible, then to shrink as if suddenly conscious of wrong-doing,

and seize every possible pretext for absenting herself from the
"girls' corner," as the pretty recess was called.

The concert plan afforded excellent opportunities for doing
this; and evening after evening she slipped away to practise her
songs upstairs, while Archie sat staring disconsolately at the
neglected work-basket and mute piano. Rose pitied him, and
longed to say a word of comfort, but felt shy,—he was such a
reserved fellow,—so left him to conduct his quiet wooing in
his own way, feeling that the crisis would soon arrive.

She was sure of this, as she sat beside him on the evening of
the concert; for while the rest of the family nodded and smiled,
chatted and laughed in great spirits, Archie was as mute as a
fish, and sat with his arms tightly folded, as if to keep in any
unruly emotions which might attempt to escape. He never
looked at the programme; but Rose knew when Phebe's turn
came by the quick breath he drew, and the intent look that
came into his eyes so absent before.

But her own excitement prevented much notice of his; for
Rose was in a flutter of hope and fear, sympathy and delight,
about Phebe and her success. The house was crowded; the
audience sufficiently mixed to make the general opinion impartial; and the stage full of little orphans with shining faces, a
most effective reminder of the object in view.

"Little dears, how nice they look!" "Poor things, so young
to be fatherless and motherless." "It will be a disgrace to the
city, if those girls are not taken proper care of." "Subscriptions
are always in order, you know; and pretty Miss Campbell will
give you her sweetest smile if you hand her a handsome check."
"I've heard this Phebe Moore, and she really has a delicious
voice: such a pity she won't fit herself for opera!" "Only sings
three times to-night; that's modest I'm sure, when she is the
chief attraction; so we must give her an encore after the Italian
piece." "The orphans lead off, I see: stop your ears if you like;
but don't fail to applaud, or the ladies will never forgive you."

Chat of this sort went on briskly, while fans waved, pro-
grammes rustled, and ushers flew about distractedly; till an
important gentleman appeared, made his bow, skipped upon
the leader's stand, and with a wave of his bâton caused a general uprising of white pinafores, as the orphans led off with
that much-enduring melody, "America," in shrill small voices,

but with creditable attention to time and tune. Pity and patriotism produced a generous round of applause; and the little girls sat down, beaming with innocent satisfaction.

An instrumental piece followed, and then a youthful gentleman, with his hair in picturesque confusion, and what his friends called a "musical brow," bounded up the steps, and, clutching a roll of music with a pair of tightly gloved hands, proceeded to inform the audience, in a husky tenor voice, that

"It was a lovely violet."

What else the song contained in the way of sense or sentiment it was impossible to discover; as the three pages of music appeared to consist of variations upon that one line, ending with a prolonged quaver, which flushed the musical brow, and left the youth quite breathless when he made his bow.

"Now she's coming! O uncle, my heart beats as if it was myself!" whispered Rose, clutching Dr. Alec's arm with a little gasp, as the piano was rolled forward, the leader's stand pushed back, and all eyes turned toward the anteroom door.

She forgot to glance at Archie, and it was as well perhaps; for his heart was thumping almost audibly, as he waited for his Phebe. Not from the anteroom, but out from among the children, where she had sat unseen in the shadow of the organ, came stately Phebe in her wine-colored dress, with no ornament but her fine hair and a white flower at her throat. Very pale, but quite composed, apparently; for she stepped slowly through the narrow lane of upturned faces, holding back her skirts, lest they should rudely brush against some little head. Straight to the front she went, bowed hastily, and, with a gesture to the accompanist, stood waiting to begin, her eyes fixed on the great gilt clock at the opposite end of the hall.

They never wandered from that point while she sung; but, as she ended, they dropped for an instant on an eager, girlish countenance, bending from a front seat; then, with her hasty little bow, she went quickly back among the children, who clapped and nodded as she passed, well pleased with the ballad she had sung.

Every one courteously followed their example; but there was no enthusiasm, and it was evident that Phebe had not produced a particularly favorable impression.

"Never sang so badly in her life," muttered Charlie, irefully.

"She was frightened, poor thing. Give her time, give her time," said Uncle Mac, kindly.

"I saw she was, and I glared like a gorgon, but she never looked at me," added Steve, smoothing his gloves and his brows at the same time.

"That first song was the hardest, and she got through much better than I expected," put in Dr. Alec, bound not to show the disappointment he felt.

"Don't be troubled. Phebe has courage enough for any thing, and she'll astonish you before the evening's over," prophesied Mac, with unabated confidence; for he knew something that the rest did not.

Rose said nothing, but, under cover of her burnous, gave Archie's hand a sympathetic squeeze; for his arms were unfolded now, as if the strain was over, and one lay on his knee, while with the other he wiped his hot forehead with an air of relief.

Friends about them murmured complimentary fibs, and affected great delight and surprise at Miss Moore's "charming style," "exquisite simplicity," and "undoubted talent." But strangers freely criticised, and Rose was so indignant at some of their remarks she could not listen to any thing upon the stage, though a fine overture was played, a man with a remarkable bass voice growled and roared melodiously, and the orphans sang a lively air with a chorus of "Tra, la, la," which was a great relief to little tongues unused to long silence.

"I've often heard that women's tongues were hung in the middle and went at both ends: now I'm sure of it," whispered Charlie, trying to cheer her up by pointing out the comical effect of some seventy-five open mouths, in each of which the unruly member was wagging briskly.

Rose laughed and let him fan her, leaning from his seat behind with the devoted air he always assumed in public; but her wounded feelings were not soothed, and she continued to frown at the stout man on the left, who had dared to say with a shrug and a glance at Phebe's next piece, "That young woman can no more sing this Italian thing than she can fly, and they ought not to let her attempt it."

Phebe did, however; and suddenly changed the stout man's

opinion by singing it grandly; for the consciousness of her first failure pricked her pride and spurred her to do her best with the calm sort of determination which conquers fear, fires ambition, and changes defeat to success. She looked steadily at Rose now, or the flushed, intent face beside her; and throwing all her soul into the task let her voice ring out like a silver clarion, filling the great hall and setting the hearers' blood a-tingle with the exulting strain.

That settled Phebe's fate as cantatrice; for the applause was genuine and spontaneous this time, and broke out again and again with the generous desire to atone for former coldness. But she would not return, and the shadow of the great organ seemed to have swallowed her up; for no eye could find her, no pleasant clamor win her back.

"Now I can die content," said Rose, beaming with heart-felt satisfaction; while Archie looked steadfastly at his programme, trying to keep his face in order, and the rest of the family assumed a triumphant air, as if *they* had never doubted from the first.

"Very well, indeed," said the stout man, with an approving nod. "Quite promising for a beginner. Shouldn't wonder if in time they made a second Cary or Kellogg of her."

"Now you'll forgive him, won't you?" murmured Charlie, in his cousin's ear.

"Yes; and I'd like to pat him on the head. But take warning and never judge by first appearances again," whispered Rose, at peace now with all mankind.

Phebe's last song was another ballad; for she meant to devote her talent to that much neglected but always attractive branch of her art. It was a great surprise, therefore, to all but one person in the hall, when, instead of singing "Auld Robin Grey," she placed herself at the piano, and, with a smiling glance over her shoulder at the children, broke out in the old bird-song which first won Rose. But the chirping, twittering, and cooing were now the burden to three verses of a charming little song, full of springtime and the awakening life that makes it lovely. A rippling accompaniment flowed through it all, and a burst of delighted laughter from the children filled up the first pause with a fitting answer to the voices that seemed calling to them from the vernal woods.

It was very beautiful, and novelty lent its charm to the surprise; for art and nature worked a pretty miracle, and the clever imitation, first heard from a kitchen hearth, now became the favorite in a crowded concert room. Phebe was quite herself again; color in the cheeks now; eyes that wandered smiling to and fro; and lips that sang as gaily and far more sweetly than when she kept time to her blithe music with a scrubbing brush.

This song was evidently intended for the children, and they appreciated the kindly thought; for, as Phebe went back among them, they clapped ecstatically, flapped their pinafores, and some caught her by the skirts with audible requests to "do it again, please; do it again."

But Phebe shook her head and vanished; for it was getting late for such small people, several of whom "lay sweetly slumbering there," till roused by the clamor round them. The elders, however, were not to be denied, and applauded persistently, especially Aunt Plenty, who seized Uncle Mac's cane and pounded with it as vigorously as "Mrs. Nubbles" at the play.

"Never mind your gloves, Steve; keep it up till she comes," cried Charlie, enjoying the fun like a boy; while Jamie lost his head with excitement, and standing up called "Phebe! Phebe!" in spite of his mother's attempts to silence him.

Even the stout man clapped, and Rose could only laugh delightedly as she turned to look at Archie, who seemed to have let himself loose at last, and was stamping with a dogged energy funny to see.

So Phebe had to come, and stood there meekly bowing, with a moved look on her face, that showed how glad and grateful she was, till a sudden hush came; then, as if inspired by the memory of the cause that brought her there, she looked down into the sea of friendly faces before her, with no trace of fear in her own, and sung the song that never will grow old.

That went straight to the hearts of those who heard her: for there was something inexpressibly touching in the sight of this sweet-voiced woman singing of home for the little creatures who were homeless; and Phebe made her tuneful plea irresistible by an almost involuntary gesture of the hands which had hung loosely clasped before her; till, with the last echo of the beloved word, they fell apart and were half-outstretched as if pleading to be filled.

It was the touch of nature that works wonders; for it made full purses suddenly weigh heavily in pockets slow to open, brought tears to eyes unused to weep, and caused that group of red-gowned girls to grow very pathetic in the sight of fathers and mothers who had left little daughters safe asleep at home. This was evident from the stillness that remained unbroken for an instant after Phebe ended; and before people could get rid of their handkerchiefs she would have been gone, if the sudden appearance of a mite in a pinafore, climbing up the stairs from the anteroom, with a great bouquet grasped in both hands, had not arrested her.

Up came the little creature, intent on performing the mission for which rich bribes of sugar-plums had been promised, and trotting bravely across the stage, she held up the lovely nosegay, saying in her baby voice, "Dis for you, ma'am;" then, startled by the sudden outburst of applause, she hid her face in Phebe's gown, and began to sob with fright.

An awkward minute for poor Phebe; but she showed unexpected presence of mind, and left behind her a pretty picture of the oldest and the youngest orphan, as she went quickly down the step, smiling over the great bouquet with the baby on her arm.

Nobody minded the closing piece; for people began to go, sleepy children to be carried off, and whispers grew into a buzz of conversation. In the general confusion, Rose looked to see if Steve had remembered his promise to help Phebe slip away before the rush began. No, there he was putting on Kitty's cloak, quite oblivious of any other duty; and, turning to ask Archie to hurry out, Rose found that he had already vanished, leaving his gloves behind him.

"Have you lost any thing?" asked Dr. Alec, catching a glimpse of her face.

"No, sir, I've found something," she whispered back, giving him the gloves to pocket along with her fan and glass, adding hastily as the concert ended, "Please, uncle, tell them all not to come with us. Phebe has had enough excitement, and ought to rest."

Rose's word was law to the family in all things concerning Phebe. So word was passed that there were to be no congratulations till to-morrow, and Dr. Alec got his party off as soon as

"SHE HELD UP THE LOVELY NOSEGAY, SAYING IN HER BABY
VOICE, 'DIS FOR YOU, MA'AM.'"

possible. But all the way home, while he and Aunt Plenty were prophesying a brilliant future for the singer, Rose sat rejoicing over the happy present of the woman. She was sure that Archie had spoken, and imagined the whole scene with feminine delight,—how tenderly he had asked the momentous question, how gratefully Phebe had given the desired reply, and now how both were enjoying that delicious hour which Rose had been given to understand never came but once. Such a pity to shorten it, she thought; and begged her uncle to go home the longest way: the night was so mild, the moonlight so clear, and herself so in need of fresh air after the excitement of the evening.

"I thought you would want to rush into Phebe's arms the instant she got done," said Aunt Plenty, innocently wondering at the whims girls took into their heads.

"So I should if I consulted my own wishes; but as Phebe asked to be let alone I want to gratify her," answered Rose, making the best excuse she could.

"A little piqued," thought the doctor, fancying he understood the case.

As the old lady's rheumatism forbade their driving about till midnight, home was reached much too soon, Rose thought, and tripped away to warn the lovers the instant she entered the house. But study, parlor, and boudoir were empty; and, when Jane appeared with cake and wine, she reported that "Miss Phebe went right upstairs, and wished to be excused, please, being very tired."

"That isn't at all like Phebe: I hope she isn't ill," began Aunt Plenty, sitting down to toast her feet.

"She may be a little hysterical; for she is a proud thing, and represses her emotions as long as she can. I'll step up and see if she doesn't need a soothing draught of some sort," and Dr. Alec threw off his coat as he spoke.

"No, no, she's only tired. I'll run up to her: she won't mind me; and I'll report if any thing is amiss."

Away went Rose, quite trembling with suspense; but Phebe's door was shut, no light shone underneath, and no sound came from the room within. She tapped, and, receiving no answer, went on to her own chamber, thinking to herself,—

"Love always makes people queer, I've heard; so I suppose they settled it all in the carriage, and the dear thing ran away to think about her happiness alone. I'll not disturb her. Why, Phebe!" added Rose, surprised; for, entering her room, there was the cantatrice, busy about the nightly services she always rendered her little mistress.

"I'm waiting for you, dear. Where have you been so long?" asked Phebe, poking the fire as if anxious to get some color into cheeks that were unnaturally pale.

The instant she spoke, Rose knew that something was wrong, and a glance at her face confirmed the fear. It was like a dash of cold water, and quenched her happy fancies in a moment; but being a delicate-minded girl she respected Phebe's mood, and asked no questions, made no comments, and left her friend to speak or be silent as she chose.

"I was so excited I would take a turn in the moonlight to calm my nerves. O dearest Phebe, I am *so* glad, so proud, so full of wonder at your courage and skill and sweet ways altogether, that I cannot half tell you how I love and honor you!" she cried, kissing the white cheeks with such tender warmth they could not help glowing faintly, as Phebe held her little mistress close, sure that nothing could disturb this innocent affection.

"It is all your work, dear; because but for you I might still be scrubbing floors, and hardly dare to dream of any thing like this," she said, in her old grateful way; but in her voice there was a thrill of something deeper than gratitude, and at the last two words her head went up with a gesture of soft pride as if it had been newly crowned.

Rose heard and saw and guessed the meaning of both tone and gesture; feeling that her Phebe deserved both the singer's laurel and the bride's myrtle wreath. But she only looked up, saying very wistfully,—

"Then it *has* been a happy night for you as well as for us."

"The happiest of my life, and the hardest," answered Phebe briefly, as she looked away from the questioning eyes.

"You should have let us come nearer and help you through. I'm afraid you are very proud, my Jenny Lind."

"I have to be; for sometimes I feel as if I had nothing else to keep me up." She stopped short there, fearing that her voice would prove traitorous if she went on. In a moment, she asked in a tone that was almost hard,—

"You think I did well to-night?"

"They all think so, and were so delighted they wanted to come in a body and tell you so; but I sent them home, because I knew you'd be tired out. Perhaps I ought not to have done it, and you'd rather have had a crowd about you than just me?"

"It was the kindest thing you ever did, and what could I like better than 'just you,' my darling?"

Phebe seldom called her that, and when she did her heart was in the little word, making it so tender that Rose thought it the sweetest in the world, next to Uncle Alec's "my little girl." Now it was almost passionate, and Phebe's face grew rather tragical as she looked down at Rose. It was impossible to seem unconscious any longer, and Rose said, caressing Phebe's cheek, which burned with a feverish color now,—

"Then don't shut me out if you have a trouble; but let me share it as I let you share all mine."

"I will! Little mistress, I've got to go away, sooner even than we planned."

"Why, Phebe?"

"Because—Archie loves me."

"That's the very reason you should stay and make him happy."

"Not if it caused dissension in the family, and you know it would."

Rose opened her lips to deny this impetuously, but checked herself and answered honestly,—

"Uncle and I would be heartily glad; and I'm sure Aunt Jessie never could object, if you loved Archie as he does you."

"She has other hopes, I think; and kind as she is it *would* be a disappointment if he brought me home. She is right; they all are, and I alone am to blame. I should have gone long ago: I knew I should; but it was so pleasant I couldn't bear to go away alone."

"I kept you, and I am to blame if any one; but indeed, dear Phebe, I cannot see why you should care even if Aunt Myra croaks, and Aunt Clara exclaims, or Aunt Jane makes disagreeable remarks. Be happy, and never mind them," cried Rose; so much excited by all this that she felt the spirit of revolt rise up

within her, and was ready to defy even that awe-inspiring institution "the family" for her friend's sake.

But Phebe shook her head with a sad smile; and answered,
still with the hard tone in her voice as if forcing back all emotion that she might see her duty clearly,—

"*You* could do that, but *I* never can. Answer me this, Rose,
and answer truly as you love me. If you had been taken into a
house, a friendless, penniless, forlorn girl, and for years been
heaped with benefits, trusted, taught, loved, and made, oh, so
happy! could you think it right to steal away something that
these good people valued very much? To have them feel that
you had been ungrateful, had deceived them, and meant to
thrust yourself into a high place not fit for you; when they had
been generously helping you in other ways, far more than you
deserved. Could you then say as you do now, 'Be happy and
never mind them'?"

Phebe held Rose by the shoulders now, and searched her
face so keenly that the other shrunk a little; for the black eyes
were full of fire, and there was something almost grand about
this girl who seemed suddenly to have become a woman. There
was no need of words to answer the questions so swiftly asked;
for Rose put herself in Phebe's place in the drawing of a breath,
and her own pride made her truthfully reply,—

"No: I could not!"

"I knew you'd say that, and help me do my duty;" and all
the coldness melted out of Phebe's manner, as she hugged her
little mistress close, feeling the comfort of sympathy even
through the blunt sincerity of Rose's words.

"I will if I know how. Now come and tell me all about it;"
and, seating herself in the great chair which had often held
them both, Rose stretched out her hands as if glad and ready
to give help of any sort.

But Phebe would not take her accustomed place; for, as if
coming to confession, she knelt down upon the rug, and,
leaning on the arm of the chair, told her love-story in the
simplest words.

"I never thought he cared for me until a little while ago. I
fancied it was you, and even when I knew he liked to hear me
sing I supposed it was because you helped; and so I did my

best, and was glad you were to be a happy girl. But his eyes told the truth; then I saw what I had been doing, and was frightened. He did not speak; so I believed, what is quite true, that he felt I was not a fit wife for him, and would never ask me. It was right: I was glad of it, yet I *was* proud; and, though I did not ask or hope for any thing, I did want him to see that I respected myself, remembered my duty, and could do right as well as he. I kept away; I planned to go as soon as possible, and resolved that at this concert I would do so well he should not be ashamed of poor Phebe and her one gift."

"It was this that made you so strange, then; preferring to go alone, and refusing every little favor at our hands?" asked Rose, feeling very sure now about the state of Phebe's heart.

"Yes; I wanted to do every thing myself, and not owe one jot of my success, if I had any, to even the dearest friend I've got. It was bad and foolish of me, and I was punished by that first dreadful failure. I was so frightened, Rose! My breath was all gone, my eyes so dizzy I could hardly see, and that great crowd of faces seemed so near I dared not look. If it had not been for the clock, I never should have got through; and when I did, not knowing in the least how I'd sung, one look at your distressed face told me that I'd failed."

"But I smiled, Phebe,—indeed I did,—as sweetly as I could; for I was sure it was only fright," protested Rose, eagerly.

"So you did: but the smile was full of pity, not of pride, as I wanted it to be; and I rushed into a dark place behind the organ, feeling ready to kill myself. How angry and miserable I was! I set my teeth, clenched my hands, and vowed that I would do well next time, or never sing another note. I was quite desperate when my turn came, and felt as if I could do almost any thing, for I remembered that *he* was there. I'm not sure how it was, but it seemed as if I was all voice; for I let myself go, trying to forget every thing except that two people must *not* be disappointed, though I died when the song was done."

"O Phebe, it was splendid! I nearly cried, I was so proud and glad to see you do yourself justice at last."

"And he?" whispered Phebe, with her face half hidden on the arm of the chair.

"Said not a word: but I saw his lips tremble and his eyes shine; and I knew he was the happiest creature there, because *I* was sure he did think you fit to be his wife, and did mean to speak very soon."

Phebe made no answer for a moment, seeming to forget the small success in the greater one which followed, and to comfort her sore heart with the knowledge that Rose was right.

"*He* sent the flowers; *he* came for me, and, on the way home, showed me how wrong I had been to doubt him for an hour. Don't ask me to tell that part, but be sure *I* was the happiest creature in the world then." And Phebe hid her face again, all wet with tender tears, that fell soft and sudden as a summer shower.

Rose let them flow undisturbed, while she silently caressed the bent head; wondering, with a wistful look in her own wet eyes, what this mysterious passion was, which could so move, ennoble, and beautify the beings whom it blessed.

An impertinent little clock upon the chimney-piece striking eleven broke the silence, and reminded Phebe that she could not indulge in love-dreams there. She started up, brushed off her tears, and said resolutely,—

"That is enough for to-night. Go happily to bed, and leave the troubles for to-morrow."

"But, Phebe, I must know what you said," cried Rose, like a child defrauded of half its bedtime story.

"I said 'No.'"

"Ah! but it will change to 'Yes' by and by; I'm sure of that: so I'll let you go to dream of 'him.' The Campbells *are* rather proud of being descendants of Robert Bruce; but they have common-sense and love you dearly, as you'll see to-morrow."

"Perhaps." And, with a good-night kiss, poor Phebe went away, to lie awake till dawn.

# Chapter VIII

## BREAKERS AHEAD

Anxious to smooth the way for Phebe, Rose was up betimes, and slipped into Aunt Plenty's room before the old lady had got her cap on.

"Aunty, I've something pleasant to tell you; and, while you listen, I'll brush your hair, as you like to have me," she began, well aware that the proposed process was a very soothing one.

"Yes, dear: only don't be too particular, because I'm late and must hurry down, or Jane won't get things straight; and it does fidget me to have the salt-cellars uneven, the tea-strainer forgotten, and your uncle's paper not aired," returned Miss Plenty, briskly unrolling the two gray curls she wore at her temples.

Then Rose, brushing away at the scanty back-hair, led skilfully up to the crisis of her tale by describing Phebe's panic and brave efforts to conquer it; all about the flowers Archie sent her; and how Steve forgot, and dear, thoughtful Archie took his place. So far it went well, and Aunt Plenty was full of interest, sympathy, and approbation; but when Rose added, as if it was quite a matter of course, "So, on the way home, he told her he loved her," a great start twitched the gray locks out of her hands as the old lady turned round, with the little curls standing erect, exclaiming, in undisguised dismay,—

"Not seriously, Rose?"

"Yes, Aunty, very seriously. He never jokes about such things."

"Mercy on us! what *shall* we do about it?"

"Nothing, ma'am, but be as glad as we ought, and congratulate him as soon as she says 'Yes.'"

"Do you mean to say she didn't accept at once?"

"She never will if we don't welcome her as kindly as if she belonged to one of our best families, and I don't blame her."

"I'm glad the girl has so much sense. Of course we can't do any thing of the sort; and I'm surprised at Archie's forgetting what he owes to the family in this rash manner. Give me my cap, child: I must speak to Alec at once." And Aunt Plenty twisted her hair into a button at the back of her head with one energetic twirl.

"Do speak kindly, Aunty, and remember that it was not Phebe's fault. She never thought of this till very lately, and began at once to prepare for going away," said Rose, pleadingly.

"She ought to have gone long ago. I told Myra we should have trouble somewhere as soon as I saw what a good-looking creature she was; and here it is as bad as can be. Dear, dear! why can't young people have a little prudence?"

"I don't see that any one need object if Uncle Jem and Aunt Jessie approve; and I do think it will be very, very unkind to scold poor Phebe for being well-bred, pretty, and good, after doing all we could to make her so."

"Child, you don't understand these things yet; but you ought to feel your duty toward your family, and do all you can to keep the name as honorable as it always has been. What do you suppose our blessed ancestress, Lady Marget, would say to our oldest boy taking a wife from the poor-house?"

As she spoke, Miss Plenty looked up, almost apprehensively, at one of the wooden-faced old portraits with which her room was hung, as if asking pardon of the severe-nosed matron, who stared back at her from under the sort of blue dish-cover which formed her head-gear.

"As Lady Marget died about two hundred years ago, I don't care a pin what she would say; especially as she looks like a very narrow-minded, haughty woman. But I do care very much what Miss Plenty Campbell says; for *she* is a very sensible, generous, discreet, and dear old lady, who wouldn't hurt a fly, much less a good and faithful girl who has been a sister to me. Would she?" entreated Rose, knowing well that the elder aunt led all the rest more or less.

But Miss Plenty had her cap on now, and consequently felt herself twice the woman she was without it; so she not only gave it a somewhat belligerent air by setting it well up, but she shook her head decidedly, smoothed down her stiff white apron, and stood up as if ready for battle.

"I shall do my duty, Rose, and expect the same of others. Don't say any more now: I must turn the matter over in my mind; for it has come upon me suddenly, and needs serious consideration."

With which unusually solemn address, she took up her keys and trotted away, leaving her niece to follow with an anxious countenance, uncertain whether her championship had done good or ill to the cause she had at heart.

She was much cheered by the sound of Phebe's voice in the study; for Rose was sure that if Uncle Alec was on their side all would be well. But the clouds lowered again when they came in to breakfast: for Phebe's heavy eyes and pale cheeks did not look encouraging; while Dr. Alec was as sober as a judge, and sent an inquiring glance toward Rose now and then as if curious to discover how she bore the news.

An uncomfortable meal, though all tried to seem as usual, and talked over last night's events with all the interest they could. But the old peace was disturbed by a word, as a pebble thrown into a quiet pool sends tell-tale circles rippling its surface far and wide. Aunt Plenty, while "turning the subject over in her mind," also seemed intent on upsetting every thing she touched, and made sad havoc in her tea-tray; Dr. Alec unsociably read his paper; Rose, having salted instead of sugared her oatmeal, absently ate it feeling that the sweetness had gone out of every thing; and Phebe, after choking down a cup of tea and crumbling a roll, excused herself, and went away, sternly resolving not to be a bone of contention to this beloved family.

As soon as the door was shut, Rose pushed away her plate, and going to Dr. Alec peeped over the paper with such an anxious face that he put it down at once.

"Uncle, this is a serious matter, and *we* must take our stand at once; for you are Phebe's guardian and I am her sister," began Rose, with pretty solemnity. "You have often been disappointed in me," she continued, "but I know I never shall be in you; because you are too wise and good to let any worldly pride or prudence spoil your sympathy with Archie and our Phebe. You won't desert them, will you?"

"Never!" answered Dr. Alec, with gratifying energy.

"Thank you! thank you!" cried Rose. "Now, if I have you and aunty on my side, I'm not afraid of anybody."

"Gently, gently, child. I don't intend to desert the lovers; but I certainly shall advise them to consider well what they are about. I'll own I *am* rather disappointed; because Archie is young to decide his life in this way, and Phebe's career seemed settled in another fashion. Old people don't like to have their plans upset, you know," he added, more lightly; for Rose's face fell as he went on.

"Old people shouldn't plan too much for the young ones then. We are very grateful, I'm sure; but we cannot always be disposed of in the most prudent and sensible way; so don't set your hearts on little arrangements of that sort, I beg," and Rose looked wondrous wise; for she could not help suspecting even her best uncle of "plans" in her behalf.

"You are quite right: we shouldn't; yet it is very hard to help it," confessed Dr. Alec, with a conscious air; and, returning hastily to the lovers, he added kindly,—

"I was much pleased with the straightforward way in which Phebe came to me this morning, and told me all about it, as if I really was her guardian. She did not own it in words: but it was perfectly evident that she loves Archie with all her heart; yet, knowing the objections which will be made, very sensibly and bravely proposes to go away at once, and end the matter,— as if that were possible, poor child," and the tender-hearted man gave a sigh of sympathy that did Rose good to hear, and mollified her rising indignation at the bare idea of ending Phebe's love affairs in such a summary way.

"You don't think she ought to go, I hope?"

"I think she will go."

"We must not let her."

"We have no right to keep her."

"O uncle! surely we have! Our Phebe, whom we all love so much."

"You forget that she is a woman now, and we have no claim upon her. Because we've befriended her for years is the very reason we should not make our benefits a burden, but leave her free; and, if she chooses to do this in spite of Archie, we must let her with a God-speed."

Before Rose could answer, Aunt Plenty spoke out like one having authority; for old-fashioned ways were dear to her soul, and she thought even love affairs should be conducted with a proper regard to the powers that be.

"The family must talk the matter over and decide what is

best for the children, who of course will listen to reason and do nothing ill-advised. For my part, I am quite upset by the news, but shall not commit myself till I've seen Jessie and the boy. Jane, clear away, and bring me the hot water."

That ended the morning conference; and, leaving the old lady to soothe her mind by polishing spoons and washing cups, Rose went away to find Phebe, while the doctor retired to laugh over the downfall of brother Mac's match-making schemes.

The Campbells did not gossip about their concerns in public; but, being a very united family, it had long been the custom to "talk over" any interesting event which occurred to any member thereof, and every one gave his or her opinion, advice, or censure with the utmost candor. Therefore the first engagement, if such it could be called, created a great sensation, among the aunts especially; and they were in as much of a flutter as a flock of maternal birds when their young begin to hop out of the nest. So at all hours the excellent ladies were seen excitedly nodding their caps together, as they discussed the affair in all its bearings, without ever arriving at any unanimous decision.

The boys took it much more calmly. Mac was the only one who came out strongly in Archie's favor. Charlie thought the Chief ought to do better, and called Phebe "a siren, who had bewitched the sage youth." Steve was scandalized, and delivered long orations upon one's duty to society, keeping the old name up, and the danger of *mésalliances*; while all the time he secretly sympathized with Archie, being much smitten with Kitty Van himself. Will and Geordie, unfortunately home for the holidays, considered it "a jolly lark;" and little Jamie nearly drove his elder brother distracted by curious inquiries as to "how folks felt when they were in love."

Uncle Mac's dismay was so comical that it kept Dr. Alec in good spirits; for he alone knew how deep was the deluded man's chagrin at the failure of the little plot which he fancied was prospering finely.

"I'll never set my heart on any thing of the sort again; and the young rascals may marry whom they like. I'm prepared for any thing now: so if Steve brings home the washerwoman's daughter, and Mac runs away with our pretty chamber-maid, I shall say, 'Bless you my children,' with mournful resignation; for, upon my soul, that is all that's left for a modern parent to do."

With which tragic burst, poor Uncle Mac washed his hands of the whole affair, and buried himself in the counting-house while the storm raged.

About this time, Archie might have echoed Rose's childish wish, that she had not *quite* so many aunts; for the tongues of those interested relatives made sad havoc with his little romance, and caused him to long fervently for a desert island, where he could woo and win his love in delicious peace. That nothing of the sort was possible soon became evident; since every word uttered only confirmed Phebe's resolution to go away, and proved to Rose how mistaken she had been in believing that she could bring every one to her way of thinking.

Prejudices are unmanageable things; and the good aunts, like most women, possessed a plentiful supply: so Rose found it like beating her head against a wall to try and convince them that Archie was wise in loving poor Phebe. His mother, who had hoped to have Rose for her daughter,—not because of her fortune, but the tender affection she felt for her,—put away her disappointment without a word, and welcomed Phebe as kindly as she could for her boy's sake. But the girl felt the truth with the quickness of a nature made sensitive by love, and clung to her resolve all the more tenaciously, though grateful for the motherly words that would have been so sweet if genuine happiness had prompted them.

Aunt Jane called it romantic nonsense, and advised strong measures,—"kind, but firm, Jessie." Aunt Clara was sadly distressed about "what people would say" if one of "our boys" married a nobody's daughter. And Aunt Myra not only seconded her views by painting portraits of Phebe's unknown relations in the darkest colors, but uttered direful prophecies regarding the disreputable beings who would start up in swarms the moment the girl made a good match.

These suggestions so wrought upon Aunt Plenty that she turned a deaf ear to the benevolent emotions native to her breast, and taking refuge behind "our blessed ancestress, Lady Marget," refused to sanction any engagement which could bring discredit upon the stainless name which was her pride.

So it all ended where it began; for Archie steadily refused to listen to any one but Phebe, and she as steadily reiterated her bitter "No;" fortifying herself half unconsciously with the hope that, by and by, when she had won a name, fate might be kinder.

While the rest talked, she had been working; for every hour showed her that her instinct had been a true one, and pride would not let her stay, though love pleaded eloquently. So, after a Christmas any thing but merry, Phebe packed her trunks, rich in gifts from those who generously gave her all but the one thing she desired; and, with a pocketful of letters to people who could further her plans, she went away to seek her fortune, with a brave face and a very heavy heart.

"Write often, and let me know all you do, my Phebe; and remember I shall never be contented till you come back again," whispered Rose, clinging to her till the last.

"She *will* come back; for in a year I'm going to bring her home, please God," said Archie, pale with the pain of parting, but as resolute as she.

"I'll earn my welcome: then perhaps it will be easier for them to give and me to receive it," answered Phebe, with a backward glance at the group of caps in the hall, as she went down the steps on Dr. Alec's arm.

"You earned it long ago, and it is always waiting for you while I am here. Remember that, and God bless you, my good girl," he said, with a paternal kiss that warmed her heart.

"I never shall forget it!" and Phebe never did.

# Chapter IX

"Now I'm going to turn over a new leaf, as I promised. I wonder what I shall find on the next page?" said Rose, coming down on New-Year's morning, with a serious face, and a thick letter in her hand.

"Tired of frivolity, my dear?" asked her uncle, pausing, in his walk up and down the hall, to glance at her with a quick, bright look she liked to bring into his eyes.

"No, sir, and that's the sad part of it; but I've made up my mind to stop while I can, because I'm sure it is not good for me. I've had some very sober thoughts lately; for, since my Phebe went away, I've had no heart for gayety: so it is a good place to stop and make a fresh start," answered Rose, taking his arm, and walking on with him.

"An excellent time! Now, how are you going to fill the aching void?" he asked, well pleased.

"By trying to be as unselfish, brave, and good as she is." And Rose held the letter against her bosom with a tender touch, for Phebe's strength had inspired her with a desire to be as self-reliant. "I'm going to set about living in earnest, as she has; though I think it will be harder for me than for her, because she stands alone, and has a career marked out for her. I'm nothing but a common-place sort of girl, with no end of relations to be consulted every time I wink, and a dreadful fortune hanging like a millstone round my neck, to weigh me down if I try to fly. It is a hard case, uncle, and I get low in my mind when I think about it," sighed Rose, oppressed with her blessings.

"Afflicted child! how can I relieve you?" And there was amusement as well as sympathy in Dr. Alec's face, as he patted the hand upon his arm.

"Please don't laugh, for I really *am* trying to be good. In the first place, help me to wean myself from foolish pleasures, and show me how to occupy my thoughts and time so that I may not idle about and dream, instead of doing great things."

"Good! we'll begin at once. Come to town with me this morning, and see your houses. They are all ready, and Mrs. Gardener has half a dozen poor souls waiting to go in as soon as you give the word," answered the doctor, promptly, glad to get his girl back again, though not surprised that she still looked with regretful eyes at the Vanity Fair, always so enticing when we are young.

"I'll give it to-day, and make the new year a happy one to those poor souls at least. I'm so sorry that it's impossible for me to go with you, but you know I must help Aunty Plen receive. We haven't been here for so long that she has set her heart on having a grand time to-day; and I particularly want to please her, because I have not been as amiable as I ought lately. I really couldn't forgive her for siding against Phebe."

"She did what she thought was right: so we must not blame her. I am going to make my New-Year's calls to-day; and, as my friends live down that way, I'll get the list of names from Mrs. G., and tell the poor ladies, with Miss Campbell's compliments, that their new home is ready. Shall I?"

"Yes, uncle, but take all the credit to yourself; for I never should have thought of it if you had not proposed the plan."

"Bless your heart! I'm only your agent, and suggest now and then. I've nothing to offer but advice: so I lavish that on all occasions."

"You have nothing because you've given your substance all away as generously as you do your advice. Never mind: you shall never come to want while I live. I'll save enough for us two, though I do make 'ducks and drakes of my fortune.'"

Dr. Alec laughed at the toss of the head with which she quoted Charlie's offensive words, then offered to take the letter, saying, as he looked at his watch,—

"I'll post that for you in time for the early mail. I like a run before breakfast."

But Rose held her letter fast, dimpling with sudden smiles, half merry and half shy.

"No, thank you, sir: Archie likes to do that, and never fails to call for all I write. He gets a peep at Phebe's in return, and I cheer him up a bit; for, though he says nothing, he has a hard time of it, poor fellow."

"How many letters in five days?"

"Four, sir, to me: she doesn't write to him, uncle."

"As yet. Well, you show hers: so it's all right; and you are a set of sentimental youngsters." And the doctor walked away, looking as if he enjoyed the sentiment as much as any of them.

Old Miss Campbell was nearly as great a favorite as young Miss Campbell; so a succession of black coats and white gloves flowed in and out of the hospitable mansion pretty steadily all day. The clan were out in great force, and came by instalments to pay their duty to Aunt Plenty, and wish the compliments of the season to "our cousin." Archie appeared first, looking sad but steadfast, and went away with Phebe's letter in his left breast-pocket; feeling that life was still endurable, though his love was torn from him: for Rose had many comfortable things to say, and read him delicious bits from the voluminous correspondence lately begun.

Hardly was he gone, when Will and Geordie came marching in, looking as fine as gray uniforms with much scarlet piping could make them, and feeling peculiarly important, as this was their first essay in New-Year's call-making. Brief was their stay, for they planned to visit every friend they had; and Rose could not help laughing at the droll mixture of manly dignity and boyish delight with which they drove off in their own carriage, both as erect as ramrods, arms folded, and caps stuck at exactly the same angle on each blonde head.

"Here comes the other couple,—Steve, in full feather, with a big bouquet for Kitty; and poor Mac, looking like a gentleman and feeling like a martyr, I'm sure," said Rose, watching one carriage turn in as the other turned out of the great gate, with its arch of holly, ivy, and evergreen.

"Here he is: I've got him in tow for the day, and want you to cheer him up with a word of praise; for he came without a struggle, though planning to bolt somewhere with uncle," cried Steve, falling back to display his brother, who came in, looking remarkably well in his state and festival array; for polishing began to tell.

"A happy New Year, aunty; same to you, cousin, and best wishes for as many more as you deserve," said Mac, heeding Steve no more than if he had been a fly, as he gave the old lady a hearty kiss, and offered Rose a quaint little nosegay of pansies.

"Heart's-ease: do you think I need it?" she asked, looking up with sudden sobriety.

"We all do. Could I give you any thing better on a day like this?"

"No: thank you very much," and a sudden dew came to Rose's eyes; for, though often blunt in speech, when Mac did do a tender thing, it always touched her; because he seemed to understand her moods so well.

"Has Archie been here? He said he shouldn't go anywhere else; but I hope you talked that nonsense out of his head," said Steve, settling his tie before the mirror.

"Yes, dear, he came; but looked so out of spirits, I really felt reproached. Rose cheered him up a little: but I don't believe he will feel equal to making calls, and I hope he won't; for his face tells the whole story much too plainly," answered Aunt Plenty, rustling about her bountiful table in her richest black silk, with all her old lace on.

"Oh, he'll get over it in a month or two, and Phebe will soon find another lover; so don't be worried about him, aunty," said Steve, with the air of a man who knew all about that sort of thing.

"If Archie does forget, I shall despise him; and I know Phebe won't try to find another lover, though she'll probably have them: she is so sweet and good!" cried Rose, indignantly; for, having taken the pair under her protection, she defended them valiantly.

"Then you'd have Arch hope against hope, and never give up, would you?" asked Mac, putting on his glasses to survey the thin boots which were his especial abomination.

"Yes, I would! for a lover is not worth having if he's not in earnest."

"Exactly: so you'd like them to wait and work and keep on loving till they made you relent, or plainly proved that it was no use."

"If they were good as well as constant, I think I should relent in time."

"I'll mention that to Pemberton; for he seemed to be hit the hardest, and a ray of hope will do him good, whether he is equal to the ten years' wait or not," put in Steve, who liked to rally Rose about her lovers.

"I'll never forgive you if you say a word to any one. It is only Mac's odd way of asking questions, and I ought not to answer them. You *will* talk about such things, and I can't stop you; but I don't like it," said Rose, much annoyed.

"Poor little Penelope! she shall not be teased about her suitors, but left in peace till her Ulysses comes home," said Mac, sitting down to read the mottoes sticking out of certain fanciful bonbons on the table.

"It is this fuss about Archie which has demoralized us all. Even the owl waked up, and hasn't got over the excitement yet, you see. He's had no experience, poor fellow; so he doesn't know how to behave," observed Steve, regarding his bouquet with tender interest.

"That's true; and I asked for information, because I may be in love myself some day, and all this will be useful, don't you see?"

"You in love!" and Steve could not restrain a laugh at the idea of the bookworm a slave to the tender passion.

Quite unruffled, Mac leaned his chin in both hands, regarding them with a meditative eye, and he answered in his whimsical way,—

"Why not? I intend to study love as well as medicine; for it is one of the most mysterious and remarkable diseases that afflict mankind, and the best way to understand it is to have it. I may catch it some day, and then I should like to know how to treat and cure it."

"If you take it as badly as you did measles and hooping-cough, it will go hard with you, old fellow," said Steve, much amused with the fancy.

"I want it to: no great experience comes or goes easily; and this is the greatest we can know, I believe, except death."

Something in Mac's quiet tone and thoughtful eyes made Rose look at him in surprise; for she had never heard him speak in that way before. Steve also stared for an instant, equally amazed; then said below his breath, with an air of mock anxiety,—

"He's been catching something at the hospital, typhoid probably, and is beginning to wander. I'll take him quietly away before he gets any wilder. Come, old lunatic, we must be off."

"Don't be alarmed: I'm all right and much obliged for your advice; for I fancy I shall be a desperate lover when my time comes, if it ever does. You don't think it impossible, do you?" and Mac put the question so soberly that there was a general smile.

"Certainly not: you'll be a regular Douglas, tender and true," answered Rose, wondering what queer question would come next.

"Thank you. The fact is, I've been with Archie so much in his trouble lately that I've got interested in this matter, and very naturally want to investigate the subject as every rational man must, sooner or later: that's all. Now, Steve, I'm ready," and Mac got up as if the lesson was over.

"My dear, that boy is either a fool or a genius, and I'm sure I should be glad to know which," said Aunt Plenty, putting her bonbons to rights with a puzzled shake of her best cap.

"Time will show; but I incline to think that he is not a fool by any means," answered the girl, pulling a cluster of white roses out of her bosom to make room for the pansies, though they did not suit the blue gown half so well.

Just then Aunt Jessie came in to help them receive, with Jamie to make himself generally useful; which he proceeded to do by hovering round the table like a fly about a honey-pot, when not flattening his nose against the window-panes, to announce excitedly, "Here's another man coming up the drive!"

Charlie arrived next, in his most sunshiny humor; for any thing social and festive was his delight, and when in this mood the Prince was quite irresistible. He brought a pretty bracelet for Rose, and was graciously allowed to put it on, while she chid him gently for his extravagance.

"I am only following your example; for, you know, 'nothing is too good for those we love, and giving away is the best thing one can do,'" he retorted, quoting words of her own.

"I wish you would follow my example in some other things as well as you do in this," said Rose, soberly, as Aunt Plenty called him to come and see if the punch was right.

"Must conform to the customs of society. Aunty's heart would be broken, if we did not drink her health in the good old fashion. But don't be alarmed: I've a strong head of my own, and that's lucky; for I shall need it before I get through,"

laughed Charlie, showing a long list, as he turned away to
gratify the old lady with all sorts of merry and affectionate
compliments as the glasses touched.

Rose did feel rather alarmed; for, if he drank the health of all
the owners of those names, she felt sure that Charlie would
need a very strong head indeed. It was hard to say any thing,
then and there, without seeming disrespect to Aunt Plenty: yet
she longed to remind her cousin of the example she tried to set
him in this respect; for Rose never touched wine, and the boys
knew it. She was thoughtfully turning the bracelet with its
pretty device of turquoise forget-me-nots, when the giver came
back to her, still bubbling over with good spirits.

"Dear little saint, you look as if you'd like to smash all the
punch-bowls in the city, and save us jolly young fellows from
to-morrow's headache."

"I should; for such headaches sometimes end in heartaches,
I'm afraid. Dear Charlie, don't be angry; but you know better
than I that this is a dangerous day for such as you: so do be
careful for my sake," she added, with an unwonted touch of
tenderness in her voice; for, looking at the gallant figure before
her, it was impossible to repress the womanly longing to keep
it always as brave and blithe as now.

Charlie saw that new softness in the eyes that never looked
unkindly on him, fancied that it meant more than it did, and,
with a sudden fervor in his own voice, answered quickly,—

"My darling, I will!"

The glow which had risen to his face was reflected in hers;
for at that moment it seemed as if it would be possible to love
this cousin, who was so willing to be led by her, and so much
needed some helpful influence to make a noble man of him.
The thought came and went like a flash; but gave her a quick
heartthrob, as if the old affection was trembling on the verge
of some warmer sentiment, and left her with a sense of responsibility never felt before. Obeying the impulse, she said, with a
pretty blending of earnestness and playfulness,—

"If I wear the bracelet to remember you by, you must wear
this to remind you of your promise."

"And you," whispered Charlie, bending his head to kiss the
hands that put a little white rose in his button-hole.

Just at that most interesting moment, they became aware of

an arrival in the front drawing-room, whither Aunt Plenty had discreetly retired. Rose felt grateful for the interruption; because, not being at all sure of the state of her heart as yet, she was afraid of letting a sudden impulse lead her too far. But Charlie, conscious that a very propitious instant had been spoilt, regarded the newcomer with any thing but a benignant expression of countenance; and whispering, "Good-by, my Rose, I shall look in this evening to see how you are after the fatigues of the day," he went away, with such a cool nod to poor Fun See that the amiable Asiatic thought he must have mortally offended him.

Rose had little leisure to analyze the new emotions of which she was conscious: for Mr. Tokio came up at once to make his compliments with a comical mingling of Chinese courtesy and American awkwardness; and before he had got his hat on Jamie shouted with admiring energy,—

"Here's another! Oh, such a swell!"

They now came thick and fast for many hours; and the ladies stood bravely at their posts till late into the evening. Then Aunt Jessie went home, escorted by a very sleepy little son, and Aunt Plenty retired to bed used up. Dr. Alec had returned in good season; for *his* friends were not fashionable ones: but Aunt Myra had sent up for him in hot haste, and he had good-naturedly obeyed the summons. In fact, he was quite used to them now; for Mrs. Myra, having tried a variety of dangerous diseases, had finally decided upon heart-complaint as the one most likely to keep her friends in a chronic state of anxiety, and was continually sending word that she was dying. One gets used to palpitations as well as every thing else; so the doctor felt no alarm, but always went, and prescribed some harmless remedy with the most amiable sobriety and patience.

Rose was tired, but not sleepy, and wanted to think over several things; so instead of going to bed she sat down before the open fire in the study to wait for her uncle, and perhaps Charlie, though she did not expect him so late.

Aunt Myra's palpitations must have been unusually severe; for the clock struck twelve before Dr. Alec came, and Rose was preparing to end her reverie, when the sound of some one fumbling at the hall-door made her jump up, saying to herself,—

"Poor man! his hands are so cold he can't get his latch-key in. Is that you, uncle?" she added, running to admit him; for Jane was slow, and the night as bitter as it was brilliant.

A voice answered "Yes," and as the door swung open in walked,—not Dr. Alec, but Charlie, who immediately took one of the hall chairs, and sat there with his hat on, rubbing his gloveless hands, and blinking as if the light dazzled him, as he said in a rapid, abrupt sort of tone,—

"I told you I'd come—left the fellows keeping it up gloriously —going to see the old year out, you know. But I promised— never break my word—and here I am. Angel in blue, did you slay your thousands?"

"Hush! the waiters are still about: come to the study fire and warm yourself; you must be frozen," said Rose, going before to roll up the easy-chair.

"Not at all—never warmer—looks very comfortable, though. Where's uncle?" asked Charlie, following with his hat still on, his hands in his pockets, and his eye fixed steadily on the bright head in front of him.

"Aunt Myra sent for him, and I was waiting up to see how she was," answered Rose, busily mending the fire.

Charlie laughed, and sat down upon a corner of the library table. "Poor old soul! what a pity she doesn't die before he is quite worn out. A little too much ether some of these times would send her off quite comfortably, you know."

"Don't speak in that way. Uncle says imaginary troubles are often as hard to bear as real ones," said Rose, turning round displeased.

Till now she had not fairly looked at him; for recollections of the morning made her a little shy. His attitude and appearance surprised her as much as his words, and the quick change in her face seemed to remind him of his manners. Getting up, he hastily took off his hat, and stood looking at her with a curiously fixed yet absent look, as he said in the same rapid, abrupt way, as if, when once started, he found it hard to stop,—

"I beg pardon—only joking—very bad taste I know, and won't do it again. The heat of the room makes me a little dizzy, and I think I got a chill coming out. It *is* cold—I *am* frozen, I dare say—though I drove like the devil."

"Not that bad horse of yours, I hope? I know it is dangerous, so late and alone," said Rose, shrinking behind the big chair, as Charlie approached the fire, carefully avoiding a footstool in his way.

"Danger is exciting—that's why I like it. No man ever called me a coward—let him try it once. I never give in—and that horse shall *not* conquer me. I'll break his neck, if he breaks my spirit doing it. No—I don't mean that—never mind—it's all right," and Charlie laughed in a way that troubled her, because there was no mirth in it.

"Have you had a pleasant day?" asked Rose, looking at him intently, as he stood pondering over the cigar and match which he held, as if doubtful which to strike and which to smoke.

"Day? oh, yes, capital. About two thousand calls, and a nice little supper at the Club. Randal can't sing any more than a crow; but I left him with a glass of champagne upside-down trying to give them my old favorite,—

"'Tis better to laugh than be sighing;'"

and Charlie burst forth in that bacchanalian melody at the top of his voice, waving an allumette-holder over his head to represent Randal's inverted wine-glass.

"Hush! you'll wake aunty," cried Rose, in a tone so commanding that he broke off in the middle of a *roulade* to stare at her with a blank look, as he said apologetically,—

"I was merely showing how it should be done. Don't be angry, dearest—look at me as you did this morning, and I'll swear never to sing another note if you say so. I'm only a little gay—we drank your health handsomely, and they all congratulated me. Told 'em it wasn't out yet. Stop, though—I didn't mean to mention that. No matter—I'm always in a scrape; but you always forgive me in the sweetest way. Do it now, and don't be angry, little darling;" and, dropping the vase, he went toward her with a sudden excitement that made her shrink behind the chair.

She was not angry, but shocked and frightened; for she knew now what the matter was, and grew so pale he saw it, and asked pardon before she could utter a rebuke.

"We'll talk of that to-morrow: it is very late; go home, now, please, before uncle comes," she said, trying to speak naturally;

yet betraying her distress by the tremor of her voice, and the sad anxiety in her eyes.

"Yes, yes, I will go—you are tired—I'll make it all right to-morrow;" and, as if the sound of his uncle's name steadied him for an instant, Charlie made for the door with an unevenness of gait which would have told the shameful truth, if his words had not already done so. Before he reached it, however, the sound of wheels arrested him; and, leaning against the wall, he listened with a look of dismay mingled with amusement creeping over his face. "Brutus has bolted—now I *am* in a fix. Can't walk home with this horrid dizziness in my head. It's the cold, Rose, nothing else, I do assure you; and a chill— yes, a chill. See here! let one of those fellows there lend me an arm—no use to go after that brute. Won't mother be frightened though, when he gets home?" and with that empty laugh again, he fumbled for the door-handle.

"No, no: don't let them see you! don't let any one know! Stay here till uncle comes, and he'll take care of you. O Charlie! how could you do it! how could you when you promised?" and, forgetting fear in the sudden sense of shame and anguish that came over her, Rose ran to him, caught his hand from the lock, and turned the key; then, as if she could not bear to see him standing there with that vacant smile upon his lips, she dropped into a chair and covered up her face.

The cry, the act, and more than all, the sight of the bowed head would have sobered poor Charlie, if it had not been too late. He looked about the room, with a vague, despairing look, as if to find the reason fast slipping from his control: but heat and cold, excitement and reckless pledging of many healths, had done their work too well to make instant sobriety possible; and owning his defeat with a groan, he turned away and threw himself face-downward on the sofa; one of the saddest sights the new year looked upon as it came in.

As she sat there with hidden eyes, Rose felt that something dear to her was dead forever. The ideal, which all women cherish, look for, and too often think they have found when love glorifies a mortal man, is hard to give up, especially when it comes in the likeness of the first lover who touches a young girl's heart. Rose had just begun to feel that perhaps this cousin, despite his faults, might yet become the hero that he sometimes looked; and the thought that she might be his inspiration was growing sweet to her, although she had not entertained it until very lately. Alas, how short the tender dream had been, how rude the awakening! how impossible it would be ever again to surround that fallen figure with all the romance of an innocent fancy, or gift it with the high attributes beloved by a noble nature!

Breathing heavily in the sudden sleep that kindly brought a brief oblivion of himself, he lay with flushed cheeks, disordered hair, and at his feet the little rose, that never would be fresh and fair again,—a pitiful contrast now to the brave, blithe young man who went so gayly out that morning to be so ignominiously overthrown at night.

Many girls would have made light of a trespass so readily forgiven by the world; but Rose had not yet learned to offer temptation with a smile, and shut her eyes to the weakness that makes a man a brute. It always grieved or disgusted her to see it in others, and now it was very terrible to have it brought so near,—not in its worst form, by any means, but bad enough to wring her heart with shame and sorrow, and fill her mind with dark forebodings for the future. So she could only sit mourning for the Charlie that might have been, while watching the Charlie that was, with an ache in her heart which found no relief till, putting her hands there as if to ease the pain, they touched the pansies, faded, but still showing gold among the sombre purple; and then two great tears dropped on them as she sighed,—

"Ah me! I do need heart's-ease sooner than I thought!"

Her uncle's step made her spring up and unlock the door, showing him such an altered face that he stopped short, ejaculating in dismay,—

"Good heavens, child! what's the matter?" adding, as she pointed to the sofa in pathetic silence, "Is he hurt?—ill?—dead?"

"No, uncle: he is—" She could not utter the ugly word, but whispered, with a sob in her throat, "Be kind to him," and fled away to her own room, feeling as if a great disgrace had fallen on the house.

# *Chapter X*

## THE SAD AND SOBER PART

"How will he look? what will he say? can any thing make us forget and be happy again?" were the first questions Rose asked herself as soon as she woke from the brief sleep which followed a long, sad vigil. It seemed as if the whole world must be changed, because a trouble darkened it for her. She was too young yet to know how possible it is to forgive much greater sins than this, forget far heavier disappointments, outlive higher hopes, and bury loves compared to which hers was but a girlish fancy. She wished it had not been so bright a day, wondered how her birds could sing with such shrill gayety, put no ribbon in her hair, and said, as she looked at the reflection of her own tired face in the glass,—

"Poor thing! you thought the new leaf would have something pleasant on it. The story has been very sweet and easy to read so far, but the sad and sober part is coming now."

A tap at the door reminded her that, in spite of her afflictions, breakfast must be eaten; and the sudden thought that Charlie might still be in the house made her hurry to the door, to find Dr. Alec waiting for her with his morning smile. She drew him in, and whispered anxiously, as if some one lay dangerously ill near by,—

"Is he better, uncle? Tell me all about it: I can bear it now."

Some men would have smiled at her innocent distress, and told her this was only what was to be expected and endured; but Dr. Alec believed in the pure instincts that make youth beautiful, desired to keep them true, and hoped his girl would never learn to look unmoved by pain and pity upon any human being vanquished by a vice, no matter how trivial it seemed, how venial it was held. So his face grew grave, though his voice was cheerful as he answered,—

"All right, I dare say, by this time; for sleep is the best medicine in such cases. I took him home last night, and no one knows he came but you and I."

"No one ever shall. How did you do it, uncle?"

"Just slipped out of the long study-window, and got him cannily off; for the air and motion, after a dash of cold water, brought him round, and he was glad to be safely landed at home. His rooms are below, you know: so no one was disturbed, and I left him sleeping nicely."

"Thank you so much," sighed Rose. "And Brutus? weren't they frightened when he got back alone?"

"Not at all: the sagacious beast went quietly to the stable, and the sleepy groom asked no questions; for Charlie often sends the horse round by himself when it is late or stormy. Rest easy, dear: no eye but ours saw the poor lad come and go, and we'll forgive it for love's sake."

"Yes, but not forget it. *I* never can; and he will never be again to me the Charlie I've been so proud and fond of all these years. O uncle, such a pity! such a pity!"

"Don't break your tender heart about it, child; for it is not incurable, thank God! I don't make light of it; but I am sure that under better influences Charlie will redeem himself, because his impulses are good, and this his only vice. I can hardly blame him for what he is, because his mother did the harm. I declare to you, Rose, I sometimes feel as if I must break out against that woman, and thunder in her ears that she is ruining the immortal soul for which she is responsible to heaven."

Dr. Alec seldom spoke in this way, and when he did it was rather awful; for his indignation was of the righteous sort, and much thunder often rouses up a drowsy soul when sunshine has no effect. Rose liked it, and sincerely wished Aunt Clara had been there to get the benefit of the outbreak; for she needed just such an awakening from the self-indulgent dream in which she lived.

"Do it, and save Charlie before it is too late!" she cried, kindling herself as she watched him; for he looked like a roused lion, as he walked about the room, with his hand clenched and a spark in his eye, evidently in desperate earnest, and ready to do almost any thing.

"Will you help?" he asked, stopping suddenly, with a look that made her stand up straight and strong as she answered with an eager voice,—

"I will."

"Then don't love him—yet."

That startled her; but she asked steadily, though her heart began to beat and her color to come,—

"Why not?"

"Firstly, because no woman should give her happiness into the keeping of a man without fixed principles; secondly, because the hope of being worthy of you will help him more than any prayers or preaching of mine. Thirdly, because it will need all our wit and patience to undo the work of nearly four and twenty years. You understand what I mean?"

"Yes, sir."

"Can you say 'No' when he asks you to say 'Yes,' and wait a little for your happiness?"

"I can."

"And will you?"

"I will."

"Then I'm satisfied, and a great weight taken off my heart. I can't help seeing what goes on, or trembling when I think of you setting sail with no better pilot than poor Charlie. Now you answer as I hoped you would, and I am proud of my girl!"

They had been standing with the width of the room between them, Dr. Alec looking very much like a commander issuing orders, Rose like a well-drilled private obediently receiving them; and both wore the air of soldiers getting ready for a battle, with the bracing of nerves and quickening of the blood brave souls feel as they put on their armor. At the last words he went to her, brushed back the hair, and kissed her on the forehead with a tender sort of gravity, and a look that made her feel as if he had endowed her with the Victoria cross for courage on the field.

No more was said then; for Aunt Plenty called them down, and the day's duties began. But that brief talk showed Rose what to do, and fitted her to do it; for it set her to thinking of the duty one owes one's self in loving as in all the other great passions or experiences which make or mar a life.

She had plenty of time for quiet meditation that day, because every one was resting after yesterday's festivity; and she sat in her little room planning out a new year, so full of good works, grand successes, and beautiful romances, that if it could have been realized the Millennium would have begun. It was a great comfort to her, however, and lightened the long hours haunted by a secret desire to know when Charlie would come, and a secret fear of the first meeting. She was sure he would be bowed down with humiliation and repentance, and a struggle took place in her mind between the pity she could not help feeling, and the disapprobation she ought to show. She decided to be gentle, but very frank; to reprove, but also to console, and try to improve the softened moment by inspiring the culprit with a wish for all the virtues which make a perfect man.

The fond delusion grew quite absorbing, and her mind was full of it as she sat watching the sun set from her western window, and admiring with dreamy eyes the fine effect of the distant hills clear and dark against a daffodil sky, when the bang of a door made her sit suddenly erect in her low chair, and say with a catch in her breath,—

"He is coming! I must remember what I promised uncle, and be very firm."

Usually Charlie announced his approach with music of some sort: now he neither whistled, hummed, nor sung, but came so quietly Rose was sure that he dreaded the meeting as much as she did, and, compassionating his natural confusion, did not look round as the steps drew near. She thought perhaps he would go down upon his knees, as he used to after a boyish offence, but hoped not; for too much humility distressed her: so she waited for the first demonstration anxiously.

It was rather a shock when it came, however; for a great nosegay dropped into her lap, and a voice, bold and gay as usual, said lightly,—

"Here she is, as pretty and pensive as you please. Is the world hollow, our doll stuffed with sawdust, and do we want to go into a nunnery to-day, cousin?"

Rose was so taken aback by this unexpected coolness that the flowers lay unnoticed, as she looked up with a face so full of surprise, reproach, and something like shame, that it was impossible to mistake its meaning. Charlie did not; and had the grace to redden deeply, and his eyes fell, as he said quickly, though in the same light tone,—

"I humbly apologize for—coming so late last night. Don't be hard upon me, cousin: you know America expects every man to do his duty on New-Year's day."

"I am tired of forgiving! You make and break promises as easily as you did years ago, and I shall never ask you for another," answered Rose, putting the bouquet away; for the apology did not satisfy her, and she would not be bribed to silence.

"But, my dear girl, you are so very exacting, so peculiar in your notions, and so angry about trifles, that a poor fellow can't please you, try as he will," began Charlie, ill at ease, but too proud to show half the penitence he felt, not so much for the fault as for her discovery of it.

"I am not angry: I am grieved and disappointed; for *I* expect every man to do his duty in another way, and keep his word to the uttermost, as I try to do. If that is exacting, I'm sorry, and won't trouble you with my old-fashioned notions any more."

"Bless my soul! what a rout about nothing! I own that I forgot: I know I acted like a fool, and I beg pardon; what more *can* I do?"

"Act like a man, and never let me be so terribly ashamed of you again as I was last night," and Rose gave a little shiver as she thought of it.

That involuntary act hurt Charlie more than her words, and it was his turn now to feel "terribly ashamed;" for the events of the previous evening were very hazy in his mind, and fear magnified them greatly. Turning sharply away, he went and stood by the fire, quite at a loss how to make his peace this time, because Rose was so unlike herself. Usually a word of excuse sufficed, and she seemed glad to pardon and forget; now, though very quiet, there was something almost stern about her that surprised and daunted him; for how could he know that all the while her pitiful heart was pleading for him, and the very effort to control it made her seem a little hard and cold? As he stood there, restlessly fingering the little ornaments upon the chimney-piece, his eye brightened suddenly; and, taking up the pretty bracelet lying there, he went slowly back to her, saying in a tone that was humble and serious enough now,—

"I *will* act like a man, and you shall never be ashamed again. Only be kind to me: let me put this on, and promise afresh; this time I swear I'll keep it. Won't you trust me, Rose?"

It was very hard to resist the pleading voice and eyes: for this humility was dangerous; and, but for Uncle Alec, Rose would have answered "Yes." The blue forget-me-nots reminded her of her own promise; and she kept it with difficulty now, to be glad always afterward. Putting back the offered trinket with a gentle touch, she said firmly, though she dared not look up into the anxious face bending toward her,—

"No, Charlie: I can't wear it yet. My hands must be free if I'm to help you as I ought. I will be kind; I will trust you: but don't swear any thing, only try to resist temptation, and we'll all stand by you."

Charlie did not like that, and lost the ground he had gained by saying impetuously,—

"I don't want any one but you to stand by me, and I must be sure you won't desert me, else, while I'm mortifying soul and body to please you, some stranger will come and steal your heart away from me. I couldn't bear that; so I give you fair warning, in such a case I'll break the bargain, and go straight to the devil."

The last sentence spoilt it all; for it was both masterful and defiant. Rose had the Campbell spirit in her, though it seldom showed; as yet she valued her liberty more than any love offered her, and she resented the authority he assumed too soon, —resented it all the more warmly, because of the effort she was making to reinstate her hero, who would insist on being a very faulty and ungrateful man. She rose straight out of her chair, saying with a look and tone which rather startled her hearer, and convinced him that she was no longer a tender-hearted child, but a woman with a will of her own, and a spirit as proud and fiery as any of her race,—

"My heart is my own, to dispose of as I please. Don't shut yourself out of it by presuming too much; for you have no claim on me but that of cousinship, and you never will have unless you earn it. Remember that, and neither threaten nor defy me any more."

For a minute it was doubtful whether Charlie would answer this flash with another, and a general explosion ensue; or wisely quench the flame with the mild answer which turneth away wrath. He chose the latter course, and made it very effective by throwing himself down before his offended goddess, as he had often done in jest; this time it was not acting, but serious

earnest, and there was real passion in his voice, as he caught
Rose's dress in both hands, saying eagerly,—

"No, no! don't shut your heart against me, or I shall turn
desperate. I'm not half good enough for such a saint as you,
but you can do what you will with me. I only need a motive to
make a man of me, and where can I find a stronger one than in
trying to keep your love?"

"It is not yours yet," began Rose, much moved, though all
the while she felt as if she were on a stage, and had a part to
play; for Charlie had made life so like a melodrama that it was
hard for him to be quite simple even when most sincere.

"Let me earn it, then. Show me how, and I'll do any thing:
for you are my good angel, Rose; and, if you cast me off, I feel
as if I shouldn't care how soon there was an end of me," cried
Charlie, getting tragic in his earnestness, and putting both
arms round her, as if his only safety lay in clinging to this beloved fellow-creature.

Behind footlights it would have been irresistible; but somehow it did not touch the one spectator, though she had neither
time nor skill to discover why. For all their ardor the words did
not ring quite true: despite the grace of the attitude, she would
have liked him better manfully erect upon his feet; and, though
the gesture was full of tenderness, a subtle instinct made her
shrink away, as she said with a composure that surprised herself,
even more than it did him,—

"Please don't. No, I will promise nothing yet; for I must
respect the man I love."

That brought Charlie to his feet, pale with something deeper
than anger; for the recoil told him more plainly than the words
how much he had fallen in her regard since yesterday. The
memory of the happy moment when she gave the rose with
that new softness in her eyes, the shy color, the sweet "for my
sake," came back with sudden vividness, contrasting sharply
with the now averted face, the hand outstretched to put him
back, the shrinking figure: and in that instant's silence poor
Charlie realized what he had lost; for a girl's first thought of
love is as delicate a thing as the rosy morning-glory, that a
breath of air can shatter. Only a hint of evil, only an hour's
debasement for him, a moment's glimpse for her of the coarser
pleasures men know, and the innocent heart, just opening to

bless and to be blessed, closed again like a sensitive plant, and shut him out perhaps for ever.

The consciousness of this turned him pale with fear: for his love was deeper than she knew; and he proved this when he said in a tone so full of mingled pain and patience that it touched her to the heart,—

"You *shall* respect me if I can make you; and when I've earned it may I hope for something more?"

She looked up then, saw in his face the noble shame, the humble sort of courage, that shows repentance to be genuine, and gives promise of success, and, with a hopeful smile that was a cordial to him, answered heartily,—

"You may."

"Bless you for that! I'll make no promises, I'll ask for none: only trust me, Rose; and, while you treat me like a cousin, remember that no matter how many lovers you may have, you'll never be to any of them as dear as you are to me."

A traitorous break in his voice warned Charlie to stop there: and, with no other good-by, he very wisely went away, leaving Rose to put the neglected flowers into water with remorseful care, and lay away the bracelet, saying to herself,—

"I'll never wear it till I feel as I did before; then he shall put it on, and I'll say 'Yes.'"

# Chapter XI

## SMALL TEMPTATIONS

"O ROSE, I've got something *so* exciting to tell you!" cried Kitty Van Tassel, skipping into the carriage next morning when her friend called for her to go shopping.

Kitty always did have some "perfectly thrilling" communication to make, and Rose had learned to take them quietly: but the next demonstration was a new one; for, regardless alike of curious observers outside and disordered hats within, Kitty caught Rose round the neck, exclaiming in a rapturous whisper,—

"My dearest creature, I'm engaged!"

"I'm so glad! Of course it is Steve?"

"Dear fellow, he did it last night in the nicest way, and mamma is *so* delighted. Now what *shall* I be married in?" and Kitty composed herself with a face full of the deepest anxiety.

"How can you talk of that so soon? Why, Kit, you unromantic girl, you ought to be thinking of your lover and not your clothes," said Rose, amused, yet rather scandalized at such want of sentiment.

"I *am* thinking of my lover; for he says he will *not* have a long engagement, so I *must* begin to think about the most important things at once, mustn't I?"

"Ah, he wants to be sure of you; for you are such a slippery creature he is afraid you'll treat him as you did poor Jackson and the rest," interrupted Rose, shaking her finger at her prospective cousin, who had tried this pastime twice before, and was rather proud than otherwise of her brief engagements.

"You needn't scold, for I know I'm right; and, when you've been in society as long as I have, you'll find that the only way to really know a man is to be engaged to him. While they want you, they are all devotion; but when they think they've got you, then you find out what wretches they are," answered Kitty, with an air of worldly wisdom which contrasted oddly with her youthful face and giddy manners.

"A sad prospect for poor Steve, unless I give him a hint to look well to his ways."

"Oh my dear child, I'm sure of him; for my experience has made me very sharp, and I'm convinced I can manage him without a bit of trouble. We've known each other for ages" (Steve was twenty and Kitty eighteen), "and always been the best of friends. Besides he is quite my ideal man: I never *could* bear big hands and feet, and his are simply adorable. Then he's the best dancer I know, and dresses in perfect taste. I really do believe I fell in love with his pocket-handkerchiefs first; they were so enchanting I couldn't resist," laughed Kitty, pulling a large one out of her pocket, and burying her little nose in the folds, which shed a delicious fragrance upon the air.

"Now that looks promising, and I begin to think you *have* got a little sentiment after all," said Rose, well pleased; for the merry brown eyes had softened suddenly, and a quick color came up in Kitty's cheek, as she answered, still half hiding her face in the beloved handkerchief,—

"Of course I have, lots of it; only I'm ashamed to show it to most people, because it's the style to take every thing in the most nonchalant way. My gracious, Rose, you'd have thought me a romantic goose last night while Steve proposed in the back parlor: for I actually cried; he was so dreadfully in earnest when I pretended that I didn't care for him, and so very dear and nice when I told the truth. I didn't know he had it in him; but he came out delightfully, and never cared a particle, though I dropped tears all over his lovely shirt-front. Wasn't that good of him? for you know he hates his things to be mussed."

"He's a true Campbell, and has got a good warm heart of his own under those fine fronts of his. Aunt Jane doesn't believe in sentiment, so he has been trained never to show any: but it is there, and you must encourage him to let it out; not foolishly, but in a way to make him more manly and serious."

"I will if I can; for, though I wouldn't own this to everybody, I like it in him very much, and feel as if Steve and I should get on beautifully. Here we are: now be sure not to breathe a word if we meet any one; I want it to be a profound secret for a week at least," added Kitty, whisking the handkerchief out of sight, as the carriage stopped before the fashionable store they were about to visit.

Rose promised with a smile; for Kitty's face betrayed her

without words, so full was it of the happiness which few eyes
fail to understand wherever they see it.

"Just a glance at the silks. You ask my opinion about white
ones, and I'll look at the colors. Mamma says satin; but that is
out now, and I've set my heart on the heaviest corded thing I
can find," whispered Kitty, as they went rustling by the long
counters strewn with all that could delight the feminine eye,
and tempt the feminine pocket.

"Isn't that opal the loveliest thing you ever saw? I'm afraid
I'm too dark to wear it, but it would just suit you. You'll need
a variety you know," added Kitty in a significant aside, as Rose
stood among the white silks, while her companion affected
great interest in the delicate hues laid before her.

"But I have a variety now, and don't need a new dress of any
sort."

"No matter, get it; else it will be gone: you've worn all yours
several times already, and *must* have a new one whether you
need it or not. Dear me! if I had as much pocket-money as you
have, I'd come out in a fresh toilet at every party I went to,"
answered Kitty, casting an envious eye upon the rainbow piles
before her.

The quick-witted shopman saw that a wedding was afoot;
for when two pretty girls whisper, smile, and blush over their
shopping, clerks scent bridal finery, and a transient gleam of
interest brightens their imperturbable countenances, and lends
a brief energy to languid voices weary with crying, "Cash!"
Gathering both silks with a practised turn of the hand, he held
them up for inspection, detecting at a glance which was the
bride-elect and which the friend; for Kitty fell back to study
the effect of the silvery white folds with an absorbing interest
impossible to mistake, while Rose sat looking at the opal as if
she scarcely heard a bland voice saying, with the rustle of silk
so dear to girlish ears,—

"A superb thing; just opened; all the rage in Paris; very rare
shade; trying to most, as the lady says, but quite perfect for a
blonde."

Rose was not listening to those words, but to others which
Aunt Clara had lately uttered; laughed at then, but thought
over more than once since.

"I'm tired of hearing people wonder why Miss Campbell

does not dress more. Simplicity is all very well for school-girls and women who can't afford any thing better, but *you* can, and you really ought. Your things are pretty enough in their way, and I rather like you to have a style of your own; but it looks odd, and people will think you are mean if you don't make more show. Besides, you don't do justice to your beauty, which would be both peculiar and striking, if you'd devote your mind to getting up ravishing costumes."

Much more to the same effect did her aunt say, discussing the subject quite artistically, and unconsciously appealing to several of Rose's ruling passions. One was a love for the delicate fabrics, colors, and ornaments which refined tastes enjoy, and whose costliness keeps them from ever growing common; another, her strong desire to please the eyes of those she cared for, and gratify their wishes in the smallest matter if she could. And last, but not least, the natural desire of a young and pretty woman to enhance the beauty which she so soon discovers to be her most potent charm for the other sex, her passport to a high place among her maiden peers.

She had thought seriously of surprising and delighting every one, by appearing in a costume which should do justice to the loveliness which was so modest that it was apt to forget itself in admiring others,—what girls call a "ravishing" dress, such as she could imagine and easily procure by the magic of the Fortunatus' purse in her pocket. She had planned it all; the shimmer of pale silk through lace like woven frost-work, ornaments of some classic pattern, and all the dainty accessories as perfect as time, taste, and money could make them.

She knew that Uncle Alec's healthful training had given her a figure that could venture on any fashion, and Nature blessed her with a complexion that defied all hues. So it was little wonder that she felt a strong desire to use these gifts, not for the pleasure of display, but to seem fair in the eyes that seldom looked at her without a tender sort of admiration, all the more winning when no words marred the involuntary homage women love.

These thoughts were busy in Rose's mind, as she sat looking at the lovely silk, and wondering what Charlie would say if she should some night burst upon him in a pale, rosy cloud, like the Aurora to whom he often likened her. She knew it would please him very much, and she longed to do all she honestly could to gratify the poor fellow; for her tender heart already felt some remorseful pangs, remembering how severe she had been the night before. She could not revoke her words, because she meant them every one; but she might be kind, and show that she did not wholly shut him out from her regard, by asking him to go with her to Kitty's ball, and gratify his artistic taste by a lovely costume. A very girlish but kindly plan; for that ball was to be the last of her frivolities, so she wanted it to be a pleasant one, and felt that "being friends" with Charlie would add much to her enjoyment. This idea made her fingers tighten on the gleaming fabric so temptingly upheld, and she was about to take it when, "If ye please, sir, would ye kindly tell me where I'd be finding the flannel place?" said a voice behind her; and, glancing up, she saw a meek little Irishwoman looking quite lost and out of place among the luxuries around her.

"Downstairs, turn to the left," was the clerk's hasty reply, with a vague wave of the hand which left the inquirer more in the dark than ever.

Rose saw the woman's perplexity, and said kindly, "I'll show you: this way."

"I'm ashamed to be throublin' ye, miss; but it's strange I am in it, and wouldn't be comin' here at all, at all, barrin' they tould me I'd get the bit I'm wantin' chaper in this big shop than the little ones more becomin' the like o' me," explained the little woman humbly.

Rose looked again, as she led the way through a well-dressed crowd of busy shoppers: and something in the anxious, tired face under the old woollen hood; the bare, purple hands, holding fast a meagre wallet and a faded scrap of the dotted flannel little children's frocks are so often made of,—touched the generous heart, that never could see want without an impulse to relieve it. She had meant only to point the way; but, following a new impulse, she went on, listening to the poor soul's motherly prattle about "me baby," and the "throuble" it was to "find clothes for the growin' childer, when me man is out av work, and the bit and sup inconvaynient these hard times," as they descended to that darksome lower world, where necessities take refuge when luxuries crowd them out from the gayer place above.

The presence of a lady made Mrs. Sullivan's shopping very easy now; and her one poor "bit" of flannel grew miraculously into yards of several colors, since the shabby purse was no lighter when she went away, wiping her eyes on the corner of a big, brown bundle. A very little thing, and no one saw it but a wooden-faced clerk, who never told; yet it did Rose good, and sent her up into the light again with a sober face, thinking self-reproachfully,—

"What right have I to more gay gowns, when some poor babies have none; or to spend time making myself fine, while there is so much bitter want in the world?"

Nevertheless the pretty things were just as tempting as ever, and she yearned for the opal silk with a renewed yearning when she got back. I am not sure that it would not have been bought in spite of her better self, if a good angel in the likeness of a stout lady with silvery curls about the benevolent face, enshrined in a plain bonnet, had not accosted her as she joined Kitty, still brooding over the wedding gowns.

"I waited a moment for you, my dear, because I'm in haste, and very glad to save myself a journey or a note," began the newcomer in a low tone, as Rose shook hands with the most affectionate respect. "You know the great box factory was burned a day or two ago, and over a hundred girls thrown out of work. Some were hurt and are in the hospital, many have no homes to go to, and nearly all need temporary help of some sort. We've had so many calls this winter I hardly know which way to turn; for the want is pressing, and I've had my finger in so many purses I'm almost ashamed to ask again. Any little contribution—ah, thank you; I was sure you wouldn't fail me, my good child," and Mrs. Gardener warmly pressed the hand that went so quickly into the little portemonnaie, and came out so generously filled.

"Let me know how else I can help, and thank you very much for allowing me to have a share in your good works," said Rose, forgetting all about gay gowns, as she watched the black bonnet go briskly away, with an approving smile on the fine old face inside it.

"You extravagant thing! how could you give so much?" whispered Kitty, whose curious eye had seen three figures on the single bill which had so rapidly changed hands.

"I believe if Mrs. Gardener asked me for my head I should give it to her," answered Rose lightly; then turning to the silks she asked, "Which have you decided upon; the yellow white or the blue, the corded or the striped?"

"I've decided nothing, except that *you* are to have the pink, and wear it at my—ahem! ball," said Kitty, who *had* made up her mind, but could not give her orders till mamma had been consulted.

"No, I can't afford it just yet. I never overstep my allowance, and I shall have to if I get any more finery. Come, we ought not to waste time here, if you have all the patterns you want," and Rose walked quickly away, glad that it was out of her power to break through two resolutions which hitherto had been faithfully kept,—one to dress simply for example's sake, the other not to be extravagant for charity's sake.

As Rosamond had her day of misfortunes, so this seemed to be one of small temptations to Rose. After she had set Kitty down at home and been to see her new houses, she drove about doing various errands for the aunts; and, while waiting in the carriage for the execution of an order, young Pemberton came by.

As Steve said, this gentleman had been "hard hit," and still hovered moth-like about the forbidden light. Being the most eligible *parti* of the season, his regard was considered a distinction to be proud of; and Rose had been well scolded by Aunt Clara for refusing so honorable a mate. The girl liked him; and he was the suitor of whom she had spoken so respectfully to Dr. Alec, because he had no need of the heiress, and had sincerely loved the woman. He had been away, and she hoped had got over his disappointment as happily as the rest; but now when he saw her, and came hurrying up so hungry for a word, she felt that he had not forgotten, and was too kind to chill him with the bow which plainly says, "Don't stop."

A personable youth was Pemberton, and had brought with him from the wilds of Canada a sable-lined overcoat, which was the envy of every masculine and the admiration of every feminine friend he had; and, as he stood at her carriage window, Rose knew that this luxurious garment and its stalwart wearer were objects of interest to the passers-by. It chanced that the tide of shoppers flowed in that direction; and, as she chatted, familiar faces often passed with glances, smiles, and nods of varying curiosity, significance, and wonder.

She could not help feeling a certain satisfaction in giving him a moment's pleasure, since she could do no more; but it was not that amiable desire alone which made her ignore the neat white parcels which the druggist's boy deposited on the front seat, and kept her lingering a little longer to enjoy one of the small triumphs which girls often risk more than a cold in the head to display. The sight of several snow-flakes on the broad shoulders which partially obstructed her view, as well as the rapidly increasing animation of Pemberton's chat, reminded her that it was high time to go.

"I mustn't keep you: it is beginning to storm," she said, taking up her muff, much to old Jacob's satisfaction; for small talk is not exciting to a hungry man whose nose feels like an icicle.

"Is it? I thought the sun was shining." And the absorbed gentleman turned to the outer world with visible reluctance, for it looked very warm and cosey in the red-lined carriage.

"Wise people say we must carry our sunshine with us," answered Rose, taking refuge in commonplaces; for the face at the window grew pensive suddenly, as he answered, with a longing look,—

"I wish I could:" then, smiling gratefully, he added, "Thank you for giving me a little of yours."

"You are very welcome." And Rose offered him her hand, while her eyes mutely asked pardon for withholding her leave to keep it.

He pressed it silently, and, shouldering the umbrella which he forgot to open, turned away, with an "up-again-and-take-another" expression, which caused the soft eyes to follow him admiringly.

"I ought not to have kept him a minute longer than I could help: for it wasn't all pity; it was my foolish wish to show off and do as I liked for a minute, to pay for being good about the gown. Oh me! how weak and silly I am in spite of all my trying!" And Miss Campbell fell into a remorseful reverie, which lasted till she got home.

"Now, young man, what brought you out in this driving storm?" asked Rose, as Jamie came stamping in that same afternoon.

"Mamma sent you a new book,—thought you'd like it: *I* don't mind your old storms!" replied the boy, wrestling his way out of his coat, and presenting a face as round and red and shiny as a well-polished Baldwin apple.

"Much obliged: it is just the day to enjoy it, and I was longing for something nice to read," said Rose, as Jamie sat down upon the lower stair for a protracted struggle with his rubber boots.

"Here you are, then—no—yes—I do believe I've forgotten it, after all!" cried Jamie, slapping his pockets one after the other, with a dismayed expression of countenance.

"Never mind: I'll hunt up something else. Let me help with those: your hands are so cold." And Rose good-naturedly gave a tug at the boots, while Jamie clutched the banisters; murmuring somewhat incoherently, as his legs flew up and down,—

"I'll go back if you want me to. I'm so sorry! It's very good of you, I'm sure. Getting these horrid things on made me forget. Mother would make me wear 'em, though I told her they'd stick like—like gumdrops," he added, inspired by recollections of certain dire disappointments when the above-mentioned sweetmeat melted in his pockets, and refused to come out.

"Now what shall we do?" asked Rose, when he was finally extricated. "Since I've nothing to read, I may as well play."

"I'll teach you to pitch and toss. You catch very well for a girl, but you can't throw worth a cent," replied Jamie, gambading down the hall in his slippers, and producing a ball from some of the mysterious receptacles in which boys have the art of storing rubbish enough to fill a peck measure.

Of course Rose agreed, and cheerfully risked getting her eyes blackened and her fingers bruised, till her young preceptor gratefully observed that "it was no fun playing where you had to look out for windows and jars and things; so I'd like that jolly book about Captain Nemo and the 'Nautilus,' please."

Being gratified, he spread himself upon the couch, crossed his legs in the air, and without another word dived "Twenty

Thousand Leagues Under the Sea," where he remained for two mortal hours, to the general satisfaction of his relatives.

Bereft both of her unexpected playfellow and the much-desired book, Rose went into the parlor, there to discover a French novel, which Kitty had taken from a library and left in the carriage among the bundles. Settling herself in her favorite lounging-chair, she read as diligently as Jamie, while the wind howled and snow fell fast without.

For an hour, nothing disturbed the cosey quiet of the house; for Aunt Plenty was napping upstairs, and Dr. Alec writing in his own sanctum; at least, Rose thought so, till his step made her hastily drop the book, and look up with very much the expression she used to wear when caught in mischief years ago.

"Did I startle you? Have a screen: you are burning your face before this hot fire." And Dr. Alec pulled one forward.

"Thank you, uncle; I didn't feel it." And the color seemed to deepen in spite of the screen, while the uneasy eyes fell upon the book in her lap.

"Have you got the 'Quarterly' there? I want to glance at an article in it, if you can spare it for a moment," he said, leaning toward her with an inquiring glance.

"No, sir: I am reading—" And, without mentioning the name, Rose put the book into his hand.

The instant his eye fell on the title, he understood the look she wore, and knew what "mischief" she had been in. He knit his brows: then smiled, because it was impossible to help it; Rose looked so conscience-stricken in spite of her twenty years.

"How do you find it?—interesting?"

"Oh, very! I felt as if I was in another world, and forgot all about this."

"Not a very good world, I fancy, if you were afraid or ashamed to be found in it. Where did this come from?" asked Dr. Alec, surveying the book with great disfavor.

Rose told him, and added slowly,—

"I particularly wanted to read it, and fancied I might, because you did when it was so much talked about the winter we were in Rome."

"I did read it to see if it was fit for you."

"And decided that it was not, I suppose; since you never gave it to me?"

"Yes."

"Then I won't finish it. But, uncle, I don't see why I should not," added Rose, wistfully; for she had reached the heart of the romance and found it wonderfully fascinating.

"You may not *see*, but don't you *feel* why not?" asked Dr. Alec, gravely.

Rose leaned her flushed cheek on her hand and thought a minute; then looked up, and answered honestly,—

"Yes, I do: but can't explain it; except that I know something *must* be wrong, because I blushed and started when you came in."

"Exactly," and the doctor gave an emphatic nod, as if the symptoms pleased him.

"But I really don't see any harm in the book so far. It is by a famous author, wonderfully well written as you know, and the characters so life-like that I feel as if I should really meet them somewhere."

"I hope not!" ejaculated the doctor, shutting the book quickly, as if to keep the objectionable beings from escaping.

Rose laughed, but persisted in her defence; for she did want to finish the absorbing story, yet would not without leave.

"I have read French novels before, and you gave them to me. Not many to be sure, but the best; so I think I know what is good, and shouldn't like this if it was harmful."

Her uncle's answer was to reopen the volume and turn the leaves an instant as if to find a particular place; then he put it into her hand, saying quietly,—

"Read a page or two aloud, translating as you go. You used to like that: try it again."

Rose obeyed, and went glibly down a page, doing her best to give the sense in her purest English. Presently she went more slowly, then skipped a sentence here and there, and finally stopped short, looking as if she needed a screen again.

"What's the matter?" asked her uncle, who had been watching her with a serious eye.

"Some phrases are untranslatable, and it only spoils them to try. They are not amiss in French, but sound coarse and bad in our blunt English," she said a little pettishly; for she felt annoyed by her failure to prove the contested point.

"Ah, my dear! if the fine phrases won't bear putting into

honest English, the thoughts they express won't bear putting into your innocent mind. That chapter is the key to the whole book; and if you had been led up, or rather down, to it artfully and artistically, you might have read it to yourself without seeing how bad it is. All the worse for the undeniable talent which hides the evil so subtly and makes the danger so delightful."

He paused a moment, then added with an anxious glance at the book, over which she was still bending,—

"Finish it if you choose: only remember, my girl, that one may read at forty what is unsafe at twenty, and that we never can be too careful what food we give that precious yet perilous thing called imagination."

And taking his "Review" he went away to look over a learned article which interested him much less than the workings of a young mind near by.

Another long silence, broken only by an occasional excited bounce from Jamie, when the sociable cuttlefish looked in at the windows, or the "Nautilus" scuttled a ship or two in its terrific course. A bell rang, and the doctor popped his head out to see if he was wanted. It was only a message for Aunt Plenty, and he was about to pop in again when his eye was caught by a square parcel on the slab.

"What's this?" he asked, taking it up.

"Rose wants me to leave it at Kitty Van's when I go. I forgot to bring her book from mamma; so I shall go and get it as soon as ever I've done this," replied Jamie, from his nest.

As the volume in his hands was a corpulent one, and Jamie only a third of the way through, Dr. Alec thought Rose's prospect rather doubtful; and, slipping the parcel into his pocket, he walked away, saying with a satisfied air,—

"Virtue doesn't always get rewarded; but it shall be this time, if I can do it."

More than half an hour afterward, Rose woke from a little nap, and found the various old favorites, with which she had tried to solace herself, replaced by the simple, wholesome story promised by Aunt Jessie.

"Good boy! I'll go and thank him," she said, half-aloud; jumping up, wide awake and much pleased.

But she did not go; for, just then, she espied her uncle

standing on the rug warming his hands with a generally fresh and breezy look about him, which suggested a recent struggle with the elements.

"How did this come?" she asked suspiciously.

"A man brought it."

"This man? O uncle! why did you take so much trouble just to gratify a wish of mine?" she cried, taking both the cold hands in hers, with a tenderly reproachful glance from the storm without to the ruddy face above her.

"Because, having taken away your French bonbons with the poisonous color on them, I wanted to get you something better. Here it is, all pure sugar; the sort that sweetens the heart as well as the tongue, and leaves no bad taste behind."

"How good you are to me! I don't deserve it; for I didn't resist temptation, though I tried. Uncle, after I'd put the book away, I thought I *must* just see how it ended, and I'm afraid I should have read it all if it had not been gone," said Rose, laying her face down on the hands she held, as humbly as a repentant child.

But Uncle Alec lifted up the bent head, and looking into the eyes that met his frankly, though either held a tear, he said, with the energy that always made his words remembered,—

"My little girl, I would face a dozen storms far worse than this to keep your soul as stainless as snow; for it is the small temptations which undermine integrity, unless we watch and pray, and never think them too trivial to be resisted."

Some people would consider Dr. Alec an over-careful man: but Rose felt that he was right; and, when she said her prayers that night, added a meek petition to be kept from yielding to three of the small temptations which beset a rich, pretty, and romantic girl,—extravagance, coquetry, and novel-reading.

# Chapter XII

---

ROSE had no new gown to wear on this festive occasion, and gave one little sigh of regret as she put on the pale blue silk, refreshed with clouds of *gaze de Chambrey*. But a smile followed, very bright and sweet, as she added the clusters of forget-me-not which Charlie had conjured up through the agency of an old German florist: for one part of her plan *had* been carried out, and Prince was invited to be her escort, much to his delight; though he wisely made no protestations of any sort, and showed his gratitude by being a model gentleman. This pleased Rose; for the late humiliation and a very sincere desire to atone for it, gave him an air of pensive dignity which was very effective.

Aunt Clara could not go; for a certain new cosmetic, privately used to improve the once fine complexion, which had been her pride till late hours impaired it, had brought out an unsightly eruption, reducing her to the depths of woe, and leaving her no solace for her disappointment but the sight of the elegant velvet dress spread forth upon her bed in melancholy state.

So Aunt Jessie was chaperon, to Rose's great satisfaction, and looked as "pretty as a pink," Archie thought, in her matronly pearl-colored gown, with a dainty trifle of rich lace on her still abundant hair. He was very proud of his little mamma, and as devoted as a lover, "to keep his hand in against Phebe's return," she said laughingly, when he brought her a nosegay of blush-roses to light up her quiet costume.

A happier mother did not live than Mrs. Jessie, as she sat contentedly beside Sister Jane (who graced the frivolous scene in a serious black gown with a diadem of purple asters nodding above her severe brow), both watching their boys with the maternal conviction that no other parent could show such remarkable specimens as these. Each had done her best according to her light; and years of faithful care were now beginning to bear fruit in the promise of goodly men, so dear to the hearts of true mothers.

Mrs. Jessie watched her three tall sons with something like wonder; for Archie was a fine fellow, grave and rather stately, but full of the cordial courtesy and respect we see so little of now-a-days, and which is the sure sign of good home-training. "The cadets," as Will and Geordie called themselves, were there as gorgeous as you please; and the agonies they suffered that night with tight boots and stiff collars no pen can fitly tell. But only to one another did they confide these sufferings, in the rare moments of repose when they could stand on one aching foot with heads comfortably sunken inside the excruciating collars, which rasped their ears and made the lobes thereof a pleasing scarlet. Brief were these moments, however; and the Spartan boys danced on with smiling faces, undaunted by the hidden anguish which preyed upon them "fore and aft," as Will expressed it.

Mrs. Jane's pair were an odd contrast, and even the stern disciplinarian herself could not help smiling as she watched them. Steve was superb, and might have been married on the spot, so superfine was his broadcloth, glossy his linen, and perfect the fit of his gloves; while pride and happiness so fermented in his youthful bosom, that there would have been danger of spontaneous combustion if dancing had not proved a safety-valve; for his strong sense of the proprieties would not permit him to vent his emotions in any other way.

Kitty felt no such restraint, and looked like a blissful little gypsy, with her brunette prettiness set off by a dashing costume of cardinal and cream color, and every hair on her head curled in a Merry Pecksniffian crop; for youth was her strong point, and she much enjoyed the fact that she had been engaged three times before she was nineteen.

To see her and Steve spin round the room was a sight to bring a smile to the lips of the crustiest bachelor or saddest spinster; for happy lovers are always a pleasing spectacle, and two such merry little grigs as these are seldom seen.

Mac, meantime, with glasses astride of his nose, surveyed his brother's performances "on the light fantastic" very much as a benevolent Newfoundland would the gambols of a toy terrier, receiving with thanks the hasty hints for his guidance which

Steve breathed into his ear as he passed, and forgetting all about them the next minute. When not thus engaged, Mac stood about with his thumbs in his vest pockets, regarding the lively crowd like a meditative philosopher of a cheerful aspect, often smiling to himself at some whimsical fancy of his own, knitting his brows as some bit of ill-natured gossip met his ear, or staring with undisguised admiration as a beautiful face or figure caught his eye.

"I hope that girl knows what a treasure she has got. But I doubt if she ever fully appreciates it," said Mrs. Jane, bringing her spectacles to bear upon Kitty, as she whisked by, causing quite a gale with her flying skirts.

"I think she will: for Steve has been so well brought up, she cannot but see and feel the worth of what she has never had; and being so young she will profit by it," answered Mrs. Jessie, softly; thinking of the days when she and her Jem danced together, just betrothed.

"I've done my duty by both the boys, and done it *thoroughly*: or their father would have spoilt them; for he's no more idea of discipline than a child," and Aunt Jane gave her own palm a smart rap with her closed fan, emphasizing the word "thoroughly" in a most suggestive manner.

"I've often wished I had your firmness, Jane: but, after all, I'm not sure that I don't like my own way best, at least with my boys; for plenty of love, and plenty of patience, seem to have succeeded pretty well;" and Aunt Jessie lifted the nosegay from her lap, feeling as if that unfailing love and patience were already blooming into her life, as beautifully as the sweet-breathed roses given by her boy refreshed and brightened these long hours of patient waiting in a corner.

"I don't deny that you've done well, Jessie; but you've been let alone, and had no one to hold your hand or interfere. If my Mac had gone to sea as your Jem did, I never should have been as severe as I am. Men are so perverse and short-sighted, they don't trouble about the future as long as things are quiet and comfortable in the present," continued Mrs. Jane, quite forgetting that the short-sighted partner of the firm, physically speaking at least, was herself.

"Ah, yes! we mothers love to foresee and foretell our children's lives even before they are born, and are very apt to be disappointed if they do not turn out as we planned. I know I am: yet I really have no cause to complain, and am learning to see that all we can do is to give the dear boys good principles, and the best training we may, then leave them to finish what we have begun;" and Mrs. Jessie's eye wandered away to Archie, dancing with Rose, quite unconscious what a pretty little castle in the air tumbled down when he fell in love with Phebe.

"Right, quite right: on that point we agree exactly. I have spared nothing to give my boys good principles and good habits, and I am willing to trust them anywhere. Nine times did I whip my Steve to cure him of fibbing, and over and over again did Mac go without his dinner rather than wash his hands. But I whipped and starved them both into obedience, and *now* I have my reward," concluded the "stern parent," with a proud wave of the fan, which looked very like a ferule, being as big, hard, and uncompromising as such an article could be.

Mrs. Jessie gave a mild murmur of assent, but could not help thinking, with a smile, that, in spite of their early tribulations, the sins for which the boys suffered had got a little mixed in their results; for fibbing Steve was now the tidy one, and careless Mac the truth-teller. But such small contradictions will happen in the best-regulated families, and all perplexed parents can do is to keep up a steadfast preaching and practising, in the hope that it will bear fruit sometime; for according to the old proverb,—

> "'Children pick up words as pigeons pease,
>    To utter them again as God shall please.'"

"I hope they won't dance the child to death among them; for each one seems bound to have his turn, even your sober Mac," said Mrs. Jessie, a few minutes later, as she saw Archie hand Rose over to his cousin, who carried her off with an air of triumph from several other claimants.

"She's very good to him, and her influence is excellent; for he is of an age now when a young woman's opinion has more weight than an old one's. Though he is always good to his mother, and I feel as if I should take great comfort in him. He's one of the sort who will not marry till late, if ever, being fond of books and a quiet life," responded Mrs. Jane, remembering how often her son had expressed his belief that philosophers should not marry, and brought up Plato as an example of the serene wisdom only to be attained by a single man, while her husband sided with Socrates, for whom he felt a profound sympathy, though he didn't dare to own it.

"Well, I don't know about that. Since my Archie surprised me by losing his heart as he did, I'm prepared for any thing, and advise you to do likewise. I really shouldn't wonder if Mac did something remarkable in that line, though he shows no signs of it yet, I confess," answered Mrs. Jessie, laughing.

"It won't be in that direction, you may be sure; for *her* fate is sealed. Dear me, how sad it is to see a superior girl, like that, about to throw herself away on a handsome scapegrace. I won't mention names, but you understand me;" and Mrs. Jane shook her head, as if she *could* mention the name of one superior girl who had thrown herself away, and now saw the folly of it.

"I'm very anxious, of course, and so is Alec: but it may be the saving of one party, and the happiness of the other; for some women love to give more than they receive," said Mrs. Jessie, privately wondering, for the thousandth time, why brother Mac ever married the learned Miss Humphries.

"You'll see that it won't prosper; and I shall always maintain that a wife cannot entirely undo a mother's work. Rose will have her hands full if she tries to set all Clara's mistakes right," answered Aunt Jane, grimly; then began to fan violently as their hostess approached to have a dish of chat about "our dear young people."

Rose was in a merry mood that night, and found Mac quite ready for fun, which was fortunate, since her first remark set them off on a droll subject.

"O Mac! Annabel has just confided to me that she is engaged to Fun See! Think of her going to housekeeping in Canton some day, and having to order rats, puppies, and birds'-nest soup for dinner," whispered Rose, too much amused to keep the news to herself.

"By Confucius! isn't that a sweet prospect?" and Mac burst out laughing, to the great surprise of his neighbors, who wondered what there was amusing about the Chinese sage. "It is rather alarming, though, to have these infants going on at this rate. Seems to be catching; a new sort of scarlet-fever, to judge by Annabel's cheeks and Kitty's gown," he added, regarding the aforesaid ladies with eyes still twinkling with merriment.

"Don't be ungallant, but go and do likewise; for it is all the fashion. I heard Mrs. Van tell old Mrs. Joy that it was going to be a marrying year; so you'll be sure to catch it," answered Rose, reefing her skirts; for, with all his training, Mac still found it difficult to keep his long legs out of the man-traps.

"It doesn't look like a painful disease; but I must be careful, for I've no time to be ill now. What are the symptoms?" asked Mac, trying to combine business with pleasure, and improve his mind while doing his duty.

"If you ever come back I'll tell you," laughed Rose, as he danced away into the wrong corner, bumped smartly against another gentleman, and returned as soberly as if that was the proper figure.

"Well, tell me 'how not to do it,'" he said, subsiding for a moment's talk when Rose had floated to and fro in her turn.

"Oh! you see some young girl who strikes you as particularly charming,—whether she really is or not doesn't matter a bit,— and you begin to think about her a great deal, to want to see her, and to get generally sentimental and absurd," began Rose, finding it difficult to give a diagnosis of the most mysterious disease under the sun.

"Don't think it sounds enticing. Can't I find an antidote somewhere; for if it is in the air this year I'm sure to get it, and it may be fatal," said Mac, who felt pretty lively and liked to make Rose merry; for he suspected that she had a little trouble from a hint Dr. Alec had given him.

"I hope you will catch it, because you'll be so funny."

"Will you take care of me as you did before, or have you got your hands full?"

"I'll help; but really with Archie and Steve and—Charlie, I shall have enough to do. You'd better take it lightly the first time, and so won't need much care."

"Very well, how shall I begin? Enlighten my ignorance and start me right, I beg."

"Go about and see people; make yourself agreeable, and not sit in corners observing other people as if they were puppets dancing for your amusement. I heard Mrs. Van once say that propinquity works wonders; and she ought to know, having married off two daughters, and just engaged a third to 'a most charming young man.'"

"Good lack! the cure sounds worse than the disease. Propinquity, hey? Why, I may be in danger this identical moment, and can't flee for my life," said Mac, gently catching her round the waist for a general waltz.

"Don't be alarmed, but mind your steps; for Charlie is looking at us, and I want you to do your best. That's perfect: take me quite round; for I love to waltz, and seldom get a good turn except with you boys," said Rose, smiling up at him approvingly, as his strong arm guided her among the revolving couples, and his feet kept time without a fault.

"This certainly is a great improvement on the chair business, to which I have devoted myself with such energy that I've broken the backs of two partners and dislocated the arm of the old rocker. I took an occasional turn with that heavy party, thinking it good practice in case I ever happen to dance with stout ladies," and Mac nodded toward Annabel, pounding gaily away with Mr. Tokio, whose yellow countenance beamed as his beady eyes rested on his plump *fiancée*.

Pausing in the midst of her merriment at the image of Mac and the old rocking-chair, Rose said reprovingly,—

"Though a heathen Chinee, Fun puts you to shame; for *he* did not ask foolish questions, but went a wooing like a sensible little man; and I've no doubt Annabel will be very happy."

"Choose me a suitable divinity, and I will try to adore. Can I do more than that to retrieve my character?" answered Mac, safely landing his partner, and plying the fan according to instructions.

"How would Emma do?" inquired Rose, whose sense of the ludicrous was strong, and who could not resist the temptation of horrifying Mac by the suggestion.

"Never! It sets my teeth on edge to look at her to-night. I suppose that dress is 'a sweet thing just out;' but, upon my word, she reminds me of nothing but a harlequin ice," and Mac turned his back on her with a shudder; for he was sensitive to discords of all kinds.

"She certainly does; and that mixture of chocolate, pea green, and pink is simply detestable, though many people would consider it decidedly 'chic,' to use her favorite word. I suppose you will dress your wife like a Spartan matron of the time of Lycurgus," added Rose, much tickled by his new conceit.

"I'll wait till I get her before I decide. But one thing I'm sure of,—she shall *not* dress like a Greek dancer of the time of Pericles," answered Mac, regarding with great disfavor a young lady who, having a statuesque figure, affected drapery of the scanty and clinging description.

"Then it is of no use to suggest that classic creature; so, as you reject my first attempts, I won't go on, but look about me quietly, and you had better do the same. Seriously, Mac, more gayety and less study would do you good; for you will grow old before your time, if you shut yourself up and pore over books so much."

"I don't believe there is a younger or a jollier feeling fellow in the room than I am, though I may not conduct myself like a dancing dervish. But I own you may be right about the books; for there are many sorts of intemperance, and a library is as irresistible to me as a bar-room to a toper. I shall have to sign a pledge, and cork up the only bottle that tempts me,—my inkstand."

"I'll tell you how to make it easier to abstain. Stop studying, and write a novel into which you can put all your wise things, and so clear your brains for a new start by and by. Do: I should *so* like to read it," cried Rose, delighted with the project; for she was sure Mac could do any thing he liked in that line.

"First live, then write. How can I go to romancing till I know what romance means?" he asked soberly, feeling that so far he had had very little in his life.

"Then you must find out, and nothing will help you more than to love some one very much. Do as I've advised, and be a modern Diogenes going about with spectacles, instead of a lantern, in search, not of an honest man, but a perfect woman. I do hope you will be successful," and Rose made her courtesy as the dance ended.

"I don't expect perfection, but I *should* like one as good as they ever make them now-a-days. If you are looking for the honest man, I wish you success in return," said Mac, relinquishing her fan with a glance of such sympathetic significance that a quick flush of feeling rose to the girl's face, as she answered very low,—

"If honesty was all I wanted, I certainly have found it in you."

Then she went away with Charlie, who was waiting for his turn, and Mac roamed about, wondering if anywhere in all that crowd his future wife was hidden, saying to himself, as he glanced from face to face, quite unresponsive to the various allurements displayed,—

> "What care I how fair she be,
> If she be not fair for me?"

Just before supper, several young ladies met in the dressing-room to repair damages; and, being friends, they fell into discourse, as they smoothed their locks, and had their tattered furbelows sewed or pinned up by the neat-handed Phillis in waiting.

When each had asked the other, "How do I look to-night, dear?" and been answered with reciprocal enthusiasm, "Perfectly lovely, darling!" Kitty said to Rose, who was helping her to restore order out of the chaos to which much exercise had reduced her curls,—

"By the way, young Randal is dying to be presented to you. May I after supper?"

"No, thank you," answered Rose, very decidedly.

"Well, I'm sure I don't see why not," began Kitty, looking displeased, but not surprised.

"I think you do, else why didn't you present him when he asked? You seldom stop to think of etiquette: why did you now?"

"I didn't like to do it till I had—you are so particular—I thought you'd say 'No;' but I couldn't tell him so," stammered Kitty, feeling that she had better have settled the matter herself; for Rose *was* very particular, and had especial reason to dislike this person, because he was not only a dissipated young reprobate himself, but seemed possessed of Satan to lead others astray likewise.

"I don't wish to be rude, dear: but I really must decline; for I cannot know such people, even though I meet them here," said Rose, remembering Charlie's revelations on New-Year's night, and hardening her heart against the man who had been his undoing on that as well as on other occasions, she had reason to believe.

"I couldn't help it! Old Mr. Randal and papa are friends; and, though I spoke of it, brother Alf wouldn't hear of passing that bad boy over," explained Kitty, eagerly.

"Yet Alf forbade your driving or skating with him; for he knows better than we how unfit he is to come among us."

"I'd drop him to-morrow if I could; but I must be civil in my own house. His mother brought him, and he won't dare to behave here as he does at their bachelor parties."

"She ought not to have brought him till he had shown some desire to mend his ways. It is none of my business, I know; but I do wish people wouldn't be so inconsistent, letting boys go to destruction, and then expecting us girls to receive them like decent people." Rose spoke in an energetic whisper, but Annabel heard her, and exclaimed, as she turned round with a powder-puff in her hand,—

"My goodness, Rose! what is all that about going to destruction?"

"She is being strong-minded; and I don't very much blame her in this case. But it leaves me in a dreadful scrape," said Kitty, supporting her spirits with a sniff of aromatic vinegar.

"I appeal to you, since you heard me, and there's no one here but ourselves: do you consider young Randal a nice person to know?" and Rose turned to Annabel and Emma with an anxious eye; for she did not find it easy to abide by her principles when so doing annoyed friends.

"No, indeed: he's perfectly horrid! Papa says he and Gorham are the wildest young men he knows, and enough to spoil the whole set. I'm so glad I've got no brothers," responded Annabel, placidly powdering her pink arms, quite undeterred by the memory of sundry white streaks left on sundry coat-sleeves.

"*I* think that sort of scrupulousness is very ill-bred, if you'll excuse my saying so, Rose. *We* are not supposed to know any thing about fastness, and wildness, and so on; but to treat every man alike, and not be fussy and prudish," said Emma, settling her many-colored streamers with the superior air of a woman of the world, aged twenty.

"Ah! but we do know; and, if our silence and civility have no effect, we ought to try something else, and not encourage wickedness of any kind. We needn't scold and preach, but we *can* refuse to know such people; and that will do some good, for

they don't like to be shunned and shut out from respectable society. Uncle Alec told me not to know that man, and I won't."
Rose spoke with unusual warmth, forgetting that she could not
tell the real reason for her strong prejudice against "that man."

"Well, *I* know him: *I* think him very jolly, and I'm engaged
to dance the German with him after supper. He leads quite as
well as your cousin Charlie, and is quite as fascinating, some
people think," returned Emma, tossing her head disdainfully;
for Prince Charming did not worship at her shrine, and it
piqued her vanity.

In spite of her quandary, Rose could not help smiling as she
recalled Mac's comparison; for Emma turned so red with spiteful chagrin, she seemed to have added strawberry-ice to the
other varieties composing the Harlequin.

"Each must judge for herself. I shall follow Aunt Jessie's
advice, and try to keep my atmosphere as pure as I can; for she
says every woman has her own little circle, and in it can use her
influence for good, if she will. I do will heartily; and I'll prove
that I'm neither proud nor fussy by receiving, here or at home,
any respectable man you like to present to me, no matter how
poor or plain or insignificant he may be."

With which declaration Rose ended her protest, and the
four damsels streamed downstairs together like a wandering
rainbow. But Kitty laid to heart what she had said; Annabel
took credit to herself for siding with her; and Emma owned
that *she* was not trying to keep her atmosphere pure when she
came to dance with the objectionable Randal. So Rose's "little
circle" was the better for the influence she tried to exert, although she never knew it.

All supper-time, Charlie kept near her, and she was quite
content with him; for he drank only coffee, and she saw him
shake his head with a frown when young Van beckoned him
toward an anteroom, from whence the sound of popping corks
had issued with increasing frequency as the evening wore on.

"Dear fellow, he does try," thought Rose, longing to show
how she admired his self-denial; but she could only say, as they
left the supper-room with the aunts, who were going early,—

"If I had not promised uncle to get home as soon after
midnight as possible, I'd stay and dance the German with you;
for you deserve a reward to-night."

"A thousand thanks! but I am going when you do," answered Charlie, understanding both her look and words, and very grateful for them.

"Really?" cried Rose, delighted.

"Really. I'll be in the hall when you come down." And Charlie thought the Fra Angelico angel was not half so bright and beautiful as the one who looked back at him out of a pale-blue cloud, as Rose went upstairs as if on wings.

When she came down again, Charlie was not in the hall, however; and, after waiting a few minutes, Mac offered to go and find him, for Aunt Jane was still hunting a lost rubber above.

"Please say I'm ready, but he needn't come if he doesn't want to," said Rose, not wishing to demand too much of her promising penitent.

"If he has gone into that bar-room, I'll have him out, no matter who is there!" growled Mac to himself, as he made his way to the small apartment whither the gentlemen retired for a little private refreshment when the spirit moved, as it often did.

The door was ajar, and Charlie seemed to have just entered; for Mac heard a familiar voice call out, in a jovial tone,—

"Come, Prince! you're just in time to help us drink Steve's health with all the honors."

"Can't stop; only ran in to say good-night, Van. Had a capital time; but I'm on duty, and must go."

"That's a new dodge. Take a stirrup-cup anyway, and come back in time for a merry-go-rounder when you've disposed of the ladies," answered the young host, diving into the wine-cooler for another bottle.

"Charlie's going in for sanctity, and it doesn't seem to agree with him," laughed one of the two other young men, who occupied several chairs apiece, resting their soles in every sense of the word.

"Apron-strings are coming into fashion,—the bluer the better: hey, Prince?" added the other, trying to be witty, with the usual success.

"You'd better go home early yourself, Barrow, or that tongue of yours will get you into trouble," retorted Charlie, conscious that he ought to take his own advice, yet lingering, nervously putting on his gloves, while the glasses were being filled.

"Now, brother-in-law, fire away! Here you are, Prince." And Steve handed a glass across the table to his cousin, feeling too much elated with various pleasurable emotions to think what he was doing; for the boys all knew Charlie's weakness, and usually tried to defend him from it.

Before the glass could be taken, however, Mac entered in a great hurry, delivering his message in an abbreviated and rather peremptory form,—

"Rose is waiting for you. Hurry up!"

"All right. Good-night, old fellows!" And Charlie was off, as if the name had power to stop him in the very act of breaking the promise made to himself.

"Come, Solon, take a social drop, and give us an epithalamium in your best Greek. Here's to you!" And Steve was lifting the wine to his own lips, when Mac knocked the glass out of his hand, with a flash of the eye that caused his brother to stare at him, with his mouth open, in an imbecile sort of way, which seemed to excite Mac still more; for, turning to his young host, he said, in a low voice, and with a look that made the gentlemen on the chairs sit up suddenly,—

"I beg pardon, Van, for making a mess; but I can't stand by and see my own brother tempt another man beyond his strength, or make a brute of himself. That's plain English: but I can't help speaking out; for I know not one of you would willingly hurt Charlie, and you will if you don't let him alone."

"What do you pitch into me for? I've done nothing. A fellow must be civil in his own house, mustn't he?" asked Van, good-humoredly, as he faced about, corkscrew in hand.

"Yes, but it is not civil to urge or joke a guest into doing what you know and he knows is bad for him. That's only a glass of wine to you, but it is perdition to Charlie; and, if Steve knew what he was about, he'd cut his right hand off before he'd offer it."

"Do you mean to say I'm tipsy?" demanded Steve, ruffling up like a little game-cock; for, though he saw now what he had done and was ashamed of it, he hated to have Mac air his peculiar notions before other people.

"With excitement, not champagne, I hope; for I wouldn't

own you if you were," answered Mac, in whom indignation was effervescing like the wine in the forgotten bottle; for the men were all young, friends of Steve's and admirers of Charlie's. "Look here, boys," he went on more quietly: "I know I ought not to explode in this violent sort of way, but upon my life I couldn't help it, when I heard what you were saying and saw what Steve was doing. Since I *have* begun I may as well finish, and tell you straight out that Prince can't stand this sort of thing. He is trying to flee temptation, and whoever leads him into it does a cowardly and sinful act; for the loss of one's own self-respect is bad enough, without losing the more precious things that make life worth having. Don't tell him I've said this, but lend a hand if you can, and never have to reproach yourselves with the knowledge that you helped to ruin a fellow-creature, soul and body."

It was well for the success of Mac's first crusade, that his hearers were gentlemen and sober: so his outburst was not received with jeers or laughter, but listened to in silence, while the expression of the faces changed from one of surprise to regret and respect; for earnestness is always effective, and championship of this sort seldom fails to touch hearts as yet unspoiled. As he paused with an eloquent little quiver in his eager voice, Van corked the bottle at a blow, threw down the corkscrew, and offered Mac his hand, saying heartily, in spite of his slang,—

"You are a first-class old brick! I'll lend a hand for one, and do my best to back up Charlie; for he's the finest fellow I know, and shan't go to the devil like poor Randal if *I* can help it."

Murmurs of applause from the others seemed to express a general assent to this vigorous statement; and, giving the hand a grateful shake, Mac retreated to the door, anxious to be off now that he had freed his mind with such unusual impetuosity.

"Count on me for any thing I can do in return for this, Van. I'm sorry to be such a marplot, but you can take it out in quizzing me after I'm gone. I'm fair game, and Steve can set you going."

With that, Mac departed as abruptly as he came, feeling that he *had* "made a mess" of it; but comforting himself with the thought that perhaps he had secured help for Charlie at his own expense, and thinking with a droll smile as he went back to his mother,—

"My romance begins by looking after other girls' lovers instead of finding a sweetheart for myself; but I can't tell Rose, so *she* won't laugh at me."

# Chapter XIII

## BOTH SIDES

S TEVE's engagement made a great stir in the family: a pleasant one this time; for nobody objected, every thing seemed felicitous, and the course of true love ran very smoothly for the young couple, who promised to remove the only obstacle to their union by growing old and wise as soon as possible. If he had not been so genuinely happy, the little lover's airs would have been unbearable; for he patronized all mankind in general, his brother and elder cousins in particular.

"Now that is the way to manage matters," he declared, standing before the fire in Aunt Clara's billiard room a day or two after the ball, with his hands behind his back,—"no nonsense, no delay, no domestic rows or tragic separations. Just choose with taste and judgment, make yourself agreeable through thick and thin; and, when it is perfectly evident that the dear creature adores the ground you walk on, say the word like a man, and there you are."

"All very easy to do that with a girl like Kitty, who has no confounded notions to spoil her and trip you up every time you don't exactly toe the mark," muttered Charlie, knocking the balls about as if it were a relief to hit something; for he was in a gloriously bad humor that evening, because time hung heavy on his hands since he had forsworn the company he could not keep without danger to himself.

"You should humor those little notions; for all women have them, and it needs tact to steer clear of them. Kitty's got dozens; but I treat them with respect, have my own way when I can, give in without growling when I can't, and we get on like a couple of—"

"Spoons," put in Charlie, who felt that he had *not* steered clear, and so suffered shipwreck in sight of land.

Steve meant to have said "doves," but his cousin's levity caused him to add with calm dignity, "reasonable beings," and then revenged himself by making a good shot which won him the game.

"You always were a lucky little dog, Steve. I don't begrudge you a particle of your happiness, but it does seem as if things weren't quite fair sometimes," said Archie, suppressing an envious sigh; for, though he seldom complained, it was impossible to contrast his own and his cousin's prospects with perfect equanimity.

> "'His worth shines forth the brightest who in hope
> Always confides: the abject soul despairs,'"

observed Mac, quoting Euripides in a conversational tone, as he lay upon a divan reposing after a hard day's work.

"Thank you," said Archie, brightening a little; for a hopeful word from any source was very comfortable.

"That's your favorite Rip, isn't it? He was a wise old boy, but you could find advice as good as that nearer home," put in Steve, who just then felt equal to slapping Plato on the shoulder; so elated was he at being engaged "first of all the lot," as he gracefully expressed it.

"Don't halloo till you are out of the wood, Dandy: Mrs. Kit has jilted two men, and may a third; so you'd better not brag of your wisdom too soon; for she may make a fool of you yet," said Charlie, cynically, his views of life being very gloomy about this time.

"No, she won't, Steve, if you do your part honestly. There's the making of a good little woman in Kitty, and she has proved it by taking you instead of those other fellows. You are not a Solomon, but you're not spoilt yet; and she had the sense to see it," said Mac, encouragingly from his corner; for he and his brother were better friends than ever since the little scene at the Van Tassels.

"Hear! hear!" cried Steve, looking more than ever like a cheerful young cockerel trying to crow, as he stood upon the hearth-rug with his hands under his coat-tails, rising and falling alternately upon the toes and heels of his neat little boots.

"Come, you've given them each a pat on the head: haven't you got one for me? I need it enough; for if ever there was a poor devil born under an evil star, it is C. C. Campbell," exclaimed Charlie, leaning his chin on his cue with a discontented expression of countenance; for trying to be good is often very hard work till one gets used to it.

"Oh, yes! I can accommodate you;" and, as if his words suggested the selection, Mac, still lying flat upon his back, repeated one of his favorite bits from Beaumont and Fletcher; for he had a wonderful memory, and could reel off poetry by the hour together.

> "'Man is his own star: and the soul that can
> Render an honest and a perfect man
> Commands all light, all influence, all fate;
> Nothing to him falls early or too late.
> Our acts our angels are; or good or ill,
> Our fatal shadows that walk by us still.'"

"Confoundedly bad angels they are too," muttered Charlie, ruefully; remembering the one that undid him.

His cousins never knew exactly what occurred on New-Year's night, but suspected that something was amiss; for Charlie had the blues, and Rose, though as kind as ever, expressed no surprise at his long absences. They had all observed and wondered at this state of things, yet discreetly made no remark, till Steve, who was as inquisitive as a magpie, seized this opportunity to say in a friendly tone, which showed that he bore no malice for the dark prophecy regarding his Kitty's faithfulness,—

"What's the trouble, Prince? You are so seldom in a bad humor that we don't know what to make of it, and all feel out of spirits when you have the blues. Had a tiff with Rose?"

"Never you mind, little boy; but this I will say,—the better women are, the more unreasonable they are. They don't require us to be saints like themselves, which is lucky; but they do expect us to render 'an honest and a perfect man' sometimes, and that is asking rather too much in a fallen world like this," said Charlie, glad to get a little sympathy, though he had no intention of confessing his transgressions.

"No, it isn't," said Mac, decidedly.

"Much you know about it," began Charlie, ill pleased to be so flatly contradicted.

"Well, I know this much," added Mac, suddenly sitting up with his hair in a highly dishevelled condition. "It is very unreasonable in us to ask women to be saints, and then expect them to feel honored when we offer them our damaged hearts, or, at best, ones not half as good as theirs. If they weren't blinded by love, they'd see what a mean advantage we take of them, and not make such bad bargains."

"Upon my word, the philosopher is coming out strong upon the subject! We shall have him preaching 'Women's Rights' directly," said Steve, much amazed at this outburst.

"I've begun you see, and much good may it do you," answered Mac, laying himself placidly down again.

"Well, but look here, man: you are arguing on the wrong side," put in Archie, quite agreeing with him, but feeling that he must stand by his order at all costs.

"Never mind sides, uphold the right wherever you find it. You needn't stare, Steve: I told you I was going to look into this matter, and I am. You think I'm wrapt up in books: but I see a great deal more of what is going on round me than you imagine; and I'm getting on in this new branch, let me tell you; quite as fast as is good for me, I dare say."

"Going in for perfection, are you?" asked Charlie, both amused and interested; for he respected Mac more than he owned even to himself, and though he had never alluded to the timely warning, neither forgot.

"Yes, I think of it."

"How will you begin?"

"Do my best all round: keep good company, read good books, love good things, and cultivate soul and body as faithfully and wisely as I can."

"And you expect to succeed, do you?"

"Please God, I will."

The quiet energy of Mac's last words produced a momentary silence. Charlie thoughtfully studied the carpet; Archie, who had been absently poking the fire, looked over at Mac as if he thanked him again; and Steve, forgetting his self-conceit, began to wonder if it was not possible to improve himself a little for Kitty's sake. Only a minute; for young men do not give much time to thoughts of this kind, even when love stirs up the noblest impulses within them. To act rather than to talk is more natural to most of them, as Charlie's next question showed; for, having the matter much at heart, he ventured to ask in an offhand way, as he laughed and twirled his cue,—

"Do you intend to reach the highest point of perfection before you address one of the fair saints, or shall you ask her to lend a hand somewhere short of that?"

"As it takes a long lifetime to do what I plan, I think I shall ask some good woman 'to lend a hand' when I've got any thing worth offering her. Not a saint, for I never shall be one myself, but a gentle creature who will help me, as I shall try to help her; so that we can go on together, and finish our work hereafter, if we haven't time to do it here."

If Mac had been a lover, he would not have discussed the subject in this simple and sincere fashion, though he might have felt it far more deeply; but being quite heart-free he frankly showed his interest, and, curiously enough, out of his wise young head unconsciously gave the three lovers before him counsel which they valued, because he practised what he preached.

"Well, I hope you'll find her!" said Charlie, heartily, as he went back to his game.

"I think I shall," and, while the others played, Mac lay staring at the window-curtain, as contentedly as if, through it, he beheld "a dream of fair women," from which to choose his future mate.

A few days after this talk in the billiard-room, Kitty went to call upon Rose; for, as she was about to enter the family, she felt it her duty to become acquainted with all its branches. This branch, however, she cultivated more assiduously than any other, and was continually running in to confer with "Cousin Rose," whom she considered the wisest, dearest, kindest girl ever created. And Rose, finding that, in spite of her flighty head, Kitty had a good heart of her own, did her best to encourage all the new hopes and aspirations springing up in it under the warmth of the first genuine affection she had ever known.

"My dear, I want to have some serious conversation with you upon a subject in which I take an interest for the first time in my life," began Miss Kitty, seating herself and pulling off her gloves, as if the subject was one which needed a firm grasp.

"Tell away, and don't mind if I go on working, as I want to finish this job to-day," answered Rose, with a long-handled paint-brush in her hand, and a great pair of shears at her side.

"You are always so busy! What is it now? Let me help: I can talk faster when I'm doing something," which seemed hardly possible; for Kitty's tongue went like a mill-clapper at all hours.

"Making picture-books for my sick babies at the hospital. Pretty work, isn't it? You cut out, and I'll paste them on these squares of gay cambric: then we just tie up a few pages with a ribbon; and there is a nice, light, durable book for the poor dears to look at as they lie in their little beds."

"A capital idea. Do you go there often? How ever do you find the time for such things?" asked Kitty, busily cutting from a big sheet the touching picture of a parent bird with a red head and a blue tail, offering what looked like a small boa-constrictor to one of its nestlings; a fat young squab with a green head, yellow body, and no tail at all.

"I have plenty of time now I don't go out so much; for a party uses up two days generally,—one to prepare for it, and one to get over it, you know."

"People think it is so odd of you to give up society all of a sudden. They say you have 'turned pious,' and it is owing to your peculiar bringing up. I always take your part, and say it is a pity other girls haven't as sensible an education; for I don't know one who is as satisfactory on the whole as you are."

"Much obliged. You may also tell people I gave up gayety because I valued health more. But I haven't forsworn every thing of the kind, Kit. I go to concerts and lectures, and all sorts of early things, and have nice times at home, as you know. I like fun as well as ever: but I'm getting on, you see, and must be preparing a little for the serious part of life; one never knows when it may come," said Rose, thoughtfully, as she pasted a squirrel upside-down on the pink cotton page before her.

"That reminds me of what I wanted to say. If you'll believe me, my dear, Steve has got that very idea into his head! Did you or Mac put it there?" asked Kitty, industriously clashing her shears.

"No, I've given up lecturing the boys lately: they are so big now they don't like it, and I fancy I'd got into a way that was rather tiresome."

"Well, then, *he* is 'turning pious' too. And what is very singular, I like it. Now don't smile: I really do; and I want to be getting ready for the 'serious part of life,' as you call it. That is,

I want to grow better as fast as I can; for Steve says he isn't half good enough for me. Just think of that!"

Kitty looked so surprised and pleased and proud, that Rose felt no desire to laugh at her sudden fancy for sobriety, but said in her most sympathetic tone,—

"I'm very glad to hear it; for it shows that he loves you in the right way."

"Is there more than one way?"

"Yes, I fancy so; because some people improve so much after they fall in love, and others do not at all. Have you never observed that?"

"I never learned how to observe. Of course, I know that some matches turn out well and some don't; but I never thought much about it."

"Well, I have; for I was rather interested in the subject lately, and had a talk with Aunt Jessie and uncle about it."

"Gracious! you don't talk to them about such things, do you?"

"Yes, indeed; I ask any questions I like, and always get a good answer. It is such a nice way to learn, Kitty; for you don't have to poke over books, but as things come along you talk about them, and remember; and when they are spoken of afterward you understand and are interested, though you don't say a word," explained Rose.

"It must be nice; but I haven't any one to do so for me. Papa is too busy, and mamma always says when I ask questions, 'Don't trouble your head with such things, child;' so I don't. What did you learn about matches turning out well? I'm interested in that, because I want mine to be quite perfect in all respects."

"After thinking it over, I came to the conclusion that uncle *was* right, and it is *not* always safe to marry a person just because you love him," began Rose, trying to enlighten Kitty without betraying herself.

"Of course not: if they haven't money or are bad. But otherwise I don't see what more is needed," said Kitty, wonderingly.

"One should stop and see if it is a wise love, likely to help both parties, and wear well; for you know it ought to last all one's lifetime, and it is very sad if it doesn't."

"I declare it quite scares me to think of it; for I don't usually go beyond my wedding-day in making plans. I remember, though, that when I was engaged the first time (you don't know the man: it was just after you went away, and I was only sixteen), some one very ill-naturedly said I should 'marry in haste and repent at leisure;' and that made me try to imagine how it would seem to go on year after year with Gustavus (who had a dreadful temper, by the way), and it worried me so to think of it that I broke the engagement, and was so glad ever afterward."

"You were a wise girl; and I hope you'll do it again, if you find, after a time, that you and Steve do not truly trust and respect as well as love one another. If you don't, you'll be miserable when it is too late, as so many people are who do marry in haste and have a lifetime to repent it. Aunt Jessie says so, and she knows."

"Don't be solemn, Rose. It fidgets me to think about lifetimes, and respecting, and all those responsible things. I'm not used to it, and I don't know how to do it."

"But you *must* think, and you must learn how before you take the responsibility upon yourself. That is what your life is for; and you mustn't spoil it by doing a very solemn thing without seeing if you are ready for it."

"Do you think about all this?" asked Kitty, shrugging up her shoulders as if responsibility of any sort did not sit comfortably on them.

"One has to sometimes, you know. But is that all you wanted to tell me?" added Rose, anxious to turn the conversation from herself.

"Oh, dear, no! The most serious thing of all is this. Steve is putting himself in order generally, and so I want to do my part; and I must begin right away before my thoughts get distracted with clothes, and all sorts of dear, delightful, frivolous things that I can't help liking. Now I wish you'd tell me where to begin. Shouldn't I improve my mind by reading something solid?" and Kitty looked over at the well-filled book-case, as if to see if it contained any thing large and dry enough to be considered "solid."

"It would be an excellent plan, and we'll look up something. What do you feel as if you needed most?"

"A little of every thing I should say; for when I look into my mind there really doesn't seem to be much there but odds and ends, and yet I'm sure I've read a great deal more than some girls do. I suppose novels don't count, though, and are of no use; for, goodness knows, the people and things they describe aren't a bit like the real ones."

"Some novels are very useful and do as much good as sermons, I've heard uncle say; because they not only describe truly, but teach so pleasantly that people like to learn in that way," said Rose, who knew the sort of books Kitty had read, and did not wonder that she felt rather astray when she tried to guide herself by their teaching.

"You pick me out some of the right kind, and I'll apply my mind to them. Then I ought to have some 'serious views' and 'methods' and 'principles;' Steve said 'principles,' good firm ones, you know," and Kitty gave a little pull at the bit of cambric she was cutting, as housewives pull cotton or calico when they want "a good firm article."

Rose could not help laughing now, though much pleased; for Kitty was so prettily in earnest, and yet so perfectly ignorant how to begin on the self-improvement she very much needed, that it was pathetic as well as comical to see and hear her.

"You certainly want some of those, and must begin at once to get them: but Aunt Jessie can help you there better than I can; or Aunt Jane, for she has very 'firm' ones, I assure you," said Rose, sobering down as quickly as possible.

"Mercy on us! I should never dare to say a word about it to Mrs. Mac: for I'm dreadfully afraid of her, she is so stern; and how I'm ever to get on when she is my mother-in-law I don't know!" cried Kitty, clasping her hands in dismay at the idea.

"She isn't half as stern as she looks; and if you go to her without fear, you've no idea how sensible and helpful she is. I used to be frightened out of my wits with her, but now I'm not a bit, and we get on nicely: indeed I'm fond of her, she is so reliable and upright in all things."

"She certainly is the straightest woman I ever saw, and the most precise. I never shall forget how scared I was when Steve took me up to see her that first time. I put on all my plainest things, did my hair in a meek knob, and tried to act like a sober, sedate young woman. Steve would laugh at me, and say I looked like a pretty nun, so I couldn't be as proper as I wished. Mrs. Mac was very kind, of course; but her eye was so sharp I felt as if she saw right through me, and knew that I'd pinned on my bonnet-strings, lost a button off my boot, and didn't brush my hair for ten minutes every night," said Kitty, in an awe-stricken tone.

"She likes you, though, and so does uncle, and he's set his heart on having you live with them by and by; so don't mind her eyes, but look straight up at her, and you'll see how kind they can grow."

"Mac likes me too, and that did please me; for he doesn't like girls generally. Steve told me he said I had the 'making of a capital little woman in me.' Wasn't it nice of him? Steve was *so* proud, though he does laugh at Mac sometimes."

"Don't disappoint them, dear. Encourage Steve in all the good things he likes or wants, make friends with Mac, love Aunt Jane, and be a daughter to uncle, and you'll find yourself a very happy girl."

"I truly will, and thank you very much for not making fun of me. I know I'm a little goose; but lately I've felt as if I might come to something if I had the right sort of help. I'll go up and see Aunt Jessie to-morrow; I'm not a bit afraid of her: and then if you'll just quietly find out from Uncle Doctor what I must read, I'll work as hard as I can. Don't tell any one, please; they'll think it odd and affected, and I can't bear to be laughed at, though I dare say it is good discipline."

Rose promised, and both worked in silence for a moment; then Kitty asked rather timidly,—

"Are you and Charlie trying this plan too? Since you've left off going out so much, he keeps away also; and we don't know what to make of it."

"He has had what he calls an 'artistic fit' lately, set up a studio, and is doing some crayon sketches of us all. If he'd only finish his things, they would be excellent; but he likes to try a great variety at once. I'll take you in sometime, and perhaps he will do a portrait of you for Steve. He likes girls' faces, and gets the likenesses wonderfully well."

"People say you are engaged: but I contradict it; because, of course, *I* should know if you were."

"We are not."

"I'm glad of it; for really, Rose, I'm afraid Charlie hasn't got 'firm principles,' though he is a fascinating fellow and one can't scold him. You don't mind my saying so, do you, dear?" added Kitty; for Rose did not answer at once.

"Not in the least: for you are one of us now, and I can speak frankly, and I will; for I think in one way you *can* help Steve very much. You are right about Charlie, both as to the principles and the fascination: Steve admires him exceedingly, and always from a boy liked to imitate his pleasant ways. Some of them are very harmless and do Steve good, but some are not. I needn't talk about it, only you must show your boy that you depend on him to keep out of harm, and help him do it."

"I will, I will! and then perhaps, when he is a perfect model, Charlie will imitate him. I really begin to feel as if I had a great deal to do," and Kitty looked as if she was beginning to like it also.

"We all have; and the sooner we go to work the better for us and those we love. You wouldn't think now that Phebe was doing any thing for Archie, but she is; and writes such splendid letters, they stir him up wonderfully, and make us all love and admire her more than ever."

"How is she getting on?" asked Kitty, who, though she called herself a "little goose," had tact enough to see that Rose did not care to talk about Charlie.

"Nicely; for you know she used to sing in our choir, so that was a good recommendation for another. She got a fine place in the new church at L——; and that gives her a comfortable salary, though she has something put away. She was always a saving creature and kept her wages carefully; uncle invested them, and she begins to feel quite independent already. No fear but my Phebe will get on: she has such energy, and manages so well. I sometimes wish I could run away and work with her."

"Ah, my dear! we rich girls have our trials as well as poor ones, though we don't get as much pity as they do," sighed Kitty. "Nobody knows what I suffer sometimes from worries that I can't talk about, and I shouldn't get much sympathy if I did; just because I live in a big house, wear good gowns, and have lots of lovers. Annabel used to say she envied me above all created beings; but she doesn't now, and is perfectly absorbed in her dear little Chinaman. Do you see how she ever could like him?"

So they began to gossip, and the sober talk was over for that time; but when Kitty departed, after criticising all her dear friends and their respective sweethearts, she had a helpful little book in her muff, a resolute expression on her bright face, and so many excellent plans for self-improvement in her busy brain, that she and Steve bid fair to turn out the model couple of the century.

# Chapter XIV

AUNT CLARA'S PLAN

BEING seriously alarmed by the fear of losing the desire of his heart, Charlie had gone resolutely to work, and, like many another young reformer, he rather overdid the matter; for, in trying to keep out of the way of temptation, he denied himself much innocent enjoyment. The artistic fit was a good excuse for the seclusion which he fancied would be a proper penance; and he sat listlessly plying crayon or paint-brush, with daily wild rides on black Brutus, which seemed to do him good; for danger of that sort was his delight.

People were used to his whims, and made light of what they considered a new one; but, when it lasted week after week and all attempts to draw him out were vain, his jolly comrades gave him up, and the family began to say approvingly,—"Now he really *is* going to settle down and do something." Fortunately, his mother let him alone; for though Dr. Alec had not "thundered in her ear" as he threatened, he *had* talked with her in a way which first made her very angry, then anxious, and, lastly, quite submissive; for her heart was set on the boy's winning Rose, and she would have had him put on sackcloth and ashes if that would have secured the prize. She made light of the cause of Rose's displeasure, considering her extremely foolish and straitlaced; "for all young men of any spirit had their little vices, and came out well enough when the wild oats were sowed." So she indulged Charlie in his new vagary, as she had in all his others, and treated him like an ill-used being, which was neither an inspiring nor helpful course on her part. Poor soul! she saw her mistake by and by, and when too late repented of it bitterly.

Rose wanted to be kind, and tried in various ways to help her cousin, feeling very sure she should succeed as many another hopeful woman has done, quite unconscious how much stronger an undisciplined will is than the truest love; and what a difficult task the wisest find it to undo the mistakes of a bad education. But it was a hard thing to do: for, at the least hint of commendation or encouragement, he looked so hopeful that she was afraid of seeming to promise too much; and, of all things, she desired to escape the accusation of having trifled with him.

So life was not very comfortable to either just then; and, while Charlie was "mortifying soul and body" to please her, she was studying how to serve him best. Aunt Jessie helped her very much, and no one guessed, when they saw pretty Miss Campbell going up and down the hill with such a serious face, that she was intent upon any thing except taking, with praise-worthy regularity, the constitutionals which gave her such a charming color.

Matters were in this state, when one day a note came to Rose from Mrs. Clara.

> "MY SWEET CHILD,—Do take pity on my poor boy, and cheer him up with a sight of you; for he is so *triste* it breaks my heart to see him. He has a new plan in his head, which strikes me as an excellent one, if you will only favor it. Let him come and take you for a drive this fine afternoon, and talk things over. It will do him a world of good and deeply oblige
> "Your ever loving
> "AUNT CLARA."

Rose read the note twice, and stood a moment pondering, with her eyes absently fixed on the little bay before her window. The sight of several black figures moving briskly to and fro across its frozen surface seemed to suggest a mode of escape from the drive she dreaded in more ways than one. "That will be safer and pleasanter," she said, and going to her desk wrote her answer.

> "DEAR AUNTY,—I'm afraid of Brutus; but, if Charlie will go skating with me, I should enjoy it very much, and it would do us both good. I can listen to the new plan with an undivided mind there; so give him my love, please, and say I shall expect him at three.
> "Affectionately,
> "ROSE."

Punctually at three, Charlie appeared with his skates over his arm, and a very contented face, which brightened wonderfully as Rose came downstairs in a seal-skin suit and scarlet skirt, so like the one she wore years ago that he involuntarily exclaimed as he took her skates,—

"You look so like little Rose I hardly know you; and it seems so like old times I feel sixteen again."

"That is just the way one ought to feel such a day as this. Now let us be off and have a good spin before any one comes. There are only a few children there now; but it is Saturday, you know, and everybody will be out before long," answered Rose, carefully putting on her mittens as she talked: for her heart was not as light as the one little Rose carried under the brown jacket; and the boy of sixteen never looked at her with the love and longing she read in the eyes of the young man before her.

Away they went, and were soon almost as merry and warm as the children round them; for the ice was in good condition, the February sunshine brilliant, and the keen wind set their blood a-tingle with a healthful glow.

"Now tell me the plan your mother spoke of," began Rose, as they went gliding across the wide expanse before them; for Charlie seemed to have forgotten every thing but the bliss of having her all to himself for a little while.

"Plan? Oh, yes! it is simply this. I'm going out to father next month."

"Really?" and Rose looked both surprised and incredulous; for this plan was not a new one.

"Really. You don't believe it, but I am; and mother means to go with me. We've had another letter from the governor, and he says if she can't part from her big baby to come along too, and all be happy together. What do you think of that?" he asked, eying her intently; for they were face to face, as she went backward and he held both her hands to steer and steady her.

"I like it immensely, and I do believe it now: only it rather takes my breath away to think of aunty's going, when she never would hear of it before."

"She doesn't like the plan very well now, and consents to go only on one condition."

"What is that?" asked Rose, trying to free her hands; for a look at Charlie made her suspect what was coming.

"That you go with us;" and, holding the hands fast, he added rapidly, "Let me finish before you speak. I don't mean that any thing is to be changed till you are ready; but if *you* go I'm willing to give up every thing else, and live anywhere as long as you like. Why shouldn't you come to us for a year or two? We've never had our share. Father would be delighted, mother contented, and I the happiest man alive."

"Who made this plan?" asked Rose, as soon as she got the breath which certainly *had* been rather taken away by this entirely new and by no means agreeable scheme.

"Mother suggested it: I shouldn't have dared to even dream of such richness. I'd made up my mind to go alone; and when I told her she was in despair, till this superb idea came into her head. After that, of course it was easy enough for me to stick to the resolution I'd made."

"Why did *you* decide to go, Charlie?" and Rose looked up into the eyes that were fixed beseechingly on hers.

They wavered and glanced aside; then met hers honestly, yet full of a humility which made her own fall as he answered very low,—

"Because I don't *dare* to stay."

"Is it so hard?" she said pitifully.

"Very hard. I haven't the moral courage to own up and face ridicule, and it seems so mean to hide for fear of breaking my word. I *will* keep it this time, Rose, if I go to the ends of the earth to do it."

"It is not cowardly to flee temptation; and nobody whose opinion is worth having will ridicule any brave attempt to conquer one's self. Don't mind it, Charlie, but stand fast; and I am sure you will succeed."

"You don't know what it is, and I can't tell you; for till I tried to give it up I never guessed what a grip it had on me. I thought it was only a habit, easy to drop when I liked: but it is stronger than I; and sometimes I feel as if possessed of a devil that *will* get the better of me, try as I may."

He dropped her hands abruptly as he said that, with the energy of despair; and, as if afraid of saying too much, he left her for a minute, striking away at full speed, as if in truth he would "go to the ends of the earth" to escape the enemy within himself.

Rose stood still, appalled by this sudden knowledge of how much greater the evil was than she had dreamed. What ought she to do? Go with her cousin, and by so doing tacitly pledge herself as his companion on that longer journey for which he was as yet so poorly equipped? Both heart and conscience protested against this so strongly that she put the thought away. But compassion pleaded for him tenderly; and the spirit of self-sacrifice, which makes women love to give more than they receive, caused her to feel as if in a measure this man's fate lay in her hands, to be decided for good or ill through her. How should she be true both to him and to herself?

Before this question could be answered, he was back again, looking as if he had left his care behind him; for his moods varied like the wind. Her attitude, as she stood motionless and alone with downcast face, was so unlike the cheerful creature who came to meet him an hour ago, it filled him with self-reproach; and, coming up, he drew one hand through his arm, saying, as she involuntarily followed him,—

"You must not stand still. Forget my heroics, and answer my question. Will you go with us, Rose?"

"Not now: that is asking too much, Charlie, and I will promise nothing, because I cannot do it honestly," she answered, so firmly that he knew appeal was useless.

"Am I to go alone, then, leaving all I care for behind me?"

"No, take your mother with you, and do your best to re-unite your parents. You could not give yourself to a better task."

"She won't go without you."

"I think she will if you hold fast to your resolution. You won't give that up, I hope?"

"No: I must go somewhere, for I can't stay here; and it may as well be India, since that pleases father," answered Charlie, doggedly.

"It will more than you can imagine. Tell him all the truth, and see how glad he will be to help you, and how sincerely he will respect you for what you've done."

"If you respect me, I don't care much about the opinion of any one else," answered Charlie, clinging with a lover's pertinacity to the hope that was dearest.

"I shall, if you go manfully away, and do the duty you owe your father and yourself."

"And, when I've done it, may I come back to be rewarded, Rose?" he asked, taking possession of the hand on his arm, as if it was already his.

"I wish I could say what you want me to. But how can I promise when I am not sure of any thing? I don't love you as I ought, and perhaps I never shall: so why persist in making me bind myself in this way? Be generous, Charlie, and don't ask it," implored Rose, much afflicted by his persistence.

"I thought you did love me: it looked very like it a month ago, unless you have turned coquette, and I can't quite believe that," he answered bitterly.

"I *was* beginning to love you, but you made me afraid to go on," murmured Rose, trying to tell the truth kindly.

"That cursed custom! What *can* a man do when his hostess asks him to drink wine with her?" And Charlie looked as if he could have cursed himself even more heartily.

"He can say 'No.'"

"I can't."

"Ah, that's the trouble! You never learned to say it even to yourself; and now it is so hard you want me to help you."

"And you won't."

"Yes, I will, by showing you that I *can* say it to myself, for your sake." And Rose looked up with a face so full of tender sorrow he could not doubt the words which both reproached and comforted him.

"My little saint! I don't deserve one half your goodness to me; but I will, and go away without one complaint to do my best, for your sake," he cried, touched by her grief, and stirred to emulation by the example of courage and integrity she tried to set him.

Here Steve and Kitty bore down upon them; and, obeying the impulse to put care behind them which makes it possible for young hearts to ache one minute and dance the next, Rose and Charlie banished their troubles, joined in the sport that soon turned the lonely little bay into a ballroom, and enjoyed the splendors of a winter sunset, forgetful of separation and Calcutta.

# Chapter XV

---

IN spite of much internal rebellion, Charlie held fast to his resolution; and Aunt Clara, finding all persuasions vain, gave in, and prepared to accompany him, in a state of chronic indignation against the world in general and Rose in particular. The poor girl had a hard time of it, and, but for her uncle, would have fared still worse. He was a sort of shield, upon which Mrs. Clara's lamentations, reproaches, and irate glances fell unavailingly, instead of wounding the heart against which they were aimed.

The days passed very quickly now; for every one seemed anxious to have the parting over, and preparations went on rapidly. The big house was made ready to shut up for a year at least, comforts for the long voyage laid in, and farewell visits paid. The general activity and excitement rendered it impossible for Charlie to lead the life of an artistic hermit any longer: and he fell into a restless condition, which caused Rose to long for the departure of the "Rajah," when she felt that he would be safe; for these farewell festivities were dangerous to one who was just learning to say "No."

"Half the month safely gone. If we can only get well over these last weeks, a great weight will be off my mind," thought Rose, as she went down one wild, wet morning toward the end of February.

Opening the study-door to greet her uncle, she exclaimed, "Why, Archie!" then paused upon the threshold, transfixed by fear; for in her cousin's white face she read the tidings of some great affliction.

"Hush! don't be frightened. Come in and I'll tell you," he whispered, putting down the bottle he had just taken from the doctor's medicine-closet.

Rose understood and obeyed; for Aunt Plenty was poorly with her rheumatism, and depended on her morning doze.

"What is it?" she said, looking about the room with a shiver, as if expecting to see again what she saw there New-Year's night. Archie was alone, however, and, drawing her toward the closet, answered, with an evident effort to be quite calm and steady,—

"Charlie is hurt! Uncle wants more ether, and the wide bandages in some drawer or other. He told me, but I forget. You keep this place in order: find them for me. Quick!"

Before he had done, Rose was at the drawer, turning over the bandages with hands that trembled as they searched.

"All narrow! I must make some. Can you wait?" And, catching up a piece of old linen, she tore it into wide strips, adding, in the same quick tone, as she began to roll them,—

"Now tell me."

"I can wait: those are not needed just yet. I didn't mean any one should know, you least of all," began Archie, smoothing out the strips as they lay across the table, and evidently surprised at the girl's nerve and skill.

"I can bear it: make haste! Is he much hurt?"

"I'm afraid he is. Uncle looks sober, and the poor boy suffers so I couldn't stay," answered Archie, turning still whiter about the lips that never had so hard a tale to tell before.

"You see, he went to town last evening to meet the man who is going to buy Brutus—"

"And Brutus did it? I knew he would!" cried Rose, dropping her work to wring her hands, as if she guessed the ending of the story now.

"Yes, and if he wasn't shot already I'd do it myself with pleasure; for he's done his best to kill Charlie," muttered Charlie's mate with a grim look; then gave a great sigh, and added with averted face,—

"I shouldn't blame the brute; it wasn't his fault: he needed a firm hand, and—" he stopped there, but Rose said quickly,—

"Go on. I *must* know."

"Charlie met some of his old cronies, quite by accident; there was a dinner-party, and they made him go, just for a good-by they said. He couldn't refuse, and it was too much for him. He would come home alone in the storm, though they tried to keep him as he wasn't fit. Down by the new bridge,— that high embankment you know,—the wind had put the lantern out—he forgot—or something scared Brutus, and all went down together."

Archie had spoken fast and brokenly; but Rose understood, and at the last word hid her face with a little moan, as if she saw it all.

"Drink this and never mind the rest," he said, dashing into the next room and coming back with a glass of water, longing to be done and away; for this sort of pain seemed almost as bad as that he had left.

Rose drank, but held his arm tightly as he would have turned away, saying in a tone of command he could not disobey,—

"Don't keep any thing back: tell me the worst at once."

"We knew nothing of it," he went on obediently. "Aunt Clara thought he was with me, and no one found him till early this morning. A workman recognized him; and he was brought home, dead they thought. I came for uncle an hour ago. Charlie is conscious now, but awfully hurt; and I'm afraid from the way Mac and uncle look at one another that—Oh! think of it, Rose! crushed and helpless, alone in the rain all night, and I never knew, I never knew!"

With that poor Archie broke down entirely; and, flinging himself into a chair, laid his face on the table, sobbing like a girl. Rose had never seen a man cry before, and it was so unlike a woman's gentler grief that it moved her very much. Putting by her own anguish, she tried to comfort his, and going to him lifted up his head and made him lean on her; for in such hours as this women are the stronger. It was a very little to do, but it did comfort Archie; for the poor fellow felt as if fate was very hard upon him just then, and into this faithful bosom he could pour his brief but pathetic plaint.

"Phebe's gone, and now if Charlie's taken I don't see how I *can* bear it!"

"Phebe will come back, dear, and let us hope poor Charlie isn't going to be taken yet. Such things always seem worse at first, I've heard people say; so cheer up and hope for the best," answered Rose, seeking for some comfortable words to say, and finding very few.

They took effect, however; for Archie did cheer up like a man. Wiping away the tears which he so seldom shed that they did not know where to go, he got up, gave himself a little shake, and said with a long breath, as if he had been under water,—

"Now I'm all right, thank you. I couldn't help it: the shock of being waked suddenly to find the dear old fellow in such a pitiful state upset me. I ought to go: are these ready?"

"In a minute. Tell uncle to send for me if I can be of any use. Oh, poor Aunt Clara! how does she bear it?"

"Almost distracted. I took mother to her, and she will do all that anybody can. Heaven only knows what aunt will do if—"

"And Heaven only can help her," added Rose, as Archie stopped at the words he could not utter. "Now take them, and let me know often."

"You brave little soul, I will," and Archie went away through the rain with his sad burden, wondering how Rose could be so calm, when the beloved Prince might be dying.

A long dark day followed, with nothing to break its melancholy monotony except the bulletins that came from hour to hour, reporting little change either for better or for worse. Rose broke the news gently to Aunt Plenty, and set herself to the task of keeping up the old lady's spirits; for, being helpless, the good soul felt as if every thing would go wrong without her. At dusk she fell asleep, and Rose went down to order lights and fire in the parlor, with tea ready to serve at any moment; for she felt sure some of the men would come, and that a cheerful greeting and creature comforts would suit them better than tears, darkness, and desolation.

Presently Mac arrived, saying the instant he entered the room,—

"More comfortable, cousin."

"Thank Heaven!" cried Rose, unclasping her hands. Then seeing how worn out, wet, and weary Mac looked as he came into the light, she added in a tone that was a cordial in itself, "Poor boy, how tired you are! Come here, and let me make you comfortable."

"I was going home to freshen up a bit; for I must be back in an hour. Mother took my place so I could be spared, and came off, as uncle refused to stir."

"Don't go home; for if aunty isn't there it will be very dismal. Step into uncle's room and refresh, then come back and I'll give you your tea. Let me, let me! I can't help in any other way; and I *must* do something, this waiting is so dreadful."

Her last words betrayed how much suspense was trying her;

and Mac yielded at once, glad to comfort and be comforted. When he came back, looking much revived, a tempting little tea-table stood before the fire; and Rose went to meet him, saying with a faint smile, as she liberally bedewed him with the contents of a cologne flask,—

"I can't bear the smell of ether: it suggests such dreadful things."

"What curious creatures women are! Archie told us you bore the news like a hero, and now you turn pale at a whiff of bad air. I can't explain it," mused Mac, as he meekly endured the fragrant shower-bath.

"Neither can I; but I've been imagining horrors all day, and made myself nervous. Don't let us talk about it; but come and have some tea."

"That's another queer thing. Tea is your panacea for all human ills; yet there isn't any nourishment in it. I'd rather have a glass of milk, thank you," said Mac, taking an easy-chair and stretching his feet to the fire.

She brought it to him and made him eat something; then, as he shut his eyes wearily, she went away to the piano, and having no heart to sing, played softly till he seemed asleep. But, at the stroke of six, he was up and ready to be off again.

"He gave me that: take it with you and put some on his hair; he likes it, and I do so want to help a little," she said, slipping the pretty flagon into his pocket, with such a wistful look, Mac never thought of smiling at this very feminine request.

"I'll tell him. Is there any thing else I can do for you, cousin?" he asked, holding the cold hand that had been serving him so helpfully.

"Only this: if there is any sudden change, promise to send for me, no matter at what hour it is: I *must* say 'Good-by.'"

"I will come for you. But, Rose, I am sure you may sleep in peace to-night; and I hope to have good news for you in the morning."

"Bless you for that! Come early, and let me see him soon. I will be very good, and I know it will not do him any harm."

"No fear of that: the first thing he said when he could speak was, 'Tell Rose carefully;' and, as I came away, he guessed where I was going, and tried to kiss his hand in the old way, you know."

Mac thought it would cheer her to hear that Charlie remembered her; but the sudden thought that she might never see that familiar little gesture any more was the last drop that made her full heart overflow, and Mac saw the "hero" of the morning sink down at his feet in a passion of tears that frightened him. He took her to the sofa, and tried to comfort her; but, as soon as the bitter sobbing quieted, she looked up and said quite steadily, great drops rolling down her cheeks the while,—

"Let me cry: it is what I need, and I shall be all the better for it by and by. Go to Charlie now, and tell him I said with all my heart, 'Good-night!'"

"I will!" and Mac trudged away, marvelling in his turn at the curiously blended strength and weakness of womankind.

That was the longest night Rose ever spent; but joy came in the morning with the early message, "He is better. You are to come by and by." Then Aunt Plenty forgot her lumbago and arose; Aunt Myra, who had come to have a social croak, took off her black bonnet as if it would not be needed at present, and the girl made ready to go and say "Welcome back," not the hard "Good-by."

It seemed very long to wait; for no summons came till afternoon, then her uncle arrived, and at the first sight of his face Rose began to tremble.

"I came for my little girl myself, because we must go back at once," he said, as she hurried toward him hat in hand.

"I'm ready, sir;" but her hands shook as she tried to tie the ribbons, and her eyes never left the face that was so full of tender pity for her.

He took her quickly into the carriage, and, as they rolled away, said with the quiet directness which soothes such agitation better than any sympathetic demonstration,—

"Charlie is worse. I feared it when the pain went so suddenly this morning; but the chief injuries are internal, and one can never tell what the chances are. He insists that he is better, but will soon begin to fail, I fear; become unconscious, and slip away without more suffering. This is the time for you to see him; for he has set his heart on it, and nothing can hurt him now. My child, it is very hard; but we must help each other bear it."

Rose tried to say, "Yes, uncle," bravely; but the words would not come; and she could only slip her hand into his with a look of mute submission. He laid her head on his shoulder, and went on talking so quietly that any one who did not see how worn and haggard his face had grown with two days and a night of sharp anxiety might have thought him cold.

"Jessie has gone home to rest, and Jane is with poor Clara, who has dropped asleep at last. I've sent for Steve and the other boys. There will be time for them later; but he so begged to see you now, I thought it best to come while this temporary strength keeps him up. I have told him how it is, but he will not believe me. If he asks you, answer honestly; and try to fit him a little for this sudden ending of so many hopes."

"How soon, uncle?"

"A few hours, probably. This tranquil moment is yours: make the most of it; and, when we can do no more for him, we'll comfort one another."

Mac met them in the hall: but Rose hardly saw him; she was conscious only of the task before her; and, when her uncle led her to the door, she said quietly,—

"Let me go in alone, please."

Archie, who had been hanging over the bed, slipped away into the inner room as she appeared; and Rose found Charlie waiting for her with such a happy face, she could not believe what she had heard, and found it easy to say almost cheerfully, as she took his eager hand in both of hers,—

"Dear Charlie, I'm so glad you sent for me. I longed to come, but waited till you were better. You surely are?" she added, as a second glance showed her the indescribable change which had come upon the face which at first seemed to have both light and color in it.

"Uncle says not: but I think he is mistaken, because the agony is all gone; and, except for this odd sinking now and then, I don't feel so much amiss," he answered feebly, but with something of the old lightness in his voice.

"You will hardly be able to sail in the 'Rajah,' I fear; but you won't mind waiting a little, while we nurse you," said poor Rose, trying to talk on quietly, with her heart growing heavier every minute.

"I shall go if I'm carried! I'll keep that promise, though it costs me my life. O Rose! you know? they've told you?" and, with a sudden memory of what brought him there, he hid his face in the pillow.

"You broke no promise; for I would not let you make one, you remember. Forget all that, and let us talk about the better time that may be coming for you."

"Always so generous, so kind!" he murmured, with her hand against his feverish cheek; then, looking up, he went on in a tone so humbly contrite it made her eyes fill with slow, hot tears.

"I tried to flee temptation: I tried to say 'No;' but I am so pitiably weak, I couldn't. You must despise me. But don't give me up entirely: for, if I live, I'll do better; I'll go away to father and begin again."

Rose tried to keep back the bitter drops; but they would fall, to hear him still speak hopefully when there was no hope. Something in the mute anguish of her face seemed to tell him what she could not speak; and a quick change came over him as he grasped her hand tighter, saying in a sharp whisper,—

"Have I really got to die, Rose?"

Her only answer was to kneel down and put her arms about him, as if she tried to keep death away a little longer. He believed it then, and lay so still, she looked up in a moment, fearing she knew not what.

But Charlie bore it manfully; for he had the courage which can face a great danger bravely, though not the strength to fight a bosom-sin and conquer it. His eyes were fixed, as if trying to look into the unseen world whither he was going, and his lips firmly set that no word of complaint should spoil the proof he meant to give that, though he had not known how to live, he did know how to die. It seemed to Rose as if for one brief instant she saw the man that might have been, if early training had taught him how to rule himself; and the first words he uttered with a long sigh, as his eye came back to her, showed that he felt the failure and owned it with pathetic candor.

"Better so, perhaps; better go before I bring any more sorrow to you, and shame to myself. I'd like to stay a little longer, and try to redeem the past; it seems so wasted now: but, if I can't, don't grieve, Rose; I'm no loss to any one, and perhaps it *is* too late to mend."

"Oh, don't say that! no one will fill your place among us: we never can forget how much we loved you; and you must believe how freely we forgive as we would be forgiven," cried Rose, steadied by the pale despair that had fallen on Charlie's face with those bitter words.

"'Forgive us our trespasses!' Yes, I should say that. Rose, I'm not ready; it is so sudden: what can I do?" he whispered, clinging to her, as if he had no anchor except the creature whom he loved so much.

"Uncle will tell you: I am not good enough; I can only pray for you," and she moved as if to call in the help so sorely needed.

"No, no, not yet! stay by me, darling: read something; there, in grandfather's old book, some prayer for such as I. It will do me more good from you than any minister alive."

She got the venerable book,—given to Charlie because he bore the good man's name,—and, turning to the "Prayer for the Dying," read it brokenly; while the voice beside her echoed now and then some word that reproved or comforted.

"The testimony of a good conscience." "By the sadness of his countenance may his heart be made better." "Christian patience and fortitude." "Leave the world in peace." "Amen."

There was silence for a little; then Rose, seeing how wan he looked, said softly, "Shall I call uncle now?"

"If you will; but first—don't smile at my foolishness, dear— I want my little heart. They took it off: please give it back, and let me keep it always," he answered, with the old fondness strong as ever, even when he could only show it by holding fast the childish trinket which she found and gave him,—the old agate heart with the faded ribbon. "Put it on, and never let them take it off," he said; and, when she asked if there was any thing else she could do for him, he tried to stretch out his arms to her with a look which asked for more.

She kissed him very tenderly on lips and forehead; tried to say "Good-by," but could not speak, and groped her way to the door. Turning for a last look, Charlie's hopeful spirit rose for a moment, as if anxious to send her away more cheerful, and he said with a shadow of the old blithe smile, a feeble attempt at the familiar farewell gesture,—

"Till to-morrow, Rose."

Alas, for Charlie! his to-morrow never came: and, when she saw him next, he lay there looking so serene and noble, it seemed as if it must be well with him: for all the pain was past; temptation ended; doubt and fear, hope and love, could no more stir his quiet heart, and in solemn truth he *had* gone to meet his Father, and begin again.

# Chapter XVI

## GOOD WORKS

The "Rajah" was delayed awhile, and when it sailed poor Mrs. Clara was on board; for every thing was ready, all thought she had better go to comfort her husband, and since her boy died she seemed to care very little what became of her. So, with friends to cheer the long voyage, she sailed away, a heavy-hearted woman, yet not quite disconsolate; for she knew her mourning was excessively becoming, and felt sure that Stephen would not find her altered by her trials as much as might have been expected.

Then nothing was left of that gay household but the empty rooms, silence never broken by a blithe voice any more, and pictures full of promise, but all unfinished, like poor Charlie's life.

There was much mourning for the bonny Prince, but no need to tell of it except as it affected Rose; for it is with her we have most to do, the other characters being of secondary importance.

When time had soothed the first shock of sudden loss, she was surprised to find that the memory of his faults and failings, short life and piteous death, grew dim as if a kindly hand had wiped out the record, and gave him back to her in the likeness of the brave, bright boy she had loved, not as the wayward, passionate young man who had loved her.

This comforted her very much; and, folding down the last blotted leaf where his name was written, she gladly turned back to reopen and reread the happier chapters which painted the youthful knight before he went out to fall in his first battle. None of the bitterness of love bereaved marred this memory for Rose, because she found that the warmer sentiment, just budding in her heart, had died with Charlie, and lay cold and quiet in his grave. She wondered, yet was glad; though sometimes a remorseful pang smote her when she discovered how possible it was to go on without him, feeling almost as if a burden had been lifted off, since his happiness was taken out of her hands. The time had not yet come when the knowledge that a man's heart was in her keeping would make the pride and joy of her life; and while she waited for that moment she enjoyed the liberty she seemed to have recovered.

Such being her inward state, it much annoyed her to be regarded as a broken-hearted girl, and pitied for the loss of her young lover. She could not explain to all the world, so let it pass, and occupied her mind with the good works which always lie ready to be taken up and carried on. Having chosen philanthropy as her profession, she felt that it was high time to begin the task too long neglected.

Her projects were excellent, but did not prosper as rapidly as she hoped; for, having to deal with people, not things, unexpected obstacles were constantly arising. The "Home for Decayed Gentlewomen," as the boys insisted on calling her two newly repaired houses, started finely; and it was a pleasant sight to see the comfortable rooms filled with respectable women busy at their various tasks, surrounded by the decencies and many of the comforts which make life endurable. But, presently, Rose was disturbed to find that the good people expected her to take care of them in a way she had not bargained for. Buffum, her agent, was constantly reporting complaints, new wants, and general discontent if they were not attended to. Things were neglected, water-pipes froze and burst, drains got out of order, yards were in a mess, and rents behindhand. Worst of all, outsiders, instead of sympathizing, only laughed and said, "We told you so," which is a most discouraging remark to older and wiser workers than Rose.

Uncle Alec, however, stood by her staunchly, and helped her out of many of her woes by good advice, and an occasional visit of inspection, which did much to impress upon the dwellers there the fact that, if they did not do their part, their leases would be short ones.

"I didn't expect to make any thing out of it, but I did think they would be grateful," said Rose, on one occasion when several complaints had come in at once, and Buffum had reported great difficulty in collecting the low rents.

"If you do this thing for the sake of the gratitude, then it *is* a failure: but if it is done for the love of helping those who need help it is a success; for in spite of their worry every one of those women feel what privileges they enjoy and value them highly," said Dr. Alec, as they went home after one of these unsatisfactory calls.

"Then the least they can do is to say 'Thank you.' I'm afraid I *have* thought more of the gratitude than the work; but if there isn't any I must make up my mind to go without," answered Rose, feeling defrauded of her due.

"Favors often separate instead of attracting people nearer to one another, and I've seen many a friendship spoilt by the obligation being all on one side. Can't explain it, but it is so; and I've come to the conclusion that it is as hard to give in the right spirit as it is to receive. Puzzle it out, my dear, while you are learning to do good for its own sake."

"I know one sort of people who *are* grateful, and I'm going to devote my mind to them. They thank me in many ways, and helping them is all pleasure and no worry. Come in to the hospital and see the dear babies, or the Asylum and carry oranges to Phebe's orphans: *they* don't complain and fidget one's life out, bless their hearts!" cried Rose, clearing up suddenly.

After that she left Buffum to manage the "Retreat," and devoted her energies to the little folks, always so ready to receive the smallest gift, and repay the giver with their artless thanks. Here she found plenty to do, and did it with such sweet goodwill that she won her way like sunshine, making many a little heart dance over splendid dolls, gay picture-books, and pots of flowers, as well as food, fire, and clothes for the small bodies pinched with want and pain.

As spring came, new plans sprung up as naturally as dandelions. The poor children longed for the country; and, as the green fields could not come to them, Rose carried them to the green fields. Down on the Point stood an old farmhouse, often used by the Campbell tribe for summer holidays. That spring it was set to rights unusually early, several women installed as housekeeper, cook, and nurses; and, when the May days grew bright and warm, squads of pale children came to toddle in the grass, run over the rocks, and play upon the smooth sands of the beach. A pretty sight, and one that well repaid those who brought it to pass.

Every one took an interest in the "Rose Garden," as Mac named it; and the women-folk were continually driving over to the Point with something for the "poor dears." Aunt Plenty sowed gingerbread broadcast; Aunt Jessie made pinafores by the dozen; while Aunt Jane "kept her eye" on the nurses, and Aunt Myra supplied medicines so liberally that the mortality would have been awful, if Dr. Alec had not taken them in charge. To him this was the most delightful spot in the world: and well it might be; for he suggested the idea, and gave Rose all the credit of it. He was often there, and his appearance was always greeted with shrieks of rapture, as the children gathered from all quarters: creeping, running, hopping on crutches, or carried in arms which they gladly left to sit on "Uncle Doctor's" knee; for that was the title by which he went among them.

He seemed as young as any of his comrades, though the curly head was getting gray; and the frolics that went on when he arrived were better than any medicine to children who had never learned to play. It was a standing joke among the friends that the bachelor brother had the largest family, and was the most domestic man of the remaining four; though Uncle Mac did his part manfully, and kept Aunt Jane in a constant fidget, by his rash propositions to adopt the heartiest boys and prettiest girls to amuse him and employ her.

On one occasion she had a very narrow escape; and the culprit being her son, not her husband, she felt free to repay herself for many scares of this sort by a good scolding; which, unlike many, produced excellent results.

One bright June day, as Rose came cantering home from the Point on her pretty bay pony, she saw a man sitting on a fallen tree beside the road, and something in his despondent attitude arrested her attention. As she drew nearer, he turned his head, and she stopped short, exclaiming in great surprise,—

"Why, Mac! what *are* you doing here?"

"Trying to solve a problem," he answered, looking up with a whimsical expression of perplexity and amusement in his face, which made Rose smile, till his next words turned her sober in a twinkling,—

"I've eloped with a young lady, and don't know what to do with her. I took her home, of course; but mother turned her out of the house, and I'm in a quandary."

"Is that her baggage?" asked Rose, pointing with her whip

to the large bundle which he held; while the wild idea flashed through her head that perhaps he really *had* done some rash deed of this sort.

"No, this is the young lady herself;" and, opening a corner of the brown shawl, he displayed a child of three,—so pale, so thin, and tiny, that she looked like a small scared bird just fallen from the nest, as she shrunk away from the light with great frightened eyes, and a hand like a little claw tightly clutching a button of Mac's coat.

"Poor baby! where did it come from?" cried Rose, leaning down to look.

"I'll tell you the story, and then you shall advise me what to do. At our hospital, we've had a poor woman who got hurt, and died two days ago. I had nothing to do with her, only took her a bit of fruit once or twice; for she had big, wistful sort of eyes that haunted me. The day she died I stopped a minute, and the nurse said she'd been wanting to speak to me, but didn't dare. So I asked if I could do any thing for her; and, though she could hardly breathe for pain,—being almost gone, —she implored me to take care of baby. I found out where the child was, and promised I'd see after her; for the poor soul couldn't seem to die till I'd given her that comfort. I never can forget the look in her eyes, as I held her hand, and said, 'Baby shall be taken care of.' She tried to thank me, and died soon after quite peacefully. Well, I went to-day and hunted up the poor little wretch. Found her in a miserable place, left in the care of an old hag, who had shut her up alone to keep her out of the way, and there this mite was, huddled in a corner crying, 'Marmar, marmar!' fit to touch a heart of stone. I blew up the woman, and took baby straight away, for she had been abused; and it was high time. Look there, will you?"

Mac turned the little skinny arm, and showed a blue mark which made Rose drop her reins, and stretch out both hands, crying with a tender sort of indignation,—

"How dared they do it? Give her to me; poor, little, mother-less thing!"

Mac laid the bundle in her arms, and Rose began to cuddle it in the fond, foolish way women have,—a most comfortable and effective way, nevertheless; and baby evidently felt that things were changing for the better, when warm lips touched her cheeks, a soft hand smoothed her tumbled hair, and a womanly face bent over her, with the inarticulate cooings and purrings mothers make. The frightened eyes went up to this gentle countenance, and rested there as if reassured; the little claw crept to the girl's neck, and poor baby nestled to her with a long sigh, and a plaintive murmur of "Marmar, marmar," that certainly would have touched a stony heart.

"Now, go on. No, Rosa, not you," said the new nurse, as the intelligent animal looked round to see if things were all right before she proceeded.

"I took the child home to mother, not knowing what else to do; but she wouldn't have it at any price, even for a night. She doesn't like children, you know, and father has joked so much about the Pointers that she is quite rampant at the mere idea of a child in the house. She told me to take it to the Rose Garden. I said it was running over now, and no room even for a mite like this. 'Go to the Hospital,' says she. 'Baby isn't ill, ma'am,' says I. 'Orphan Asylum,' says she. 'Not an orphan: got a father who can't take care of her,' says I. 'Take her to the Foundling place, or Mrs. Gardener, or some one whose business it is. I will *not* have the creature here, sick and dirty and noisy. Carry it back, and ask Rose to tell you what to do with it.' So my cruel parent cast me forth; but relented as I shouldered baby, gave me a shawl to put her in, a jumble to feed her with, and money to pay her board in some good place. Mother's bark is always worse than her bite, you know."

"And you were trying to think of the 'good place' as you sat here?" asked Rose, looking down at him with great approval, as he stood patting Rosa's glossy neck.

"Exactly. I didn't want to trouble you, for you have your house full already; and I really couldn't lay my hand on any good soul who would be bothered with this little forlornity. She has nothing to recommend her, you see,—not pretty, feeble, and shy as a mouse; no end of care, I dare say: yet she needs every bit she can get to keep soul and body together, if I'm any judge."

Rose opened her lips impulsively, but closed them without speaking, and sat a minute looking straight between Rosa's ears, as if forcing herself to think twice before she spoke. Mac watched her out of the corner of his eye, as he said, in a musing tone, tucking the shawl round a pair of shabby little feet the while,—

"This seems to be one of the charities that no one wants to undertake; yet I can't help feeling that my promise to the mother binds me to something more than merely handing baby over to some busy matron or careless nurse in any of our over-crowded institutions. She is such a frail creature she won't trouble any one long, perhaps; and I *should* like to give her just a taste of comfort, if not love, before she finds her 'Marmar' again."

"Lead Rosa: I'm going to take this child home; and, if uncle is willing, I'll adopt her, and she *shall* be happy!" cried Rose, with the sudden glow of feeling that always made her lovely. And, gathering poor baby close, she went on her way like a modern Britomart, ready to redress the wrongs of any who had need of her.

As he led the slowly stepping horse along the quiet road, Mac could not help thinking that they looked a little like the Flight into Egypt: but he did not say so, being a reverent youth,—only glanced back now and then at the figure above him; for Rose had taken off her hat to keep the light from baby's eyes, and sat with the sunshine turning her uncovered hair to gold, as she looked down at the little creature resting on the saddle before her, with the sweet thoughtfulness one sees in some of Correggio's young Madonnas.

No one else saw the picture, but Mac long remembered it; and ever after there was a touch of reverence added to the warm affection he had always borne his cousin Rose.

"What is the child's name?" was the sudden question which disturbed a brief silence, broken only by the sound of pacing hoofs, the rustle of green boughs overhead, and the blithe carolling of birds.

"I'm sure I don't know," answered Mac, suddenly aware that he had fallen out of one quandary into another.

"Didn't you ask?"

"No: the mother called her 'Baby;' the old woman, 'Brat.' And that is all I know of the first name: the last is Kennedy. You can Christen her what you like."

"Then I shall name her Dulcinea, as you are her knight, and

call her Dulce for short. That is a sweet diminutive, I'm sure," laughed Rose, much amused at the idea.

Don Quixote looked pleased, and vowed to defend his little lady stoutly, beginning his services on the spot by filling the small hands with buttercups, thereby winning for himself the first smile baby's face had known for weeks.

When they got home, Aunt Plenty received her new guest with her accustomed hospitality, and, on learning the story, was as warmly interested as even enthusiastic Rose could desire, bustling about to make the child comfortable with an energy pleasant to see; for the grandmotherly instincts were strong in the old lady, and of late had been beautifully developed.

In less than half an hour from the time baby went upstairs, she came down again on Rose's arm, freshly washed and brushed, in a pink gown much too large, and a white apron decidedly too small; an immaculate pair of socks, but no shoes; a neat bandage on the bruised arm, and a string of spools for a plaything hanging on the other. A resigned expression sat upon her little face; but the frightened eyes were only shy now, and the forlorn heart evidently much comforted.

"There! how do you like your Dulce now?" said Rose, proudly displaying the work of her hands, as she came in with her habit pinned up, and carrying a silver porringer of bread and milk.

Mac knelt down, took the small, reluctant hand, and kissed it as devoutly as ever good Alonzo Quixada did that of the Duchess; while he said, merrily quoting from the immortal story,—

"'High and Sovereign Lady, thine till death, the Knight of the Rueful Countenance.'"

But baby had no heart for play, and, withdrawing her hand, pointed to the porringer, with the suggestive remark,—

"Din-din, *now*."

So Rose sat down and fed the Duchess, while the Don stood by and watched the feast with much satisfaction.

"How nice she looks! Do you consider shoes unhealthy?" he asked, surveying the socks with respectful interest.

"No: her shoes are drying. You must have let her go in the mud."

"I only put her down for a minute when she howled; and she made for a puddle, like a duck. I'll buy her some new ones,—clothes too. Where do I go, what do I ask for, and how much do I get?" he said, diving for his pocket-book, amiably anxious, but pitiably ignorant.

"I'll see to that. We always have things on hand for the Pointers as they come along, and can soon fit Dulce out. You may make some inquiries about the father if you will; for I don't want to have her taken away just as I get fond of her. Do you know any thing about him?"

"Only that he is in State Prison for twenty-one years, and not likely to trouble you."

"How dreadful! I really think Phebe was better off to have none at all. I'll go to work at once, then, and try to bring up the convict's little daughter to be a good woman; so that she will have an honest name of her own, since he has nothing but disgrace to give her."

"Uncle can show you how to do that, if you need any help. He has been so successful in his first attempt I fancy you won't require much," said Mac, picking up the spools for the sixth time.

"Yes, I shall; for it is a great responsibility, and I do not undertake it lightly," answered Rose, soberly; though the double-barrelled compliment pleased her very much.

"I'm sure Phebe has turned out splendidly, and you began very early with her."

"So I did! that's encouraging. Dear thing, how bewildered she looked when I proposed adopting her. I remember all about it; for uncle had just come, and I was quite crazy over a box of presents, and rushed at Phebe as she was cleaning brasses. How little I thought my childish offer would end so well!" and Rose fell a musing with a happy smile on her face, while baby picked the last morsels out of the porringer with her own busy fingers.

It certainly had ended well; for Phebe at the end of six months not only had a good place as choir-singer, but several young pupils, and excellent prospects for the next winter.

"'Accept the blessing of a poor young man,
    Whose lucky steps have led him to your door,'

and let me help as much as I can. Good-by, my Dulcinea," and, with a farewell stroke of the smooth head, Mac went away to report his success to his mother, who, in spite of her seeming harshness, was already planning how she could best befriend this inconvenient baby.

# Chapter XVII

## AMONG THE HAY-COCKS

Uncle Alec did not object; and, finding that no one had any claim upon the child, permitted Rose to keep it for a time at least. So little Dulce, newly equipped even to a name, took her place among them and slowly began to thrive. But she did not grow pretty, and never was a gay, attractive child; for she seemed to have been born in sorrow and brought up in misery. A pale, pensive little creature, always creeping into corners and looking timidly out, as if asking leave to live, and, when offered playthings, taking them with a meek surprise that was very touching.

Rose soon won her heart, and then almost wished she had not; for baby clung to her with inconvenient fondness, changing her former wail of "Marmar" into a lament for "Aunty Wose" if separated long. Nevertheless, there was great satisfaction in cherishing the little waif; for she learned more than she could teach, and felt a sense of responsibility which was excellent ballast for her enthusiastic nature.

Kitty Van, who made Rose her model in all things, was immediately inspired to go and do likewise, to the great amusement as well as annoyance of her family. Selecting the prettiest, liveliest child in the Asylum, she took it home on trial for a week. "A perfect cherub" she pronounced it the first day, but an "*enfant terrible*" before the week was over; for the young hero rioted by day, howled by night, ravaged the house from top to bottom, and kept his guardians in a series of panics by his hair-breadth escapes. So early on Saturday, poor, exhausted Kitty restored the "cherub" with many thanks, and decided to wait till her views of education were rather more advanced.

As the warm weather came on, Rose announced that Dulce needed mountain air; for she dutifully repeated as many of Dr. Alec's prescriptions as possible, and, remembering how much good Cosy Corner did her long ago, resolved to try it on her baby. Aunt Jessie and Jamie went with her, and Mother Atkinson received them as cordially as ever. The pretty daughters were all married and gone, but a stout damsel took their place; and nothing seemed changed except that the old heads were grayer and the young ones a good deal taller than six years ago.

Jamie immediately fraternized with neighboring boys, and devoted himself to fishing with an ardor which deserved greater success. Aunt Jessie revelled in reading, for which she had no time at home; and lay in her hammock a happy woman, with no socks to darn, buttons to sew, or housekeeping cares to vex her soul.

Rose went about with Dulce like a very devoted hen with one rather feeble chicken; for she was anxious to have this treatment work well, and tended her little patient with daily increasing satisfaction. Dr. Alec came up to pass a few days, and pronounced the child in a most promising condition. But the grand event of the season was the unexpected arrival of Phebe.

Two of her pupils had invited her to join them in a trip to the mountains, and she ran away from the great hotel to surprise her little mistress with a sight of her, so well and happy that Rose had no anxiety left on her account.

Three delightful days they spent, roaming about together, talking as only girls can talk after a long separation, and enjoying one another like a pair of lovers. As if to make it quite perfect, by one of those remarkable coincidences which sometimes occur, Archie happened to run up for the Sunday; so Phebe had *her* surprise, and Aunt Jessie and the telegraph kept their secret so well, no one ever knew what maternal machinations brought the happy accident to pass.

Then Rose saw a very pretty, pastoral bit of love-making, and long after it was over, and Phebe gone one way, Archie another, the echo of sweet words seemed to linger in the air, tender ghosts to haunt the pine-grove, and even the big coffee-pot had a halo of romance about it; for its burnished sides reflected the soft glances the lovers interchanged, as one filled the other's cup at that last breakfast.

Rose found these reminiscences more interesting than any novel she had read, and often beguiled her long leisure by planning a splendid future for her Phebe, as she trotted about after her baby in the lovely July weather.

On one of the most perfect days, she sat under an old apple-tree on the slope behind the house where they used to play. Before her opened the wide intervale, dotted with hay-makers at their picturesque work. On the left, flowed the swift river fringed with graceful elms in their bravest greenery; on the right, rose the purple hills serene and grand; and overhead glowed the midsummer sky which glorified it all.

Little Dulce tired of play, lay fast asleep in the nest she had made in one of the hay-cocks close by; and Rose leaned against the gnarled old tree, dreaming day-dreams with her work at her feet. Happy and absorbing fancies they seemed to be; for her face was beautifully tranquil, and she took no heed of the train which suddenly went speeding down the valley, leaving a white cloud behind. Its rumble concealed the sound of approaching steps, and her eyes never turned from the distant hills, till the abrupt appearance of a very sunburnt but smiling young man made her jump up, exclaiming joyfully,—

"Why Mac! where did you drop from?"

"The top of Mount Washington. How do you do?"

"Never better. Won't you go in? You must be tired after such a fall."

"No, thank you; I've seen the old lady. She told me Aunt Jessie and the boy had gone to town, and that you were 'settin' round' in the old place; so I came on at once, and will take a lounge here, if you don't mind," answered Mac, unstrapping his knapsack, and taking a hay-cock as if it were a chair.

Rose subsided into her former seat, surveying her cousin with much satisfaction, as she said,—

"This is the third surprise I've had since I came. Uncle popped in upon us first, then Phebe, and now you. Have you had a pleasant tramp? Uncle said you were off."

"Delightful! I feel as if I'd been in heaven, or near it, for about three weeks; and thought I'd break the shock of coming down to the earth by calling here on my way home."

"You look as if heaven suited you. Brown as a berry; but so fresh and happy, I should never guess you had been scrambling down a mountain," said Rose, trying to discover why he looked so well in spite of the blue-flannel suit and dusty shoes; for there was a certain sylvan freshness about him, as he sat there full of the reposeful strength the hills seemed to have given, the wholesome cheerfulness days of air and sunshine put into a man, and the clear, bright look of one who had caught glimpses of a new world from the mountain-top.

"Tramping agrees with me. I took a dip in the river as I came along, and made my toilet in a place where Milton's Sabrina might have lived," he said, shaking back his damp hair, and settling the knot of scarlet bunch-berries stuck in his button-hole.

"You look as if you found the nymph at home," said Rose, knowing how much he liked the Comus.

"I found her *here*," and he made a little bow.

"That's very pretty; and I'll give you one in return. You grow more like Uncle Alec every day, and I think I'll call you Alec, Jr."

"Alexander the Great wouldn't thank you for that," and Mac did not look as grateful as she had expected.

"Very like, indeed, except the forehead. His is broad and benevolent; yours high and arched. Do you know if you had no beard, and wore your hair long, I really think you'd look like Milton," added Rose, sure that would please him.

It certainly did amuse him; for he lay back on the hay and laughed so heartily that his merriment scared the squirrel on the wall and woke Dulce.

"You ungrateful boy! will nothing suit you? When I say you look like the best man I know, you give a shrug; and, when I liken you to a great poet, you shout: I'm afraid you are very conceited, Mac;" and Rose laughed too, glad to see him so gay.

"If I am, it is your fault. Nothing I can do will ever make a Milton of me, unless I go blind some day," he said, sobering at the thought.

"You once said a man could be what he liked if he tried hard enough; so why shouldn't you be a poet?" asked Rose, liking to trip him up with his own words, as he often did her.

"I thought I was to be an M.D."

"You might be both. There have been poetical doctors, you know."

"Would you like me to be such an one?" asked Mac, looking at her as seriously as if he really thought of trying it.

"No: I'd rather have you one or the other. I don't care

which, only you must be famous in either you choose. I'm very ambitious for you; because, I insist upon it, you are a genius of some sort. I think it is beginning to simmer already, and I've a great curiosity to know what it will turn out to be."

Mac's eyes shone as she said that, but before he could speak a little voice said, "Aunty Wose!" and he turned to find Dulce sitting up in her nest, staring at the broad blue back before her with round eyes.

"Do you know your Don?" he asked, offering his hand with respectful gentleness; for she seemed a little doubtful whether he was friend or stranger.

"It is 'Mat,'" said Rose, and that familiar word seemed to reassure the child at once; for, leaning forward, she kissed him as if quite used to doing it.

"I picked up some toys for her by the way, and she shall have them at once to pay for that. I didn't expect to be so graciously received by this shy mouse," said Mac, much gratified; for Dulce was very chary of her favors.

"She knew you; for I always carry my home-album with me, and when she comes to your picture she always kisses it, because I never want her to forget her first friend," explained Rose, pleased with her pupil.

"First, but not best," answered Mac, rummaging in his knapsack for the promised toys, which he set forth upon the hay before delighted Dulce.

Neither picture-books nor sweeties; but berries strung on long stems of grass, acorns and pretty cones, bits of rock shining with mica, several bluebirds' feathers, and a nest of moss with white pebbles for eggs.

"Dearest Nature, strong and kind," knows what children love, and has plenty of such playthings ready for them all, if one only knows how to find them. These were received with rapture; and, leaving the little creature to enjoy them in her own quiet way, Mac began to tumble the things back into his knapsack again. Two or three books lay near Rose, and she took up one which opened at a place marked by a scribbled paper.

"Keats? I didn't know you condescended to read any thing so modern," she said, moving the paper to see the page beneath.

Mac looked up, snatched the book out of her hand, and shook down several more scraps; then returned it with a curiously shame-faced expression, saying, as he crammed the papers into his pocket,—

"I beg pardon, but it was full of rubbish. Oh, yes! I'm fond of Keats; don't you know him?"

"I used to read him a good deal; but uncle found me crying over the 'Pot of Basil,' and advised me to read less poetry for a while or I should get too sentimental," answered Rose, turning the pages without seeing them; for a new idea had just popped into her head.

"'The Eve of St. Agnes' is the most perfect love-story in the world, I think," said Mac, enthusiastically.

"Read it to me. I feel just like hearing poetry, and you will do it justice if you are fond of it," said Rose, handing him the book with an innocent air.

"Nothing I'd like better; but it is rather long."

"I'll tell you to stop if I get tired. Baby won't interrupt; she will be contented for an hour with those pretty things."

As if well pleased with his task, Mac laid himself comfortably on the grass, and leaning his head on his hand read the lovely story as only one could who entered fully into the spirit of it. Rose watched him closely, and saw how his face brightened over some quaint fancy, delicate description, or delicious word; heard how smoothly the melodious measures fell from his lips, and read something more than admiration in his eyes, as he looked up now and then to mark if she enjoyed it as much as he.

She could not help enjoying it; for the poet's pen painted as well as wrote, and the little romance lived before her: but she was not thinking of John Keats as she listened; she was wondering if this cousin was a kindred spirit, born to make such music and leave as sweet an echo behind him. It seemed as if it might be; and, after going through the rough caterpillar and the pent-up chrysalis changes, the beautiful butterfly would appear to astonish and delight them all. So full of this fancy was she that she never thanked him when the story ended; but, leaning forward, asked in a tone that made him start and look as if he had fallen from the clouds,—

"Mac, do you ever write poetry?"

"Never."

"What do you call the song Phebe sang with her bird chorus?"

"That was nothing till she put the music to it. But she promised not to tell."

"She didn't; I suspected, and now I know," laughed Rose, delighted to have caught him.

Much discomfited, Mac gave poor Keats a fling, and leaning on both elbows tried to hide his face; for it had reddened like that of a modest girl when teased about her lover.

"You needn't look so guilty; it is no sin to write poetry," said Rose, amused at his confusion.

"It's a sin to call that rubbish poetry," muttered Mac, with great scorn.

"It is a greater sin to tell a fib, and say you never write it."

"Reading so much sets one thinking about such things, and every fellow scribbles a little jingle when he is lazy or in love, you know," explained Mac, looking very guilty.

Rose could not quite understand the change she saw in him, till his last words suggested a cause which she knew by experience was apt to inspire young men. Leaning forward again, she asked solemnly, though her eyes danced with fun,—

"Mac, are you in love?"

"Do I look like it?" and he sat up with such an injured and indignant face, that she apologized at once; for he certainly did not look lover-like with hay-seed in his hair, several lively crickets playing leap-frog over his back, and a pair of long legs stretching from tree to hay-cock.

"No, you don't; and I humbly beg your pardon for making such an unwarrantable insinuation. It merely occurred to me that the general upliftedness I observe in you might be owing to that, since it wasn't poetry."

"It is the good company I've been keeping, if any thing. A fellow can't spend 'A Week' with Thoreau, and not be the better for it. I'm glad I show it; because in the scramble life is to most of us, even an hour with such a sane, simple, and sagacious soul as his must help one," said Mac, taking a much worn book out of his pocket with the air of introducing a dear and honored friend.

"I've read bits, and liked them: they are so original and fresh and sometimes droll," said Rose, smiling to see what natural and appropriate marks of approbation the elements seemed to set upon the pages Mac was turning eagerly; for one had evidently been rained on, a crushed berry stained another, some appreciative field-mouse or squirrel had nibbled one corner, and the cover was faded with the sunshine, which seemed to have filtered through to the thoughts within.

"Here's a characteristic bit for you:—

"'I would rather sit on a pumpkin, and have it all to myself, than be crowded on a velvet cushion. I would rather ride on earth in an ox-cart, with free circulation, than go to heaven in the fancy car of an excursion train, and breathe malaria all the way.'

"I've tried both and quite agree with him," laughed Mac; and, skimming down another page, gave her a paragraph here and there.

"'Read the best books first, or you may not have a chance to read them at all.'

"'We do not learn much from learned books, but from sincere human books: frank, honest biographies.'

"'At least let us have healthy books. Let the poet be as vigorous as a sugar-maple, with sap enough to maintain his own verdure, besides what runs into the trough; and not like a vine which, being cut in the spring, bears no fruit, but bleeds to death in the endeavor to heal its wounds.'"

"That will do for you," said Rose, still thinking of the new suspicion which pleased her by its very improbability.

Mac flashed a quick look at her and shut the book, saying quietly, though his eyes shone, and a conscious smile lurked about his mouth,—

"We shall see, and no one need meddle; for, as my Thoreau says,—

> "'Whate'er we leave to God, God does
>      And blesses us:
>   The work we choose should be our own
>      God lets alone.'"

Rose sat silent, as if conscious that she deserved his poetical reproof.

"Come, you have catechised me pretty well; now I'll take my turn and ask why *you* look 'uplifted,' as you call it. What have you been doing to make yourself more like your name-sake than ever?" asked Mac, carrying war into the enemy's camp with the sudden question.

"Nothing but live, and enjoy doing it. I actually sit here, day after day, as happy and contented with little things as Dulce is, and feel as if I wasn't much older than she," answered the girl, feeling as if some change was going on in that pleasant sort of pause, but unable to describe it.

"'As if a rose should shut and be a bud again,'"

murmured Mac, borrowing from his beloved Keats.

"Ah, but I can't do that! I must go on blooming whether I like it or not, and the only trouble I have is to know what leaf I ought to unfold next," said Rose, playfully smoothing out the white gown, in which she looked very like a daisy among the green.

"How far have you got?" asked Mac, continuing his cate-chism as if the fancy suited him.

"Let me see. Since I came home last year, I've been gay, then sad, then busy, and now I am simply happy. I don't know why; but seem to be waiting for what is to come next, and getting ready for it, perhaps unconsciously," she said, looking dreamily away to the hills again, as if the new experience was coming to her from afar.

Mac watched her thoughtfully for a minute, wondering how many more leaves must unfold, before the golden heart of this human flower would lie open to the sun. He felt a curious de-sire to help in some way, and could think of none better than to offer her what he had found most helpful to himself. Picking up another book, he opened it at a place where an oak-leaf lay, and, handing it to her, said, as if presenting something very excellent and precious,—

"If you want to be ready to take whatever comes in a brave and noble way, read that, and the one where the page is turned down."

Rose took it, saw the words "Self-Reliance," and, turning the leaves, read here and there a passage which was marked:—

"'My life is for itself, and not for a spectacle.'

"'Insist on yourself: never imitate. That which each can do best, none but his Maker can teach him.'

"'Do that which is assigned to you, and you cannot hope or dare too much.'

Then coming to the folded leaf, whose title was "Heroism," she read, and brightened as she read,—

"'Let the maiden, with erect soul, walk serenely on her way; accept the hint of each new experience; search in turn all the objects that solicit her eye, that she may learn the power and the charm of her new-born being.'

"'The fair girl who repels interference by a decided and proud choice of influences inspires every beholder with something of her own nobleness; and the silent heart encourages her. O friend, never strike sail to a fear! Come into port greatly, or sail with God the seas.'

"You understand that, don't you?" asked Mac, as she glanced up with the look of one who had found something suited to her taste and need.

"Yes, but I never dared to read these *Essays*, because I thought they were too wise for me."

"The wisest things are sometimes the simplest, I think. Every one welcomes light and air, and cannot do without them; yet very few could explain them truly. I don't ask you to read or understand all of that,—don't myself,—but I do recommend the two essays I've marked, as well as 'Love' and 'Friendship.' Try them, and let me know how they suit. I'll leave you the book."

"Thanks. I wanted something fine to read up here; and, judging by what I see, I fancy this *will* suit. Only Aunt Jessie may think I'm putting on airs, if I try Emerson."

"Why should she? He has done more to set young men and women thinking, than any man in this century at least. Don't you be afraid: if it is what you want, take it, and go ahead as he tells you,—

> "'Without halting, without rest,
> Lifting Better up to Best.'"

"I'll try," said Rose, meekly; feeling that Mac had been going ahead himself much faster than she had any suspicion.

Here a voice exclaimed "Hallo!" and, looking round, Jamie was discovered surveying them critically, as he stood in an independent attitude, like a small Colossus of Rhodes in brown linen, with a bundle of molasses-candy in one hand, several new fish-hooks cherished carefully in the other, and his hat well on the back of his head, displaying as many freckles as one somewhat limited nose could reasonably accommodate.

"How are you, young one?" said Mac, nodding.

"Tip-top. Glad it's you: thought Archie might have turned up again, and he's no fun. Where did you come from? What did you come for? How long are you going to stay? Want a bit? It's jolly good."

With which varied remarks Jamie approached, shook hands in a manly way, and, sitting down beside his long cousin, hospitably offered sticks of candy all round.

"Did you get any letters?" asked Rose, declining the sticky treat.

"Lots: but mamma forgot to give 'em to me, and I was rather in a hurry; for Mrs. Atkinson said somebody had come, and I couldn't wait," explained Jamie, reposing luxuriously with his head on Mac's legs, and his mouth full.

"I'll step and get them. Aunty must be tired, and we should enjoy reading the news together."

"She is the most convenient girl that ever was," observed Jamie, as Rose departed, thinking Mac might like some more substantial refreshment than sweetmeats.

"I should think so, if you let her run your errands, you lazy little scamp," answered Mac, looking after her as she went up the green slope; for there was something very attractive to him about the slender figure in a plain white gown, with a black sash about the waist, and all the wavy hair gathered to the top of the head with a little black bow.

"Sort of pre-Raphaelite, and quite refreshing after the furbelowed creatures at the hotels," he said to himself, as she vanished under the arch of scarlet-runners over the garden-gate.

"Oh, well! she likes it. Rose is fond of me, and I'm very good to her when I have time," continued Jamie, calmly explaining. "I let her cut out a fish-hook, when it caught in my leg, with a sharp pen-knife; and you'd better believe it hurt: but I never squirmed a bit, and she said I was a brave boy. And then, one day I got left on my desert island,—out in the pond, you know,—the boat floated off, and there I was for as much as an hour before I could make any one hear. But Rose thought

I might be there; and down she came, and told me to swim ashore. It wasn't far; but the water was horrid cold, and I didn't like it. I started though, just as she said, and got on all right, till about half way, then cramp or something made me shut up and howl, and she came after me slapdash, and pulled me ashore. Yes, sir, as wet as a turtle, and looked so funny, I laughed; and that cured the cramp. Wasn't I good to mind when she said, 'Come on?'"

"She was, to dive after such a scapegrace. I guess you lead her a life of it, and I'd better take you home with me in the morning," suggested Mac, rolling the boy over, and giving him a good-natured pummelling on the hay-cock, while Dulce applauded from her nest.

When Rose returned with ice-cold milk, gingerbread, and letters, she found the reader of Emerson up in the tree, pelting and being pelted with green apples, as Jamie vainly endeavored to get at him. The siege ended when Aunt Jessie appeared; and the rest of the afternoon was spent in chat about home affairs.

Early the next morning Mac was off, and Rose went as far as the old church with him.

"Shall you walk all the way?" she asked, as he strode along beside her, in the dewy freshness of the young day.

"Only about twenty miles, then take car and whisk back to my work," he answered, breaking a delicate fern for her.

"Are you never lonely?"

"Never: I take my best friends along, you know," and he gave a slap to the pocket from which peeped the volume of Thoreau.

"I'm afraid you leave your very best behind you," said Rose, alluding to the book he had lent her yesterday.

"I'm glad to share it with you. I have much of it here; and a little goes a great way, as you will soon discover," he answered, tapping his head.

"I hope the reading will do as much for me as it seems to have done for you. I'm happy; but you are wise and good: I want to be, also."

"Read away, and digest it well; then write, and tell me what you think of it. Will you?" he asked, as they paused where the four roads met.

"If you will answer. Shall you have time with all your other work? Poetry—I beg pardon—medicine is very absorbing, you know," answered Rose, mischievously; for just then, as he stood bareheaded with the shadows of the leaves playing over his fine forehead, she remembered the chat among the hay-cocks, and he did not look at all like an M.D.

"I'll make time."

"Good-by, Milton."

"Good-by, Sabrina."

# *Chapter XVIII*

---

ROSE did read and digest, and found her days much richer for the good company she kept; for an introduction to so much that was wise, beautiful, and true, could not but make that month a memorable one. It is not strange that while the young man most admired "Heroism" and "Self-Reliance," the girl preferred "Love" and "Friendship," reading them over and over like prose poems, as they are, to the fitting accompaniment of sunshine, solitude, and sympathy; for letters went to and fro, with praiseworthy regularity.

Rose much enjoyed this correspondence, and found herself regretting that it was at an end when she went home in September; for Mac wrote better than he talked, though he could do that remarkably well when he chose. But she had no chance to express either pleasure or regret; for, the first time she saw him after her return, the great change in his appearance made her forget every thing else. Some whim had seized him to be shaven and shorn, and when he presented himself to welcome Rose she hardly knew him; for the shaggy hair was nicely trimmed and brushed, the cherished brown beard entirely gone, showing a well cut mouth and handsome chin, and giving a new expression to the whole face.

"Are you trying to look like Keats?" she asked after a critical glance, which left her undecided whether the change was an improvement or not.

"I am trying not to look like uncle," answered Mac, coolly.

"And why, if you please?" demanded Rose, in great surprise.

"Because I prefer to look like myself, and not resemble any other man, no matter how good or great he may be."

"You haven't succeeded then; for you look now very much like the Young Augustus," returned Rose, rather pleased, on the whole, to see what a finely shaped head appeared after the rough thatch was off.

"Trust a woman to find a comparison for every thing under the sun!" laughed Mac, not at all flattered by the one just made.

"What do you think of me, on the whole?" he asked a minute later, as he found Rose still scrutinizing him with a meditative air.

"Haven't made up my mind. It is such an entire change I don't know you, and feel as if I ought to be introduced. You certainly look much more tidy; and I fancy I *shall* like it, when I'm used to seeing a somewhat distinguished-looking man about the house instead of my old friend Orson," answered Rose, with her head on one side to get a profile view.

"Don't tell uncle why I did it, please: he thinks it was for the sake of coolness, and likes it, so take no notice; they are all used to me now, and don't mind," said Mac, roving about the room as if rather ashamed of his whim after all.

"No, I won't; but you mustn't mind if I'm not as sociable as usual for a while. I never can be with strangers, and you really do seem like one. That will be a punishment for your want of taste and love of originality," returned Rose, resolved to punish him for the slight put upon her beloved uncle.

"As you like. I won't trouble you much anyway; for I'm going to be very busy. May go to L. this winter, if uncle thinks best; and then my 'originality' can't annoy you."

"I hope you won't go. Why, Mac, I'm just getting to know and enjoy you, and thought we'd have a nice time this winter reading something together. Must you go?" and Rose seemed to forget his strangeness, as she held him still by one button while she talked.

"That *would* be nice. But I feel as if I must go: my plans are all made, and I've set my heart on it," answered Mac, looking so eager that Rose released him, saying sadly,—

"I suppose it is natural for you all to get restless, and push off; but it is hard for me to let you go one after the other, and stay here alone. Charlie is gone, Archie and Steve are wrapt up in their sweethearts, the boys away, and only Jamie left to 'play with Rose.'"

"But I'll come back, and you'll be glad I went if I bring you my—" began Mac, with sudden animation; then stopped abruptly to bite his lips, as if he had nearly said too much.

"Your what?" asked Rose, curiously; for he neither looked nor acted like himself.

"I forgot how long it takes to get a diploma," he said, walking away again.

"There will be one comfort if you go: you'll see Phebe, and can tell me all about her; for she is so modest she doesn't half do it. I shall want to know how she gets on, if she is engaged to sing ballads in the concerts they talk of for next winter. You will write, won't you?"

"Oh, yes! no doubt of that," and Mac laughed low to himself, as he stooped to look at the little Psyche on the mantelpiece. "What a pretty thing it is!" he added soberly, as he took it up.

"Be careful. Uncle gave it to me last New-Year, and I'm very fond of it. She is just lifting her lamp to see what Cupid is like; for she hasn't seen him yet," said Rose, busy putting her work-table in order.

"You ought to have a Cupid for her to look at. She has been waiting patiently a whole year, with nothing but a bronze lizard in sight," said Mac, with the half-shy, half-daring look which was so new and puzzling.

"Cupid fled away as soon as she woke him, you know, and she had a bad time of it. She must wait longer till she can find and keep him."

"Do you know she looks like you? Hair tied up in a knot, and a spiritual sort of face. Don't you see it?" asked Mac, turning the graceful little figure toward her.

"Not a bit of it. I wonder whom I shall resemble next! I've been compared to a Fra Angelico angel, Saint Agnes, and now 'Syke,' as Annabel once called her."

"You'd see what I mean, if you'd ever watched your own face when you were listening to music, talking earnestly, or much moved; then your soul gets into your eyes and you are—like Psyche."

"Tell me the next time you see me in a 'soulful' state, and I'll look in the glass; for I'd like to see if it is becoming," said Rose, merrily, as she sorted her gay worsteds.

> "'Your feet in the full-grown grasses,
>     Moved soft as a soft wind blows;
> You passed me as April passes,
>     With a face made out of a rose,'"

murmured Mac, under his breath, thinking of the white figure going up a green slope one summer day; then, as if chiding himself for sentimentality, he set Psyche down with great care, and began to talk about a course of solid reading for the winter.

After that, Rose saw very little of him for several weeks, as he seemed to be making up for lost time, and was more odd and absent than ever when he did appear. As she became accustomed to the change in his external appearance, she discovered that he was altering fast in other ways, and watched the "distinguished-looking gentleman" with much interest; saying to herself, when she saw a new sort of dignity about him alternating with an unusual restlessness of manner, and now and then a touch of sentiment, "Genius is simmering, just as I predicted."

As the family were in mourning, there were no festivities on Rose's twenty-first birthday, though the boys had planned all sorts of rejoicings. Every one felt particularly tender toward their girl on that day, remembering how "poor Charlie" had loved her; and they tried to show it in the gifts and good wishes they sent her. She found her sanctum all aglow with autumn leaves, and on her table so many rare and pretty things she quite forgot she was an heiress, and only felt how rich she was in loving friends.

One gift greatly pleased her, though she could not help smiling at the source from whence it came; for Mac sent her a Cupid,—not the chubby child with a face of naughty merriment, but a slender, winged youth, leaning on his unstrung bow, with a broken arrow at his feet. A poem, "To Psyche," came with it: and Rose was much surprised at the beauty of the lines; for, instead of being witty, complimentary, or gay, there was something nobler than mere sentiment in them, and the sweet old fable lived again in language which fitly painted the maiden Soul looking for a Love worthy to possess it.

Rose read them over and over, as she sat among the gold and scarlet leaves which glorified her little room, and each time found new depth and beauty in them; looking from the words that made music in her ear to the lovely shapes that spoke with their mute grace to her eye. The whole thing suited her exactly, it was so delicate and perfect in its way; for she was tired of costly gifts, and valued very much this proof of her cousin's taste and talent, seeing nothing in it but an affectionate desire to please her.

All the rest dropped in at intervals through the day to say a loving word, and last of all came Mac. Rose happened to be alone with Dulce, enjoying a splendid sunset from her western window; for October gave her child a beautiful good-night.

Rose turned round as he entered, and, putting down the little girl, went to him with the evening red shining on her happy face, as she said gratefully,—

"Dear Mac, it was *so* lovely! I don't know how to thank you for it in any way but this." And, drawing down his tall head, she gave him the birthday kiss she had given all the others.

But this time it produced a singular effect: for Mac turned scarlet, then grew pale; and when Rose added playfully, thinking to relieve the shyness of so young a poet, "Never again say you don't write poetry, or call your verses rubbish: I *knew* you were a genius, and now I'm sure of it," he broke out, as if against his will,—

"No. It isn't genius: it is—love!" Then, as she shrunk a little, startled at his energy, he added, with an effort at self-control which made his voice sound strange,—

"I didn't mean to speak, but I can't suffer you to deceive yourself so. I *must* tell the truth, and not let you kiss me like a cousin when I love you with all my heart and soul!"

"Oh Mac, don't joke!" cried Rose, bewildered by this sudden glimpse into a heart she thought she knew so well.

"I'm in solemn earnest," he answered, steadily, in such a quiet tone that, but for the pale excitement of his face, she might have doubted his words. "Be angry, if you will. I expect it, for I know it is too soon to speak. I ought to wait for years, perhaps; but you seemed so happy I dared to hope you had forgotten."

"Forgotten what?" asked Rose, sharply.

"Charlie."

"Ah! you all will insist on believing that I loved him better than I did!" she cried, with both pain and impatience in her voice; for the family delusion tried her very much at times.

"How could we help it, when he was every thing women most admire?" said Mac, not bitterly, but as if he sometimes wondered at their want of insight.

"*I* do not admire weakness of any sort: I could never love

without either confidence or respect. Do me the justice to believe that, for I'm tired of being pitied."

She spoke almost passionately, being more excited by Mac's repressed emotion than she had ever been by Charlie's most touching demonstration, though she did not know why.

"But he loved you so!" began Mac; feeling as if a barrier had suddenly gone down, but not daring to venture in as yet.

"That was the hard part of it! That was why I tried to love him,—why I hoped he would stand fast for my sake, if not for his own; and why I found it so sad sometimes not to be able to help despising him for his want of courage. I don't know how others feel, but, to me, love isn't all. I must look up, not down, trust and honor with my whole heart, and find strength and integrity to lean on. I have had it so far, and I know I could not live without it."

"Your ideal is a high one. Do you hope to find it, Rose?" Mac asked, feeling, with the humility of a genuine love, that *he* could not give her all she desired.

"Yes," she answered, with a face full of the beautiful confidence in virtue, the instinctive desire for the best which so many of us lose too soon, to find again after life's great lessons are well learned. "I do hope to find it, because I try not to be unreasonable and expect perfection. Smile if you will, but I won't give up my hero yet," and she tried to speak lightly, hoping to lead him away from a more dangerous topic.

"You'll have to look a long while, I'm afraid," and all the glow was gone out of Mac's face; for he understood her wish, and knew his answer had been given.

"I have uncle to help me; and I think my ideal grew out of my knowledge of him. How can I fail to believe in goodness, when he shows me what it can be and do?"

"It is no use for me to say any more; for I have very little to offer. I did not mean to say a word, till I'd earned a right to hope for something in return. I cannot take it back; but I can wish you success, and I do, because you deserve the very best," and Mac moved, as if he was going away without more words, accepting the inevitable as manfully as he could.

"Thank you: that makes me feel very ungrateful and unkind. I wish I could answer as you want me to; for, indeed, dear Mac, I'm very fond of you in my own way," and Rose looked up with such tender pity and frank affection in her face, it was no wonder the poor fellow caught at a ray of hope, and, brightening suddenly, said in his own odd way,—

"Couldn't you take me on trial, while you are waiting for the true hero? It may be years before you find him; meantime, you could be practising on me in ways that would be useful when you get him."

"O Mac! what *shall* I do with you?" exclaimed Rose, so curiously affected by this very characteristic wooing, that she did not know whether to laugh or cry; for he was looking at her with his heart in his eyes, though his proposition was the queerest ever made at such a time.

"Just go on being fond of me in your own way, and let me love you as much as I like in mine. I'll try to be satisfied with that," and he took both her hands so beseechingly that she felt more ungrateful than ever.

"No, it would not be fair: for you would love the most; and, if the hero did appear, what would become of you?"

"I should resemble Uncle Alec in one thing at least,—fidelity; for my first love would be my last."

That went straight to Rose's heart; and for a minute she stood silent, looking down at the two strong hands that held hers so firmly, yet so gently; and the thought went through her mind, "Must he too be solitary all his life? I have no dear lover as my mother had, why cannot I make him happy and forget myself?"

It did not seem very hard; and she owned that, even while she told herself to remember that compassion was no equivalent for love. She wanted to give all she could, and keep as much of Mac's affection as she honestly might; because it seemed to grow more sweet and precious when she thought of putting it away.

"You will be like uncle in happier ways than that, I hope; for you, too, must have a high ideal, and find her and be happy," she said, resolving to be true to the voice of conscience, not be swayed by the impulse of the moment.

"I *have* found her, but I don't see any prospect of happiness, do you?" he asked, wistfully.

"Dear Mac, I cannot give you the love you want, but I do trust and respect you from the bottom of my heart, if that is any comfort," began Rose, looking up with eyes full of contrition, for the pain her reply must give.

She got no further, however; for those last words wrought a marvellous change in Mac. Dropping her hands, he stood erect, as if inspired with sudden energy and hope, while over his face there came a brave, bright look, which for the moment made him a nobler and a comelier man than ever handsome Prince had been.

"It *is* a comfort!" he said, in a tone of gratitude, that touched her very much. "You said your love must be founded on respect, and that you have given me: why can I not earn the rest? I'm nothing now; but every thing is possible when one loves with all his heart and soul and strength. Rose, *I* will be your hero if a mortal man can, even though I have to work and wait for years. I'll *make* you love me, and be glad to do it. Don't be frightened. I've not lost my wits: I've just found them. I don't ask any thing: I'll never speak of my hope, but it is no use to stop me; I *must* try it, and I *will* succeed!"

With the last words, uttered in a ringing voice, while his face glowed, his eyes shone, and he looked as if carried out of himself by the passion that possessed him, Mac abruptly left the room, like one eager to change words to deeds and begin his task at once.

Rose was so amazed by all this, that she sat down trembling a little, not with fear or anger, but a feeling half pleasure, half pain; and a sense of some new power—subtle, strong, and sweet—that had come into her life. It seemed as if another Mac had taken the place of the one she had known so long,— an ardent, ambitious man, ready for any work, now that the magical moment had come, when every thing seems possible to love. If hope could work such a marvellous change for a moment, could not happiness do it for a lifetime? It would be an exciting experiment to try, she thought, remembering the sudden illumination which made that familiar face both beautiful and strange.

She could not help wondering how long this unsuspected sentiment had been growing in his heart, and felt perplexed by its peculiar demonstration; for she had never had a lover like this before. It touched and flattered her, nevertheless: and she could not but feel honored by a love so genuine and generous;

for it seemed to make a man of Mac all at once, and a manly man too, who was not daunted by disappointment, but could "hope against hope," and resolve to *make* her love him if it took years to do it.

There was the charm of novelty about this sort of wooing, and she tried to guess how he would set about it, felt curious to see how he would behave when next they met, and was half angry with herself for not being able to decide how she ought to act. The more she thought the more bewildered she grew; for, having made up her mind that Mac was a genius, it disturbed all her plans to find him a lover, and such an ardent one. As it was impossible to predict what would come next, she gave up trying to prepare for it; and, tired with vain speculations, carried Dulce off to bed, wishing she could tuck away her love-troubles as quietly and comfortably as she did her sleepy little charge.

Simple and sincere in all things, Mac gave Rose a new surprise by keeping his promise to the letter,—asked nothing of her, said nothing of his hope, and went on as if nothing had happened, quite in the old friendly way. No, not quite; for now and then, when she least expected it, she saw again that indescribable expression in his face, a look that seemed to shed a sudden sunshine over her, making her eyes fall involuntarily, her color rise, and her heart beat quicker for a moment. Not a word did he say, but she felt that a new atmosphere surrounded her when he was by; and, although he used none of the little devices most lovers employ to keep the flame alight, it was impossible to forget that underneath his quietude there was a hidden world of fire and force, ready to appear at a touch, a word from her.

This was rather dangerous knowledge for Rose, and she soon began to feel that there were more subtle temptations than she had expected; for it was impossible to be unconscious of her power, or always to resist the trials of it which daily came unsought. She had never felt this desire before: for Charlie was the only one who had touched her heart; and he was constantly asking as well as giving, and wearied her by demanding too much, or oppressed by offering more than she could accept.

Mac did neither: he only loved her, silently, patiently,

hopefully; and this generous sort of fidelity was very eloquent to a nature like hers. She could not refuse or chide, since nothing was asked or urged: there was no need of coldness, for he never presumed; no call for pity, since he never complained. All that could be done was to try and be as just and true as he was, and to wait as trustfully for the end, whatever it was to be.

For a time she liked the new interest it put into her life, yet did nothing to encourage it; and thought that if she gave this love no food it would soon starve to death. But it seemed to thrive on air; and presently she began to feel as if a very strong will was slowly but steadily influencing her in many ways. If Mac had never told her that he meant to "*make* her love him," she might have yielded unconsciously; but now she mistook the impulse to obey this undercurrent for compassion, and resisted stoutly, not comprehending yet the reason for the unrest which took possession of her about this time.

She had as many moods as an April day; and would have much surprised Dr. Alec by her vagaries, had he known them all. He saw enough, however, to guess what was the matter, but took no notice; for he knew this fever must run its course, and much medicine only does harm. The others were busy about their own affairs, and Aunt Plenty was too much absorbed in her rheumatism to think of love; for the cold weather set in early, and the poor lady kept her room for days at a time, with Rose as nurse.

Mac had spoken of going away in November, and Rose began to hope he would; for she decided that this silent sort of adoration was bad for her, as it prevented her from steadily pursuing the employments she had marked out for that year. What was the use of trying to read useful books, when her thoughts continually wandered to those charming essays on "Love and Friendship?" to copy antique casts, when all the masculine heads looked like Cupid, and the feminine ones like the Psyche on her mantel-piece? to practise the best music, if it ended in singing over and over the pretty spring-song without Phebe's bird-chorus? Dulce's company was pleasantest now; for Dulce seldom talked, so much meditation was possible. Even Aunt Plenty's red flannel, camphor, and Pond's Extract were preferable to general society; and long solitary rides on Rosa seemed the only thing to put her in tune after one of her attempts to find out what she ought to do or leave undone.

She made up her mind at last; and arming herself with an unmade pen, like Fanny Squeers, she boldly went into the study to confer with Dr. Alec, at an hour when Mac was usually absent.

"I want a pen for marking: can you make me one, uncle?" she asked, popping in her head to be sure he was alone.

"Yes, my dear," answered a voice so like the doctor's that she entered without delay.

But before she had taken three steps she stopped, looking rather annoyed; for the head that rose from behind the tall desk was not rough and gray, but brown and smooth, and Mac, not Uncle Alec, sat there writing. Late experience had taught her that she had nothing to fear from a *tête-à-tête*; and, having with difficulty taken a resolution, she did not like to fail of carrying it out.

"Don't get up: I won't trouble you if you are busy; there is no hurry," she said, not quite sure whether it were wiser to stay or run away.

Mac settled the point, by taking the pen out of her hand and beginning to cut it, as quietly as Nicholas did on that "thrilling" occasion. Perhaps he was thinking of that; for he smiled as he asked,—

"Hard or soft?"

Rose evidently had forgotten that the family of Squeers ever existed, for she answered,—

"Hard, please," in a voice to match. "I'm glad to see you doing that," she added, taking courage from his composure, and going as straight to her point as could be expected of a woman.

"And I am very glad to do it."

"I don't mean making pens, but the romance I advised," and she touched the closely written page before him, looking as if she would like to read it.

"That is my abstract of a lecture on the circulation of the blood," he answered, kindly turning it so that she could see. "I don't write romances: I'm living one," and he glanced up with the happy, hopeful expression which always made her feel as if he was heaping coals of fire on her head.

"I wish you wouldn't look at me in that way: it fidgets me," she said a little petulantly; for she had been out riding, and knew that she did not present a "spiritual" appearance, after the frosty air had reddened nose as well as cheeks.

"I'll try to remember. It does itself before I know it. Perhaps this may mend matters," and, taking out the blue glasses he sometimes wore in the wind, he gravely put them on.

Rose could not help laughing: but his obedience only aggravated her; for she knew he could observe her all the better behind his ugly screen.

"No, it won't: they are not becoming; and I don't want to look blue when I do not feel so," she said, finding it impossible to guess what he would do next, or to help enjoying his peculiarities.

"But you don't to me; for in spite of the goggles every thing is rose-colored now," and he pocketed the glasses, without a murmur at the charming inconsistency of his idol.

"Really, Mac, I'm tired of this nonsense: it worries me and wastes your time."

"Never worked harder. But does it *really* trouble you to know I love you?" he asked anxiously.

"Don't you see how cross it makes me?" and she walked away, feeling that things were not going as she intended to have them at all.

"I don't mind the thorns if I get the rose at last; and I still hope I may, some ten years hence," said this persistent suitor, quite undaunted by the prospect of a "long wait."

"I think it is rather hard to be loved whether I like it or not," objected Rose, at a loss how to make any headway against such indomitable hopefulness.

"But you can't help it, nor can I: so I must go on doing it with all my heart till you marry; and then—well, then I'm afraid I may hate somebody instead," and Mac spoilt the pen by an involuntary slash of his knife.

"Please don't, Mac!"

"Don't which, love or hate?"

"Don't do either: go and care for some one else; there are plenty of nice girls who will be glad to make you happy," said Rose, intent upon ending her disquiet in some way.

"That is too easy. I enjoy working for my blessings; and the harder I have to work the more I value them when they come."

"Then if I suddenly grew very kind would you stop caring about me?" asked Rose, wondering if that treatment would free her from a passion which both touched and tormented her.

"Try and see;" but there was a traitorous glimmer in Mac's eyes which plainly showed what a failure it would be.

"No, I'll get something to do, so absorbing I shall forget all about you."

"Don't think about me if it troubles you," he said tenderly.

"I can't help it." Rose tried to catch back the words: but it was too late; and she added hastily, "That is, I cannot help wishing you would forget *me*. It is a great disappointment to find I was mistaken when I hoped such fine things of you."

"Yes, you were very sure that it was love when it was poetry; and now you want poetry when I've nothing on hand but love. Will both together please you?"

"Try and see."

"I'll do my best. Any thing else?" he asked, forgetting the small task she had given him, in his eagerness to attempt the greater.

"Tell me one thing. I've often wanted to know; and now you speak of it I'll venture to ask. Did you care about me when you read Keats to me last summer?"

"No."

"When *did* you begin?" asked Rose, smiling in spite of herself at his unflattering honesty.

"How can I tell? Perhaps it did begin up there, though; for that talk set us writing, and the letters showed me what a beautiful soul you had. I loved that first: it was so quick to recognize good things, to use them when they came, and give them out again as unconsciously as a flower does its breath. I longed for you to come home, and wanted you to find me altered for the better in some way as I had found you. And when you came it was very easy to see why I needed you,—to love you entirely, and to tell you so. That's all, Rose."

A short story, but it was enough: the voice that told it with such simple truth made the few words so eloquent Rose felt strongly tempted to add the sequel Mac desired. But her eyes had fallen as he spoke; for she knew his were fixed upon her, dark and dilated, with the same repressed emotion that put such fervor into his quiet tones, and, just as she was about to look up, they fell on a shabby little footstool. Trifles affect women curiously, and often most irresistibly when some agitation sways them: the sight of the old hassock vividly recalled Charlie; for he had kicked it on the night she never liked to remember; like a spark it fired a long train of recollections, and the thought went through her mind,—

"I fancied I loved him, and let him see it; but I deceived myself, and he reproached me for a single look that said too much. This feeling is very different, but too new and sudden to be trusted. I'll neither look nor speak till I am quite sure; for Mac's love is far deeper than poor Charlie's, and I must be very true."

Not in words did the resolve shape itself, but in a quick impulse, which she obeyed,—certain that it was right, since it was hard to yield to it. Only an instant's silence followed Mac's answer, as she stood looking down with fingers intertwined, and color varying in her cheeks. A foolish attitude; but Mac thought it a sweet picture of maiden hesitation, and began to hope that a month's wooing was about to end in winning for a lifetime. He deceived himself, however; and cold water fell upon his flame, subduing but by no means quenching it, when Rose looked up with an air of determination, which could not escape eyes that were growing wonderfully far-sighted lately.

"I came in here to beg uncle to advise you to go away soon. You are very patient and forbearing, and I feel it more than I can tell. But it is not good for you to depend on any one so much for your happiness, I think; and I know it is bad for me to feel that I have so much power over a fellow-creature. Go away, Mac, and see if this isn't all a mistake. Don't let a fancy for me change or delay your work, because it may end as suddenly as it began, and then we should both reproach ourselves and each other. Please do! I respect and care for you so much, I can't be happy to take all and give nothing. I try to, but I'm not sure—I want to think—it is too soon to know yet—"

Rose began bravely, but ended in a fluttered sort of way, as she moved toward the door; for Mac's face, though it fell at first, brightened as she went on, and at the last word, uttered almost involuntarily, he actually laughed low to himself, as if this order into exile pleased him much.

"Don't say that you give nothing, when you've just shown

me that I'm getting on. I'll go; I'll go at once; and see if absence won't help you 'to think, to know, and to be sure,' as it did me. I wish I could do something more for you; as I can't, good-by."

"Are you going *now*?" and Rose paused in her retreat, to look back with a startled face, as he offered her a badly made pen, and opened the door for her just as Dr. Alec always did; for, in spite of himself, Mac did resemble the best of uncles.

"Not yet; but you seem to be."

Rose turned as red as a poppy, snatched the pen, and flew upstairs, to call herself hard names, as she industriously spoiled all Aunt Plenty's new pocket-handkerchiefs by marking them "A. M. C."

Three days later Mac said "Good-by" in earnest; and no one was surprised that he left somewhat abruptly, such being his way, and a course of lectures by a famous physician the ostensible reason for a trip to L. Uncle Alec deserted most shamefully at the last moment by sending word that he would be at the station to see the traveller off: Aunt Plenty was still in her room; so, when Mac came down from his farewell to her, Rose met him in the hall, as if anxious not to delay him. She was a little afraid of another *tête-à-tête*, as she fared so badly at the last, and had assumed a calm and cousinly air, which she flattered herself would plainly show on what terms she wished to part.

Mac apparently understood, and not only took the hint, but surpassed her in cheerful composure; for, merely saying, "Good-by, cousin; write when you feel like it," he shook hands, and walked out of the house as tranquilly as if only a day instead of three months were to pass before they met again. Rose felt as if a sudden shower-bath had chilled her, and was about to retire, saying to herself with disdainful decision,—

"There's no love about it after all; only one of the eccentricities of genius," when a rush of cold air made her turn, to find herself in what appeared to be the embrace of an impetuous overcoat, which wrapt her close for an instant, then vanished as suddenly as it came, leaving her to hide in the sanctum, and confide to Psyche with a tender sort of triumph in her breathless voice,—

"No, no, it isn't genius: *that* must be love!"

# Chapter XIX

## BEHIND THE FOUNTAIN

---

Two days after Christmas, a young man of a serious aspect might have been seen entering one of the large churches at L——. Being shown to a seat, he joined in the services with praiseworthy devotion, especially the music, to which he listened with such evident pleasure that a gentleman who sat near by felt moved to address this appreciative stranger after church.

"Fine sermon to-day. Ever heard our minister before, sir?" he began, as they went down the aisle together among the last; for the young man had lingered as if admiring the ancient building.

"Very fine. No, sir, I have never had that pleasure. I've often wished to see this old place, and am not at all disappointed. Your choir, too, is unusually good," answered the stranger, glancing up at several bonnets bobbing about behind the half-drawn curtains above.

"Finest in the city, sir. We pride ourselves on our music, and always have the best. People often come for that alone," and the old gentleman looked as satisfied as if a choir of cherubim and seraphim "continually did cry" in his organ-loft.

"Who is the contralto? That solo was beautifully sung," observed the younger man, pausing to read a tablet on the wall.

"That is Miss Moore. Been here about a year, and is universally admired. Excellent young lady: couldn't do without her. Sings superbly in oratorios. Ever heard her?"

"Never. She came from X——, I believe?"

"Yes; highly recommended. She was brought up by one of the first families there. Campbell is the name. If you come from X——, you doubtless know them."

"I have met them. Good morning." And with bows the gentlemen parted; for at that instant the young man caught sight of a tall lady going down the church-steps, with a devout expression in her fine eyes, and a prayer-book in her hand.

Hastening after her, the serious-minded young man accosted her just as she turned into a quiet street.

"Phebe!"

Only a word, but it wrought a marvellous change; for the devout expression vanished in the drawing of a breath, and the quiet face blossomed suddenly with color, warmth, and "the light that never was on sea or land," as she turned to meet her lover, with an answering word as eloquent as his,—

"Archie!"

"The year is out to-day. I told you I should come. Have you forgotten?"

"No: I knew you'd come."

"And you are glad?"

"How can I help it?"

"You can't: don't try. Come into this little park, and let us talk." And, drawing her hand through his arm, Archie led her into what to other eyes was a very dismal square, with a boarded-up fountain in the middle, sodden grass-plots, and dead leaves dancing in the wintry wind.

But to them it was a summery Paradise; and they walked to and fro in the pale sunshine, quite unconscious that they were objects of interest to several ladies and gentlemen waiting anxiously for their dinner, or yawning over the dull books kept for Sunday reading.

"Are you ready to come home now, Phebe?" asked Archie, tenderly, as he looked at the downcast face beside him, and wondered why all women did not wear delightful little black velvet bonnets, with one deep-red flower against their hair.

"Not yet. I haven't done enough," began Phebe, finding it very hard to keep the resolution made a year ago.

"You have proved that you can support yourself, make friends, and earn a name, if you choose. No one can deny that; and we are all getting proud of you. What more can you ask, my dearest?"

"I don't quite know, but I am very ambitious. I want to be famous, to do something for you all, to make some sacrifice for Rose, and, if I can, to have something to give up for your sake. Let me wait and work longer: I know I haven't earned my welcome yet," pleaded Phebe, so earnestly that her lover knew it would be vain to try and turn her; so wisely contented himself with half, since he could not have the whole.

"Such a proud woman! Yet I love you all the better for it, and understand your feeling. Rose made me see how it seems to you; and I don't wonder that you cannot forget the unkind things that were looked, if not said, by some of my amiable aunts. I'll try to be patient on one condition, Phebe."

"And what is that?"

"You are to let me come sometimes while I wait, and wear this lest you should forget me," he said, pulling a ring from his pocket, and gently drawing a warm, bare hand out of the muff where it lay hidden.

"Yes, Archie, but not here,—not now!" cried Phebe, glancing about her, as if suddenly aware that they were not alone.

"No one can see us here: I thought of that. Give me one happy minute, after this long, long year of waiting," answered Archie, pausing just where the fountain hid them from all eyes, for there were houses only on one side.

Phebe submitted; and never did a plain gold ring slip more easily to its place than the one he put on in such a hurry that cold December day. Then one hand went back into the muff red with the grasp he gave it, and the other to its old place on his arm, with a confiding gesture, as if it had a right there.

"Now I feel sure of you," said Archie, as they went on again, and no one the wiser for that tender transaction behind the ugly pyramid of boards. "Mac wrote me that you were much admired by your church people, and that certain wealthy bachelors evidently had designs on the retiring Miss Moore. I was horribly jealous, but now I defy every man of them."

Phebe smiled with the air of proud humility that was so becoming, and answered briefly,—

"There was no danger: kings could not change me, whether you ever came or not. But Mac should not have told you."

"You shall be revenged on him, then; for, as he told secrets about you, I'll tell you one about him. Phebe, he loves Rose!" And Archie looked as if he expected to make a great sensation with his news.

"I know it." And Phebe laughed at his sudden change of countenance, as he added inquiringly,—

"She told you, then?"

"Not a word. I guessed it from her letters: for lately she says nothing about Mac, and before there was a good deal; so I suspected what the silence meant, and asked no questions."

"Wise girl! then you think she does care for the dear old fellow?"

"Of course she does. Didn't he tell you so?"

"No, he only said when he went away, 'Take care of my Rose, and I'll take care of your Phebe,' and not another thing could I get out of him; for *I* did ask questions. He stood by me like a hero, and kept Aunt Jane from driving me stark mad with her 'advice.' I don't forget that, and burned to lend him a hand somewhere; but he begged me to let him manage his wooing in his own way. And from what I see, I should say he knew how to do it," added Archie, finding it very delightful to gossip about love affairs with his sweetheart.

"Dear little mistress! how does she behave?" asked Phebe, longing for news, but too grateful to ask at headquarters; remembering how generously Rose had tried to help her, even by silence, the greatest sacrifice a woman can make at such interesting periods.

"Very sweet and shy and charming. I try not to watch: but upon my word I cannot help it sometimes; she is so 'cunning,' as you girls say. When I carry her a letter from Mac she tries so hard to show how glad she is, that I want to laugh, and tell her I know all about it. But I look as sober as a judge, and as stupid as an owl by daylight; and she enjoys her letter in peace, and thinks I'm so absorbed by my own passion that I'm blind to hers."

"But why did Mac come away? He says lectures brought him, and he goes; but I am sure something else is in his mind, he looks so happy at times. I don't see him very often, but when I do I'm conscious that he isn't the Mac I left a year ago," said Phebe, leading Archie away: for inexorable propriety forbade a longer stay, even if prudence and duty had not given her a reminding nudge; as it was very cold, and afternoon church came in an hour.

"Well, you see Mac was always peculiar, and he cannot even grow up like other fellows. I don't understand him yet, and am sure he's got some plan in his head that no one suspects, unless it is Uncle Alec. Love makes us all cut queer capers; and I've an idea that the Don will distinguish himself in some uncommon way. So be prepared to applaud whatever it is. We owe him that, you know."

"Indeed we do! If Rose ever speaks of him to you, tell her I shall see that he comes to no harm, and she must do the same for my Archie."

That unusual demonstration of tenderness from reserved Phebe very naturally turned the conversation into a more personal channel; and Archie devoted himself to building castles in the air so successfully that they passed the material mansion without either being aware of it.

"Will you come in?" asked Phebe, when the mistake was rectified, and she stood on her own steps looking down at her escort, who had discreetly released her before a pull at the bell caused five heads to pop up at five different windows.

"No, thanks. I shall be at church this afternoon, and the Oratorio this evening. I must be off early in the morning, so let me make the most of precious time, and come home with you to-night as I did before," answered Archie, making his best bow, and quite sure of consent.

"You may," and Phebe vanished, closing the door softly, as if she found it hard to shut out so much love and happiness as that in the heart of the sedate young gentleman, who went briskly down the street, humming a verse of old "Clyde" like a tuneful bass viol.

> "'Oh, let our mingling voices rise
> In grateful rapture to the skies,
> Where love has had its birth.
>
> Let songs of joy this day declare
> That spirits come their bliss to share
> With all the sons of earth.'"

That afternoon Miss Moore sang remarkably well, and that evening quite electrified even her best friends by the skill and power with which she rendered "Inflammatus" in the oratorio.

"If that is not genius, I should like to know what it is?" said one young man to another, as they went out just before the general crush at the end.

"Some genius and a great deal of love. They are a grand

team, and, when well driven, astonish the world by the time they make in the great race," answered the second young man, with the look of one inclined to try his hand at driving that immortal span.

"Dare say you are right. Can't stop now: she's waiting for me. Don't sit up, Mac."

"The gods go with you, Archie."

And the cousins separated: one to write till midnight, the other to bid his Phebe good-by, little dreaming how unexpectedly and successfully she was to earn her welcome home.

# Chapter XX

## WHAT MAC DID

ROSE, meantime, was trying to find out what the sentiment was with which she regarded her cousin Mac. She could not seem to reconcile the character she had known so long with the new one lately shown her; and the idea of loving the droll, bookish, absent-minded Mac of former times appeared quite impossible and absurd: but the new Mac, wide awake, full of talent, ardent and high-minded, was such a surprise to her she felt as if her heart was being won by a stranger, and it became her to study him well before yielding to a charm which she could not deny.

Affection came naturally, and had always been strong for the boy; regard for the studious youth easily deepened to respect for the integrity of the young man: and now something warmer was growing up within her; but at first she could not decide whether it was admiration for the rapid unfolding of talent of some sort, or love answering to love.

As if to settle that point, Mac sent her on New-Year's day a little book plainly bound and modestly entitled "Songs and Sonnets." After reading this with ever-growing surprise and delight, Rose never had another doubt about the writer's being a poet; for, though she was no critic, she had read the best authors and knew what was good. Unpretending as it was, this had the true ring, and its very simplicity showed conscious power; for, unlike so many first attempts, the book was not full of "My Lady," neither did it indulge in Swinburnian convulsions about

"The lilies and languors of peace,
The roses and raptures of love;"

or contain any of the highly colored mediæval word-pictures so much in vogue. "My book should smell of pines, and resound with the hum of insects," might have been its motto: so sweet and wholesome was it with a spring-like sort of freshness, which plainly betrayed that the author had learned some of

Nature's deepest secrets, and possessed the skill to tell them in tuneful words. The songs went ringing through one's memory long after they were read; and the sonnets were full of the subtle beauty, insight, and half-unconscious wisdom, which seem to prove that "genius is divine when young."

Many faults it had, but was so full of promise that it was evident Mac had not "kept good company, read good books, loved good things, and cultivated soul and body as faithfully as he could," in vain. It all told now; for truth and virtue had blossomed into character, and had a language of their own more eloquent than the poetry to which they were what the fragrance is to the flower. Wiser critics than Rose felt and admired this; less partial ones could not deny their praise to a first effort, which seemed as spontaneous and aspiring as a lark's song; and, when one or two of these Jupiters had given a nod of approval, Mac found himself, not exactly famous, but much talked about. One set abused, the other set praised, and the little book was sadly mauled among them: for it was too original to be ignored, and too robust to be killed by hard usage; so it came out of the fray none the worse, but rather brighter, if any thing, for the friction which proved the gold genuine.

This took time, however, and Rose could only sit at home reading all the notices she could get, as well as the literary gossip Phebe sent her: for Mac seldom wrote, and never a word about himself; so Phebe skilfully extracted from him in their occasional meetings all the personal news her feminine wit could collect, and faithfully reported it.

It was a little singular that without a word of inquiry on either side, the letters of the girls were principally filled with tidings of their respective lovers. Phebe wrote about Mac; Rose answered with minute particulars about Archie; and both added hasty items concerning their own affairs, as if these were of little consequence.

Phebe got the most satisfaction out of the correspondence; for, soon after the book appeared, Rose began to want Mac home again, and to be rather jealous of the new duties and delights that kept him. She was immensely proud of her poet, and had little jubilees over the beautiful fulfilment of her prophecies; for even Aunt Plenty owned now with contrition that "the boy was not a fool." Every word of praise was read aloud on the house-tops, so to speak, by happy Rose; every adverse criticism was hotly disputed; and the whole family were in a great state of pleasant excitement over this unexpectedly successful first flight of the Ugly Duckling, now generally considered by his relatives as the most promising young swan of the flock.

Aunt Jane was particularly funny in her new position of mother to a callow poet, and conducted herself like a proud but bewildered hen when one of her brood takes to the water. She pored over the poems trying to appreciate them, but quite failing to do so; for life was all prose to her, and she vainly tried to discover where Mac got his talent from. It was pretty to see the new respect with which she treated his possessions now; the old books were dusted with a sort of reverence; scraps of paper laid carefully by lest some immortal verse be lost; and a certain shabby velvet jacket fondly smoothed, when no one was by to smile at the maternal pride which filled her heart, and caused her once severe countenance to shine with unwonted benignity.

Uncle Mac talked about "my son" with ill-concealed satisfaction, and evidently began to feel as if his boy was going to confer distinction upon the whole race of Campbell, which had already possessed one poet. Steve exulted with irrepressible delight, and went about quoting "Songs and Sonnets," till he bored his friends dreadfully by his fraternal raptures.

Archie took it more quietly, and even suggested that it was too soon to crow yet; for the dear old fellow's first burst might be his last, since it was impossible to predict what he would do next. Having proved that he *could* write poetry, he might drop it for some new world to conquer, quoting his favorite Thoreau, who, having made a perfect pencil, gave up the business, and took to writing books with the sort of indelible ink which grows clearer with time.

The aunts of course had their "views," and enjoyed much prophetic gossip, as they wagged their caps over many social cups of tea. The younger boys thought it "very jolly, and hoped the Don would go ahead and come to glory as soon as possible," which was all that could be expected of "Young America," with whom poetry is not usually a passion.

But Dr. Alec was a sight for "sair een:" so full of concentrated contentment was he. No one but Rose, perhaps, knew how proud and pleased the good man felt at this first small success of his godson; for he had always had high hopes of the boy, because in spite of his oddities he had such an upright nature, and promising little did much, with the quiet persistence which foretells a manly character. All the romance of the doctor's heart was stirred by this poetic bud of promise, and the love that made it bloom so early; for Mac had confided his hopes to uncle, finding great consolation and support in his sympathy and advice. Like a wise man, Dr. Alec left the young people to learn the great lesson in their own way, counselling Mac to work, and Rose to wait, till both were quite certain that their love was built on a surer foundation than admiration or youthful romance.

Meantime he went about with a well-worn little book in his pocket, humming bits from a new set of songs, and repeating with great fervor certain sonnets which seemed to him quite equal, if not superior, to any that Shakspeare ever wrote. As Rose was doing the same thing, they often met for a private "read and warble," as they called it; and, while discussing the safe subject of Mac's poetry, both arrived at a pretty clear idea of what Mac's reward was to be when he came home.

He seemed in no hurry to do this, however, and continued to astonish his family by going into society, and coming out brilliantly in that line. It takes very little to make a lion, as every one knows who has seen what poor specimens are patted and petted every year, in spite of their bad manners, foolish vagaries, and very feeble roaring. Mac did not want to be lionized, and took it rather scornfully, which only added to the charm that people suddenly discovered about the nineteenth cousin of Thomas Campbell, the poet. He desired to be distinguished in the best sense of the word, as well as to look so, and thought a little of the polish society gives would not be amiss, remembering Rose's efforts in that line. For her sake he came out of his shell, and went about seeing and testing all sorts of people with those observing eyes of his, which saw so much in spite of their near-sightedness. What use he meant to make of these new experiences no one knew; for he wrote short letters, and, when questioned, answered with imperturbable patience,—

"Wait till I get through; then I'll come home and talk about it."

So every one waited for the poet, till something happened which produced a greater sensation in the family than if all the boys had simultaneously taken to rhyming.

Dr. Alec got very impatient, and suddenly announced that he was going to L. to see after those young people; for Phebe was rapidly singing herself into public favor, with the sweet old ballads which she rendered so beautifully that hearts were touched as well as ears delighted, and her prospects brightening every month.

"Will you come with me, Rose, and surprise this ambitious pair, who are getting famous so fast they'll forget their home-keeping friends if we don't remind them of us now and then?" he said, when he proposed the trip one wild March morning.

"No, thank you, sir; I'll stay with auntie: that is all I'm fit for; and I should only be in the way among those fine people," answered Rose, snipping away at the plants blooming in the study window.

There was a slight bitterness in her voice and a cloud on her face, which her uncle heard and saw at once, half-guessed the meaning of, and could not rest till he had found out.

"Do you think Phebe and Mac would not care to see you?" he asked, putting down a letter in which Mac gave a glowing account of a concert at which Phebe surpassed herself.

"No, but they must be very busy," began Rose, wishing she had held her tongue.

"Then what is the matter?" persisted Dr. Alec.

Rose did not speak for a moment, and decapitated two fine geraniums with a reckless slash of her scissors, as if pent-up vexation of some kind must find a vent. It did in words also; for, as if quite against her will, she exclaimed impetuously,—

"The truth is, I'm jealous of them both!"

"Bless my soul! what now?" ejaculated the doctor, in great surprise.

Rose put down her watering-pot and shears, came and stood before him with her hands nervously twisted together, and said, just as she used to do when she was a little girl confessing some misdeed,—

"Uncle, I must tell you; for I've been getting very envious, discontented, and bad lately. No, don't be good to me yet; for you don't know how little I deserve it. Scold me well, and make me see how wicked I am."

"I will as soon as I know what I am to scold about. Unburden yourself, child, and let me see all your iniquity; for, if you begin by being jealous of Mac and Phebe, I'm prepared for any thing," said Dr. Alec, leaning back as if nothing could surprise him now.

"But I am not jealous in that way, sir. I mean I want to be or do something splendid as well as they. I can't write poetry or sing like a bird; but I *should* think I might have my share of glory in some way. I thought perhaps I could paint, and I've tried, but I can only copy: I've no power to invent lovely things, and I'm so discouraged; for that is my one accomplishment. Do you think I have *any* gift that could be cultivated, and do me credit like theirs?" she asked so wistfully that her uncle felt for a moment as if he never could forgive the fairies, who endow babies in their cradles, for being so niggardly to his girl. But one look into the sweet, open face before him, reminded him that the good elves *had* been very generous, and he answered cheerfully,—

"Yes, I do; for you have one of the best and noblest gifts a woman can possess. Music and poetry are fine things; and I don't wonder you want them, or that you envy the pleasant fame they bring. I've felt just so, and been ready to ask why it didn't please heaven to be more generous to some people; so you needn't be ashamed to tell me all about it."

"I know I ought to be contented, but I'm not. My life is very comfortable, but so quiet and uneventful I get tired of it, and want to launch out as the others have, and do something, or at least try. I'm glad you think it isn't very bad of me, and I'd like to know what my gift is," said Rose, looking less despondent already.

"The art of living for others so patiently and sweetly that we enjoy it as we do the sunshine, and are not half grateful enough for the great blessing."

"It is very kind of you to say so, but I think I'd like a little fun and fame, nevertheless," and Rose did not look as thankful as she ought.

"Very natural, dear; but the fun and the fame do not last; while the memory of a real helper is kept green long after poetry is forgotten and music silent. Can't you believe that, and be happy?"

"But I do so little, nobody sees or cares, and I don't feel as if I was really of any use," sighed Rose, thinking of the long, dull winter, full of efforts that seemed fruitless.

"Sit here, and let us see if you really do very little, and if no one cares," and, drawing her to his knee, Dr. Alec went on, telling off each item on one of the fingers of the soft hand he held.

"First, an infirm old aunt is kept very happy by the patient, cheerful care of this good-for-nothing niece. Secondly, a crotchety uncle, for whom she reads, runs, writes, and sews so willingly that he cannot get on without her. Thirdly, various relations who are helped in various ways. Fourthly, one dear friend never forgotten, and a certain cousin cheered by praise which is more to him than the loudest blast Fame could blow. Fifthly, several young girls find her an example of many good works and ways. Sixthly, a motherless baby is cared for as tenderly as if she was a little sister. Seventhly, half a dozen poor ladies made comfortable; and, lastly, some struggling boys and girls with artistic longings are put into a pleasant room furnished with casts, studies, easels, and all manner of helpful things, not to mention free lessons given by this same idle girl, who now sits upon my knee owning to herself that her gift *is* worth having after all."

"Indeed, I am! Uncle, I'd no idea I had done so many things to please you, or that any one guessed how hard I try to fill my place usefully. I've learned to do without gratitude: now I'll learn not to care for praise, but to be contented to do my best, and have only God know."

"He knows, and He rewards in His own good time. I think a quiet life like this often makes itself felt in better ways than one that the world sees and applauds; and some of the noblest are never known till they end, leaving a void in many hearts. Yours may be one of these if you choose to make it so, and no one will be prouder of this success than I, unless it be—Mac."

The clouds were quite gone now, and Rose was looking straight into her uncle's face with a much happier expression, when that last word made it color brightly, and the eyes glance away for a second. Then they came back full of a tender sort of resolution, as she said,—

"That will be the reward I work for," and rose, as if ready to be up and doing with renewed courage.

But her uncle held her long enough to ask quite soberly, though his eyes laughed,—

"Shall I tell him that?"

"No, sir, please don't! When he is tired of other people's praise, he will come home, and then—I'll see what I can do for him," answered Rose, slipping away to her work with the shy, happy look that sometimes came to give her face the charm it needed.

"He is such a thorough fellow he never is in a hurry to go from one thing to another. An excellent habit, but a trifle try-ing to impatient people like me," said the doctor, and picking up Dulce, who sat upon the rug with her dolly, he composed his feelings by tossing her till she crowed with delight.

Rose heartily echoed that last remark, but said nothing aloud, only helped her uncle off with dutiful alacrity, and, when he was gone, began to count the days till his return, wishing she had decided to go too.

He wrote often, giving excellent accounts of the "great creatures," as Steve called Phebe and Mac, and seemed to find so much to do in various ways that the second week of absence was nearly over before he set a day for his return, promising to astonish them with the account of his adventures.

Rose felt as if something splendid was going to happen, and set her affairs in order, so that the approaching crisis might find her fully prepared. She had "found out" now, was quite sure, and put away all doubts and fears to be ready to welcome home the cousin whom she was sure uncle would bring as her reward. She was thinking of this one day, as she got out her paper to write a long letter to poor Aunt Clara, who pined for news far away there in Calcutta.

Something in the task reminded her of that other lover whose wooing ended so tragically, and opening the little drawer of keepsakes, she took out the blue bracelet, feeling that she owed Charlie a tender thought in the midst of her new happi-ness; for of late she *had* forgotten him.

She had worn the trinket hidden under her black sleeve for a long time after his death, with the regretful constancy one sometimes shows in doing some little kindness all too late. But her arm had grown too round to hide the ornament, the forget-me-nots had fallen one by one, the clasp had broken; and that autumn she laid the bracelet away, acknowledging that she had outgrown the souvenir as well as the sentiment that gave it.

She looked at it in silence for a moment, then put it softly back, and, shutting the drawer, took up the little gray book which was her pride, thinking as she contrasted the two men and their influence on her life,—the one sad and disturbing, the other sweet and inspiring,—"Charlie's was passion: Mac's is love."

"Rose! Rose!" called a shrill voice, rudely breaking the pensive reverie, and with a start she shut the desk exclaiming as she ran to the door,—

"They have come! They have come!"

# Chapter XXI

---

D<small>R.</small> A<small>LEC</small> had not arrived, but bad tidings had, as Rose guessed the instant her eye fell upon Aunt Plenty, hobbling downstairs with her cap awry, her face pale, and a letter flapping wildly in her hand, as she cried distractedly,—

"Oh, my boy! my boy! sick, and I not there to nurse him! Malignant fever, so far away. What can those children do? why did I let Alec go?"

Rose got her into the parlor; and, while the poor old lady lamented, she read the letter which Phebe had sent to her that she might "break the news carefully to Rose."

> "D<small>EAR</small> M<small>ISS</small> P<small>LENTY</small>,—Please read this to yourself first, and tell my little mistress as you think best. The dear doctor is very ill; but I am with him, and shall not leave him day or night till he is safe. So trust me, and do not be anxious; for every thing shall be done that care and skill and entire devotion can do. He would not let us tell you before, fearing you would try to come at the risk of your health. Indeed it would be useless; for only one nurse is needed, and I came first, so do not let Rose or anybody else rob me of my right to the danger and the duty. Mac has written to his father; for Dr. Alec is now too ill to know what we do, and we both felt that you ought to be told without further delay. He has a bad malignant fever, caught no one can tell how, unless among some poor emigrants whom he met wandering about quite forlorn in a strange city. He understood Portuguese, and sent them to a proper place when they had told their story. But I fear he has suffered for his kindness; for this fever came on rapidly, and before he knew what it was I was there, and it was too late to send me away.
>
> "*Now* I can show you how grateful I am, and if need be give my life so gladly for this friend who has been a father to me. Tell Rose his last conscious word and thought

were for her. 'Don't let her come; keep my darling safe.'
Oh, do obey him! Stay safely at home; and, God helping
me, I'll bring Uncle Alec back in time. Mac does all I will
let him. We have the best physicians, and every thing is
going as well as can be hoped till the fever turns.

"Dear Miss Plenty, pray for him and for me, that I
may do this one happy thing for those who have done
so much for

"Your ever dutiful and loving<br>"PHEBE."

As Rose looked up from the letter, half stunned by the sudden news and the great danger, she found that the old lady had
already stopped useless bewailing, and was praying heartily,
like one who knew well where help was to be found. Rose
went and knelt down at her knee, laying her face on the clasped
hands in her lap, and for a few minutes neither wept nor spoke.
Then a stifled sob broke from the girl, and Aunt Plenty gathered the young head in her arms, saying, with the slow tears of
age trickling down her own withered cheeks,—

"Bear up, my lamb, bear up. The good Lord won't take him
from us I am sure: and that brave child *will* be allowed to pay
her debt to him; I feel she will."

"But I want to help. I *must* go, aunty, I must: no matter
what the danger is," cried Rose, full of a tender jealousy of
Phebe for being first to brave peril for the sake of him who had
been a father to them both.

"You can't go, dear, it's no use now; and she is right to say,
'Keep away.' I know those fevers, and the ones who nurse often
take it, and fare worse for the strain they've been through.
Good girl to stand by so bravely, to be so sensible, and not let
Mac go too near! She's a grand nurse: Alec couldn't have a
better, and she'll never leave him till he's safe," said Miss Plenty,
excitedly.

"Ah, you begin to know her now, and value her as you
ought. *I* think few would have done as she has; and if she does
get ill and die it will be our fault partly; because she'd go
through fire and water to make us do her justice, and receive
her as we ought," cried Rose, proud of an example which she
longed to follow.

"If she brings my boy home, I'll never say another word. She may marry every nephew I've got, if she likes, and I'll give her my blessing," exclaimed Aunt Plenty, feeling that no price would be too much to pay for such a deed.

Rose was going to clap her hands, but wrung them instead; remembering with a sudden pang that the battle was not over yet, and it was much too soon to award the honors.

Before she could speak Uncle Mac and Aunt Jane hurried in; for Mac's letter had come with the other, and dismay fell upon the family at the thought of danger to the well-beloved Uncle Alec. His brother decided to go at once, and Aunt Jane insisted on accompanying him: though all agreed that nothing could be done but wait, and leave Phebe at her post as long as she held out; since it was too late to save her from danger now, and Mac reported her quite equal to the task.

Great was the hurry and confusion till the relief party was off. Aunt Plenty was heart-broken that she could not go with them, but felt that she was too infirm to be useful; and, like a sensible old soul, tried to content herself with preparing all sorts of comforts for the invalid. Rose was less patient, and at first had wild ideas of setting off alone, and forcing her way to the spot where all her thoughts now centred. But, before she could carry out any rash project, Aunt Myra's palpitations set in so alarmingly that they did good service for once, and kept Rose busy taking her last directions, and trying to soothe her dying-bed; for each attack was declared fatal, till the patient demanded toast and tea, when hope was again allowable and the rally began.

The news flew fast, as such tidings always do: and Aunt Plenty was constantly employed in answering inquiries; for her knocker kept up a steady tattoo for several days. All sorts of people came; gentle-folk and paupers, children with anxious little faces, old people full of sympathy, pretty girls sobbing as they went away, and young men who relieved their feelings by swearing at all emigrants in general and Portuguese in particular. It was touching and comforting to see how many loved the good man who was known only by his benefactions, and now lay suffering far away, quite unconscious how many unsuspected charities were brought to light by this grateful solicitude, as hidden flowers spring up when warm rains fall.

If Rose had ever felt that the gift of living for others was a poor one, she saw now how beautiful and blest it was,—how rich the returns, how wide the influence, how much more precious the tender tie which knit so many hearts together, than any breath of fame, or brilliant talent, that dazzled, but did not win and warm. In after years she found how true her uncle's words had been; and, listening to eulogies of great men, felt less moved and inspired by praises of their splendid gifts than by the sight of some good man's patient labor for the poorest of his kind. Her heroes ceased to be the world's favorites; and became such as Garrison fighting for his chosen people; Howe restoring lost senses to the deaf, the dumb, and blind; Sumner unbribable, when other men were bought and sold: and many a large-hearted woman working as quietly as Abby Gibbons, who for thirty years has made Christmas merry for two hundred little paupers in a city almshouse, beside saving Magdalens and teaching convicts.

The lesson came to Rose when she was ready for it, and showed her what a noble profession philanthropy is, made her glad of her choice, and helped fit her for a long life full of the loving labor, and sweet satisfaction unostentatious charity brings to those who ask no reward, and are content if "only God knows."

Several anxious weeks went by with wearing fluctuations of hope and fear; for Life and Death fought over the prize each wanted, and more than once Death seemed to have won. But Phebe stood at her post, defying both danger and death with the courage and devotion women often show. All her soul and strength were in her work; and, when it seemed most hopeless, she cried out with the passionate energy which seems to send such appeals straight up to Heaven,—

"Grant me this one boon, dear Lord, and I will never ask another for myself!"

Such prayers avail much, and such entire devotion often seems to work miracles when other aids are vain. Phebe's cry was answered; her self-forgetful task accomplished, and her long vigil rewarded with a happy dawn. Dr. Alec always said that she kept him alive by the force of her will; and that, during the hours when he seemed to lie unconscious, he felt a strong, warm hand holding his, as if keeping him from the swift current trying to sweep him away. The happiest hour of all her life was that in which he knew her, looked up with the shadow of a smile in his hollow eyes, and tried to say in his old cheery way,—

"Tell Rose I've turned the corner, thanks to you, my child."

She answered very quietly, smoothed the pillow, and saw him drop asleep again, before she stole away into the other room, meaning to write the good news; but could only throw herself down, and find relief for a full heart in the first tears she had shed for weeks. Mac found her there, and took such care of her that she was ready to go back to her place,—now indeed a post of honor,—while he ran off to send home a telegram which made many hearts sing for joy, and caused Jamie, in his first burst of delight, to propose to ring all the city bells and order out the cannon.

"Saved: thanks to God and Phebe."

That was all; but every one was satisfied, and every one fell a-crying, as if hope needed much salt water to strengthen it. That was soon over, however, and then people went about smiling and saying to one another, with hand-shakes or embraces, "He is better: no doubt of it now!" A general desire to rush away and assure themselves of the truth pervaded the family for some days; and nothing but awful threats from Mac, stern mandates from the doctor, and entreaties from Phebe not to undo her work, kept Miss Plenty, Rose, and Aunt Jessie at home.

As the only way in which they could ease their minds and bear the delay, they set about spring cleaning, with an energy which scared the spiders, and drove char-women distracted. If the old house had been infected with small-pox, it could not have been more vigorously scrubbed, aired, and refreshed. Early as it was, every carpet was routed up, curtains pulled down, cushions banged, and glory-holes turned out, till not a speck of dust, a last year's fly, or stray straw could be found. Then they all sat down and rested in such an immaculate mansion that one hardly dared to move for fear of destroying the shining order everywhere visible.

It was late in April before this was accomplished, and the necessary quarantine of the absentees well over. The first mild days seemed to come early, so that Dr. Alec might return with safety from the journey which had so nearly been his last. It was perfectly impossible to keep any member of the family away on that great occasion. They came from all quarters in spite of express directions to the contrary; for the invalid was still very feeble, and no excitement must be allowed. As if the wind had carried the glad news, Uncle Jem came into port the night before; Will and Geordie got a leave on their own responsibility; Steve would have defied the entire Faculty, had it been necessary; and Uncle Mac and Archie said simultaneously, "Business be hanged to-day."

Of course, the aunts arrived all in their best; all cautioning everybody else to keep quiet, and all gabbling excitedly at the least provocation. Jamie suffered most during that day, so divided was he between the desire to behave well and the frantic impulse to shout at the top of his voice, turn somersaults, and race all over the house. Occasional bolts into the barn, where he let off steam by roaring and dancing jigs, to the great dismay of the fat old horses and two sedate cows, helped him to get through that trying period.

But the heart that was fullest beat and fluttered in Rose's bosom, as she went about putting spring flowers everywhere; very silent, but so radiant with happiness that the aunts watched her, saying softly to one another, "Could an angel look sweeter?"

If angels ever wore pale-green gowns and snowdrops in their hair, had countenances full of serenest joy, and large eyes shining with an inward light that made them very lovely, then Rose did look like one. But she felt like a woman: and well she might; for was not life very rich that day, when uncle, friend, and lover were coming back to her together? Could she ask any thing more, except the power to be to all of them the creature they believed her, and to return the love they gave her with one as faithful, pure, and deep?

Among the portraits in the hall hung one of Dr. Alec, taken soon after his return by Charlie, in one of his brief fits of inspiration. Only a crayon, but wonderfully life-like and carefully finished, as few of the others were. This had been handsomely framed, and now held the place of honor, garlanded with green wreaths, while the great Indian jar below blazed with a pyramid of hot-house flowers sent by Kitty. Rose was giving

these a last touch, with Dulce close by, cooing over a handful
of sweet "daffydowndillies," when the sound of wheels sent
her flying to the door. She meant to have spoken the first welcome and had the first embrace; but when she saw the altered
face in the carriage, the feeble figure being borne up the steps
by all the boys, she stood motionless till Phebe caught her in
her arms, whispering with a laugh and a cry struggling in her
voice,—

"I did it for you, my darling, all for you!"

"O Phebe, never say again you owe me any thing! I never
can repay you for this," was all Rose had time to answer, as
they stood one instant cheek to cheek, heart to heart, both too
full of happiness for many words.

Aunt Plenty had heard the wheels also, and, as everybody
rose *en masse*, had said as impressively as extreme agitation
would allow, while she put her glasses on upside-down, and
seized a lace tidy instead of her handkerchief,—

"Stop! all stay here, and let *me* receive Alec. Remember his
weak state, and be calm, quite calm, as I am."

"Yes, aunt, certainly," was the general murmur of assent: but
it was as impossible to obey as it would have been to keep
feathers still in a gale; and one irresistible impulse carried the
whole roomful into the hall, to behold Aunt Plenty beautifully
illustrate her own theory of composure by waving the tidy
wildly, rushing into Dr. Alec's arms, and laughing and crying
with an hysterical abandonment which even Aunt Myra could
not have surpassed.

The tearful jubilee was soon over, however; and no one
seemed the worse for it: for the instant his arms were at liberty
Uncle Alec forgot himself, and began to make other people
happy, by saying seriously, though his thin face beamed pater-
nally, as he drew Phebe forward,—

"Aunt Plenty, but for this good daughter I never should
have come back to be so welcomed. Love her for my sake."

Then the old lady came out splendidly, and showed her mettle; for, turning to Phebe, she bowed her gray head as if saluting
an equal; and, offering her hand, answered with repentance,
admiration, and tenderness trembling in her voice,—

"I'm proud to do it for her own sake. I ask pardon for my silly
prejudices, and I'll prove that I'm sincere by—where's that boy?"

There were six boys present: but the right one was in exactly the right place at the right moment; and, seizing Archie's hand, Aunt Plenty put Phebe's into it, trying to say something appropriately solemn, but could not; so hugged them both, and sobbed out,—

"If I had a dozen nephews, I'd give them *all* to you, my dear, and dance at the wedding, though I had rheumatism in every limb."

That was better than any oration; for it set them all to laughing, and Dr. Alec was floated to the sofa on a gentle wave of merriment. Once there, every one but Rose and Aunt Plenty was ordered off by Mac, who was in command now, and seemed to have sunk the poet in the physician.

"The house must be perfectly quiet, and he must go to sleep as soon as possible after the journey; so all say 'Good-by' now, and call again to-morrow," he said, watching his uncle anxiously, as he leaned in the sofa corner, with four women taking off his wraps, three boys contending for his overshoes, two brothers shaking hands at short intervals, and Aunt Myra holding a bottle of strong salts under his devoted nose every time there was an opening anywhere.

With difficulty the house was partially cleared: and then, while Aunt Plenty mounted guard over her boy, Rose stole away to see if Mac had gone with the rest; for as yet they had hardly spoken in the joyful flurry, though eyes and hands had met.

# Chapter XXII

## SHORT AND SWEET

IN the hall she found Steve and Kitty; for he had hidden his little sweetheart behind the big couch, feeling that she had a right there, having supported his spirits during the late anxiety with great constancy and courage. They seemed so cosey, billing and cooing in the shadow of the gay vase, that Rose would have slipped silently away if they had not seen and called to her.

"He's not gone: I guess you'll find him in the parlor," said Steve, divining with a lover's instinct the meaning of the quick look she had cast at the hat-rack, as she shut the study-door behind her.

"Mercy, no! Archie and Phebe are there, so he'd have the sense to pop into the sanctum and wait; unless you'd like me to go and bring him out?" added Kitty, smoothing Rose's ruffled hair, and settling the flowers on the bosom where Uncle Alec's head had laid until he fell asleep.

"No, thank you, I'll go to him when I've seen my Phebe. She won't mind me," answered Rose, moving on to the parlor.

"Look here," called Steve, "do advise them to hurry up and all be married at once. We were just ready when uncle fell ill, and now we can *not* wait a day later than the first of May."

"Rather short notice," laughed Rose, looking back with the door-knob in her hand.

"We'll give up all our splendor, and do it as simply as you like, if *you* will only come too. Think how lovely! three weddings at once! Do fly round and settle things: there's a dear," implored Kitty, whose imagination was fired with this romantic idea.

"How can I, when I have no bridegroom yet?" began Rose, with conscious color in her tell-tale face.

"Sly creature! you know you've only got to say a word and have a famous one. Una and her lion will be nothing to it," cried Steve, bent on hastening his brother's affair, which was much too dilatory and peculiar for his taste.

"He has been in no haste to come home, and I am in no haste to leave it. Don't wait for me, 'Mr. and Mrs. Harry Walmers, Jr.;' I shall be a year at least making up my mind: so you may lead off as splendidly as you like, and I'll profit by your experience;" and Rose vanished into the parlor, leaving Steve to groan over the perversity of superior women, and Kitty to comfort him by promising to marry him on May-day "all alone."

A very different couple occupied the drawing-room, but a happier one; for they had known the pain of separation, and were now enjoying the bliss of a reunion which was to last unbroken for their lives. Phebe sat in an easy-chair, resting from her labors, pale and thin and worn, but lovelier in Archie's eyes than ever before. It was very evident that he was adoring his divinity; for, after placing a footstool at her feet, he had forgotten to get up, and knelt there, with his elbow on the arm of her chair, looking like a thirsty man drinking long draughts of the purest water.

"Shall I disturb you if I pass through?" asked Rose, loth to spoil the pretty tableau.

"Not if you stop a minute on the way and congratulate me, cousin; for she says 'Yes' at last!" cried Archie, springing up to go and bring her to the arms Phebe opened as she appeared.

"I knew she would reward your patience, and put away her pride when both had been duly tried," said Rose, laying the tired head on her bosom, with such tender admiration in her eyes that Phebe had to shake some bright drops from her own before she could reply in a tone of grateful humility, that showed how much her heart was touched,—

"How can I help it, when they all are so kind to me? Any pride would melt away under such praise and thanks and loving wishes as I've had to-day; for every member of the family has taken pains to welcome me, to express far too much gratitude, and to beg me to be one of you. I needed very little urging; but, when Archie's father and mother came and called me 'daughter,' I would have promised any thing to show my love for them."

"And him," added Rose; but Archie seemed quite satisfied, and kissed the hand he held as if it had been that of a beloved princess, while he said with all the pride Phebe seemed to have lost,—

"Think what she gives up for me: fame and fortune and the admiration of many a better man. You don't know what a splendid prospect she has of becoming one of the sweet singers who are loved and honored everywhere; and all this she puts away for my sake, content to sing for me alone, with no reward but love."

"I am so glad to make a little sacrifice for a great happiness: I never shall regret it or think my music lost, if it makes home cheerful for my mate. Birds sing sweetest in their own nests, you know," and Phebe bent toward him with a look and gesture which plainly showed how willingly she offered up all ambitious hopes upon the altar of a woman's happy love.

Both seemed to forget that they were not alone, and in a moment they were; for a sudden impulse carried Rose to the door of her sanctum, as if the south wind which seemed to have set in was wafting this little ship also toward the Islands of the Blest, where the others were safely anchored now.

The room was a blaze of sunshine and a bower of spring freshness and fragrance: for here Rose had let her fancy have free play; and each garland, fern, and flower had its meaning. Mac seemed to have been reading this sweet language of symbols, to have guessed why Charlie's little picture was framed in white roses, why pansies hung about his own, why Psyche was half hidden among feathery sprays of maiden's-hair, and a purple passion-flower lay at Cupid's feet. The last fancy evidently pleased him; for he was smiling over it, and humming to himself, as if to beguile his patient waiting, the burden of the air Rose so often sung to him,—

> "Bonny lassie, will ye gang, will ye gang
>   To the birks of Aberfeldie?"

"Yes, Mac, anywhere!"

He had not heard her enter, and wheeling round looked at her with a radiant face, as he said, drawing a long breath,—

"At last! you were so busy over the dear man, I got no word. But I can wait: I'm used to it."

Rose stood quite still, surveying him with a new sort of

reverence in her eyes, as she answered with a sweet solemnity, that made him laugh and redden with the sensitive joy of one to whom praise from her lips was very precious.

"You forget that you are not the Mac who went away. I should have run to meet my cousin, but I did not dare to be familiar with the poet whom all begin to honor."

"You like the mixture then? You know I said I'd try to give you love and poetry together."

"Like it! I'm so glad, so proud, I haven't any words strong and beautiful enough to half express my wonder and my admiration. How *could* you do it, Mac?" and a whole face full of smiles broke loose, as Rose clapped her hands, looking as if she could dance with sheer delight at his success.

"It did itself, up there among the hills, and here with you, or out alone upon the sea. I could write a heavenly poem this very minute, and put you in as Spring; you look like her in that green gown with snowdrops in your bonny hair? Rose, am I getting on a little? Does a hint of fame help me nearer to the prize I'm working for? Is your heart more willing to be won?"

He did not stir a step, but looked at her with such intense longing that his glance seemed to draw her nearer like an irresistible appeal; for she went and stood before him, holding out both hands, as if she offered all her little store, as she said with simplest sincerity,—

"It is not worth so much beautiful endeavor; but, if you still want so poor a thing, it is yours."

He caught the hands in his, and seemed about to take the rest of her, but hesitated for an instant, unable to believe that so much happiness was true.

"Are you sure, Rose,—very sure? Don't let a momentary admiration blind you: I'm not a poet yet; and the best are but mortal men, you know."

"It is not admiration, Mac."

"Nor gratitude for the small share I've taken in saving uncle? I had my debt to pay, as well as Phebe, and was as glad to risk my life."

"No: it is not gratitude."

"Nor pity for my patience? I've only done a little yet, and am as far as ever from being like your hero. I can work and wait still longer, if you are not sure; for I must have all or nothing."

"O Mac! why will you be so doubtful? You said you'd make me love you, and you've done it. Will you believe me now?" And, with a sort of desperation, she threw herself into his arms, clinging there in eloquent silence, while he held her close; feeling, with a thrill of tender triumph, that this was no longer little Rose, but a loving woman, ready to live and die for him.

"Now I'm satisfied!" he said presently, when she lifted up her face, full of maidenly shame at the sudden passion which had carried her out of herself for a moment. "No: don't slip away so soon; let me keep you for one blessed minute, and feel that I have really found my Psyche."

"And I my Cupid," answered Rose, laughing, in spite of her emotion, at the idea of Mac in that sentimental character.

He laughed too, as only a happy lover could; then said, with sudden seriousness,—

"Sweet Soul! lift up your lamp, and look well before it is too late; for I'm no god, only a very faulty man."

"Dear Love! I will. But I have no fear, except that you will fly too high for me to follow, because I have no wings."

"You shall live the poetry, and I will write it; so my little gift will celebrate your greater one."

"No: you shall have all the fame, and I'll be content to be known only as the poet's wife."

"And I'll be proud to own that my best inspiration comes from the beneficent life of a sweet and noble woman."

"O Mac! we'll work together, and try to make the world better by the music and the love we leave behind us when we go."

"Please God, we will!" he answered fervently; and, looking at her as she stood there in the spring sunshine, glowing with the tender happiness, high hopes, and earnest purposes that make life beautiful and sacred, he felt that now the last leaf had folded back, the golden heart lay open to the light, and his Rose had bloomed.

END.

# OTHER WRITINGS

# Address of the Republican
# Women of Massachusetts

TO THE WOMEN OF AMERICA

The time has come, in the progress of Civilization, when the women of America may make themselves felt in politics as a recognized and beneficent power. This manifestation will naturally precede the establishment of the Equal Rights of Woman, as cause precedes effect.

The National Republican Convention recently held in Philadelphia unanimously adopted the following, as a part of its declaration of principles:—

> 14. The Republican party is mindful of its obligations to the loyal women of America for their noble devotion to the cause of freedom; their admission to wider fields of usefulness is viewed with satisfaction; and the honest demand of any class of citizens for additional rights should be treated with respectful consideration.

The cause of Woman is the cause of Civilization; and, in the providence of God, the Republican party has been preeminently the party of Civilization. It has effectually suppressed a most formidable rebellion, excited and carried on to perpetuate the worst form of tyranny ever inflicted upon mankind, and has maintained the Union and its free institutions at a priceless cost. It has liberated four million slaves,—one half of whom were women. It has lifted them from the auction block to the plane of American citizenship. It has essentially aided a grand educational movement at the South, which must ultimately be of inestimable value to that depressed and impoverished section of our country in all that pertains to popular enlightenment, general industry, business enterprise, accumulative prosperity, and public order. It has conferred political equality upon four hundred thousand colored men, once bought and sold in the market like cattle. It has gathered to itself an overwhelming proportion of the intelligence, virtue,

787

patriotism, and piety of the land. It has evinced a disposition to enlarge its sphere of action for the furtherance of equal rights to the extent of its possibilities, in accordance with the progressive spirit of the Age. While, in all these and other matters of vital importance to our national unity and stability, it has been persistently and virulently opposed by the Democratic party, to the imperiling of our dearest rights and most precious interests as a people.

Therefore we hail the Republican recognition of woman's devotion to freedom in the past as a tribute well-timed and well-deserved. We accept the Republican congratulation upon Woman's admission to wider fields of usefulness as opportune and statesman-like; we receive the Republican assurance of respectful consideration for Woman's rights in the future as a sincere expression of good-will, and as an initiatory step toward securing the elective franchise for all citizens irrespective of sex.

In submitting this grave issue to the "respectful consideration" of all parties, the Republican party has not only indicated an increasing sense of justice, but has done much towards hastening the hour for its satisfactory solution. Already, the Republicans of Massachusetts have responded by adopting a platform containing the following explicit declaration:—

> 8. *Resolved*—That we heartily approve of the recognition of the rights of Woman contained in the fourteenth clause of the National Republican Platform; that the Republican Party of Massachusetts, as the representative of liberty and progress, is in favor of extending suffrage on equal terms to all American citizens, irrespective of sex, and will hail the day when the educated intellect and enlightened conscience of woman will find direct expression at the ballot-box.

In marked and dishonorable contrast with this advanced action of the Republican Conventions at Philadelphia and Worcester, was the refusal of the so-called Liberal Convention at Cincinnati, and the Democratic Convention at Baltimore, to admit women as delegates, or to give the slightest heed to Woman's claim which was respectfully submitted to them, thus evincing a settled purpose to discountenance any consideration of the "honest demand" of American women "for additional rights" or political enfranchisement.

We believe the utmost reliance may be placed upon the readiness of President Grant to sustain any Congressional action that may be taken, under his administration, in favor of basing the right of suffrage upon personality, and not upon sex; so that whatever may be the limitations to the exercise of that right, they shall cease to be proscriptive in reference to a natural distinction which ought not to affect the liberties and interests of a human being. In his numerous appointments of women to the superintendence of post-offices, and other public trusts, he has given practical proof that he is in favor of Woman's admission to "wider fields of usefulness;" and in the employment of thousands of women in the various departments of the general government, a similar spirit has been indicated on an unexampled scale.

In the person of his Presidential competitor, Horace Greeley, we see one who formerly gave his hearty approval to the Woman's Rights movement, but who has since treated it with hostility and contempt; and whose journal, the *Tribune*, has dealt it many an unmerited blow. It behooves every woman, therefore, who sees in the success of that movement the removal of an odious proscription and the abolishment of class legislation, to exert her utmost personal, social and moral influence to prevent his election.

In the nomination of Henry Wilson for the Vice-Presidency of the United States, we have additional evidence of the purpose of the Republican party to take no step backward, but to advance the standard of impartial liberty. In him we recognize the upright and sagacious statesman, the early and devoted advocate of the oppressed, and the outspoken supporter of the claim of Woman to a just share of political representation.

We are willing to trust the Republican party and its candidates as saying what they mean, and meaning what they say; and, in view of their honorable record, we have no fear of a betrayal on their part.

Let us show our country and the world that the women of America are capable of political responsibility, by wisely accepting the progressive platform of the Philadelphia Convention as prophetic of our complete enfranchisement at a day not far distant. Let us everywhere co-operate to create an overwhelming public sentiment in favor of the party that deems our claim to the ballot worthy of respectful consideration wherever fairly and properly presented, and to defeat the party that ignores our claim.

So shall the cause of Equal Rights continue to march on until its shining goal is attained, and A PEOPLE'S GOVERNMENT is established on the indestructible basis of "THE CONSENT OF THE GOVERNED."

Signed in behalf of the Republican women of Massachusetts in Convention assembled,

> LYDIA MARIA CHILD,
> HARRIET BEECHER STOWE,
> ELIZABETH STUART PHELPS,
> LOUISA M. ALCOTT,
> GRACE GREENWOOD,
> JULIA WARD HOWE,
> MARY A. LIVERMORE,
> HELEN E. GARRISON,
> ABBY W. MAY,
> CAROLINE M. SEVERANCE,
> HARRIET H. ROBINSON,
> MARGARET W. CAMPBELL,
> MARY F. EASTMAN,
> ADA C. BOWLES,
> ELIZABETH P. PEABODY,
> HARRIET W. SEWALL,
> LUCY STONE,
>                         Committee.

BOSTON, Sept. 25, 1872.

# Kate's Choice

"WELL, what do you think of her?"

"I think she's a perfect dear, and not a bit stuck up with all her money."

"A real little lady, and ever so pretty."

"She kissed me lots, and don't tell me to run away, so I love her."

The group of brothers and sisters standing round the fire laughed as little May finished the chorus of praise with these crowning virtues.

Tall Alf asked the question, and seemed satisfied with the general approval of the new cousin just come from England to live with them. They had often heard of Kate, and rather prided themselves on the fact that she lived in a fine house, was very rich, and sent them charming presents. Now pity was added to the pride, for Kate was an orphan, and all her money could not buy back the parents she had lost. They had watched impatiently for her arrival, had welcomed her cordially, and after a day spent in trying to make her feel at home they were comparing notes in the twilight, while Kate was having a quiet talk with mamma.

"I hope she will choose to live with us. You know she can go to any of the uncles she likes best," said Alf.

"We are nearer her age than any of the other cousins, and papa is the oldest uncle, so I guess she will," added Milly, the fourteen-year-old daughter of the house.

"She said she liked America," said quiet Frank.

"Wonder if she will give us a lot of her money?" put in practical Fred, who was always in debt.

"Stop that!" commanded Alf. "Mind now, if you ever ask her for a penny I'll shake you out of your jacket."

"Hush! she's coming," cried Milly, and a dead silence followed the lively chatter.

A fresh-faced bright-eyed girl of fifteen came quietly in, glanced at the group on the rug, and paused as if doubtful whether she was wanted.

"Come on!" said Fred, encouragingly.

"Shall I be in the way?"

"Oh! dear, no, we were only talking," answered Milly, drawing her cousin nearer with an arm about her waist.

"It sounded like something pleasant," said Kate, not exactly knowing what to say.

"We were talking about you," began little May, when a poke from Frank made her stop to ask, "What's that for? We *were* talking about Kate, and we all said we liked her, so it's no matter if I do tell."

"You are very kind," and Kate looked so pleased that the children forgave May's awkward frankness.

"Yes, and we hoped you'd like us and stay with us," said Alf, in the lofty and polite manner which he thought became the young lord of the house.

"I am going to try all the uncles in turn, and then decide; papa wished it," answered Kate, with a sudden tremble of the lips, for her father was the only parent she could remember, and had been unusually dear for that reason.

"Can you play billiards?" asked Fred, who had a horror of seeing girls cry.

"Yes, and I'll teach you."

"You had a pony-carriage at your house, didn't you?" added Frank, eager to help on the good work.

"At grandma's,—I had no other home, you know," answered Kate.

"What shall you buy first with your money?" asked May, who *would* ask improper questions.

"I'd buy a grandma if I could," and Kate both smiled and sighed.

"How funny! We've got one somewhere, but we don't care much about her," continued May, with the inconvenient candor of a child.

"Have you? Where is she?" and Kate turned quickly, looking full of interest.

"Papa's mother is very old, and lives ever so far away in the country, so of course we don't see much of her," explained Alf.

"But papa writes sometimes, and mamma sends her things every Christmas. We don't remember her much, because we never saw her but once, ever so long ago; but we do care for her, and May mustn't say such rude things," said Milly.

"I shall go and see her. I can't get on without a grand-mother," and Kate smiled so brightly that the lads thought her prettier than ever. "Tell me more about her. Is she a dear old lady?"

"Don't know. She is lame, and lives in the old house, and has a maid named Dolly, and—that's all I can tell you about her," and Milly looked a little vexed that she could say no more on the subject that seemed to interest her cousin so much.

Kate looked surprised, but said nothing, and stood looking at the fire as if turning the matter over in her mind, and trying to answer the question she was too polite to ask,—how could they live without a grandmother? Here the tea-bell rang, and the flock ran laughing downstairs; but, though she said no more, Kate remembered that conversation, and laid a plan in her resolute little mind which she carried out when the time came.

According to her father's wish she lived for a while in the family of each of the four uncles before she decided with which she would make her home. All were anxious to have her, one because of her money, another because her great-grandfather had been a lord, a third hoped to secure her for his son, while the fourth and best family loved her for herself alone. They were worthy people, as the world goes,—busy, ambitious, and prosperous; and every one, old and young, was fond of bright, pretty, generous Kate. Each family was anxious to keep her, a little jealous of the rest, and very eager to know which she would choose.

But Kate surprised them all by saying decidedly when the time came,—

"I must see grandma before I choose. Perhaps I ought to have visited her first, as she is the oldest. I think papa would wish me to do it. At any rate, I want to pay my duty to her before I settle anywhere, so please let me go."

Some of the young cousins laughed at the idea, and her old-fashioned, respectful way of putting it, which contrasted strongly with their free-and-easy American speech. The uncles were surprised, but agreed to humor her whim, and Uncle George, the eldest, said softly,—

"I ought to have remembered that poor Anna was mother's only daughter, and the old lady would naturally love to see the girl. But, my dear, it will be desperately dull. Only two old women and a quiet country town. No fun, no company, you won't stay long."

"I shall not mind the dulness if grandma likes to have me there. I lived very quietly in England, and was never tired of it. Nursey can take care of me, and I think the sight of me will do the dear old lady good, because they tell me I am like mamma."

Something in the earnest young face reminded Uncle George of the sister he had almost forgotten, and recalled his own youth so pleasantly that he said, with a caress of the curly head beside him,—

"So it would, I'm sure of it, and I've a great mind to go with you and 'pay my duty' to mother, as you prettily express it."

"Oh, no, please don't, sir; I want to surprise her, and have her all to myself for a little while. Would you mind if I went quite alone with Nursey? You can come later."

"Not a bit; you shall do as you like, and make sunshine for the old lady as you have for us. I haven't seen her for a year, but I know she is well and comfortable, and Dolly guards her like a dragon. Give her my love, Kitty, and tell her I send her something she will value a hundred times more than the very best tea, the finest cap, or the handsomest tabby that ever purred."

So, in spite of the lamentations of her cousins, Kate went gayly away to find the grandma whom no one else seemed to value as she did.

You see, grandpa had been a farmer, and lived contentedly on the old place until he died; but his four sons wanted to be something better, so they went away one after the other to make their way in the world. All worked hard, got rich, lived splendidly, and forgot as far as possible the old life and the dull old place they came from. They were good sons in their way, and had each offered his mother a home with him if she cared to come. But grandma clung to the old home, the simple ways, and quiet life, and, thanking them gratefully, she had remained in the big farm-house, empty, lonely, and plain though it was, compared to the fine homes of her sons.

Little by little the busy men forgot the quiet, uncomplaining old mother, who spent her years thinking of them, longing to see and know their children, hoping they would one day remember how she loved them all, and how solitary her life must be.

Now and then they wrote or paid her a hasty visit, and all sent gifts of far less value to her than one loving look, one hour of dutiful, affectionate companionship.

"If you ever want me, send and I'll come. Or, if you ever need a home, remember the old place is here always open, and you are always welcome," the good old lady said. But they never seemed to need her, and so seldom came that the old place evidently had no charm for them.

It was hard, but the sweet old woman bore it patiently, and lived her lonely life quietly and usefully, with her faithful maid Dolly to serve and love and support her.

Kate's mother, her one daughter, had married young, gone to England, and, dying early, had left the child to its father and his family. Among them little Kate had grown up, knowing scarcely any thing of her American relations until she was left an orphan and went back to her mother's people. She had been the pet of her English grandmother, and, finding all the aunts busy, fashionable women, had longed for the tender fostering she had known, and now felt as if only grandmothers could give.

With a flutter of hope and expectation, she approached the old house after the long journey was over. Leaving the luggage at the inn, and accompanied by faithful Nurse, Kate went up the village street, and, pausing at the gate, looked at the home where her mother had been born.

A large, old-fashioned farm-house, with a hospitable porch and tall trees in front, an orchard behind, and a capital hill for blackberries in summer, and coasting in winter, close by. All the upper windows were curtained, and made the house look as if it was half-asleep. At one of the lower windows sat a portly puss, blinking in the sun, and at the other appeared a cap, a regular grandmotherly old cap, with a little black bow perked up behind. Something in the lonely look of the house and the pensive droop of that cap made Katy hurry up the walk and tap eagerly at the antique knocker. A brisk little old woman peered out, as if startled at the sound, and Kate asked, smiling, "Does Madam Coverley live here?"

"She does, dear. Walk right in," and throwing wide the

door, the maid trotted down a long, wide hall, and announced in a low tone to her mistress,—

"A nice, pretty little girl wants to see you, mum."

"I shall love to see a young face. Who is it, Dolly?" asked a pleasant voice.

"Don't know, mum."

"Grandma must guess," and Kate went straight up to the old lady with both hands out, for the first sight of that sweet old face won her heart.

Lifting her spectacles, grandma looked silently a minute, then opened her arms without a word, and in the long embrace that followed Kate felt assured that she was welcome to the home she wanted.

"So like my Anna! And this is her little girl? God bless you, my darling! So good to come and see me!" said the old lady when she could speak.

"Why, grandma, I couldn't get on without you, and as soon as I knew where to find you I was in a fidget to be off; but had to do my other visits first, because the uncles had planned it so. This is Dolly, I am sure, and that is my good nurse. Go and get my things, please, Nursey. I shall stay here until grandma sends me away."

"That will never be, deary. Now tell me every thing. It is like an angel coming to see me all of a sudden. Sit close, and let me feel sure it isn't one of the dreams I make to cheer myself when I'm lonesome."

Kate sat on a little stool at grandma's feet, and, leaning on her knee, told all her little story, while the old lady fed her hungry eyes with the sight of the fresh young face, listened to the music of a loving voice, and felt the happy certainty that some one had remembered her, as she longed to be remembered.

Such a happy day as Kate spent talking and listening, looking at her new home, which she found delightful, and being petted by the two old women, who would hardly let Nursey do any thing for her. Kate's quick eyes read the truth of grandma's lonely life very soon; her warm heart was full of tender pity, and she resolved to devote herself to making the happiness of the dear old lady's few remaining years, for at eighty one should have the prop of loving children, if ever.

To Dolly and madam it really did seem as if an angel had come, a singing, smiling, chattering sprite, who danced all over the old house, making blithe echoes in the silent room, and brightening every corner she entered.

Kate opened all the shutters and let in the sun, saying she must see which room she liked best before she settled. She played on the old piano, that wheezed and jangled, all out of tune; but no one minded, for the girlish voice was as sweet as a lark's. She invaded Dolly's sacred kitchen, and messed to her heart's content, delighting the old soul by praises of her skill, and petitions to be taught all she knew. She pranced to and fro in the long hall, and got acquainted with the lives of painted ancestors hanging there in big wigs or short-waisted gowns. She took possession of grandma's little parlor, and made it so cosey the old lady felt as if she was bewitched, for cushioned arm-chairs, fur foot-stools, soft rugs, and delicate warm shawls appeared like magic. Flowers bloomed in the deep, sunny window-seats, pictures of lovely places seemed to break out on the oaken walls, a dainty work-basket took its place near grandma's quaint one, and, best of all, the little chair beside her own was seldom empty now.

The first thing in the morning a kiss waked her, and the beloved voice gave her a gay "Good-morning, grandma dear!" All day Anna's child hovered about her with willing hands and feet to serve her, loving heart to return her love, and the tender reverence which is the beautiful tribute the young should pay the old. In the twilight, the bright head always was at her knees; and, in either listening to the stories of the past or making lively plans for the future, Kate whiled away the time that used to be so sad.

Kate never found it lonely, seldom wished for other society, and grew every day more certain that here she could find the cherishing she needed, and do the good she hoped.

Dolly and Nurse got on capitally; each tried which could sing "Little Missy's" praises loudest, and spoil her quickest by unquestioning obedience to every whim or wish. A happy family, and the dull November days went by so fast that Christmas was at hand before they knew it.

All the uncles had written to ask Kate to pass the holidays with them, feeling sure she must be longing for a change. But she had refused them all, saying she should stay with grandma, who could not go anywhere to join other people's merry-makings, and must have one of her own at home. The uncles urged, the aunts advised, and the cousins teased; but Kate denied them all, yet offended no one, for she was inspired by a grand idea, and carried it out with help from Dolly and Nurse, unsuspected by grandma.

"We are going to have a little Christmas fun up here among ourselves, and you mustn't know about it until we are ready. So just sit all cosey in your corner, and let me riot about as I like. I know you won't mind, and I think you'll say it is splendid when I've carried out my plan," said Kate, when the old lady wondered what she was thinking about so deeply, with her brows knit and her lips smiling.

"Very well, dear, do any thing you like, and I shall enjoy it, only don't get tired, or try to do too much," and with that grandma became deaf and blind to the mysteries that went on about her.

She was lame, and seldom left her own rooms; so Kate, with her devoted helpers, turned the house topsy-turvy, trimmed up hall and parlors and great dining-room with shining holly and evergreen, laid fires ready for kindling on the hearths that had been cold for years, and had beds made up all over the house.

What went on in the kitchen, only Dolly could tell; but such delicious odors as stole out made grandma sniff the air, and think of merry Christmas revels long ago. Up in her own room Kate wrote lots of letters, and sent orders to the city that made Nursey hold up her hands. More letters came in reply, and Kate had a rapture over every one. Big bundles were left by the express, who came so often that the gates were opened and the lawn soon full of sleigh-tracks. The shops in the village were ravaged by Mistress Kate, who laid in stores of gay ribbon, toys, nuts, and all manner of queer things.

"I really think she's lost her mind," said the postmaster as she flew out of the office one day with a handful of letters.

"Pretty creter! I wouldn't say a word against her, not for a mint of money. She's so good to old Mrs. Coverley," answered his fat wife, smiling as she watched Kate ride up the village street on an ox-sled.

If grandma had thought the girl out of her wits, no one could have blamed her, for on Christmas day she really did behave in the most singular manner.

"You are going to church with me this morning, grandma. It's all arranged. A close carriage is coming for us, the sleighing is lovely, the church all trimmed up, and I must have you see it. I shall wrap you in fur, and we will go and say our prayers together, like good girls, won't we?" said Kate, who was in a queer flutter, while her eyes shone, her lips were all smiles, and her feet kept dancing in spite of her.

"Anywhere you like, my darling. I'd start for Australia tomorrow, if you wanted me to go with you," answered grandma, who obeyed Kate in all things, and seemed to think she could do no wrong.

So they went to church, and grandma did enjoy it; for she had many blessings to thank God for, chief among them the treasure of a dutiful, loving child. Kate tried to keep herself quiet, but the odd little flutter would not subside, and seemed to get worse and worse as time went on. It increased rapidly as they drove home, and, when grandma was safe in her little parlor again, Kate's hands trembled so she could hardly tie the strings of the old lady's state and festival cap.

"We must take a look at the big parlor. It is all trimmed up, and I've got my presents in there. Is it ready, Doll?" asked Kate, as the old servant appeared, looking so excited that grandma said, laughing,—

"We have been quiet so long, poor Dolly don't know what to make of a little gayety."

"Lord bless us, my dear mum! It's all so beautiful and kinder surprisin', I feel as ef merrycles had come to pass agin," answered Dolly, actually wiping away tears with her best white apron.

"Come, grandma," and Kate offered her arm. "Don't she look sweet and dear?" she added, smoothing the soft, silken shawl about the old lady's shoulders, and kissing the placid old face that beamed at her from under the new cap.

"I always said madam was the finest old lady a-goin', ef folks only knew it. Now, Missy, ef you don't make haste, that parlor-door will bust open, and spoil the surprise; for they are just bilin' over in there," with which mysterious remark Dolly vanished, giggling.

Across the hall they went, but at the door Kate paused, and said with a look grandma never forgot,—

"I hope I have done right. I hope you'll like my present, and not find it too much for you. At any rate, remember I meant to please you and give you the thing you need and long for most, my dear old grandma."

"My good child, don't be afraid. I shall like any thing you do, and thank you for your thought of me. What a curious noise! I hope the fire hasn't fallen down."

Without another word, Kate threw open the door and led grandma in. Only a step or two—for the old lady stopped short and stared about her, as if she didn't know her own best parlor. No wonder she didn't, for it was full of people, and such people! All her sons, their wives and children, rose as she came in, and turned to greet her with smiling faces. Uncle George went up and kissed her, saying, with a choke in his voice, "A merry Christmas, mother!" and everybody echoed the words in a chorus of good-will that went straight to the heart.

Poor grandma could not bear it, and sat down in her big chair, trembling, and sobbing like a little child. Kate hung over her, fearing the surprise had been too much; but joy seldom kills, and presently the old lady was calm enough to look up and welcome them all by stretching out her feeble hands and saying, brokenly yet heartily,—

"God bless you, my children! This *is* a merry Christmas, indeed! Now tell me all about it, and who everybody is; for I don't know half the little ones."

Then Uncle George explained that it was Kate's plan, and told how she had made every one agree to it, pleading so eloquently for grandma that all other plans were given up. They had arrived while she was at church, and had been with difficulty kept from bursting out before the time.

"Do you like your present?" whispered Kate, quite calm and happy now that the grand surprise was safely over.

Grandma answered with a silent kiss that said more than the warmest words, and then Kate put every one at ease by leading up the children, one by one, and introducing each with some lively speech. Everybody enjoyed this and got acquainted quickly; for grandma thought the children the most remarkable she had ever seen, and the little people soon made up their minds that an old lady who had such a very nice, big house, and such a dinner waiting for them (of course they had peeped everywhere), was a most desirable and charming grandma.

By the time the first raptures were over Dolly and Nurse and Betsey Jane (a girl hired for the occasion) had got dinner on the table; and the procession, headed by Madam proudly escorted by her eldest son, filed into the dining-room where such a party had not met for years.

It would be quite impossible to do justice to that dinner: pen and ink are not equal to it. I can only say that every one partook copiously of every thing; that they laughed and talked, told stories, and sang songs; and when no one could do any more, Uncle George proposed grandma's health, which was drunk standing, and followed by three cheers. Then up got the old lady, quite rosy and young, excited and gay, and said in a clear strong voice,—

"I give you in return the best of grandchildren, little Kate."

I give you my word the cheer they gave grandma was nothing to the shout that followed these words; for the old lady led off with amazing vigor, and the boys roared so tremendously that the sedate tabby in the kitchen flew off her cushion, nearly frightened into a fit.

After that, the elders sat with grandma in the parlor, while the younger part of the flock trooped after Kate all over the house. Fires burned everywhere, and the long unused toys of their fathers were brought out for their amusement. The big nursery was full of games, and here Nursey collected the little ones when the larger boys and girls were invited by Kate to go out and coast. Sleds had been provided, and until dusk they kept it up, the city girls getting as gay and rosy as Kate herself in this healthy sport, while the lads frolicked to their hearts' content, building snow forts, pelting one another, and carousing generally without any policeman to interfere or any stupid old ladies to get upset, as at home in the park.

A cosey tea and a dance in the long hall followed, and they were just thinking what they would do next when Kate's second surprise came.

There were two great fireplaces in the hall: up the chimney of one roared a jolly fire, but the other was closed by a tall fire-board. As they sat about, resting after a brisk contra dance, a queer rustling and tapping was heard behind this fire-board.

"Rats!" suggested the girls, jumping up into the chairs.

"Let's have 'em out!" added the boys, making straight for the spot, intent on fun.

But before they got there, a muffled voice cried, "Stand from under!" and down went the board with a crash, out bounced Santa Claus, startling the lads as much as the rumor of rats had the girls.

A jolly old saint he was, all in fur, with sleigh-bells jingling from his waist and the point of his high cap, big boots, a white beard, and a nose as red as if Jack Frost had had a good tweak at it. Giving himself a shake that set all the bells ringing, he stepped out upon the hearth, saying in a half-gruff, half-merry tone,—

"I call this a most inhospitable way to receive me! What do you mean by stopping up my favorite chimney? Never mind, I'll forgive you, for this is an unusual occasion. Here, some of you fellows, lend a hand and help me out with my sack."

A dozen pair of hands had the great bag out in a minute, and, lugging it to the middle of the hall, left it beside St. Nick, while the boys fell back into the eager, laughing crowd that surrounded the newcomer.

"Where's my girl? I want my Kate," said the saint, and when she went to him he took a base advantage of his years, and kissed her in spite of the beard.

"That's not fair," whispered Kate, as rosy as the holly-berries in her hair.

"Can't help it,—must have some reward for sticking in that horrid chimney so long," answered Santa Claus, looking as roguish as any boy. Then he added aloud, "I've got something for everybody, so make a big ring, and the good fairy will hand round the gifts."

With that he dived into his bag and brought out treasure after treasure, some fine, some funny, many useful, and all appropri-ate, for the good fairy seemed to have guessed what each one wanted. Shouts of laughter greeted the droll remarks of the jolly saint, for he had a joke about every thing, and people were quite exhausted by the time the bottom of the sack was reached.

"Now, then, a rousing good game of blind man's buff, and then this little family must go to bed, for it's past eleven."

As he spoke, the saint cast off his cap and beard, fur coat, and big boots, and proceeded to dance a double shuffle with great vigor and skill; while the little ones, who had been thoroughly mystified, shouted, "Why, it's Alf!" and fell upon him *en masse* as the best way of expressing their delight at his successful performance of that immortal part.

The game of blind man's buff that followed was a "rouser" in every sense of the word, for the gentlemen joined, and the children flew about like a flock of chickens when hawks are abroad. Such peals of laughter, such shouts of fun, and such racing and scrambling that old hall had never seen before. Kate was so hunted that she finally took refuge behind grandma's chair, and stood there looking at the lively scene, her face full of happiness as she remembered that it was her work.

The going to bed that night was the best joke of all; for, though Kate's arrangements were peculiar, every one voted that they were capital. There were many rooms, but not enough for all to have one apiece. So the uncles and aunts had the four big chambers, all the boys were ordered into the great playroom, where beds were made on the floor, and a great fire blazing that the camping out might be as comfortable as possible. The nursery was devoted to the girls, and the little ones were sprinkled round wherever a snug corner was found.

How the riotous flock were ever got into their beds no one knows. The lads caroused until long past midnight, and no knocking on the walls of paternal boots, or whispered entreaties of maternal voices through key-holes, had any effect, for it was impossible to resist the present advantages for a grand Christmas rampage.

The girls giggled and gossiped, told secrets, and laid plans more quietly; while the small things tumbled into bed, and went to sleep at once, quite used up with the festivities of this remarkable day.

Grandma, down in her own cosey room, sat listening to the blithe noises with a smile on her face, for the past seemed to

have come back again, and her own boys and girls to be frolicking above there, as they used to do forty years ago.

"It's all so beautiful I can't go to bed, Dolly, and lose any of
it. They'll go away to-morrow, and I may never see them any
more," she said, as Dolly tied on her night-cap and brought
her slippers.

"Yes, you will, mum. That dear child has made it so pleasant
they can't keep away. You'll see plenty of 'em, if they carry out
half the plans they have made. Mrs. George wants to come up
and pass the summer here; Mr. Tom says he shall send his boys
to school here, and every girl among them has promised Kate
to make her a long visit. The thing is done, mum, and you'll
never be lonely any more."

"Thank God for that!" and grandma bent her head as if she
had received a great blessing. "Dolly, I want to go and look at
those children. It seems so like a dream to have them here, I
must be sure of it," said grandma, folding her wrapper about
her, and getting up with great decision.

"Massy on us, mum, you haven't been up them stairs for
months. The dears are all right, warm as toasts, and sleepin'
like dormice, I'll warrant," answered Dolly, taken aback at this
new whim of old madam's.

But grandma would go, so Dolly gave her an arm, and together the two old friends hobbled up the wide stairs, and
peeped in at the precious children. The lads looked like a camp
of weary warriors reposing after a victory, and grandma went
laughing away when she had taken a proud survey of this
promising portion of the rising generation. The nursery was
like a little convent full of rosy nuns sleeping peacefully; while
a pictured Saint Agnes, with her lamb, smiled on them from
the wall, and the firelight flickered over the white figures and
sweet faces, as if the sight were too fair to be lost in darkness.
The little ones lay about promiscuously, looking like dissipated
Cupids with sugar hearts and faded roses still clutched in their
chubby hands.

"My darlings!" whispered grandma, lingering fondly over
them to cover a pair of rosy feet, put back a pile of tumbled
curls, or kiss a little mouth still smiling in its sleep.

But when she came to the coldest corner of the room, where
Kate lay on the hardest mattress, under the thinnest quilt, the

old lady's eyes were full of tender tears; and, forgetting the stiff joints that bent so painfully, she knelt slowly down, and, putting her arms about the girl, blessed her in silence for the happiness she had given one old heart.

Kate woke at once, and started up, exclaiming with a smile,—

"Why, grandma, I was dreaming about an angel, and you look like one with your white gown and silvery hair!"

"No, dear, you are the angel in this house. How can I ever give you up?" answered madam, holding fast the treasure that came to her so late.

"You never need to, grandma, for I have made my choice."

*May 18 and 25, 1872*

# How I Went Out to Service

WHEN I was eighteen I wanted something to do. I had tried teaching for two years, and hated it; I had tried sewing, and could not earn my bread in that way, at the cost of health; I tried story-writing and got five dollars for stories which now bring a hundred; I had thought seriously of going upon the stage, but certain highly respectable relatives were so shocked at the mere idea that I relinquished my dramatic aspirations.

"What *shall* I do?" was still the question that perplexed me. I was ready to work, eager to be independent, and too proud to endure patronage. But the right task seemed hard to find, and my bottled energies were fermenting in a way that threatened an explosion before long.

My honored mother was a city missionary that winter, and not only served the clamorous poor, but often found it in her power to help decayed gentlefolk by quietly placing them where they could earn their bread without the entire sacrifice of taste and talent which makes poverty so hard for such to bear. Knowing her tact and skill, people often came to her for companions, housekeepers, and that class of the needy who do not make their wants known through an intelligence office.

One day, as I sat dreaming splendid dreams, while I made a series of little petticoats out of the odds and ends sent in for the poor, a tall, ministerial gentleman appeared, in search of a companion for his sister. He possessed an impressive nose, a fine flow of language, and a pair of large hands, encased in black kid gloves. With much waving of these somber members, Mr. R. set forth the delights awaiting the happy soul who should secure this home. He described it as a sort of heaven on earth. "There are books, pictures, flowers, a piano, and the best of society," he said. "This person will be one of the family in all respects, and only required to help about the lighter work, which my sister has done herself hitherto, but is now a martyr to neuralgia and needs a gentle hand to assist her."

My mother, who never lost her faith in human nature, spite of many impostures, believed every word, and quite beamed with benevolent interest as she listened and tried to recall some needy young woman to whom this charming home would be a blessing. I also innocently thought:

"That sounds inviting. I like housework and can do it well. I should have time to enjoy the books and things I love, and D—— is not far away from home. Suppose I try it."

So, when my mother turned to me, asking if I could suggest any one, I became as red as a poppy and said abruptly:

"Only myself."

"Do you really mean it?" cried my astonished parent.

"I really do if Mr. R. thinks I should suit," was my steady reply, as I partially obscured my crimson countenance behind a little flannel skirt, still redder.

The Reverend Josephus gazed upon me with the benign regard which a bachelor of five and thirty may accord a bashful damsel of eighteen. A smile dawned upon his countenance, "sicklied o'er with the pale cast of thought," or dyspepsia; and he softly folded the black gloves, as if about to bestow a blessing, as he replied, with emphasis:

"I am sure you would, and we should think ourselves most fortunate if we could secure your society, and—ahem—services for my poor sister."

"Then I'll try it," responded the impetuous maid.

"We will talk it over a little first, and let you know to-morrow, sir," put in my prudent parent, adding, as Mr. R—— arose: "What wages do you pay?"

"My dear madam, in a case like this let us not use such words as those. Anything you may think proper we shall gladly give. The labor is very light, for there are but three of us and our habits are of the simplest sort. I am a frail reed and may break at any moment; so is my sister, and my aged father cannot long remain; therefore, money is little to us, and any one who comes to lend her youth and strength to our feeble household will not be forgotten in the end, I assure you." And, with another pensive smile, a farewell wave of the impressive gloves, the Reverend Josephus bowed like a well-sweep and departed.

"My dear, are you in earnest?" asked my mother.

"Of course, I am. Why not try this experiment? It can but fail, like all the others."

"I have no objection; only I fancied you were rather too proud for this sort of thing."

"I am too proud to be idle and dependent, ma'am. I'll scrub floors and take in washing first. I do housework at home for love; why not do it abroad for money? I like it better than teaching. It is healthier than sewing and surer than writing. So why not try it?"

"It is going out to service, you know, though you are called a companion. How does that suit?"

"I don't care. Every sort of work that is paid for is service; and I don't mind being a companion, if I can do it well. I may find it is my mission to take care of neuralgic old ladies and lackadaisical clergymen. It does not sound exciting, but it's better than nothing," I answered, with a sigh; for it *was* rather a sudden downfall to give up being a Siddons and become a Betcinder.

How my sisters laughed when they heard the new plan! But they soon resigned themselves, sure of fun, for Lu's adventures were the standing joke of the family. Of course, the highly respectable relatives held up their hands in holy horror at the idea of one of the clan degrading herself by going out to service. Teaching a private school was the proper thing for an indigent gentlewoman. Sewing even, if done in the seclusion of home and not mentioned in public, could be tolerated. Story-writing was a genteel accomplishment and reflected credit upon the name. But leaving the paternal roof to wash other people's teacups, nurse other people's ails, and obey other people's orders for hire—this, this was degradation; and headstrong Louisa would disgrace her name forever if she did it.

Opposition only fired the revolutionary blood in my veins, and I crowned my iniquity by the rebellious declaration:

"If doing this work hurts my respectability, I wouldn't give much for it. My aristocratic ancestors don't feed or clothe me and my democratic ideas of honesty and honor won't let me be idle or dependent. You need not know me if you are ashamed of me, and I won't ask you for a penny; so, if I never do succeed in anything, I shall have the immense satisfaction of knowing I am under no obligation to any one."

In spite of the laughter and the lamentation, I got ready my small wardrobe, consisting of two calico dresses and one delaine, made by myself, also several large and uncompromising blue aprons and three tidy little sweeping-caps; for I had some English notions about housework and felt that my muslin hair-protectors would be useful in some of the "light labors" I was to undertake. It is needless to say they were very becoming. Then, firmly embracing my family, I set forth one cold January day, with my little trunk, a stout heart, and a five-dollar bill for my fortune.

"She will be back in a week," was my sister's prophecy, as she wiped her weeping eye.

"No, she won't, for she has promised to stay the month out and she will keep her word," answered my mother, who always defended the black sheep of her flock.

I heard both speeches, and registered a tremendous vow to keep that promise, if I died in the attempt—little dreaming, poor innocent, what lay before me.

Josephus meantime had written me several remarkable letters, describing the different members of the family I was about to enter. His account was peculiar; but I believed every word of it and my romantic fancy was much excited by the details he gave. The principal ones are as follows, condensed from the voluminous epistles which he evidently enjoyed writing:

"You will find a stately mansion, fast falling to decay, for my father will have nothing repaired, preferring that the old house and its master should crumble away together. I have, however, been permitted to rescue a few rooms from ruin; and here I pass my recluse life, surrounded by the things I love. This will naturally be more attractive to you than the gloomy apartments my father inhabits, and I hope you will here allow me to minister to your young and cheerful nature when your daily cares are over. I need such companionship and shall always welcome you to my abode.

"Eliza, my sister, is a child at forty, for she has lived alone with my father and an old servant all her life. She is a good creature, but not lively, and needs stirring up, as you will soon see. Also I hope by your means to rescue her from the evil influence of Puah, who, in my estimation, is a *wretch*. She has gained entire control over Eliza, and warps her mind with great skill, prejudicing her against *me*, and thereby desolating my home. Puah hates *me* and always has. Why I know not, except that I will not yield to her control. She ruled here for years while I was away, and my return upset all her nefarious plans. It will always be my firm opinion that she has tried to *poison me*, and may again. But even this dark suspicion will not deter me from my duty. I cannot send her away, for both my deluded father and my sister have entire faith in her, and I cannot shake it. She is faithful and kind to them, so I submit and remain to guard them, even at the risk of my life.

"I tell you these things because I wish you to know all and be warned, for this old hag has a specious tongue, and I should grieve to see you deceived by her lies. Say nothing, but watch her silently, and help me to thwart her evil plots; but do not trust her, or beware."

Now this was altogether romantic and sensational, and I felt as if about to enter one of those delightfully dangerous houses we read of in novels, where perils, mysteries, and sins freely disport themselves, till the newcomer sets all to rights, after unheard of trials and escapes.

I arrived at twilight, just the proper time for the heroine to appear; and, as no one answered my modest solo on the rusty knocker, I walked in and looked about me. Yes, here was the long, shadowy hall, where the ghosts doubtless walked at midnight. Peering in at an open door on the right, I saw a parlor full of ancient furniture, faded, dusty, and dilapidated. Old portraits stared at me from the walls and a damp chill froze the marrow of my bones in the most approved style.

"The romance opens well," I thought, and, peeping in at an opposite door, beheld a luxurious apartment, full of the warm glow of firelight, the balmy breath of hyacinths and roses, the white glimmer of piano keys, and tempting rows of books along the walls.

The contrast between the two rooms was striking, and, after an admiring survey, I continued my explorations, thinking that I should not mind being "ministered to" in that inviting place when my work was done.

A third door showed me a plain, dull sitting-room, with an old man napping in his easy-chair. I heard voices in the kitchen beyond, and, entering there, beheld Puah the fiend. Unfortunately for the dramatic effect of the tableaux, all I saw was a mild-faced old woman, buttering toast, while she conversed with her familiar, a comfortable gray cat.

The old lady greeted me kindly, but I fancied her faded blue eye had a weird expression and her amiable words were all a snare, though I own I was rather disappointed at the commonplace appearance of this humble Borgia.

She showed me to a tiny room, where I felt more like a young giantess than ever, and was obliged to stow away my possessions as snugly as in a ship's cabin. When I presently descended, armed with a blue apron and "a heart for any fate," I found the old man awake and received from him a welcome full of ancient courtesy and kindliness. Miss Eliza crept in like a timid mouse, looking so afraid of her buxom companion that I forgot my own shyness in trying to relieve hers. She was so enveloped in shawls that all I could discover was that my mistress was a very nervous little woman, with a small button of pale hair on the outside of her head and the vaguest notions of work inside. A few spasmodic remarks and many awkward pauses brought us to teatime, when Josephus appeared, as tall, thin, and cadaverous as ever. After his arrival there was no more silence, for he preached all suppertime something in this agreeable style.

"My young friend, our habits, as you see, are of the simplest. We eat in the kitchen, and all together, in the primitive fashion; for it suits my father and saves labor. I could wish more order and elegance; but *my* wishes are not consulted and I submit. I live above these petty crosses, and, though my health suffers from bad cookery, I do not murmur. Only, I must say, in passing, that if you *will* make your battercakes green with saleratus, Puah, I shall feel it my duty to throw them out of the window. *I* am used to poison; but I cannot see the coats of this blooming girl's stomach destroyed, as mine have been. And, speaking of duties, I may as well mention to you, Louisa (I call you so in a truly fraternal spirit), that I like to find my study in order when I come down in the morning; for I often need a few moments of solitude before I face the daily annoyances of my life. I shall permit *you* to perform this light task, for *you* have some idea of order (I see it in the formation of your brow), and feel sure that *you* will respect the sanctuary of thought. Eliza is so blind she does not see dust, and Puah enjoys devastating the one poor refuge I can call my own this side the grave. We are all waiting for you, sir. My father keeps up the old formalities, you observe; and I endure them, though *my* views are more advanced."

The old gentleman hastily finished his tea and returned thanks, when his son stalked gloomily away, evidently oppressed with the burden of his wrongs, also, as I irreverently fancied, with the seven "green" flapjacks he had devoured during the sermon.

I helped wash up the cups, and during that domestic rite Puah chatted in what I should have considered a cheery, social way had I not been darkly warned against her wiles.

"You needn't mind half Josephus says, my dear. He likes to hear himself talk and always goes on so before folks. I sometimes thinks his books and new idees have sort of muddled his wits, for he is as full of notions as a paper is of pins; and he gets dreadfully put out if we don't give in to 'em. But, gracious me! they are so redicklus sometimes and so selfish I can't allow him to make a fool of himself or plague Lizy. She don't dare to say her soul is her own; so I have to stand up for her. His pa don't know half his odd doings; for I try to keep the old gentleman comfortable and have to manage 'em all, which is not an easy job, I do assure you."

I had a secret conviction that she was right, but did not commit myself in any way, and we joined the social circle in the sitting-room. The prospect was not a lively one, for the old gentleman nodded behind his newspaper; Eliza, with her head pinned up in a little blanket, slumbered on the sofa, Puah fell to knitting silently; and the plump cat dozed under the stove. Josephus was visible, artistically posed in the luxurious recesses of his cell, with the light beaming on his thoughtful brow, as he pored over a large volume or mused with upturned eye.

Having nothing else to do, I sat and stared at him, till, emerging from a deep reverie, with an effective start, he became conscious of my existence and beckoned me to approach the "sanctuary of thought" with a melodramatic waft of his large hand.

I went, took possession of an easy-chair, and prepared myself for elegant conversation. I was disappointed, however; for Josephus showed me a list of his favorite dishes, sole fruit of all that absorbing thought, and, with an earnestness that flushed his saffron countenance, gave me hints as to the proper preparation of these delicacies.

I mildly mentioned that I was not a cook; but was effectually silenced by being reminded that I came to be generally useful, to take his sister's place, and see that the flame of life which burned so feebly in this earthly tabernacle was fed with proper fuel. Mince pies, Welsh rarebits, sausages, and strong coffee did not strike me as strictly spiritual fare; but I listened meekly and privately resolved to shift this awful responsibility to Puah's shoulders.

Detecting me in gape, after an hour of this high converse, he presented me with an overblown rose, which fell to pieces before I got out of the room, pressed my hand, and dismissed me with a fervent "God bless you, child. Don't forget the dropped eggs for breakfast."

I was up betimes next morning and had the study in perfect order before the recluse appeared, enjoying a good prowl among the books as I worked and becoming so absorbed that I forgot the eggs, till a gusty sigh startled me, and I beheld Josephus, in dressing gown and slippers, languidly surveying the scene.

"Nay, do not fly," he said, as I grasped my duster in guilty haste. "It pleases me to see you here and lends a sweet, domestic charm to my solitary room. I like that graceful cap, that housewifely apron, and I beg you will wear them often; for it refreshes my eye to see something tasteful, young, and womanly about me. Eliza makes a bundle of herself and Puah is simply detestable."

He sank languidly into a chair and closed his eyes, as if the mere thought of his enemy was too much for him. I took advantage of this momentary prostration to slip away, convulsed with laughter at the looks and words of this bald-headed sentimentalist.

After breakfast I fell to work with a will, eager to show my powers and glad to put things to rights, for many hard jobs had evidently been waiting for a stronger arm than Puah's and a more methodical head than Eliza's.

Everything was dusty, moldy, shiftless, and neglected, except the domain of Josephus. Up-stairs the paper was dropping

from the walls, the ancient furniture was all more or less dilapidated, and every hole and corner was full of relics tucked away
by Puah, who was a regular old magpie. Rats and mice reveled
in the empty rooms and spiders wove their tapestry undisturbed, for the old man would have nothing altered or repaired
and his part of the house was fast going to ruin.

I longed to have a grand "clearing up"; but was forbidden
to do more than to keep things in livable order. On the whole,
it was fortunate, for I soon found that my hands would be kept
busy with the realms of Josephus, whose ethereal being shrank
from dust, shivered at a cold breath, and needed much cosset-
ing with dainty food, hot fires, soft beds, and endless service,
else, as he expressed it, the frail reed would break.

I regret to say that a time soon came when I felt supremely
indifferent as to the breakage, and very skeptical as to the fra-
gility of a reed that ate, slept, dawdled, and scolded so energetically. The rose that fell to pieces so suddenly was a good
symbol of the rapid disappearance of all the romantic delusions
I had indulged in for a time. A week's acquaintance with the
inmates of this old house quite settled my opinion, and further
developments only confirmed it.

Miss Eliza was a nonentity and made no more impression on
me than a fly. The old gentleman passed his days in a placid
sort of doze and took no notice of what went on about him.
Puah had been a faithful drudge for years, and, instead of
being a "wretch," was, as I soon satisfied myself, a motherly
old soul, with no malice in her. The secret of Josephus's dislike
was that the reverend tyrant ruled the house, and all obeyed
him but Puah, who had nursed him as a baby, boxed his ears as
a boy, and was not afraid of him even when he became a man
and a minister. I soon repented of my first suspicions, and grew
fond of her, for without my old gossip I should have fared ill
when my day of tribulation came.

At first I innocently accepted the fraternal invitations to visit
the study, feeling that when my day's work was done I earned
a right to rest and read. But I soon found that this was not the
idea. I was not to read; but to be read to. I was not to enjoy
the flowers, pictures, fire, and books; but to keep them in
order for my lord to enjoy. I was also to be a passive bucket,
into which he was to pour all manner of philosophic, meta-

physical, and sentimental rubbish. I was to serve his needs, soothe his sufferings, and sympathize with all his sorrows—be a galley slave, in fact.

As soon as I clearly understood this, I tried to put an end to it by shunning the study and never lingering there an instant after my work was done. But it availed little, for Josephus demanded much sympathy and was bound to have it. So he came and read poems while I washed dishes, discussed his pet problems all meal-times, and put reproachful notes under my door, in which were comically mingled complaints of neglect and orders for dinner.

I bore it as long as I could, and then freed my mind in a declaration of independence, delivered in the kitchen, where he found me scrubbing the hearth. It was not an impressive attitude for an orator, nor was the occupation one a girl would choose when receiving calls; but I have always felt grateful for the intense discomfort of that moment, since it gave me courage to rebel outright. Stranded on a small island of mat, in a sea of soapsuds, I brandished a scrubbing brush, as I indignantly informed him that I came to be a companion to his sister, not to him, and I should keep that post or none. This I followed up by reproaching him with the delusive reports he had given me of the place and its duties, and assuring him that I should not stay long unless matters mended.

"But I offer you lighter tasks, and you refuse them," he begun, still hovering in the doorway, whither he had hastily retired when I opened my batteries.

"But I don't like the tasks, and consider them much worse than hard work," was my ungrateful answer, as I sat upon my island, with the softsoap conveniently near.

"Do you mean to say you prefer to scrub that hearth to sitting in my charming room while I read Hegel to you?" he demanded, glaring down upon me.

"Infinitely," I responded promptly, and emphasized my words by beginning to scrub with a zeal that made the bricks white with foam.

"Is it possible!" and, with a groan at my depravity, Josephus retired, full of ungodly wrath.

I remember that I immediately burst into jocund song, so that no doubt might remain in his mind, and continued to warble cheerfully till my task was done. I also remember that I cried heartily when I got to my room, I was so vexed, disappointed, and tired. But my bower was so small I should soon have swamped the furniture if I had indulged copiously in tears; therefore I speedily dried them up, wrote a comic letter home, and waited with interest to see what would happen next.

Far be it from me to accuse one of the nobler sex of spite or the small revenge of underhand annoyances and slights to one who could not escape and would not retaliate; but after that day a curious change came over the spirit of that very unpleasant dream. Gradually all the work of the house had been slipping into my hands; for Eliza was too poorly to help or direct, and Puah too old to do much besides the cooking. About this time I found that even the roughest work was added to my share, for Josephus was unusually feeble and no one was hired to do his chores. Having made up my mind to go when the month was out, I said nothing, but dug paths, brought water from the well, split kindlings, made fires, and sifted ashes, like a true Cinderella.

There never had been any pretense of companionship with Eliza, who spent her days mulling over the fire, and seldom exerted herself except to find odd jobs for me to do—rusty knives to clean, sheets to turn, old stockings to mend, and, when all else failed, some paradise of moths and mice to be cleared up; for the house was full of such "glory holes."

If I remonstrated, Eliza at once dissolved into tears and said she must do as she was told; Puah begged me to hold on till spring, when things would be much better; and pity pleaded for the two poor souls. But I don't think I could have stood it if my promise had not bound me, for when the fiend said "Budge" honor said "Budge not," and I stayed.

But, being a mortal worm, I turned now and then when the ireful Josephus trod upon me too hard, especially in the matter of boot-blacking. I really don't know why that is considered such humiliating work for a woman; but so it is, and there I drew the line. I would have cleaned the old man's shoes without a murmur; but he preferred to keep their native rustiness intact. Eliza never went out, and Puah affected carpet-slippers of the Chinese-junk pattern. Josephus, however, plumed himself upon his feet, which, like his nose, were large, and never took his walks abroad without having his boots in a high state of polish. He had brushed them himself at first; but soon after the explosion I discovered a pair of muddy boots in the shed, set suggestively near the blacking-box. I did not take the hint, feeling instinctively that this amiable being was trying how much I would bear for the sake of peace.

The boots remained untouched; and another pair soon came to keep them company, whereat I smiled wickedly as I chopped just kindlings enough for my own use. Day after day the collection grew, and neither party gave in. Boots were succeeded by shoes, then rubbers gave a pleasing variety to the long line, and then I knew the end was near.

"Why are not my boots attended to?" demanded Josephus, one evening, when obliged to go out.

"I'm sure I don't know," was Eliza's helpless answer.

"I told Louizy I guessed you'd want some of 'em before long," observed Puah, with an exasperating twinkle in her old eye.

"And what did she say?" asked my lord with an ireful whack of his velvet slippers as he cast them down.

"Oh! she said she was so busy doing your other work you'd have to do that yourself; and I thought she was about right."

"Louizy" heard it all through the slide, and could have embraced the old woman for her words, but kept still till Josephus had resumed his slippers with a growl and retired to the shed, leaving Eliza in tears, Puah chuckling, and the rebellious handmaid exulting in the china-closet.

Alas! for romance and the Christian virtues, several pairs of boots were cleaned that night, and my sinful soul enjoyed the spectacle of the reverend bootblack at his task. I even found my "fancy work," as I called the evening job of paring a bucketful of hard russets with a dull knife, much cheered by the shoe-brush accompaniment played in the shed.

Thunder-clouds rested upon the martyr's brow at breakfast, and I was as much ignored as the cat. And what a relief that was! The piano was locked up, so were the bookcases, the newspapers mysteriously disappeared, and a solemn silence reigned at table, for no one dared to talk when that gifted tongue was mute. Eliza fled from the gathering storm and had a comfortable fit of neuralgia in her own room, where Puah nursed her, leaving me to skirmish with the enemy.

It was not a fair fight, and that experience lessened my respect for mankind immensely. I did my best, however—grubbed about all day and amused my dreary evenings as well as I could; too proud even to borrow a book, lest it should seem like a surrender. What a long month it was, and how eagerly I counted the hours of that last week, for my time was up Saturday, and I hoped to be off at once. But when I announced my intention such dismay fell upon Eliza that my heart was touched, and Puah so urgently begged me to stay till they could get some one that I consented to remain a few days longer, and wrote posthaste to my mother, telling her to send a substitute quickly or I should do something desperate.

That blessed woman, little dreaming of all the woes I had endured, advised me to be patient, to do the generous thing, and be sure I should not regret it in the end. I groaned, submitted, and did regret it all the days of my life.

Three mortal weeks I waited; for, though two other victims came, I was implored to set them going, and tried to do it. But both fled after a day or two, condemning the place as a very hard one and calling me a fool to stand it another hour. I entirely agreed with them on both points, and, when I had cleared up after the second incapable lady, I tarried not for the coming of a third, but clutched my property and announced my departure by the next train.

Of course, Eliza wept, Puah moaned, the old man politely regretted, and the younger one washed his hands of the whole affair by shutting himself up in his room and forbidding me to say farewell because he "could not bear it." I laughed, and fancied it done for effect then; but I soon understood it better and did not laugh.

At the last moment, Eliza nervously tucked a sixpenny pocketbook into my hand and shrouded herself in the little blanket with a sob. But Puah kissed me kindly and whispered, with an odd look: "Don't blame us for anything. Some folks is liberal and some ain't." I thanked the poor old soul for her kindness to me and trudged gayly away to the station, whither my property had preceded me on a wheelbarrow, hired at my own expense.

I never shall forget that day. A bleak March afternoon, a sloppy, lonely road, and one hoarse crow stalking about a field, so like Josephus that I could not resist throwing a snowball at him. Behind me stood the dull old house, no longer either mysterious or romantic in my disenchanted eyes; before me rumbled the barrow, bearing my dilapidated wardrobe; and in my pocket reposed what I fondly hoped was, if not a liberal, at least an honest return for seven weeks of the hardest work I ever did.

Unable to resist the desire to see what my earnings were, I opened the purse and beheld *four dollars.*

I have had a good many bitter minutes in my life; but one of the bitterest came to me as I stood there in the windy road, with the sixpenny pocket-book open before me, and looked from my poor chapped, grimy, chill-blained hands to the paltry sum that was considered reward enough for all the hard and humble labor they had done.

A girl's heart is a sensitive thing. And mine had been very full lately; for it had suffered many of the trials that wound deeply yet cannot be told; so I think it was but natural that my first impulse was to go straight back to that sacred study and fling this insulting money at the feet of him who sent it. But I was so boiling over with indignation that I could not trust myself in his presence, lest I should be unable to resist the temptation to shake him, in spite of his cloth.

No, I would go home, show my honorable wounds, tell my pathetic tale, and leave my parents to avenge my wrongs. I did so; but over that harrowing scene I drop a veil, for my feeble pen refuses to depict the emotions of my outraged family. I will merely mention that the four dollars went back and the reverend Josephus never heard the last of it in that neighborhood.

My experiment seemed a dire failure and I mourned it as such for years; but more than once in my life I have been grateful for that serio-comico experience, since it has taught me many lessons. One of the most useful of these has been the power of successfully making a companion, not a servant, of those whose aid I need, and helping to gild their honest wages with the sympathy and justice which can sweeten the humblest and lighten the hardest task.

*June 4, 1874*

# Woman's Part in the Concord Celebration

B EING frequently asked "what part the women took in the Concord Centennial celebration?" I give herewith a brief account of our share on that occasion.

Having set our houses in order, stored our larders, and filled our rooms with guests, we girded up our weary souls and bodies for the great day, feeling that we must do or die for the honor of old Concord.

We had no place in the procession, but such women as wished to hear the oration were directed to meet in the town hall at half past nine, and there wait till certain persons, detailed for the service, should come to lead them to the tent, where a limited number of seats had been provided for the weaker vessels.

This seemed a sensible plan, and as a large proportion of ladies chose the intellectual part of the feast the hall was filled with a goodly crowd at the appointed hour. No one seemed to know what to do except wait, and that we did with the patience born of long practice. But it was very trying to the women of Concord to see invited guests wandering forlornly about or sitting in chilly corners meekly wondering why the hospitalities of the town were not extended to them as well as to their "men folks" who were absorbed into the pageant in one way or another.

For an hour we women waited, but no one came, and the sound of martial music so excited the patient party that with one accord we moved down to the steps below, where a glimpse of the approaching procession might cheer our eyes. Here we stood with the north wind chilling us to the marrow of our bones, a flock of feminine Casabiancas with the slight difference of freezing instead of burning at our posts.

Some wise virgins, who put not their trust in men, departed to shift for themselves, but fifty or more obeyed orders and stood fast till, just as the procession appeared, an agitated gentleman with a rosette at his buttonhole gave the brief command,

"Ladies cross the common and wait for your escort:"

Then he vanished and was seen no more.

Over we went, like a flock of sheep, leaving the show behind us, but comforting ourselves with the thought of the seats "saving up" for us and of the treat to come. A cheerful crowd, in spite of the bitter wind, the rude comments of the men swarming by, and the sad certainty which slowly dawned upon us that we were entirely forgotten. The gay and gallant presence of a granddaughter of the Dr. Ripley who watched the fight from the old Manse, kept up our spirits; for this indomitable lady circulated among us like sunshine, inspiring us with such confidence that we rallied round the little flag she bore, and followed where it led.

Patience has its limits, and there came a moment when the revolutionary spirit of '76 blazed up in the bosoms of these long suffering women; for, when some impetuous soul cried out "Come on and let us take care of ourselves!" there was a general movement; the flag fluttered to the front, veils were close reefed, skirts kilted up, arms locked, and with one accord the Light Brigade charged over the red bridge, up the hill, into the tented field, rosy and red-nosed, disheveled but dauntless.

The tent was closely packed, and no place appeared but a corner of the platform. Anxious to seat certain grey-haired ladies weary with long waiting, and emboldened by a smile from Senator Wilson, a nod from Representative May, and a pensive stare from Orator Curtis, I asked the President of the day if a few ladies could occupy that corner till seats could be found for them?

"They can sit or stand anywhere in the town except on this platform; and the quicker they get down the better, for gentlemen are coming in to take these places."

This gracious reply made me very glad to descend into the crowd again, for there at least good-nature reigned; and there we stood, placidly surveyed by the men (who occupied the seats set apart for us,) not one of whom stirred, though the grandmother of Boston waited in the ranks.

My idea of hospitality may be old-fashioned, but I must say I felt ashamed of Concord that day, when all I could offer my guests, admiring pilgrims to this "Mecca of the mind," was the extreme edge of an unplaned board; for, when the gods were settled, leave was given us to sit on the rim of the platform.

Perched there, like a flock of tempest tossed pigeons, we had the privilege of reposing among the sacred boots of the Gamaliels at whose feet we sat, and of listening to the remarks of the reporters, who evidently felt that the elbow room of the almighty press should not be encroached upon even by a hair's breadth.

"No place for women," growled one.

"Never was a fitter," answered a strong-minded lady standing on one foot.

"Ought to have come earlier, if they come at all."

"So they would, if they had not obeyed orders. Never will again."

"Don't see why they couldn't be contented with seeing the procession."

"Because they preferred poetry and patriotism to fuss and feathers."

"Better have it all their own way next time."

"No doubt they will, and I hope we shall all be there to see."

So the dialogue ended in a laugh, and the women resigned themselves to cold shoulders all round. But as I looked about me, it was impossible to help thinking that there should have been a place for the great granddaughters of Prescott, William Emerson, John Hancock and Dr. Ripley, as well as for Isaac Davis's old sword, the scissors that cut the immortal cartridges, and the ancient flag some woman's fingers made. It seemed to me that their presence on that platform would have had a deeper significance than the gold lace which adorned one side, or the senatorial ponderosity under which it broke down on the other; and that the men of Concord had missed a grand opportunity of imitating those whose memory they had met to honor.

The papers have told the tale of that day's exploits and experiences, but the papers did not get all the little items, and some of them were rather funny. Just before the services began, a distracted usher struggled in to inform Judge Hoar that the wives of several potentates had been left out in the cold, and must be accommodated. Great was the commotion then, for these ladies being bobs to political kites, could not be neglected; so a part of the seats reserved for women were with much difficulty cleared, and the "elect precious" set thereon.

Dear ladies! how very cold and wretched they were when they got there, and how willingly the "free and independent citizenesses" of Concord forgave them for reducing their limited quarters to the point of suffocation, as they spread their cloaks over the velvet of their guests, still trying to be hospitable under difficulties.

When order was restored, what might be called "the Centennial Break Down" began. The President went first—was it an omen? and took refuge among the women, who I am happy to say received him kindly and tried to temper the wind to His Imperturbability, as he sat among them looking so bored that I longed to offer him a cigar.

The other gentleman stood by the ship, which greatly diversified the performances by slowly sinking with all on board but the captain. Even the orator tottered on the brink of ruin more than once, and his table would have gone over if a woman had not held up one leg of it for an hour or so. No light task, she told me afterward, for when the inspired gentleman gave an impressive thump, it took both hands to sustain the weight of his eloquence. Another lady was pinned down by the beams falling on her skirts, but cheerfully sacrificed them, and sat still, till the departure of the presidential party allowed us to set her free.

Finding us bound to hear it out, several weary gentlemen offered us their seats, after a time; but we had the laugh on our side now, and sweetly declined, telling them their platform was not strong enough to hold us.

It was over at last, and such of us as had strength enough left went to the dinner, and enjoyed another dish of patriotism "cold without;" others went home to dispense hot comforts, and thaw the congealed visitors who wandered to our doors.

Then came the ball, and there all went well, for Woman was in her sphere, her "only duty was to please," and the more there were, the merrier; so the deserted damsels of the morning found themselves the queens of the evening, and, forgetting and forgiving, bore their part as gaily as if they had put on the vigor of their grandmothers with the old brocades that became them so well.

Plenty of escorts, ushers and marshals at last, and six chairs apiece if we wanted them. Gentlemen who had been as grim as griffins a few hours before were all devotion now, and spectacles that had flashed awful lightning on the women who dared prefer poetry to polkas now beamed upon us benignly, and hoped we were enjoying ourselves, as we sat nodding along the walls while our guests danced.

That was the end of it, and by four A. M., peace fell upon the exhausted town, and from many a welcome pillow went up the grateful sigh:

"Thank heaven we shall not have to go through this again!"

No, not quite the end; for by and by there will come a day of reckoning, and then the tax-paying women of Concord will not be forgotten I think, will not be left to wait uncalled upon, or be considered in the way; and *then*, I devoutly wish that those who so bravely bore their share of that day's burden without its honor, will rally round their own flag again, and, following in the footsteps of their forefathers, will utter another protest that shall be "heard round the world."

*Concord, Mass.*                    LOUISA M. ALCOTT.

*May 1, 1875*

# *Letter to the* Woman's Journal, *June 29, 1876*

---

D EAR MRS. STONE:—One should be especially inspired this Centennial year before venturing to speak or write. I am not so blest, and find myself so busy trying to get ready for the good time that is surely coming, I can only in a very humble way, help on the cause all women should have at heart.

As reports are in order, I should like to say a word for the girls, on whom in a great measure, depends the success of the next generation.

My lines fell in pleasant places last year, and I looked well about me as I went among the young people, who unconsciously gave me some very cheering facts in return for very poor fictions.

I was both surprised and delighted with the nerve and courage, the high aims and patient persistence, which appeared, not only among the laborious young women whose teacher is necessity, but among tenderly nurtured girls who cherished the noblest ambitions and had learned to earn the happiness no wealth could buy them.

Having great faith in young America, it gave me infinite satisfaction to find such eager interest in all good things, and to see how irresistably the spirit of our new revolution, stirring in the hearts of sisters and daughters, was converting the fathers and brothers who loved them. One shrewd, business man said, when talking of Woman Suffrage, "How *can* I help believing in it, when I've got a wife and six girls who are *bound* to have it?"

And many a grateful brother declared he could not be mean enough to shut any door in the face of the sister who had made him what he was.

So I close this hasty note by proposing three cheers for the girls of 1876—and the hope that they will prove themselves worthy descendants of the mothers of this Revolution, remembering that

> "Earth's fanatics make
> Too often Heaven's saints."

*Concord, June 29*                               L. M. ALCOTT.

# Anna's Whim

"Now just look at that!" cried a young lady, pausing suddenly in her restless march to and fro on one of the wide piazzas of a seaside hotel.

"At what?" asked her companion, lazily swinging in a hammock.

"The difference in those two greetings. It's perfectly disgraceful!" was the petulant reply.

"I didn't see any thing. Do tell me about it," said Clara, opening her drowsy eyes with sudden interest.

"Why, young Barlow was lounging up the walk, and met pretty Miss Ellery. Off went his hat; he gave her a fine bow, a gracious smile, a worn-out compliment, and then dawdled on again. The next minute Joe King came along. Instantly Barlow woke up, laughed out like a pleased boy, gave him a hearty grip of the hand, a cordial 'How are you, old fellow? I'm no end glad to see you!' and, linking arms, the two tramped off, quite beaming with satisfaction."

"But, child, King is Barlow's best friend; Kitty Ellery only an acquaintance. Besides, it wouldn't do to greet a woman like a man."

"Yes, it would, especially in this case; for Barlow adores Kate, and might, at least, treat her to something better than the nonsense he gives other girls. But, no, it's proper to simper and compliment; and he'll do it till his love gets the better of 'prunes and prisms,' and makes him sincere and earnest."

"This is a new whim of yours. You surely wouldn't like to have any man call out 'How are you, Anna?' slap you on the shoulder, and nearly shake your hand off, as Barlow did King's, just now," said Clara, laughing at her friend.

"Yes, I would," answered Anna, perversely, "if he really meant it to express affection or pleasure. A good grip of the hand and a plain, hearty word would please me infinitely better than all the servile bowing down and sweet nonsense I've had lately. I'm not a fool; then, why am I treated like one?" she continued, knitting her handsome brows and pacing to and fro like an angry leopardess. "Why don't men treat me like a reasonable being?—talk sense to me, give me their best ideas, tell me their plans and ambitions, let me enjoy the real man in them, and know what they honestly are? I don't want to be a goddess stuck up on a pedestal. I want to be a woman down among them, to help and be helped by our acquaintance."

"It wouldn't do, I fancy. They wouldn't like it, and would tell you to keep to your own sex."

"But my own sex don't interest or help me one bit. Women have no hope but to be married, and that is soon told; no ideas but dress and show, and I'm tired to death of both; no ambition but to outshine their neighbors, and I despise that."

"Thank you, love," blandly murmured Clara.

"It is true, and you know it. There *are* sensible women; but not in my set. And I don't seem to find them. I've tried the life set down for girls like me, and for three years I've lived and enjoyed it. Now I'm tired of it. I want something better, and I mean to have it. Men *will* follow, admire, flatter, and love me; for I please them and they enjoy my society. Very well. Then it's fair that I should enjoy theirs. And I should if they would let me. It's perfectly maddening to have flocks of brave, bright fellows round me, full of every thing that is attractive, strong, and helpful, yet not be able to get at it, because society ordains twaddle between us, instead of sensible conversation and sincere manners."

"What shall we do about it, love?" asked Clara, enjoying her friend's tirade.

"*You* will submit to it, and get a mental dyspepsia, like all the other fashionable girls. I won't submit, if I can help it; even if I shock Mrs. Grundy by my efforts to get plain bread and beef instead of confectionery."

Anna walked in silence for a moment, and then burst out again, more energetically than ever.

"Oh! I do wish I could find one sensible man, who would treat me as he treats his male friends,—even roughly, if he is honest and true; who would think me worthy of his confidence, ask my advice, let me give him whatever I have that is wise and excellent, and be my friend in all good faith."

"Ahem!" said Clara, with a significant laugh, that angered Anna.

"You need not try to abash me with your jeers. I know what

I mean, and I stand by my guns, in spite of your 'hems.' I do *not* want lovers. I've had dozens, and am tired of them. I will not marry till I know the man thoroughly; and how *can* I know him with this veil between us? They don't guess what I really am; and I want to prove to them and to myself that I possess brains and a heart, as well as 'heavenly eyes,' a 'queenly figure,' and a 'mouth made for kissing.'"

The scorn with which Anna uttered the last words amused her friend immensely, for the petulant beauty had never looked handsomer than at that moment.

"If any man saw you now, he'd promise whatever you ask, no matter how absurd. But don't excite yourself, dear child; it is too warm for heroics."

Anna leaned on the wide baluster a moment, looking thoughtfully out upon the sea; and as she gazed a new expression stole over her charming face, changing its disdainful warmth to soft regret.

"This is not all a whim. I know what I covet, because I had it once," she said, with a sigh. "I had a boy friend when I was a girl, and for several years we were like brother and sister. Ah! what happy times we had together, Frank and I. We played and studied, quarrelled and made up, dreamed splendid dreams, and loved one another in our simple child fashion, never thinking of sex, rivalry, or any of the forms and follies that spoil maturer friendships."

"What became of him? Did he die angelically in his early bloom, or outgrow his Platonics with round jackets?" asked Clara.

"He went to college. I went abroad, to be 'finished off;' and when we met a year ago the old charm was all gone, for we were 'in society' and had our masks on."

"So the boy and girl friendship did not ripen into love and end the romance properly?"

"No, thank Heaven! no flirtation spoilt the pretty story. Frank was too wise, and I too busy. Yet I remember how glad I was to see him; though I hid it properly, and pretended to be quite unconscious that I was any thing but a belle. I got paid for my deceit, though; for, in spite of his admiration, I saw he was disappointed in me. I should not have cared if I had been disappointed in him; but I was quick to see that he was growing into one of the strong, superior men who command respect. I wanted to keep his regard, at least; and I seemed to have nothing but beauty to give in return. I think I never was so hurt in my life as I was by his not coming to see me after a week or two, and hearing him say to a friend, one night, when I thought I was at my very best, 'She is spoilt, like all the rest.'"

"I do believe you loved him, and that is why you won't love any one else," cried Clara, who had seen her friend in her moods before; but never understood them, and thought she had found a clew now.

"No," said Anna, with a quiet shake of the head. "No, I only wanted my boy friend back, and could not find him. The fence between us was too high; and I could not climb over, as I used to do when I leaped the garden-wall to sit in a tree and help Frank with his lessons."

"Has the uncivil wretch never come back?" asked Clara, interested in the affair.

"Never. He is too busy shaping his life bravely and successfully to waste his time on a frivolous butterfly like Anna West."

An eloquent little gesture of humility made the words almost pathetic. Kind-hearted Clara was touched by the sight of tears in the "heavenly eyes," and tumbling out of the hammock she embraced the "queenly figure" and warmly pressed the "lips that were made for kissing," thereby driving several approaching gentlemen to the verge of distraction.

"Now don't be tragical, darling. You have nothing to cry for, I'm sure. Young, lovely, rich, and adored, what more *can* any girl want?" said Clara, gushingly.

"Something besides admiration to live for," answered Anna, adding, with a shrug, as she saw several hats fly off and several manly countenances beam upon her, "Never mind, my fit is over now; let us go and dress for tea."

Miss West usually took a brisk pull in her own boat before breakfast; a habit which lured many indolent young gentlemen out of their beds at unaccustomed hours, in the hope that they might have the honor of splashing their legs helping her off, the privilege of wishing her "*Bon voyage*," or the crowning rapture of accompanying her.

On the morning after her "fit," as she called the discontent of a really fine nature with the empty life she led, she was up and out unusually early; for she had kept her room with a headache all the evening, and now longed for fresh air and exercise.

As she prepared the "Gull" for a start, she was idly wondering what early bird would appear eager to secure the coveted worm, when a loud and cheerful voice was heard calling,—

"Hullo, Anna!" and a nautically attired gentleman hove in sight, waving his hat as he hailed her.

She started at the unceremonious salute and looked back. Then her whole face brightened beautifully as she sprang up the bank, saying, with a pretty mixture of hesitation and pleasure,—

"Why, Frank, is that you?"

"Do you doubt it?"

And the new-comer shook both her hands so vigorously that she winced a little as she said, laughing,—

"No, I don't. That is the old squeeze with extra power in it."

"How are you? Going for a pull? Take me along and show me the lions. There's a good soul."

"With pleasure. When did you come?" asked Anna, settling the black ribbon under the sailor collar which set off her white throat charmingly.

"Last night. I caught a glimpse of you at tea; but you were surrounded then and vanished immediately afterward. So when I saw you skipping over the rocks just now, I gave chase, and here I am. Shall I take an oar?" asked Frank, as she motioned him to get in.

"No, thank you. I prefer to row myself and don't need any help," she answered, with an imperious little wave of the hand; for she was glad to show him she could do something besides dance, dress, and flirt.

"All right. Then I'll do the luxurious and enjoy myself." And, without offering to help her in, Frank seated himself, folded his arms, stretched out his long legs, and placidly remarked,—

"Pull away, skipper."

Anna was pleased with his frank and friendly greeting, and, feeling as if old times had come again, sprang in, prepared to astonish him with her skill.

"Might I suggest that you"—began Frank, as she pushed off.

"No suggestions or advice allowed aboard this ship. I know what I'm about, though I *am* a woman," was the severe answer, as the boat glided from the wharf.

"Ay, ay, sir!" And Frank meekly subsided, with a twinkle of amusement in the eyes that rested approvingly on the slender figure in a blue boating suit and the charming face under the sailor hat.

Anna paddled her way dexterously out from among the fleet of boats riding at anchor in the little bay; then she seated herself, adjusted one oar, and looked about for the other rowlock. It was nowhere visible; and, after a silent search, she deigned to ask,—

"Have you seen the thing anywhere?"

"I saw it on the bank."

"Why didn't you tell me before?"

"I began to, but was quenched; so I obeyed orders."

"You haven't forgotten how to tease," said Anna, petulantly.

"Nor you to be wilful."

She gave him a look that would have desolated most men; but only made Frank smile affably as she paddled laboriously back, recovered the rowlock and then her temper, as, with a fine display of muscle, she pulled out to sea.

Getting into the current, she let the boat drift, and soon forgot time and space in the bewildering conversation that followed.

"What have you been doing since I saw you last?" she asked, looking as rosy as a milkmaid, as she stopped rowing and tied up her wind-tossed hair.

"Working like a beaver. You see"—and then, to her utter amazement, Frank entered into an elaborate statement of his affairs, quite as if she understood all about it and her opinion was valuable. It was all Greek to Anna, but she was immensely gratified; for it was just the way the boy used to tell her his small concerns in the days when each had firm faith in the other's wisdom. She tried to look as if she understood all about "investments, percentage, and long credit;" but she was out of her depth in five minutes, and dared say nothing, lest she should betray her lamentable ignorance on all matters of business. She got out of the scrape by cleverly turning the conversation to old times, and youthful reminiscences soon absorbed them both.

The faint, far-off sound of a gong recalled her to the fact that breakfast was nearly ready; and, turning the boat, she was dismayed to see how far they had floated. She stopped talking and rowed her best; but wind and tide were against her, she was faint with hunger, and her stalwart passenger made her task doubly hard. He offered no help, however; but did the luxurious to the life, leaning back, with his hat off, and dabbling his hands in the way that most impedes the progress of a boat.

Pride kept Anna silent till her face was scarlet, her palms blistered, and her breath most gone. Then, and not till then, did she condescend to say, with a gasp, poorly concealed by an amiable smile,—

"Do you care to row? I ought to have asked you before."

"I'm very comfortable, thank you," answered Frank. Then, as an expression of despair flitted over poor Anna's face, he added bluntly, "I'm getting desperately hungry, so I don't care if I do shorten the voyage a bit."

With a sigh of relief, she rose to change seats, and, expecting him to help her, she involuntarily put out her hands, as she passed. But Frank was busy turning back his cuffs, and never stirred a finger; so that she would have lost her balance and gone overboard if she had not caught his arm.

"What's the matter, skipper?" he asked, standing the sudden grip as steadily as a mast.

"Why didn't you help me? You have no more manners than a turtle!" cried Anna, dropping into the seat with the frown of a spoiled beauty, accustomed to be gallantly served and supported at every step.

Frank only added to his offence by laughing, as he said carelessly,—

"You seemed so independent, I didn't like to interfere."

"So, if I had gone overboard, you would not have fished me out, unless I asked you to do it, I suppose?"

"In that case, I'm afraid I shouldn't have waited for orders. We can't spare you to the mermen yet."

Something in the look he gave her appeased Anna's resentment; and she sat silently admiring the strong, swift strokes that sent the "Gull" skimming over the water.

"Not too late for breakfast, after all," she said graciously, as they reached the wharf, where several early strollers stood watching their approach.

"Poor thing! You look as if you needed it," answered Frank. But he let her get out alone, to the horror of Messrs. Barlow, King, & Co.; and, while she fastened the boat, Frank stood settling his hatband, with the most exasperating unconsciousness of his duty.

"What are you going to do with yourself this morning?" she asked, as she walked up the rocky path, with no arm to lean upon.

"Fish. Will you come along?"

"No, thank you. One gets so burnt. I shall go to my hammock under the pine," was the graciously suggestive reply of the lady who liked a slave to fan or swing her, and seldom lacked several to choose from.

"See you at dinner, then. My room is in the Cottage. So by-by for the present." And, with a nod, Frank strolled away, leaving the lovely Miss West to mount the steps and cross the hall unescorted.

"The dear fellow's manners need polish. I must take him in hand, I see. And yet he is very nice, in spite of his brusque ways," thought Anna, indulgently. And more than once that morning she recalled his bluff "Hullo, Anna!" as she swung languidly in her hammock, with a devoted being softly reading Tennyson to her inattentive ears.

At dinner she appeared in unusual spirits, and kept her end of the table in a ripple of merriment by her witty and satirical sallies, privately hoping that her opposite neighbor would discover that she could talk well when she chose to do so. But Frank was deep in politics, discussing some new measure with such earnestness and eloquence that Anna, pausing to listen for a moment, forgot her lively gossip in one of the great questions of the hour.

She was listening with silent interest, when Frank suddenly appealed to her to confirm some statement he had just made; and she was ignominiously obliged to confess she knew too little about the matter to give any opinion. No compliment ever paid her was more flattering than his way of turning to her now and then, as if including her in the discussion as a matter of course; and never had she regretted any thing more keenly than she did her ignorance on a subject that every man and woman should understand and espouse.

She did her best to look intelligent; racked her brain to remember facts which she had heard discussed for weeks, without paying any attention to them; and, thanks to her quick wit and womanly sympathy, she managed to hold her own, saying little, but looking much.

The instant dinner was over, she sent a servant to the reading-room for a file of late papers, and, retiring to a secluded corner, read up with a diligence that not only left her with clearer ideas on one subject, but also a sense of despair at her own deficiencies in the knowledge of many others.

"I really must have a course of solid reading. I do believe that is what I need; and I'll ask Frank where to begin. He always was an intelligent boy; but I was surprised to hear how well he talked. I was actually proud of him. I wonder where he is, by the way. Clara wants to be introduced, and I want to see how he strikes her."

Leaving her hiding-place, Anna walked forth in search of her friends, looking unusually bright and beautiful, for her secret studies had waked her up and lent her face the higher charm it needed. Clara appeared first. The new-comer had already been presented to her, and she professed herself "perfectly fascinated." "Such a personable man! Quite distinguished, you know, and so elegant in his manners! Devoted, graceful, and altogether charming."

"You like his manners, do you?" and Anna smiled at Clara's enthusiasm.

"Of course I do; for they have all the polish of foreign travel, with the indescribable something which a really fine character lends to every little act and word."

"Frank has never been abroad, and if I judged his character by his manners I should say he was rather a rough customer," said Anna, finding fault because Clara praised.

"You are so fastidious, nothing ever suits you, dear. I didn't expect to like this old friend of yours. But I frankly confess I do immensely; so, if you are tired of him, I'll take him off your hands."

"Thank you, love. You are welcome to poor Frank, if you can win him. Men are apt to be more loyal to friendship than women; and I rather fancy, from what I saw this morning, that he is in no haste to change old friends for new."

Anna spoke sweetly, but at heart was ill pleased with Clara's admiration of her private property, as she considered "poor Frank," and inwardly resolved to have no poaching on her preserves.

Just then the gentleman in question came up, saying to Anna, in his abrupt way,—

"Every one is going to ride, so I cannot get the best horses; but I've secured two, and now I want a companion. Will you come for a good old-time gallop?"

Anna thought of her blistered hands, and hesitated, till a look at Clara's hopeful face decided her to accept. She did so, and rode like an Amazon for several hours, in spite of heat, dust, and a hard-mouthed horse, who nearly pulled her arms out of the sockets.

She hoped to find a chance to consult Frank about her course of useful reading; but he seemed intent on the "old-time gallop," and she kept up gallantly till the ride was over, when she retired to her room, quite exhausted, but protesting with heroic smiles that she had had a delightful time.

She did not appear at tea; but later in the evening, when an informal dance was well under way, she sailed in on the arm of a distinguished old gentleman, "evidently prepared to slay her thousands," as young Barlow said, observing the unusual brilliancy of her eyes and the elaborate toilette she had made.

"She means mischief to-night. Who is to be the victim, I wonder?" said another man, putting up his glass for a survey of the charmer.

"Not the party who came last evening. He is only an old friend, she says."

"He might be her brother or her husband, judging by the cavalier way in which he treats her. I could have punched his head this morning, when he let her pull up that boat alone," cried a youthful adorer, glaring irefully at the delinquent, lounging in a distant doorway.

"If she said he was an old friend, you may be sure he is an accepted lover. The dear creatures all fib in these matters; so I'll lay wagers to an enormous amount that all this splendor is for the lord and master, not for our destruction," answered

Barlow, who was wise in the ways of women and wary as a moth should be who had burnt his wings more than once at the same candle.

Clara happened to overhear these pleasing remarks, and five minutes after they were uttered she breathed them tenderly into Anna's ear. A scornful smile was all the answer she received; but the beauty was both pleased and annoyed, and awaited with redoubled interest the approach of the old friend, who was regarded in the light of a successful lover. But he seemed in no haste to claim his privileges, and dance after dance went by, while he sat talking with the old general or absently watching the human teetotums that spun about before him.

"I can't stand this another moment!" said Anna to herself, at last, and beckoned the recreant knight to approach, with a commanding gesture.

"Why don't you dance, sir?"

"I've forgotten how, ma'am."

"After all the pains I took with you when we had lessons together, years ago?"

"I've been too busy to attend to trifles of that sort."

"Elegant accomplishments are not trifles, and no one should neglect them who cares to make himself agreeable."

"Well, I don't know that I do care, as a general thing."

"You ought to care; and, as a penance for that rude speech, you must dance this dance with me. I cannot let you forget all your accomplishments for the sake of business; so I shall do my duty as a friend and take you in hand," said Anna, severely.

"You are very kind; but is it worth the trouble?"

"Now, Frank, don't be provoking and ungrateful. You know you like to give pleasure, to be cared for, and to do credit to your friends; so just rub up your manners a bit, and be as well-bred as you are sensible and brave and good."

"Thank you, I'll try. May I have the honor, Miss West?" and he bowed low before her, with a smile on his lips that both pleased and puzzled Anna.

They danced the dance, and Frank acquitted himself respectably, but relapsed into his objectionable ways as soon as the trial ended; for the first thing he said, with a sigh of relief, was,—

"Come out and talk; for upon my life I can't stand this oven any longer."

Anna obediently followed, and, seating herself in a breezy corner, waited to be entertained. But Frank seemed to have forgotten that pleasing duty; for, perching himself on the wide baluster of the piazza, he not only proceeded to light a cigarette, without even saying, "By your leave," but coolly offered her one also.

"How dare you!" she said, much offended at this proceeding. "I am not one of the fast girls who do such things, and I dislike it exceedingly."

"You used to smoke sweet-fern in corn-cob pipes, you remember; and these are not much stronger," he said, placidly restoring the rejected offering to his pocket.

"I did many foolish things then which I desire to forget now."

"And some very sweet and sensible ones, also. Ah, well! it can't be helped, I suppose."

Anna sat silent a moment, wondering what he meant; and when she looked up, she found him pensively staring at her, through a fragrant cloud of smoke.

"What is it?" she asked, for his eyes seemed seeking something.

"I was trying to see some trace of the little Anna I used to know. I thought I'd found her again this morning in the girl in the round hat; but I don't find her anywhere to-night."

"Indeed, Frank, I'm not so much changed as I seem. At least, to you I am the same, as far as I can be. Do believe it, and be friends, for I want one very much?" cried Anna, forgetting every thing but the desire to reestablish herself in his good opinion. As she spoke, she turned her face toward the light and half extended her hand, as if to claim and hold the old regard that seemed about to be withdrawn from her.

Frank bent a little and scanned the upturned face with a keen glance. It flushed in the moonlight and the lips trembled like an anxious child's; but the eyes met his with a look both proud and wistful, candid and sweet,—a look few saw in those lovely eyes, or, once seeing, ever forgot. Frank gave a little nod, as if satisfied, and said, with that perplexing smile of his,—

"Most people would see only the beautiful Miss West, in a remarkably pretty gown; but I think I catch a glimpse of little Anna, and I am very glad of it. You want a friend? Very good. I'll do my best for you; but you must take me as I am, thorns and all."

"I will, and not mind if they wound sometimes. I've had roses till I'm tired of them, in spite of their sweetness."

As he spoke, Frank had taken the hand she offered, and, having gravely shaken it, held the "white wonder" for an instant, glancing from the little blisters on the delicate palm to the rings that shone on several fingers.

"Are you reading my fortune?" asked Anna, wondering if he was going to be sentimental and kiss it.

"After a fashion; for I am looking to see if there is a suspicious diamond anywhere about. Isn't it time there was one?"

"That is not a question for you to ask;" and Anna caught away her hand, as if one of the thorns he spoke of had suddenly pricked.

"Why not? We always used to tell each other every thing; and, if we are to go on in the old friendly way, we must be confidential and comfortable, you know."

"You can begin yourself then, and I'll see how I like it," said Anna, aroused and interested, in spite of her maidenly scruples about the new arrangement.

"I will, with all my heart. To own the truth, I've been longing to tell you something; but I wasn't sure that you'd take any interest in it," began Frank, eating rose-leaves with interesting embarrassment.

"I can imagine what it is," said Anna, quickly, while her heart began to flutter curiously, for these confidences were becoming exciting. "You have found your fate, and are dying to let everybody know how happy you are."

"I think I have. But I'm not happy yet. I'm desperately anxious, for I cannot decide whether it is a wise or foolish choice."

"Who is it?"

"Never mind the name. I haven't spoken yet, and perhaps never shall; so I may as well keep that to myself,—for the present, at least."

"Tell me what you like then, and I will ask no more

questions," said Anna, coldly; for this masculine discretion annoyed her.

"Well, you see, this dear girl is pretty, rich, accomplished, and admired. A little spoilt, in fact; but very captivating, in spite of it. Now, the doubt in my mind is whether it is wise to woo a wife of this sort; for I know I shall want a companion in all things, not only a pretty sweetheart or a graceful mistress for my house."

"I should say it was *not* wise," began Anna, decidedly; then hastened to add, more quietly: "But perhaps you only see one side of this girl's character. She may have much strength and sweetness hidden away under her gay manner, waiting to be called out when the right mate comes."

"I often think so myself, and long to learn if I am the man; but some frivolous act, thoughtless word, or fashionable folly on her part dampens my ardor, and makes me feel as if I had better go elsewhere before it is too late."

"You are not madly in love, then?"

"Not yet; but I should be if I saw much of her, for when I do I rather lose my head, and am tempted to fall upon my knees, regardless of time, place, and consequences."

Frank spoke with sudden love and longing in his voice, and stretched out his arms so suggestively that Anna started. But he contented himself with gathering a rose from the clusters that hung all about, and Anna slapped an imaginary mosquito as energetically as if it had been the unknown lady, for whom she felt a sudden and inexplicable dislike.

"So you think I'd better not say to my love, like the mad gentleman to Mrs. Nickleby, 'Be mine, be mine'?" was Frank's next question, as he sat with his nose luxuriously buried in the fragrant heart of the rose.

"Decidedly not. I'm sure, from the way you speak of her, that she is not worthy of you; and your passion cannot be very deep if you can quote Dickens's nonsense at such a moment," said Anna, more cheerfully.

"It grows rapidly, I find; and I give you my word, if I should pass a week in the society of that lovely butterfly, it would be all over with me by Saturday night."

"Then don't do it."

"Ah! but I want to desperately. Do say that I may, just for a last nibble at temptation, before I take your advice and go back to my bachelor life again," he prayed beseechingly.

"Don't go back, love somebody else, and be happy. There are plenty of superior women in the world who would be just the thing for you. I am sure you are going to be a man of mark, and you *must* have a good wife,—not a silly little creature, who will be a clog upon you all your life. So *do* take my advice, and let me help you, if I can."

Anna spoke earnestly, and her face quite shone with friendly zeal; while her eyes were full of unspoken admiration and regard for this friend, who seemed tottering on the verge of a precipice. She expected a serious reply,—thanks, at least, for her interest; and great was her surprise to see Frank lean back against the vine-wreathed pillar behind him, and laugh till a shower of rose-leaves came fluttering down on both their heads.

"I don't see any cause for such unseemly merriment," was her dignified reproof of this new impropriety.

"I beg your pardon. I really couldn't help it, for the comical contrast between your sage counsels and your blooming face upset me. Your manner was quite maternal and most impressive, till I looked at you in your French finery, and then it was all up with me," said Frank, penitently, though his eyes still danced with mirth.

The compliment appeased Anna's anger; and, folding her round white arms on the railing in front of her, she looked up at him with a laugh as blithe as his own.

"I dare say I was absurdly sober and important; but you see it is so long since I have had a really serious thought in my head or felt a really sincere interest in any one's affairs but my own that I overdid the matter. If you don't care for my advice, I'll take it all back; and you can go and marry your butterfly as soon as you like."

"I rather think I shall," said Frank, slowly. "For I fancy she *has* got a hidden self, as you suggested, and I'd rather like to find it out. One judges people so much by externals that it is not fair. Now, you, for instance, if you won't mind my saying it, don't show half your good points; and a casual observer would consider you merely a fashionable woman,—lovely, but shallow."

"As you did the last time we met," put in Anna, sharply.

If she expected him to deny it, she was mistaken; for he answered, with provoking candor,—

"Exactly. And I quite grieved about it; for I used to be very fond of my little playmate and thought she'd make a fine woman. I'm glad I've seen you again; for I find I was unjust in my first judgment, and this discovery gives me hope that I may have been mistaken in the same way about my—well, we'll say sweetheart. It's a pretty old word and I like it."

"If he only *would* forget that creature a minute and talk about something more interesting!" sighed Anna to herself. But she answered, meekly enough: "I knew you were disappointed in me, and I did not wonder; for I am not good for much, thanks to my foolish education and the life I have led these last few years. But I do sincerely wish to be more of a woman, only I have no one to tell me how. Everybody flatters me and"—

"I don't!" cried Frank, promptly.

"That's true." And Anna could not help laughing in the middle of her confessions at the tone of virtuous satisfaction with which he repelled the accusation. "No," she continued, "you are honest enough for any one; and I like it, though it startles me now and then, it is so new."

"I hope I'm not disrespectful," said Frank, busily removing the thorns from the stem of his flower.

"Oh, no! Not that exactly. But you treat me very much as if I was a sister or a—masculine friend." Anna meant to quote the expression Clara had reported; but somehow the word "wife" was hard to utter, and she finished the sentence differently.

"And you don't like it?" asked Frank, lifting the rose to hide the mischievous smile that lurked about his mouth.

"Yes, I do,—infinitely better than the sentimental homage other men pay me or the hackneyed rubbish they talk. It does me good to be a little neglected; and I don't mind it from you, because you more than atone for it by talking to me as if I could understand a man's mind and had one of my own."

"Then you don't quite detest me for my rough ways and egotistical confidences?" asked Frank, as if suddenly smitten with remorse for the small sins of the day.

"No, I rather fancy it, for it seems like old times, when you and I played together. Only then I could help you in many ways, as you helped me; but now I don't seem to know any thing, and can be of no use to you or any one else. I should like to be; and I think, if you would kindly tell me what books to read, what people to know, and what faculties to cultivate, I might become something besides 'a fashionable woman, lovely but shallow.'"

There was a little quiver of emotion in Anna's voice as she uttered the last words that did not escape her companion's quick ear. But he only smiled a look of heartfelt satisfaction to the rose, and answered soberly:

"Now that is a capital idea, and I'll do it with pleasure. I have often wondered how you bright girls *could* be contented with such an empty sort of life. We fellows are just as foolish for a time, I know,—far worse in the crops of wild oats we sow; but we have to pull up and go to work, and that makes men of us. Marriage ought to do that for women, I suppose; but it doesn't seem to nowadays, and I do pity you poor little things from the bottom of my heart."

"I'm ready now to 'pull up and go to work.' Show me how, Frank, and I'll change your pity into respect," said Anna, casting off her lace shawl, as if preparing for immediate action; for his tone of masculine superiority rather nettled her.

"Come, I'll make a bargain with you. I'll give you something strong and solid to brace up your mind, and in return you shall polish my manners, see to my morals, and keep my heart from wasting itself on false idols. Shall we do this for one another, Anna?"

"Yes, Frank," she answered heartily. Then, as Clara was seen approaching, she added playfully, "All this is *sub rosa*, you understand."

He handed her the flower without a word, as if the emblem of silence was the best gage he could offer. Many flowers had been presented to the beauty; but none were kept so long and carefully as the thornless rose her old friend gave her, with a cordial smile that warmed her heart.

A great deal can happen in a week, and the seven days that followed that moonlight *tête-à-tête* seemed to Anna the fullest and the happiest she had ever known. She had never worked so hard in her life; for her new tutor gave her plenty to do, and she studied in secret to supply sundry deficiencies which she was too proud to confess. No more novels now; no more sentimental poetry, lounging in a hammock. She sat erect upon a hard rock and read Buckle, Mill, and Social Science Reports with a diligence that appalled the banished dawdlers who usually helped her kill time. There was early boating, vigorous horse exercise, and tramps over hill and dale, from which she returned dusty, brown, and tired, but as happy as if she had discovered something fairer and grander than wild flowers or the ocean in its changeful moods. There were afternoon concerts in the breezy drawing-rooms, when others were enjoying siestas, and Anna sang to her one listener as she had never sung before. But best of all were the moonlight *séances* among the roses; for there they interchanged interesting confidences and hovered about those dangerous but delightful topics that need the magic of a midsummer night to make the charm quite perfect.

Anna intended to do her part honorably; but soon forgot to correct her pupil's manners, she was so busy taking care of his heart. She presently discovered that he treated other women in the usual way; and at first it annoyed her that she was the only one whom he allowed to pick up her own fan, walk without an arm, row, ride, and take care of herself as if she was a man. But she also discovered that she was the only woman to whom he talked as to an equal, in whom he seemed to find sympathy, inspiration, and help, and for whom he frankly showed not admiration alone, but respect, confidence, and affection.

This made the loss of a little surface courtesy too trifling for complaint or reproof; this stimulated and delighted her; and, in striving to deserve and secure it, she forgot every thing else, prouder to be one man's true friend than the idol of a dozen lovers.

What the effect of this new league was upon the other party was less evident; for, being of the undemonstrative sex, he kept his observations, discoveries, and satisfaction to himself, with no sign of especial interest, except now and then a rapturous allusion to his sweetheart, as if absence was increasing his passion.

Anna tried to quench his ardor, feeling sure, she said, that it was a mistake to lavish so much love upon a person who was so entirely unworthy of it. But Frank seemed blind on this one point; and Anna suffered many a pang, as day after day showed her some new virtue, grace, or talent in this perverse man, who seemed bent on throwing his valuable self away. She endeavored to forget it, avoided the subject as much as possible, and ignored the existence of this inconvenient being entirely. But as the week drew to an end a secret trouble looked out at her eyes, a secret unrest possessed her, and every moment seemed to grow more precious as it passed, each full of a bitter sweet delight never known before.

"I must be off to-morrow," said Frank, on the Saturday evening, as they strolled together on the beach, while the sun set gloriously and the great waves broke musically on the sands.

"Such a short holiday, after all those months of work!" answered Anna, looking away, lest he should see how wistful her tell-tale eyes were.

"I may take a longer holiday, the happiest a man can have, if somebody will go with me. Anna, I've made up my mind to try my fate," he added impetuously.

"I have warned you; I can do no more." Which was quite true, for the poor girl's heart sunk at his words, and for a moment all the golden sky was a blur before her eyes.

"I won't be warned, thank you; for I'm quite sure now that I love her. Nothing like absence to settle that point. I've tried it, and I can't get on without her; so I'm going to 'put my fortune to the touch and win or lose it all.'"

"If you truly love her, I hope you will win, and find her the wife you deserve. But think well before you put your happiness into any woman's hands," said Anna, bravely trying to forget herself.

"Bless you! I've hardly thought of any thing else this week! I've enjoyed myself, though; and am very grateful to you for making my visit so pleasant," Frank added warmly.

"Have I? I'm so glad!" said Anna, as simply as a pleased child; for real love had banished all her small coquetries, vanities, and affectations, as sunshine absorbs the mists that hide a lovely landscape.

"Indeed, you have. All the teaching has not been on my side, I assure you; and I'm not too proud to own my obligation to a woman. We lonely fellows, who have neither mother, sister, nor wife, need some gentle soul to keep us from getting selfish, hard, and worldly; and few are so fortunate as I in having a friend like little Anna."

"Oh, Frank! what have I done for you? I haven't dared to teach one so much wiser and stronger than myself. I've only wanted to, and grieved because I was so ignorant, so weak, and silly," cried Anna, glowing beautifully with surprise and pleasure at this unexpected revelation.

"Your humility blinded you; yet your unconsciousness was half the charm. I'll tell you what you did, dear. A man's moral sense gets blunted knocking about this rough-and-tumble world, where the favorite maxim is, 'Every man for himself and the Devil take the hindmost.' It is so with me; and in many of our conversations on various subjects, while I seemed to be teaching you, your innocent integrity was rebuking my worldly wisdom, your subtle instincts were pointing out the right which is above all policy, your womanly charity softening my hard judgments, and your simple faith in the good, the beautiful, the truly brave was waking up the high and happy beliefs that lay, not dead, but sleeping, in my soul. All this you did for me, Anna, and even more; for, in showing me the hidden side of your nature, I found it so sweet and deep and worshipful that it restores my faith in womankind, and shows me all the lovely possibilities that may lie folded up under the frivolous exterior of a fashionable woman."

Anna's heart was so full she could not speak for a moment; then like a dash of cold water came the thought, "And all this that I have done has only put him further from me, since it has given him courage to love and trust that woman." She tried to show only pleasure at his praise; but for the life of her she could not keep a tone of bitterness out of her voice as she answered gratefully,—

"You are too kind, Frank. I can hardly believe that I have so many virtues; but if I have, and they, like yours, have been asleep, remember you helped wake them up, and so you owe me nothing. Keep your sweet speeches for the lady you go to woo. I am contented with honest words that do not flatter."

"You shall have them;" and a quick smile passed over Frank's face, as if he knew what thorn pricked her just then, and was not ill pleased at the discovery. "Only, if I lose my sweetheart, I may be sure that my old friend won't desert me?" he asked, with a sincere anxiety that was a balm to Anna's sore heart.

She did not speak, but offered him her hand with a look which said much. He took it as silently, and, holding it in a firm, warm grasp, led her up to a cleft in the rocks, where they often sat to watch the great breakers thunder in. As she took her seat, he folded his plaid about her so tenderly that it felt like a friendly arm shielding her from the fresh gale that blew up from the sea. It was an unusual attention on his part, and coming just then it affected her so curiously that, when he lounged down beside her, she felt a strong desire to lay her head on his shoulder and sob out,—

"Don't go and leave me! No one loves you half as well as I, or needs you half so much!"

Of course, she did nothing of the sort; but began to sing, as she covertly whisked away a rebellious tear. Frank soon interrupted her music, however, by a heavy sigh; and followed up that demonstration with the tragical announcement,—

"Anna, I've got something awful to tell you."

"What is it?" she asked, with the resignation of one who has already heard the worst.

"It is so bad that I can't look you in the face while I tell it. Listen calmly till I am done, and then pitch me overboard if you like, for I deserve it," was his cheerful beginning.

"Go on." And Anna prepared herself to receive some tremendous shock with masculine firmness.

Frank pulled his hat over his eyes, and, looking away from her, said rapidly, with an odd sound in his voice,—

"The night I came I was put in a room opening on the back piazza; and, lying there to rest and cool after my journey, I heard two ladies talking. I knocked my boots about to let them know I was near; but they took no notice, so I listened. Most women's gabble would have sent me to sleep in five minutes; but this was rather original, and interested me, especially when I found by the names mentioned that I knew one of the parties. I've been trying your experiment all the week. Anna, how do you like it?"

She did not answer for a moment, being absorbed in swift retrospection. Then she colored to her hat-brim, looked angry, hurt, amused, gratified, and ashamed, all in a minute, and said slowly, as she met his laughing eyes,—

"Better than I thought I should."

"That's good! Then you forgive me for my eavesdropping, my rudeness, and manifold iniquities? It was abominable; but I could not resist the temptation of testing your sincerity. It was great fun; but I'm not sure that I shall not get the worst of it, after all," said Frank, sobering suddenly.

"You have played so many jokes upon me in old times that I don't find it hard to forgive this one; though I think it rather base in you to deceive me so. Still, as I have enjoyed and got a good deal out of it, I don't complain, and won't send you overboard yet," said Anna, generously.

"You always were a forgiving angel." And Frank settled the plaid again more tenderly than before.

"It was this, then, that made you so brusque to me alone, so odd and careless? I could not understand it and it hurt me at first; but I thought it was because we had been children together and soon forgot it, you were so kind and confidential, so helpful and straightforward. It *was* 'great fun,' for I always knew you meant what you said; and that was an unspeakable comfort to me in this world of flattery and falsehood. Yes, you may laugh at me, Frank, and leave me to myself again. I can bear it, for I've proved that my whim was a possibility. I see my way now, and can go on alone to a truer, happier life than that in which you found me."

She spoke out bravely, and looked above the level sands and beyond the restless sea, as if she had found something worth living for and did not fear the future. Frank watched her an instant, for her face had never worn so noble an expression before. Sorrow as well as strength had come into the lovely features, and pain as well as patience touched them with new beauty. His own face changed as he looked, as if he let loose some deep and tender sentiment, long held in check, now ready to rise and claim its own.

"Anna," he said penitently, "I've got one other terrible confession to make, and then my conscience will be clear. I want to tell you who my sweetheart is. Here's her picture. Will you look at it?"

She gave a little shiver, turned steadily, and looked where he pointed. But all she saw was her own astonished face reflected in the shallow pool behind them. One glance at Frank made any explanation needless; indeed, there was no time for her to speak before something closer than the plaid enfolded her, something warmer than tears touched her cheek, and a voice sweeter to her than wind or wave whispered tenderly in her ear,—

"All this week I have been studying and enjoying far more than you; for I have read a woman's heart and learned to trust and honor what I have loved ever since I was a boy. Absence proved this to me: so I came to look for little Anna, and found her better and dearer than ever. May I ask her to keep on teaching me? Will she share my work as well as holiday, and be the truest friend a man can have?"

And Anna straightway answered, "Yes."

*December 18, 1873*

# *My Girls*

O NCE upon a time I wrote a little account of some of the agreeable boys I had known, whereupon the damsels reproached me with partiality, and begged me to write about them. I owned the soft impeachment, and promised that I would not forget them if I could find any thing worth recording.

That was six years ago, and since then I have been studying girls whenever I had an opportunity, and have been both pleased and surprised to see how much they are doing for themselves now that their day has come.

Poor girls always had my sympathy and respect, for necessity soon makes brave women of them if they have any strength or talent in them; but the well-to-do girls usually seemed to me like pretty butterflies, leading easy, aimless lives when the world was full of work which ought to be done.

Making a call in New York, I got a little lesson, which caused me to change my opinion, and further investigation proved that the rising generation was wide awake, and bound to use the new freedom well. Several young girls, handsomely dressed, were in the room, and I thought, of course, that they belonged to the butterfly species; but on asking one of them what she was about now school was over, I was much amazed to hear her reply, "I am reading law with my uncle." Another said, "I am studying medicine;" a third, "I devote myself to music," and the fourth was giving time, money, and heart to some of the best charities of the great city.

So my pretty butterflies proved to be industrious bees, making real honey, and I shook hands with sincere respect, though they did wear jaunty hats; my good opinion being much increased by the fact that not one was silly enough to ask for an autograph.

Since then I have talked with many girls, finding nearly all intent on some noble end, and as some of them have already won the battle, it may be cheering to those still in the thick of the fight, or just putting on their armor, to hear how these sisters prospered in their different ways.

Several of them are girls no longer; but as they are still

unmarried, I like to call them by their old name, because they are so young at heart, and have so beautifully fulfilled the promise of their youth, not only by doing, but being excellent and admirable women.

A is one in whom I take especial pride. Well-born, pretty, and bright, she, after a year or two of society, felt the need of something more satisfactory, and, following her taste, decided to study medicine. Fortunately she had a father who did not think marriage the only thing a woman was created for, but was ready to help his daughter in the work she had chosen, merely desiring her to study as faithfully and thoroughly as a man, if she undertook the profession that she might be an honor to it. A *was* in earnest, and studied four years, visiting the hospitals of London, Paris, and Prussia; being able to command private lessons when the doors of public institutions were shut in her face because she was a woman. More study and work at home, and then she had the right to accept the post of resident physician in a hospital for women. Here she was so successful that her outside practice increased rapidly, and she left the hospital to devote herself to patients of all sorts, beloved and valued for the womanly sympathy and cheerfulness that went hand in hand with the physician's skill and courage.

When I see this woman, young still, yet so independent, successful, and contented, I am very proud of her; not only because she has her own house, with a little adopted daughter to make it home-like, her well-earned reputation, and a handsome income, but because she has so quietly and persistently carried out the plan of her life, undaunted by prejudice, hard work, or the solitary lot she chose. She may well be satisfied; for few women receive so much love and confidence, few mothers have so many children to care for, few physicians are more heartily welcomed and trusted, few men lead a freer, nobler life, than this happy woman, who lives for others and never thinks of any fame but that which is the best worth having, a place in the hearts of all who know her.

B is another of my successful girls; but her task has been a harder one than A's, because she was as poor as she was ambitious. B is an artist, loving beauty more than any thing else in the world; ready to go cold and hungry, shabby and lonely, if she can only see, study, and try to create the loveliness she worships. It was so even as a child; for flowers and fairies grew on her slate when she should have been doing sums, painted birds and butterflies perched on her book-covers, Flaxman's designs, and familiar faces appeared on the walls of her little room, and clay gods and goddesses were set upon the rough altar of her moulding board, to be toiled over and adored till they were smashed in the "divine despair" all true artists feel.

But winged things will fly sooner or later, and patient waiting, persistent effort, only give sweetness to the song and strength to the flight when the door of the cage opens at last. So, after years of hard work with pencil and crayon, plaster and clay, oil and water colors, the happy hour came for B when the dream of her life was realized; for one fine spring day, with a thousand dollars in her pocket and a little trunk holding more art materials than clothes, she sailed away, alone, but brave and beaming, for a year in England.

She knew now what she wanted and where to find it, and "a heavenly year" followed, though to many it would have seemed a very dull one. All day and every day but the seventh was spent in the National Gallery, copying Turner's pictures in oil and water colors. So busy, so happy, so wrapt up in delightsome work, that food and sleep seemed impertinencies, friends were forgotten, pleasuring had no charms, society no claims, and life was one joyful progress from the blue Giudecca to the golden Sol de Venezia, or the red glow of the old Temeraire. "Van Tromp entering the mouth of the Texel" was more interesting to her than any political event transpiring in the world without; ancient Rome eclipsed modern London, and the roar of a great city could not disturb the "Datur Hora Quieti" which softly grew into beauty under her happy brush.

A spring-tide trip to Stratford, Warwick, and Kenilworth was the only holiday she allowed herself; and even this was turned to profit; for, lodging cheaply at the Shakespearian baker's, she roamed about, portfolio in hand, booking every lovely bit she saw, regardless of sun or rain, and bringing away a pictorial diary of that week's trip which charmed those who beheld it, and put money in her purse.

When the year was out, home came the artist, with half her little fortune still unspent, and the one trunk nearly as empty as it went, but there were two great boxes of pictures, and a golden saint in a coffin five feet long, which caused much interest at the Custom House, but was passed duty-free after its owner had displayed it with enthusiastic explanations of its charms.

"They are only attempts and studies, you know, and I dare say you'll all laugh at them; but I feel that I *can* in time *do* something, so my year has not been wasted," said the modest damsel, as she set forth her work, glorifying all the house with Venetian color, English verdure, and, what was better still, the sunshine of a happy heart.

But to B's great surprise and delight, people did *not* laugh; they praised and bought, and ordered more, till, before she knew it, several thousand dollars were at her command, and the way clear to the artist-life she loved.

To some who watched her, the sweetest picture she created was the free art-school which B opened in a very humble way; giving her books, copies, casts, time, and teaching to all who cared to come. For with her, as with most who *earn* their good things, the generous desire to share them with others is so strong it is sure to blossom out in some way, blessing as it has been blessed. Slowly, but surely, success comes to the patient worker, and B, being again abroad for more lessons, paints one day a little still life study so well that her master says she "does him honor," and her mates advise her to send it to the Salon. Never dreaming that it will be accepted, B, for the joke of it, puts her study in a plain frame, and sends it, with the eight thousand others, only two thousand of which are received.

To her amazement the little picture is accepted, hung "on the line" and noticed in the report. Nor is that all, the Committee asked leave to exhibit it at another place, and desired an autobiographical sketch of the artist. A more deeply gratified young woman it would be hard to find than B, as she now plans the studio she is to open soon, and the happy independent life she hopes to lead in it, for she has earned her place, and, after years of earnest labor, is about to enter in and joyfully possess it.

There was C,—alas, that I must write *was!* beautiful, gifted, young, and full of the lovely possibilities which give some girls such an indescribable charm. Placed where it would have been natural for her to have made herself a young queen of society, she preferred something infinitely better, and so quietly devoted herself to the chosen work that very few guessed she had any.

I had known her for some years before I found it out, and then only by accident; but I never shall forget the impression it made upon me. I had called to get a book, and something led me to speak of the sad case of a poor girl lately made known to me, when C, with a sudden brightening of her whole face, said, warmly, "I wish I had known it, I could have helped her."

"You? what can a happy creature like you know about such things?" I answered, surprised.

"That is my work." And in a few words which went to my heart, the beautiful girl, sitting in her own pretty room, told me how, for a long time, she and others had stepped out of their safe, sunshiny homes to help and save the most forlorn of our sister women. So quietly, so tenderly, that only those saved knew who did it, and such loyal silence kept, that, even among the friends, the names of these unfortunates were not given, that the after life might be untroubled by even a look of reproach or recognition.

"Do not speak of this," she said. "Not that I am ashamed; but we are able to work better in a private way, and want no thanks for what we do."

I kept silence till her share of the womanly labor of love, so delicately, dutifully done, was over. But I never saw that sweet face afterward without thinking how like an angel's it must have seemed to those who sat in darkness till she came to lift them up.

Always simply dressed, this young sister of charity went about her chosen task when others of her age and position were at play; happy in it, and unconsciously preaching a little sermon by her lovely life. Another girl, who spent her days reading novels and eating confectionery, said to me, in speaking of C,—

"Why doesn't she dress more? She is rich enough, and so handsome I should think she would."

Taking up the reports of several charities which lay on my table, I pointed to C's name among the generous givers, saying,—

"Perhaps *that* is the reason;" and my visitor went away with a new idea of economy in her frivolous head, a sincere respect for the beautiful girl who wore the plain suit and loved her neighbor *better* than herself.

A short life; but one so full of sweetness that all the bitter waters of the pitiless sea cannot wash its memory away, and I am sure that white soul won heaven sooner for the grateful prayers of those whom she had rescued from a blacker ocean.

D was one of a large family all taught at home, and all of a dramatic turn; so, with a witty father to write the plays, an indulgent mother to yield up her house to destruction, five boys and seven girls for the *corps dramatique*, it is not to be wondered at that D set her heart on being an actress.

Having had the honor to play the immortal Pillicoddy on that famous stage, I know whereof I write, and what glorious times that little company of brothers and sisters had safe at home. But D burned for a larger field, and at length found a chance to appear on the real boards with several of her sisters. Being very small and youthful in appearance they played children's parts, fairies in spectacles and soubrettes in farce or vaudeville. Once D had a benefit, and it was a pretty sight to see the long list of familiar names on the bill; for the brothers and sisters all turned out and made a jolly play of "Parents and Guardians," as well as a memorable sensation in the "Imitations" which they gave.

One would think that the innocent little girls might have come to harm singing in the chorus of operas, dancing as peasants, or playing "Nan the good-for-nothing." But the small women were so dignified, well-mannered, and intent on their duties that no harm befell them. Father and brothers watched over them; there were few temptations for girls who made "Mother" their confidante, and a happy home was a safe refuge from the unavoidable annoyances to which all actresses are exposed.

D tried the life, found it wanting, left it, and put her experiences into a clever little book, then turned to less pleasant but more profitable work. The father, holding a public office, was allowed two clerks; but, finding that his clear-headed daughter could do the work of both easily and well, gave her the place, and she earned her thousand a year, going to her daily duty looking like a school girl; while her brain was busy with figures and statistics which would have puzzled many older heads.

This she did for years, faithfully earning her salary, and meanwhile playing her part in the domestic drama; for real tragedy and comedy came into it as time went on; the sisters married or died, brothers won their way up, and more than one Infant Phenomenon appeared on the household stage.

But through all changes my good D was still "leading lady," and now, when the mother is gone, the other birds all flown, she remains in the once overflowing nest, the stay and comfort of her father, unspoiled by either poverty or wealth, unsaddened by much sorrow, unsoured by spinsterhood. A wise and witty little woman, and a happy one too, though the curly locks are turning gray; for the three Christian graces, faith, hope, and charity, abide with her to the end.

Of E I know too little to do justice to her success; but as it has been an unusual one, I cannot resist giving her a place here, although I never saw her, and much regret that now I never can, since she has gone to plead her own cause before the wise Judge of all.

Her story was told me by a friend, and made so strong an impression upon me that I wrote down the facts while they were fresh in my mind. A few words, added since her death, finish the too brief record of her brave life.

At fourteen, E began to read law with a legal friend. At eighteen she began to practise, and did so well that this friend offered her half his business, which was very large. But she preferred to stand alone, and in two years had a hundred cases of all sorts in different courts, and never lost one.

In a certain court-room, where she was the only woman present, her bearing was so full of dignity that every one treated her with respect. Her opponent, a shrewd old lawyer, made many sharp or impertinent remarks, hoping to anger her and make her damage her cause by some loss of self-control. But she merely looked at him with such a wise, calm smile, and answered with such unexpected wit and wisdom, that the man was worsted and young Portia won her suit, to the great satisfaction of the spectators, men though they were.

She used to say that her success was owing to hard work,—

too hard, I fear, if she often studied eighteen hours a day. She asked no help or patronage, only fair play, and one cannot but regret that it ever was denied a creature who so womanfully proved her claim to it.

A friend says, "she was a royal girl, and did all her work in a royal way. She broke down suddenly, just as she had passed the last hostile outpost; just as she had begun to taste the ineffable sweetness of peace and rest, following a relative life-time of battle and toil."

But, short as her career has been, not one brave effort is wasted, since she has cleared the way for those who come after her, and proved that women have not only the right but the ability to sit upon the bench as well as stand at the bar of justice.

Last, but by no means least, is F, because her success is the most wonderful of all, since every thing was against her from the first, as you will see when I tell her little story.

Seven or eight years ago, a brave woman went down into Virginia with a friend, and built a schoolhouse for the freed people, who were utterly forlorn; because, though the great gift of liberty was theirs, it was so new and strange they hardly understood how to use it. These good women showed them, and among the first twenty children who began the school, which now has hundreds of pupils, white as well as black, came little F.

Ignorant, ragged and wild, yet with such an earnest, resolute face that she attracted the attention of her teachers at once, and her eagerness to learn touched their hearts; for it was a hard fight with her to get an education, because she could only be spared now and then from corn-planting, pulling fodder, toting water, oyster-shucking or grubbing the new land.

She must have made good use of those "odd days," for she was among the first dozen who earned a pictorial pocket-handkerchief for learning the multiplication table, and a proud child was F when she bore home the prize. Rapidly the patient little fingers learned to write on the first slate she ever saw, and her whole heart went into the task of reading the books which opened a new world to her.

The instinct of progression was as strong in her as the love of light in a plant, and when the stone was lifted away, she sprang up and grew vigorously.

At last the chance to go North and earn something, which all freed people desire, came to F; and in spite of many obstacles she made the most of it. At the very outset she had to fight for a place in the steamer, since the captain objected to her being admitted to the cabin on account of her color; though any lady could take her black maid in without any trouble. But the friend with whom she travelled insisted on F's rights, and won them by declaring that if the child was condemned to pass the night on deck, she would pass it with her.

F watched the contest with breathless interest, as well she might; for this was her first glimpse of the world outside the narrow circle where her fourteen years had been spent. Poor little girl! there seemed to be no place for her anywhere; and I cannot help wondering what her thoughts were, as she sat alone in the night, shut out from among her kind for no fault but the color of her skin.

What could she think of "white folks'" religion, intelligence, and courtesy? Fortunately she had one staunch friend beside her to keep her faith in human justice alive, and win a little place for her among her fellow beings. The captain for very shame consented at last, and F felt that she was truly free when she stepped out of the lonely darkness of the night into the light and shelter of the cabin, a harmless little girl, asking only a place to lay her head.

That was the first experience, and it made a deep impression on her; but those that followed were pleasanter, for nowhere in the free North was she refused her share of room in God's world.

I saw her in New York, and even before I learned her story I was attracted to the quiet, tidy, door-girl by the fact that she was always studying as she sat in the noisy hall of a great boarding-house, keeping her books under her chair and poring over them at every leisure moment. Kindly people, touched by her patient efforts, helped her along; and one of the prettiest sights I saw in the big city was a little white girl taking time from her own sports to sit on the stairs and hear F recite. I think Bijou Heron will never play a sweeter part than that, nor have a more enthusiastic admirer than F was when we went together to see the child-actress play "The Little Treasure" for charity.

To those who know F it seems as if a sort of miracle had been wrought, to change in so short a time a forlorn little Topsy into this intelligent, independent, ambitious girl, who not only supports and educates herself, but sends a part of her earnings home, and writes such good letters to her mates that they are read aloud in school. Here is a paragraph from one which was a part of the Christmas festival last year:—

"I have now seen what a great advantage it is to have an education. I begin to feel the good of the little I know, and I am trying hard every day to add more to it. Most every child up here from ten to twelve years old can read and write, colored as well as white. And if you were up here, I think you would be surprised to see such little bits of children going to school with their arms full of books. I do hope you will all learn as much as you can; for an Education is a great thing."

I wonder how many white girls of sixteen would do any better, if as well, as this resolute F, bravely making her way against fate and fortune, toward the useful, happy womanhood we all desire. I know she will find friends, and I trust that if she ever knocks at the door of any college, asking her sisters to let her in, they will not disgrace themselves by turning their backs upon her; but prove themselves worthy of their blessings, by showing them Christian gentlewomen.

Here are my six girls; doctor, artist, philanthropist, actress, lawyer, and freedwoman; only a few among the hundreds who work and win, and receive their reward, seen of men or only known to God. Perhaps some other girl reading of these may take heart again, and travel on cheered by their example; for the knowledge of what has been done often proves wonderfully inspiring to those who long to do.

I felt this strongly when I went to a Woman's Congress not long ago; for on the stage was a noble array of successful women, making the noblest use of their talents in discussing all the questions which should interest and educate their sex. I was particularly proud of the senators from Massachusetts, and, looking about the crowded house to see how the audience stirred and glowed under their inspiring words, I saw a good omen for the future.

Down below were grown people, many women, and a few men; but up in the gallery, like a garland of flowers, a circle of girlish faces looked down eager-eyed; listening, with quick smiles and tears, to the wit or eloquence of those who spoke, dropping their school books to clap heartily when a good point was made, and learning better lessons in those three days than as many years of common teaching could give them.

It was close and crowded down below, dusty and dark; but up in the gallery the fresh October air blew in, mellow sunshine touched the young heads, there was plenty of room to stir, and each day the garland seemed to blossom fuller and brighter, showing how the interest grew. There they were, the future Mary Livermores, Ednah Cheneys, Julia Howes, Maria Mitchells, Lucy Stones, unconsciously getting ready to play their parts on the wider stage which those pioneers have made ready for them, before gentler critics, a wiser public, and more enthusiastic friends.

Looking from the fine gray heads which adorned the shadowy platform, to the bright faces up aloft, I wanted to call out,—

"Look, listen, and learn, my girls; then, bringing your sunshine and fresh air, your youth and vigor, come down to fill nobly the places of these true women, and earn for yourselves the same success which will make their names long loved and honored in the land."

1878

CHRONOLOGY

NOTE ON THE TEXTS

NOTES

# Chronology

1832    Born November 29 in Germantown, Pennsylvania, the second child of Abigail May Alcott (known as "Abba") and Amos Bronson Alcott. (Father, known as Bronson, was born in poverty in rural Connecticut in 1799 and left school at thirteen to work as an itinerant peddler; an autodidact, he became a schoolteacher and education reformer, publishing *Observations on the Principles and Methods of Infant Instruction* in 1830. Mother, born 1800 into a Boston Unitarian family, married Bronson in Boston in 1830; they moved to Germantown in 1831 to open a school. Their first child, Anna, was born in Philadelphia on March 16, 1831.)

1833–35    Father meticulously records his observations of Alcott's infancy and early education. The family returns to Boston in July 1834 in financial distress. In September, with the help of his wife's family and school reformer Elizabeth Peabody, father founds the experimental Temple School; students include relatives or relatives-in-law of Melville, Hawthorne, Emerson, and John Quincy Adams. Sister Elizabeth Sewall Alcott ("Lizzie") is born on June 24, 1835. Father becomes a vegetarian; meets Ralph Waldo Emerson and visits him at Concord.

1836–37    Accompanies father to the Temple School, where he reads Wordsworth and the Gospels to students. Father joins Emerson, Henry David Thoreau, George Ripley, Orestes Brownson, and others to start the Transcendentalist Club. Margaret Fuller begins teaching at the Temple School. Father's *Conversations with Children on the Gospels* is published in 1837; its liberal theology and discussion of pregnancy create a scandal that, along with the financial panic of 1837, forces the Temple School to close.

1838    Father teaches school in the family home; Emerson encourages him to write. Mother suffers a miscarriage. Alcott runs away from home about this time; is punished by being tied to the sofa.

1839    Father admits an African American girl, Susan Robinson, to his school and loses nearly all of his students; gives up professional teaching. Mother gives birth to a son, who dies after only a few hours.

1840    Family moves to Concord, where they live in a cottage on two acres near the Concord River. Sister Abigail May Alcott ("May") is born July 26.

1841    Writes her first poem, "The Robin." Attends school with Lizzie in Emerson's home, and visits her mother's family in Boston. Father lectures in Concord and nearby towns.

1842    Father travels to England for six months, where he visits Alcott House, an experimental school named in his honor, and returns home in October with Henry Wright, the director of Alcott House, and a disciple, Charles Lane. Mother notices Alcott's fondness for writing and gives her a pencil case for her tenth birthday.

1843    In June, the family moves with Charles Lane and his son William to a farm near Harvard, Massachusetts, where they found Fruitlands, a utopian community, and attempt to live as a "consociate family"; others, including a dietary reformer and an advocate of nudism, join them for varying intervals. They live mainly on bread, apples, potatoes, and water; the burden of farmwork falls mainly on Abba. Alcott helps with housework, chores, and childcare; acts out plays with her sisters; reads Plutarch, Byron, Dickens, Maria Edgeworth, and Oliver Goldsmith.

1844    Fruitlands fails in January. Charles Lane and his son join a Shaker community; the Alcotts move to rented rooms in Still River, Massachusetts, and live on Abba's inheritance from her father and donations from the Mays and Emerson. Alcott attends the Still River village school in the summer.

1845–46  In January, with mother's inheritance and help from Emerson, family buys a house in Concord, which father names "Hillside." Alcott is given a bedroom of her own; she is educated at home by her father and Sophia Foord, a young teacher who subsequently opens a schoolroom in Emerson's barn. Acts out Bunyan's *Pilgrim's Progress* at home with sisters.

1847    In February, family shelters a fugitive slave from Maryland, who spends a week at Hillside. Alcott reads Hawthorne,

Charlotte Brontë, Shakespeare, Dante, Carlyle, and Goethe (Emerson lends her *Wilhelm Meister*). In July, family visits Thoreau at Walden Pond, where father had helped him build a cabin. Mother takes a job at a water-cure hotel in Waterford, Maine, in the fall; Anna teaches in Walpole, New Hampshire.

1848 Alcott reads and supports the "Declaration of Sentiments" of the Seneca Falls women's rights convention. Family moves to Boston. Mother is hired to serve as missionary to the poor by the South Friendly Society, a philanthropic group. Alcott runs the household while Anna teaches.

1849 Writes novel *The Inheritance* (it is not published until after her death); earns money teaching and sewing. Alcott sisters found Pickwick Club and publish a family newspaper, *The Olive Leaf*.

1850 Alcott teaches reading and Sunday school classes in the South End of Boston; dreams of becoming an actress. Reads Frederika Bremer's *Easter Offering* and Hawthorne's *The Scarlet Letter*, both just published. Entire family afflicted with smallpox, but all recover. In August, mother starts an "Intelligence Service," or employment agency.

1851 Alcott is inspired by speakers at an antislavery meeting, including William Henry Channing and Wendell Phillips: "I felt ready to do anything,—fight or work, hoot or cry." Works as a domestic servant in Dedham, Massachusetts, but is "starved & frozen" there, and quits. Earns a total of $40 as governess for the Lovering family, and $40 by sewing and seamstress work. Her first publication, "Sunlight," a poem, appears in September in *Peterson's Magazine* under pseudonym Flora Fairfield.

1852 Publishes story "The Rival Painters" in *Olive Branch*, a weekly paper enjoyed by the Alcott sisters. Hears transcendentalist Theodore Parker preach on "The Public Function of Women." Teaches school with Anna at home. Reads *Uncle Tom's Cabin*. Hillside purchased by the Hawthornes; mother gives up employment agency and takes in lodgers in their rented house in Beacon Hill. Story "The Masked Marriage" published in December.

1853 In January starts a small school in the family parlor, with around ten pupils. Spends summer in Leicester, Massachusetts, working as a domestic; returns to teaching in October.

Anna takes a job teaching in Syracuse, New York. Father embarks on a midwestern speaking tour.

1854        Father returns in February, without having earned the money the family had hoped for. In May, father joins the Vigilance Committee, which makes a failed attempt to rescue Anthony Burns, a fugitive slave, from the Boston courthouse. Alcott visits Anna in Syracuse. "The Rival Prima Donnas" published in November in the *Saturday Evening Gazette*. *Flower Fables*, a collection of fairy stories written for Emerson's daughter and dedicated to Abba, is published in December in an edition of 1,600 copies by George Briggs. The book earns Alcott only $32, but receives good reviews.

1855        Attends plays in Boston. Family spends the summer rent-free in a relative's house in Walpole, New Hampshire. Fanny Kemble visits; Alcott and Anna act in amateur theatricals. Family returns to Boston in the fall. Alcott hears William Makepeace Thackeray lecture in December.

1856        Publishes stories and poems in the *Saturday Evening Gazette*; earns money sewing. Lizzie and May contract scarlet fever from a poor family that their mother is taking care of, and Lizzie never fully recovers. Alcott attends Theodore Parker's Sunday evening discussions and meets William Lloyd Garrison. In December, works as tutor for Alice Lovering, a young invalid. Wears her first silk dress (a gift from an aunt) on New Year's Eve.

1857        Works as a tutor, writer, and seamstress; sends money to her mother. Reads a biography of Charlotte Brontë, and notes in her journal, "I can't be a C.B., but I may do a little something yet." In September, family buys a house in Concord and begins renovations.

1858        Alcott and her mother nurse Lizzie, whose illness worsens; Lizzie dies in March. In April, Anna becomes engaged to John Pratt, son of Minot Pratt, the director of Brook Farm; they agree to postpone the wedding until the family has recovered from Lizzie's death. Alcott acts in productions of the Concord Dramatic Society: "Perhaps it is acting, not writing, I'm meant for." Family moves into new home in July; Alcott returns to Boston as Alice Lovering's tutor.

1859        Writes in March: "Busy life teaching, writing, sewing, getting all I can from lectures, books, and good people. Life is my college. May I graduate well, and earn some honors!" Father appointed Superintendent of Schools in Concord. John Brown speaks at Concord Town Hall in May; family celebrates his attack at Harpers Ferry in October and mourns his execution in December.

1860    Publishes a poem, "With a Rose That Bloomed on the Day of John Brown's Martyrdom," in *The Liberator*; an antislavery story, "M.L.," is rejected by an editor afraid of offending southern readers. Begins work on novel *Moods*. Anna marries John Pratt in May. Alcott sees her farce *Nat Bachelor's Pleasure Trip* performed in Boston. Theodore Parker dies in June. Family hosts John Brown's widow when she visits Concord in July. Attends lecture by health reformer Dr. Dio Lewis; notes Concord is "convulsed just now with a Gymnastic fever." Story "A Modern Cinderella: or, The Little Old Shoe," based on Anna's romance with John Pratt, is published in *The Atlantic Monthly*.

1861    Begins writing novel *Work* (at first titled "Success"), and revises *Moods*. Writes a song for Concord school festival hailing "our John Browns" that causes controversy; Emerson defends her and reads the song to the assembly. When the Civil War begins in April, writes: "I've often longed to see a war, and now I have my wish. I long to be a man; but as I can't fight, I will content myself with working for those who can." John Brown's daughters board at Orchard House, parents' house in Concord. Alcott reads Fanny Burney's *Evelina*, Fielding's, *Amelia*, and Carlyle's *The French Revolution*. Visits cousins in the White Mountains of New Hampshire.

1862    Alcott shows publisher James T. Fields manuscript of "How I Went Out to Service"; he tells her, "Stick to your teaching, Miss Alcott. You can't write." Teaches at a Boston kindergarten from January to April. Meets writer Rebecca Harding: "A handsome, fresh, quiet woman, who says she never had any troubles, though she writes about woes. I told her I had had lots of troubles; so I write jolly tales; and we wondered why we each did so." Attends Thoreau's funeral in May. On December 11, travels to Washington, D.C., where she serves as an army nurse at Union Hotel Hospital.

1863    Story "Pauline's Passion and Punishment" wins $100 prize and appears in *Frank Leslie's Illustrated Newspaper*. At the

hospital, contracts typhoid fever and suffers hallucinations;
is treated with calomel, a compound containing mercury,
which possibly permanently damages her health. Father
brings her home, where she recovers over several months.
Anna's first son born in March. Letters about Alcott's
nursing experience, printed in *The Boston Commonwealth*
beginning in May, are unexpectedly popular; in August,
James Redpath publishes them as *Hospital Sketches*. A
poem, "Thoreau's Flute," and an antislavery story, "My
Contraband; or, The Brothers," appear in *Atlantic
Monthly*. Encouraged by praise for *Hospital Sketches* and
new demand for her work, finishes *Moods*.

1864    *On Picket Duty, and Other Tales* published in January.
        Reads Sir Walter Scott, Goethe, Fanny Burney, Dickens, and
        Longfellow's *Tales of a Wayside Inn*. Continues writing
        *Work*. In July, publishes a collection of "Colored Soldiers'
        Letters" in *The Commonwealth*. At her publisher J. K. Lor-
        ing's suggestion, cuts ten chapters from *Moods*; the novel is
        published in late December and "makes a little stir."

1865    Attends January convention of Massachusetts Anti-
        Slavery Society. Thriller "V.V.: or, Plots and Counterplots"
        is serialized (under pseudonym A. M. Barnard) in *The
        Flag of Our Union* in February; several other "sensation
        stories" appear later in the year. In March, is invited to
        dinner by Henry James Sr. and "treated like the Queen of
        Sheba"; Henry James Jr., who is "very friendly" at dinner,
        gives *Moods* a mixed review in the July *North American
        Review*. Travels to Europe in July as a companion to Anna
        Weld, an invalid; visits England, Belgium, Holland, Ger-
        many, Switzerland, and France. In Switzerland befriends
        Ladislas Wisniewski, a young traveler who had fought in
        the Polish rebellion against Russia in 1863.

1866    Spends January through April in Nice; decides to come
        home early, as Anna Weld is not interested in travel and
        "my time is too valuable to be wasted." In May joins
        Ladislas Wisniewski in Paris; sees sights and attends the
        theater. Travels to London, where she meets a wide circle
        of people including Mathilde Blind, a poet; Barbara Bodi-
        chon, an advocate for women's rights and education;
        Frances Cobbe, an essayist, philanthropist, and feminist
        reformer; Elizabeth Garrett, a pioneering doctor; philoso-
        pher John Stuart Mill; and political leaders Benjamin Dis-

raeli and William Gladstone. Returns to Concord in July. Novel "A Modern Mephistopheles, or the Long Fatal Love Chase" rejected as "too sensational."

1867      Thriller "The Abbot's Ghost; or, Maurice Treherne's Temptation" serialized in January. Overworked and ill, is unable to write from January to June. In August, travels to Clarke's Island, in the Connecticut River near Northfield, Massachusetts, with May and a group of Concord friends. In September, is commissioned by Thomas Niles of Roberts Brothers to write a story for girls, and agrees to try. Accepts editorship of the children's magazine *Merry's Museum*. *Morning-Glories, and Other Stories* published in December. Hears Charles Dickens lecture, and is "disappointed."

1868      In February, writes article "Happy Women": "I put in my list all the busy, useful, independent spinsters I know, for liberty is a better husband than love to many of us." Acts in a charity church fair. From May to June, writes the first part of *Little Women*, doubtful of its chances. Published by Roberts Brothers in September, the book is a popular and critical success, and quickly sells out its first printing. Niles asks for a sequel, which Alcott begins in November. Attends lecture by Unitarian minister John Weiss on "Woman Suffrage." An English edition of the first part of *Little Women* is published in December.

1869      Sends the second part of *Little Women* to Roberts Brothers on January 1; it is published in April. Puts her family's financial affairs in order: "Paid up all the debts, thank the Lord!—every penny that money can pay,—and now I feel as if I could die in peace." Spends July at Rivière de Loup, Quebec, and August, with May, at Mt. Desert, Maine. Roberts Brothers publishes *Hospital Sketches and Camp and Fireside Stories*. Continues to suffer from ill health.

1870      Novel *An Old-Fashioned Girl* published by Roberts Brothers in March. In April, sails for Europe with May and May's friend Alice Bartlett; travels through France to Switzerland (which she finds "crammed with refugees" from the Franco-Prussian War), and then throughout Italy to Rome, where she takes an apartment. Brother-in-law John Pratt dies in late November, leaving two sons.

1871      In January, in Rome, begins *Little Men: Life at Plumfield*

*With Jo's Boys*; feels she "must be a father now" to her nephews and writes the novel in order to support them. Spends March in Albano and part of April in Venice; travels to London via Munich, Cologne, and Antwerp. *Little Men* is published in London in May. Returns to Boston in June, leaving May in Europe to pursue her study of art; by the end of the month, Roberts Brothers in Boston prints 38,000 copies of *Little Men*. Falls ill soon after she arrives home; takes morphine to sleep.

1872 *Aunt Jo's Scrap Bag: My Boys* published in January. Writes "Shawl Straps," an account of her 1870–71 European tour, for the *Christian Union*; it appears as a book in November. Attends lectures by Thomas Wentworth Higginson, Octavius Brooks Frothingham, and Rabbi Max Lilienthal. Continues writing *Work*.

1873 Visits Newport, Rhode Island; meets writer Helen Hunt Jackson. Finishes *Work*. Gives May $1,000 to return to London to study art. Spends summer in Boston with sick mother. Roberts Brothers publishes *Work: A Story of Experience* in June; "Transcendental Wild Oats," a fictionalized account of the family's life at Fruitlands in the 1840s, is published in December, along with a story collection, *Aunt Jo's Scrap Bag. Cupid and Chow Chow, Etc.*

1874 In January, writes: "When I had the youth I had no money; now I have the money I have no time; and when I get the time, if I ever do, I shall have no health to enjoy life. . . . Life always was a puzzle to me, and gets more mysterious as I go on." In February, meets English novelist Charles Kingsley, who is on an American tour. Publishes "How I Went Out to Service," an account of her early experience as a domestic, in June. Suffers from poor health while working on novel *Eight Cousins* ("was in such pain could not do much . . . no sleep without morphine"), but finishes in December.

1875 Father, on a western speaking tour, writes that he is "adored as the grandfather of *Little Women*." Alcott signs autographs at Vassar, is "rather lionized" in New York, and at home receives a constant stream of celebrity-seeking visitors. ("Fame is an expensive luxury. I can do without it," she writes.) Attends Woman's Congress in Syracuse in the fall; is surrounded by autograph hunters. *Eight Cousins: or, The Aunt-Hill* published by Roberts Brothers.

Stays at a New York hotel in November and December; visits literary salons, clubs, and theaters, "very gay for a country-mouse."

1876　Travels to Philadelphia in January. Hears Henry Ward Beecher preach, but does not like him. Attends Centennial Ball in Boston. Nurses mother. In September, again sends May to Europe to study art: "The money I invest in her pays the sort of interest I like." Novel *Rose in Bloom. A Sequel to "Eight Cousins"* published by Roberts Brothers in November; the first printing of 10,000 copies quickly sells out.

1877　*A Modern Mephistopheles* published anonymously in the Roberts Brothers' No Name Series. ("It has been simmering ever since I read Faust last year. Enjoyed doing it, being tired of providing moral pap for the young," she writes in her journal; the book bears the same title as the novel rejected in 1866, but is a different work.) Helps Anna purchase a house in Concord. Is bedridden for several weeks in July. Finishes *Under the Lilacs* as she takes care of her mother, who is ill; in November, mother dies. Roberts Brothers publishes *Aunt Jo's Scrap Bag. My Girls, Etc.*

1878　Stays with Anna while they mourn their mother. May marries Ernest Nieriker, a Swiss businessman, in Paris in March. Alcott attempts to write a memoir of Abba, but finds "it is too soon, and I am not well enough." Nurses Anna, who has a broken leg. Roberts Brothers publishes *Under the Lilacs.* In November, begins novella "Diana and Persis," based on May's romance and marriage.

1879　Acts at an authors' carnival at the Boston Music Hall in January. Reads Mary Wollstonecraft. Sets up trust funds for the education of Anna's children. Honored along with Frances Hodgson Burnett at a gala dinner of Boston's Papyrus Club in February. Enjoys Gilbert and Sullivan's *H.M.S. Pinafore.* Reads for an audience of 400 men at Concord Prison. Registers to vote in local elections, the first woman in Concord to do so, and in September canvasses for woman suffrage. Reads at a women's prison in Sherborn, Massachusetts, preferring it to the "armed wardens & 'knock down & drag out' methods" of the Concord Prison. In October, Roberts Brothers publishes *Aunt Jo's Scrap Bag: Jimmy's Cruise in the Pinafore.* Father, who had hosted a school of philosophy in July, embarks on a two-month western tour. May dies in Paris on December 29, six weeks after giving birth to Louise Marie (called Louisa May, or "Lulu") Nieriker.

1880    Mourns May: "the wave of sorrow kept rolling over me & I could only weep & wait till the tide ebbed again." Finishes novel *Jack and Jill* in February; attends Emerson's 100th lecture at the Concord Lyceum. In March, joins nineteen women in voting at Concord town meeting. Writes a stage version of Jules Verne's *Michel Strogoff*, but does not attempt to have it published or produced. Spends July and August in York, Maine. Roberts Brothers publishes a new edition of *Little Women*, with illustrations by Frank T. Merrill. Adopts niece Lulu Nieriker, who arrives from Europe in September. Pays poll taxes for the first time. *Jack and Jill: A Village Story* is published by Roberts Brothers in October.

1881    Spends July in Nonquitt, on the Massachusetts coast. In October, attempts to form a woman suffrage club: "the women need so much coaxing it is hard work." Writes preface for an edition of Theodore Parker's prayers. Suffers increasingly from ill health.

1882    Helps found a temperance society in Concord, and writes short articles to aid its cause. Revised edition of *Moods* published. Emerson dies in April: "Our best & greatest American gone. . . . I can never tell all he has been to me from the time I sang Mignon's song under his window, a little girl, & wrote letters à la Bettine to him, my Goethe, at 15, up through my hard years when his essays on Self-Reliance, Character, Compensation, Love & Friendship helped me to understand myself & life & God & Nature." Writes article on Emerson for *The Youth's Companion*. Spends summer at Nonquitt. Begins work on *Jo's Boys* in October. Father is left paralyzed by stroke, and never fully recovers. Roberts Brothers publishes *Aunt Jo's Scrap Bag: An Old-Fashioned Thanksgiving* and *Proverb Stories*.

1883    Cares for her father and Lulu. Spends summer at Nonquitt. Attends lectures by Pratap Chunder Mozoomdar ("Curious to hear a Hindoo tell how the life of Christ impressed him") and Matthew Arnold.

1884    Sends niece to kindergarten. In June, sells Orchard House and buys a beach house in Nonquitt, where she spends the summer. Tries to work on *Jo's Boys* but finds "my head won't bear work yet," and puts it aside. Roberts Brothers publishes *Spinning-Wheel Stories* in November.

1885    Sees Boston "mind-cure" practitioner Anna B. Newman, but after many visits finds the treatment unsuccessful: "my ills are not imaginary." Contributes a letter to the April 18 *Woman's Journal* about her experience. Reads *George Eliot's Life as Related in Her Letters and Journals*, just published, and Charles de Montalembert's *Life of St. Elizabeth*. Spends summer in Concord and Nonquitt. Rereads old letters and decides to burn many of them. Rents a large house for family in Boston's Louisburg Square.

1886    In July, finishes *Jo's Boys, and How They Turned Out*, the concluding novel in the March family trilogy, which is published by Roberts Brothers in September. Hears Julia Ward Howe lecture on "Women in Plato's Republic." Her doctor, Rhoda Lawrence, forbids her to work on novels "or anything that will need much thought." Suffers from pain and insomnia. Spends December at Dr. Lawrence's nursing home in Roxbury. Reviews Frances Hodgson Burnett's *Little Lord Fauntleroy*.

1887    Plans to adopt her nephew John Pratt. Visits Princeton for a month with Dr. Lawrence; her health improves in the summer, and she is able to take long walks again and ride. Suffers from weakness and pain in her limbs, and returns to Dr. Lawrence's in the fall for treatment. *A Garland for Girls* is published in December.

1888    Writes occasionally, and sews clothes for poor children when she is unable to write. In early March visits father, whose health has worsened; is herself in violent pain the next day, and lapses into unconsciousness. Dies, probably of intestinal cancer or an autoimmune disease such as lupus, on March 6, two days after her father. Buried in the family plot at Sleepy Hollow Cemetery in Concord.

# Note on the Texts

This volume contains three novels by Louisa May Alcott: *Work: A Story of Experience* (1873), *Eight Cousins; or, The Aunt-Hill* (1875), and *Rose in Bloom. A Sequel to "Eight Cousins"* (1876), as well as seven stories and articles.

Alcott began writing the novel that became *Work* in January 1861 under the title "Success," putting it away after less than a month. She intended it to be autobiographical, basing episodes on her stints as a domestic servant, governess, and seamstress and her experiences in private and benefit theatricals. Some characters were modeled on her friends and acquaintances: for example, Henry David Thoreau became David Sterling, Theodore Parker became Mr. Power, and Harriet Tubman was transformed into Hepsey Johnson. Alcott added to it sporadically during 1863–65 and then again set the manuscript aside. In November 1872, the owners of *The Christian Union* asked Alcott for a serial, offering $3,000. Alcott renamed the manuscript "Work," revising some stories she had written previously and incorporating them into the novel. For example, a thriller she had written anonymously in 1865, "A Nurse's Story," became the chapter "Companion"; and an episode from *Hospital Sketches* (1863), Alcott's popular Civil War memoir based on the letters she wrote to her family when she worked as a nurse at the Union Hospital in Washington, D.C., was reused as the basis for the death of David Sterling. Alcott wrote using a steel pen on impression paper, akin to modern carbon paper, to produce three manuscripts: for *The Christian Union*, her U.S. publisher, and her London publisher. In the process she permanently damaged her right thumb and taught herself to write with her left hand. *Work* was serialized in *The Christian Union* as "Work; or Christie's Experiment," December 18, 1872–June 18, 1873, and was published in book form in June 1873 by Roberts Brothers in Boston and (without authorial revision) by Sampson Low in London as *Work: A Story of Experience*. This volume uses the first American edition as the source for its text.

Alcott had considered writing a novel for children championing education reform since she visited Dr. Dio Lewis's school for girls in Lexington, Massachusetts, in mid-1864, and the Bellerive School in Vevey, Switzerland, run by Frédéric Edouard Sillig, in fall 1865. She began writing *Eight Cousins* as a serial for *St. Nicholas*, a children's magazine edited by Mary Mapes Dodge, in summer 1874, originally calling it either "The Aunt Hill" or "Rose & the Rest." It appeared in *St. Nicholas* from January to October 1875. In order to secure her copyright in Great Britain, it was also serialized in *Good Things: A Picturesque Magazine*, a British children's magazine edited by George MacDonald, from December 5, 1874 to November 27, 1875. The novel (including two chapters Dodge had deleted to save space) was published by Roberts Brothers in Boston in late September 1875 as *Eight Cousins; or, The Aunt-Hill*. An identical British edition was published in London at about the same time by Sampson Low.

In August and September 1876 Alcott wrote a sequel at the request of Thomas Niles at Roberts Brothers, which published it in November as *Rose in Bloom. A Sequel to "Eight Cousins"*; Sampson Low brought out a British edition (without authorial revision) almost immediately. This volume uses the first American edition of each novel as the source for its text.

The following is a list of the stories and articles included in this volume, in the order of their appearance, giving the source of each text.

"Address of the Republican Women of Massachusetts" (Boston, September 25, 1872) is a self-published broadside signed by Alcott, along with Lydia Maria Child, Harriet Beecher Stowe, and Julia Ward Howe.

"Kate's Choice" was first serialized in *Hearth and Home* on May 18 and 25, 1872. Alcott then collected it in *Aunt Jo's Scrap-Bag. Cupid and Chow-Chow, Etc.* (Boston: Roberts Brothers; London: Sampson Low, 1874), the American edition of which is the source for the text in this volume.

"How I Went Out to Service. A Story," was published in *The Independent* on June 4, 1874. An autobiographical account of Alcott's seven weeks spent as a servant in 1851 (which also inspired a chapter in *Work*), it was not collected by Alcott. The text from *The Independent* is used in this volume.

"Woman's Part in the Concord Celebration" was published in *Woman's Journal and Suffrage News*, a magazine published by the American Woman Suffrage Association that was edited by Lucy Stone, on May 1, 1875; and "Letter to the Woman's Journal, June 29, 1876," was published in the same magazine on July 15, 1876. Neither letter was collected by Alcott, and the texts from the *Woman's Journal* are used in this volume.

"Anna's Whim" was first serialized in *The Independent* on December 18, 1873, and reprinted in the *Woman's Journal* on February 21, 1874, before being collected by Alcott in *Silver Pitchers: and Independence, A Centennial Love Story* (Boston: Roberts Brothers; London: Sampson Low, 1876), the American edition of which is the source for the text in this volume.

"My Girls" was published for the first time in *Aunt Jo's Scrap-Bag. My Girls, Etc.* (Boston: Roberts Brothers, 1878), which is the source for the text in the present volume.

This volume presents the texts of the original printings chosen for inclusion here, but it does not attempt to reproduce features of their typographic design. The texts are presented without change, except for the correction of typographical errors. Spelling, punctuation, and capitalization are often expressive features, and they are not altered, even when inconsistent or irregular. The following is a list of typographical errors corrected, cited by page and line number: 41.5, Peg. and; 48.17, eight-year old; 118.32, home.; 123.17, mite; 132.3, out of window; 136.8, on't,; 136.36, nourishin,'; 149.3, men. and; 164.11, bit"; 164.13, look, he; 168.4, neglected.'; 209.36, Florida,"; 225.6, heauty; 245.6, married:"; 293.1, WORK; 334.23, melody.'"; 345.21, at sound; 374.16, workbox; 405.19, the night before; 488.27, fast But; 586.3, hearts; 648.25, will!; 737.23–24, 'Love and Friendship.'; 804.21, warrant,'; 808.8, know though; 809.21, gave The; 816.2, heartly; 817.25, tears Puah; 820.35, gentlemen; 821.22, Anxcious; 822.2–3, Gamalials; 829.1, growing one; 835.31, friend," she says.

# *Notes*

In the notes below, the reference numbers denote page and line of this volume (the line count includes headings). No note is made for material included in standard desk-reference books. Quotations from Shakespeare are keyed to *The Riverside Shakespeare*, ed. G. Blakemore Evans (Boston: Houghton Mifflin, 1974). Biblical quotations are keyed to the King James Version. For references to other studies and further information than is included in the Chronology, see Ednah D. Cheney, ed., *Louisa May Alcott: Her Life, Letters, and Journals* (Boston: Roberts Brothers, 1889); Joel Myerson and Daniel Shealy, eds., *The Selected Letters of Louisa May Alcott* (Boston: Little, Brown, 1987); Joel Myerson and Daniel Shealy, eds., *The Journals of Louisa May Alcott* (Boston: Little, Brown, 1989); Martha Saxton, *Louisa May Alcott: A Modern Biography* (Boston: Houghton Mifflin, 1997); Daniel Lester Shealy, "The Author-Publisher Relationships of Louisa May Alcott" (Ph.D. dissertation, University of South Carolina, 1985); Susan Cheever, *Louisa May Alcott: A Personal Biography* (New York: Simon & Schuster, 2010); Gregory Eiselein and Anne K. Phillips, eds., *The Louisa May Alcott Encyclopedia* (Westport, CT: Greenwood Press, 2001).

WORK

8.19 "The Farmer's Friend,"] *The Farmer's Friend: A Record of Recent Discoveries, Improvements, and Practical Suggestions in Agriculture* (London: Smith, Elder and Co., 1847).

8.29 a Mrs. Fry, a Florence Nightingale] Elizabeth Fry (1780–1845), English prison reformer who opened a training school for nurses in 1840 that inspired Florence Nightingale (1820–1910), English reformer considered to be the founder of modern nursing.

15.2 SERVANT] In 1853 Alcott had briefly worked as "second girl," or laundress, for her uncle Samuel May. See also note 806.1.

17.4 intelligence office] Alcott's mother, Abba May Alcott, started an "Intelligence Service," or employment agency, in 1850 in Boston.

18.2–3 Turner's "Rain, Wind, and Hail," . . . upside down] An allusion to Joseph Mallord William Turner's "Rain, Steam and Speed—The Great Western Railway" (1844). A critic for *The Art-Union*, an art magazine published in London, had said of Turner's two paintings in the 1841 British Institution Exhibition that "they would be equally effective, equally pleasing, and equally comprehensible if turned upside-down; indeed, we are not quite sure that one of them has not actually been reversed." Alcott's sister May's copies of Turner's works had been praised by John Ruskin.

18.11–12   Zenobia . . . Aspasia] Zenobia (240–c. 274 C.E.), queen of Palmyra in Roman Syria, led a revolt against the Roman Empire and conquered Egypt. She was defeated by the emperor Aurelian and taken as a prisoner to Rome. A character in Nathaniel Hawthorne's *Blithedale Romance* (1852) is named for her. Aspasia (470–400 B.C.E.), the highly educated consort (or wife) of Athenian orator Pericles, taught rhetoric and conversed with Socrates and is a major character in Lydia Maria Child's novel *Philothea* (1835).

20.2   Hepsey Johnson] Alcott based this character on Harriet Tubman (c. 1820–1913), whom she had met when Tubman visited Concord in 1860. Tubman had escaped from slavery in Maryland in 1849 and then returned to the state several times, leading dozens of slaves to freedom on the Underground Railroad. During the Civil War, she volunteered as a nurse in the Sea Islands of South Carolina and had organized a network of African American spies and scouts who aided the Union army in raids along the coast.

26.9   "The Abbot."] Novel (1820) by Sir Walter Scott about Mary, Queen of Scots.

29.12   Micawber] Wilkins Micawber, impecunious character in *David Copperfield* (1849–50) by Charles Dickens.

30.2   ACTRESS] Alcott made her stage debut in the spring of 1855 in Boston in a benefit performance for the Federal Street Church, playing "Oronthy Bluggage," a character she created, who delivered a burlesque monologue on "Woman, and Her Position." At the invitation of comedian William Warren (1812–1888) she then repeated her performance in a paid appearance at the Howard Atheneum. However, in a letter to her father on November 28, 1855 (the day before their birthday), she wrote, "After being on the stage & seeing more nearly the tinsel & brass of actor life, (much as I should love to be a great star *if* I could,) I have come to the conclusion that its not worth trying for at the expense of health & peace of mind."

34.29   Boadicea] Queen of the Iceni, a Celtic British tribe, who led an uprising in circa 60 C.E. against occupying Roman forces and burned the city of Londinium (modern London). According to Tacitus, she committed suicide after her army was defeated by the Romans.

35.12   Britomarte] Female Knight of Chastity representing military virtue in Spenser's *The Faerie Queene* (1590).

36.29–30   Siddons and Rachel] Sarah Siddons (1755–1831), English Shakespearean actress, and Elisabeth Rachel Félix (1821–1858), French actress known as Mademoiselle Rachel.

38.12–13   Tilly Slowboy] Clumsy nursemaid in Dickens's *The Cricket on the Hearth* (1845).

38.13–14   Kent, the comedian] Based on William Warren; see note 30.2.

39.13   Miggs] Lady's maid and later a jailor in a women's prison in Dickens's *Barnaby Rudge* (1841).

41.5   'Masks and Faces.' . . . Peg] Play (1852) by Charles Reade and Tom Taylor based on the scandalous life of Irish actress Margaret "Peg" Woffington (1720–1760).

42.28   the Rival Queens] Tragedy (1677) by English dramatist Nathaniel Lee about the jealousy between Roxana and Statira, the first and second wives of Alexander the Great.

45.2   GOVERNESS] From 1851 to 1859, Alcott worked intermittently for Mr. and Mrs. Joseph S. Lovering as governess and teacher for their five children, and especially for Alice Lovering, an invalid, to whom she taught reading, math, and other subjects.

56.8   Bedlam] Bethlem Hospital, founded in London in 1247 and known colloquially as Bedlam, Europe's oldest institution for the mentally ill.

59.29   "John Halifax,"] Dinah Mulock Craik, *John Halifax, Gentleman* (1857), in which the hero, an orphan, shows himself to be a gentleman by merit rather than by birth, and is helped by Phineas Fletcher, the invalid son of Halifax's employer.

70.2   COMPANION] In July 1865 Alcott traveled to Europe as the nurse and companion of Anna Minot Weld (1835–1924), an invalid; they were also accompanied by Weld's half brother, George Weld. The two women had little in common and Alcott resigned in April 1866, spent two months travelling in France and England, and returned to the U.S. in July 1866.

85.19–20   David's music brought repose to Saul.] Cf. 1 Samuel 16:14–23.

90.22   the tragic death she had chosen] In writing about the despair and suicide of Helen, Alcott may also have drawn on the experiences of members of her own family. Her uncle, Junius Alcott, had struggled with mental instability before committing suicide in April 1852, and her cousin Louisa May Willis had committed suicide in November 1862 after, according to her obituary, repeated "attacks" of the "disease" of insanity. Alcott's father, Bronson, had experienced episodes of hallucination in 1844 and 1849. John Matteson, biographer of Bronson and Louisa Alcott, suggests that members of the Alcott family suffered from bipolar disorder, an illness with a significant genetic component. On September 4, 1873, responding to a letter from the five Lukens sisters, who regularly corresponded with Alcott after they solicited her subscription to their homemade magazine *Little Things*, Alcott wrote: "I did not like the suicide in 'Work,' but as much of that chapter was true I let it stand as a warning to several people who need it to my knowledge, & to many whom I do not know. I have already had letters from strangers thanking me for it, so I am not sorry it went in. One must have both the dark & the light side to paint life truly."

102.18–19　Magdalen Asylums] Institutions ostensibly existing to house and rehabilitate "fallen women" and prostitutes, but which forced women to perform heavy labor, such as laundry or sewing, without compensation. They were named for Mary Magdalene, a figure from the Gospels conventionally identified in the Roman Catholic church with the converted prostitute in Luke 7:36–50.

112.36–37　a present the ladies are going to give the minister;] In November 1855 Alcott wrote her father that she was "sewing busily for friends & am expecting the high honor of making a set of shirts for the Reverend Dr Gannett a present from his worshippers."

115.7–8　that sorrowful bewilderment . . . over her] In October 1858, after the death of her sister Lizzie in March and the betrothal of her sister Anna in April, Alcott was overwhelmed with a "fit of despair" and wrote to her family that "last week was a busy, anxious time, & my courage most gave out, for every one was so busy, & cared so little whether I got work or jumped into the river that I thought seriously of doing the latter. In fact did go over the Mill Dam & look at the water. But it seemed so mean to turn & run away before the battle was over that I went home, set my teeth & vowed I'd *make* things work in spite of the world, the flesh & the devil."

119.30–31　Bridge of Sighs] Poem (1844) by Thomas Hood, concerning the suicide of a pregnant and homeless young woman who jumped from Waterloo Bridge in London.

125.30–31　Indian-pudding] Traditional New England dessert similar to hasty pudding, made with cornmeal, milk, and molasses or maple syrup and baked until it gains the texture of custard.

129.21　Pickwickian] Evincing an expansive, idiosyncratic interest in the world, in the manner of Samuel Pickwick, protagonist of Dickens's *The Posthumous Papers of the Pickwick Club* (1836–37), which chronicles the adventures of Pickwick and three members of his eponymous club who travel throughout England "enlarging [their] sphere of observation; to the advancement of knowledge, and the diffusion of learning."

131.26　Casabianca] "Casabianca," poem (1826) by British poet Felicia Dorothea Hemans, commemorating an incident during the British naval victory in the battle of the Nile in 1798, in which a young son of Louis de Casabianca, commander of the French flagship *L'Orient*, remained at his post even as the ship burned around him.

132.20　"John Gilpin"] "The Diverting History of John Gilpin," comic ballad (1782) by William Cowper.

132.21　"The Bay of Biscay, O,"] Song (c. 1805) by Irish dramatist and songwriter Andrew Cherry.

132.22　"Chevy Chase"] "The Ballad of Chevy Chase," sixteenth-century traditional English ballad.

144.5   *blanchisseuse*] French: laundress.

144.12   Lindley Murray,] Author and grammarian (1745–1826); his *English Grammar* (1795) was for many years the most widely used grammar textbook in the U.S.

144.39–40   Fuller quaintly says . . . them,"] Thomas Fuller (1608–1661) in *The Holy State and the Prophane State* (1642), of the qualities of a good widow.

145.27–28   Thomas Power] Alcott based Power on Theodore Parker (1810–1860), a Unitarian minister, social reformer, and radical abolitionist who led the Twenty-Eighth Congregational Society of Boston during the 1850s, while Alcott was living and working there. She frequently attended Sunday evening gatherings at Parker's home and called him one of her most important teachers, along with Emerson and her father.

146.32   suz] I.e., sirs.

154.32–37   "Nearer, my God . . . to thee!"] "Nearer, My God, To Thee," hymn (1841) by English poet Sarah Flower Adams (1805–1848) with music by her sister Eliza Flower (1803–1846).

155.33–34   Mr. Sterling] Alcott modeled David Sterling on Henry David Thoreau (1817–1862), who was a neighbor of the Alcotts in Concord, and whose school Louisa May Alcott briefly attended. From Thoreau, Alcott took Sterling's connection to nature, his brown beard, and his flute, as well as his dislike of travel and dependence on his mother. Mr. Hyde in *Little Men*, Adam Warwick in *Moods*, and Mac in *Rose in Bloom* also owe their characterizations to Thoreau.

162.39   mould] Garden soil.

164.19   Pimlico order] I.e., clean and orderly. Pimlico, a middle-class neighborhood of London, was known for its white stucco terrace houses and gardens.

167.17–168.4   "Welcome, maids . . . neglected."] "To Violets," by English poet Robert Herrick (1591–1674).

192.18–19   "'Tell them, dear, that . . . for being.'"] From "The Rhodora," poem (1847) by Ralph Waldo Emerson (1803–1882).

194.28–29   "Heroes and Hero-worship,"] *On Heroes, Hero-Worship, and The Heroic in History* (1841) by Scottish philosopher Thomas Carlyle (1795–1881).

195.5   Tilly Slowboy, Miss Miggs, and Mrs. Gummage] For Tilly Slowboy, see note 38.12–13. For Miss Miggs, see note 39.13. Mrs. Gummidge, a self-pitying widow in Dickens's *David Copperfield* (1849–50).

195.13   Miss St. Clair as Juliet] Sallie St. Clair (1831–1867), popular English-born American actress.

195.35   the dagger scene] *Macbeth*, II.i.33–64.

197.7–23   "You see me, . . . her king."] *The Merchant of Venice*, III.ii.149–165.

207.10–12   "Not the first . . . love."] From "A Temple to Friendship," by Irish poet Thomas Moore (1779–1852).

207.34–37   As George Macdonald . . . her window."] In *Adela Cathcart* (1864).

225.25   Orson-like] Bearlike.

225.25–26   meerschaums] Clay used for tobacco pipes.

228.27–28   Beau Brummel] George Bryan "Beau" Brummell (1778–1840), fashion icon and friend of the Prince Regent, later George IV, who is credited with introducing the modern men's suit and well-tailored, fitted clothing.

231.36   "So let me seem until I be"] From the first line of a song, sung by the child Mignon, in *Wilhelm Meisters Lehrjahre* (1795–96), by Johann Wolfgang von Goethe (book 8, chapter 2).

243.15   "The nunnery of a chaste heart and quiet mind."] Cf. "To Lucasta, Going to the Warres" (1649), poem by English poet Richard Lovelace (1618–1657).

257.16   Claude Melnotte] In *The Lady of Lyons; or, Love and Pride* (1838) by Edward Bulwer-Lytton, a gardener's son who disguises himself as a foreign prince in order to trick the heroine into marrying him. She discovers the trick when Melnotte takes her to his widowed mother's home after their marriage.

258.23   The gun fired . . . Fort Sumter] Confederate forces fired on the federal garrison at Fort Sumter, in Charleston Harbor, South Carolina, on April 12, 1861, starting the Civil War.

263.11   cross of the Legion of Honor] The highest decoration awarded in France.

275.33–34   "I could not love thee, . . . honor more."] From "To Lucasta, Going to the Warres," by Richard Lovelace.

290.24   this shot through the lungs] David's death is based on that of the Virginia blacksmith John Suhre in Alcott's *Hospital Sketches*.

296.40   south wind whispering in David's flute] Cf. Alcott's poem "Thoreau's Flute": "Then from the flute, untouched by hands, / There came a low, harmonious breath: / 'For such as he there is no death;—"

306.24   Aspasia] See note 18.11–12.

306.25–26   Hypatia . . . Tyrian purple curtain] Hypatia (c. 370–415), mathematician and head of the Neoplatonist school in Alexandria, who was murdered by a mob incited by Cyril, archbishop of Alexandria. Harriet Beecher Stowe, in *The Chimney-Corner* (1866), wrote that Hypatia, known for her beauty, "gave lectures on philosophy behind a curtain, lest her charms should distract the attention of too impressible young men." Tyrian purple, also known as royal purple, is an expensive dye made from mollusks, restricted in ancient Greece and Rome for the use of royalty.

313.26  a De Staël] Madame de Staël (1766–1817), French Romantic novelist who hosted a celebrated literary and intellectual salon.

316.22–24  Mr. Greatheart . . . Christiana] In the second part of John Bunyan's *Pilgrim's Progress* (1684), Mr. Greatheart leads Christiana and Mercy from their home in the City of Destruction to the Celestial City.

316.35–36  John Brown and Colonel Shaw] John Brown (1800–1859), militant abolitionist who was executed for his raid on the federal arsenal at Harpers Ferry, Virginia, which was intended to spark a massive slave rebellion. Robert Gould Shaw (1837–1863) commanded the black 54th Massachusetts Infantry regiment during the Civil War and was killed in the unsuccessful Union assault on Fort Wagner in Charleston Harbor on July 18, 1863.

EIGHT COUSINS

324.6  Ariadne Blish] Ariadne Blish taught in public schools in Cambridge, Massachusetts, for eleven years, and ran a school in her home. After the publication of *Eight Cousins*, Alcott learned of her objection to the use of her name and wrote to her that "five & thirty years ago I heard the name of Ariadne Blish & because of its peculiarity have remembered it ever since, although all knowledge of the child who bore it ended then & there. . . . if there should be a sequel Ariadne will be rechristened." She later wrote to Caroline Healey Dall, "I remember nothing about little Ariadne except that she was a very well behaved child who was held up to naughty Louisa as a model girl." Ariadne was renamed Annabel in *Rose in Bloom*.

326.29–30  Arabella Montgomery in the 'Gypsy's Child.'] Most likely in a story by Elizabeth Stuart Phelps Ward.

330.29  top-knot] A knob or tuft of hair worn on the crown of the head.

334.11  Highland Fling] Scottish solo dance popular in the early nineteenth century involving flicking of the feet.

334.22–23  'Sing for you . . . dulcy melody.'"] From the chorus of "Nelly Bly" (1850), song by Stephen Foster.

334.38  Fitzjames . . . Roderick Dhu] See Canto V of *The Lady of the Lake*, narrative poem (1810) by Sir Walter Scott.

335.18  Wallace and Montrose] William Wallace defeated the army of Edward I at Stirling Bridge in 1297 and continued to oppose English rule in Scotland until his capture and execution in 1305. James Graham, 1st Marquess of Montrose (1612–1650), won a series of victories over the Scottish opponents of Charles I, 1644–45, before being defeated and forced into exile. He returned to Scotland in 1650 to fight for Charles II, but was captured and executed at Edinburgh.

336.37   "Bonnie Dundee;"] Song (1825) by Sir Walter Scott.

338.14–15   "All the blue bonnets are over the border"] Traditional Scottish tune with lyrics by Sir Walter Scott, from *The Monastery* (1820).

344.35   quassia cup] Cup made of quassia wood, which imparts a bitter flavor to water placed in it. The resulting liquid was drunk as a tonic.

351.30   Blimber hot-bed . . . feminine Toots.] Dr. Blimber is a schoolmaster and Toots a scatterbrained classmate of Paul Dombey in Charles Dickens's novel *Dombey and Son* (1846–48).

357.9   "Where are you going . . . a-milking, sir, she said,"] Nursery rhyme.

358.3   Prunes and Prisms] Propriety in speech and behavior (from a phrase used in elocution exercises).

358.38–39   Hebe, goddess of health,] In Greek mythology, daughter of Hera and Zeus, cup-bearer to the gods and wife of Heracles.

362.18   Morgiana] A slave of Ali Baba who repeatedly saves his life from the Forty Thieves in *The Arabian Nights' Entertainments.*

363.7   paroquet.] Parakeet.

364.2   Arabella] See note 326.29–30.

370.10–11   "'Puss-tat, puss-tat, . . . Tween.'"] Nursery rhyme.

383.3–12   "Oh, Timballoo! . . . in a sieve."] From "The Jumblies" (1871), poem by English nonsense poet Edward Lear.

389.27–29   Lapsing Souchong, . . . green Twankey.] Lapsang Souchong, black tea with a smoky flavor grown in southern China; Assam Pekoe, high-grade malty black tea from Assam, northeastern India; rare Ankoe, or Ankay, variety of oolong tea grown in Anxi County in the Fujian province of China; Flower Pekoe, term for high grade of tea with long leaves; Howqua's mixture, tea blend sold beginning in the 1830s and supposedly created by Chinese businessman Howqua (1769–1843); Scented Caper, scented tea with round closely twisted leaf; Padral, or Padrae, tea, strongly flavored black tea grown in southern China; black Congou, black tea grown in northern China that was once used in English breakfast blends; and green Twankay, low-grade green tea with a ragged leaf.

389.31   'Chops'] Large flat-bottomed barges used to load and unload ships, owned by Chinese merchants and hired out to foreign traders.

389.35   in Canton is the Dwelling of the Holy Pigs] At the Honan temple in Canton, now Guangzhou, the capital of Guangdong province.

392.30–33   "'Look only,' . . . little shoe,'"] From "Mabel on Midsummer Day" (1839) by English poet Mary Howitt.

398.14   'spondulics,'] Slang: money.

399.8   Cleopatra landing from her golden galley] Cf. *Antony and Cleopatra*, II.ii.191–226.

402.16–17   famous dancing party in "Alice's Adventures in Wonderland."] See Chapter X, "The Lobster Quadrille."

402.20–21   "Water Babies"] *The Water-Babies, A Fairy Tale for a Land Baby* (1863), children's novel by the Reverend Charles Kingsley.

402.36   Captain Cook . . . Owhyhee] Captain James Cook (1728–1779), British explorer, cartographer, and officer in the Royal Navy who was killed in a fight with Hawaiians during his third voyage to the Pacific.

403.1   Captain Kidd] Captain William Kidd (c. 1645–1701), Scottish sailor tried and executed for piracy who was popularly believed to have left behind buried treasure.

403.4   Sinbad] Sinbad the Sailor, in *The Arabian Nights' Entertainments*.

416.14–15   "Bonny lassie, . . . Aberfeldie?"] "The Birks of Aberfeldy," song (1787) by Robert Burns, to a traditional melody.

426.31–32   "Coo," said . . . pine-tree."] From "The Little Doves," song by American clergyman and hymnist John Henry Hopkins Jr., in *Carols, Hymns and Songs* (1863).

427.7   catamount] A wildcat such as a cougar or lynx.

431.33–34   Gig-lamps] Slang: spectacles.

474.28   this little book] Abba Goold Woolson, *Dress-Reform: A Series of Lectures Delivered in Boston, on Dress as It Affects the Health of Women* (Boston: Roberts Brothers, 1874).

475.29   Hebe] See note 358.38–39.

475.31–32   Gabrielle dress] One-piece dress with no seam at the waist and skirts a little above the ankle.

491.3   Stenie] Nickname for Stephen.

494.20–21   "Sweet Home,"] "Home! Sweet Home!" song by Sir Henry Bishop with lyrics by John Howard Payne, adapted from his 1823 opera *Clari, or the Maid of Milan*.

505.20–23   "The way into my parlor . . . Phebe dear?"] From "The Spider and the Fly" (1829) by English poet Mary Howitt.

509.35–36   'the birds begin to sing?'] From "Sing a Song of Sixpence," a nursery rhyme.

528.15   'Codlin's your friend,'] Thomas Codlin is a Punch & Judy showman in Dickens's *The Old Curiosity Shop* (1840–41) who attempts to gain Little Nell's confidence in order to collect the reward for information on her whereabouts.

ROSE IN BLOOM

537.2    bodkin-wise] Sitting wedged between two other persons in a seat meant for two people.

548.26    "The Birks of Aberfeldie,"] See note 416.14–15.

556.39    Atalanta] In Greek mythology, huntress who would marry only if she could be beaten in a footrace. Hippomenes got three golden apples from Aphrodite and delayed Atalanta long enough to win the race by throwing the apples down in front of her so that she stopped to pick them up.

558.22–25    "Chide me not, . . . thought."] "The Apology" (1847) by Ralph Waldo Emerson.

560.23    Annabel Blish] See note 324.6.

561.17    Worth] Charles Frederick Worth (1825–1895), English-born fashion designer who created the House of Worth in Paris and dominated Parisian fashion in the late nineteenth century.

564.10–11    Lady Hester Stanhope] British socialite and traveler (1776–1839).

564.25–26    Aurora] Roman goddess of the dawn.

564.30    "'Sleeping I dreamed, love, dreamed, love, of thee,'"] From "Sleeping I Dreamed, Love," 1847 song with lyrics by M. E. Hewitt and music by W. V. Wallace.

566.10    Fra Angelico angel] Italian Renaissance painter (c. 1395–1455) whose paintings of angels are delicate and golden-haired, often with rainbow-colored wings.

567.33–36    "While our rosy fillets . . . we beguile."] "Ode XLIII" by Irish poet Thomas Moore, from *Odes of Anacreon* (1800).

568.2    St. Francis] St. Francis of Assisi (c. 1181–1226), Catholic saint who practiced and celebrated poverty.

568.8–9    St. Martin] St. Martin of Tours (316–397), patron saint of France and of innkeepers.

573.25    ''tis their nature to,'] Popular, much-parodied phrase originally from Isaac Watt's "Song XVI. Against Quarreling and Fighting" from *Divine Songs Attempted in Easy Language, for the Use of Children* (1715).

581.8    Lady Bountiful] A character in George Farquhar's 1707 comedy *The Beaux' Stratagem* well-known for her generosity.

583.3–4    all that glitters is not gold,] Cf. *The Merchant of Venice*, II.vii.65.

584.10    wheat among the tares] Cf. Matthew 13:24–30.

588.6–13    "As he was walkin' . . . laddie in?"] "Charlie Is My Darling," song by Robert Burns (1794).

588.29   Psyche] Maiden who marries Cupid without knowing his identity and on the condition that she can never see him. Encouraged by her sisters to disobey, she lights a lamp and he leaves her.

588.31–34   "He set his Jenny . . . bonny lass."] See note 588.6–13.

591.7–8   Paul Pry] Nosy or prying person, from the title character of the popular 1825 farce *Paul Pry*, by English author John Poole.

591.11   "Mysteries of Udolpho,"] Novel (1794) by Ann Radcliffe, often called the archetypal Gothic novel.

591.13–15   'here's your straw color, . . . your perfect yellow' Shakspeare.] Cf. *A Midsummer Night's Dream*, I.ii.93–96.

592.38–39   "Will you let me . . . heart of flesh?"] Cf. Ezekiel 36:26.

594.5–6   Guy Carleton, Count Altenberg, and John Halifax] Guy Carleton is an honest, sensitive gentleman who eventually marries the heroine in *Queechy* (1852), novel by Elizabeth Wetherell (pseudonym of Susan Warner). Count Altenberg is the romantic hero who loves the heroine for her modesty and dignity in Maria Edgeworth's novel *Patronage* (1814). In *John Halifax, Gentleman* (1856) by Dinah Mulock Craik, the hero becomes a gentleman by merit, not birth (see note 59.29).

594.7   Guy Livingston, Beauclerc, and Rochester] In *Guy Livingstone, or Thorough* (1857) by George Alfred Lawrence, Livingstone is physically strong, temperamental, and thinks little of ruining the reputations of women. Beauclerc is a young and handsome man in Maria Edgeworth's *Helen* (1834) who fights a duel in defense of his fiancée's honor. Edward Rochester is the romantic hero of Charlotte Brontë's *Jane Eyre* (1847), who woos Jane by pretending to love another woman and who tries to marry her while his first wife is still living.

597.25–31   "Oh were thou . . . wad be my queen."] "O Wert Thou In The Cauld Blast" (1796) by Robert Burns.

597.33   Orpheus] In Greek mythology, a singer able to charm even stones with his music.

603.11   Adonis] In Greek mythology, a beautiful youth, love of Aphrodite, who was killed by a boar while hunting.

607.3   Turveydrop] Character in Dickens's *Bleak House* (1852–53), known for his perfect manners and deportment.

611.1   Evelina] Heroine of *Evelina*, 1778 novel by Fanny Burney.

615.29   teetotum] A spinning top similar to a dreidel.

615.32   a 'glass of fashion and a mould of form'] *Hamlet*, III.i.153.

616.4–6   'Woe! woe! . . . mortal blow!'] From Aeschylus's *Agamemnon*, translated (1849) by Theodore Alois William Buckley.

621.31 Dummy for a partner] In whist games, the exposed hand is known as the dummy.

621.32–33 Wall . . . chinks.] Cf. *A Midsummer Night's Dream*, V.i.155–205.

626.18 "Mrs. Nubbles"] Kit's mother in Dickens's *The Old Curiosity Shop* (1840–41).

630.38 Jenny Lind] Johanna Maria Lind (1820–1887), known as Jenny Lind, Swedish opera singer popular in the United States and Europe.

643.6 Vanity Fair] In *The Pilgrim's Progress* (1678) by John Bunyan, a fair that is perpetually held in the town of Vanity, representing attachment to worldly things.

647.6–7 Douglas, tender and true] Refrain of popular poem "Too Late" by Dinah Mulock Craik (c. 1860).

651.18 "'Tis better to laugh than be sighing;'"] Chorus of drinking song from the opera *Lucrezia Borgia* (1833), with music by Gaetano Donizetti and libretto by Felice Romani after the play by Victor Hugo.

656.28 Victoria cross] The highest military decoration in the United Kingdom, instituted in 1856 and awarded for valor "in the presence of the enemy."

665.24–25 Fortunatus' purse] Fortunatus, a German folk hero, received a purse from the goddess of Fortune that was continually refilled.

667.33 portemonnaie] French: wallet.

676.30 Merry Pecksniffian crop] Heavily curled, à la Mercy "Merry" Pecksniff in Dickens's *Martin Chuzzlewit* (1843–44).

682.1–2 Lycurgus] Spartan lawgiver (c. 820–730 B.C.E.) who instituted a variety of reforms aimed against luxury and extolling austerity.

682.31–32 Diogenes . . . lantern] Diogenes (c. 412–323 B.C.E.), a Greek philosopher and one of the founders of Cynicism. He reputedly conducted a search for an honest man in broad daylight with a lantern.

683.8–9 "What care I . . . for me?"] From "Shall I, Wasting in Despair" (1615) by English poet George Wither.

687.15 Solon] Athenian lawgiver (c. 638–558 B.C.E.) and moral reformer.

691.7–8 "'His worth shines forth . . . despairs,'"] From Euripides's tragedy *Herakles* (c. 415 B.C.E.), translated by the Reverend Robert Potter in 1781–83.

692.6–11 "'Man is his own star . . . us still.'"] The epilogue to *The Honest Man's Fortune* (1613), tragicomedy by Nathan Field, John Fletcher, and Philip Massinger; also the epigraph to Emerson's essay "Self-Reliance" (1841).

716.17–18 "Prayer for the Dying,"] Taken from the prayer for a sick person in *A Liturgy Collected for the Use of the Church at King's Chapel, Boston* (1785, multiple editions).

724.15   Britomart] See note 35.12.

726.38–39   "'Accept the blessing . . . your door,'] Cf. "The Beggar's Petition" (1769) by English poet and minister Thomas Moss.

731.5–6   Milton's Sabrina] A water nymph in John Milton's masque *Comus* (1634).

732.30   "Dearest Nature, strong and kind,"] From poem "Experience" in Emerson's *Essays: Second Series* (1844).

735.8–12   "'I would rather sit . . . the way.'] From Thoreau's *Walden* (1854). Alcott had briefly attended Thoreau's school and followed him on nature walks and on boating trips to Walden Pond. Thoreau served as a pall-bearer at Elizabeth Alcott's funeral and was a guest at Anna Alcott's wedding.

735.16–24   "'Read the best . . . wounds.'] Thoreau, *A Week on the Concord and Merrimack Rivers* (1849).

735.32–35   "'Whate'er we leave to God, . . . lets alone.'"] Thoreau, "Inspiration" (1841).

736.9   "'As if a rose should shut and be a bud again,'"] John Keats, "The Eve of St. Agnes" (1819), stanza 27.

736.35–737.3   "Self-Reliance," . . . "Heroism,"] Essays by Ralph Waldo Emerson.

737.33–34   "'Without halting . . . Best.'"] From Emerson's "May-Day" (1867).

737.39   Colossus of Rhodes] One of the Seven Wonders of the Ancient World, a statue of the Greek Titan Helios in the city of Rhodes that was almost one hundred feet tall and was once thought to have bestrode the harbor entrance. The statue was completed c. 280 B.C.E. and stood for fifty-six years before being destroyed by an earthquake c. 224 B.C.E.

741.32   Young Augustus] Augustus Caesar (63 B.C.E.–14 C.E.)

742.7   Orson] A bear.

742.19   L.] London.

743.7   Psyche] See note 588.29.

743.25   Fra Angelico angel] See note 566.10.

743.25   Saint Agnes] Catholic martyr (c. 291–304), the patron saint of chastity and girls, often pictured with a lamb.

743.34–37   "'Your feet in . . . a rose,'"] From "An Interlude" (1866) by Algernon Charles Swinburne.

750.38–39   Pond's Extract] Patent medicinal tea made of witch hazel used to cure small cuts and other ailments.

751.4    Fanny Squeers] In Dickens's *Life and Adventures of Nicholas Nickleby* (1838–39), the schoolmaster's daughter who falls in love with Nicholas. Having heard that the new teacher is handsome, she comes into his classroom, ostensibly to have her father mend a pen, but really to meet Nicholas.

751.26    Rose evidently had forgotten . . . Squeers] In *Nicholas Nickleby*, Fanny requests a soft pen and sighs, "to give Nicholas to understand that her heart was soft, and that the pen was wanted to match."

760.26–31    "'Oh, let our mingling voices . . . songs of earth.'"] Cf. "O Let Your Mingling Voices Rise," Christmas hymn (1845) by Mary Ann Roscoe Jevons.

762.27–30    Swinburnian convulsions . . . of love;"] Cf. "Dolores (Notre-Dame des Sept Douleurs),'" poem (1866) by Algernon Charles Swinburne, known for his florid style.

774.11–15    Garrison . . . Abby Gibbons] William Lloyd Garrison (1805–1879) edited *The Liberator*, 1831–65; helped found the American Anti-Slavery Society in 1833; and served as its president, 1843–65. Samuel Gridley Howe (1801–1876), the husband of Julia Ward Howe, was a physician who founded the Perkins School for the Blind, the oldest school for the blind in the United States. Charles Sumner (1811–1874), Republican senator from Massachusetts, 1851–74, who denounced corruption in the Grant administration and in Congress. Abigail Hopper Gibbons (1801–1893), reformer who worked for civil rights and education for blacks, women's prison reform, and aid for veterans.

779.34    Una and her lion] In Book One of *The Faerie Queene* (1590) by Edmund Spenser, Una's innocence and beauty pacify a lion that is about to attack her, and the beast becomes her protector.

780.2–3    'Mr. and Mrs. Harry Walmers, Jr.;'] In Dickens's Christmas story "The Boots at the Holly-Tree Inn," a young couple of seven and eight years old who attempt to elope.

781.18–19    Islands of the Blest] In Greek mythology, a paradise reserved for heroes and men and women favored by the gods.

781.31–32    "Bonny lassie, . . . Aberfeldie?"] See note 416.14–15.


OTHER WRITINGS

790.10    LYDIA MARIA CHILD,] Author, abolitionist, and women's rights activist (1802–1880) who edited the *National Anti-Slavery Standard* from 1841 to 1843 and was the close friend of Alcott's mother Abby May Alcott.

790.11    HARRIET BEECHER STOWE,] Abolitionist and author (1811–1896) of *Uncle Tom's Cabin* and other novels, children's books, women's literature, and journalism.

790.12    ELIZABETH STUART PHELPS,] Author (1844–1911) and advocate for clothing reform and women's financial independence from men.

790.14 GRACE GREENWOOD,] Sarah Jane Lippincott (1823–1904), author, abolitionist, and women's rights advocate who wrote under the pseudonym Grace Greenwood, was the first woman reporter on the *New York Times* payroll and one of the first women to gain admittance to the congressional press galleries.

790.15 JULIA WARD HOWE,] Author and activist for suffrage, prison reform, and international peace, Howe (1819–1910), best known as the author of "The Battle Hymn of the Republic," edited the antislavery newspaper *Commonwealth* with her husband, Samuel Gridley Howe, and helped found the New England Woman Suffrage Association. In 1907 she became the first woman to be elected to the American Academy of Arts and Sciences.

790.16 MARY A. LIVERMORE,] Woman suffrage and temperance reformer (1820–1905) who edited *The Agitator* and *Woman's Journal.*

790.17 HELEN E. GARRISON,] Helen Eliza Garrison (1811–1876), the wife of abolitionist William Lloyd Garrison.

790.18 ABBY W. MAY,] Abigail Williams May (1829–1888), abolition, education, and women's rights reformer, a cofounder of the New England Women's Club, and one of the first women to serve on the Boston School Committee and the Massachusetts Board of Education. She was the first cousin of Alcott's mother Abigail May Alcott.

790.19 CAROLINE M. SEVERANCE,] Abolitionist and suffragist (1820–1914) who helped found the first women's club in the United States, the New England Women's Club.

790.20 HARRIET H. ROBINSON,] Poet and author (1825–1911) who helped organize the National Woman Suffrage Association of Massachusetts and the New England Women's Club.

790.21 MARGARET W. CAMPBELL,] Suffragist (1827–post-1903) who worked for the American Woman Suffrage Association and wrote for the *Woman's Journal.*

790.22 MARY F. EASTMAN,] Suffragist orator and educator (1833–1908), the first female high school graduate in Massachusetts, and secretary of the Association for Advancement of Women.

790.23 ADA C. BOWLES,] Universalist minister Ada C. Burpee Bowles (1836–1928), abolitionist, suffragist, and temperance reformer. She later moved to San Francisco, where she edited a newspaper column on women's suffrage and served as president of the San Francisco Woman's Suffrage Society.

790.24 ELIZABETH P. PEABODY,] Educator (1804–1894) and author of elementary grammar and history textbooks. Opened the first American kindergarten in Boston in 1860 and lectured at Bronson Alcott's Concord School of Philosophy (1879–84).

790.25   HARRIET W. SEWALL,] Poet and suffragist (1819–1889) and the editor of the collected letters of Lydia Maria Child.

790.26   LUCY STONE,] Abolitionist, orator, and leader of the women's rights movement (1818–1893) who helped organize the first National Women's Rights Convention and was the first woman from Massachusetts to earn a college degree. Elizabeth Cady Stanton wrote: "Lucy Stone was the first person by whom the heart of the American public was deeply stirred on the woman question." Stone founded and edited the *Woman's Journal*, for which Alcott wrote, with her husband Henry Browne Blackwell.

806.1   *How I Went Out to Service*] Based on her uncomfortable, sexually charged experiences as a companion at a house in Dedham for James Richardson, a demanding and abusive elderly lawyer who had been a classmate of Thoreau's at Harvard and an admirer of Bronson Alcott. Alcott had imagined a genteel job whose duties would include reading to Richardson; instead she was told to black his boots. When she finally left, Richardson added insult to injury by paying her only four dollars. Alcott showed this essay to the Boston publisher James T. Fields two years later, hoping Fields would launch her writing career; instead he advised her to "stick to your teaching, Miss Alcott. You can't write."

808.15–16   Siddons . . . Betcinder.] For Siddons, see note 36.29–30. Betcinder is Cinderella.

808.40–809.1   delaine] From French *de laine* ("of wool"); also a breed of Merino sheep producing high-quality wool for women's dresses.

811.6   Borgia] The Borgia family in Renaissance Italy were notoriously power hungry.

820.30   feminine Casabiacas] See note 131.26.

820.32   wise virgins] Cf. Matthew 25:1–13.

821.8   Dr. Ripley] The Reverend Ezra Ripley (1751–1841), Ralph Waldo Emerson's step-grandfather.

821.24–26   Senator Wilson . . . President of the day] Henry Wilson (1812–1875), senator from Massachusetts, 1855–1873, and vice president of the U.S., 1873–75. Alcott's cousin, the Reverend Samuel May Jr. (1810–1899), had been a member of the Massachusetts house of representatives in 1874. George William Curtis (1824–1892), a writer and the political editor of *Harper's Weekly*, delivered the keynote speech of the celebration. The president of the centennial celebration was Ebenezer Rockwood Hoar (1816–1895), a lawyer and judge from Concord who was U.S. Attorney General, 1869–70.

822.2–3   the Gamalials at whose feet we sat] Cf. Acts 22:3.

822.22–24   Prescott, . . . Isaac Davis's] Samuel Prescott (1751–c. 1777), Revolutionary War patriot who with Paul Revere was part of the "midnight ride" to warn the people of Concord about the approaching British army. The Reverend William Emerson Sr. (1743–1776), grandfather of Ralph Waldo Emerson, served as a chaplain in the Continental Army. John Hancock (1737–1793), president of the Second Continental Congress and signer of the Declaration of Independence. For Dr. Ripley, see note 821.8. Isaac Davis (1745–1775) led a militia company in the battle of Concord and was the first American officer to die in the Revolution.

822.35   Judge Hoar] See note 821.24–26.

823.8–11   The President . . . His Imperturbability] President Ulysses S. Grant.

825.3   Mrs. Stone] Lucy Stone; see note 790.26.

827.29   Mrs. Grundy] A narrowly conventional or priggish person, after a character in Thomas Morton's 1798 play *Speed the Plough.*

839.29   like the mad gentleman to Mrs. Nickleby, 'Be mine, be mine'] In Dickens's *Life and Adventures of Nicholas Nickleby* (1838–39), Nicholas's mother rejects the advances of their neighbor and becomes convinced that he went mad because of her rejection.

844.26–27   'put my fortune to the touch . . . lose it all.'"] Cf. "My dear and only love" (1643) by James Graham, Marquess of Montrose.

845.13–14   'Every man for himself . . . hindmost.'] Early sixteenth-century proverb.

850.5   A] Possibly Laura Whiting Hosmer (1833–1896), Concord homeopathic physician and Alcott's close friend, or Lucy Sewall (1837–1890), the daughter of Samuel E. Sewall, Abba Alcott's cousin and Alcott's financial advisor. Lucy Sewall was resident physician at the New England Hospital for Women and Children and became its director in 1869.

850.36   B] Based on Alcott's sister May.

851.24–25   Guidecca . . . Sol de Venezia . . . Temeraire.] *Venice, seen from the Giudecca Canal* (1840), *The Sun of Venice Going to Sea* (1843), and *The Fighting Temeraire* (1839), paintings by Joseph Mallord William Turner.

851.26   "Van Tromp entering the mouth of the Texel"] 1831 painting by J. M. W. Turner.

851.29   "Datur Hora Quieti"] Watercolor (c. 1830–32) by J. M. W. Turner.

854.12   Pillicoddy] Character in the nautical comedy *Poor Pillicoddy: A Farce in One Act* (1843) by English dramatist John Maddison Morton.

855.7   Infant Phenomenon] Byname of Ninetta Crummles, character in Dickens's *Nicholas Nickleby*, a member of the theatrical troupe in which Nicholas performs.

857.37  Bijou Heron . . . "The Little Treasure"] Born Helen Wallace Stoepel (1863–1937), famous child actress; *The Little Treasure*, short comedic play (1855) by Augustus Glossop Harris and Thomas J. Williams.

858.3  Topsy] A slave girl in Harriet Beecher Stowe's *Uncle Tom's Cabin* (1852) whose famous response to the catechistical question "Who made you?"—"I spect I grow'd. Don't think nobody never made me."—inspired the popular figure of speech "it grow'd like Topsy," used to suggest development without the benefit of guidance or direction.

859.11–12  Mary Livermores, . . . Lucy Stones,] For Livermore, see note 790.16. Ednah Cheney (1824–1904), writer, suffragist, abolitionist, and lecturer at Bronson Alcott's Concord School of Philosophy; she also wrote two biographies of Louisa May Alcott. For Howe, see note 790.15. Maria Mitchell (1818–1889), astronomer, the first woman elected to the American Academy of Arts and Sciences, and professor at Vassar College. For Stone, see note 790.26.

*This book is set in 10 point ITC Galliard Pro, a*
*face designed for digital composition by Matthew Carter*
*and based on the sixteenth-century face Granjon. The paper*
*is acid-free lightweight opaque and meets the requirements*
*for permanence of the American National Standards Institute.*
*The binding material is Brillianta, a woven rayon cloth made*
*by Van Heek–Scholco Textielfabrieken, Holland.*
*Composition by Dedicated Book Services. Printing and*
*binding by Edwards Brothers Malloy, Ann Arbor.*
*Designed by Bruce Campbell.*

# THE LIBRARY OF AMERICA SERIES

The Library of America fosters appreciation and pride in America's literary heritage by publishing, and keeping permanently in print, authoritative editions of America's best and most significant writing. An independent nonprofit organization, it was founded in 1979 with seed funding from the National Endowment for the Humanities and the Ford Foundation.

To subscribe to the series or to order individual copies, please visit www.loa.org or call (800) 964-5778.